Jilly Cooper is a journalist, writer and media superstar. The author of many number one bestselling novels, including *Riders*, *Rivals*, *Polo*, *The Man Who Made Husbands Jealous*, *Appassionata*, *Score!*, *Pandora* and *Wicked!*, she lives in Gloucestershire with her husband, Leo, her rescue greyhound, Feather, and five cats. She was appointed OBE in the 2004 Queen's Birthday Honours List for her contribution to literature.

Find out more about Jilly Cooper and her novels by visiting her website: www.jillycooper.co.uk

THE MAN WHO MADE HUSBANDS JEALOUS

'A blockie with real style'
Good Housekeeping

'Latest compulsive sooper-Cooper'
Kate Saunders, *Cosmopolitan*

'A seductive new novel from Jilly Cooper . . .
The prose fizzes with pun, wit and orgasmic
dalliance'
She

'Jilly's lusty tales are such a thumping – or
should I say humping – good read that you
keep turning the pages until you have raced to
the end of the last racy chapter . . .
unputdownable'
Jane Ducas, *Woman's Journal*

'A great roistering read in the best Cooper
tradition'
The Times

'Wonderful array of characters ... Jilly's best hero yet ... the action is the hottest Jilly has yet produced ... the whole thing is vintage Cooper, full of the romping humour and spot-on observations"
Katy Bravery, *Today*

'A new Jilly Cooper novel always produces mixed emotions in our family. Excitement and anticipation from me and gloom and despair from my husband, our three children and the guinea pig who know they will be ignored and neglected for however long it will take me to read. The Man Who Made Husbands Jealous proved no exception. There has been no hot food in our house and precious little conversation for the last three days'
Charlotte Joll, *Spectator*

'Jilly Cooper rides again, with her raunchiest novel yet'
Woman and Home

'addictive'
Independent

'Cooper's touch is supreme ... The Tolstoy of the shires has done it again'
Midweek

By Jilly Cooper

FICTION	Wicked!
	Pandora
	The Rutshire Chronicles:
	Riders
	Rivals
	Polo
	The Man Who Made Husbands Jealous
	Appassionata
	Score!
NON-FICTION	Animals in War
	Class
	How to Survive Christmas
	Hotfoot to Zabriskie Point (with Patrick Lichfield)
	Intelligent and Loyal
	Jolly Marsupial
	Jolly Super
	Jolly Superlative
	Jolly Super Too
	Super Cooper
	Super Jilly
	Super Men and Super Women
	The Common Years
	Turn Right at the Spotted Dog
	Work and Wedlock
	Angels Rush In
	Araminta's Wedding
CHILDREN'S BOOKS	Little Mabel
	Little Mabel's Great Escape
	Little Mabel Saves the Day
	Little Mabel Wins
ROMANCE	Bella
	Emily
	Harriet
	Imogen
	Lisa & Co
	Octavia
	Prudence
ANTHOLOGIES	The British in Love
	Violets and Vinegar

THE MAN WHO MADE HUSBANDS JEALOUS

Jilly Cooper

CORGI BOOKS

TRANSWORLD PUBLISHERS
61–63 Uxbridge Road, London W5 5SA
a division of The Random House Group Ltd
www.booksattransworld.co.uk

THE MAN WHO MADE HUSBANDS JEALOUS
A CORGI BOOK : 9780552156394

First published in Great Britain
in 1991 by Bantam Press
a division of Transworld Publishers
Corgi edition published 1994
Corgi edition reissued 2007

Addresses for Random House Group Ltd companies outside the UK
can be found at: www.randomhouse.co.uk
The Random House Group Ltd Reg. No. 954009

Typeset in 10 pt Linotype Plantin by
Chippendale Type Ltd.

6 8 10 9 7

The Random House Group Limited supports The Forest Stewardship
Council® (FSC®), the leading international forest-certification organisation.
Our books carrying the FSC label are printed on FSC®-certified paper.
FSC is the only forest-certification scheme supported by the leading
environmental organisations, including Greenpeace. Our
paper procurement policy can be found at
www.randomhouse.co.uk/environment

MIX
Paper from
responsible sources
FSC® C016897

Printed and bound in Great Britain by Clays Ltd, St Ives plc

To Emily

with love and gratitude

for so much happiness

Acknowledgements

One of the delights of writing *The Man Who Made Husbands Jealous* has been the kindness and enthusiasm of the people who helped me. These include in particular John Lodge, Managing Director of Lodge Securities, who initiated me into the mysteries of highly sophisticated security systems; trainer Nigel Twiston-Davies and his wife Cathy, who took me racing and allowed me to spend several days at their yard; Emily Gardiner and Alicia Winter who advised me on the pop music front; and Ian Maclay, the former Managing Director of The Royal Philharmonic Orchestra and the orchestra themselves, who provided me with much joy and enlightenment, both at rehearsal and concerts.

I should also like to thank Martin Stephen for telling me about headmasters; composer Geoffrey Burgon and master cellist Bobby Kok for talking to me about music; Andrew Parker-Bowles and John Oaksey for being brilliant about racing; Shirley Bevan for advising me on the illnesses of horses; Simon Cowley for walking the Cheltenham course with me in a deluge; and Raymond and Jenny Mould for inviting me into their box to see Tipping Tim win gloriously at Cheltenham. Peter and Alexandra Hunter and Sally Reygate also told me wonderful stories about their horses Esperanta and Regal, both now sadly departed.

Many other people helped me. Like those referred to above, they are all skilled in their own fields, but as I was writing fiction, I only followed their advice as far as it fitted my own story, and their expertise is in no way reflected by the accuracy of this book. They include:

Anthony and Mary Abrahams, Richard Bell, Sebastian Birkhead, John Bowes-Lyon, Charlie Brooks, Peter Cadbury, Edith and Jack Clarkson, Peter Clarkson, Father Damian of Prinknash Abbey, Jim Davidson, Herbert Despard, Fiona Feeley, Dennis Foot, Miriam Francombe, Susannah and William Franklyn, Judy Gaselee, E. W. Gillespie, Managing Director, Cheltenham Racecourse, Tony Hoskins, George and Huw Humphreys, John Irvin, Geoffrey and Jorie Kent, Carl Llewellyn, Roger and Rowena Luard, David Marchwood, Managing Director, Moët & Chandon (London) Ltd., Pussy Minchin, Sharon Morgan, Lana Myers, Peter Norman, Managing Director, Parfums Givenchy, Rosemary Nunneley, Guy Ralls, Henry Sallitt, Lottie Sjögren, Edward Smith, Pauline Stanbury, Diane Stevens, Harry Turner, Barry Watts, Madeline and Malcolm White, Kate Whitehouse and Francis Willey.

I should also like to thank the National Canine Defence League and in particular Mrs Clarissa Baldwin for allowing me to use their slogan – 'A Dog is for Life . . . Not Just for Christmas'.

The subconscious mind works in strange ways. Almost from conception, *The Man Who Made Husbands Jealous* was set in Paradise, a mythical village in the mythical county of Rutshire. Paradise Village in the book has a population of around eight hundred, an Anglo-Saxon church, a pub, a restaurant, a handful of shops and lies on a river at the bottom of a beautiful valley surrounded by steeply sloping woodland studded with beautiful houses.

During a driving lesson, when the book was well under way, I told my instructor, Peter Clarkson, about my fictional village. Did I know there was a Paradise in Gloucestershire, he asked, and promptly drove me to a tiny hamlet which looked down into a valley, even more beautiful than the one of my imagination. Charles II is alleged to have named the place Paradise. Arriving by night while escaping from the Roundheads, he gazed out of the window the following morning and asked in rapture if he had arrived in Paradise. As I had written so much of the book by then, and because the two 'Paradises' are totally different, except in their rare beauty, I decided to keep the name, but would stress that no-one living nor any of the locations in Paradise, Rutshire, bear any resemblance or are based on anyone living or any of the places in Paradise, Gloucestershire.

I must also reiterate that *The Man Who Made Husbands Jealous* is a work of fiction and none of the characters is based on anyone. Any resemblance to any living person is purely coincidental and wholly unintended.

An author is only as good as her publishers. Mine have been magnificent. I would like to say a massive thank you to Paul Scherer, Mark Barty-King, Patrick Janson-Smith, of Transworld Publishers Ltd., and all their staff for their continued encouragement and advice while I was writing the book. Once it was delivered I had marvellous editorial advice from Diane Pearson, Broo Doherty and Tom Hartman. Nor could anyone have a more charming, merry or skilful agent than Desmond Elliott. I also owe a special debt of gratitude to my son Felix, who in January 1992 restored the gazebo at the bottom of the garden so I was able to write in blissful seclusion uninterrupted by doorbells or telephones.

Finishing a big book is tremendously exciting and consequently I owe a further huge debt of gratitude to my friends Annette Xuereb-Brennan, Annalise Dobson, Anna Gibbs-Kennet and Marjorie Williams for entering into the spirit by working late into the night typing huge chunks of the manuscript, and often correcting factual mistakes and fearful spelling. Ann Mills was equally marvellous at clearing up after us all without throwing away any vital scribbling.

Nor could the book have been written without the wonderfully soothing presence of my PA, Jane Watts, who listened when I was in despair, provided numerous funny lines and spent hours collating and photostating the manuscript.

Finally, I would most of all like to thank my family, Leo, Felix, Emily, Barbara and Hero. All provided comfort, tolerance and inspiration. Few writers are as privileged.

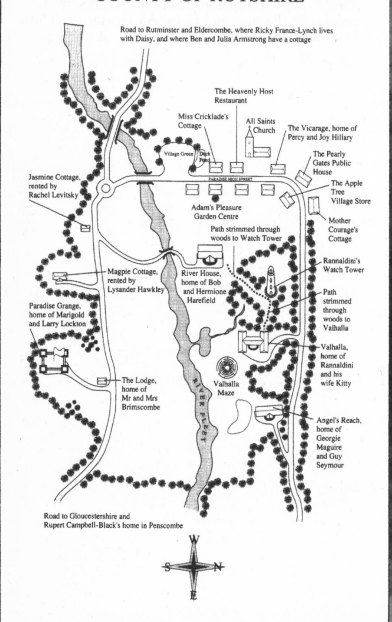

THE VALLEY OF PARADISE IN THE COUNTY OF RUTSHIRE

Road to Rutminster and Eldercombe, where Ricky France-Lynch lives with Daisy, and where Ben and Julia Armstrong have a cottage

The Heavenly Host Restaurant

Miss Cricklade's Cottage

All Saints Church

The Vicarage, home of Percy and Joy Hillary

Village Green
Duck Pond

The Pearly Gates Public House

PARADISE HIGH STREET

The Apple Tree Village Store

Jasmine Cottage, rented by Rachel Levitsky

Adam's Pleasure Garden Centre

Mother Courage's Cottage

Path strimmed through woods to Watch Tower

Rannaldini's Watch Tower

Magpie Cottage, rented by Lysander Hawkley

River House, home of Bob and Hermione Harefield

Path strimmed through woods to Valhalla

Paradise Grange, home of Marigold and Larry Lockton

Valhalla, home of Rannaldini and his wife Kitty

The Lodge, home of Mr and Mrs Brimscombe

Valhalla Maze

RIVER FLEET

Angel's Reach, home of Georgie Maguire and Guy Seymour

Road to Gloucestershire and Rupert Campbell-Black's home in Penscombe

W
S — N
E

CHARACTERS

EDWARD BARTHOLOMEW ALDERTON	A significant grandchild.
ARCHANGEL MIKE	Landlord of The Pearly Gates Public House and captain of Paradise Cricket XI.
JULIA ARMSTRONG	A passionate painter.
BEN ARMSTRONG	Her husband – a caring beard in computers.
ASTRID	A comely Palm Beach groom.
MISS BATES	A temp with tempting ankles.
BEATRICE	A fair flautist misused by Rannaldini.
JAMES BENSON	A very smooth private doctor.
BONNY	A Palm Beach polo groupie.
SABINE BOTTOMLEY	Headmistress of Bagley Hall – a less caring beard.
TEDDY BRIMSCOMBE	Larry Lockton's gardener.
MRS BRIMSCOMBE	His wife.
BUNNY	An ace Gloucestershire vet.
RUPERT CAMPBELL-BLACK	Multi-millionaire owner/ trainer, ex-world show-jumping champion, Mecca for most women.
TAGGIE CAMPBELL-BLACK	His second wife – an angel.
MARCUS CAMPBELL-BLACK	His son – an embryo concert pianist.
TABITHA CAMPBELL-BLACK	His daughter – a teenage tearaway.

13

SEB AND DOMMIE CARLISLE	The heavenly twins. Vastly brave professional polo players, whose serious wildness has been tempered by the recession.
CHLOE CATFORD	Talented mezzo-soprano and Boris Levitsky's mistress.
BLUEY CHARTERIS	Rupert Campbell-Black's first jockey.
LADY CHISLEDEN	An old boot and a pillar of Paradise.
CLIVE	Rannaldini's sinister black-leather-clad henchman.
MRS COLMAN	David Hawkley's secretary – nicknamed 'Mustard' by the boys because she's so keen on him.
CAMERON COOK	A talented television termagent.
MISS CRICKLADE	Winner of the home-made wine class at Paradise Church fête for ten years running.
DANNY	One of Rupert Campbell-Black's stable lads.
DIZZY	Rupert Campbell-Black's head groom. A glamorous divorcée.
FERDINAND FITZGERALD	Fat Ferdie. Lysander Hawkley's best friend and minder. Estate agent and fixer who is riding the recession with a cowboy's skill.
RICKY FRANCE-LYNCH	Polo captain of England.
DAISY FRANCE-LYNCH	His painter wife, a friend of Julia Armstrong.
GERALDINE	Guy Seymour's London secretary.
GRAYDON GLUCKSTEIN	Chairman of the New World Philharmonic Orchestra.
HELEN GORDON	Rupert Cambell-Black's first wife.
BOB HAREFIELD	Orchestra manager of the London Met. A saint.

HERMIONE HAREFIELD	His seriously tiresome wife. Rannaldini's mistress. One of the world's leading sopranos and an applause junkie.
LITTLE COSMO HAREFIELD	A four-year-old fiend.
LYSANDER HAWKLEY	A hero of our time.
DAVID 'HATCHET' HAWKLEY	Lysander's father and an unmerry widower. Headmaster of Fleetley – a top English public school.
DINAH HAWKLEY	An old soak, and the widow of David Hawkley's much older brother, Alastair.
HEINZ	A colourless assistant conductor at the London Met.
THE REVEREND PERCIVAL HILLARY	A portly parson who confines his pastoral visits to drinks time.
JOY HILLARY	His wife. A bossy boots.
BEATTIE JOHNSON	A seductive, totally unprincipled journalist.
FREDDIE JONES	Electronics supremo and director of Venturer Television.
BORIS LEVITSKY	A glamorous, temperamental composer who defected from Russia in the eighties. Assistant conductor at the London Met and lover of red wine, red meat and red-blooded women.
RACHEL LEVITSKY	His English wife. A concert pianist who has sacrificed her career to bring up two children: Vanya and Masha. Performs under her maiden name, Rachel Grant.
LARRY LOCKTON	Chief Executive of Catchitune Records and a rough diamond.

15

MARIGOLD LOCKTON	His once-ravishing wife, who is finding to her cost that rough diamonds are not for ever.
ISAAC LOVELL	A brilliant jump jockey.
SHERRY MACARTHY	A ravishing neglected American wife.
GEORGIE MAGUIRE	A sixties singer/songwriter and sex symbol. Slightly long-in-the-capped tooth, but poised for a massive come-back.
DANCER MAITLAND	A rock star.
MARCIA MELLING	A susceptible divorcée, one of Rupert Campbell-Black's owners.
OSWALDO	A colourful guest conductor of the London Met.
MR PANDOPOULOS	Another of Rupert Campbell-Black's owners.
MRS PIGGOTT	Georgie Maguire's daily. Nicknamed Mother Courage because of her fondness for a pint of beer.
ROBERTO RANNALDINI	One of the world's greatest conductors. Musical director of the London Met and a very evil genius.
KITTY RANNALDINI	His much younger third wife who runs his life like clockwork.
WOLFGANG RANNALDINI	Rannaldini's son from his first marriage, a good sort.
NATASHA RANNALDINI	Rannaldini's daughter from his second marriage: a handful in all senses of the word.
CECILIA RANNALDINI	Rannaldini's second wife and a world famous diva. Given to throwing plates and tantrums.

GUY SEYMOUR   A bishop's son and Georgie Maguire's very decent and rather unlikely husband. Owner of London art gallery and nurser of talent.

FLORA SEYMOUR   Guy's and Georgie's wild child.

MEREDITH WHALEN   A highly expensive gay interior designer, known as the Ideal Homo because he's always being asked as a spare man for deserted wives at Paradise dinner parties.

ELMER WINTERTON   American Security billionaire. Chief executive of Safus Houses Inc. and a philandering Palm Beach polo patron.

MARTHA WINTERTON   His ravishing neglected second wife.

I

Lysander Hawkley appeared to have everything. At twenty-two, he was tall, broad-shouldered, heart-stoppingly handsome, wildly affectionate, with a wall-to-wall smile that withered women. In January 1990 at the finals of a Palm Beach polo tournament, this hero of our time was lying slumped on a Prussian-blue rug in the pony lines sleeping off the excesses of the night before.

The higher the standard of polo the better looking tend to be both grooms and ponies. On this punishingly hot, muggy day, all around Lysander beautiful girls in Prussian-blue shirts and baseball caps were engaged in the frantic activity of getting twenty-four ponies ready for the match. But, trying not to wake him, they swore under their breaths as they bandaged and tacked-up charges driven demented by an invasion of mosquitoes. And, if they could, these beautiful girls would have hushed the thunder that grumbled irritably along the flat, palm-tree fringed horizon.

But Lysander didn't stir – not even when an Argentine groom working for the opposition jumped a pony clean over him on the way to the warm-up area, nor when two of his team mates, the Carlisle twins, Sebastian and Dominic, roared up in a dark green Aston Martin yelling in rage and relief that they'd finally tracked him down.

People loved doing things for Lysander. The grooms had kept their voices down. In the same way Seb and Dommie, both England polo internationals, had persuaded Elmer Winterton, the security billionaire who employed them for the Palm Beach season, to fly Lysander out as a substitute when the fourth member of the team had broken his shoulder in the semi-finals.

'The little fucker,' howled Seb, leaping out of the car, 'after all the trouble we took getting him the job.'

'He rewards us by getting rat-assed,' said Dommie.

Together they gazed indignantly down at Lysander, sprawled lean-hipped and loose-limbed as a lurcher puppy. Lazily he stretched out and raked a mosquito bite in his sleep.

'No-one looking at that angelic inertia,' went on Dommie grimly, 'could imagine his ability for wanton destruction when he's awake.'

'Well, if he channels some of that ability against the opposition we'll be OK,' said Seb, and, picking up a Prussian-blue bucket, he dashed the contents into Lysander's face. 'Come on, Mr Hawkley. This is your wake-up call.'

'What the fuck?' Leaping as though he'd been electrocuted, frantically wiping dirty water out of his eyes, Lysander slowly and painfully focused on two, round, ruffian faces and four dissipated blue eyes glaring down at him from under thick blond fringes.

'Oh, it's you two,' he groaned. 'For a terrible moment I thought I was seeing double. What the hell are you trying to do to me?'

'Nothing to what you're doing to yourself,' said Seb briskly. 'Game starts in half an hour. Get your ass into gear.'

'Did you pull that blonde?' asked Dommie, unbuttoning his grey-striped shirt and selecting a Prussian-blue polo shirt from the back of the Aston Martin.

'I'm not sure,' Lysander's wonderfully smooth, wide forehead wrinkled for a second. 'I went back to her place, certainly, but I've got a terrible feeling I fell asleep on the job. I'd better ring and apologize.'

'Later.' Seb chucked him a polo shirt.

'I bloody can't,' complained Lysander, taking a sodden piece of paper from his shirt pocket. 'She gave me her number but the ink's run. I'd like a tan like that,' he added, admiring Dommie's solidly muscled conker-brown back.

'Well, you won't get one unless you play bloody well this afternoon,' said Seb, stepping out of his jeans. 'Elmer's threatening to send you home on the next plane. The fax in the barn is for business use only. Elmer is desperate for details of some massive Jap deal, and all morning the machine has been spewing out the racing pages of every English newspaper.'

'Oh, great! They've arrived.' Leaping to his feet, Lysander tore off his shirt without bothering to undo any buttons. 'If I get changed quickly, I can have a bet. If Elmer won't let me use the telephone in the barn, can I borrow yours?'

'No, you cannot!' Grabbing Lysander's arm, Seb yanked him back. 'Bloody get dressed and warmed up. We didn't bring you all the way from Fulham to make fools of us.'

'Foolham,' said Lysander. For a moment, his head went back and his big mouth stretched in a roar of laughter showing off wonderfully even teeth. Then he looked perplexed.

'Now, where did I leave my polo gear?'

The opposition team, who were called 'Mr Beefy', consisted of a fast-food tycoon, Butch Murdoch, a good consistent player, and his three Argentine professionals, one of whom, Juan O'Brien, was the greatest player in the world. Wearing red shirts, they were already hitting balls across a field which rippled beneath its heat haze like a vast green lake. A red mobile canteen was handing out free hamburgers to Mr Beefy supporters. Inhaling a waft of frying onions, as he and the twins rode onto the field, Lysander retched and clamped his mouth shut. Unable to find his kit, he was wearing boots that wouldn't zip up, borrowed knee-pads and a too-large hat which kept falling over his perfect nose and which did nothing to deflect a white-hot sun from his murderous headache.

An utterly instinctive horseman, Lysander's polo career had been held back in the past by his ability to be distracted during matches.

'Oh wow, oh wow,' he was now muttering as he took in the glamorous, gold-limbed female supporters, crowding the stands and lolling on the burning bonnets of the Cadillacs and Lincolns lining the field.

'God, I've got a hangover. This horse is *so* over the top,' he grumbled, trying to stop a madly excited chestnut mare taking off as Butch Murdoch's private ambulance manned by an army of paramedics, stormed past to take up position at mid-field.

'Kerr-ist!' Lysander nearly lost his hat as he swung round. 'Look at the legs on that brunette in the pink skirt.'

'More to the point,' Seb lowered his voice, 'see that man in the panama in the second row of the stands. He's an England selector flown specially over to watch you.'

'Really!' Lysander's blue-green eyes widened in wonder.

'So get your finger out.'

'You bet!' Squeezing the chestnut, Lysander galloped off in a cloud of dust, tapping a practice ball effortlessly ahead of him.

'That's not true,' said Dommie who had slightly more principles than Seb.

'Of course it's not,' said Seb. 'But it might take his mind off fieldside crumpet!'

The twins were basically amused by Lysander's antics. In their youth, when they had made more money ripping off rich patrons than by their polo skills, their own wildness had been legendary. But the chill hand of the recession was making patrons more parsimonious and hot horse deals less easy and, as Elmer Winterton paid them a long salary and picked up their expenses, it was very much in their interest that Lysander distinguished himself that afternoon.

And here at last, trailing security guards, and perennially late because he liked to give the impression of being delayed by matters of state, came Elmer Winterton. He was followed by a private ambulance even larger than Mr Beefy's and manned by more paramedics.

Elmer's company, Safus, not only produced the Safus House which was allegedly so well secured that no intruder could break in, but also specialized in screening high-risk computers for the American government and industry. Elmer could frequently be heard boasting that only he knew the passwords to the nation's most crucial secrets.

Having flown several senators and their wives down from Washington by private jet to watch him play, he was desperate that his team should win the cup under the Prussian-blue Safus colours.

Dark, swarthy, squat, with eyebrows that without ferocious plucking would have met in the middle, Elmer had mean, small eyes and a long nose that jerked up at the end like a white rhinoceros. He also displayed the rhino's erratic belligerence and was so unable to control his overbred ponies that he was as likely to crash into his own side as the opposition.

It would be hard to have been uglier or a worse rider than Elmer, as he lumbered on to the field intolerably pounding the kidneys of his delicate dapple-grey pony, but such were his power and riches that the gold-limbed girl groupies licked their lips and rolled their shorts up an inch or two higher as he passed.

The heat was stifling. To the west, sinister black clouds advanced like a procession of Benedictine monks. Shaggy palm trees quivered with stillness above the mushroom-brown houses that flanked the outfield. As sweating ponies lined up and the umpire chucked the ball into a shifting forest of legs, Lysander could be heard saying, 'I wonder if Elmer's paramedics have got any Fernet-Branca.'

By half-time, Safus was trailing 2–8 and Lysander was dying of shame. Not having played since last summer, he was scuppered by hangover and the cauldron heat of Palm Beach after a freezing English winter. Unused to such fast well-bred ponies or such hard dry ground, he had had a terrible three chukkas. Mr Beefy's three Argentine hired assassins hadn't allowed him near the ball. Nor were matters helped by Elmer barging around like some geriatric in an ancient Mini, who keeps pulling in front of faster drivers on the motorway. Of the eight goals scored by Mr Beefy, six had been penalties awarded against Elmer. Elmer was also aware that a photographer, hired by the Safus PR Department, was videoing the entire game to show at the sales conference next month and he hadn't touched the ball once.

'I pay for this fucking team,' he was now yelling at Seb and Dommie in the pony lines, 'and I'm going to fucking well hit the fucking ball as much as I fucking well like, and as for him,' he stabbed a stubby finger at a cringing Lysander, 'hired assassin indeed. Hired asshole more likely, that son of a bitch couldn't assassinate a fly.'

Matching Elmer's mood, the black clouds now hovered above the pony lines like a vast impenetrable yew hedge. Lysander's eyes and throat were lined with dust. He'd towelled off a bucket of sweat as he came off the field, and now he was wringing wet again.

Comfort, however, was at hand from a honey-blond groom called Astrid.

'Don't listen to Elmer,' she told Lysander, 'and don't be fooled by this mare. She doesn't have brakes, but she sure is fast,' she added as she pulled down the stirrups of a mean-looking yellow pony, whose coat quivered irritably against the flies.

'What's she called?' Lysander asked listlessly as he put his foot in the stirrup.

'Mrs Ex, after Elmer's ex-wife,' said Astrid, jumping to avoid the mare's darting teeth, 'because she's always bombing around causing trouble.'

'Surprised he got anyone to marry him,' shuddered Lysander, gathering up his reins and his stick.

In defence of her master Mrs Ex put in a terrific buck. Next moment Lysander was sitting on the ground.

'See what I mean,' bellowed Elmer, 'that asshole can't even stay on a fucking horse. Get the paramedic. He'll certify the guy injured and we can put in a sub.'

But the fall had sobered Lysander. Vaulting on to Mrs Ex, he galloped back into the fray. In the fourth chukka, Dommie and Seb both scored twice, and Lysander once. Then Mr Beefy's Argentines rallied and Lysander was so transfixed with admiration for Juan O'Brien's forehand pass that he completely forgot to mark the number two player to whom Juan was passing.

'Take the bloody man, Lysander,' screamed Dommie. But he was too late, the number two had scored.

Three minutes later to placate Elmer, who was belly-aching about being the only member of the Safus team not to have scored, Dommie dropped a ball a foot in front of him and bang in front of the goal.

'Take your time, Elmer,' he shouted, galloping upfield in support.

'Elmer Winterton is looking awful good,' said the commentator.

Elmer took a swipe, missed, and, losing his temper, started to beat his pony.

'Hi,' yelled Lysander, thundering across the field, 'that is absolutely not on.'

'It absolutely isn't on, is it, you little fuckwit.' Elmer mimicked Lysander's English accent. 'I can hit anything I want,' and raising his stick he took a furious swipe at Lysander who promptly lifted his stick in retaliation.

'Stop it,' roared Seb.

Fortunately, like a bucket of water over a dogfight, the dense black cloud keeled over in a tidal wave. Like cats, the spectators shot into their cars. Most of the players, particularly the Argentines, who detested rain, would have followed suit. But Lysander felt only blessed relief. For the first time in forty-eight hours he was cool and he was utterly used to playing in the rain.

'Lysander Hawkley is looking awful good,' crackled the loudspeaker a minute later. 'He's got the line and he's really motoring on Elmer Winterton's yellow pony. Oh, where are you going, Lysander?'

Shying at one of Mr Beefy's white-and-red paper napkins which had blown on to the field, Mrs Ex had taken off through the downpour carting Lysander, who was whooping with laughter, past Elmer's and Mr Beefy's ambulances, beyond the goal posts and goal judge off into the Everglades. Three minutes later, he cantered back, still roaring his head off.

'When a horse takes off, there's not much you can do. The only thing that stopped Mrs Ex was a huge croc on the river bank. I thought it was one of your security guards. Sir,' he added hastily seeing the sudden fury in Elmer's beady little eyes.

Fortunately Mrs Ex's turn of speed proved more effective going the other way. Hanging on Lysander's hands like an express train, she whisked him past three outraged Argentines, which enabled him to lean right out of the saddle and flick the ball between the red-and-white posts with a glorious, offside cut shot.

As the bell went for the end of the fifth chukka the crowd hooted approval from the inside of their cars. Riding back to the pony lines through the deluge Lysander noticed a lone spectator huddling in the stands beneath the totally inadequate protection of a Prussian-blue Safus umbrella. Catching a glimpse of long brown legs Lysander recognized the brunette in the pink skirt he'd admired earlier. Returning for the last chukka, he carried a spare blue rug which had kept dry in Elmer's trailer.

'Oh, how darling of you,' said the brunette as he jumped off and spread it over her legs.

Her hair, the rich brown of soy sauce, fell in dripping rats' tails. The rain intensified the dark freckles that polka-dotted her thin face and arms. She was shivering like a dog in a vet's waiting room.

'You should be inside your car,' reproved Lysander.

'My husband likes to know where I am, in case he breaks a mallet.' The girl pointed to three spare polo

26

sticks propped against the low white fence in front of her.

'Lucky bloke,' sighed Lysander.

'Lysander,' called Seb sharply.

Glancing round, Lysander saw the other players were already lined up for the throw-in and galloped over to join them.

'Don't chat up girls in the middle of a game,' said Seb in a furious undertone, 'particularly when they're the patron's wife.'

'She's married to Elmer?' asked Lysander, appalled.

'Yup, and unless we win, he'll take it out on her afterwards.'

In the last chukka, with Mr Beefy only one goal ahead, the tension got to both sides. Then Juan O'Brien swore so badly at the umpire for ignoring one of Elmer's more blatant fouls that the umpire retaliated by awarding a penalty against Juan.

As Seb took the hit for Safus, Lysander belted back to the pony lines to change horses and have another look at Elmer's wife. The way her white silk shirt was clinging to her body was nothing short of spectacular. How could she have married such an ape?

While Seb circled his pony then clouted the ball between the posts, Juan O'Brien came off the back line and blocked the shot with his pony's shoulder. Lysander winced. He'd seen players stop goals with their pony's heads. Enraged, he galloped upfield, picked up the ball, played cat and mouse with it, hit it in the air, before slamming it between the posts. The spectators honked their horns in ecstasy.

The storm had passed. Ponies steamed. Bits, stirrups and the huge silver cup on its red tablecloth glittered in the returning sun.

'I guess Safus is going to stage a come-back situation,' said the commentator.

Juan O'Brien guessed otherwise. In the closing seconds of the game he roared downfield, black curls streaming under his hat, swinging his stick, driving the ball gloriously before him, then, unmarked and overconfident, just in front of goal he hit wide.

Pouncing, Lysander backed the ball upfield to Seb who passed to Dommie, who carried on through the puddles until he encountered a wall of Argentine resistance and hastily cut the ball to a furiously racing-up Lysander, who met it gloriously. With twenty seconds on the clock, Lysander was perfectly poised to score the winning goal but, seeing Elmer scowling red-faced in front of the posts, and remembering Elmer's drenched wife, who would get hell after the game, he passed instead to Elmer. The twins groaned in disbelief, but, by some miracle, on the bell Elmer managed to coax the ball between the posts.

All Elmer's senators, flown down by private jet, who'd been wondering what the hell to say to him after the game, cheered with deafening relief. The company cameraman decided not to shoot himself after all. At last he had a clip he could show at the sales conference and later he was able to film Elmer brandishing the huge silver cup while his beautiful wife clapped so enthusiastically that she spilled champagne down her pink skirt.

Back at Elmer's barn, Lysander, having drunk a great deal of Moët from the cup, hazily checked the legs of his ponies, thanking them profusely as he plied them with Polo mints. He then thanked the grooms with equal enthusiasm and passed round the individual magnum of Moët he'd been given as a member of the winning team.

'You're certainly flavour of the month,' said Astrid. 'Elmer reckons you're the best Brit he's ever played with. He wants you to stay on for the Rolex next month.'

In moments of excitement Lysander could do little more than open and shut his mouth.

'Really?' he gasped finally.

'Really!' Pretending to buckle under the weight, Astrid handed him a sheaf of faxes. 'Here are your racing pages.'

'I'd forgotten those!' Lysander gave a whoop of joy. 'Now I can have a bet.'

'No you can't!' Seb marched in, already changed, with his hair slicked back from the shower. 'It's nearly midnight in England and the only thing racing at the moment is the very unblue blood through Elmer's veins. In between copies of *Sporting Life* the fax managed to spew out confirmation of his Jap deal. Elmer is several million bucks richer now and he wants to party. So move it.'

'But I want to get pissed with this lot.' Lysander gazed wistfully at Astrid.

'Lysander,' said Seb wearily, 'you want to play polo for a living. If you're prepared to be charming and diplomatic, you can brownnose your way into riding some of the most fabulous horses in the world, but for a start lay off Elmer's wife and his grooms.'

'He sure is the cutest guy,' sighed Astrid as Lysander was dragged protesting away.

2

The party was held in one of the soft brown houses clustering round the polo field. Male guests ranged from lithe, bronzed, professional polo players of all nationalities to rich businessmen, some of them patrons, some of who merely liked to be part of the polo scene. The women included glamorous groupies of all ages, wearing everything from T-shirts and jeans to strapless dresses showing off massive jewels.

The feeling of jungle warfare was intensified by the forest of glossy green tropical plants in every room and by the fact that all the professionals were on the prowl for rich patrons, and the patrons, despite having wives present, were stalking the prettiest groupies who were, in turn, hunting anything in trousers.

Loud cheers greeted the arrival of the Safus team.

'If you have oats, prepare to sow them now,' murmured Seb as the cheering died away and a hush fell over the room.

'Talk about Elmer's angels,' drawled a predatory blonde in a fire-engine-red dress licking her scarlet lips.

Elmer, mean little eyes flickering with rage, was the only person who didn't laugh. He'd kept on his brown boots and white breeches which the game had hardly marked, so that everyone should know he was a polo player, but had changed into a clean blue Safus polo shirt. As groupies started edging through the vegetation towards the rest of his team, Elmer, competitive as ever, was determined to annex the prettiest. Soon he was bosom to pectorals with a mettlesome brunette called Bonny whose bottom lip protruded more than any of the scented orchids massed in the centre of the living room, and whose buttocks swelled out of the briefest white shorts like an inverted Nell Gwyn.

Refusing to admit how blind he was without glasses, Elmer had to peer very closely to see the logo on her jutting orange T-shirt.

'*If you can read this,*' he spelled out slowly, then peering even closer, '*You're a dirty old man.*'

Bonny shrieked with laughter. Reluctantly Elmer decided to join in. 'That's kinda neat.'

'Yours is neater,' said Bonny. 'That deep blue is just great with your eyes. Has anyone told you how like Richard Gere you are? I'd give anything for a Safus T-shirt.'

'Swappyer then,' said Elmer.

'He'd never have stripped off in public,' muttered Seb, 'if he hadn't got a Barbados suntan and just lost ten pounds, none of it admittedly off his ego, on a pre-season crash diet. Jeees-us.' He choked on his drink as Bonny's head disappeared into the orange T-shirt and her upstretched wriggling arms showed off a pair of magnificent brown breasts.

Elmer's eyes were popping like a garrotted Pekinese. The orange T-shirt, once he had wriggled into it, clashed with his port-wine face but in no way doused his lust.

'I see your picture every time I pick up the *Wall Street Journal*,' Bonny was now telling him. 'But you are so much cuter in the flesh.'

'The flesh is weak where lovely young women like you are concerned,' said Elmer thickly.

The logo on Lysander's faded grey T-shirt read:

Sex is evil,
Evil is sin,
Sin's forgiven
So get stuck in.

He was getting drunker by the minute and had now been

cornered by two stunning but interchangeable suntanned blondes.

'Did you fly commercial?' asked the first.

Lysander looked blank.

'She's trying to figure if you came over by private jet, preferably your own,' explained the second.

'Oh, right,' said Lysander. 'No, I flew Virgin. The air hostesses were really sweet.'

'Surprised they were still intacta with you on board,' said the first.

Glancing round for a waitress with a bottle, Lysander caught sight of Martha Winterton. Shaded by a vast yucca, she was chatting mindlessly to a senator's wife and trying not to watch Elmer. Her desolation was tangible.

'You're not really a good friend of George Bush?' Bonny was growing more raucous. 'I would just love to meet him.'

'It could be arranged.' Elmer's pudgy right hand was surreptitiously stroking her left buttock as they leant side by side against a dragged yellow wall.

The senator's wife had drifted off to talk to Butch Murdoch. Martha was gazing despairingly into her empty glass. Oblivious of Seb's stern warning that trespassers would be put on the next plane, Lysander crossed the room.

'Have you dried off?'

Martha jumped. Her huge eyes, the clear brown of Tio Pepe held up to the light, were swimming with tears. It was a second before she recognized him.

'Oh sure – it was so dear of you to bring me that blanket.'

She had a husky, hesitant voice. Her creased white shirt still clung to her body. Her dark hair, which had dried all fluffy, was pulled back in a bandeau making her freckled face look even thinner.

'You needed a lifeboat,' said Lysander.

'I could use one now.'

'Have a drink first.'

As Lysander grabbed a bottle from a passing waitress, Martha noticed a badge saying: 'Birthday Boy' pinned to his grey T-shirt. Clutching her glass of champagne as though it was boiling tea and she a shipwreck victim, she took a great gulp.

'There's a nice fire in the garden,' said Lysander seeing the goose-flesh on her thin freckled arms.

Outside, the dull aquamarine of the swimming-pool reflected a few faint stars. Rain had bowed down the hibiscus and the oleander bushes, but their flowers, pink, red, amethyst and yellow, glistened jewel-like in the flood-lighting. Great drenched pelts of purple and magenta bougainvillaea clung to the house and the garden fences.

To an almost overpowering scent of orange and lemon blossom was added a tempting smell of roast pork, garlic and rosemary as half a dozen sucking pigs jerked above the glowing coals of the barbecue. Apart from an inscrutable Mexican houseboy who occasionally plunged a skewer into their shining gold sides, the place was deserted.

Caressed by the warm night air Lysander gave a sigh of pure joy.

'Such bliss to go outside and not shiver, but I expect it's cold for you.' Solicitously, he edged her towards the fire.

'Poor little things,' Martha looked sadly at the sucking pigs, then, pulling herself together, 'You're kinda tanned for someone just arrived from England.'

'It's fake,' confessed Lysander, lifting the light brown hair flopping over his forehead. 'Look how it's streaked on the hairline and turned my eyebrows orange. I borrowed the stuff from Dolly, my girlfriend. She's a model and always having to turn herself strange colours. I wanted to terrorize everyone into thinking I'd got brown playing in Argentina all winter. But I was pissed when I put it on last night.'

She's so sweet when she smiles, he thought. To hell with Seb and Dommie.

'And it's your birthday?' she asked.

'No,' Lysander glanced down at his birthday-boy badge, 'but it gets me lots of free drinks.' He opened his blue-green eyes very wide and then roared with such infectious laughter that people standing in doorways and sitting in windows and even the inscrutable Mexican houseboy looked up and smiled.

'When is your birthday?' asked Martha.

'25 February, I shall be twenty-three.'

'You're a Pisces.'

Lysander nodded. 'Friendly, warm, considerate, easy-going, but cross me and you'll see how tough I can be. My father who's a classical scholar pronounces it, "Piss-ces".'

'What does your daddy do?'

'He's a headmaster. Supposed to be a great teacher, but he spends most of his time raising funds and wowing mothers.'

'Does your mother wow the fathers?'

For a second an expression of utter anguish spilled over the boy's sunny, innocent, charming face. Shutting his eyes he took a couple of deep breaths as though trying to survive some horrific torture without crying out.

'She just died,' he mumbled, 'last October.'

'Ohmigod!' Martha put a hand on his arm which was clenched like cast iron, 'Whatever happened?'

'She had a fall on the road. The horse went up. She wasn't wearing a hard hat.'

As the Mexican plunged in another skewer the boiling fat dripped on to the red coals which hissed and flared up, lighting Lysander's face like a soul in hell.

'You poor little guy,' said Martha. 'Were you very close?'

Lysander nodded. 'She was more like my sister. All my friends were in love with her.'

'Your father must have been devastated.'

Lysander's face hardened. 'Dad doesn't show his feelings. Basically we don't talk. He prefers my brothers, Hector and Alexander. They're better at things.'

From inside the house the band struck up. 'I get no kick from champagne,' crooned a mellow tenor.

'I do,' said Lysander, emptying the bottle into Martha's glass.

'What d'you do?' asked Martha.

'Estate agent.'

'Not much fun with the recession.'

'Best thing that ever happened to him.'

Gliding up, Seb Carlisle topped up both their glasses. 'Recession enables Rip-Off Van Winkle here to sleep and sober up all day in the office when he's not ringing Ladbroke's or sloping off home to watch *Neighbours*. He couldn't do any of that if he had to sell houses.'

'Oh shut up, Seb,' said Lysander. 'Now guard Martha for a minute.'

Turning, he was nearly sent flying by the predatory blonde in the fire-engine-red dress.

'If you've finished with your toy boy,' she said pointedly to Martha, 'I'd love to dance with him.'

'You're sweet,' said Lysander, 'but I must have a slash.'

'He's just adorable.' Martha watched Lysander drifting gracefully as smoke across the lawn.

'Isn't he?' agreed Seb. 'Unfortunately his boss put him on commission only and as he's not selling any houses he's running up terrible debts, betting and going out clubbing every night.'

'He ought to do something else.'

'He's about to go to a new job working in the City for some merchant bank which specializes in pretty, personable young men; but he'll never last. He's not cut out for the City. He ought to be a jump jockey or a polo player. You saw what a beautiful horseman he was this afternoon, but it took him four chukkas to get his act together.'

'He's very upset about his mother.'

'Devastated,' agreed Seb. 'Completely lost his base, drinking himself stupid; can't settle to anything. Unlike his pompous achieving brothers, he's pretty dyslexic and he left school without an O level. His mother spoilt him rotten – the worse the prank the more she laughed, but she always bailed him out when he ran out of money. Pity Elmer can't sign him up for the whole season. Pedro Cavanali broke his leg falling on the boards this afternoon. He plays medium goal with Elmer.'

'I'll see what I can do,' said Martha.

The Mexican had carved two of the sucking pigs. Maids were carrying bowls of salad and baked potatoes through to the dining room as Lysander bounded through the french windows brandishing another bottle.

'Clear the lawn for ballet,' he shouted, then standing on one leg executed a pirouette, spilling a lot of champagne and only just avoided collapsing on the grass.

'You need an early night,' said Seb pointedly.

Inside the house, Lysander could see Elmer bending over Bonny, playing with the ends of her hair, no doubt boasting that Mrs Ex's equine ancestors had come over in the *Mayflower*.

'I'll stick around,' said Lysander.

'Well, at least behave yourself,' warned Seb.

'Some hope,' said Dommie, who wandered over tearing the flesh off the leg of a sucking pig with very white teeth. 'Grub's up. It's very good, although,' he dropped his voice so only Seb could hear, 'our patron seems to have started already. He's eating that slag alive.'

Going towards the house, Martha caught sight of Elmer and went into reverse.

'That Bonny's a bucket,' said Lysander in outrage. 'You're much, much prettier.'

'She's newer.' Martha took out a cigarette with a trembling hand. 'Have you got a light?'

Lysander hadn't, but, before Martha could stop him he'd plunged a twenty-dollar bill into the coals of the barbecue.

'You're crazy but awful sweet,' reproached Martha, as he almost burnt his fingers getting the charred paper to her cigarette in time, but she was too immersed in her own misery.

'It's my fault,' she confessed. 'My last husband was faithful and dull and I was bored out of my skull, so I ran off with Elmer, who had a roving eye and I haven't slept since.'

'Elmer's a shit,' said Lysander with such disapproval that Martha looked up. 'Dad was a shit to my mother and he's already found someone else, a Mrs Colman, an army widow. She's got veiny ankles and wears shirts with pie-frill collars,' he went on in disgust. 'The boys call her "Mustard" because she's so keen on Dad. She helps him fund-raise. They're turning the stables where Mum kept her horses into a new music school.'

'The speed with which Mrs Ex carted you this afternoon,' said Martha bitterly, 'is only equalled by the haste with which men shack up if they're divorced or widowed, or bored with their wives. Oh God, no!'

Following her gaze, Lysander saw Bonny run off shrieking excitedly into the wet depths of the shrubbery followed by Elmer.

'Could you bear to take me home?'

'Oh wow, that's like offering me a ride in the National,' said Lysander. 'Could I bear? I certainly could.' Then, seeing Seb beadily advancing on them with two platefuls of food, 'Look, I don't want the twins getting heavy. Let's escape through the garden.'

3

The full moon was rising rose-coloured like the inside of a pink grapefruit. Martha's limo was apple green, open and very long with the number plate: MARTHA 30.

'Elmer gave it me for my thirtieth birthday. That was when he was doing everything to prise me away from my ex. Hardly the ideal gift to hide under one's mattress!'

In her distress Martha grazed an incoming Cadillac as she stormed out of the car-park. Lysander slumped beside her, gazing at the stars, which seemed to be shooting around a lot, tunelessly singing: 'A Groovy Kind of Love'.

Elmer's house in the heart of smart Palm Beach was surrounded by a thick, impenetrable ficus hedge. Two scowling security guards, restraining snarling Dobermanns, gave Lysander a malevolent once-over as they opened massive electric gates.

'Friendly fellows,' observed Lysander as they glided through a huge shadowy garden filled with darkly dipping trees. 'What are those dishes on those big black poles?'

'Microwave units to pick up on any intruder. There are also sensors under the lawn. Not a rabbit or a racoon goes undetected. Inside the ficus hedge is hidden a chain-link fence topped with razor wire and an electronic intrusion detector.'

'I'd guard someone like you,' said Lysander.

'Not me, himself,' said Martha flatly. 'Safus screens high-risk computers, Elmer's sewn up most of the Government contracts. As only he holds the password to all the computer installations, he needs protection twenty-four hours a day. No-one breaks in here.'

Ahead, ghostly in the moonlight, rose Elmer's pale pink fortress, so like nougat that Lysander felt he ought to take a large bite out of it to sober himself up.

'Amazing place.'

'Was,' said Martha bitterly. 'One of the oldest houses in Palm Beach stood on this site. Elmer razed it and built another. He's not into longevity.'

Going into the living room, Lysander found himself gazing into the mouth of a cannon and ducked.

'That thing was fired in the Civil War,' said Martha.

'Nearly as old as Elmer. Why the hell did you marry him?'

'I was called in to redecorate his office. Underneath a big desk you don't see a guy's clay feet.'

Only marred by too many photographs of Elmer fraternizing with the famous, the room was charmingly decorated in pale golds as though Midas had idly trailed his fingers over sofas, carpets, walls and huge bunches of deeply scented yellow roses. On an easel was a half-finished portrait of Elmer looking virile. The two ponies he was riding and leading were only roughly sketched in.

'God, you've flattered him,' grumbled Lysander.

'It's not finished. He can't decide which pony he wants to ride.'

'Cut out holes; then he can ride a different one each day. Did you do that?' Lysander turned to the waving corn field above the fireplace.

'No, that's by Van Gogh.'

'Yours is better. And much better than that one.'

'That's Paul Klee,' said Martha in gentle reproof. 'It cost several million dollars.'

'Really.' Astounded, Lysander peered at it again. 'Perhaps I should take up painting.'

They were interrupted by another huge Dobermann hurtling into the room, fangs bared, growling horribly.

39

'Stay, Tyson,' screamed Martha. 'Don't touch him.'

But Lysander went straight up to the dog, hand outstretched.

'Hallo boy, aren't you beautiful?'

Disarmed by such genuine admiration, Tyson, after a few dubious growls, started wagging his stubby tail and writhing his shiny solid black body against Lysander.

'That dog is a serial killer,' said Martha in amazement. 'Elmer and Nancy, his ex, have endless legal tussles over him. Nancy has custody and Elmer visitation rights on weekends, but he's always playing polo so the dog goes crazy. Now Nancy's threatening to take it to a dog shrink in New York so that's another two thousand dollars a month. She should pay you instead,' she added as Tyson collapsed in an ecstatic heap at Lysander's feet.

After a very disapproving butler had opened a bottle of Dom Perignon for them, Martha, who was still shivering uncontrollably, went off to change, leaving Lysander with the telephone. Instinctively he started to dial the number at home, then stopped with a moan of pain, remembering that the only person in the world he really wanted to talk to would never pick up a telephone again.

The only changing Martha had done when she returned twenty minutes later was to put on an old olive-green cardigan with the buttons done up all wrong. Lysander was encouraged that she smelled of toothpaste, but her eyes were very red.

'Did you get through?' she asked.

'I did. I rang Ferdie my flatmate in Fulham to see if my dog Jack was OK. He is, and Dolly, my girlfriend, is modelling in Paris.' Lysander looked cast down. 'Neither of them was remotely pleased.'

'Hardly surprising. It's four o'clock in the morning in Europe.'

'That must be it,' said Lysander, cheering up. 'Anyway Ferdie did read out Mystic Meg – she does the horoscopes in the *News of the World* and she's seriously on the crystal ball. She says Pisces will find happiness with someone with freckles.'

Martha didn't register. Chain-smoking, she jumped every time the telephone rang, then, because the butler answered, bit her lip when it wasn't Elmer and slumped back on the yellow and crimson striped sofa.

'All husbands have mistresses these days like they have faxes and mobiles and they can't think how they ever existed without them.' The drink was really getting to her now, her soft husky voice was shrill, with the words rattling out like machine-gun fire.

'D'you know what's really causing the recession?' she demanded. 'Pandemic adultery – Tom Wolfe's "tidal wave of concupiscence". A guy is so busy deceiving his wife and his PA, who's probably another mistress anyway, he can't concentrate. How can you put your back into work when you're sticking your dick into some bimbo all the time?'

Although his hands were busy stroking an ecstatic Tyson, Lysander found his knees edging towards Martha's.

'I'd never have taken up with Elmer,' she went on hysterically, 'if he hadn't painted such a dire picture of his marriage; how Nancy neglected him and never slept with him. Then after Elmer and I were married Nancy dumped in *Vanity Fair* and I realized she'd adored him and been absolutely wiped out. She called me one evening when she was drunk, to tell me he was a clinical narcissist and I'd never satisfy him. All her friends were there this evening. They'll be on to her first thing: "You held him for twenty-five years, Nancy, Martha couldn't hold him for as many weeks".' She gave a sob.

'What's pandemic?' asked Lysander.

But Martha had beaten the butler to the telephone.

'Oh, hi.' She was poised between tears and a screaming match. 'I didn't want to spoil your fun. No, no.' She was apologetic now. 'I wasn't implying anything.'

Lysander could now hear Elmer yelling. Martha seemed to slump.

'OK, right, sleep well.' Slowly she replaced the receiver.

41

'Elmer's over the limit. He's spending the night at the barn.'

'Yippee.' Lysander hugged Tyson. 'Let's have another bottle.'

'And he's got a dozen guards who could drive him home if he wanted. He's only drunk with lust. I guess he and that tramp were bouncing around in the Jacuzzi when he called me. That would have given him a charge.'

She burst into tears.

Lysander was a shining example of the continued existence of the age of chivalry. He hadn't read endless articles in the women's pages about the caddish chauvinism of his sex, he had never heard of New Man or sexual harassment. His heart entirely ruled his head. Anything in distress moved him and just as he had gathered up poor, miserably disturbed, aggressively insecure Tyson, now he bounded over to Martha.

'Don't cry. You're so beautiful and he's such a toad.'

Folding her into his warm, tender embrace, he tried to still her trembling body, smoothing away tears and mascara with his thumbs; then, when she still sobbed, comforting her in the only way he understood by kissing her smudged quivering mouth. For a second she fought him off, then, desperate for reassurance, she gradually responded to his wonderful enthusiasm.

Her skin was as smooth and silken as her shirt but, as he started undoing her buttons, she jumped away.

'I'm too skinny. Elmer says I'm like an ironing board with two buttons sewn on to tell you which the front is.'

Lysander winced, then drew her back into his arms. 'All the better to press my suit on.' Then, as Martha smiled, 'I'm going to kiss every freckle.'

'You'll be here for a thousand years.'

'Wouldn't be long enough. Let's go upstairs.'

'We shouldn't.'

'We can't fight Mystic Meg.'

Tyson, however, in true Dobermann fashion, refused to let Lysander out of the room until his basket had been carried up to the bedroom and he'd been settled in with strokes and Bonios which gave Martha time to undress and hide herself under the ivy-green silk sheets of the vast emerald and white striped four-poster. Books were piled high on her bedside table. On the other side there stood only a digital clock and a silver-framed photograph of Elmer and George Bush.

'Elmer only reads balance sheets and the messages on T-shirts,' said Martha with a sob.

'Hush, don't think about him.'

Still in his clothes, Lysander waded through a pampas-grass of long white carpet and gently drew back the sheets. Instantly Martha's thin arms flew to her tiny breasts. But, like Aladdin stumbling on his cave and touching each gold bar, precious stone and rope of pearls with amazed joy and excitement, Lysander slowly examined her body, stroking her nipples and her concave belly and breathing in the remains of Diorella behind her ears and inside her wrists.

'Christ, you're gorgeous!' He ran his hands up the inside of her long slender legs. 'I freaked when I first saw these in the stands.'

Dropping his clothes on the floor, he stripped off with total unselfconsciousness and rightly so because he was glorious, with a body as white, firmly curved and inviting on those emerald-green sheets, as early morning mushrooms in a dew-drenched field. His well-developed chest with a slight down of light brown hair narrowed to the flattest stomach and more downy hair from which his cock reared up as jaunty and as confident of bringing joy as a conductor's baton raised for action.

'I've only been married five months,' mumbled Martha. 'We really shouldn't.'

'We should, too.'

'Wouldn't Dolly be upset?'

'Probably, but basically I can't help myself.'

His fake tan was turning orange, his bluey-green eyes were crossing with drink, but, as the big laughing mouth

43

came down on hers, Martha was reduced to the same slobbering ecstasy as Tyson.

Wriggling down the bed, Lysander kissed the arch of her instep, each coral-painted toe, then slowly, slowly up the velvet thighs, feeling the increasing tension as his hands grazed her breasts and shaven armpits, never stopping caressing.

'We really shouldn't,' said Martha faintly.

Reaching out Lysander turned the photograph of Elmer and George Bush to the wall.

'We don't need an audience.'

Then, plunging his face into her pubic hair, snuffling as appreciatively as a truffle pig, he mumbled, 'As I was saying to Martha's bush.'

Feeling him helpless with laughter, she had to join in, but soon her laughter turned to gasps. Only when he knew she'd come did he keep her pleasure on the boil with half a minute of slowly stabbing fingers.

'Come inside me,' urged Martha.

'Just wait a sec, while I slip into something tight,' murmured Lysander, reaching for a condom from the back pocket of his jeans. Then as joyously as an otter diving into a summer stream he plunged his cock inside her.

'Oh wow, that was terrific,' said Martha as they lay back afterwards, sharing a cigarette.

'I didn't get a Christmas bonus because I didn't sell any houses so it's been worth waiting till January. You are so lovely.' Lysander kissed her hand.

'How come you are such an incredible lover?'

'Basically, Dolly taught me a lot. One of the advantages of having an older woman.'

'How old is she?' Martha snuggled against his chest.

'Twenty-four.'

'Ouch.'

'But she started at fourteen, so there's a lot of mileage. Look, I just adored sleeping with you.'

'Me too.' Martha found she couldn't keep her hands off him.

Noticing polo bruises darkening his ribs, arms and thighs like the purple markings on a white violet, she wanted to kiss them all better and explore in return his wonderful body.

'You're a really sweet guy with the softest heart and the hardest cock.'

'Better than the other way round.' Lysander dropped ash on the pampas-grass. 'I wish I was someone who could go on for hours, but I get so excited, particularly when it's someone like you. Dolly always makes me stay awake afterwards and stroke her for ages. I find that the most difficult part.' His voice was slurring, his eyelids drooping. 'Let's do it again in a minute. Will you come with me to Disneyland tomorrow? I want to get Donald Duck's autograph.'

Martha removed the cigarette as he fell asleep.

4

Elmer Winterton's evening had deteriorated. Bonny, having consumed too much champagne and sucking pig, had suddenly lurched out of the Jacuzzi and for want of a bowl had thrown up in Elmer's fish-tank. Whereupon his piranhas had swarmed up to the surface and eaten the lot which had turned Elmer's stomach. Feeling a longing for his shy slender wife, he had been prevented from going straight home by Bonny passing out. Not trusting his guards at the barn not to blab he was reduced to driving her thirty miles home himself.

None of his guards in the gate house felt like telling Elmer he had a houseguest. It was only after he had noticed a T-shirt warning him: *Sex is Evil* on his bedroom carpet that he glanced up and found his number one player and his wife as enchantingly entwined as Cupid and Psyche.

For the second time in twenty-four hours, Lysander was roused from sleep. But Elmer, red and roaring, was a considerably less attractive alarm clock than the twins.

'I don't employ you on my team to hump my wife,' he howled.

'Didn't secure her very well, you fat ape,' howled back Lysander. 'How can you chase disgusting slags like that when you've got something so beautiful at home?'

That Lysander was right didn't improve Elmer's temper. Gathering up a bowl from a table by the door, he was about to hurl it at Lysander.

'Not the Ming, Elmer,' wailed Martha.

Elmer paused, which gave Lysander time to wriggle over Martha, scoop up her pale pink silk knickers as a

46

fig leaf, and shoot round the bed out of the room just as a glass bottle of Jolie Madame missing him by inches, smashed against the dragged green wall.

'Not out,' squealed Lysander, belting across the landing and down the stairs three steps at a time to find the front door quadrupally locked, whichever way he pulled and tugged it. For an agonizing second he was reminded how his father used to bolt the great oak door at home and his mother used to steal down the back stairs to let him in through the kitchen. Then he jumped out of his totally unprotected skin as shots rang out, shattering the chandelier in the hall. Grabbing a bronze of Elmer astride a polo pony from the hall table, like a weightlifter on a second surge of strength, he hurled it at the window. But the bullet-proof glass didn't even dent. Instead, like a mass castration of howler monkeys, an ear-splitting alarm blasted the house.

'Oh, shut up.' Lysander clutched his head, then jumped as steel shutters clanged like guillotines across the windows and the outside doors.

Frantically checking the ground floor, he found every exit blocked and himself back in the hall.

'Try and escape, you son of a bitch,' bellowed Elmer, reappearing on the landing.

As Lysander ducked behind a large fern, bullets buried themselves in the panelling behind him. Diving for a side door, he raced up some stairs. Behind him he could hear shouting and dogs baying; he was going to be ripped apart. Bolting round the circular landing, deterring an approaching Dobermann by hurling a cheese plant, he shot into Martha's bedroom.

'Dum, di di, dum di, dum di dum di.'

Giggling hysterically, gasping out the James Bond tune, Lysander snaked under the green silk sheet, pulling a pillow over his head.

'Gemme out of here.'

In answer, half-crying, half-laughing, Martha ripped off the sheet, shoved a swipe card into his hands, then, sliding open a wardrobe, dived through a dense forest of dresses to a secret door at the back.

'Through here,' she hissed. 'At the bottom of the stairs, turn right. At the end of the passage next to the Samuel Palmer of haymaking by a full moon, you'll find a little door. Put my swipe card in the slot then dial this number, thirty (for my age, remember), forty-nine (for Elmer's). Hurry, for God's sake. Elmer won't take any prisoners.'

'Thanks for everything.' Leaning back through the forests of scented taffetas and silks for a last kiss, Lysander raced down the stairs and found the painting. The full moon was honey gold not grapefruit pink this time. And there was the little door.

His hands were trembling so badly it took three goes to slot in the swipe card. Now, what was the number? His brain froze. Martha's age? He punched up a three then a nought, but what was Elmer's? About a hundred. The frenzied growling grew closer; any second they'd realize he'd escaped this way. Elmer? Elmer? Would the thirty be still working or would it run out like a half-rung telephone number? That was it. He punched a four and a nine. Nothing happened. Perhaps he'd put the card in back to front or upside down.

'Oh please God,' he moaned, 'I'm sorry I screwed Martha, but you'd have done the same, God, she was *so* beautiful.' As he hurled himself against the door it caved in and he was out in the dripping garden, darker now because the moon had vanished behind a big black cloud.

The smell of orange blossom was suffocating. Venus blazed above the ficus rampart. As Lysander bolted, white and leggy as a unicorn, across the perfect lawn he triggered off the underground sensors. Suddenly 1000-watt lamps lit up the garden brighter than day and closed-circuit television cameras swung round to trap him on a dozen monitors in the house and at the gate. Elmer's guards had simply to pick him off. Hearing the blood-curdling barking as the pack of dogs was unleashed, Lysander ducked behind a traveller's palm to avoid a hail of bullets.

The ficus hedge topped by razor wire was twenty yards away. Streaming as he was with rain and sweat, it would electrocute him instantly. Ahead loomed a vast individual ficus tree, Falstaffian in girth and so old that its lower branches rested their elbows on the ground. Scuttling up the nearest branch like a squirrel, Lysander managed to wriggle round the trunk just as the dogs began leaping for his feet with gnashing teeth. Swinging out on to another branch, he dropped into the street.

Heart hammering, legs trembling and giving way, sobbing with terror, Lysander collapsed against the huge hedge wondering what the hell to do next. The practical answer was to put as much distance between himself and Elmer as possible, but, bollock-naked with no identification except bruises, he'd probably get arrested and slapped into a loony bin and get his brains sawn open like *One Flew Over the Cuckoo's Nest*.

The streets were deserted, but the sky was lightening. Loping eastwards he was overtaken by yet another open stretch and, as he cringed into the nearest hedge, feeling the clipped twigs scraping his bare back, the driver stopped and reversed.

A blonde in a black strapless dress with huge sapphires hanging from her ears and circling her neck and wrists, she was a good deal older than Martha but almost as stunning.

'What happened to you?' she asked, looking him up and down in amusement.

'The husband came home.'

'Well, at least you're not armed. You'd better get in.'

Lysander shot into the car.

Seeing the *Wall Street Journal* lying on the back seat, Lysander covered himself with the front page like a car rug.

'Phew – it's really kind of you.'

'I figured I heard shots, or was that Elmer Winterton cracking his knee joints?'

49

'He tried to kill me,' said Lysander, perking up.

'The guy's an animal.'

'No animal is that nasty. Christ!' Glancing down at the *Wall Street Journal* Lysander saw Elmer's photograph glaring up at him. 'He's following me. I could tear him out, then my cock would stick through.'

'Feel free,' said the blonde.

'Martha said he was a clinical Nazi.'

'I thought he was Dutch.'

'Good thing that tree I shinned up didn't have Dutch Elmer disease or the branch would have given way.' Having started giggling, Lysander found he couldn't stop. 'I'm sorry. It's nervous hysteria. Have you got a cigarette?'

'Sure, in my purse. The name's Sherry by the way, Sherry Macarthy.'

Protected back and front by more pages of the *Wall Street Journal*, Lysander slid into Sherry's house which was bigger and more lushly decorated than Elmer's with a back garden falling straight into the ocean.

'I guess you'd like some breakfast and a pair of my husband's shorts?'

'You got a husband?' Lysander shot into reverse.

'He's in San Francisco,' said Sherry soothingly.

Lysander crept back. 'Could I possibly have a shower? After all that sex and fear I must stink like a polecat.'

Upstairs he admired another vast four-poster, this time swathed in primrose-yellow silk and topped at its four corners by gilded cherubs, none of whom was protected by the *Wall Street Journal*.

'Amazing room.'

'It's Franco's, my husband's,' said Sherry, who was turning on the gold taps of a vast marble bath next door. 'Help yourself.'

The doors of a fitted cupboard which took up a whole wall, and which had been lavishly handpainted with pale yellow and coral-pink roses, slid back to reveal hundreds of shirts. There were more scent bottles massed on the bathroom shelves than a duty-free shop. Franco

50

also must have the snakiest of hips. Lysander had the greatest difficulty finding a pair of shorts he could zip up.

'God, this is great! I haven't eaten for forty-eight hours.'

Having downed three glasses of orange juice, Lysander was tucking into a huge plate of bacon, eggs, tomatoes, mushrooms and hashbrowns, while Sherry filled yellow-and-white cups with very black coffee.

They were sitting beside a beautiful blue pool guarded by four big blue china dragons. White geraniums spilled over the faded terracotta pots and little waves gambolled idly on the pale sand below them. Above, the palm trees rattled in their diffident fashion.

Sherry had also showered and had swapped her black taffeta and her sapphires for a flamingo-pink sarong which left bare her almost too brown shoulders. Her still-wet, short blond hair was slicked back Rudolph Valentino style, but was softened by a pink hibiscus behind her left ear. There were crow's feet round her warmly smiling eyes and the skin was beginning to crêpe on her breast bones and her arms, but she was in great shape and a terrific listener.

'You can kiss goodbye to that job with Elmer,' she said when Lysander had finished his account of the night's escapades.

'I wouldn't mind if I hadn't got Jack, Arthur and Tiny to support,' sighed Lysander as he spread black-cherry jam on a croissant.

'You've got three kids?'

'Jack's my Jack Russell.'

'Original name.'

The irony was lost on Lysander.

'Arthur's my horse. He's a steeplechaser. He won a lot of races but he's having a year off with leg trouble. I'm hoping to ride him next season. He's such a character. Tiny's a shetland. She's Arthur's stable-mate.'

'They must miss you.' Sherry edged nearer Lysander.

'Not as much as I miss them. I've got another job to go to,' he went on gloomily, 'with Ballensteins, the merchant bank, but that doesn't start till the first of March. Playing polo for Elmer would have paid off my overdraft and a few bills – and I wanted a suntan to wow the Ballenstein typing pool on the first day.'

'You'll wow them anyway,' murmured Sherry. The boy was positively edible. 'At least you can get brown round the pool today.'

'I won't be in the way?'

'Have you looked in the mirror recently? But you mustn't burn.'

The climbing sun had already given a pink glow to his white shoulders. Surreptitiously he undid the top button of Franco's shorts; they'd castrate him in a minute. Having cleared away breakfast the maid returned with bottles of champagne and Ambre Solaire. Sherry patted the blue-and-white pool-lounger.

'After such a disturbed night, you must be pooped. Lie down and I'll oil you.'

Sherry had been trained as a masseuse and her provocative smiling eyes made Lysander even hotter than the sun as she kneeded and stroked his body. As her braceleted hands moved downwards, her sarong seemed to work loose so he could see straight down her deep brown cleavage and feel her bare thighs against his hip bone.

Only the constricting tightness of Franco's shorts had hidden a large erection.

'Do my back.' Embarrassed, he rolled over.

Sherry laughed softly. 'The maid's going shopping in a minute, then you can get brown *all* over.'

Sticky with oil, her hand slid down his backbone and disappeared under Franco's shorts. Lysander moaned. God, her fingers were going everywhere. She was doing such magical things any moment his cock would lift him into the air like a one-handed press-up. Then, as the sarong fell apart, he felt soft fur caressing his thighs and realized she was wearing no knickers.

52

Lysander never got a suntan. He and Sherry spent a lazy, boozy day, making love, watching racing on satellite, having outlandish bets and feeding each other spoonfuls of caviar and strawberries dipped in Dom Perignon.

Around five o'clock Lysander had given himself enough Dutch courage to go back to Elmer's barn and collect his luggage and polo sticks. Hopefully, Elmer would be safely in Washington drinking vodka and electronics with George and Barbara. As Lysander could only pull up Franco's jeans mid-thigh, Sherry drove him to Worth Avenue and, despite his protests, kitted him out in boxer shorts, Lacoste polo shirts, chinos, several pairs of loafers and a dark blue baseball cap with SAINTS on the front. She tried to buy him half a dozen suits.

'You shouldn't. I've had a really good time,' he told her as she drove him back to Elmer's.

'Me, too. Franco's gay, as you probably gathered,' said Sherry. 'He'd die of jealousy if he knew who I'd spent the day with.'

Lysander, who'd drunk a lot of Dom Perignon, had tears in his eyes. 'But that's awful. A beautiful woman like you wasted on some shirtlifter. Why don't you leave him?'

Sherry shook her head. 'Guys are like gold dust after you're forty,' she said, drawing up outside Elmer's barn. 'At least Franco's a husband and as a couple you get asked out so you get the chance to meet new guys. The wages of single life is social death, I promise you.'

Flinging his arms round her bare neck, Lysander collapsed on her warm, gold, scented breasts. 'As soon as I've sorted out things here, I'll get a taxi back to your place.'

If she hadn't dropped him at the bottom of the long white rose colonnade leading up to Elmer's barn, he would have bolted straight back into her car.

Reluctant to admit he'd been cuckolded and that his impregnable security system had been violated, Elmer had tried to hush up last night's escapade. But he'd reckoned without the Press, particularly when one of the maids, seeing such a stunning streaker, had leaked the story.

As Lysander weaved into the yard, a dozen camera lenses were turned on him and an immigration officer grabbed him, pinning his arms behind his back. 'You're going back to the UK, Lover Boy.'

'I can't,' protested Lysander, 'I'm going to Disneyland tomorrow. I've got to get Donald Duck's autograph. Hallo, Mrs Ex.' He waved at the long yellow face peering out of a nearby box.

'You're not going anywhere. Now walk.'

'I'll run if you like,' said Lysander as a gun jabbed his spine.

'Don't smartass me, Pretty Boy.'

'What about my polo sticks?'

'All your gear's packed.'

'But I haven't said goodbye to Martha or Sherry. Talk about coming down to earth without a bang. Oh, Mr Deporter, whatever shall I do?' sang Lysander tunelessly as he danced a few steps. 'I wanted to go to Disneyland and you sent me back to—'

'Walk,' howled the immigration officer and all Elmer's security guards.

In the end they locked him up for the night to sober up in order to smuggle him on to the first plane the next morning. Just as he was leaving, the twins came racing up with a large envelope. Inside was a silver pen from Tiffany's with a clip in the shape of a polo stick, ten thousand dollars and a scrawled note from Martha:

'Darling Lysander, I'm sorry it's all over the papers, but at least Elmer's been all over me since you left. You sure know how to make husbands jealous. I'll call you when I'm coming to the UK, probably for Ascot. Love, Martha.'

Feeling like a billionaire with hundred-dollar bills spilling out of his pockets, Lysander boarded first class. He tried to concentrate on the air hostess's pep-talk about exits and life-jackets. If the plane crashed he wouldn't have Martha's swipe card to help him.

Then, glancing down at the paper another hostess had handed him with a distinct smirk, only his seat-belt stopped him hitting the plane roof. For there was Martha smiling up at him. The photograph had been taken before she lost weight. She looked gorgeous and there was Elmer looking absolutely repulsive and there was Elmer's pink palace with a large caption: FORT KNOCKS-UP, and there, oh Christ, was Lysander himself, surrounded by immigration officers and giggling and waving like the village idiot.

Being dyslexic it took him some time to wade through the copy. There was a lot of guff about Safus security system being violated and national secrets being in jeopardy. Elmer was quoted as saying: *'It was just a lover's tiff, Martha and I are now reconciled.'*

Lysander shook his head in bewilderment. Then, as the plane started taxiing down the runway, jumped out of his skin again, for across the gangway a glamorous blonde was reading another newspaper with a front-page headline: MARTHA'S TOY BOY DEPORTED AT GUNPOINT and a huge picture of him looking mercifully less asinine. What the hell were Dolly and his father going to say? Perhaps the story wouldn't reach England. No-one knew Elmer over there. He did hope the bastard wasn't being beastly to Martha.

The only answer when the champagne started to flow after take-off was to get drunk again. One of the freebies handed out by the airline was a pack of cards. Getting into conversation with a foxy smiling Irishman beside him, Lysander discovered a fellow drinker and poker player.

By the time they reached Heathrow Lysander had managed to lose the Tiffany pen and most of Martha's ten thousand dollars, but he had enough left to buy a slab of Toblerone for Jack the dog, Fracas for Dolly and a bottle of whisky for Ferdie, his flatmate.

Before landing, the blonde across the gangway vanished into the lavatory for ages and emerged looking even more stunning – obviously tarting herself up for someone meeting her. Then, as she passed, Lysander's pleasure turned to pain. For a second he couldn't locate it. Then he recognized her scent: Diorissimo. His mother had never worn anything else.

When he'd first gone away to prep school he was so distraught she had drenched a handkerchief with it to comfort him at night. Now he leant back in his seat trying to handle the appalling feeling of desolation. Instinctively on landing he would have nipped into a telephone box to reassure her he was safe.

'I'm only happy when all my children are back in England,' she used to say, but he'd always known that his return made her happiest of all.

The post-champagne downer, plus a dank, dark, cold January evening did nothing to improve his spirits. As he slid through customs out into the airport, there was a firework display of camera bulbs exploding and cries of: 'That's him', 'Over here, Sandy'.

Fortunately Lysander was fitter than any of the paparazzi. Escaping them was a doddle compared to shaking off Elmer's guard-dogs.

'Can you drive like hell to Fountain Street in Fulham,' he gasped to a taxi driver, 'and can I possibly borrow your *Evening Standard*?'

Only when he'd finished the racing pages did Lysander turn to the front of the paper to find another vast picture of himself and the headline: MYSTERY STREAKER A BRIT. SENATE CALL FOR PUBLIC INQUIRY.

Digesting the details, Lysander had to leave the back-seat light on all the way into London.

'You better charge me extra for electricity,' he said, handing back the *Standard*.

'Worf it for a fantastic bird like that,' said the driver, as the taxi jolted over discarded vegetables littering the North End Road.

Thank Christ Dolly was still in Paris. London was at its most tatty. Most of the shops had sales on, the bitter east wind was rattling frozen litter along pavements and gutters.

'Fink we've lost them,' said the driver as he turned into Fountain Street.

5

Fountain Street was a charming Victorian terrace lined with cherry trees. Number 10 had been taken by Ferdie for a low rent because it was on the market and would sell better if lived in. Ferdie had repainted the bottle-green door and tied back the red rose which swarmed up the pink-washed front of the house. Ignoring the empty dustbins by the gate and the frantic waving of the two gays opposite, Lysander let himself in. Among the leaflets for decorators, window cleaners and minicabs was a postcard from Dolly saying she missed him and would be home tomorrow. There was also a mountain of brown envelopes which he didn't open. Thank goodness he was starting his new job with Ballensteins in March. His father had fiddled it for him as a quid pro quo for taking Rodney Ballenstein's son into his smart public school. The good-luck cards from all Lysander's old office cronies were still up in the drawing room.

The house looked awfully tidy – and it wasn't even the Filipino cleaner's day. Lysander switched on the simulated log fire which sent shadows flickering over the dark red wallpaper. In the fridge next door he found Bio Yoghurt and pink grapefruit juice (Ferdie must be on one of his endless diets), ham, Scotch eggs and a bottle of Moët.

He'd just helped himself to most of the ham and the last of Ferdie's whisky when a white envelope thudded through the letter-box. Addressed to him it was marked: URGENT AND CONFIDENTIAL.

'*Dear Hawkley*,' read Lysander with a giggle, again it took him several seconds to take in the fact that Ballensteins

58

was an old-established firm who prided themselves on their utter discretion. In view of Lysander's recent very unfortunate publicity, the job was no longer open.

The truth was that Rodney Ballenstein was not only a business friend of Elmer's but also had a new bimbo wife, whom he didn't entirely trust, and an equally glamorous PA on whom he had long-range designs. There was no way Rodney was going to have Lysander lounging round his office causing havoc.

'Fucking hell!' Lysander screwed up the letter and threw it on the gas logs.

At that moment the front door opened, there was a frantic scampering of paws and Jack the Jack Russell hurtled in like a bullet, yapping and jumping with all four feet off the ground, to greet his master.

Jack was followed by Ferdie bringing in the emptied dustbins.

'Hi,' he said, chucking the *Evening Standard* on the hall table, 'I was expecting you.'

Ferdinand Fitzgerald was a fixer, as fly and commercially orientated as Lysander was ingenuous and unmaterialistic. A schoolfriend of Lysander's, he was also an estate agent who, despite the recession, was doing very well. In addition to selling houses, he charged for dinner parties and for friends to stay the night in Fountain Street and let out properties on his firm's books by the afternoon for chums visiting London to bonk in. Ferdie's Achilles' heel was Lysander, whom he adored and had protected both from the bullying and the advances of older boys at school and beyond and whom he let get away with murder.

Very plump with a double chin and pink cheeks hiding an excellent bone structure, Ferdie looked like a clean-shaven Laughing Cavalier who'd slicked back his hair in an attempt to pass as a Roundhead. Cheerfulness, however, kept breaking in. He and Lysander were known to their friends as Mr Fixit and Mr Fucksit.

Today as he hung up his long navy-blue coat in the hall, the Roundhead mood predominated, particularly when Lysander, who always poured out everything at once, immediately told him he had lost both the Palm Beach and the Ballenstein jobs.

'Pretty stinking, getting fired before I've even got there,' grumbled Lysander, feeding Scotch eggs to a slavering Jack.

'You should have signed the contract before you left,' reproved Ferdie. 'It's still on the kitchen table.'

'There must be some party to go to,' said Lysander, 'I feel very depressed. How am I going to support Jack and the horses?'

As Ferdie read the Ballenstein letter looking for loopholes, Lysander opened the bottle of champagne from the fridge and threw the cork on to the floor. Ferdie picked it up.

'You live in a cork-lined room, Lysander. Sadly you lack Proust's application. This house has been tidy since you've been away. Annunciata took two days to muck out your room. No self-respecting pig would have dossed down in it. And you'll have to sleep on the sofa tonight. I've rented it to Matt Gibson and that's his Moët and his Scotch eggs you're feeding to that seriously spoilt dog. Look at the way he's scratched every door. And that is disgusting.' Ferdie removed two strips of ham fat from the gas logs with a shudder. 'How many times do I have to tell you? This is not a real fire.'

'Don't you want to hear about Palm Beach?'

'Not particularly. I've read most of it in the *Standard*. Look, we've got to talk about dosh.'

'I've just got in.' Lysander was now feeding Jack Toblerone and trying to read Ferdie's *Evening Standard*, which was a later edition, upside down.

'*EastEnders* is on in a minute.' He got up to turn on the television. 'Then let's go clubbing later, Ferd. My overdraft's so big I might as well make it bigger. I must just check my horoscope,' he added, switching over to Ceefax and Patric Walker.

'It'll tell you the debtors' prison is looming,' said Ferdie.

Turning off the television, he sat Lysander down and made him open the brown envelopes. The bills were horrific.

'Barclaycard, Ladbroke's, Foxtrot Oscar, Tramps, British Telecom,' intoned Ferdie. 'Christ, your telephone bill's longer than your telephone number.'

'It's not all me.'

'The long-distance calls are itemized and all to Dolly. And how in hell did you spend seven hundred pounds at Janet Reger?'

'That was Dolly's Christmas present.'

'Not to mention bills for bootmakers, saddlers, vets, feed bills, livery fees, blacksmith, Interflora; and here's a letter from the off-licence complaining your cheque bounced. How did you manage to run up a bill for five hundred pounds at an off-licence?'

'The girl with the big boobs lets me have it on tick. It's useful when we have parties.' Having filled up his glass, Lysander filled up Jack's water-bowl. 'I watched satellite in Palm Beach. You can watch racing twenty-four hours a day. Turn on the telly. It'll be *The Bill* in a minute.'

'You are not going to watch anything,' snapped Ferdie, stacking the bills tidily and chucking the brown envelopes in the waste-paper basket. 'You owe me four months' rent and you can at least sign on tomorrow.'

Lysander shuddered. 'They might find me a job. Basically, I need a holiday.'

'Matt Gibson saved his dole money for six months and went skiing,' said Ferdie sternly.

'I've never saved anything in my life. OK, I'll go and tap Dad tomorrow.'

Knowing how Lysander loathed going to see his father, Ferdie relented. Ringing a head-hunting friend called Roger Westwood, he arranged for Lysander to see him the following day.

'There's a PR job going,' said Ferdie switching off the telephone. 'The firm's got two bloodstock agencies and a polo club. At least you know something about horses.'

But turning round, he found Lysander had fallen asleep with Jack clutched in his arms like a teddy bear. He looked about twelve. He could sleep anywhere, curling up in patches of sunlight like a cat. Sighing, Ferdie removed his shoes and covered him with his own duvet.

Ferdie had a rotten morning taking some Arabs (who had no idea what they were looking for and who hardly spoke any English) round a big block of luxury flats in Chelsea Harbour. The weather was even meaner than yesterday. There were no meters and Ferdie had to put his BMW convertible in a car-park, forcing the Arabs to walk two hundred yards with a bitter east wind whipping up their robes. They were then so picky that Ferdie's good nature ran out. Shoving them into a taxi instead of driving them back to Claridge's, he returned to bung the porter, who often tipped him off if people were moving out, about new flats coming on to the market.

Ringing the office from his car, he learnt that a Greek couple had ratted on a deal on a half a million pound Radnor Walk house.

Twelve thousand pounds the poorer, Ferdie abandoned his perennial diet and mindlessly devoured two bacon rolls. Ringing Lysander to check he was on course for the interview with Roger Westwood he got no answer. Ferdie cursed. Roger was a vital contact because people he placed in jobs were often moving and needed to sell houses and buy new ones. Ferdie was putting his own reputation on the line, sending Lysander to see him. He'd better go back to Fountain Street to see what was going on.

Lysander appeared compliant but ended up doing exactly what he chose. Ferdie was reminded of an English Setter his family had once owned, who was beautiful, sweet natured, thick but also cunning, with a nose on elastic for bitches, and virtually untrainable.

He found the place in chaos. Lysander shed possessions like leaves in autumn. Records, tapes, telephone books, glasses, the remains of breakfast, over-flowing ashtrays, the racing pages of the *Sun* and several discarded ties littered the sitting room. Lysander, already dressed for the interview, was ringing Ladbroke's.

'Why the hell can't you shut my bedroom door?' Ferdie retrieved a Gucci loafer from Jack's ravening jaws. 'And what *do* you look like?'

Lysander glanced down at the crumpled grey suit and the blue and white striped shirt.

'Basically I put on the thing that least needed ironing,' he said apologetically.

He'd have pinched one of my shirts if they hadn't been too big, thought Ferdie darkly, then caught sight of an empty bottle of Moët in the waste-paper basket.

'You've been drinking.'

'Only half the bottle.'

'You can't fucking afford champagne.'

'I didn't,' said Lysander smugly. 'An incredibly nice girl turned up with it from *The Scorpion*. She left me her card.'

Examining it, Ferdie gave a groan.

'Beattie Johnson! Are you crazy? She's the most bent journalist in England.'

'Well, she was sweet to me. Said she'd read all the Palm Beach stuff and wanted me to have the chance to tell my side of the story, and if I told her all about Martha and Sherry, *The Scorpion* might give me a Ferrari.'

Ferdie went white. 'You didn't?'

'Course not.' Lysander assumed an air of great virtue. 'I couldn't do that to Martha. Besides, Dolly would do her nut. Off the record I did tell her how funny it was escaping from Elmer's and being picked up by Sherry. She took some pictures. She said she could get me some modelling work.'

'Christ, when will you learn?' Ferdie was in despair, but there was no time for reproaches.

Sighing, he straightened Lysander's tie, gave his shoes a last polish and brushed Jack's white hairs off his suit. He then put a couple of Roger Westwood's cards in both

Lysander's breast and inside pockets and turned down the *A–Z* with the relevant road ringed. Finally he gave Lysander an Extra Strong mint to hide the champagne fumes and his last twenty-pound note in case he needed some cash.

'Now, don't forget to steer Roger on to racing. That's the only thing you know anything about, and try and look interested. No, you haven't got time to watch *Neighbours*. Move it.'

An insanely fast driver, Lysander reached Roger's office near Holborn ten minutes early and pulled up his battered dark green Golf outside a television shop to watch the end of *Neighbours* and the runners going down to the start for the 2.15. He'd been right to back that dark brown mare, she looked really well. *Neighbours* ended on a clinch, which reminded Lysander that Dolly was due back this evening. Worried about the side-effects of being on the Pill since she was fourteen, Dolly had recently come off it, so he had better nip into the next door chemist's shop to buy some condoms. He was just waiting at the counter wondering if rainbow ones would improve his performance – Dolly was very demanding – when a girl swept into the shop sending a rack of bath caps flying.

She was very tall and thin, with fine pale hair drawn back from a long, beautiful unmade-up face into a tortoise-shell clip. Very inadequately dressed in a grey wool midi-dress, she had the gangling panicky air of a giraffe who'd escaped from the zoo into rush-hour traffic.

'I want some eye-gel,' she announced in a high, trembling voice. 'No, not that one, it's tested on animals. In fact I want three tubes. I'm going to be doing a lot of crying in the next few days. My husband's just left me.' And she burst into tears.

The pharmacist forced to serve her, because his assistant was late back from lunch, was totally thrown. His scrubbed face turned dark crimson, as his little eyes darted round looking for a way of escape. Lysander showed no such reticence. Leaping forwards, knocking over a rack of tweezers, he put an arm round the girl's shuddering shoulders. Gently steering her towards the chair kept for pensioners awaiting prescriptions, he broke into a nearby box of pale blue Kleenex and started to blot up the tears. Unlike Martha, there was no mascara to run.

'You poor thing, what a bastard. He'll come back.'

'Never, never,' gulped the girl.

'Go and make a cup of tea, Diane,' snapped the chemist to his assistant who, buckling beneath carrier bags, had tried to sidle in undetected and was now gazing at Lysander in wonder.

Gradually between sobs and sniffs, Lysander elicited the information that the distressed beauty's name was Rachel and that her husband Boris was a Russian dissident and an assistant conductor of the London Metropolitan Orchestra.

'But he never gets to conduct in public because that bastard Rannaldini – he's the London Met's musical director – never gives him the chance. Boris's compositions are wonderful, too, but no-one will programme them because they're rather difficult.'

'Dropped saucepan sort of stuff?' asked Lysander helpfully.

'If you mean atonal,' said the girl bridling slightly, 'yes, it is. Rannaldini could help; but he's jealous of Boris's genius. He actually told Boris, Boris's compositions emptied concert halls. Thank you,' she added as Diane, the assistant, now in a white coat, returned newly made-up and reeking of scent, and handed her a cup of pallid tea.

'You're all being so kind. Boris is kind really,' she went on despairingly, 'but being Russian he gets frustrated trying to communicate and we've got young children and they get on his nerves in a small flat.'

'That's no reason to walk out,' said Lysander indignantly. 'Have a slug of that tea, although you really need something stronger.'

Lifting the cup, Rachel's shaking hand spilled so much, she put it down again.

'Boris is in love with a mezzo called Chloe,' she announced miserably. 'The London Met's recording *Otello* at the moment. She's singing Emilia, so he sees her all the time and Rannaldini's positively encouraging it.'

'What a shit.' Lysander tugged out another wadge of blue Kleenex.

'I was so desperate,' continued Rachel with a sob, 'I went to see Rannaldini this morning, just barged past his secretary. Rannaldini had the temerity to offer me a gin and tonic, saying he couldn't understand why I was making a fuss. He feels the "affaire",' Rachel choked on the word, 'has added a new depth to Boris's compositions, and Chloe has never sung so well. He's a fiend, Rannaldini, he corrupts everyone.' She broke into noisier sobs.

Having exhausted one box of Kleenex, Lysander broke into another. Due to the slow service of Diane, who was not the only one transfixed with interest by this beautiful couple, a long queue had formed – many of whom were beginning to chunter. The pharmacist also noticed that several regulars, who were too embarrassed to ask so publicly for cures for piles or chronic constipation, had sidled out again. He cleared his throat, then when Lysander took no notice, told him and Rachel they couldn't stay indefinitely.

'No, of course not.' Rachel rubbed her forehead in bewilderment. 'My God, I should have picked up the children.'

'Where are they?' asked Lysander, who'd been squatting down beside her, rising stiffly to his feet.

'With a girlfriend.'

'Well, we'll find a pub and ring her. Then I'll run you over there.'

Ferdie's afternoon had been no more rewarding than his morning. A mega-rich German, for whom he'd been searching for months, had suddenly been found a two million pound property by a rival agent and an appalling survey had scuppered a deal that looked certain. Returning home that evening frozen and exhausted, Ferdie caught the telephone on its last ring.

It was Roger Westwood in a rage. He'd lunched with the Chief Executive of the PR firm and asked him back to the office to meet Lysander.

'And the little fucker never showed. Didn't even bother to call. Christ – what kind of idiot did that make me look?'

Ferdie had to crawl. 'He left here at half-past one, Roger. I don't see how he could have lost the address.'

'Well, he's lost the fucking job. After all the business I've put your way, Ferdie, you could have come up with someone better.'

'Look, I'm really sorry.'

But Roger had hung up.

I am too young to have a coronary, thought Ferdie. How the hell could Lysander do this to me?

Fumbling to turn on the lamp by the fire, he once more surveyed the chaos. Jack, fed up with being alone, had chewed several tapes. Ferdie put the rest back in their box.

In the kitchen, nothing had been returned to the fridge. The milk had gone off, the pink grapefruit juice was tepid. Lysander had polished off his whisky last night. In a fury Ferdie ate quarter of a pound of cheese and the last of the Scotch eggs. His brooding was interrupted by Jack leaping on to the sofa, bristling with rage and wagging his stumpy tail as he peered out of the window.

Wearily joining him, Ferdie swore in disbelief. There, staggering down the street, was Lysander, arm in arm with a blind man, both of them being led by a resigned-looking guide-dog. Ferdie threw up the window.

'We are two little lambs that have gone astray, Baa, Baa, Baa,' sang the blind man and Lysander tunelessly as they tottered across the road.

Windows were going up all along the street. The gays opposite were nearly falling off their balcony. Passers-by stopped and stared as Lysander paused, swaying, outside the front door. Breaking a bar of chocolate into pieces he gave it to the drooling guide-dog, then handed Ferdie's last fiver to the blind man. He took so long getting his key into the latch that Ferdie let him in. Lysander's hair was flopping all over his face. The faded orange tan had a blue tinge.

'Christ, it's cold!' Bending down to gather up an ecstatically yapping Jack, Lysander had great difficulty getting up again.

'Where the fuck have you been?' yelled Ferdie.

'In The Goat and Boots,' said Lysander with a hiccup.

'Why didn't you go to that interview?'

'Ohmigod!' Lysander's palm smote his wide-open mouth. 'I completely forgot. I'm *really* sorry. I'll ring and explain. Basically I just nipped into the chemist to get some condoms, when this poor, poor girl rushed in to buy some eye-gel. Can you beat it? Her husband had just left her.'

'Oh no,' moaned Ferdie.

'Well, I had to look after her.' Gently putting Jack down Lysander wandered into the kitchen fretfully upending the empty whisky bottle. 'Honestly, she was so sad and so beautiful, and she had adorable children – God, I love kids – and her husband's a Russian diffident. We went back to the flat. We got a bottle on the way and she was just telling me all about this bastard Rannaldini, who's led her husband astray. She said he was legendary.'

'Legendarily difficult,' snapped Ferdie.

With mounting anger he watched Lysander get a tin of Pedigree Chum out of the fridge, fork it into a blue bowl of Bristol glass which normally lived in the sitting room, and scatter dog biscuits all over the floor.

'Who is he?' asked Lysander.

'Rannaldini. About the greatest conductor in the world. Jesus, you're a philistine.'

'Well, he's Boris's boss. Rachel played some of Boris's music. It sounded quite awful – like a lot of buffaloes in a labour ward. But it reminded her of him so she started crying, and I was comforting her when Boris walked in. He'd decided not to leave her. He wasn't at all diffident when he saw me, and he's a big bugger so I legged it before he blacked my eye.'

'Then you could have used the eye-gel,' said Ferdie, sourly sweeping up dog biscuits. 'Well, you screwed up that bloodstock account job.'

'I'm desperately sorry, Ferd, I couldn't just leave her. The other problem is basically my car's been nicked. When I came out of her flat in Drake Street it had gone.'

'Probably towed away.' Ferdie was furiously crashing plates and mugs into the dishwasher.

'It wasn't. I stopped off at a champagne tasting at Oddbins on the way home. They let me use their telephone. Then I went to The Goat and Boots. That's where I met Syd, that blind bloke. His guide-dog was incredible; she was called Bessie. You'd have loved her, Jacko.'

As he opened the kitchen door, Jack rushed out and an icy blast rushed in.

'We'd better call the police about your car,' said Ferdie.

'Rachel was so pretty in a leggy sort of way.' Lysander glanced at his watch. 'Hell, I've missed *Coronation Street*.' Going into the sitting room he switched on the television. 'I must find out who won the 2.15. Where's the remote control?'

But, as he up-ended a box of tapes on to the floor in an attempt to find it, Ferdie flipped.

'Just shut up for once,' he howled, 'and go to fucking bed.'

69

6

Next morning Ferdie had to relent because Lysander woke up, as he so often did, crying for his mother.

'Oh Ferd, I dreamt she was alive, the fog came down and I couldn't find her.'

Dripping with sweat, reddened eyes rolling in terror, bedclothes thrown all over the sitting room, Lysander reached for a cigarette with a shaking hand.

Slumped in despair, he let the bubbles subside in the Alka Seltzer Ferdie brought him. The cartoons on TV AM which usually produced whoops of joy failed to raise a smile. He was too low even to switch over to Ceefax for the day's runners and his horoscope.

'What's the point of Russell Grant rabbiting on about a romantic day for Pisces when I've got to go and tap Dad?' He started to shake again.

Ferdie sighed. As Lysander's car hadn't been found and he'd promised to be at Fleetley, the public school in Gloucestershire where his father was headmaster, by eleven-thirty, Ferdie agreed to drive him down for a fee. Not that he'd ever get it, and he'd have to pretend to the office that he was out viewing properties.

'You ought to get something inside you,' he chided Lysander. 'You haven't eaten since yesterday morning.'

'I feel sick.'

Lysander jumped at the telephone, always hoping it might be his mother and her whole death a terrible dream.

Picking up the receiver, Ferdie listened for a minute, before snapping: 'He's not here, and if he were, he

70

wouldn't have anything to say,' and crashed it down again.

'You're going to feel even sicker. That was the *Sun*. Beattie Johnson's dumped in *The Scorpion*. They'll all be baying at the door in a second. We better move it.'

On top of *The Financial Times* and the *Estate Agent's Gazette*, the newsagent on the corner placed a copy of *The Scorpion*.

'Lover Boy's in trouble again,' he told Ferdie with a smirk. 'Remind him he owes me sixty quid for mags and fags.'

'I'm first in the queue,' said Ferdie, grabbing a packet of toffees. 'Oh my God!'

On the front of *The Scorpion* was a ludicrously, wantonly glamorous photograph of Lysander surrounded by foliage and wearing nothing but a flannel. 'WHO COULD BLAME MARTHA WINTERTON?' said the huge headline.

'What the hell possessed you to pose virtually naked for Beattie Johnson?' asked Ferdie as he got back into the car.

'I was having a bath when she arrived,' said Lysander sulkily.

Lysander, whom Ferdie described as the Geoffrey Boycott of reading, was still digesting the full horrors when the BMW shook off the remnants of rush-hour traffic and reached the M4.

'*Drop dead handsome*,' he read out laboriously. '*And he nearly did when the bullets of Elmer's guards rang out. Frozen in his tracks, Lysander could have passed for a statue of Adonis* (who's he?) *in that moonlit garden!*

'"*I aim to be a jump jockey*," *says twenty-two-year-old Lysander, who should have no trouble with Bechers, if he can clear Elmer's twenty-foot electric fence without a horse.*

'Oh Christ, it goes on about me being "*the youngest son of David 'Hatchet' Hawkley, headmaster of Fleetley, one of England's snootiest public schools (fees £12,000 a year).*

Perhaps Hatchet will give cheeky Lysander six of the best when they meet."

'Jesus, Beattie is a bitch,' said Lysander furiously. 'She promised she wouldn't print any of the things I told her off the record. I'd have taken that Ferrari if I'd known. We'd better step on it before some do-gooder shows Dad *The Scorpion*. Thank goodness it's banned at Fleetley. Dolly's going to be livid, too. I feel seriously sick.'

He groped for a cigarette and was soon coughing his lungs out and dropping ash and toffee papers all over Ferdie's very clean car.

'That is the ultimate obscenity,' he said disapprovingly as they got stuck in the fast lane behind a blonde in a Porsche going just below the speed limit, so Ferdie was forced to overtake on the inside.

'Ought to be driving funeral cars.' Lysander swung round to glare at her, then changed his mind. 'Quite pretty though. Perhaps she's just passed her test. Looks like that girl in the house next door. Did you ever bonk her?'

Ferdie nodded gloomily. 'We had a bloody good four days while you were in Palm Beach. I even took her to San Lorenzo. Then she announced she was flying back to Australia to get married, and she'd only been practising on me.'

Ferdie told it as a big joke, but Lysander sensed the hurt. He longed for Ferdie to attract girls as effortlessly as he did.

'Stupid cow,' he said crossly, then to cheer Ferdie up, as they came off the motorway, 'God, you shift this car. I've never done it this fast even at night.'

As they approached Fleetley through the bleak winter landscape with its patches of snow and icy wind flattening the pale grass on the verges, Jack started to snuffle at the window at familiar territory and Lysander grew lower and lower.

'I can't believe she won't be here,' he muttered, pulling Sherry's blue baseball cap further over his nose.

He could never understand why his mother had stayed married to his stiff-upper-lipped, rigidly conventional, father. But, as a gesture of conciliation, he stopped in Fleetley Village to buy him a bottle of port and a packet of Swoop for his parrot, Simonides.

Fleetley School had once been inhabited by dukes. Now only the iron gates flanked by rampant stone lions and the avenue of towering flat-bottomed horse-chestnuts, and the great house itself, square, yellowy-grey and Georgian, remained. All round like mushrooms had sprung up classrooms, science labs, gyms and houses for masters and boys. The great lake had been turned into a swimming pool.

Nowhere for Arthur and Tiny to graze now, thought Lysander, gazing at the silvery-green stretches of playing field.

'Oh no!' He gave a whimper. The stables where he and his mother had kept their horses had already been flattened to make way for the new music school towards which, Mrs Colman, his father's secretary, had helped raise £300,000.

'You coming in?' he asked Ferdie.

Ferdie shook his head: 'I've got some calls to make.'

Although Ferdie had got straight As in four A levels, and David Hawkley had privately admitted he would be the first old boy to make a million, David had never forgiven his son's best friend for flogging booze, cigarettes and condoms on the black market to other boys.

'I'll leave Jack with you then,' said Lysander. 'Simonides always gives him a nervous breakdown, imitating his bark. Christ, I hope Dad's in a good mood.'

David Hawkley ran one of the best schools in the country. Nicknamed 'Hatchet' by the boys for the sharpness of his tongue, he was as brilliant a teacher as administrator, but tended ruthlessly to suppress the romantic intuition which had made him the finest classical scholar of his generation. Extremely good-looking, pale, patrician, tight-lipped, like the first Duke of Wellington, with black Regency curls brushed flat and streaked with grey, he gave an impression of banked fires under colossal control – as though the battles of the Peninsula and Waterloo were being fought internally against despair and the powers of darkness.

Inflexible by nature, he had been particularly tough with his youngest son because Pippa, his late wife, had adored the boy so much. And Lysander was so agonizingly like Pippa with his wide-apart, blue-green eyes, which always opened wider when he was thinking what to say, the thick glossy brown hair falling over his forehead, and the sweet sleepy smile that totally transformed his face. Like Pippa he had the same air of helplessness, of not being responsible for his actions, of retreating into a dream world and laughing at all the wrong moments.

Lysander was so different from David's older sons, Alexander and Hector, who, like their father, had got firsts at Cambridge, and were now doing brilliantly in the BBC and the Foreign Office. Both had made suitable marriages, and, unlike their father, hugged their children, cooked Sunday lunch, knew the difference between puff and shortcrust pastry, and changed nappies without any loss of masculinity. Like their father, however, they had endless discussions on what to do for and about Lysander.

Awaiting his son that morning, David Hawkley was in a particularly savage mood. Normally in January, he would have been basking in the glow of getting half the sixth form into Oxbridge. But such was the bias against public schools that this year only ten boys had scraped in and none of them with scholarships, resulting in endless re-criminatory telephone calls from parents. Having been up most of the night, ruthlessly marking down Mocks papers, he didn't think next year's lot would fare any better.

His mood was even worse because a fox had killed his beloved parrot, Simonides, that morning. Simonides had barked at dogs, chattered away in Greek and Latin, and shouted 'Fuck Off', probably taught to him by Lysander, at parents who wouldn't leave. He had also perched on

74

David's shoulders as he worked, hopped on to his bed, snuggling into his neck at dawn and been his only solace since Pippa died.

David was also livid because stories of Lysander's Palm Beach exploits were plastered all over *The Scorpion*, which had been slyly left around by the boys – even on his pew in chapel.

Worst of all, Lysander in his vagueness had put the two letters he'd laboriously written in Palm Beach in the wrong envelopes. Thus instead of receiving a cheery note saying his son was getting on well and would visit him next month, David opened the letter Lysander had written to his highly dubious girlfriend, Dolly. This not only told her of the disgusting things Lysander was intending to do to her sexually when they met up again, but also how he would probably be forced to tap his battleaxe of a father and that he was sure his father in turn was keen on his secretary, 'Mustard', and what a dog she was.

David Hawkley was almost more outraged by the deterioration in Lysander's spelling and grammar. But he was not prepared to hand the letter back with Sps in the margin, nor tell his son that the word 'lick' did not have two Ks, and that swuzzont-nerve certainly wasn't spelt like that, nor ask what the hell was 'growler guzzling'.

Icy with rage, David watched his youngest son getting out of a flash car, driven by that fat, deeply unsuitable friend, who should surely have been at work in some office. He then wandered up the path, wincing at the cacophony of the eleven-thirty bell, and stopped to stroke Hesiod, the school cat, who'd been shut out yet again by Mrs Colman, who didn't approve of pets in the office.

It was Mrs Colman who had drawn David's attention to *The Scorpion* first thing that morning.

'I never read that beastly rag, but my Mrs Mop brought it in. I'm so sorry, David,' – never 'David' except when they were alone.

Now orgasmic with disapproval, Mrs Colman was ushering Lysander into the study. Handsome, big nosed, high complexioned and hearty, she got quite skittish when Alexander or Hector visited their father: 'Mr Hawkley, Mr Hector Hawkley to see you.' But Lysander was too hauntingly like his mother, of whom Mrs Colman had been inordinately jealous.

Lysander noticed that 'Mustard' was very glammed up in cherry-red lambswool with matching colour on what could be seen of her pursed lips. Catching a discreet waft of Chanel No 5, he afforded her equal coolness.

'Hi, Dad.' He dumped the carrier bag on his father's vast green-leather desk beside the neatly stacked Mocks papers. 'The Swoop's for Simonides.'

Timeo Danaos, thought David, peering into the bag. Unable to trust his voice not to quiver, he didn't tell Lysander about Simonides, and merely said: 'Thank you. You'd better sit down.'

For a man outwardly as bleak as the day, his study was an unexpectedly charming and welcoming room. Most of the wallspace was covered with books, well worn and thumbed in faded crimsons, blues, dark greens and browns, mostly in the original Greek and Latin, with their gold lettering glinting in the flames that glowed from the apple logs in the grate. Within reach were Aristotle's *Ethics* and the seven volumes of Gibbon's *Decline and Fall*. And because David Hawkley was not a vain man, tucked away on a top shelf were his own much-admired translations of Plato, Ovid and Euripides. He had been translating Catullus when Pippa died and had done no work on it since.

On the remaining walls were some good English water-colours, exquisite French engravings of Aesop's fables, a photograph of the Headmasters' Conference last year in Aberdeen, and yet another far more faded photograph of himself winning his blue at Cambridge, breast against the tape, dark head thrown back.

Over the fireplace was the Poussin of rioting nymphs and shepherds left to him by Aunt Amy, who had also left twenty thousand pounds to Lysander rather than his elder brothers because she felt the boy needed a helping hand. Lysander, to his father's fury, had instantly blued the lot on a steeplechaser called King Arthur, who had promptly gone lame and not run since.

Unlike Elmer Winterton, David Hawkley believed in longevity, so the holes in the carpet were mostly covered by good rugs. The springs had completely gone in the ancient sofa upholstered in a dark green Liberty print to match the wallpaper. Mrs Colman kept urging him to replace the sofa with something modern, and relaxing, but David didn't want parents to linger, particularly the beautiful, divorced or separated mothers – God, there were enough of them – who came to talk about their sons and ended up talking about themselves, their eyes pleading for a chance to find comfort in comforting him.

And now Lysander was sprawled on the same low sofa, huddled in Ferdie's long, dark blue overcoat, re-adjusting his long legs, yet as seductive in his drooping passivity as Narcissus or Balder the Beautiful. But, modest like his father, he always seemed unaware of his miraculous looks.

David didn't offer Lysander a glass of the medium-dry sherry he kept for parents, although he could have done with one himself, because he didn't want any conviviality to creep in.

Lysander, who always had difficulty meeting his father's cold, penetrating grey eyes, noticed he was wearing a new Hawkes tie, and that his black scholar's gown, now green with age, was no longer full of holes where it had kept catching on door handles. His mother had only used needles to remove rose thorns, so the invisible stitches must be Mustard's work, as was the posy of mauve and blue freesias on his father's desk, whose sweet, delicate scent fought with the blasts of lunchtime curry drifting from the school kitchens.

There was a long, awkward pause. Lysander tried not to yawn. Noticing how the lines had deepened round his father's mouth and how the dark rings beneath his eyes nearly joined his arched black brows, as though he was wearing glasses, Lysander felt a wave of compassion.

'How are you, Dad?'

'Coping,' snapped David.

Then a pigeon landed on the window-sill and for a blissful second, David thought it was Simonides. Then, as reality reasserted itself, he channelled his misery into a furious attack on Lysander for sending the wrong letter.

'How dare you refer to Mrs Colman in those offensive terms,' he said finally, 'after all she's done for the school? Quite by chance, recognizing your illiterate scrawl, I opened the letter. Imagine the hurt it would have caused Mrs Colman if she'd seen it.'

Crossing the room, he threw the vile document on the fire, putting a log on top to bury it.

'What the hell have you got to say for yourself? And take off that ridiculous baseball cap.'

Flushing like a girl, Lysander opened his eyes wide and launched into a flurry of apology.

'I'm really, really sorry, Dad, I honestly am. Basically it's very expensive living in London, and I honestly didn't mean to upset you and Mustard . . . I mean Mrs Colman, but basically my car's been nicked and I'd no idea Arthur's vet's bills were going to be so high, and I honestly promise to do better, and basically my attitude towards money is—' He got to his feet to let in the school cat who was mewing piteously on the window-ledge.

'Sit down,' thundered his father.

'But it's freezing. Hesiod always came in when Mum—'. Then, seeing his father's face, he sat down. He desperately needed some money. 'As I was saying, basically my attitude—'

'That's enough,' David interrupted him. 'You have used the words basically and honestly about twenty times in the last five minutes. There is absolutely nothing honest about your promises to do better, nor basic about your attitude to money. You roll up here, plainly hungover to the teeth. You bring disrepute on the family getting your exploits plastered all over the papers. I hoped you would have learnt that no gentleman ever discusses the women with whom he's been to bed.'

With a shudder, Lysander wondered if his father had bonked Mustard yet. The fumes of curry were really awful. He hoped the bursar had ordered a consignment of three-ply bog-paper to deal with it. Poor Hesiod was still mewing.

'What is worse,' went on his father, 'is that in order to secure that job in the City – which I gather Roddy Ballenstein has already withdrawn – can't say I blame him – I have been forced to admit the stupidest boy I have ever come across.'

'Stupider than me?' said Lysander in amazement.

'It is *not* funny!'

'I'm really sorry, Dad.' Lysander noticed with a stab of pain that his father had removed his mother's photograph from the mantelpiece. Probably Mustard's doing. Dragging his mind back to the present he heard his father saying:

'I realize from your letter that you only came down to tap me. Well, I'm not helping you. You've got to learn to stand on your own feet. I suggest you send that horse on which you're always squandering money to the knackers, and get yourself a decent job. Now if you'll excuse me, I have a governors' meeting.'

Lysander went quietly outside, but when he saw a gloating Mustard peering round the net curtains, something snapped. Raising two fingers at her, he scooped up Hesiod, who was now weaving and mewing round his feet, and bolting down the garden path, shoved the cat into Ferdie's car and jumped in after it.

In the ensuing pandemonium with Jack nearly getting his eyes clawed out as he tried to swallow Hesiod whole and Lysander trying to separate them and Mustard running down the drive in her medium high heels, crying, 'Stop thief', Hesiod started shitting with terror and was forcibly ejected by Ferdie outside the Science Lab.

'I expect they'll start experimenting on him as soon as they've cut his vocal chords,' said Ferdie as he stormed down the drive.

Then, seeing Lysander's stricken face, 'I'm only winding you up. Quite resourceful of Jacko though, trying to eat that mog. Obviously knows he's going to have to fend for himself from now on.'

'What you talking about?'

'Hatchet didn't cough up.'

'He didn't.' Lysander rubbed his bloody, lacerated hands on his jeans. 'Can I borrow another fiver? I must put some flowers on Mum's grave.'

Unclothed as yet by any lichen or the grime of age, Pippa Hawkley's headstone looked poignantly white and defenceless beside all the other gravestones lurching higgledy-piggledy in Fleetley Village churchyard.

Almost as white and defenceless as her son, thought Ferdie, as he watched Lysander chuck out some dead chrysanthemums which had blown over and refill their vase with four bunches of snowdrops.

Philippa Hawkley 1942–89, *Requiescat in Pace*, read Ferdie, and tears stung his eyes as he wondered how anyone so vivid and vital as his ex-headmaster's wife could ever rest peacefully. Worried that Lysander, who was now swaying beside him, was going to black out, he urged him back into the car and turned up the heat. He ought to belt straight back to London. Yesterday's Arabs had rung his boss and complained about being bundled into a taxi. Instead he decided to take Lysander for a drive.

7

The sun, an even later riser than Lysander, at last put in an appearance, lighting up frost-bleached fields, yellow stone walls and striping the drying road ahead with tree shadows. As the countryside grew more hilly and deeply wooded, Ferdie drove past a beautiful house on the side of the valley with smooth grey trunks of beeches like the Albert Hall organ pipes soaring behind it.

Lysander was temporarily roused out of his gloom, when Ferdie said the estate belonged to Rupert Campbell-Black, ex-world show-jumping champion and now one of the most successful owner-trainers in the country.

'Look at those fences! God, I wish Rupert'd give me a job.' Lysander craned his neck to gaze into the yard. 'I could ride all his horses and he'd know how to get Arthur sound again. Sometimes I think Arthur's enjoying retirement and doesn't want to get sound at all. I can't work in London any more, Ferdie, I'm having a mid-life crisis at twenty-two.'

'I realize that,' said Ferdie. 'I've got plans for you.'

Driving on another ten miles, through tree tunnels and woods carpeted with fading beech leaves and lit by the occasional sulphur-yellow cloud of hazel catkins, they passed a tiny hamlet on the right called Paradise. Five minutes later, Ferdie crossed over into the county of Rutshire, and pulled up on the top of a steep hill.

Climbing out, almost swept away into a dance of death by the violence of the wind, they found themselves looking down into a most beautiful valley. From the top, vast trees descended the steep sides like passengers on a moving staircase. Over the trees were flung great silken waterfalls of travellers' joy. These seemed to flow directly into a hundred little streams, which flashed like sword blades in the sunshine as they hurtled through rich brown ploughed fields or bright green water meadows into the River Fleet which ran along the bottom of the valley. Ahead, a mile downriver, a little village of pale gold Cotswold cottages gathered round an Early English church like parishioners respectfully listening to a sermon.

'Below you,' shouted Ferdie over the wind, 'lies Rutshire's valley of Paradise, much larger and more ostentatious than its Gloucestershire namesake. But where everyone wants to live, and where house prices go up rather than down.

'Here,' – Ferdie indicated several splendid houses peeping like lions out of the woods on either side – 'you will find the most Des-Reses in England, because of the magnificent views and the money that's been spent on them. Rupert Campbell-Black refers to the area as Non-U-Topia because so many Nouveaux have moved in. It's also been nicknamed the Rift Valley because so many marriages break up.'

'So what?' grumbled Lysander, who was cold and having to hang on to his baseball cap and to poor Jack whose ears were getting blown inside out.

'I did a bit of research while you were unsuccessfully tapping your father,' yelled Ferdie, who being fat, felt the cold less. 'You know your friend Rachel? Well, this is the empire of her husband's conductor-boss, Rannaldini. His is the biggest house up on the right. It's called Valhalla. The garden's sensational in summer. You can see the maze and there deep in the woods you can see a little gazebo – Rannaldini's out-of-control tower – where he has total privacy to edit tapes, study scores and bonk ladies who approach unseen from the other side of the wood.

'Rannaldini only spends a few weeks a year here,' explained Ferdie, 'because he's always jetting round the world avoiding tax and outraged mistresses, when he's not terrifying the London Met into submission. Rumour has it,' he added knowingly, 'that if things get too hot in England, Rannaldini's got his sights on the New York or Berlin Philharmonics.'

'I get it,' said Lysander, shoving Jack inside his coat. 'Rannaldini's house might go on the market and you'd get it on your books first and make a killing.'

'Exactly,' said Ferdie, getting back into the car. 'It's always worth watching this area.'

Driving down the hill he turned off at a signpost saying: PARADISE 2 MILES.

'You make a killing,' he went on, 'selling a house here to a couple. Then, when the marriage breaks up in a few years, you make another killing finding them two separate houses and, if you're lucky, flogging the old one for them.'

Paradise, which had been voted Best-Kept Village in Rutshire for the last ten years, lived up to its name. Even on the bleakest day it was sheltered by the towering tree-covered hills. The churchyard and the gardens that lined the main street were already crowded with aconites, snowdrops and early crocuses. Winter jasmine and evergreen honeysuckle climbed to the roofs of the cottages, from whose chimneys, opal-blue smoke rose straight up, hardly ruffled by the wind. Although the duck pond was frozen, there were fat ruby buds on the black spiky branches of the lime trees which framed the village green.

Next to the church behind ancient stone walls hung with tuffets of mauve aubrietia lurked a charming rectory. As well as an excellent village shop called The Apple Tree, which stocked everything from videos to vine leaves, Paradise boasted a garden centre called Adam's Pleasure which sold petrol, and a restaurant, called The Heavenly Host, with its duck-egg-blue shutters drawn, which opened only in the evenings.

Ferdie and Lysander, however, shot with indecent haste into the saloon bar of The Pearly Gates Public House.

'Morning, Ferdie,' said the landlord who had tipped him off about local houses on several previous visits.

Sustained by a couple of large whiskies and a plate of very hot steak-and-kidney pie and chips in front of a roaring fire, Lysander began to feel slightly more cheerful.

Apart from a couple of pensioners gazing at half-pints of beer, the place was deserted except for the vicar, who, in between drinking large glasses of red wine and writing Sunday's sermon, gazed surreptitiously at Lysander.

'They ought to invent a killer cocktail called the Holy Spirit,' murmured Ferdie, whose pink cheeks had turned bright scarlet in the warmth.

On the walls, dominating the coaching scenes, village cricket elevens and gleaming horse brasses, were two framed photographs. One was of a haughty-looking, grey-haired man with his eyes shut waving a stick, the other of a strikingly handsome woman with dark, curly hair and her mouth so wide open that Lysander was tempted to toss her the piece of the pastry he was feeding to Jack.

'Who are they?' he asked Ferdie.

'Rannaldini conducting Mahler and Hermione Harefield, his mistress, singing it. That's her house on the left.'

Out of the window, Lysander could see tall yellow chimneys, beckoning like fingers between two great black yew trees.

'She's a world-famous diva,' continued Ferdie mopping up gravy with a third piece of bread. 'She met Rannaldini when he was conducting *Rigoletto* in Milan ten years ago. It's been a staggeringly successful partnership in and out of bed. You must have heard of Harefield and Rannaldini – no, perhaps not.' He shook his head. 'They almost outsell Nigel Kennedy.

'Hermione's incredibly beautiful and a pain in the ass, which Rannaldini probably enjoys because he's rumoured to go both ways. Hermione's husband, Bob, is the orchestra manager of the London Met. He's a seriously nice guy with the flattest stomach in Rutshire. He should have the narrowest shoulders, shrunk by so many musicians sobbing on them as a result of Rannaldini's tantrums.'

Ignoring Lysander's reproachful glances at his empty glass, Ferdie picked up the car keys.

'Come on, I haven't finished the tour.'

Outside, the sun had gone in. The cottages along the High Street huddled together for warmth. As they drove out of the village up the south side of the valley, they passed a cottage with a waterfall and a swing hanging from a bent apple tree.

'That's Jasmine Cottage,' said Ferdie slowing down, 'which also belongs to Hermione and Bob Harefield. Last year they rented it out to your pianist friend Rachel and her Russian husband Boris. Then Rachel went abroad on a concert tour, and Boris was left behind, babysitting and writing incomprehensible music no-one wanted, so he started looking around sexually. In the autumn they moved back to London hoping it might be easier to find work, but it doesn't seem to have helped the marriage, if yesterday's eye-gel incident is anything to go by.

'And that ravishing house, hidden in the willows on the left belongs to Valentine Hardman. He's a top lawyer with a mistress up in London, so his wife Annabel threatens daily to throw herself into the River Fleet.

'And that vulgar pile up on the left,' Ferdie nearly ran over a pheasant as he peered through vast electric gates up a long drive, 'is Paradise Grange. It belongs to Larry Lockton, chief executive of Catchitune Records who make a fortune out of Rannaldini and Harefield. Larry keeps buying companies, but I suspect he's hopelessly overleveraged and riding for a fall.

'Now Larry's another bloke Rannaldini's led astray,' added Ferdie, driving on. 'Larry used to be a fat little man who never smiled because he had bad teeth. But he was so jealous of all Rannaldini's mistresses, he wanted one, too. So he had his teeth fixed, lost three stone and got a new haircut like Mel Gibson and started bonking his secretary. He's even bought her a bonkerie in Pelham Crescent. I sold it to him,' explained Ferdie, not without complacency. 'Ground floor with a nice garden and fitted cupboards for all the skeletons. Larry's wife, Marigold, used to be very pretty. She was his childhood sweetheart, but once he started to make his pile and began climbing socially, she got Weybridged and dressed like the Queen, eating too many white chocolates, and throwing herself into charity work like a rugger ball with a difficult bounce.'

'Why are you telling me all this?'

'Hang on – there *is* a reason.'

Driving on up the hill Ferdie pulled into a gap. Through the trees across the valley half a mile to the right of Valhalla they could see a Georgian house, smaller than Fleetley, but exquisitely proportioned, with soaring stone angels on each corner of the roof.

'That house, Angel's Reach, was totally unmodernized with a fantastic wild garden,' said Ferdie. 'It's been bought by Georgie Maguire and her husband, Guy Seymour, who are spending an absolute fortune on it.'

Lysander opened a bloodshot eye. 'Even I've heard of her. Wasn't she a pop singer in the sixties? Mum had all her records.'

'That's right. Now she writes songs as well.'

'I've always thought she was seriously attractive,' said Lysander.

'Georgie and Guy paid a million five.' Ferdie edged the car on until they could see a long lake glinting gold in the falling sun below the house.

'My guess is they can't afford it, but they're gambling on her new album, which is produced by Larry Lockton and Catchitune, being a massive hit.'

'Aren't Georgie and Guy supposed to be the happiest couple in show business?' sighed Lysander enviously.

'Which probably means they're both screwing around,' said Ferdie cynically.

Lysander shook his head in bewilderment. 'It's quite awful. What's the point of getting married if you spend your time bonking other people?'

'This monstrous regiment of womanizers,' said Ferdie with a shrug. 'Paradise husbands ring up from London on Thursdays to remind the housekeepers to get their wives out of the freezer so they'll be unfrosted by the time the master returns on Friday night.'

'Why the hell do the wives put up with it?' asked Lysander with a shudder. 'At least Dad didn't bonk other women.'

'When your husband's as rich as Croesus, you get used to a certain lifestyle and you can't bear to give it up.'

'I've got Croesus in my face,' said Lysander, peering gloomily in the driving mirror. 'Let's go home, Ferd, I want to see Dolly and explain about *The Scorpion* before she goes into orbit. This place is seriously depressing.'

'It is,' said Ferdie, swinging the car round, 'particularly for someone like Marigold Lockton. She loves that shit Larry to distraction, and that's where you come in. You're going to be her toy boy.'

'How old is she?'

'About thirty-eight.'

'I can't bonk an old wrinkly like that,' said Lysander in outrage.

'You're not going to bonk her, just hang about and rattle her husband, and make him so jealous he'll come roaring back. It worked with Boris Levitsky and Elmer Winterton. This time you're going to get paid.'

'Don't be ridiculous,' snapped Lysander. 'I can't get a husband back if the marriage is dead. You can't reheat baked potatoes.'

'First you've got to look at the wife,' said Ferdie. 'If she's gone to seed, you unseed her, and make her look like a mistress. Put back the gleam in her eye, let her taunt her husband with a scented body that's quivering with lust for someone else.' Ferdie rubbed the windscreen which was steaming up. 'Get the weight off, get her some decent clothes (I bet there's a raver lurking beneath Marigold's polyester V-necks). Above all, make her stop nagging and act detached. No more flying leaps to catch the telephone on the first ring.'

'You've really studied this.' Lysander looked at Ferdie with new respect as they drew up outside the big electric gates of Paradise Grange.

'We are about to repackage and remarket a product,' said Ferdie. 'Let's go see Marigold.'

8

Up a long drive through splendid parkland dotted with noble trees, Paradise Grange reared up, a sprawling bulk of grey stone topped by turrets and battlements. On the perfect lawns still-frozen patches merged with great sheets of snowdrops and on the roof a flag flying the famous yellow-and-purple Catchitune colours was fretted by the bitter wind. Although it was still early afternoon, carriage lamps blazed on either side of the great oak front door. There was no answer when Ferdie rang the bell which played the Hallelujah Chorus. But as he pushed open the door he bumped into Marigold Lockton, deliriously excited that he might be a returning Larry and followed by an overweight, furiously barking, spaniel.

There's no way I'm going to get Larry Lockton back for that, thought Lysander. Marigold looked absolutely dreadful, rather like a Beryl Cook lady masquerading as Mrs Thatcher. She was twenty pounds overweight, with red eyes and red veins criss-crossing her unhealthily white cheeks. An Alice band on her mousy permed hair emphasized a corrugated forehead. A V-necked polyester dress in overcooked-sprouts-green showed off a neck and arms as opaque and pudgy as the white chocolates with which she constantly stuffed herself. She had clearly also been stuck into the vodka for several hours.

Her first carefully elocuted words to Ferdie were that he could forget about the house he was finding her in Tregunter Road.

'Even if Larry's plannin' to put Paradise Grange on the

market, Ay'm not movin'. The kiddies love their 'ome; whay should they lose it and whay should Ay after all the work Ay've put into redecoratin' it?' She pointed to the oak panelling in the hall which had been painted a rather startling flamingo pink.

'Larry wanted the kiddies brought up in the country.' Her voice rattled like a sliver of bone in the Hoover as she led them into a vast drawing room. 'So he stuck me down 'ere, mayles away from the shops. Now he's packed them off to boardin' school to get a posh accent and some smart friends, and he's given may daily help and Mr and Mrs Brimscombe, our couple what live at the bottom of the drayve, a month's notice to force me out.

'Poor Mr B's tended this garden for nearly forty years. Look at the poor old chap.' Marigold pointed out of the window at an ancient gardener morosely clipping a yew hedge. 'Ay can't lay him off, it'd break his 'eart. Even more than mine's broke.'

'Marigold,' interrupted Ferdie, 'this is Lysander Hawkley.'

'Pleased to meet you,' said Marigold unenthusiastically, then pulling herself together, 'I suppose you want a noggin.'

'Please,' said Ferdie, then, seeing Lysander's appalled face, whispered, 'Hang about, I promise you it's worth it.'

'She's gross,' hissed Lysander. 'I'd need serious beer goggles to get within a hundred yards.'

'Lovely view,' enthused Ferdie loudly, squeezing between a large harp and a wind-up gramophone to look out of the huge window stretching the length of the room. 'You can see Valhalla and Angel's Reach from here, and Rachel's cottage behind those Wellingtonias.'

'I don't care,' grumbled Lysander, 'I want to go home.'

Despite several bright Persian rugs tossed over a pink wall-to-wall carpet, a matching pink dog basket, a super-abundance of silk cushions on their points like a Kirov line-up and enough tartan chairs and sofas to do the

Highland fling, the room was as cosy as the furniture department of an Oxford Street store. There were too many dark cumbersome pieces, too many chandeliers, too much gilt on the mirrors and too few logs bravely burning in the vast stone cave of a fireplace.

On the walls, equally disparate, were several gold discs won by Catchitune, a lugubrious Stubbs spaniel, a Hogarth etching of a musical evening, a framed manuscript of the first page of a Beethoven Sonata, and a Picasso of grapes and a violin. The grand piano was weighed down with various recording awards and photographs of Larry Lockton fratting with the famous – mostly Mrs Thatcher. All round the room, busts of the great composers looked dourly down from their pedestals at such a visual mishmash.

Poor Marigold was in a frightful state. First she forgot the water for the whisky, then going back to fetch it, she forgot what she wanted it for, and proceeded to water a bowl of lurid pink hyacinths, not even noticing when it overflowed.

'At least you've got lots of flowers,' said Lysander looking around at the massed bunches of salmon-pink gladioli.

'Ay sent them to myself,' confessed Marigold, and burst into tears.

While Ferdie shot off to refill the jug and collect some kitchen roll, Lysander, who was beginning to feel really sorry for Marigold, asked her how she had found out about Larry's bimbo.

'It was at the office party in December. Ay always used to be the prettiest girl at office parties.' Grabbing a piece of kitchen roll, she thrust it into her eyes. 'All the bosses chased after me when we were first married, now Ay'm the old trout, what everyone has to suck up to because Ay'm the boss's waife.'

She blew her nose noisily and took a slug of the replenished vodka and tonic.

'May word, that's strong, Ferdie. Anyway, I was chattin' to the company secretary's wife when I looked across the room and there was Nikki – she's Larry's PA – sitting on a leather sofa. Larry was standin' besaide her chattin' to the financial director and she was rubbin' his . . . er – the front of his trousers.'

'Perhaps she was brushing off a bit of fluff,' said Lysander.

'She's the bit of fluff,' said Marigold disdainfully. 'Then Larry saw Ay was looking and kicked her on the shins. When Ay tackled him, he shouted that Ay was imaginin' things and should get some glasses. Next day Ay was so distraught, Ay'd just set off to the Distressed Gentlefolks AGM.'

Coals to Newcastle, thought Ferdie.

'Lady Chisleden was in the chair, I recall,' went on Marigold, 'and I got all the way to Rutminster before I re-alized I'd forgotten the minutes. I always type them, I used to be a secretary, so I rushed home. Patch came running down the stairs, which is unusual, she always stays in her basket in the kitchen if we go out, so I ran upstairs. I'd just had the guest bedroom redecorated in peach Draylon, with peach damask curtains, and Ay thought Ay'd take another peek, it looked so lovely, and Ay caught them at it.'

'How awful,' said Lysander, appalled. 'What did you do?'

'Ay was so shocked, Ay said, "I've just had this room redecorated." And Nikki asked why didn't Ay have the walls dragged. Ay said, "Ay don't care for draggin', it always looks as though it should have another coat." Then Ay said, "How long have you been sleepin' with may husband?" She said, "Ay must just look it up in may faylo-fax," the cheeky cow.'

'What's she like?' asked Lysander. Seeing Marigold was shivering he got up and put more logs on the fire.

'Nikki? Spelt with a double K for Kleptomania, only she lifts husbands rather than shops,' Marigold sniffed. 'She looks like one of those girls who guides folk towards wheels of fortune in game shows. Very, very pretty, in fact she's so pretty Ay never suspected she'd be interested in may Larry. Ay thought the only woman Larry admired was Margaret Thatcher. Nikki asked me why Ay didn't have the walls dragged.'

'You told us that,' said Ferdie, who was anxious to get down to business.

'Ay'm sorry, I keep repeatin' myself. I trayed so hard to be a good wife. I got lonely in the country, but I kept busy with may committees, and Ay always washed may hair on Frayday and had a candlelit dinner waitin' for Larry when he got back from town.' She started to cry again.

'I wish someone would do that for me.' Lysander reached for more kitchen roll.

'I worked so hard in the early years, darnin' his socks, studying cheap cuts and going without lunch. We were so happy then.'

'Can we see your wedding photographs?' interrupted Ferdie briskly. 'And some when you were first married.'

Collapsing heavily between him and Lysander on the sofa, Marigold opened a red photograph album.

'You look terrific,' said Lysander gazing in amazement at a sixties snapshot of Marigold in Hyde Park. 'Great legs, and that chain belt's very sexy.'

'I gave up lunch for a whole fortnight to pay for that dress,' sighed Marigold. 'I had a handspan waist then.'

'Well, you better give up a few more lunches,' reproved Ferdie. 'You've hardly got a legspan waist now, and your skin's awful.'

Lysander winced, and wished he could go next door and watch the 3.15. Outside a gaudy pheasant with a red face and staring eyes, trailing awkwardly round the frozen lawn looking for refuge, reminded him of Marigold.

'It's nothing personal,' said Ferdie kindly. 'It's exactly like getting a horse fit for a big race. You need a month on the road and two on the gallops. Lysander'll take you jogging and when it gets lighter in the evenings and you're frantic for that forbidden first drink of the day, you can both play tennis.'

'It'll never work,' moaned Marigold. 'If it weren't for Patch, I'd kill myself.'

Patch stared balefully at them through the strings of the harp.

When Ferdie started to discuss money, Lysander was so embarrassed Ferdie had to take him off to Larry's den, where he was very excited to find a bar in the corner with every drink known to man hanging upside down with rightway-up labels.

'Oh, can I play with it?'

'Of course, and watch the end of Lingfield on the big screen. If you get bored with that, Larry's got all Donald Duck's cartoons up on the right,' said Ferdie, shutting the door firmly.

'It's going to cost you,' he told Marigold, going back into the sitting room.

'Ay haven't got any money. Larry's keepin' me so short.'

'Well, you'll have to pawn a few rings.'

'He's charmin', Lysander.'

'Charming,' agreed Ferdie. 'But very expensive. We'll have to find a cottage for him to rent down here. Not too near Paradise to preserve his air of mystery. He needs a couple of paddocks and stabling for his horses and a really sharp, fuck-off car, a Porsche or better still a red Ferrari.'

Then, ignoring Marigold's gasp of horror, 'And access to a helicopter – we can't have Larry thinking he's some tinpot gigolo – and some decent clothes: a few suits and Gucci shoes. He needs decent shoes because he has a tendency to ingrowing toenails. And you must arrange an account at The Apple Tree, and the nearest off-licence and install satellite television, so he doesn't get bored down here. Then there's the little matter of his debts.'

'How much are they?' said Marigold faintly.

'Ten grand should cover it,' said Ferdie airily. 'He'll

need pocket money of course to send you flowers and take you out on the tiles. If Larry comes back to you that's a further ten grand, and a retainer for the next year to keep Larry on his toes.'

'But Ay haven't got that kind of money,' whimpered Marigold. 'Ay shall be destitute.'

'No, you won't.' Ferdie topped up her glass. 'Insist Larry buys you that house in Tregunter, and I'll pretend it cost one hundred and fifty thousand pounds more than it does, which gives us lots of leeway.'

Marigold was so distraught, and by this time so awash with vodka, that she accepted all Ferdie's conditions.

'Life is about taking chances,' said Ferdie, cosily pocketing a vast advance cheque. 'It's going to be a lark, I promise you.'

'You 'ave terrific control over Lysander,' said Marigold shaking her head.

'I'm his mind and his minder,' Ferdie reassured her. 'I'll be overseeing things all the way.'

Watching the 3.15 on Larry's ten-foot screen made the race ten times more exciting, but Lysander felt ten times more depressed when the horse he'd backed fell at the last fence.

He thought of Arthur in his last race, donkey ears flapping, big feet splaying out in all directions, but with so much heart in his great grey girth that he ran on and on, just tipping the last fence in his tiredness. He'd got to get Arthur sound again. He had no job, no money, no prospects, no mother. The snowdrops outside, like the ones on her grave, reminded him he'd never see her again. The fish-ponds under the trees were turning ruby red in the setting sun.

He was roused from his black gloom by Ferdie, quite unable to keep the smirk off his broad pink face.

'Well, you got the job.'

'What job?'

'Being Marigold's toy boy.'

'Don't be an asshole. I can't bonk for money.'

'You only get paid if you don't bonk her. We don't want you involved in a messy divorce case.'

'What about Arthur and Tiny?'

'They can move in, too.'

All Lysander's scruples were overcome when he saw his first pay cheque. On the way back to London he and Ferdie stopped to order a red Ferrari. Arriving at Fountain Street, they found the telephone ringing. It was the police.

'I think we've found your Golf GTi, Mr Hawkley. Does it have a NCDL sticker in the back saying, "A Dog is for Life . . . Not Just for Christmas"?'

'That's the one.'

'It wasn't in Drake Street where you thought you'd left it, but in Kempton Street.'

'Thanks awfully,' said Lysander, 'that's really, really kind of you, but basically I don't need it any more, because I've just got another one.'

'*Lysander!*' Ferdie grabbed the telephone in exasperation. 'We'll be over to pick it up at once,' he told the policeman.

9

Lysander, Arthur, Tiny, Jack and a red Ferrari with a top speed of 200 m.p.h. moved into a charming cottage seven miles from Paradise, and Lysander lost no time in getting Marigold into training. As they both jogged in track suits along punishingly steep footpaths, watching the first celandine and coltsfoot pushing their way through the leaf mould and the winter barley slowly turning the brown fields pale green, Lysander wished it was Arthur he was getting fit for the Rutminster Gold Cup rather than Marigold, but they made terrific progress.

Marigold was still desperately low and Lysander got bored as she endlessly bent his ear about Larry, but he began to realize the extent of her hurt and desolation, and how hard she had supported Larry in his rocket-like rise to the top.

'Ay really trayed to be a social asset,' she told Lysander one morning as they pounded up Paradise Hill. 'For years Ay struggled with those dreadful elocution lessons.' Pink from her exertions, Marigold went even pinker. 'Ay was taught by a disgustin' old Lezzie who kept touchin' may bosom to make me project from the chest.'

'How dreadful,' Lysander shuddered.

'Let's stop and look at the vista,' gasped Marigold, who was panting more from non-stop chatter than the one-in-five gradient.

Across the valley, softened by a pale sun, morning mist and the thickening buds of its army of trees, Paradise Grange rose like a fairy-tale castle.

'Ay can't bear to leave it,' she sighed. 'You should

see it in summer when the Paradise Pearl is out. That's a pinky-whaite wisteria Mr Brimscombe planted thirty years ago. We floodlaight it in the evenings. And that's Lady Chisleden's home to the left. Ay trayed so hard to dress laike Lady Chisleden.'

'I don't think that's wise,' said Lysander in alarm. 'The old trout was blocking Paradise High Street this morning with her Bentley, bawling out Adam's Pleasure for delivering manure that was more straw than shit. Perhaps she could give Arthur a job.'

Marigold smiled, but as they started off down the hill, she returned to the subject of Larry.

'Talkin' of horses, Ay always thought we had a good love laife,' her voice trembled. 'But one of the things Nikki screamed at me was that Larry told her Ay made love laike a dead horse, because Ay never moved.'

Although Marigold had told him this a dozen times, Lysander put his arm round her.

'Alive horses don't move very much,' he said consolingly. 'I've seen lots of them being covered. My Uncle Alastair ran a stud at one time, and someone always held the mare still. Anyway, men say anything to a girl when they want to get their leg over.'

To begin with Lysander used to escape to London as soon as he had supervised Marigold's frugal supper, to party all night, returning yawning at breakfast and falling asleep in the afternoon on Larry's sunbed. But gradually he spent more and more time at Paradise Grange. There was so much to do, working out in the gym, swimming in the heated pool, riding the hunters Larry abandoned after he'd been bucked off at the opening meet, watching all Larry's Walt Disney tapes, playing with Larry's bar.

'What a pity you're off the booze, Marigold. I could mix you some terrific cocktails.'

One of their first mutual projects was the restoration of Arthur, who'd been confined to box rest for three months by the vet. As soon as the old horse arrived, Lysander had driven Marigold over to his cottage to meet him.

It was a beautiful day after a night of heavy rain, the robins were singing their heads off, and the racing streams glittered in the sunshine. Marigold tried not to squeal with terror as Lysander stormed the red Ferrari along the winding country lanes, whose high hedges were filling up so quickly with buds and even leaves one had no idea who might be hurtling in the opposite direction. By contrast, barking his head off, and rattling back and forwards like a shaken dice, Jack seemed to be thoroughly enjoying himself.

'How did you acquire Arthur?' asked Marigold faintly.

'Well, it's an extraordinary story. Basically my cousin Titus was in the Army in the Oman and during some skirmish he found Arthur wandering on the edge of the desert, thin as a rake and desperately dehydrated. Well, Titus had nowhere to stable him that night and no headcollar, so he and his men made a corral by parking four army lorries, nose to tail. Even in his desperately weakened condition, Arthur jumped straight over one of the bonnets after a passing mare.

'Titus thought they'd lost him, but he was back nosing around for toast and marmalade the next morning. Anyway, he was such a distinctive-looking horse that his owner, some Arab sheik whom Titus was liberating, recognized him and was so grateful he let Titus keep him. Arthur's got quite a good pedigree.

'Titus brought him back to England, and gave him to his father, my Uncle Alastair, who was a trainer and who won a lot of races with him. I was left some money by an aunt and Alastair was in financial trouble – he was always bad with money – so I spent the lot buying Arthur from him. I'd always loved the horse. Dad was absolutely livid.'

'Ay'm not surprised,' said Marigold, shocked. 'Your uncle shouldn't have taken all your inheritance.'

'You haven't met Arthur,' said Lysander fondly. 'Anyway, poor Uncle Alastair died of a heart attack and Arthur fell first time out last September. The vet said rest him for a year, but Mum and I were determined to get him sound by next season. Then Mum died in October.' For a second Lysander's hands clenched on the wheel. Then, swinging off the road and destroying any hope that Marigold might have had that he might slow down on the stony track up to the cottage, he added, 'So, I'm going to get him sound if it kills me.'

'Yes, Ay can see that,' said Marigold, only thankful to be alive amid so much death, as Lysander drew up with a jerk outside the stables behind the cottage. 'Oh, how adorable,' she squeaked.

For the great grey horse hanging out of his box was tugging hay from a net so untidily that Tiny, his black Shetland stable-mate, who was attacking another net hung below his, had nearly vanished under a thatch of dropped hay.

'The sweet wee thing.' Marigold rushed forward to hug the little pony.

'I wouldn't,' warned Lysander.

As Tiny lashed out with a lightning off-hind, he pulled Marigold out of the way just in time.

'Tiny,' he added, giving the pony a sharp boot on the rump, 'is an absolute bitch.'

'She ought to meet Nikki,' said Marigold with a sniff. 'Nikki said—'

'Basically I only keep Tiny,' interrupted Lysander hastily, before Marigold could get into her stride, 'because Arthur's so bats about her. She henpecks him dreadfully, and she's tried to kill Jack several times.'

Scooping Jack up, Lysander held him so he could lick Arthur's nose, then plonked the little dog between the horse's huge flopping ears. Immediately Jack tightroped down Arthur's straggly mane and settled down into the small of his back.

'How adorable,' sighed Marigold, giving Tiny a very wide berth, as she stroked Arthur. 'He's 'uge, isn't he?'

'Eighteen hands,' said Lysander proudly. 'He was the biggest horse in training. The public still send him fan mail and Twix bars, because they know he loves them.'

Arthur was pure white except for his grey nose and dark eyes which were fringed with long, straight, white eyelashes and edged with white on the inside corners, as though some make-up artist had wanted to widen them.

'Arthur looks as though he's been around,' said Marigold.

'Basically he has,' said Lysander. 'He's lived in back gardens in Fulham and on Dolly's parents' lawn; there was a row about that, and he spent three days in the orchard of a woman whose house I was – er – trying to sell.'

Not anxious to expand on that, Lysander pointed to the traffic cones and rubber tyres he'd hung over Arthur's door to give him something to biff around and amuse himself with.

'He's so good about being inside.' Lysander pulled Arthur's ears. 'He just adores being petted. He never bites Tiny back and if Jack attacks his ankles, he just looks down in amazement. If he were a human, he'd put on a smoking jacket and velvet-crested slippers every night. He's such a gent.'

'Like his master,' said Marigold warmly.

'I wish Dolly thought so,' sighed Lysander. 'She's just sent me a really sarky card: CONGRATULATIONS ON YOUR RETIREMENT. Now watch this.'

As he produced a tin of Fanta out of his Barbour pocket, Arthur gave a deep Vesuvius whicker. Pulling back the tab, Lysander put the tin between Arthur's big yellow teeth and, with gurgles of ecstasy, Arthur tipped back his head and drained the lot.

'He can't get up in the morning without his bowl of coffee,' said Lysander retrieving the tin, 'but only if it has two spoonfuls of sugar.'

February 13th was a day for celebration. Marigold weighed in a stone lighter at nine stone four, and even Patch had shed five pounds and could wriggle through the cat door again. After a frugal lunch of clear soup, fennel-and-kiwi-fruit salad, Marigold was virtuously stuffing invitations to a Save the Children Bring and Buy into envelopes, instead of white chocolates into herself, and Lysander was sitting with his muddy booted legs up on the table, trying to compose a Valentine poem to Dolly who still hadn't forgiven him for his exploits in Palm Beach.

'Ferdie's brilliant at writing poems, but he's out and I must get it in the post. What rhymes with green?'

'Keen, mean, been, my queen, sheen,' suggested Marigold. 'Did you know birds choose their mates on Valentine's Day?' She peered out at the crowded bird-table. 'And that in the spring the chaffinch gets a pinker breast and the blackbird a more golden beak and look at that starlin', his feathers are all purple and green in the sunshine.'

But Lysander was looking at Marigold. Her skin was glowing pink, not dead white laced with hectic red. Her eyes, no longer bloodshot, were the same hazel as the catkins dropping their pollen on the kitchen table. There was no resemblance now to a Beryl Cook lady.

'Sod the birds! You're the one looking terrific,' he said, tipping back his chair.

'Oh, get on with you,' said Marigold, putting two invitations into the same envelope, and blushing crimson. 'Look at those sweet little great tits, swingin' on that coconut.' Then her happiness evaporated. 'That was the coconut Larry won at the village fête last year.'

'How d'you know so much about birds?' asked Lysander, anxious to distract her.

'Ay thought Ay should study wildlaife when we moved to the country. Unfortunately Larry got interested in another kaind of bird.' That's a sort of joke, if a very weak one, Marigold thought in surprise. Perhaps I'm beginning to laugh again.

'How are you getting on with your poem?' she asked. Proudly Lysander handed it across the table.

'*The rose is red, the grarse is green,*' read Marigold. '*Open your legs and i'le turn you to creem.*'

'Oh, Laysander!' Marigold was shocked rigid. 'Ay don't think that's in the raight spirit. Why don't you pop down to The Apple Tree? They've got some beautiful floral cards, with such lovely sentiments inside, or even left blank to record your message. Ay weakened,' Marigold hung her head, 'and sent one with primroses on to Larry. Ay trayed to get it back, and nearly got my hand stuck in the letter-box. Anyway, Ay don't think Nikki'll let it through, she gets the kettle out for anythin' marked prayvate and confidential.'

Lysander was so worried Marigold would get no Valentines that he rushed off to The Apple Tree and bought her the largest card in the shop, which he handed to her with a huge bunch of daffodils the next morning, so she wouldn't get all excited and think it was from Larry.

'Oh, that's beautiful,' said Marigold, deeply touched.

Inside Lysander had written: '*To Marrygold who gets prittier eech day. love Lysander.*'

I didn't marry gold, she thought sadly. It's Nikki that's going to do that, as soon as Larry divorces me.

Seeing her face cloud over, Lysander handed her another present. More Sellotape than gift wrap, thought Marigold fondly as she broke her way in, and found a size ten pair of black-velvet shorts.

'They're lovely,' she squeaked, 'but you must be jokin'.'

'Give it three weeks,' said Lysander, 'and we'll be there.'

'We,' mumbled Marigold. How very nice.

'As we can't celebrate your great weight loss by getting pissed this evening,' added Lysander, 'I bought some magic mushrooms in Rutminster.'

'Ay can't take drugs,' said Marigold, appalled. 'Ay'm hoping to become a JP.'

'It's just a natural product,' said Lysander airily. 'We can make tea out of them, you'll love it and you won't put on an ounce.'

'Ay'm supposed to be going to a Best-Kept Village committee.'

'Cancel it. *Crocodile Dundee*'s on television.'

'Ay really shouldn't,' said Marigold. That was the third committee meeting she'd cancelled that week.

What a very sweet boy, thought Marigold. When they were jogging he helped her over stiles and caught her elbow if she slipped in the mud or on the icy roads, and he always opened doors and helped her on with her coat. He was probably doing it because he thought of her as a pathetic old wrinkly, she told herself sternly, but Larry had never done any of these things in eighteen years. And Lysander never got cross.

She loved the elegant way he draped himself over sofas and window seats, and suddenly dropped off to sleep like a puppy. And he was so appreciative of her cooking even if it was clear soup, fennel and kiwi fruit.

'I got a tip-off about some seriously good dope, in Cathedral Lane in Rutminster of all unlikely places,' Lysander told Marigold as they jogged up the north side of Paradise a fortnight later, 'and this nutter pressed his face against the car window and said "Are you looking for Jesus?" I said, "No, I'm looking for No. 37." Anyway, they're offering an eighth of an ounce for the price of a sixteenth. If they're discounting drugs, the recession must be biting.'

He was trying to cheer up Marigold, who, despite the beauty and incredible mildness of the day, had been thrown into black gloom by the display of crocuses on the lawn below the house. Specially planted by herself and Mr Brimscombe, it spelled out the word: CATCHITUNE in the record company's purple-and-yellow colours.

'It was the sort of gesture Larry adored. Ay was going to floodlight them as a surprise, so he could see them from his helicopter when he landed on Frayday neight.'

And now bees were humming in the crocuses which

were arching back their petals and thrusting forward their orange stamens to welcome the sun, if not a returning Larry.

'Where's Rannaldini?' asked Lysander, as they pounded past the secretive grey abbey shrouded in its conspirator's cowl of woods.

'Whizzin' round the world avoiding ex-waives and tax,' said Marigold sourly. 'Rannaldini plays on people's weaknesses. He realized Larry was socially insecure. He made us go ex-directory for a start, said bein' unlisted was the done thing. Just meant that no-one could phone us. Then he told Larry it was common to put up the name of one's house. Ay'd just had a board carved in poker work for Larry's birthday. Larry put it in the attic. So no-one can faind the house to drop in. Then he encouraged Larry to 'ave electric gates to keep out the public, so if people could faind the house, they couldn't get in anyway. Phew, it's hot.'

Marigold's green track suit was dark with sweat.

'Is he attractive, Rannaldini?'

'In a horrid sort of way,' said Marigold disapprovingly. 'Not may taype, far too edgy makin'. Doesn't Angel's Reach look lovely in the sunshine?'

Stopping to rest on a mossy stile, they gazed down at the big Georgian house which was to be the future home of pop star Georgie Maguire. As well as the stone angels guarding the roof and the gates at the bottom of the drive, more angels had been clipped out of the lowering yew battlements which protected the house from the east wind. And, tossing their yellow locks, a row of weeping willows seemed about to tumble into the lake like glorious Swedish blondes racing down to bathe.

'It'll be lovely having another celeb in the village to vie with Hermione and Rannaldini,' said Marigold. 'I must make sure Georgie opens the church fête this summer to irritate Hermione. Georgie's my best friend,' she went on proudly. 'She and Guy bought the house so she'd know someone near by in the country. Ay don't know what she'll say when she comes back from the States and fainds out Larry's trying to chuck me out.

'People are so competitive round here,' sighed Marigold, breathing in the faint sweet heady smell of damp earth, burgeoning leaves and violets. 'Rannaldini was jealous of Larry's executive jet, so he got a bigger one. Then Larry got a Land-Rover with three telephones, so Rannaldini got a Range Rover with four.'

Below them the River Fleet lay like mother of pearl along the bottom of the valley. Black-headed gulls congregated on its banks.

'Our grounds extend to the river,' said Marigold, 'so Rannaldini bought another twenty acres so he could have a mooring, too. Then Rannaldini had Hermione and God knows who else so Larry had to have Nikki.'

'Who's Rannaldini married to at the moment?' asked Lysander, watching the gulls rising and resettling on the opposite bank like a snowstorm.

'Well, his second wife, Cecilia, was an incredibly glamorous Italian soprano, but she made scenes rather than beds, and Rannaldini likes an ordered life. And not meanin' to boast, I think he was a bit jealous that Larry's home ran more smoothly than his did.'

'I bet he was.' Lysander squeezed Marigold's shoulder. 'Basically you know how to make a man happy.'

'Well, Ay don't know, but anyway, Rannaldini divorced Cecilia and married Kitty, his PA. In her case it stands for permanently available. She's a poppet, an absolute gem, runs Rannaldini's houses, sorts out his finances, checks his contracts, protects him from importunate fans and ex-mistresses, looks after his hoards of fraightful kiddies, and whisks up supper whenever he invaites entire orchestras home without any warning.'

'I could do with someone like that,' said Lysander. 'I don't understand the poll tax at all.'

'And she puts up with Hermione treating her laike a housemaid. Oh sugar, talk of the devil.'

There was a whirl and chug like the last spin of a

huge washing-machine, as a helicopter appeared over the woods.

'That's Hermione coming home,' said Marigold furiously. 'She's also been on tour. No doubt she'll be over in a flash, boastin' what a success she's been and how many men have fallen madly in love with her – "One can never have too many men in love with one, Marigold" – and bringing me her latest tape to cheer me up, which my husband has already produced in its thousands, and saying, "How are you? How *are* you?" when she doesn't give a shit. Whoops, penny in the swear box. Hermione must be the most irritating person since the nurse in *Romeo and Juliet*.'

Next moment, the helicopter landed on the lawn of the big yellow house with beckoning chimneys, which lay between Valhalla and Paradise Village. They could see a tiny figure getting out and people running across the lawn to meet her and could hear voices and laughter echoing round the wood.

'Let's stop off at The Apple Tree and get some Mars bars,' said Marigold, through gritted teeth.

'Better not. Ferdie's coming down to weigh you tomorrow.'

Back home, Marigold changed out of her track suit and had a long, comforting bath. When she came very apprehensively into the kitchen, wearing some new jeans, Lysander gave a Tarzan howl of joy.

'My God, they're great. You've got such a terrific ass – I mean figure.'

'Not so good with all this flesh spillin' over like uncooked pastry,' said Marigold, raising her dark blue cardigan above the waistband.

'That'll be gone in a week,' said Lysander, thinking what a lovely mouth Marigold had when it was laughing and not hidden in a hard line brooding about Larry. She looked ever less like a Beryl Cook lady now the regimented curls had been straightened and streaked and fell in a shiny blond bob over one eye. The hot bath had unleashed the Arpège she had splashed all over her body.

'If Ferdie's comin' tomorrow, I better take a ton of Ex-Lax tonaight,' said Marigold.

Heavens, who would have thought she'd ever discuss laxatives with a man? But having ridden races, Lysander knew all about getting weight off. He really was a very sweet boy.

10

Half an hour later Lysander and Marigold were in Larry's study, smoking like mad to dull their appetites, and watching the runners in the 3.00 at Wincanton circling in the paddock.

'I've backed Rupert Campbell-Black's horse, Penscombe Pride,' said Lysander. 'That bay in the dark blue rug, doesn't he look well? He won both the Rutminster and the Cotchester Gold Cups last year.'

'Even I know that,' said Marigold.

'He's favourite, but he's carrying so much weight.'

Next moment Jack flew out of the basket he now shared with Patch and went into a frenzy of yapping as Hermione Harefield swept in.

'What's the point of electric gates,' muttered Marigold, 'when Mrs Brimscombe lets in the horrors?'

Hermione was fortunate to have looks that needed little maintenance. Her strong, glossy, dark brown curls fell naturally into shape. Her big eyes the colour of After Eights were fringed with thick lashes that never needed mascara. No spot nor red vein ever marred a complexion as smooth and creamy as Carnation Milk. Her splendid bosom soared above an enviously slim waist and she never wore trousers, because they would have emphasized a rather large bottom and hidden long, charmingly curved legs. She could easily have passed for the much admired younger sister of Michelangelo's David, but in Hermione's case, beauty was only rhinocerous-hide deep.

Embracing Marigold regally, she said: 'How are you, how *are* you?' in her deep, thrillingly rich voice, and presented her with a tape of herself singing sea shanties, including 'Blow the wind southerly'. She then insisted on pressing the mute button of the television, and playing the tape fortissimo, while recounting details of her wildly successful tour.

'Such love, such love, one could feel it reaching out to one,' cried Hermione. 'But it's a responsibility to be so beloved. I must take my voice increasingly into the open air and bring music to the people. So I've decided to do Hyde Park and Wembley this summer.

'But when I felt Paradise beneath my feet and little Cosmo rushed across the lawn crying, "Mummy, Mummy", I knew that here was the real world.' She smiled at Lysander, who, having risen when she came in, was now back with his feet on the table, listening to her non-stop flow with his mouth open.

Finally Marigold butted in: 'Hermione, may I introduce Lysander Hawkley, my personal exercise trainer.'

'But you never take any exercise,' said Hermione in disbelief, which turned to disapproval when Marigold despatched Lysander to get a bottle of wine and some Perrier for herself.

'You shouldn't encourage workmen to watch television and drink in the middle of the afternoon, Marigold. What's he doing here?'

'Mending my heart.'

But Hermione wasn't listening. 'I need to get in touch with Larry. I'm recording *Dido* next week, and I want to know who's singing Aeneas and which recording studio's been booked.'

'Ay haven't a clue,' snapped Marigold. 'Ring Nikki's new apartment. You'll find Larry in bed there.'

'Don't be bitter, Marigold, it's *so* ageing,' chided Hermione, who loathed her friends having marriage problems because it gave them an excuse to talk about themselves rather than her.

'I refuse to take sides,' she went on. 'I'm sure poor Larry's as confused as you are.'

'And sells millions of your records,' said Marigold furiously.

'Oh Marigold, you silly billy,' sighed Hermione, looking at Marigold properly for the first time. 'You've dyed your hair.'

'I thought I needed a change.'

Hermione put her head on one side. 'Well, if you like it that's the main thing, and I've never seen you in jeans before. We are jazzing ourselves up.'

With a trembling hand Marigold reached for a Silk Cut. Hermione, who had a singer's pathological horror of smoking, was about to reproach her when she was distracted by the tape reaching 'Blow the wind southerly'.

'This is my favourite, I never thought anyone could sing "Blow" as well as Kathleen Ferrier, but the American critics say my version is better.'

'Oh, look,' sighed Lysander, pausing in the doorway, his arms full of bottles and glasses, and nodding at an incredibly handsome man talking to a sardonic-looking jockey in blue-and-green colours. 'That's Rupert Campbell-Black. Isn't he handsome? And seriously cool? And that's Bluey Charteris who rides for him – lucky sod.'

Lysander was about to turn up the sound when the cameras switched to the latest odds. Penscombe Pride's were shortening.

'I was lucky to get that bet on early. God, I want to meet Rupert.'

Hermione refused a drink, but said pointedly that she'd like some tea, because she hadn't had any lunch.

'You're out of luck,' said Lysander. 'Marigold's on a diet.'

Hermione turned to Marigold. 'I thought you were looking awfully tired.'

'She looks great!' Lysander smiled amiably at Hermione. 'I'm afraid the only thing in the fridge is some smoked salmon.'

'For *our* supper,' said Marigold.

'I'll have that,' said Hermione, and such was the force

of her personality that she was just polishing off the lot, washed down by Earl Grey and honey, when Jack and Patch went into another frenzy of barking.

This time it was Rannaldini's young wife, Kitty. Clutching a bunch of freesias and a red-spotted tin, she blushed when she saw not only Marigold but also Hermione, her husband's mistress, plus an incredibly good-looking young man. Perhaps he was Hermione's latest.

Launching into a flurry of 'how are yous', Hermione embraced Kitty graciously, then embarrassed her by saying teasingly: 'Both sides, Kitty,' and holding out her other cheek to be kissed after Kitty had ducked away.

Marigold, who, since Larry's departure, had suffered from chronic lapse of memory, suddenly blocked on Lysander's surname and merely introduced him and Kitty by their Christian names.

Heavens, he's gorgeous, thought Kitty, he must be some young actor who's making a pop record; such a sweet sleepy smile.

'Very pleased to meet you, Ly-sunder,' she stammered, then turning to Marigold, 'you look wonderful. I love your 'air, and you're so lovely and slim.'

'I *have* been tryin',' said Marigold gratefully.

'Well, you probably won't want that,' said Kitty going even redder, as Marigold opened the red-spotted tin which contained a huge dark chocolate cake.

'Oh yum,' sighed Marigold. 'Oh, Kitty, you are kaind, but I truly mustn't. Lysander can, though.'

'And so can I,' said Hermione. 'I never have to diet.'

Having helped herself to a vast slice, Hermione rewound the tape to play 'Blow the wind southerly', which was blotted out by Lysander's howl of joy as Penscombe Pride won by a length.

'Yippee!' He hugged Marigold in ecstasy. 'I've won two fucking grand. I can buy you a gold exercise bike now.'

Looking very bootfaced, Hermione picked up a new biography of Placido Domingo, turning to the index for reference to herself.

'I must go,' said Kitty. 'I didn't mean to butt in when you'd got company, Marigold.'

'You must have a drink to celebrate,' said Lysander, letting Marigold go.

'I'll have a small sweet sherry then,' said Kitty. 'Rannaldini don't approve, but I can't drink it dry.'

'I'll have some more Perrier please, darling.' Marigold handed Lysander her glass.

'Clever to 'ave a win like that,' said Kitty, 'I'm afraid I'm terrified of 'orses. I'd 'ave walked over 'ere this afternoon, but Rannaldini's turned The Prince of Darkness – he's a big black fing with 'uge teef – out in Long Meadow, so I came by car.'

'I know The Prince of Darkness. Bloody good horse, came second in the Whitbread,' said Lysander.

''E's still got 'uge teef,' sighed Kitty.

Lysander thought Kitty was as plain as Hermione was beautiful. She was probably younger than him, but she had a round pale face and eyes far too wide apart behind disfiguringly strong spectacles. Her fuzzy light brown hair was dragged off a rather spotty forehead into a bun. With her squashed snub nose and big generous mouth, the bottom lip of which she was nervously gnawing as she listened to Hermione, she resembled an apprehensive pug on the end of a chatterbox mistress.

A gold cross round her neck and a navy-blue polyester dress with a white collar gave her a prim look, but couldn't disguise her heavy breasts and lack of waist. Plump legs were not flattered by flesh-coloured tights, nor by navy-blue high heels which thrust her forward like a plant desperately seeking the sunlight.

'Cheers.' She attacked her large glass of sherry. 'I was wondering if you'd like to come to tea, I mean supper, next week, Marigold?'

'Love to,' said Marigold. 'As long as you don't cook anything fattening. Can I bring Lysander? He's just moved into a cottage at Eldercombe.'

'That's nice. Near Ricky France-Lynch,' said Kitty.

'His wife Daisy's just 'ad the most gorgeous li-el boy,' she added wistfully.

'You'll be next,' said Marigold reassuringly.

''Eavens, I 'ope so,' said Kitty, who, unlike Marigold, made no attempt to disguise a strong cockney accent.

Hermione, having finished reading about herself in the Domingo biography, cut another massive piece of chocolate cake and asked: 'Do you play an instrument, Ly-sarnder.'

'Yarss,' said Lysander gravely. 'I learnt the piano at prep. school, but I only play with one hand because I was always fending off Mr Molesworth, the music master, with the other one.'

'What a pity,' said Hermione, ignoring Marigold's laughter. 'I'm recording Beethoven's Cycle "To the distant beloved" on Monday. I need an accompanist to rehearse with. Such a beautiful work. D'you know it?'

Lysander shook his head. 'Can't imagine anyone bicycling to see a beloved round here, particularly a distant one. The hills are so steep. It's bad enough jogging.'

For a second, Kitty's face crumpled up into a smile, then she quickly asked Hermione how little Cosmo was.

'Magic, magic,' said Hermione warmly. 'Which reminds me, Kitty. Do you know definitely when Rannaldini's getting back? I've got to learn Amelia Boccanegra at top speed so I need him to work with me on the character and the vocal demands.'

'I fink he's coming back for Georgie Maguire's launching party,' said Kitty.

'I'd forgotten we'd got to be subjected to that,' grumbled Hermione. 'One meets such awful people at pop-record launches.'

'I expect Larry needs you and Rannaldini to raise the tone,' said Marigold acidly.

'I expect he does,' agreed Hermione. 'But I still don't really like Georgie Maguire's voice.'

'I love it,' said Lysander.

'So do I,' agreed Kitty defiantly, then, seeing Hermione's glare, 'I must go.'

'I've got a great pile of contracts at home,' said Hermione to punish her, 'so perhaps you could pop over tomorrow and check them for me.'

So you don't have to fork out for a lawyer, thought Marigold furiously.

As Lysander showed Kitty out, Hermione reproached Marigold for fraternizing with young men.

'He's probably G-A-Y, the way he was going on about Rupert Campbell-Black.' Then patronizingly as she refilled her glass, 'You're not in your first youth, Marigold.'

'I'm about to be into my first youth,' muttered Marigold through clenched teeth.

'*Blow the wind southerly*,' sang Hermione on the tape.

'Who was that girl?' asked Lysander returning.

'Didn't you realize?' said Marigold. 'That's Kitty Rannaldini.'

'Rannaldini's daughter?' Lysander took a cigarette from Marigold's pack.

'No, his wife.'

'His wife!' said Lysander. 'Bloody hell, I thought Rannaldini was into fantastic-looking women.'

Hermione had been about to reproach Lysander for smoking. Instead she bowed in acknowledgement of the implied compliment, then added sententiously: 'Some people think she's rather common, but I maintain Kitty Rannaldini is very much her own woman.'

'Hardly be anyone else's, looking like that,' said Lysander. 'He must have got her from Pug Rescue.'

'That's unkind.' Hermione laughed heartily.

'Kitty's sweet,' protested Marigold angrily. 'She's such a good listener – unlaike some – and so kaind you forget how plain she is.'

Outside the setting sun, like a great red air balloon, was turning the mist which had suddenly filled the valley the softest rose-pink. Having polished off another drink, Hermione, known locally as the Great White Hinter, asked if the Ferrari outside the door was Lysander's and whether he could run her home.

'I walked here, but it's a bit chilly, and we singers are paranoid about getting colds. Goodbye, Marigold, don't take everything quite so personally.'

Lysander returned ten minutes later to find Marigold gibbering with rage. Her fury at Hermione's jibes and smugness had been exacerbated by a sudden, violent explosion of jealousy because she had waltzed off with Lysander. This was the more appalling because after all she had suffered over Larry, Marigold thought she was immune from feeling jealous about anyone else.

'The bitch,' she stormed, 'not taking saides indeed. "Don't be bitter, Marigold, if you like your hair, that's what matters." And being so patronizing about Georgie and poor darling Kitty.'

'Have a drink. One won't hurt. What's brought all this on?'

'Then insistin' you drove her home. God, I'm unhappy.'

Marigold was so upset, she unthinkingly picked up the remaining quarter of chocolate cake and was about to shove it into her face when Lysander grabbed her hand, squeezing it until she dropped the cake on the floor. Then he took her in his arms.

'Don't be miserable. She's just jealous. I think you're absolutely gorgeous.'

'You do?' whispered Marigold.

'Yarss,' said Lysander, and catching her off guard as she giggled, he kissed her, nearly losing his tongue in the process as Marigold clamped her teeth and lips together with a squeal of horrified rage.

'How dare you?' With shock fuelled by years of respectability and inhibition, she was fighting him off, pummelling his chest like Frank Bruno. 'No, no, no!'

But Lysander grabbed her arms, and much stronger than her, drew her towards him, tantalizing her with the lithe, youthful warmth of his body, refusing to let go, until, panic-stricken, she raised her leg to knee him in the groin. But somehow her leg never reached its target, for far above it, Lysander was whispering words of such affection and desire into her hair.

'I want you, Marigold. You creep into my thoughts like that pink mist stealing up the valley.'

Glancing up, amazed by such poetic sentiment, and seeing the gentleness in his adorably innocent eyes, and feeling his fingers stroking her face, seeking some loving message in braille, she let him put his beautiful mouth on hers.

As she kissed him back, the raised leg retreated and coiled itself round the other leg in ecstasy, and the pummelling Frank Bruno fists unclenched, and, 'may goodness', she was hanging from Lysander's neck like a chimpanzee because she was so dizzy with lust it was the only way she could stand up.

Slowly, slowly like a Harrods lift at Christmas, Lysander progressed downwards. Worried that her breasts might be droopy, she clamped her arms back over them, but as Lysander caressed her neck, she couldn't remember if she'd plucked out that bristle on her chin this morning. Raising her hand to check, she left her right breast exposed. Next moment it had fallen like a ripe pear into his hand, as he unhooked her bra.

'Let's go to bed.'

'We can't. Ay've never been to bed with anyone but Larry, and he says Ay fuck laike a dead . . . ' Marigold gave a wail.

'Hush, just regard it as a superior form of work-out.'

People are said never to remember how they get upstairs to the bedroom, but it was imprinted on Marigold's memory, because Lysander kissed her on every stair, but still half her mind was fretting about stretch marks and whether her body would be creased by such tight jeans and, although she'd had a bath two hours ago, whether she should wash again, so she wouldn't smell of mouldy old woman. As they reached the landing, she nearly led him into the airing cupboard.

'No, not in our bedroom,' she squeaked with a resurgence of virtue, 'and certainly not in there,' as Lysander tried another door. 'That's where I caught Larry and Nikki.'

'Good, I can lay you and the ghost.'

'But the central heating's been off for days.'

Lysander's body was warmer than any radiator as he drew her close, and slowly began to unbutton her navy-blue cardigan.

'Turn off the laight,' moaned Marigold as she shot between the peach satin sheets.

'I want to look at you,' said Lysander.

In the end they compromised by leaving the light on on Lysander's side with the lampshade tipped outwards.

'God, I love snogging. Let's go on for hours.'

And Marigold, who hadn't snogged since the Purley Odeon in the sixties, responded with alacrity.

Then with the joyful excitement of a child unpacking a Christmas stocking he began to explore her body.

'Christ, these are beautiful.' He buried his face in her heavy breasts. 'And do you like being stroked here?' He turned her over to admire her surprisingly high rounded bottom. 'This is my favourite bit.' His hands crept up the velvet inside of her thighs. 'No, it isn't quite. This is.' His long fingers disappeared into the sticky, spongy burrow.

'Aaaaaah,' sighed Marigold.

'Eureka,' said Lysander as like a doorbell in the dark his middle finger found the nub of her clitoris.

'Ay reek of what?' Marigold jumped away in horror. She knew she should have washed beforehand.

'The only Greek I know. Come here.'

'Ay truly shouldn't.'

'Isn't it nice?'

'Heavenly, but we mustn't, oh, please go on, oh, gracious me, how lovely, oh, help me, help me.' Marigold went silent and rigid, her breath came in little gasps, and she forgot to hold her tummy in. Finally she gave a contented moan.

'Oh Lay-sander, that was top 'ole.'

'It certainly was.' Opening her eyes, she saw he was smiling down at her. 'Open your legs, and I'll turn you to cream. Did you enjoy it?'

'Oh, very much, and now Ay must give you pleasure.'

Dutifully Marigold reared up on her elbow. The progress of her hand down his flat belly into the down of hair was impeded by a cock rearing up like the Tower of Pisa.

'May word.'

Marigold had never really liked Larry's cock, which was rather small and, because he preferred to make love in the morning, she'd never known after a night's sleep what was under the folds. She'd always treated it like an unexploded bomb.

But Lysander, having had a shower after their jog, smelled as fresh and sweet as the violets that had scented the valley that afternoon, and his cock tasting faintly of Pear's soap was so hard and smooth beneath her lips that she began to give it puppy licks.

Used to Dolly's snake-like flickering expertise, Lysander was curiously turned on. But when she grew bolder and tried to take his cock in her mouth he sensed her fear, and detaching himself slithered down the satin sheets, pulling her on top of him.

'Oh, that's wonderful,' gasped Marigold, feeling gloriously thrust upward. 'Oh Lay-sander, I'm flaying from your flagpole. Oh Lay-sander. LAY-SANDER!'

'That was miraculous,' said Lysander, retrieving the duvet from the floor, as he collapsed back on to the satin pillows.

'You're amazing, a complete revelation.'

'Men are supposed to go on for hours, I never last more than a minute – if I'm lucky, so I make up for it beforehand.'

'Ay should feel guilty.'

'Why – we must have lost at least five hundred calories.'

Then, suddenly, he sat up, put the fist of one hand into the palm of the other, screwed up his face engagingly like Hermione, and sang in a high falsetto: '*Blow the cock, southerly, southerly, southerly,*' and they both collapsed with giggles.

'We mustn't tell Ferdie,' said Marigold.

'No, he'd be livid,' said Lysander in alarm. 'He insisted no bonking.'

'We won't do it again.'

'We might. If we use up another five hundred calories, we could get a take-away for supper.'

'Oh, yes please.'

'How about now.'

Marigold glanced at the clock in amazement. 'But you'll miss *Neighbours*.'

'Some things are more important.'

'Oh Laysander, that's the greatest compliment Ay've ever been paid. Why don't we phone Mrs Brimscombe and ask her to record it?'

11

This and subsequent glorious couplings cheered Marigold up immensely, particularly when her two sons came home from prep school for the weekend, and fell almost more in love with Lysander than she had. Not only did he play endless billiards and darts with them, and took them to the amusement arcades in Rutminster and to the stables to mess around with Arthur and Tiny, but he also initiated them into the more dubious pleasures of poker, chemmy and betting.

Jason's shriek of delight when he won £120 on an each-way bet at Chepstow was only equalled by Mark's quiet satisfaction that, by the end of the weekend, Lysander owed him £5,225 at poker.

Marigold was wryly aware that Lysander was far nearer to the boys in age and behaviour than he was to her. But she was overjoyed to see her sons emerge from pale mono-syllabic shell-shock, no doubt induced as much by two terms at an English prep school as by the collapse of their parents' marriage. She was also gratified that whenever the boys were absorbed with anything, Lysander sloped out to the kitchen for a surreptitious, but no less passionate, embrace. He couldn't keep his hands off her.

She had lost a further seven pounds a week later when she got a telephone call on her private line. Knowing it could only be Larry, she was only just stopped by Lysander from snatching up the receiver on the first ring. The warmth of his hand over hers gave her strength.

'Make him wait ten rings, and play it cool.'

Larry was telephoning to say he'd be in the area that

evening, could he drop in for a very quick drink. Marigold was thrown into total panic.

'We'd better ask Ferdie's advice on this one,' said Lysander.

Ferdie, bored of not selling houses in London and wanting to suss out properties in Paradise, said he would be straight down to orchestrate the whole thing.

Larry Lockton was a bully with a mega-ego and no small talk, who was used to ordering around thousands at work. Having lost weight, found a decent dentist and coaxed his coarse black hair forward to hide a receding hairline, he had developed sex appeal late in life. Huge success at work and a decent tailor had accelerated the process. When addressing his social superiors, he talked with an orchard of plums in his mouth.

Landing the helicopter, he saw a blur of yellow and purple. What the hell was Marigold doing spoiling his perfect lawn with crocuses? It would take ten grand off the asking price. He must remember to remove his gold discs, the Picasso, the Stubbs and the framed Beethoven sonata, before Marigold got too grasping over the spoils. Letting himself in, Larry was surprised not to be welcomed by Marigold. Only Patch greeted him, and then with reservation. Larry meant fewer chewsticks and banishment from her mistress's bed at night. Going into the kitchen, he found a table with pink candles laid for two, pink freesias and hyacinths everywhere and two bottles of Moët in the fridge.

Oh Christ, he hoped Marigold wasn't planning to lure him into staying for dinner. Nikki was expecting him back. They were going to a party to meet Kiri Te Kanawa and Marigold's attempted candle-lit lobster thermidor last month had ended in total hysterics and both lobsters being hurled at him. He'd better watch out for flying sauceboats.

He could hear noises overhead. Finding a navy-blue overcoat covered in dog hairs hanging over the banisters,

Larry went slowly up to his former bedroom where he was shocked to discover his naked wife blow-drying her hair. Seeing him, she jumped only slightly, then languidly wrapped round herself a fluffy yellow towel which matched her eyes.

'Larry! Ay didn't hear you arrive. Let me finish my hair. You know it drays crinkly if Ay stop in the middle.'

Marigold then kept him waiting half an hour, giving him time to absorb all Lysander's clutter of drying boots, breeches, *Sporting Life*s, and a pile of beautifully ironed Harvie & Hudson shirts on the hall table. When she wandered down, still in the yellow towel, Marigold was delighted to see Larry's shirt was crumpled and missing a button.

She also noticed how old he looked – compared with Lysander – and that, with hair long enough for a pony-tail, a new black moustache, bags under his eyes and designer stubble flecked with grey (all no doubt Nikki's work), he looked seedy rather than sexy. He was also dressed uncharacteristically butchly in a studded leather jacket, and black jeans belted with a large silver buckle.

'Where's your motor bike?' she said teasingly. 'I thought you'd have got fat gobblin' up all those poor little companies, but you seem to have lost even more weight. Have a glass of bubbly. Ay'm going to.'

It's my fucking champagne, thought Larry, noticing that as she took the bottle out of the fridge, she replaced it with another, and that her hair was streaked very blond and her toenails had been newly painted scarlet. The towel was showing a great expanse of stunning, recently waxed, Duo-tanned legs. Marigold, in fact, was looking fantastic, as though she'd been restored and a picture light shone over her.

Larry then asked her if she'd mind coming to the party next week to launch Georgie Maguire's new album, *Rock Star*.

'I've brought the whole package.' Larry threw the tape, the single and the album down on the kitchen table.

The sleeve showed Georgie Maguire clinging wetly to a rock, with her head thrown back, eyes closed, nostrils flaring, long, drenched red hair snaking down her back. 'I think it looks terrific.'

'Hermione was barefoot on the sleeve of *Blow the wind southerly*,' said Marigold, who knew Nikki had worked on the design. 'Are you trying to tell folk your artistes can't afford shoes?'

Larry refused to rise. 'Album's going to be a massive hit. It's storming up the American charts, so the party'll be a celebration. Loads of names accepted already. Hermione and Rannaldini are coming.'

'And presumably Nikki to add glamour,' said Marigold sweetly.

'She might look in,' admitted Larry. 'Should be a terrific bash.'

I'll bash her, thought Marigold, narrowly missing Larry as the champagne cork flew out.

Larry adjusted his leather jacket, bought new that morning, wondering if it were over the top. He felt more at home in pin-stripe.

'Pop in for half an hour,' he said gruffly, 'just to show Georgie there's no hard feelings.'

'Because she won't sign another contract with you, if she has an inkling what an absolute shit you've been to me,' said Marigold flaring up.

'Chill out,' said Larry, which irritated Marigold more than ever. 'It's in your interest. You'll be able to screw far more maintenance out of me if Georgie signs that contract,' he added heartily. 'Besides it's her first big break in twenty years. She wants her best friend there.'

Weighing up the options, Marigold let the towel slip a fraction.

'And I'd like you to be there,' Larry was shocked to hear himself saying.

'All right, Ay'll show,' Marigold agreed flatly, 'and tray and behave.' Then, glancing at the kitchen clock, 'I must get ready. Don't hurry, finish your drink.'

Utterly thrown, expecting either abuse or pleading to stay, Larry drained his whisky, and was then even more flabbergasted when Marigold said: 'Ay've decided Ay've been horribly selfish over the kids. One must be civilized for their sakes. And they must get to know Nikki, she's so near them in age.' Let Larry experience some of the same guilt she felt about cradle-snatching. 'In fact, you can have them next weekend. I'm goin' away.'

'To your mother?' asked Larry.

'No, to Paris.' Marigold smiled beautifully. 'And Mummy would be decaydedly *de trop*.'

If Larry had looked round he would have seen the tears in his wife's eyes. Instead, trampling crocuses underfoot as he strode furiously out to his helicopter, he was incensed to see a red Ferrari, unleashed by a signal from Ferdie, storming up the drive. Larry had refused to listen to Hermione's hints about an over-familiar workman. Workmen in his experience did *not* drive Ferraris. Only when he looked back from his helicopter did he read: CATCHITUNE in yellow and purple on the lawn and almost weep.

Five days later Lysander drove Marigold up to London for Georgie Maguire's launching party. A huge sixties star, Georgie was now in her late forties. But from the posters plastered all over the walls of Hammersmith and Fulham: GEORGIE MAGUIRE – LIVE IN CONCERT, which showed her clinging to the same wet rock as on the CD sleeve, she was still seductive in a slightly blousy way.

'How can one be dead in concert?' asked Lysander, dodging and diving through end-of-rush-hour traffic.

'She'll be dead on her feet from touring and jet lag,' said Marigold.

Georgie's new album was already Number Two in America, because of the leading track, the actual 'Rock Star' of the title. The song, in fact, was not about a rock star, but a celebration of Georgie's abiding love for her husband Guy, who was not only the rock on which she built her life, but the star who guided her. The sentiment would have been mawkish had not the lyrics and melody, written and sung by Georgie herself in her husky, mezzo-soprano voice, been so beautiful. With so many marriages breaking up, such a simple public confession of love had driven the Americans wild. The young in particular adored the song, because they craved the example of a happy lasting union in the same way they had loved 'Lady in Red', which Chris de Burgh had written about his wife.

To distract herself from the terrors of Lysander's driving, and the party ahead, Marigold played the advance *Rock Star* tape all the way up to London. It still made her cry.

'What's Georgie's husband like?' asked Lysander, overtaking a startled chauffeur in a limo on the inside, as he stormed up the Lillie Road.

'Oh, very attractive, rather stern, but incredibly kaind. Georgie used to be terribly wild before she married and for quite a whayle afterward. Guy got an honours degree at Cambridge and a boxing blue. His father was a bishop in some hot African country, so Guy's used to givin' orders. His family were horrifayed when he married Georgie, but he stuck bay her. He calmed her down, understood her need for freedom, yet yanked in the reins when she went too far. He was also big enough to handle her success and her failures. He was there when she went out of fashion in the late-seventies, and stopped her drinking heavily when she had one flop after another. Ay've never forgotten her last big launch in the early eighties. They hired the Hippodrome and none of the media turned up, just Georgie dancing by herself to her own music, then collapsin' in a sozzled heap. It was terrible.'

'Poor Georgie,' Lysander was appalled. 'I'd have danced with her.'

'She's a bit scatty, too,' went on Marigold, checking her reflection for the thousandth time, 'and Guy's always given her so much back-up domestically, changing nappies, taking the kids out. He's a wonderful cook, too. He should give Larry lessons.'

'And me,' said Lysander. 'He sounds depressingly like one of my brothers. How did you and Georgie meet?'

'She came as a temp to the office where Ay was working, tryin' to support herself between gigs. She could only taype with two fingers, and used to come in and collapse on the taypewriter complainin' that she'd been trippin' all night. I tayped most of her letters. But she was such fun. She had lots of unsuitable musician boyfriends, but Guy was always in the background. Her Guyrope, she called him. Finally they got married.'

'What does he do?' asked Lysander, shooting a red light at the bottom of the North End Road.

'Well, he was thinking of going into the Church. He'd have packed them in like Billy Graham, but the thought of Georgie as a vicar's waife probably put him off, so he went into Sotheby's, he was always arty and had a terrific eye. Now he's got his own gallery. He's pretty successful, discovering obscure painters, then making a killing when they become famous.

'Their finances have always been a bit haphazard, but hopefully *Rock Star* will put them on a secure financial footing. They need it for all the money they're pourin' into Angel's Reach. The trouble is they're too generous. Guy's always helping struggling artists, and he does so much for charity.'

'Guy, Guy with the terrific eye,' said Lysander. 'When they move into Paradise, he can take your place on all those "Preservation of Rural Gentlecats" committees, and you can spend all day in bed with me.'

'Whay d'you draive so fast?' shrieked Marigold, as, narrowly avoiding a collision with an oncoming bus, Lysander screeched off right into Fountain Street.

'Because I'm desperate to bonk you before Ferdie gets home.'

Waving a friendly two fingers at the gays opposite, who were peering out of their curtains, Lysander whisked her into the flat.

*　　*　　*

127

As it was they had plenty of time. Marigold was changing and Lysander was watching *EastEnders* and giggling over a postcard of the Eiffel Tower, signed: PLASTERED OF PARIS, which he and Marigold had sent Ferdie, when Ferdie himself walked in, bringing a new dark blue pinstripe suit, made by Douglas Hayward, for Lysander.

'They'll all be bopping around in black leather and T-shirts. You'll stand out much better,' added Ferdie as he straightened Lysander's new blue silk tie.

'Oh, Laysander,' gasped Marigold from the darkness at the top of the stairs. 'Ay've never seen you in a suit before.'

'Everyone'll think I've stolen it,' Lysander squinted at himself in the hall mirror.

'You look scrumptious.'

It was true. As decent tailoring hides a multitude of tums on a middle-aged body, it can also marvellously elongate a broad-shouldered, willowy figure. On Lysander, the suit seemed to dance.

'Well, come on down, Marigold. Let's have a look at you,' ordered Ferdie. 'Jesus,' he caught his breath, 'you have worked hard.'

For the most gorgeous legs encased in black fishnet were coming down the stairs. Above them Marigold was wearing the black shorts Lysander had given her on Valentine's Day, a white silk shirt and a black velvet coat slung over her shoulders.

Meeting her at the bottom, Ferdie took her hand and raised it to his lips. 'You look sensational,' he said slowly. 'Marilyn Monroe's face and body on Marlene Dietrich's legs.'

'Whay, thank you, Ferdie.'

'And you've got into my black shorts.' Lysander gave a whoop.

'And look what I've borrowed from Cartier's for you to pretend Lysander's just given you.' Ferdie pinned a diamond brooch in the shape of a key on her velvet lapel. 'Now take off your wedding-ring, and remember to look happy.'

'It'll be strange not being a waife,' said Marigold, sliding off the huge diamond and putting it in her handbag. 'Ay tried so hard to be the perfect company waife. Ay wore Jaegar shirtwaisters and never yawned or swore or smoked too much. Ay always read *Billboard* and *The Gramophone* so Ay could talk to reviewers and distributors. Ay even trayed to laike Grand Opera.'

'Well, it's high time,' Ferdie undid two more buttons of her silk shirt, 'you kicked over the Traceys, or Nikkis.'

'Don't worry,' said Lysander, seeing Marigold trembling at Nikki's name. 'I'll stay superglued to you all evening – and so will every man in the room – you look so beautiful.'

12

The one person not allowed to make an entrance at the party, which was held in a large blacked-out film studio in Soho, was Georgie Maguire herself. Her husband, who believed punctuality was next to Godliness, made sure she was there twenty minutes before kick-off, only to find the place deserted except for a handful of technicians up ladders adjusting spotlights, and softening the filters on the camera lights which hung from the ceiling.

To emphasize the marine theme of the album, a large papier-mâché rock had been plonked in the middle of the room. A cardboard lighthouse flashed on and off in one corner. Lobster pots had been placed round the walls from which hung fishermen's nets, cut-outs of fish sea-horses with lit-up eyes and clumps of seaweed which were beginning to smell.

Monitors showed the same clip of Georgie clinging voluptuously to the rock. Waitresses wearing matelot jerseys and bell-bottoms, many of whom remembered Georgie from the sixties, crunched around a floor littered with sea-shells and sand, making up a rum punch and putting out glasses. Caterers, who were knocking up a sea-food buffet, crept out of the kitchen wiping prawn juice on their aprons to have a gawp.

'It all looks wonderful. If only I was slim enough to wear horizontal stripes! You've gone to so much trouble.' Georgie drifted among them in tearful ecstasy, captivating, flattering, signing autographs, then adding to Guy in an undertone, 'and absolutely no-one's going to turn up.'

Then, because Guy hadn't given her time to get ready she shot into the Ladies to titivate.

Immediately she was joined by a girl in a dark blue velvet dress with a pie-frill collar, which flattened her breasts and stopped at mid-calf above sensible, medium-heeled shoes. Blond hair, held in place by a black velvet band, emphasized a long nose and a thin beige predatory face, giving the distinct impression of the wolf in *Little Red Riding Hood* trying to pass himself off as Alice in Wonderland.

'Hi, Georgie,' said the blonde in a deep, put-on voice. 'I'm Nikki, Larry Lockton's PA. We met when you came to the office.'

'Oh, right,' said Georgie, who didn't remember at all. 'How nice to see you. God, I'm nervous.'

Not nearly as nervous as I am, thought Nikki, trying to soften the black kohl round her eyes with a shaking finger.

Ever since Larry had been to see Marigold last week he'd been tetchy and withdrawn and the weekend with the boys had been disastrous, not to mention the mud all over her new cream carpet. To cap it there'd been a piece in the *Daily Mail* that morning about the way the careers of high flyers took a dive when they left their wives for bimbos. Nikki's aim tonight was therefore to look even more wifely than Marigold.

Georgie, who loathed being talked to when she was getting ready, was trying to secure her newly washed hair, which Guy had insisted she wore up to banish any sixties hippy image. She wished this silly girl, who was now rabbiting on about the wonders of Paradise, would go away.

'You must drop in if you're ever in the area again,' murmured Georgie.

It was her standard response to any fan. She would have died if they'd taken her up on it.

'We'd like that, Georgie,' said Nikki. Little do you know, she thought, that I'm going to be your neighbour and the wife of your record producer, able to control your fat advances. Then she added out loud, 'I'm dead excited about meeting Rannaldini, aren't you?'

Momentarily, Georgie was roused out of her trance. 'I'd forgotten he was coming,' she said.

'They say he picks women off like ducks bobbing past in a shooting gallery,' said Nikki, adjusting the garters holding up her deliberately wifely, nutmeg-brown stockings.

Not that she'd attract Rannaldini like this. But there would be years ahead when, as the mistress of Paradise Grange, she reverted to her normal, shimmeringly sexy, black leather, tousled-blond self.

Having charmed a large Bells out of the waitresses, Guy Seymour was lining up glasses and press releases and delightedly noticing the number of Press who were signing their names in the visitors' book, when Larry Lockton stormed in.

God, he looks ridiculous, thought Guy.

Larry was wearing a scowl, a black leather jacket, a white T-shirt hanging outside black jeans. Any inches added by black, high-heeled cowboy boots were negated by the weight of gold jewellery and the black hair which was beginning to cascade in ringlets over his collar and sweating forehead.

'Of all the fucking things to happen,' he roared, flattening the waiting Catchitune publicity staff against the walls.

'We've got a lot of heavy-weight Press here already,' said Guy soothingly, reading upside down as reporters from *The Scorpion* and *The Sunday Times* Style pages signed in.

'Fat lot of good it'll do us.' Larry glared round. 'They've all turned up to see Rannaldini.' Then, as Guy drew him out of earshot of the reporters, 'The fucker phoned as I entered Old Compton Street, saying he wasn't coming, so I rammed the Merc in front.'

Rannaldini, he went on, who was on sabbatical from the London Met making a film of *Don Giovanni*, had been due to fly back for the party that afternoon. Instead he had returned secretly the day before in order to surprise the London Met who were playing Beethoven's *Ninth* at the Festival Hall under Oswaldo, their guest conductor.

'Oswaldq's too bloody good for Rannaldini's liking,' stormed Larry, grabbing one of two more large whiskies conjured up by Guy. 'Anyway, Rannaldini plonks himself down in the front row, and sits stony-faced with his eyes shut until the last moment when the singing starts. Then he stalks out, distracting everyone from the music, and telling some gleefully hovering reporter from the *Evening Standard* that he can't listen to such garbage any longer.

'So, of course, it is all over the *Standard*, and, as is his fucking wont to get himself out of trouble, Rannaldini jumps into his jet and shoves off back to LA, missing the fuss and Georgie's party. The bastard didn't even have the guts to ring me until he was safely over the Irish Sea. Even Kitty doesn't know he's buggered off. She's on her way up.'

Larry couldn't have been angrier. He or rather Catchitune had poured vast sums into Rannaldini's pocket. He and Rannaldini were supposed to be buddies, and Nikki, who was a terrific star-fucker, was dying to meet him, and besides he needed moral support in case Marigold punched Nikki on the nose.

He and Guy were interrupted by a photographer from *The Scorpion* who was loading up his camera.

'First edition goes to press any minute. What time are you expecting Rannaldini?'

As Larry opened his mouth, Guy interrupted smoothly: 'He'll be along in a minute. Traffic's terrible.' Then he murmured to Larry, 'We've got the Press here, let's use them.'

'Where's Georgie anyway?' asked Larry, suddenly remembering he had an album to launch.

'In the bog, grouting her face,' said Guy.

Larry went white. 'Nikki's in there.'

'Shit! She won't say anything to Georgie about you and her, will she?'

'She promised not to,' said Larry gloomily, 'but she's so off the wall. I run a billion-pound company and I've been answering my telephone all day, while Nikki goes to the hairdresser and tarts herself up.'

'I'll yank Georgie out of the bog,' said Guy, shooting off, 'and you keep Nikki off the drink. It gets to women.'

'How's *Rock Star* doing, Larry?' asked the *Daily Mail*.

'Breaking all records. We've already put on a massive re-press,' muttered Larry, bolting off to the Gents.

No-one could have been a less heavenly host than Larry. He had no chit-chat, only intense concentration on what temporarily interested him, which on this occasion, confusingly, was both Nikki and Marigold. He also had the nightmare of making a speech. Practice making more and more imperfect, he had been rewriting the draft given him by the publicity department all day.

Outside the Ladies, Guy roared: 'For God's sake, come out at once, Panda,' which was a nickname from when they'd first met, when he could hardly see Georgie's eyes for sooty black make-up.

'Thank you,' said Georgie loudly to the cloakroom lady, as she drifted out, to draw attention to the couple of gold pound coins she'd left beside the silver in the saucer.

Funny, observed the cloakroom lady, as she pocketed the coins, that Georgie, despite her slim top-half, had revealed plump legs when she'd raised her skirt to pull up her tights and the blonde in the ultra-respectable dress had been wearing no knickers at all.

Exhausted from the American launch, Georgie was now running on pure adrenalin. Like a long-lost lover, her American public had been flowing back in the last week of the tour. The fan letters, dried to a trickle, were beginning to pour in, workmen hailed her from scaffolding. For the first time in years, people nudged as she passed in the street.

The English launch was far more of an ordeal, because

London had been the home of her last humiliating flop and because Guy was with her today, which made her far more nervous, because he was the person she most wanted to please in the world.

She was deathly pale as she entered the party room, her earthy sensual face almost puddingy, but when she saw the waiting army of reporters and frenziedly clicking cameramen, colour seeped back into her cheeks, her long, mournful heavy-lidded eyes started to sparkle, and the deep lines, which ran from her wide snub nose past the corners of her coral-pink mouth with its huge pouting snapdragon lower lip, seemed to disappear in a wonderful, wicked, face-splitting smile.

The rigours of the American tour had knocked off seven pounds and given her back her cheek-bones. The long slinky dress, the same blue as sunlit summer seas, emphasized her slim shoulders, pretty breasts and waist and bypassed her hips and legs. As she draped herself over the papier-mâché rock for the photographers, her heavy russet hair broke away from its moorings and writhed over her shoulders – Georgie, the sex symbol, was reborn.

Soon she was wooing the Press.

'What are you working on?' asked the *Express*.

'A musical about mid-life crisis called *Ant and Cleo*.'

'Autobiographical?' asked the *Mirror*.

'Of course not,' Georgie smiled across at Guy, who said firmly, 'And Georgie's about to sign a contract for a new album for Catchitune.'

'Dar-ling,' reproached Georgie, 'I want to get shot of *Ant and Cleo* first.'

'You looking forward to living next to Rannaldini in the country?' asked *The Scorpion*.

'God, yes. I'm a colossal fan. I think he's brilliant and stunning, too.'

'Perhaps he could produce *Ant and Cleo*,' suggested the *Telegraph*.

'Paradise Productions. Wouldn't that be wonderful?' sighed Georgie.

'Look this way, Georgie,' shouted the photographers, 'To me, Georgie.' 'Smile, Georgie.' 'Climb on the rock; show us your legs,' which was the one thing Georgie was not prepared to do.

Shoved rudely aside, as so often happened, by people anxious to get to his wife, Guy Seymour moved round the room, slipping cards with the gallery's address on to anyone rich and famous who might be interested in buying paintings.

'Is Georgie Maguire here in person?' asked a pale girl from the *Independent*.

'Of course she is,' answered Guy quite sharply.

'I went to a launch at lunchtime,' said the girl huffily, 'where the pop star didn't show. The record company didn't feel it was relevant and they didn't play any of her records,' she shouted over the boom of *Rock Star*. 'Of course hype and hard sell are very unfashionable at the moment.'

'That's why we're in the middle of a recession,' snapped Guy.

'She's not bad for forty-six,' admitted the girl, consulting her hand-out. 'Which is her famous husband?'

'I am,' said Guy.

'Oh, right. D'you manage Georgie?'

'No-one manages Georgie.'

The room was filling up with record distributors, disc jockeys, Catchitune employees, musicians produced by Catchitune and the general freeloaders of the music business.

Through a fog of cigarette smoke, people drifted up and down: men in overcoats, T-shirts, designer gymshoes and baseball caps, clutching beer bottles like grenades, or in leather jackets with their shirts hanging out like Larry. Girls with scarlet lips, tangled hair, wandering eyes and pale faces like Brides of Dracula, who never saw the daylight, crunched over the sea shells, restlessly searching for celebrities or at least familiar faces.

Everyone pretended not to stare at Georgie, but they all agreed that the album was great and that, in the down light, she looked terrific. But they ignored her because big stars don't like to be pestered and it wouldn't be cool to go up to her.

The Press were getting restless.

'That's great, thank you.' One by one they closed their notebooks, switched off their tape recorders and looked around for Rannaldini.

Georgie, however, having been out of fashion a long time, desperately needed reassurance. Like a bride at her own wedding whom everyone thinks is too important to waylay, she was suddenly deserted and sought Guy out in panic.

'It's going to be a mega-flop. Everyone's leaving.'

'Don't be so bloody wet, Panda.'

'Judging by celebrity head-counts, this party is a complete wash-out,' said the girl from the *Independent*.

Then in walked Dancer Maitland, thin as a rake with his long tousled mane and black-lined eyes, one of the biggest rock stars on both sides of the Atlantic.

'Hi, darling.' He came straight up to Georgie, hugging her cautiously so as not to disturb either of their hair or make-up.

'Great album. Wish I'd written it. Bloody nice of me to be here, when you've just pushed me off Number One in the States and no doubt you'll do the same in England. I hear you're moving to Rutshire. I'll be there in April when practice chukkas start. You must come and 'ave dinner.'

'Oh, we'd love to,' said Georgie ecstatically. 'Oh, Dancer, thank you for coming, and making the party. Have you met Guy?'

Dancer looked at Guy's strong stern face, whose classical good looks were only marred by a nose broken when he was boxing for Cambridge. The warmth of the reddy-brown complexion and the friendly smile showing excellent teeth were tempered by eyes which despite laughter lines were the cold pale azure of Basildon Bond writing-paper.

A battered, gold corduroy suit, a blue-and-gold paisley silk-tie and beautifully cut, straight, white-blond hair falling on the collar of his dark blue shirt, gave him an arty look. But the overwhelming impression was of some high churchman: a man of passion but strong-willed enough to resist the overtures of the most wantonly ravishing parishioner.

Sexy but tough as shit, thought Dancer, wincing at Guy's firm handshake.

'Georgie gives you a good press,' he said. 'But I thought I was the only rock star livin' in Rutshire.'

And the photographers got their picture, because Dancer came to launching parties even less often than Rannaldini.

Dancer was followed by Andrew Lloyd Webber, Rod Stewart, Simon Bates, Steve Wright, Cilla Black, Simon Le Bon and a host of other celebs, so Rannaldini wasn't missed nearly as much as he would have liked. Hermione, on the other hand, made a deliberately late entrance with her devoted, balding husband Bob who, as the orchestra manager of the London Met, had had a punishing day dealing with Rannaldini and the Press.

Hermione was looking radiant in a rich, red Chanel suit embroidered with roses and with a built-in bra to boost her splendid breasts. To boost her sales, she carried a large crocodile bag, rattling with tapes of *Blow the wind southerly* to thrust on unsuspecting journalists.

'I thought you'd like to hear some real music,' she murmured to the music critic of *The Times*.

Although she smiled graciously round, she was pained by the fog of cigarette smoke and the photographers still clustering round Georgie and Dancer.

'Who's that striking woman in the swansdown bolero and red leather shorts? Didn't she play Susannah at the ENO?' she asked Bob. 'Her face is so familiar.'

'She's the Catchitune receptionist,' said Bob not unkindly. 'You see her each time you go into the building.'

Hermione, having spent the morning in bed with Rannaldini, was shored up in the knowledge that he had blacked the party not because he wanted to avoid the Press, but because he loathed the idea of Georgie Maguire and was violently opposed to her stealing his thunder in Paradise. He was furious that Georgie, as a pop star, would probably earn twice as much as he and Hermione put together, and he detested Georgie's mawkish celebration of marriage. Everywhere he went in LA last week, he'd heard 'Rock Star' being sung and whistled, as it raced up the charts.

Accepting, however, that this was the quickest way to get her picture in the papers, Hemione glided up to Guy whom she'd already met with Larry.

'Hallo, Mr Wonderful,' she said archly, kissing him on his firm, handsome mouth, then carefully choosing a lull in the music turned to Georgie: 'I'm simply livid with Rannaldini for crying off. I said, "Georgie Maguire's music gives pleasure to so many people." I kept telling him, "You'll love Georgie when you meet her, Maestro," but he's such an intellectual snob, and he does feel "Rock Star" is a rip-off of "Lady in Red".'

'It'll be Lady in *the* red by the time we've paid for Angel's Reach,' said Georgie lightly, but her happiness evaporated and when *Hello* magazine asked them both to turn and smile, the photographer caught Georgie looking miserable, and Hermione, who instantly composed her features, eyes open, brows raised, dazzling white teeth flashing, looking gorgeous.

'I've bought you a present,' Hermione handed Georgie *Blow the wind southerly*, 'because I wanted to cheer you up about that beastly piece in the *Guardian*.'

'I hid it from Georgie, so shut up,' hissed Guy, adding, 'You look fabulous, love your hair,' because women were always distracted by flattery, and briskly led Georgie off to meet the new music editor of *Billboard*.

'What Rannaldini actually said,' stage-whispered Hermione to Dancer Maitland, 'was that he didn't want to meet an ageing sex symbol.'

'Because he does that in the mirror every morning,' snapped Dancer.

People were dancing in corners, falling on food. Tables were filling up with glasses. Catchitune, cashing in on having the Press present, were playing records by other artistes on their books. Nikki, in her pie-frilled collared blue velvet dress and determined to prove she was a better Chief Executive's wife than Marigold, was working the room, pressing her new London address on disc jockeys and important retailers, hinting that she and Larry were together now, and would soon be throwing a lovenest warming party in Paradise.

Emerging from the Gents after yet another rewrite, desperate for a cigarette, Larry scooped up a handful of prawn vol-au-vents.

'We have given up canapés for Lent, or we won't be able to get into our new jeans,' said Nikki reprovingly as she glided up and removed the plate.

What in hell's got into her? thought Larry. She looks like a complete frump. In fact the only person in the room looking more matronly than Nikki was Kitty Rannaldini, who, like many women much younger than their husbands, tried to dress older than she was. Exhausted from spring cleaning for Rannaldini's return, she had belted up the motorway because she'd promised to support Marigold and because she longed to see her errant husband even for a couple of hours.

Kitty dreaded parties. In friends' houses, she could escape to the kitchen to help, or take round bottles and gather up dirty glasses – but these matelots in their striped jerseys looked as though they'd down tools if she picked up a plate. Being a wonderful listener, she survived socially on a one-to-one basis, or in the office where people got to know and love her. The only way to communicate over one of Catchitune's heavy rock bands, however, was with your eyes or your swaying body, which in Kitty's case were concealed by hopelessly strong spectacles and a beetroot-pink crimplene tent-dress, which she'd bought by mail order because she was too ashamed of her bulges to go into clothes shops.

Now she was being chewed out by Larry, who needed some ass to kick and who broke the news to her that Rannaldini had done a runner, as though it were her fault.

'Did he say when he was coming back to England?' stammered Kitty, trying to hide her desperate disappointment.

'No,' snapped Larry, 'and where the fuck's Marigold?'

'She's definitely coming.'

'Sorry, love.' Larry patted her arm. 'I've given up smoking. Nikki sent me to a hypnotist last week and I haven't had a fag since.'

'But that's brilliant,' said Kitty, who knew Larry had been on sixty a day. 'How d'you feel?'

'Fine, except every ten minutes I climb up the curtains and throttle the cat.' Larry was about to quiz Kitty about Marigold's bit of rough trade, but seeing Nikki bearing down, he bolted back into the Gents.

Who the hell can I talk to? thought Kitty in panic. Seeing Georgie still talking to the languid new music editor of *Billboard*, she took a deep breath and went over.

'I just come to say 'ow much we're all lookin' forward to you moving into Angel's Reach.'

Georgie looked blank. This frump, with her fuzzy hair drawn into a pony-tail and a big spot on her forehead, must have emerged from the Catchitune accounts department.

'I'm Kitty Rannaldini,' said Kitty, amused to see Georgie's wary half-smile widen into one of incredulous excitement.

'Has Rannaldini come after all?'

'He can't make it, some drama wiv *Don Giovanni*. He was ever so upset.'

The cross round Kitty's neck glittered in the moving

spotlight, then, as it moved on, darkness hid her blushes at such a thumping lie.

'Oh, I'm so pleased.' Georgie sighed with relief. 'Hermione said Rannaldini blacked it deliberately.'

'Really,' said the man from *Billboard* suddenly interested.

'I'm a triffic fan of yours, Georgie,' said Kitty hastily. 'Could I have your autograph?'

The *Billboard* man was appalled at such lack of cool, but Georgie delightedly signed a page of Kitty's autograph book. Seeing Georgie wasting valuable time on some dowdy groupie, Guy whizzed over.

'May I borrow Georgie for a minute?' he asked, and frogmarched her off to charm the manager of Tower Records, Piccadilly.

As the *Billboard* man promptly disappeared in search of more exciting prey, Kitty overheard a *Scorpion* reporter saying: 'Let's call it a day. Rannaldini's obviously not coming.'

'I gather the wife's here,' said the *Mirror*. 'Might get something out of her. Let's try the mistress first.'

Retreating hastily into the darkness, sitting on a lobster pot, poor Kitty miserably ate her way through a large plate of paella, trying to ignore the great phallic lighthouse flashing on the opposite wall. If only she could escape in her little car down the motorway to a cup of cocoa and her Danielle Steel, but she'd promised to give Marigold support. Through the darkness she caught a whiff of Chanel No. 5, and peppermint breath.

'Hi, Kitty,' said a caressing, rather common, voice, which she'd heard so often over the telephone discussing Rannaldini's contracts and recording dates.

Unlike Georgie, Kitty immediately recognized Nikki – less glamorous than she expected, but as the lighthouse beam flashed on to the vulpine features, far more predatory. What chance had poor Marigold got?

'So pleased to meet you at last.' Nikki plonked herself on

an adjoining lobster pot. 'And I was looking forward to meeting Rannaldini. I've heard such nice things about you.'

Kitty, who hadn't heard anything nice about Nikki, stared at the pieces of squid round the rim of her plate and felt sorry for them because they'd been rejected, too.

'We must have lunch,' urged Nikki.

'I don't come to town very often.'

'Then we'll meet in the country. I'll be moving into Paradise Grange very shortly.' Nikki's forked tongue was loosened by drink. 'Larry and I are getting married.'

Kitty was aghast. 'Oh, poor Marigold, and wot about the poor kids?'

'It didn't deter you that Rannaldini was a married man with children,' said Nikki sharply.

'No, I know.' Kitty hung her head. There didn't seem any point adding that Rannaldini was separated from Cecilia by the time she'd gone to work for him.

'Anyway,' went on Nikki, fishing, 'Marigold's got some rough trade in tow, hasn't she?'

Nikki, in fact, was iffy about this development. The boys had banged on and on about Lysander all weekend and, having written off Marigold as a sexless old bag, Nikki disliked any proof that she might be able to attract even rough trade. On the other hand, if she did find someone, it would save Larry a great deal of guilt and alimony. Nikki had been so certain Larry was going for a quicky divorce – she'd even planned her dress, cream silk, for the Registry Office.

And there he was scowling and clutching his speech, his hair all tousled. No-one would think he was worth billions.

'See you in a bit,' murmured Nikki, and sliding over to Larry, taking his hand in the darkness, she placed it under her gathered velvet skirt straight on to her damp pubic hair.

'Come on, make me come, I dare you,' she whispered.

That should obliterate all thoughts of Marigold.

13

'D'you think we should arraive together?' said Marigold, overcome by a sudden fit of respectability as she signed her name in the visitors' book. 'Ay mean Ay am Larry's wife. All his staff will be there. What's everyone goin' to say?'

'They'll say, "Hallo, Marigold, Hallo, Lysander," ' giggled Lysander, who'd been smoking a joint in the car.

As they entered the party, the room went still.

'Hallo, Marigold, Hallo, Lysarnder,' said Hermione loudly.

Larry whipped his hand from Nikki's bush as if it were a wasps' nest, for across the room was the Marigold he'd first fallen in love with, but ten times more beautiful.

Who is he? Who is he? Shaken out of their cool, everyone in the room was frantically trying to identify Lysander.

'Kerist,' exploded the Catchitune Sales Director. 'It's the boss's wife.'

'Lucky thing,' said Denise the receptionist.

A favourite has no friends. Nikki, since she had taken up with Larry, had snubbed senior and junior secretaries alike and banned executives from Larry's presence. Marigold, on the other hand, had always been kind. She had written to Larry's staff when they married or had babies, and been sweet even to the lowest packer at office parties. With the increasingly dark cloud of recession, they felt Marigold would not have let them starve. So they now converged on her joyfully telling her how marvellous she looked, and having a really good butcher's at Lysander. It therefore took Marigold several minutes to reach Georgie. Ignoring a hovering Larry, resisting the temptation to tuck in his shirt and throttle him with his silly gold necklace, she flung herself on her great friend, telling her how wonderful she looked and how much she adored the album.

'Oh Georgie, Ay'm so proud of you and for Guy, too. It's such a wonderful celebration of your love for each other.'

'Great party,' said Lysander, who managed to have eyes for no-one but Marigold, but also on stalks for all the famous people he wanted to meet. 'There's Dancer Maitland, and Steve Wright and Simon Bates, and all the cast of *EastEnders*, and that lovely girl from *Brookside*. Oh my,' he looked at Georgie, 'and you, too. The album's fantastic. Can I have your autograph?'

Rootling round in Marigold's bag in a gesture of casual intimacy, he found a pen and Marigold's diary, out of which he tore a page and handed it to Georgie.

'Why are they playing this junk instead of *Rock Star*?'

'It's evidently uncool to play one's own music,' sighed Georgie.

'Bollocks! It's your party.'

Georgie turned to Marigold. 'You look amazing, twenty years younger. Whatever happened?'

'He did,' said Marigold, taking Lysander's arm.

'Lucky thing,' Georgie laughed as though this was a huge joke.

'How are the children?' asked Marigold.

'Well, Flora's been at Bagley Hall since January,' said Georgie, 'so she'll be near by when we move to Paradise. It's co-ed, so I hope she's managing to do some work. Melanie's in Australia bankrupting us with reverse-charged calls. And your two?' asked Georgie, who never remembered names.

'Both at prep school,' said Marigold.

Hermione was having a bad party. None of the pop music press were remotely interested that she was doing *Dido and*

Aeneas. Once again she had to approach Georgie to get her picture taken.

'How was Paris?' she asked Marigold.

'Oh, lovely. We stayed at the Ritz.'

'Did you go to the Pompidou?'

'No.'

And when Marigold and Lysander hadn't been to any of the operas or concerts Hermione suggested, she said patronizingly, 'You must have gone to some decent restaurants?'

'We just used room service at the Ritz,' said Lysander.

'The only thing flambéeing in our suite was me,' giggled Marigold.

The next moment they were joined by Guy and Larry, both unnerved by the juxtaposition of Georgie and Marigold.

'Are you an actor?' asked Guy.

'No. Lysander plays polo and raydes in races,' said Marigold. 'He loves horses.'

'Particularly bonking dead ones,' said Lysander, kissing Marigold. Then turning to Hermione, he asked blandly, 'How's Dildo and Aeneas going, Helena?'

Determined not to betray her rage, Hermione grabbed Lysander's arm. 'Come and meet Nikki. You two must be the same age.'

The stirring cow, thought Marigold, as Lysander was dragged off into the gloom.

'What are Flora and Melanie doing now?' she said.

'You've just asked me that,' said Georgie, drawing Marigold aside. 'Are you OK?'

'Fine,' said Marigold.

'You're not. You're shaking.'

'Larry's having the most terrific affaire,' mumbled Marigold. 'He wants a divorce and me out of Paradise.'

'Christ, you poor darling. I'd no idea. Larry's a bastard. Who is she?'

'Nikki. That blonde being introduced to Lysander.'

'Oh.' Georgie peered through the gloom. 'She did a

146

number on me in the Ladies. Very plain and frumpy, I thought.'

'She's trying to look like a waife tonight,' sighed Marigold. 'Normally she exudes sex.'

'Lysander doesn't think so,' said Georgie. 'He's done a U-turn. Wow, he's good looking.'

'OK?' Lysander took Marigold's hand.

'Can I borrow you, Panda?' Guy called over, sensing trouble. 'Dempster wants a word.'

'What did you think of Nikki?' Marigold couldn't resist asking.

'Gross,' said Lysander, beckoning to a waitress to fill up Marigold's glass. 'Looks as though she fell off the back of a Larry.'

Marigold burst out laughing.

'Scuse me, Mr Maguire.' An *Evening Standard* photographer sent Guy flying as he raced to get a picture of Georgie greeting Jason Donovan.

'They also serve,' said a quiet voice at Guy's elbow. It was Bob Harefield, Hermione's long-suffering husband, who'd got hold of a whisky bottle with which he laced Guy's glass.

Balding, round-faced, bow-tied, always smiling, Bob gave the impression of a Humpty Dumpty who'd survived a great fall by the skin of his teeth.

Because of his amiable egg-like face, people tended not to notice the lean beauty of his body. No-one could understand how he could put up with Hermione and Rannaldini, but certainly his tactful handling of the latter had stopped most of the London Met committing suicide. Guy would have liked to have had a heart-to-heart with him about the Catchitune royalty system, but unfortunately Bob had that bespectacled frump in tow.

'I want you to meet the nicest lady in Paradise,' said Bob, 'Kitty Rannaldini.'

Guy nearly dropped his glass.

'Rannaldini, did you say?' He added in amazement.

'I didn't realize.' He couldn't really say, 'Love your hair, you're looking fabulous,' short of total hypocrisy, so he thanked her for being nice to Georgie. 'You *are* a brickette.'

'I was just suggesting to Kitty,' said Bob, 'that we ought to start a second-fiddle club for people married to celebs.'

'You've got the London Met to look after as well,' said Kitty.

'Well, you've got all Rannaldini's children and ex-wives. That's much worse,' said Bob, then when Kitty protested, 'you know they are.'

'I've got used to the post and the telephone always being for Georgie,' volunteered Guy. 'I don't even mind being shoved aside by people desperate to meet her. The only thing I find wearing is her constant need for reassurance, but all artists are like that.'

He watches her the whole time, thought Kitty wistfully, seeing she's got a drink and talking to the right people.

'I did like Georgie,' she said timidly. 'Will you be in London during the week?'

Guy nodded. 'I hope you and Marigold will stop her getting lonely.'

'Oh, I will,' Kitty felt impossibly flattered, 'and Angel's Reach is so beautiful. All the angels was turning pink in the sunset as I was driving up this evening. As though they was flushed with excitement about you movin' in.'

Guy smiled. 'That's sweet. I so look forward to being part of a community again. If you live in a village you must put something back.'

'Marigold'll rope you in. She does so much for others.'

'Particularly at the moment,' said Bob, looking in amusement at Marigold who was peeling Mediterranean prawns and handing them to Lysander. 'That boy is the smoothest bit of trade I've ever seen, straight out of Fortnum's toy department.'

Guy, who strongly disapproved of extra-marital frolicking, deliberately changed the subject.

'What are you doing after this?' he asked Kitty.

Kitty looked at her watch. 'Driving back to Rutshire.'

'Come dine with us, Larry's booked a table at Hero's.'

'I've already eaten a 'ole paella.'

'Have one course. I insist.'

Feeling his warm hand on her arm, Kitty thought Guy was one of the nicest men she'd ever met. It would be lovely having him in Paradise, as an island at parties who one wasn't frightened of going up to.

Seeing Georgie was nose to nose with David Frost now, Guy said, 'I've got to ring Brian Sewell of the *Evening Standard* and try and get him along to a preview tomorrow. Have you got any pound coins for a fiver?'

Returning five minutes later, he was grabbed by Georgie.

'That bastard Larry's having an affaire with that blonde.'

'It's not serious, I'll explain later,' murmured Guy. 'Larry's about to make a speech. Go and stand beside him.'

As 'Rock Star' boomed out from every speaker, people turned to watch the video on the monitor, which showed shoals of fish turning into ink-blot ghosts which, in turn, became boats being shipwrecked, sharks prowling through the deep, lusty fishermen pulling in nets. Then the waves pounded the rock to which Georgie was clinging, until there seemed no hope for her survival. Then slowly the seas calmed, the sun came out, and Georgie was draped against the rock, drenched in her grey rags but smiling.

'*Rock star, rock star, rock star, you are my rock star*,' sang Georgie in her husky haunting voice. And on the monitor appeared a close-up of Guy looking wonderfully macho in a blue denim shirt which brought out the strange light azure of his eyes, with the wind tugging at his arctic-blond hair.

Even people round the buffet, stopped eating and drinking and listened to the track, swaying and dancing to the beat.

At the end when Guy walked up to the rock, picked up

Georgie and carried her away across the sands with her wet hair trailing, and a pack of basset hounds raced after them, everyone cheered and stamped their feet. Those who were holding glasses and couldn't clap, banged their other hand on the table, and cried, 'Speech, speech'.

Sweat glistening on his forehead, Larry grasped the microphone.

'We're very happy to be producing Georgie Maguire,' he mumbled. 'We think she's a bit special, and she's going to be around for a long time to come. Catchitune hope this album is the first of many. This party isn't a hype, no big deal, but as we speak "Rock Star" is Number One in the American charts. I give you Georgie Maguire.'

That's the first draft I wrote, thought the head of publicity indignantly, and I've been fired a dozen times today for my pains.

Georgie took the microphone and in a choked voice thanked everyone at Catchitune, and particularly Larry and his lovely wife, Marigold.

'Hurrah,' bellowed the Catchitune staff glaring at Nikki.

'It's been a long time in the wilderness,' Georgie went on, 'which makes tonight even more special. This is the second happiest day of my life. The happiest was when I married my husband, Guy Seymour' – she emphasized Guy's surname – 'the loveliest, strongest man in the world. I'd like you to drink to Guy, my rock.'

Everyone clapped and cheered. Standing beside Marigold, Lysander noticed a girl in front removing her spectacles to wipe away the tears, and realized it was Kitty Rannaldini. He'd say hallo later. Then, in the lull that followed, out of the gloom, Marigold's very distinct tones could be heard saying to the man on her other side, 'Are you the chief buyer of Tower Records or a disc jockey for Radio 1? Well, take your 'and off may bottom then.'

There was a howl of mirth.

'Marigold used to be such a dutiful wife,' whispered Hermione in shocked tones. 'What *has* got into her?'

'I think that miraculous toy boy has,' said Bob.

'Larry's having an affaire with that ghastly Nikki,' hissed Georgie, as smilingly she and Guy posed for photographs.

'Shut up,' hissed back Guy. 'The boot's on the other foot.'

'Lovely speech,' said Nikki, coiling her hand into Larry's.

'Just going to check the other room,' said Larry noticing Marigold was missing.

Next door, the smell of dope and hairy male armpits spilling out of sleeveless T-shirts was suffocating.

'*Rock star, rock star, my life would be a zero, without my steadfast hero*,' sang the writhing, gyrating couples in ecstasy.

Indifferent to such proof of a mega-hit on his hands, Larry scoured the room. Then suddenly the dancers parted like clouds at night to reveal two bright stars, Lysander and Marigold, in each other's arms. Outraged, Larry watched Lysander put a joint in Marigold's mouth and her breasts swelling provocatively as she inhaled, then Lysander taking a last puff before stamping it underfoot, then French kissing her on and on, with all Catchitune's staff and distributors dancing round to have a better look. Larry was appalled at the pain. Stumbling upstairs, he roared at the General Manager to close the bar.

As Lysander and Marigold drifted back hand in hand, Georgie noticed the diamond brooch on Marigold's black velvet coat.

'Isn't that lovely?'

'Lysander took me to Cartier's this afternoon,' yelled Marigold over the din of the music as Larry joined the group. 'It's the key to freedom.'

Noticing his wife was no longer wearing a wedding-ring, Larry felt sick.

Waitresses were gathering up plates. Guests were ostentatiously up-ending empty glasses hoping for refills.

'We must go,' said Marigold.

'I thought you were coming out to dinner,' wailed Georgie.

'We've got to get back to Paradise. Patch is on her own. We just dropped in to wish you luck. Not that you're going to need it. I'll ring you first thing for a proper gossip.'

Larry and Guy exchanged uneasy glances.

On the way out, Lysander tore another page from Marigold's diary and peeled off to get Chris de Burgh's autograph.

Oblivious of Nikki's chilling, killing stare, Larry bolted after Marigold, drawing her aside. She noticed that his T-shirt could have been whiter. He noticed the softness of her thighs swelling up into the black velvet shorts and the way her breasts swung gently as bells under her white silk shirt.

Oblivious to Catchitune staff, who were handing out little papier-mâché rocks, tapes of *Rock Star* and Body Shop seaweed extract as going-home presents, he said: 'You look beautiful, Mar, I'll ring you.'

Catching them up, Lysander deliberately dropped Marigold's diary, which Larry pocketed, and was horrified to read: LYSANDER, VENICE scrawled across the next weekend. No wonder she didn't want the boys.

His evening was further ruined when he arrived with Georgie and Guy and the rest of his party at Hero's, his favourite restaurant, and was accosted by the headwaiter who was the worst gossip in Soho, and constantly feeding stories to Dempster.

'Meester Lockton, I am very pleased to see Meesis Lockton dining here the other night with your younger brother. She look very well.'

'I thought you were an only child, Larry,' said Hermione loudly.

Once again ignoring Nikki's killing stare, Larry snarled, 'Bring me a packet of Silk Cut.'

Primed beforehand, the band struck up 'Rock Star' as Georgie entered the dining room.

'Everyone in the room will be humming it in a week,

Panda,' said Guy proudly, then in an undertone to Larry, 'we've got to get that contract signed, before Marigold gives Georgie an earful tomorrow. Georgie's insanely loyal.'

But Larry could only think of his own problems. In the past, bored with Marigold, envious of Rannaldini's effortless promiscuity, he had fallen madly in love with Nikki. Now he was torn between his rapacious sexy mistress, who was at this moment deliberately flirting with Guy, and Marigold who had looked utterly ravishing this evening. How unhappy would I be without either? thought Larry. Catchitune had just recorded *The Beggar's Opera*.

Nor had he anticipated how wildly jealous he would be of this Adonis with his public-school accent. He'd been humiliated in front of his entire staff, who knew all about Nikki, because Nikki had told them, and if there were a messy divorce, he might not get his knighthood before Rannaldini, if at all.

In addition, Nikki was not as clockwork as Marigold. She was far less efficient in the office now she had to look after him at home, and last night she had shouted at him for putting his plate in the sink rather than the dishwasher. Before he met Nikki, Larry had never lifted a finger at home except to check the dust on top of a picture.

He was haunted by Rannaldini's warning:

'Once she's hooked you, the mistress becomes the wardress. She knows all the tricks you used to cheat on Marigold.'

Nikki now sat in his office, monitoring his telephone calls from all those young singers, who seemed perfectly happy for Larry to make them, if he was prepared to make their records as well. Since he'd taken up with Nikki and shattered the myth of being an utterly faithful husband, gorgeous girls had been looking at him in the most exciting way. All that promise would be nipped in the bud if he settled for Nikki.

'They keep a cosh behind their backs,' warned Rannaldini. 'You never see it until they've got the handcuffs on. I made that mistake with Cecilia. She begrudged me my old freedoms, so I ditched her.'

Larry was fed up with going to the gym, only drinking spritzers – bloody wet – and not smoking and saying 'No', to canapés. Ignoring Nikki's scowl of rage, he accepted a white roll from the waiter, and spreading it thickly with butter, ordered Spaghetti Carbonara as a first course followed by a T-bone and chips.

Georgie was now signing an autograph for an elderly couple at the next table.

'I'd much rather she signed that contract,' hissed Guy.

Looking across at Nikki being calmed down by Bob, Larry had a brainwave.

'I'll get it,' he said.

Nipping out to the Rolls, as he had so often in the past when he wanted to ring Nikki, his heart thumping, he dialled Marigold's number. Just as he was about to ring off the telephone was picked up. There was music and laughter in the background.

'We oughta talk, Princess,' Larry told Marigold roughly. 'I gotta be in Bristol tomorrow. Thought I'd spend the night at home and return your diary.'

'What took you so long?' snapped Nikki, as Larry sat down beside her and kissed her fondly on the cheek. After all, he did want a fuck later.

'Getting this,' he said, putting a sheaf of papers in front of Georgie. 'Can I have your autograph, please?'

'For your wife, your daughter, your mother or your girlfriend,' said Georgie with a laugh.

'For myself,' said Larry.

It was a Catchitune contract for a million pounds.

14

Not wanting to alert the whole of Paradise to his return, Larry drove rather than flew down the following evening. Arriving as the red flame of sunset finally gave way to the distant russet glow of the Rutminster streetlights, he caught a glimpse of Catchitune written in fading crocuses and breathed in a heady scent of polyanthus, narcissus and newly turned earth, as he got out of a borrowed Mini. The Grange might face north, but it was still the finest garden in Paradise. He noticed a ladder against the house, Mr Brimscombe, the finest gardener in Rutshire, although threatened with the sack, had been trimming the famous Paradise Pearl from around the master-bedroom windows.

Across the valley he could see a single light burning in Valhalla. Kitty was still working, sorting out the tangled skeins of her husband's life. Soon Rannaldini, too, would be home studying and settling scores in his tower in the woods. Angel's Reach was in darkness, but shortly Georgie would be burning the midnight oil earning her million pound advance as she worked on her new album to be handed in by Christmas, and to the left he could see the jewel-coloured stained-glass hall windows of the River House. Bob and Hermione must be enjoying a rare evening at home.

Larry gave a sigh of satisfaction – all these people beavering away to put money into Catchitune's coffers. Despite the doom and gloom, this year's figures had been good, next year's should be spectacular. Only when he turned towards his own house did he realize that the only lights on were the carriage lamps by the door.

Letting himself in, falling over one of Lysander's boots, he only just reached the burglar alarm in time. After initial woofing, Patch slumped back in her basket, sulking because Jack, her boyfriend, had been banished for the evening.

Larry had skipped lunch anticipating a delicious dinner cooked by Marigold, but had planned on working up a further appetite by screwing her beforehand.

In the kitchen he was welcomed by Marks & Spencer's Chicken and Asparagus and Bread and Butter Pudding, both in foil trays. He loathed asparagus.

There was also a note from Marigold:

'*Larry*,' (not even dear), '*These will take five minutes in the microwave. Gone out to dinner, back around midnight. Make yourself at home.*'

It's my fucking home, thought Larry furiously.

He couldn't even ring for someone to run him up steak and chips because he'd laid them all off, and even he wouldn't summon Mrs Brimscombe from the lodge in the middle of *Coronation Street*.

There were no curtains drawn, nor a fire in the lounge. He couldn't complain. It was so mild that in the old days, he would have bellyached about the central heating being left on or a fire lit.

Returning to the kitchen, he found an empty bottle of champagne in the bin, two glasses in the sink and a huge bunch of pink roses with a card on the draining board. '*Marigold, you were out of this world. All love, L.*'

His Harley Street consultant had warned him against stress, but Larry had never been nearer a coronary as he bolted upstairs and was knocked sideways by the smell of Joy. Marigold was tidy to the point of finickityness, but now carrier bags with new clothes littered the bed and the armchairs. In the bathroom he found the top off the scented body lotion, a razor clogged with hair that looked unpleasantly pubic, a Cellophane pack that had contained black, eight-denier, seamed stockings and a size ten label on the floor. Marigold used to be size sixteen. The hairdryer was still plugged in, and worst of all *The Joy of Sex* on the edge of the bath lay open at fellatio. It was no comfort to Larry that this was exactly the state in which Nikki left their new *en suite* bathroom in Pelham Crescent.

With a howl Larry hurled *The Joy of Sex* out of the window, whereupon the clockwork squawking of a pheasant reminded him of his clockwork wife running away. Not wanting to go home to Nikki, who thought he was looking at a new pop group in Bristol, he stormed down to The Pearly Gates and got so drunk he didn't even notice Marigold, Lysander and Ferdie coming out of The Heavenly Host across the road around eleven.

'Ay've got fraightful butterflies,' gasped Marigold as Ferdie pulled up outside The Grange.

'Should be moths at night,' said Lysander, who'd been getting gloomier as the evening progressed.

'No more lipstick,' ordered Ferdie, as Marigold opened her bag.

Ruffling her hair, he undid several buttons of her red dress – 'You've got to look as though you've been got at,' – before allowing her out of the car.

'Now play it cool, and remember no bonking. We'll stick around for a sec in case you need rescuing.'

Watching Marigold going up the steps, Lysander felt the same sickness as when his mother, trying not to cry, had walked down the platform after putting him on the school train. But a minute later Marigold came rushing back.

'He's gone, without leaving a note,' she sobbed. 'Ay've blown it, Ay've blown it.'

Appalled to find Marigold so devastated, Lysander leapt out of the car.

'He'll be back.' He put an arm round her. 'Probably just stormed out in a strop.'

'Must have been one hell of a strop, if he left the door open and the burglar alarm off with Picassos and Stubbs in the house,' mused Ferdie. 'Can you see anything missing?'

'Only Larry,' wailed Marigold, as Jack jumped into Patch's basket, snuggling up to her.

Desperate to give Marigold comfort, Lysander poured her a glass of Sancerre.

'I taped *Casualty* for you,' he said. It was Marigold's favourite programme.

'Ay'm the only casualty round 'ere.' Putting her chain-handled bag down with a clatter on the draining board, she was bashing the stems of Lysander's pink roses with a rolling pin, when the telephone rang.

'Don't answer it,' howled Ferdie. But faster than Nijinsky out of the starting gates, Marigold was across the room. The telephone stopped on the third ring.

'It's our secret code,' squeaked Marigold.

As the telephone began again, she snatched it up before Ferdie could stop her, listened for a second, then put her trembling hand over the receiver.

'Larry wants to come over. He's in The Pearly Gates.'

'That's the nearest he's going to get to heaven this evening,' said Ferdie briskly. 'Tell him no. You've got red eyes and a red nose, and you're both so wasted it'll only end in a punch or bunk-up and blow all your advantage. Say you're tired.'

Ferdie's square face could look very big and mean. His friends didn't employ him as a bouncer at their twenty-firsts for nothing.

Meekly Marigold told Larry she was shattered. They arranged to have dinner next week.

'Who's that in the background?' growled Larry, as Lysander sulkily crashed the door of the fridge.

'Only Patch,' said Marigold. 'See you next week.'

'We'll plan the whole operation when the time comes,' said Ferdie. 'Come along, Lysander.'

And because Ferdie wasn't supposed to know he'd been bonking Marigold, Lysander reluctantly had to comply. Jack, even more reluctant to be removed from Patch's paws, bit his master sharply on the hand.

*   *   *

Alone in her pink-flounced four-poster, Marigold couldn't sleep. She had envisaged a scene from *Gone with the Wind*, with herself being so provoking that Larry would sweep her upstairs like Clark Gable – well, at least the black moustache was the same – and ravish her – at this point admittedly his technique would become Lysander's. Then, becoming Larry again, he would swear she was his only love and Nikki a fearful aberration.

Hepped up for conflict, twitching with desire, Marigold longed for Lysander's tender and exuberant lovemaking after which she always fell into a wonderful sleep. Lysander was better than any pill, and he didn't leave you feeling woozy and unable to drive in the morning.

Having spent so many nights alone at the Grange, Marigold was unafraid of the dark, and always left her curtains open because no-one could see in except the birds. Outside a full moon was admiring her reflection in the fish-ponds, and a gentle west wind was scratching the bare stems of the famous Paradise Pearl against the window.

Marigold had never masturbated in her life, thinking it a disgusting habit, but Lysander had made her come so wonderfully with his fingers and tongue, she thought she'd give it a whirl and put the duvet over Patch snoring beside her, so the dog wouldn't be corrupted.

'Think about something that really turns you on,' Lysander always urged her.

So Marigold thought about Lysander. Goodness, it was nice and quite easy, her breath was coming faster and faster, when she heard a loud bang on the window, which couldn't be just windswept wisteria twigs. Then to her horror she saw a man framed in the window, the moonlight behind him. Screaming her head off she whipped her finger from her clitoris to the panic button.

Mr Brimscombe, however, who slept lightly because of his rheumatism, had already heard a car going towards the house. The driver must have had a remote control to open the electric gates, but it wasn't young Mr Hawkley because his red Ferrari always blared music.

Remembering his ladder outside Marigold's bedroom, Mr Brimscombe set out to investigate.

The Paradise Pearl, a unique silver-pink wisteria, had been propagated by Mr Brimscombe's grandfather who'd gone to the grave with the secret of its exquisite vigour and colouring. Gardeners came from all over the world to admire and attempt to copy it. Mr Brimscombe's first ignoble thought when he saw a man up the ladder was not that he was attempting to break in or rape Mrs Lockton, but that he was taking cuttings off the Paradise Pearl.

Shooting across the lawn like a crab, he seized the ladder just as Larry was peering in at the incredibly erotic sight of his beautiful slimmed-down wife playing with herself, the lamplight warming her lovely breasts. Excitement turned to horror, however, when he saw the duvet moving beside her – it must be that young puppy Lysander, not even capable of satisfying her. As Larry banged furiously on the window, his ladder was suddenly shaken down below with even more fury.

'Come down, you thieving bugger,' screached Mr Brimscombe.

Instantly obeying, Larry missed the next rung, grabbed a gnarled branch of the Paradise Pearl, bringing it and himself crashing to the ground on top of a whole bed of Crown Imperials.

If Marigold hadn't recognized Larry and rushed to open the double glazing and alert Mr Brimscombe to his master's identity, Larry would have been cudgelled to death by a fox-headed walking-stick.

Next morning Marigold rang Ferdie to tell him what had happened.

'Just a social climb,' said Ferdie.

Marigold giggled. 'Larry got off with a bruising and a sprained ankle. He's just discharged himself from Rutminster Hospital. Oh, and Ferdie, he's taking me to The Four Seasons tonaight.'

'Well, play it cool.'

The following morning Marigold summoned Ferdie to The Grange.

'We never made The Four Seasons. We ended up in bed.'

'On the first date?' Disapprovingly, Ferdie dipped a chocolate biscuit in his coffee. 'You're a slag, Marigold. When are you seeing him again?'

'Tonight. He's going to leave Nikki and come home. Oh, Ferdie, Ay can't thank you both enough.'

'We aim to please,' Ferdie pocketed a £10,000 cheque for mission accomplished and persuaded Marigold she must keep Lysander on a year's retainer, so he could whizz back if Larry started acting up. 'And we must return that diamond key to Cartier's.'

'How do I explain that to Larry?'

'That it isn't ethical to accept presents from young boys if one has made it up with one's husband. It's believing Lysander could afford one hundred thousand pounds for a brooch that rattled Larry.'

Marigold was brought up short. She was going to miss Lysander dreadfully. She had found it much easier to forgive Larry, because having Lysander around had made her realize how heady it must have been for Larry having Nikki. But at least if he was on a retainer, she'd see him occasionally. She decided to give him two polo ponies and a set of Dick Francis talking books as he was such a slow reader.

Lysander was so upset at the thought of Larry taking Marigold to The Four Seasons, and no doubt to bed, that he'd gone out and got plastered. Next morning, overwhelmed with hangover, clutching a cup of coffee, he'd gone out to see Arthur in his box.

He found the old horse had eaten all his bedding, a habit from his early days, when he didn't know where his next meal was coming from, that he only reverted to when he felt very low and neglected.

'I'm sorry, boy,' said Lysander appalled, flinging his arms round Arthur's neck, avoiding the green bits where Arthur had rolled. 'I'm sorry, Mum and Uncle Alastair. I haven't forgotten. I'll bloody well get him sound and have another crack at the Rutminster.'

He emptied his cup into a bucket, because Arthur loved drinking coffee.

Having left Marigold and picked up a hamburger from the pub, Ferdie drove over to Lysander's. He found him slumped, shivering in the corner of Arthur's stable clutching Jack like a teddy bear, with Ferdie's blue coat wrapped round him like a child's dressing gown. Lysander was deathly pale and looked absurdly young. Arthur having abandoned silent sympathy, was lying flat out with his eyes open snoring loudly to get his master's attention.

'Here's something to cheer you up,' said Ferdie.

'Marigold's divorce papers?'

'Even better.' Having taken his ten per cent commission, Ferdie handed over a cheque for £9,000, which Lysander pocketed listlessly.

'Unlike you I don't think dosh is the most important thing in the world.'

'It comes a fucking good second.' Ferdie handed Arthur a bit of hamburger bun. 'Don't be bloody ungrateful. Thanks to me you don't owe a bean, in fact you've got a fat bank balance as well as a Ferrari and some really sharp suits. In the old days, you were always grumbling that you wanted to take Dolly to decent places and become a Lanson lout.'

'I've grown out of that way of life. All those phoneys poncing around at the Catchitune party. I don't want to be part of that scene any more. Why can't I stay here and get Arthur sound?'

'Larry's coming back. It'll be easier if you're not around.'

'She can't go back to that overpaid clown.' Lysander was nearly in tears. 'He'll have her back in pie-frilled collars in a week. I'm very fond of Marigold,' he added defiantly. 'Being with her reminded me of Mum. I wouldn't mind settling down with her.'

'Don't be ridiculous,' said Ferdie more gently. 'You'd have to take her bopping on her zimmer in a few years' time. And that accent would get seriously on your nerves.'

'It would not,' said Lysander furiously.

'It's like walking hound puppies. You have to send them back. You don't have to go back to London. I've got another job for you in Cheshire rattling a drain billionaire who's cheating on his wife.'

'I'm not interested.'

'You will be when you see the wife. She's stunning. And you can take Arthur, Tiny and Jack. Evidently there's a brilliant vet up there.'

Still lying down, Arthur snored even louder, opening an eye to see if Ferdie was prepared to relinquish any more hamburger bun.

'Come on, you owe it to Arthur,' persisted Ferdie. 'Tomorrow to fresh woods and Porsches new.'

15

A fortnight later when Guy and Georgie moved into Angel's Reach, all the removal men were whistling 'Rock Star' which now topped the UK as well as the American charts.

Guy, who took a week off work, masterminded the entire operation. Georgie drifted about getting in everyone's way and going into poetic ecstasies over the lushness of the Rutshire spring. Blackthorn was breaking in dazzling white waves over the brightening green fields. On the first morning they were woken before dawn by the birds. Georgie had never seen so many lambs jumping in the fields or daffodils in a halo round their very own lake. A singer-songwriter could not but be gay in such a jocund company.

Euphoria, however, soon gave way to panic as she realized she'd lost Act One of her musical *Ant and Cleo* in the move. She daren't tell Guy as he'd insist on helping her look, and there were all sorts of old love letters and the odd recent one in her boxes of papers which she didn't want him to find. In the excitement of having a Number One record, she'd also agreed to deliver the new album by Christmas.

'I'll never get it done in time,' she wailed to Guy, who was putting up some rather startling abstracts in the kitchen. The sink was still blocked with flowers wishing them luck in their new home, which Georgie would never get round to arranging.

Putting down his hammer, Guy took Georgie in his arms.

'Larry's just rung to say he's going to bring in some whizz-kid producer to remix and revamp a lot of your old songs, so you'll only have to write half a dozen or so new ones. It's so restful here, you'll do them in your sleep.'

'No good if I can't sleep,' mumbled Georgie fretfully into Guy's chest.

Having not arranged the making of a single curtain to fit the vast Angel's Reach windows, she was getting increasingly irritated at being woken by the sun and the bloody birds at five-thirty in the morning.

So Guy, who knew where everything was, unearthed some swirling blue, olive and purple William Morris curtains which had hung in the house in Hampstead and charmed Kitty Rannaldini, who'd left a dozen new-laid eggs in the porch on their first morning, into letting them down.

As Kitty had promised to return the curtains as soon as possible, Guy, who felt sorry for her rattling around in that huge, supposedly haunted house, had invited her over for a late lunch on the Friday after they moved in. Following this, they would all drive over to the end-of-term concert at Bagley Hall, where Georgie's and Guy's younger daughter, Flora, and Kitty's stepchildren, Wolfie and Natasha, were pupils.

Georgie, who'd been failing to work, hugged Kitty in delight as she staggered through the front door, the curtains in her arms.

'Oh, you *are* kind! Put them down on the hall chair. Oh dear, you're wearing a skirt – I was hoping to get away with jeans.'

Although Kitty had never received any affection from her stepdaughter, she felt she ought to support her at the concert because Rannaldini was still away. She had put on a compost-brown suit with a full skirt, which had once looked marvellous on Hermione, but which did nothing for Kitty's figure or colouring. She had made it worse by trying to add the feminine touches of a pottery flower-brooch and a frilly white Tricel shirt.

'Guy's bound to bully me into changing,' moaned Georgie. 'Let's go and murder a huge drink. Don't worry, Guy's driving. We'll need to be pissed to sit through all those Merry Peasants and out-of-tune fiddles.'

Kitty followed her into a kitchen which had just been charmingly redecorated with a cornflower-blue tiled floor, white walls, primrose-yellow surfaces, blue-and-white plates and framed family photographs with blue mounts among Guy's abstracts on the walls.

'Ow, it's so fresh and pretty,' marvelled Kitty.

'Guy's taste,' said Georgie. 'He's awfully clever.'

The kitchen was also surprisingly tidy, except for a large tabby cat with orange eyes, who sprawled most unhygienically, Kitty thought, across a big scrubbed table. She was frightened of animals, particularly of the Rott-weilers which guarded Rannaldini, and The Prince of Darkness, the vicious black steeplechaser, who, now the National Hunt Season was over, roamed the fields terror-izing any rambler who ventured on to Rannaldini's land.

'What's he called?' Kitty tried to be polite, as the cat bopped Georgie with a fat paw as she passed.

'Charity,' said Georgie. 'It's Guy's cat. He adores her. Flora chose the name, so we could all say, "Daddy does a tremendous amount for Charity". And he does. He's already joined the Best-Kept Village Committee, and he popped down to say hallo to the vicar this morning. He should have been back hours ago.'

'It all looks lovely.' Kitty admired the crocus-yellow walls in the hall.

'And I've found a cleaner, thank God, a Mrs Piggot,' said Georgie. Then, seeing Kitty's wary look, 'I'm not sure how hot she is on cleaning, but she's ace on gossip. She's already told me the vicar's a bit of a "puff".'

She's so attractive, thought Kitty wistfully, even with her dark red hair going greasy, and last night's mascara smudged under her eyes, and a split in her jeans where they'd lost a battle with her spreading hips.

Forcing a large Bacardi and Coke on Kitty, Georgie

bore her upstairs to a bedroom so large and high that even the massive still-unmade four-poster looked like a child's cot. Blushing, Kitty averted her eyes from a damp patch on the bottom sheet. Crumpling the duvet was a large basset-hound.

'This is Dinsdale,' said Georgie, screwing up the basset's jowly face, gazing into his bloodshot eyes and kissing him on the nose. 'The one thing that can be relied on to look worse than me in the morning. Now, let's look at these curtains. Goodness, you've done them well. Although they're not really bedroomy, I've never been very good with flowered chintz. Let's put them up.'

In no time Kitty found herself standing in her stocking-inged feet, acutely ashamed of her fat ankles, amid the clutter of Georgie's dressing table, as she perilously hooked the curtains on to a big brass rail.

'A bloody girlfriend rang me this morning' – Georgie gazed moodily at the long blond tresses of the willows lining the lake – 'saying wasn't I worried about all those bimbos and separated women in London, waiting to seduce Guy while I'm down here. Guy of *all* people! He's *so* stuffy about people having affaires. Then she said, "Do watch the drink, it gets to you in the country." ' Georgie took a great slug of her Bacardi.

'I'm a bit pissed off with Marigold,' she went on, glancing across at The Grange which was in deep shadow. 'Apart from flowers when we moved in – some rather awful mauve gladioli – I've hardly heard a word. She's having problems with Larry. Nikki's proving even more difficult to give up than smoking. He should try Nikki's hypnotist again, and Nikki intends to take him to the cleaners. Funny when she always forgot to take his suits there when she was living with him. Now she's never off the telephone screaming abuse at Larry, and dropping the telephone if Marigold answers.

'And Lysander's never off the telephone from Cheshire (dropping it natch, when Larry picks it up), offering to fly down and whisk Marigold away, which must be tempting. I didn't really talk to him at the *Rock Star* launch, but he was faint-making.'

'Gorgeous,' sighed Kitty, remembering how Lysander had come over to kiss her hallo/goodbye as he was leaving the party. 'There, I fink that's OK.'

'Looks marvellous,' said Georgie drawing the curtains and plunging them into such total darkness that Kitty nearly fell off the dressing table. 'We must pay you. No, don't be silly. Let's have another drink, then I must wash my hair.'

I'm obviously not going to get any lunch, thought Kitty, which was probably a good thing. She'd totally failed to go on a diet for Rannaldini's return tomorrow.

'Just as I expected, they look terrific,' said a deep, carrying voice. 'Why am I always saying, "You're a brick, Kitty"?'

Guy looked so handsome that, as he put out a warm, strong hand to help her down, and then kissed her cheek, Kitty wished she looked less shiny from her exertions, and hastily fumbled for her high-heeled shoes.

'What kept you?' snapped Georgie, tugging the elastic band out of her hair.

'Frog-spawn in the village pond, blue-and-white violets on the bank, primroses like day-old chicks. It was such a beautiful day, I walked. I suppose you haven't remembered to put on the potatoes, Panda?'

'Hell, I forgot,' sighed Georgie. 'I'm sorry, darling, but I'm not really hungry.'

'Well, Kitty and I are,' said Guy, 'which is why I bought smoked salmon, pâté and vine leaves at The Apple Tree. It's such a sophisticated shop. I arranged for us to have an account there.'

'Which means Flora will chalk up fags and booze,' said Georgie.

'She must be told not to,' said Guy sharply. 'There was a list for ordering your hot cross buns. That's what I call a proper village shop. I can't believe it's Easter in a fortnight.'

'Ow, I love Easter,' said Kitty. 'Somehow you can't wait for Jesus to rise from the dead and walk barefooted in the white dew among the daffodils.'

Then she blushed scarlet as Georgie said rather mockingly: 'Dinsdale loves Easter, too, because it means chocolate. How was the vicar? Mrs Piggot says he's gay.'

'I had coffee with him and his wife,' said Guy, who disapproved of gossip. 'They were charming.'

'Mrs Piggot says he's a piss-artist,' went on Georgie.

'Takes one to know one,' said Guy dismissively. 'The gin's dropped three inches since she's been cleaning for you.'

'I must wash my hair,' said Georgie.

'You haven't got time,' said Guy flatly. 'You've asked Kitty to lunch. It's already three o'clock and we've got to leave by four to get decent seats.'

'The concert doesn't start till five.'

'And the rush-hour starts at four on Fridays in the country, and Flora's singing a solo. We must be on time, Panda.'

Georgie looked mutinous. She was a celebrity. Everyone would be gazing at her. She couldn't have dirty hair.

Reading her thoughts, Guy said, 'You always look lovely, Panda.'

What a wonderful husband, thought Kitty enviously, kind and concerned but so firm like a Danielle Steel hero. 'I don't need any din – I mean lunch,' she stammered.

A certain row was averted by the telephone. Georgie's work in the last week had been constantly interrupted by the Press ringing up to ask how she was adjusting to the country, or by demands to go on television or the radio, all of which had been turned down by Guy.

'My wife has shut herself away with a December deadline,' he was saying briskly. 'Well, I can answer that one. Dogs mostly.'

'Who was that? What did they want to know?' asked Georgie fretfully.

'*The Scorpion*. What do you wear in bed?'

'And you said, "Dogs"?' Georgie started to laugh. 'I do love you. People are going to think I'm even more of a slut than I am.'

'I've got an idea,' said Guy. 'As we've only time for a sandwich now and it's Flora's first night in Paradise, I'll take you all out to The Heavenly Host this evening.'

'Perfect,' said Georgie, 'as a thank-you present for the curtains.'

'I can't,' sighed Kitty, suppressing a simultaneous shiver of terror and longing, 'Rannaldini's flying in first fing tomorrow. I must see everyfink's perfect.'

16

In fact, Rannaldini was already in England, finally having finished his film of *Don Giovanni*, which he had produced, directed, conducted, edited and, according to the wags of the music world, probably played the part of the Don with every woman on the set as well.

Arriving a day early at Heathrow in his private jet, he drove straight to the recently built Mozart Hall in Holland Park in order to surprise the London Met, who were rehearsing for a televised performance of Mahler's *Fourth*, which he was to conduct on Sunday.

Not content with stalking out of the London Met's performance of Beethoven's *Ninth* three weeks earlier, Rannaldini was now outraged to learn from a rather large bird called Hermione that the guest conductor, Oswaldo, had been taking rehearsals with a joint in one hand and a baton in the other – such appalling lack of discipline. The London Met, however, were devoted to Oswaldo. He was gentle, hugely appreciative (Rannaldini had never learnt the English for thank you) and a marvellous musician. He listened to the more experienced members of the orchestra, and sought their advice on how things should be played. He also remembered his musicians' first names, bought them drinks on their birthday and tried to get them rises.

This was quite unlike Rannaldini, who had the ability to terrorize and hypnotize simultaneously, and who could reduce his entire string section to jelly by raising a jet-black eyebrow. (Telling themselves that the same eyebrow was probably dyed did nothing to reduce their terror.)

As Musical Director of the London Met, Rannaldini's job was to control the orchestra and staff, choose guest conductors, select the soloists and plan the repertoire for the whole season. But as he was also Musical Director of other orchestras in Germany and mid-America, where the London Met were concerned, he would make a series of snap decisions twice a year over a three-hour lunch with Hermione's husband, Bob Harefield, his orchestra manager. He then left Bob, and to a larger extent Kitty, to augment these decisions as he whizzed off round the world.

When Rannaldini had joined the London Met eight years ago, he had rowed constantly with the Board. Apart from being away so much, he cost them a fortune in overtime, because he was always late, and then would make the orchestra spend three hours getting three bars right. But, because he had been so successful, he now had them eating out of his very grasping hand and could do what he liked.

For Rannaldini sold records. The London Met loathed him, but he bullied them into perfection. They were the best and most famous orchestra in Europe, and they never had an empty seat.

They were also the best looking. Resplendent himself, Rannaldini liked beauty in others, and knew that audiences liked gazing at beautiful people, particularly when the music became too demanding. Bob Harefield, therefore, scoured the country for attractive young musicians, who played more vigorously, were more malleable and much cheaper. In the London Met, unless you were exceptionally gifted, over forty you were a marked man.

Biographers tended to attribute Rannaldini's machiavellian nature to his early life. His father, Wolfgang, had been a German army officer, who met Rannaldini's mother Gina, a chilly left-wing intellectual of great beauty but uncertain temper, during the last despairing days of the war, when the Germans had withdrawn up the leg of Italy.

Returning to Italy after a gruelling three years in a

POW camp, Wolfgang found Gina living on the edge of a small Umbrian hill town, unhappily and most unsuitably married to Paolo Rannaldini, an Italian gentleman farmer, who'd lost practically everything in the war. Although Gina had grown less beautiful and more cantankerous, the affaire started again, until Paolo found out, by which time Wolfgang was quite relieved to be seen off with a shotgun. Having failed to withdraw down the leg of Gina, however, the result was a baby called Roberto, who took Paolo's name but little else.

After this reversal, Paolo increasingly sought refuge in drink and other women and occasionally to beating up little Roberto. Gina, blaming her son quite wrongly for sabotaging the political career which she had always dreamed of, was terribly hard on him, frequently hitting him for displaying the same sybaritic nature as his German father. Even worse, she gave him no affection, particularly humiliating in a country where mothers hero-worship their sons, and took no pride in his achievements.

Irresistible to women, Roberto grew up fatally drawn to those who rejected him, or gave him a hard time like his mother. In return for his savage upbringing, he dealt out savage treatment to his musicians, his staff, and any woman foolish enough to fall in love with him.

In his late teens he left Italy and sought out his father, now a rich Hamburg industrialist who, proud of his unexpectedly glamorous, talented son, gave him some money and introduced him to a rich but plain wife, who supported him through three years at music school and gave him a son, little Wolfgang.

Just after leaving college, Rannaldini had another break, conducting his first performance of *Medea*, during which he fell madly in love with Cecilia, a famous but incredibly temperamental visiting soprano who was playing the leading role. He married her as soon as he could get a divorce. Cecilia bore him several children, of whom Natasha was the eldest, and helped him hugely with his career.

A musician of genius, who could play several instruments,

including the eternal triangle, Rannaldini had been persuaded by Cecilia that he would only have the ultimate control he craved if he became a conductor. Their stormy marriage lasted fifteen years, and only foundered when Rannaldini's affaire with Hermione became too public and Cecilia's jealousy too excessive. Leaving her because she was too much trouble, he married Kitty because she was absolutely no trouble at all.

An improviser of genius, Rannaldini expected his musicians to be note-perfect at a first rehearsal. He was lucky in that he had a memory instant as a Polaroid. Glanced at, a page of music was not forgotten. Thus he was always able to conduct without a score, which was good because he never lost vital eye-contact with his orchestra, and because he was too vain to wear spectacles in public.

Rannaldini was a dandy. His tailcoats were only perfect after twenty-five fittings. Women had been known to die for Rannaldini's back with its broad flat shoulders beneath the polished pelt of pewter-grey hair. The front was even better, with the sculptured, usually tanned, features, the beautifully shaped, slightly thin lips, and the dark, dark eyes that not only mesmerized orchestras, but gazed deep, deep into women's eyes until their eyeballs melted.

Apart from his childhood which still gave him nightmares, Rannaldini had two great sadnesses. He was one of the greatest conductors in the world, but he minded that he was only an interpretative artist. He had composed in his youth, but, able to absorb other people's music so effortlessly, he was terrified of being derivative and banal, and not succeeding 100 per cent. Secondly, he would have given anything to be six foot rather than five foot six.

And now he was back, padding stealthily into the new Mozart Hall a day early. The orchestra had already played Mahler's *Fourth* to a rapturous reception in Vienna the night before. Afterwards most of the musicians had stayed up for Oswaldo's birthday party, preferring to catch an early morning plane home for the rehearsal while still tight.

With the cheers of the sophisticated Viennese audience still ringing in their aching heads, they felt there was little need to do more than touch up a few difficult passages and practise with Hermione, who was to be the soloist in the fourth movement on Sunday. As Rannaldini was due back tomorrow, there was very much an elegiac feeling of the last day of the holidays, which was intensified by the players' paraphernalia of music cases, dinner-jackets, evening dresses in plastic cases and hold-alls which littered the front-stall seats and the gangway. No-one even minded that a cleaner was hoovering the red carpet up in the dress circle.

Hands floating above the music like a seagull, tall and gangling with a shock of blond hair, Oswaldo swayed on the rostrum, his ginger T-shirt showing two inches of bony white back each time he raised his arms.

'This is dancing music,' he said, calling a halt in the second movement. 'It should be a little yar.'

Short of English, he pushed his elbows upwards, swaying his narrow hips to illustrate an imaginary beat.

'Christ, I've got a hangover,' said the leader of the orchestra, calling out to a passing Bob Harefield, 'Get us an Alka-Seltzer, there's a love, and let's have a black-coffee break at the end of this movement, Ossie.'

But suddenly the musicians at the front desks started to shake, without knowing why. Then, gradually, as a faint sweet-musky scent reached the nostrils of the entire orchestra, they realized it was Rannaldini's horribly distinctive aftershave, Maestro, specially created for him by Givenchy, wafting over them, as he strolled towards the rostrum.

'A little yar,' he murmured silkily. 'What a very specific instruction. Not very OK ya in this case.'

The leader of the orchestra dropped his bow, the percussionist choked on his toffee, a bassoonist hastily put down P.D. James, the harpist stopped painting her toe-nails, a beautiful violinist in a purple shirt, deliberately placed at the desk nearest the audience, stopped reading a letter from her boyfriend. A female horn player, who'd been infatuated with Rannaldini since he'd bedded her on the orchestra's last trip to Japan, dived behind the cellist in front, frantically combing her hair, and applying blusher to her blanched cheeks. A paper dart intended for Oswaldo fell at Rannaldini's feet. Oswaldo melted away like snow in the morning sun. Bob Harefield on his way into the hall with a fizzing glass of Alka-Seltzer went sharply into reverse.

Normally chatter swelled whenever there was a halt, but now the hall was totally silent. Musicians, still trickling in because they hadn't expected Rannaldini, were greeted with a sabatier tongue which slashed through their excuses.

'Another pile-up on the motorway? The traffic was terrible from the airport?' bawled Rannaldini to a little flautist weighed down by Sainsbury carrier bags. 'The road was perfectly clear ten minutes ago.

'A train taken off? *Balderdash!*' His voice rose to a scream. 'You're late! If it happens again you're fired.'

'I'm sorry, Rannaldini, there was a bomb-scare in Sloane Square,' said a front-desk violinist scuttling in.

'Bomb-scare,' purred Rannaldini, as the man frantically tuned his violin, twiddling and twisting the nobs with a shaking hand. Then with a roar, 'I'll put a bomb under you, all of you! Just look under your cars before you leave.'

Slowly he mounted the rostrum. As gleamingly brown from the LA sun as any of the cellos in his string section, he kept on his black overcoat with the astrakhan collar because he hadn't adjusted to the cold March weather. Letting the score drop to the floor in a gesture of contempt, he removed his Rolex and laid it on the music-stand, then stood as still as one of his own Valhalla statues, establishing dominance.

The orchestra edged nearer their music-stands, wishing they could have fastened seat-belts against turbulence. Suddenly the music they'd known backwards five minutes ago seemed terrifyingly unfamiliar.

Tapping the baton given him by Toscanini, Rannaldini held out his arms. The leader put his violin under his chin, bow quaking in his hand, as Rannaldini gave the upbeat for the start of the funereally slow third movement.

Eyes missing nothing, gesticulating exquisitely with his beautiful hands, the right one keeping time, the left exhorting his musicians on, he let them have their heads. Economical with his movements, even his stick hand twitching no more than the tail of a cat watching a bird through a window, Rannaldini lulled them into a false sense of security. Perhaps the audience in Vienna had been right, after all.

Then he unleashed his fury, like a Fascist police squad moving in on a defenceless mob with cudgels, finding fault after fault with the performance until the women were in tears, the men grey and shaking, and shredded India rubber covered the floor where they'd erased Oswaldo's instructions on their scores and replaced them with Rannaldini's.

Able to identify a wrong note ten miles away, he singled out an oboe player. 'You make a hundred meestakes.'

'It's difficult that bit,' stammered the player.

'Rubbish,' thundered Rannaldini.

Strolling down from the rostrum he picked up the oboe and played it perfectly.

'You haven't practised. You're fired.' He handed back the oboe.

Then he noticed Bob Harefield's charming Humpty Dumpty face with its tired bruised eyes, and shouted that he would not conduct on Sunday unless the twenty-four musicians Bob had hired in his absence were fired as well.

'I no Okkay them,' he screamed.

'But every seat is sold, Maestro, and what about the

177

BBC and Catchitune?' said the manager of the Mozart Hall, almost in tears.

'It weel 'ave to be cancelled,' snarled Rannaldini. 'I weel not play with peegs.' Howling, he turned on his orchestra and would have kicked over a few music-stands if his handmade black shoes hadn't been new.

'I 'ear you murder Beethoven *Nine*. Poor Beethoven I 'ope they didn't restore his 'earing in 'eaven. I 'ave tape of Radio Three programme last week when you abort *The Creation*.'

'We got very good reviews for both,' protested Bob, putting a comforting arm round the shoulder of the sacked oboist.

'Reviewers are stupid peegs, and I want heem sacked,' Rannaldini pointed at the front-desk violinist who'd rushed in late.

'We can't sack him,' whispered Bob. 'His wife's just left him.'

'Sensible woman,' said Rannaldini, then, his voice rising to a shriek, 'I want heem fired.'

A diversion was caused by the cleaner who started hoovering again at the back of the stalls.

'Another sensible woman,' said Rannaldini, 'trying to obliterate this cacophony.'

A further diversion was caused by the arrival of Hermione swathed in mink to sing in the fourth movement.

'I refuse to put those poor furriers out of business,' she was saying to her entourage of agent, secretary, make-up girl, seamstress and lighting specialist. 'I, for one, believe people come before animals.'

Having kissed her on both cheeks, Rannaldini calmed down a little.

'We will move on to the last movement, since Mrs Harefield has done you the honour of turning up and, unlike you, knows the score.'

Hermione was a nightmare to work with. Beneath the façade of gushing serenity, she was ruthlessly egotistical, always making a fuss about dressing rooms and acoustics, taking against members of the orchestra, or other soloists, creating fearful anxiety as to whether she would go on at all, leaving everyone drained because she'd milked them of so many compliments. Then, once she opened her mouth, her performance would be flawless.

Today as she flapped around, fussing about being properly lit, her husband Bob went quietly round the orchestra smoothing feathers. Holding the score, eating an apple to moisten her throat, Hermione listened unmoved while Rannaldini bawled out a beautiful little blond female flautist who, out of terror, had fluffed the introductory bars before Hermione's entrance.

Waiting for the nod to bring her in, Hermione stood on Rannaldini's left, as she had so often in the past while he was making her famous in every capital in the world. It still gave Rannaldini a charge. Hermione couldn't act for the percussionist's toffee. She always sacrificed acting for beauty of tone. She irritated the hell out of Rannaldini, but when she opened her mouth and that ripple of angelic sound soared full and clear above the orchestra, he could forgive her anything. In return she seemed to be making love to him with her huge brown eyes, grateful to him for conjuring up magic she was unaware she possessed.

The orchestra watched her wonderful bosom rising and falling with a mixture of lust and dislike, but at the end they gave her a round of applause and even the odd bravo because she expected it.

'Excellent, Mrs Harefield.' Rannaldini's flat bitchy voice could sink to reverberatingly seductive depths when he was in a conciliatory mood.

'But as for you lot, go 'ome and practise. This is the score.' Picking it off the floor, he hurled it into the orchestra, narrowly missing a lady clarinetist. 'Now steek to eet, and eef you 'aven't learn it properly by tomorrow, I won't go on on Sunday.' And he stalked out, leaving Hermione, who was expecting lunch at San Lorenzo, mouthing in outrage.

'What can we do?' asked the manager of the Mozart

Hall in despair. 'You can't sack all those musicians.'

Bob shrugged. 'Rannaldini's just jackbooting around because he's been away and he can't bear his orchestra playing well for someone else. Also,' Bob dropped his voice, 'Cecilia – wife number two – is in London. She's come over for *Lucia* at Covent Garden, so he wanted an excuse to storm out early and take her to lunch and double bed at The Savoy. She lives in New York, but he always sleeps with her when she comes over, or if he's in New York.'

'What's she like?' asked the leader of the orchestra, forgetting his hangover.

'Little black mamba in little black numbers. Eats men for breakfast, or would if she wasn't always on a diet.' Bob shook with laughter.

'Goodness,' said the sacked oboe player, momentarily roused out of his despondency, 'Does Hermione know?'

'Christ, no! Why upset her? Cecilia's supposed to be going down to Bagley Hall this evening to some end-of-term concert. Boris Levitsky's the music master so the standard may have improved a little. I suppose Rannaldini may roll up as well, and Hermione. They'll all fly in different helicopters.'

'That guy's a saint,' said the leader of the orchestra, as Bob moved off to calm Hermione down.

17

Bagley Hall was a chic progressive boarding-school set amid rolling green parkland on the edge of the Rutminster–Gloucestershire border. The parents, who tended to be arty or from the media, had chosen the school mostly because they heard the music was wonderful, and they believed that their somewhat problematical darlings wouldn't come to much harm amid such remote rural surroundings. The former assumption was certainly true since Boris Levitsky had become music master. Last seen threatening to beat up Lysander for comforting his wife Rachel after they met in a London chemist's, Boris had shortly afterwards left the London Met, where he had worked as an assistant conductor, in an attempt to save his marriage.

Boris had loathed being an assistant conductor, which meant he was a glorified understudy, who took rehearsals, memorized scores and kept a tailcoat hanging in a cupboard backstage, ready to come on at a moment's notice – but alas the moment never came.

This, with the added frustration of never getting any of his compositions published or performed, had driven Boris into the ego boost of an affaire with Chloe the mezzo.

Envious of Boris's genius both as composer and conductor and not wanting competition at the London Met, Rannaldini had actively helped him to get the job at Bagley Hall, not least because he felt his daughter Natasha, and less so his son Wolfgang, who was in his last year and musically disinclined, could do with some decent teaching.

Boris found teaching much worse than being an assistant conductor. It was so draining that he had no effort left for composition. He was thirty-one and he was aware of time running out, particularly now that Europe, after the collapse of the Berlin Wall, was flooded with Russian musicians. His novelty value was ebbing away. He would never achieve recognition.

Now the concert hall was filling up. Through the thick green velvet curtains, Boris could see Kitty Rannaldini, so sweet and downtrodden being ignored by her step-daughter, Natasha. A voluptuous sixteen year old, almost incestuously in love with her father, Natasha had inherited both Cecilia's and Rannaldini's histrionic temperaments but not alas their talent. Her voice was powerful, but harsh. Assuming it must be good, however, she never listened to criticism.

Boris's best pupil was Marcus Campbell-Black, who at seventeen played the piano with such sensitivity and imagination that there was little left to teach him. Through the curtain, Boris could see Marcus's father, the legendarily handsome Rupert. Only dragged here on sufferance by his wife Taggie, Rupert was determined to leave early. He didn't want to be buttonholed by his ex-wife Helen, who was sitting in the row behind.

Rupert had not forgiven Helen for not sending Marcus to his old school, Harrow. Convinced that there was no money in playing the piano as a career, it had taken Rupert a long time to get over the shock, four years ago, when Marcus had timidly announced that he wanted to become a concert pianist.

Today Rupert was worrying about the recession. At Venturer, the local ITV company of which he was a director, advertising had slumped. The bloodstock market had also taken a dive. Finally he had been up all night with a sick filly, who was a distinct possibility for the Guineas and The Oaks and he wanted to get back to her.

He was, therefore, the only adult not thrown into turmoil because Rannaldini had just telephoned Natasha to say he would be attending the concert after all. Parents and teachers were all in a tizz in case one of their darlings was discovered. The pupils, on the other hand, were more excited by the presence of Georgie Maguire and Guy Seymour who were becoming cult figures since the launching of *Rock Star*. Natasha Rannaldini, who saw herself as the victim of a broken home, thought 'Rock Star' was the most wonderful song, and that the reason she wasn't as popular at Bagley Hall as Flora Seymour was because she didn't have parents as happy as Guy and Georgie. Amazed to see them arriving with her dreary stepmother, whom she usually passed off as the younger children's au pair, Natasha was forced to speak to Kitty in order to meet them.

'Shame your father isn't here to hear you singing,' said Guy.

'But he will be.' From under heavy eyelids, Natasha shot a spiteful glance at Kitty. 'He just rang to say he's on his way.'

For a second, Guy thought Kitty would black out with horror as she remembered she hadn't turned on the central heating in the tower, or put clean sheets on Rannaldini's bed there or in her bedroom, in case he deigned to sleep with her this evening. There was nothing special for supper, and Rannaldini's guard-dogs were still down in the village with their handler. He liked a pack welcome.

'I must go,' she mumbled white-lipped, 'I'll get a taxi.'

'You will *not*.' Firmly Guy took her arm. 'It's Rannaldini's fault for arriving a day early. He can join us at The Heavenly Host.'

Georgie, still smarting because Rannaldini had dismissed 'Rock Star' as derivative, was even more livid that Guy hadn't let her wash her hair. She'd had to make up in the car and now, in the crowded, overheated hall, was terrified that her pale skin would grow red and blotchy. She was also piqued that while everyone else's children were crowding around asking for autographs, Flora, whom she hadn't seen since before the American tour, hadn't showed up.

Although she had only been at the school one term, Flora had already established herself as the Bagley Hall wild child, determined to buck the system. Wolfie Rannaldini had a massive crush on her, so did Marcus Campbell-Black, but he was too shy to do anything about it. Like most of the girls in the school, Flora had a massive crush on Boris Levitsky, who had sallow skin, wonderful slitty dark grey eyes and high cheek-bones. With his long blue jacket and shaggy black hair in a pony-tail, he would be perfectly cast as Mr Christian in *Mutiny on the Bounty*.

The concert had been due to start at five o'clock. It was now five-thirty, and there was still no sign of Rannaldini. The orchestra had tuned up and up. Parents were looking at their watches. Many of them had long drives home and would be forced to stumble out in the middle, ruining the concert, which was probably Rannaldini's intention, thought Boris darkly. Determined to impress his old mentor, he was getting increasingly strung up. He was very tired, because sustained by vodka he was playing the fiddle in a Soho night-club to make ends meet.

Out in the hall, distraction was provided by the arrival of the great diva, Hermione Harefield, who'd just rolled up with Bob and plonked herself down between Kitty and Guy in the seat that was being kept for Rannaldini. It was twenty-five to six. Miss Bottomley, the headmistress, vast and Sapphic, had just risen furiously to announce that the concert could be delayed no longer, when Rannaldini's helicopter landed on the lawn outside, squashing a lot of daffodils. Kitty watched him jump down like a cat, bronzed and impossibly glamorous, with his thick pewter hair hardly ruffled by the wind, and her heart failed, as it always did. Georgie, prepared to detest him because of Hermione's jibes, thought he was the most attractive man she had ever seen. It was not just the good looks, but the total lack of contrition.

'Sorry to hold you up, Sabine,' he called out blithely to an apoplectic Miss Bottomley, as he swept up the aisle asphyxiating everyone with Maestro. 'We had engine trouble.' Then, glancing up at Boris, who was fuming in the wings, 'Carry on, Boris.'

Always engine trouble when Cecilia's in town, thought Kitty despairingly.

'Over here, Rannaldini. We've saved you a seat,' called Hermione in her deep thrilling voice.

In fact she hadn't. It merely meant that Helen Campbell-Black had to move into the row in front and sit next to her ex-husband, Rupert, who had in the past been infinitely more promiscuous and far later for every engagement than Rannaldini, but who was now glaring at him with all the chilling disapproval of the reformed rake.

'Fucking Casanouveau,' he murmured to Taggie. 'Can't imagine him as a schoolboy. Must have spent his time in the biology lab dissecting live rats.'

Moving down the row to join Hermione, Rannaldini's eyes fell on a cringing Kitty.

'Friday is a work day,' he murmured as he sat down beside her. 'I assume everything's in order at home for you to play truant like this.'

'I fort you was coming tomorrow,' stammered Kitty. 'I fort Natasha would like one of us to be here.'

'Hush,' said Hermione loudly, 'Boris wishes to begin.'

Boris had a hole in his dark blue jacket, buttons off his white frilled shirt, a nappy pin holding up his trousers, and his unruly black hair was escaping from its black bow. Mounting the rostrum, he bent to kiss the score of Brahms' *Academic Overture*, lifted his stick and began immediately. If Rannaldini was all icy precision, Boris was all fire and romantic enthusiasm. The orchestra played as though they were possessed. Bob Harefield, who never stopped talent-spotting and was now leaning against the wall at the back of the hall, took out his notebook.

Rannaldini, on the other hand, closed his eyes and ostentatiously winced at any wrong note. Rupert Campbell-Black was not much better behaved, his golden head lolling on his present wife's shoulder as he gently snored in counterpoint to the music, until his ex-wife woke him up to listen to Marcus playing the last movement of Mozart's *E Flat Piano Concerto*. This Marcus did so exquisitely, and looked so touching, with his faun's face, big hazel eyes and gleaming dark red hair, that the audience, despite being kept late by Rannaldini, demanded an encore.

Mopping his brow, looking much happier, Boris tapped the rostrum.

'Marcus will now play a little composition of my own. I 'op you all like him.'

The audience wasn't sure, and started looking bewildered and at their watches, not understanding the music one bit.

'Sounds as though the stable cat's got loose on the piano. Awful lot of wrong notes,' muttered Rupert.

'I think they're meant to be, because it's modern,' whispered Taggie.

'Hush,' said Rupert's ex-wife furiously.

Rannaldini, who'd repeatedly refused to programme Boris's music, felt totally vindicated, and smirking, pretended to go to sleep again. Through almost closed eyes he was aware of Kitty, plump, white and quivering like a blancmange. It was cruel to compare her with the other very young wife in the room, but Rannaldini did so. Staring at Taggie Campbell-Black, he decided she was very desirable, particularly in that red cashmere polo-neck which had brought a flush to her cheeks. And what breasts, and what legs in that black suede mini-skirt! Her succulent thighs must be twice as long and half the width of Kitty's. She was reputed to be a marvellous cook, and to be adored by all Rupert's children, which was more than could be said for Kitty. How amusing to take Taggie off Rupert, thought Rannaldini, who liked long-distance challenges. As if willed by his lust, Taggie turned round and smiled without thinking because he looked familiar. Then, realizing they hadn't been introduced, she turned away, and Rannaldini suddenly encountered such a murderous glare from Rupert that he hastily looked up the row at Helen. She was stunning, too. Rupert certainly knew how to pick them. Rannaldini wished he had brought Cecilia to redress the balance, but he had exhausted her so much at The Savoy she couldn't be bothered to get out of bed.

And now it was Natasha's turn to sing 'Hark, Hark the Lark'. Her voice was strident and she hadn't practised enough. Marcus played the accompaniment, and, being a kind boy, speeded up to get her through the difficult bits. The audience, who didn't know any better, seeing in their programme that she was a Rannaldini, gave her huge applause, led by Hermione.

Rannaldini let his thoughts wander to the little blond flautist he had reduced to tears at the rehearsal. Tomorrow he would be stern at first, then stun her with a word of praise and ultimately ask her to his flat in Hyde Park Square for a drink. 'I only bully you, dearest child, because you have talent.'

The orchestra, with Wolfie playing the clarinet, Natasha the violin and Marcus Campbell-Black the trumpet, were just murdering the 'Dove' from Respighi's *The Birds*, and plucking the poor thing as well, and Rannaldini was about to stage another of his very public walk-outs which would take all the attention off Boris, when Kitty whispered that the girl Wolfie was mad about was coming on next.

The orchestra, who were going to end the concert with an *Enigma Variation*, stayed in their seats. Rannaldini couldn't imagine his stolid rugger-playing son being mad about anyone interesting, but when Flora strolled on to the platform, he couldn't take his eyes off her. Despite having several spots, greasy red hair the colour of tabasco and a pale green complexion from drinking at lunchtime, she was the sexiest girl he'd ever seen. Her school shirt, drenched in white wine, clung almost transparently to her small jutting breasts, her tie was askew, her black stockings laddered. Gazing truculently at the back of the hall she sang 'Speed Bonny Boat' unaccompanied and the room went still. Her voice was beyond criticism, sweet, pure, piercingly distinctive and delivered in a take-it-or-leave-it manner without a quiver of nerves. Her star quality was undeniable. Georgie clutched Guy's hand. Deeply moved, Guy couldn't resist glancing sideways, delighted at the dramatic effect his daughter's voice was having on Rannaldini. He didn't want her to become a pop star, but a career in classical music would be different. Perhaps Flora was learning to behave at last.

But when Flora reached the line about winds roaring loudly and thunderclouds rending the air, she so empathized with tossing on a rough sea that she suddenly turned even greener, and, grabbing the nearest trumpet from a protesting Marcus, threw up into it.

The first person to break the long and appalled silence was Rupert Campbell-Black, quite unable to control his laughter.

Sod Wolfie, thought Rannaldini with a surge of excitement, I must have that girl.

Georgie and Guy were so overwhelmed with mortification and, in Guy's case, white-hot rage that they nearly boycotted the drinks party afterwards. Miss Bottomley, who'd been looking for an excuse all term, was poised to sack Flora on the spot when Rannaldini glided up and smoothed everything over.

Putting his beautiful suntanned hand, which was immediately shrugged off, on Miss Bottomley's wrestler's shoulders, he assured her that all creative artists suffered from stage fright.

'The girl's impossible,' spluttered Miss Bottomley.

'But on course for stardom. I never 'ear a voice like this since I first heard Hermione Harefield. Even Mrs Harefield,' Rannaldini lowered his voice suggestively, 'need endless coaxing to go on and very delicate handling.'

Frightfully excited at the thought of handling Hermione, Miss Bottomley agreed to give Flora another chance.

'I will speak to her parents,' insisted Rannaldini.

He then astounded Wolfie, Natasha and Kitty by changing his mind and staying on for the drinks party. As Rupert Campbell-Black had led the stampede of cars down the drive, he would at least have the floor to himself.

'Was "Hark, Hark" OK, Papa?' demanded Natasha, linking arms with her father as she led him down dark-panelled corridors past gawping staff and pupils.

'Excellent,' said Rannaldini abstractedly, 'you've come on a lot. What was the matter with Wolfie's little redhead?'

'Flora?'

Deliberately Natasha let the door into Miss Bottomley's private apartment slam in the face of Kitty, who was panting to keep up with them on her high heels.

'Flora got pissed at lunchtime,' explained Natasha. 'She's got this massive crush on Boris Levitsky and she saw him French, or rather,' Natasha giggled, 'Russian-kissing some strange blonde – not Rachel his wife – outside the Nat West this morning. That was Boris's trumpet Flora was sick into. Boris had lent it to Marcus.'

So Boris is back with Chloe the mezzo, thought Rannaldini. Certainly he didn't regard Flora's massive crush on the Russian as any competition.

Miss Bottomley's large study was already packed with parents falling on drink and food like the vultures culture always seems to turn people into. Most of them, Rannaldini noticed scornfully, seemed to be gathering like flies on a cowpat round that ghastly, blousy Georgie Maguire, who kept throwing him hot glances. Ignoring her totally, but accepting a glass of orange juice – he never touched cheap wine – Rannaldini spoke briefly to Boris.

'Well tried, my dear. Slightly too ambitious. They are still cheeldren, and was it wise to programme one of your own compositions in front of these Pheelistines?'

Boris, whose conducting arm was not aching too much to prevent him downing several glasses of red, wanted to smash Rannaldini's cold, fleshless, but curiously sensual face, but then Rannaldini murmured something about having a pile of freelance work. Boris needed the money badly.

'Now introduce me to Flora's parents,' he said to Natasha.

'Oh, didn't you twig, Papa? Flora's Georgie Maguire's daughter.'

Rannaldini didn't miss a beat. Gliding forward, parting parents like the Red Sea by sheer force of personality, he stopped in front of Georgie, put his hands in the pockets of his soft brown suede jacket, bowed slightly and glared aggressively into her eyes. His trick was to unnerve women by staring them out, then suddenly to smile.

'*Señora* Seymour,' he said caressingly. 'May I call you Georgie?' Then raising her hand which was clutching a soggy Ritz cracker topped with tinned pâté and chopped gherkin, he touched it with his lips.

Just one corny-etto, thought Guy.

'I am sorry I mees your launching,' went on Rannaldini, 'I 'op it is not too late to say: welcome to Paradise.'

'Oh, not at all. How lovely to meet you at last.' Georgie was totally flustered, as though a great tiger had strolled out of the jungle and was rubbing his face against her cheek. Rannaldini was even more faint-making close up.

'And I loff *Rock Star*. It is great music and your peecture don't do you any justice.'

What could Rannaldini be playing at? Hermione, who'd joined them, was looking furious.

'Oh, thank you,' gasped Georgie, then remembering her manners, 'This is Guy – my husband,' she added almost regretfully.

'I haff heard much of your gallery.' Rannaldini switched his searchlight charm on to Guy. 'You were first to exeebit Daisy France-Lynch when no-one else had 'eard of her. I 'ave several of her paintings.'

'Oh, right,' Guy was totally disarmed. 'I'd love to see them.'

'You shall,' said Rannaldini. 'First I want to get Bob over to talk about Flora.'

Seeing his endlessly compassionate and good-natured orchestra manager making too good a job of cheering up Boris Levitsky, Rannaldini clicked his fingers imperiously.

Refusing to be ruffled, Bob finished what he was saying and was fighting his way through the mob when Guy said to Rannaldini: 'You may not have been here to welcome us, but Kitty has been an absolute brick, bringing us new-laid eggs and turning down curtains. You're a lucky man,' he added rather heartily, aware that the searchlight beam had dimmed a little.

Rannaldini, who detested Kitty furthering anyone's interests but his own, much preferred it if she turned down invitations rather than curtains. He even begrudged her taking an hour off on Sunday to go to church.

Aware of a distinct chill but not understanding why, Georgie couldn't bear to lose contact.

'We wanted to take Kitty out to The Heavenly Host tonight,' she stammered.

'Why don't we all go? We were planning to celebrate Flora's first night home, although on second thoughts she seems to have pre-empted us rather too well already. Why don't you both come to dinner at Angel's Reach? How about Friday week? We should be a little less shambolic by then.'

Hermione, who was about to draw Georgie aside and explain that the protocol in Paradise was for long-term residents to invite first, awaited one of Rannaldini's legendary put-downs.

Instead, to her amazement, he accepted with enthusiasm.

On four glasses of cheap wine, Georgie proceeded to invite Bob, who'd just brought Boris over to be introduced, and Hermione who only accepted because Rannaldini had.

Then she asked Boris and his wife Rachel, if they were in the country, to make up for the sick trumpet, which Boris reassured Georgie would easily wash out. Then, to placate Miss Bottomley, she asked her as well.

'Best time to have a house-warming party when it's not all done up for people to ruin,' said Georgie happily.

As they drove home, a moon one size up from new was winging its way like a white dove towards a dying flame-red sunset. Slumped in the back Flora was fast asleep.

'I thought you wanted peace and quiet in the country,' chided Guy.

'I got carried away. I thought it would be good for Flora to meet Rannaldini. She needs an older man to direct her. One never listens to one's parents at her age. He says she's exceptional. Anyway I can't cut myself off completely. We can have sausages and mash. People will only expect a picnic as we've just moved in.'

Guy, who knew he'd be lumbered with the cooking and the organization, put his mind to the menu.

Georgie lay back in a blissful haze, convinced Rannaldini had only accepted because he fancied her. It was years since she'd felt that loin-churning excitement.

'Rannaldini's lovely, isn't he?' she couldn't help saying.

'Not terribly,' said Guy shortly. 'Not to Kitty and he's clearly terribly two-faced.'

But it was such a beautiful face, thought Georgie dreamily, you didn't mind there being two of them.

18

Guy was an ace cook and a wonderful host, but Georgie had never known him make such a fuss about a dinner party. His nose had been in Anton Mosimann for days. As the dining room was still being wallpapered, he took the Friday of the dinner party off and set the big scrubbed table in the kitchen first thing in the morning. He then got enraged when Charity the cat did bending races in and out of the glasses, decanters and flowers, and with Flora when she drifted in at lunchtime with a group of friends and started making toasted sandwiches and leaving a trail of mugs, crumbs and overflowing ashtrays.

'We met a crowd of spiders fleeing down the drive singing the theme from *Exodus*,' Flora told her father. 'You ought to put one in a glass case to remind us what they look like.'

'Don't be fatuous,' snapped Guy, bashing a lobster claw with unusual violence.

When he wasn't cooking Guy seemed to spend the whole day cleaning surfaces, tidying and re-arranging the house, and disappearing to get petrol for the mower.

Every superfluous blade of grass must be cut, like a woman waiting for her lover, thought Georgie, who, having been told she was more hindrance than help, retired to work.

She was enchanted with her new study, high up in the west tower and reached by a staircase so narrow they had to hoist her piano, her worktable and Dinsdale's ancient *chaise-longue* in through the window. Sitting at her table, pen poised over a blank page of manuscript paper, she was trying to write a song equating love to everlasting candles on a birthday cake.

'*The strongest winds may blow and rack, but I'll come burning brightly back,*' wrote Georgie. The word 'rack' was too obscure: she'd have to think of something else. She got down the rhyming dictionary.

She could see the great lichened curve of an angel's wing, and if she leant out of the window she could look over a fuzz of wood as soft as rabbit's fur to the chimneys of Valhalla and Rannaldini's grey tower beyond. Paradise lived more and more up to its name. Like quill pens plunging into inky-green spring grass, little poplar trees lined the drive. As Guy's mowing machine paused, Georgie could hear the rattle of a woodpecker.

After the morning's rain, the mist was rising milky blue down the valley like a thousand smoke signals. Dreamily she imagined herself sending a message to Rannaldini: '*Guy's home. His lunch in Bath's been cancelled. We can't meet today.*'

On the mantelpiece was an unsigned good luck card from Tancredi who'd been the lead guitarist in her first famous group of the sixties. Georgie and Tancredi had been the most passionate and fatal of lovers, and when the group split up, she had settled for Guy and stability, and Tancredi had kicked his cocaine habit and married a homespun middle-American girl and made good in Los Angeles. But they still telephoned each other occasionally, and met up and made love when Tancredi came over to England, agreeing that, although they were far better off with their present partners, there was still an undeniable bond between them. Tancredi was due back in May. Perhaps he could come down to Angel's Reach when Guy was in London. There were plainly advantages to being alone in the country mid-week, particularly if Rannaldini was around.

Then Georgie looked up at the corkboard where she'd pinned cuttings from the *Rock Star* launch. Guy –

square jawed, clear-eyed, sternly handsome – stared down at her. She must get a copy of the photograph from the *Express* and have it framed.

Guy was the one who mattered, but it was lovely to be fancied. Feeling dreadfully self-indulgent, she slotted in the tape of *Rock Star*, glorying in the smoky beauty of her own voice and picked up her pen.

Flora had only agreed to wait at the table, because Boris was coming to dinner. Now she had further enraged Guy by messing up the guest bathroom and annexing his Free Foresters' cricket sweater. Hearing shouting from downstairs, Georgie wondered if Guy was uptight because he'd picked up the vibes between her and Rannaldini. She felt very excited as she wandered downstairs reeking of Giorgio, in a clinging velvet midi-dress, the same luminous grey as the sky on a moonlit night, which streamlined her opulent body and showed off her tousled red hair.

'*No Spring, nor Summer beauty has such grace, As I have seen in one Autumnal face.*' She could imagine Rannaldini murmuring in that wonderful throbbing basso profundo.

The house certainly looked lovely. The huge rooms, although hell to heat, were a marvellous showcase for Guy's paintings. Rannaldini and Larry, and to a lesser extent, Bob were collectors, Guy even had hopes of Rupert Campbell-Black, who despite not knowing the difference between a Titian and a Tretchikoff, had one of the finest collections of paintings in the country.

Drifting into the drawing room, however, Georgie found that all their own paintings had been taken down and the stark white walls covered with vast oils of the same copulating couple, a rapacious naked girl coiled round a faceless man in a pin-stripe suit.

Flora, who was still wearing Guy's cricket sweater, and looking as trampishly sexy as her mother looked voluptuous and replete, was gazing at them in horror.

'What's this shit?' she demanded.

'Don't swear.' Guy's lips tightened, as he adjusted a

picture light. 'And don't make comments on things about which you know nothing. These are original Armstrongs.'

'You'd need strong arms to hoist up a dog like that girl. They're absolutely gross.'

'It's a moving and original interpretation of the *Kama Sutra.*'

'Pin-stripe suitra more like,' drawled Flora. 'Who's coming to this bash anyway?'

Guy looked even more bootfaced, but was not prepared to risk a row that might leave him waitressless.

'Well, I decided in for a penny in for a pound. There's Julia Armstrong and her husband Ben.' Going into the kitchen, he gave his raspberry purée, to go with the lobster mousseline, a stir.

'Who's she?' asked Georgie.

Guy sighed. 'Oh Panda, I've told you a hundred times. She's having an exhibition at the gallery next month. I thought people might enjoy a preview tonight. Ben and Julia live in Islington, but they've rented a weekend cottage in Eldercombe. They've got young children. Ben's in computers. I like him a lot. Leave those grapes alone, Flora,' he said sharply. 'And you were going to wash a couple of lettuces, Georgie, I've done the dressing. And for goodness' sake, do the placement before everyone arrives.'

Oh God, placement was more taxing than A level maths! There was Julia and Ben, Rannaldini and Kitty, Annabel Hardman, another friend of Georgie's who lived in Paradise, and Valentine, her brilliant beast of a lawyer husband, who might not turn up. Boris and Rachel, Marigold and Lysander or Larry, and for Miss Bottomley Georgie had invited Meredith Whalen, an extremely expensive, gay interior designer, who was nicknamed the Ideal Homo, because he was so often asked to make up numbers at Paradise dinner parties.

'I'll need log tables to work out this one,' grumbled Georgie.

'Bottomley'd better go on your right, Mum,' advised Flora. 'She'll need two chairs.'

'Don't be silly,' giggled Georgie. 'She goes on Daddy's right and Hermione on his left.'

But Guy, who was spooning caviar on to each plate beside the lobster mousseline, was not in the mood for frivolity.

'Put Julia Armstrong on my left. She won't know anyone, and I've got to talk shop to her, and put Ben on your left.'

With alarm Georgie suddenly noticed a dozen bottles of Dom Perignon, a battalion of Nuits St George as well as the vat of caviar and four bottles of Barsac in the fridge. They were horrendously overdrawn at the moment, but she didn't feel she could remonstrate with Guy when he'd done all the cooking and her new grey velvet dress had cost a fortune.

Following him into the drawing room she found him putting on a record. Next moment Mozart flooded the house from every speaker.

'Oh, lovely,' sighed Georgie, 'Rannaldini's *Così*.'

'It's Mozart's *Così*,' snapped Guy.

He *is* uptight about Rannaldini, thought Georgie.

Guy was wearing neither tie nor jacket, which was unusual. A cornflower-blue shirt which she hadn't seen before was tucked into very dark grey cords held up with a leather belt. He looked glowingly handsome, and Georgie told him so. 'And you're in great shape,' she added, putting her arms round his broad athletic back, and feeling his flat taut midriff.

'Must be humping all that furniture.'

'You've worked so hard,' murmured Georgie, 'particularly today. I *am* lucky. Love you, darling.'

'Love you, Panda,' said Guy. 'Now do the placement, so you can relax and enjoy yourself.'

The evening, in fact, was far from relaxed. By nine o'clock only Miss Bottomley had arrived, roaring up on a motor bike and in a foul mood because she'd got lost.

Then at a quarter-past nine Boris rang full of tearful and

mostly incomprehensible contrition. Rachel had found out that he'd been seeing his old mistress, Chloe, and issued an ultimatum. As a point of honour Boris felt he must resign from the marriage, so he couldn't make dinner, nor understandably could Rachel, which meant a frantic resetting of the table, and a rewrite of the placement – not easy when one was three Bacardis up.

Even worse, Flora, on learning Boris wasn't coming, retired to her bedroom with a bottle of Barsac and the cordless telephone, and flatly refused to do any waitressing. Bob then arrived with Hermione, looking radiant in an olive-green Chanel suit braided with rose pink. Bringing up the rear, was Meredith, the Ideal Homo.

'We're late because Rannaldini sacked two soloists this afternoon and Bob's got to find replacements by Monday,' said Hermione, handing her mink to Guy. 'Gracious, it looks different since the Jennings' day.'

She then proceeded to go into ecstasies over the dark green wallpaper in the downstairs lavatory which they hadn't changed, and on peering into the study which had been papered in dark mulberry to set off Guy's Victorian paintings, said: 'What colour are you going to paint this dreadfully dark room?'

Meredith, who looked like Christopher Robin with Shirley Temple's blond curls, and who was tiny, beautifully dressed, and a great giggler, made no comment, on the principle that any praise might do him out of a possible job.

'I think it looks wonderful,' said Bob Harefield, hugging a disconsolate Georgie.

By nine-thirty, they were still light on Rannaldini and Kitty, Julia and Ben Armstrong, Annabel and Valentine Hardman and Marigold and whoever. Georgie was so nervous and belted upstairs so often to check her face that Bob wondered if she was on something. Rannaldini's *Der Rosenkavalier* was now surging out of the speakers, and Hermione had started to sing along.

'You better put on the broccoli,' muttered Guy as

he opened another bottle of champagne. 'I can't do everything.'

Not waiting for the water to boil, Georgie was returning from the kitchen when through the door came a girl with long hair, the red of springtime copper beeches, and a lot of dark make-up round her fox-brown eyes. She was wearing a cream midi-dress, which enhanced her very pale skin, as falling snowflakes whiten the sky. Her slender neck seemed almost too delicate to support a heavy metal scorpion which hung between unexpectedly full breasts.

Lovely, thought Georgie with pleasure. Not unlike me twenty years ago, I must go on a diet.

'Panda, this is Julia Armstrong,' said Guy, 'and this,' he added even more warmly, 'is Ben.'

Ben in computers was bald with protruding eyes, full red lips emphasized by a straggling black beard, and a little frill of black hair flowing over his white collar like a draught extractor. Seeing Guy in a shirt, he promptly removed his jacket to show off a small waist and hips as wide as his shoulders. He then proceeded to explain, in his nasal, very common voice, that they were late because he'd been kept at the office on extremely important business.

'What a lovely spot, Guy,' he went on, accepting a drink. 'How did you find it?'

'With great difficulty if you had Georgie's directions,' boomed Sabine Bottomley, who was gazing in admiration at Julia.

It is sod's law, thought Georgie irritably, as Julia clapped her hands in joy as she saw her paintings on the walls, that such an enchanting girl should be on Guy's left and I should be landed with her gh-a-a-stly husband.

But next moment the balance was redressed by the arrival of Rannaldini, who'd been kept on even more important business, some multi-billion Yen record deal with the Japs, and who was livid not to be the last to arrive. Heart-stopping in a dark blue velvet smoking-jacket, he was followed by poor Kitty looking unbelievably plain in burgundy polyester, with just the wrong gathers over the hips for her bean-bag figure.

As Ben was nearest the door and shamefully because they were the two most unattractive people in the room, Georgie introduced him to Kitty.

'Do you play an instrument?' asked Ben.

'She plays the word processor,' called out Rannaldini bitchily. 'Don't give her any other ideas.'

Introduced to Julia, who, in her nervousness, Georgie called Juliet, Rannaldini was all-purring amiability, but grew less so on learning that Flora had pushed off upstairs.

'Go and get your daughter,' Guy hissed at Georgie.

Always *my* daughter, when she's acting up, thought Georgie, applying another layer of Clinique, and a squirt of Giorgio before banging on Flora's door.

'Darling, please come out and be nice. Rannaldini's bought you tickets for the *St Matthew Passion*.'

'I don't care,' sobbed Flora who'd drunk nearly a whole bottle of Barsac. 'The only passion I have is for Boris Levitsky and he's buggered off with that slag Chloe. My life is over.'

Charging downstairs, Georgie found Guy pointing out the merits of one of Julia's enmeshed couples to Rannaldini, Bob and Meredith, the Ideal Homo.

'They're very strong,' Guy said warmly. 'I'm certain Armstrong is going to be very big.'

Meredith, who inveigled vast fees out of his clients with the innocence of a schoolboy touting for pocket money, raised his little grey flannel leg three inches off the ground in imitation of the Pin-stripe Lover.

'I couldn't get myself into that position in a thousand years,' he giggled. 'He must be awfully fit.'

Irritated he wasn't taking the painting seriously enough, Guy turned on Georgie. 'Annabel Hardman has just rung and bottled out,' he whispered furiously. 'Valentine's stuck in London.'

'And in some blonde, oh, poor Annabel,' said Georgie.

'Says she can't face it on her own,' snarled Guy. 'And

where's your friend Marigold? The quails will be totally ruined.'

Next moment a disgusting smell of burnt rubber drifted in from the kitchen.

'Oh God, I forgot the broccoli,' wailed Georgie.

Guy's face tightened. Even worse, Dinsdale, fed up with being tripped over, had hoisted himself on to the big dark gold corduroy sofa in front of the fire and angrily refused to be evicted when Hermione wanted to sit down.

'No, I won't have any more champagne. I'm looking forward to a glass of wine at dinner.' Hermione looked at her Cartier watch pointedly.

She was fed up with fascinating Miss Bottomley who had even more beard than Julia's husband, with whom Kitty was making very heavy weather.

'I'm starving,' muttered Meredith to Georgie. 'I had lunch with Bob and Hermione, and the old bat just served up stale bread and mousetrap, which would have been turned down by any self-respecting rat. "Hermione," I told her, "this mousetrap's been in your larder longer than Dame Agatha's play." She wasn't amused.'

In panic, feeling as if all her guests were set in gelatine, Georgie had another drink. It was plain from the bored expression on Rannaldini's face that he wasn't remotely interested in her, and if Marigold didn't show they'd need speaking trumpets to hear each other at dinner. Her heart lifted as lights came up the drive, but they went round to the back of the house. It was Mrs Piggott, Georgie's cleaner, whom Flora had nicknamed Mother Courage, because she drank so much beer and who had already arrived to wash up.

We should never have moved to the country and got embroiled in such grandiose entertaining, thought Georgie. But just as they were seated round the kitchen table, and Ben, to his horror, found himself next to dowdy Kitty yet again, the curtainless windows were filled with flashing lights and a helicopter landed on the lawn spewing out Larry and Marigold who was looking stunning in a scarlet satin suit. Clasping hands, they ran across the lawn, nearly tripping over a molehill.

'Fraightfully sorry we're late,' said Marigold as Georgie hastily wrote Larry's name on a place card instead of Lysander's. 'Larry was closing a deal.'

'Anyone we know?' asked Bob Harefield.

After some coaxing, Larry admitted that he'd just bought 28 per cent of a vast Japanese record company.

'He also found taime to make love to me on the office carpet,' whispered Marigold to Georgie.

19

The dinner party perked up a bit after this as Larry and Marigold affected everyone with their high spirits. Idly flipping over the piece of paper on which Georgie had worked out the placement, Rannaldini found his cv, which Georgie had had faxed down from the London Met Press Office, so she would be able to talk knowledgeably about his career at dinner. Rannaldini smirked. If Georgie had the hots for him, he'd gain access to her house and Flora more easily. A gaze-hound who hunted by sight rather than scent, having once seen Flora, he wouldn't rest until he caught her, however long the chase.

On the other hand, Georgie wasn't unattractive. She looked much better today. It would be an added *frisson* to play off mother and daughter.

So he turned the charm on Georgie, praising Flora's looks and blazing talent which could only come from her mother. He then told Georgie about his guest-conducting and filming commitments all over the world, and Georgie didn't take in a word he said, because, from the way he was looking at her, she felt he'd already taken a degree in the geography of her body without removing a single garment. And that voice, husky, slow, reverberating like the molten depths of a volcano pondering whether to wipe out a nearby town just for the hell of it, made his tritest utterance sound significant.

'We are both on treadmill, my dear Georgie,' he was saying now, softly, 'I in my Lear Jet, you in your leetle study, both making music, but we will meet from time to time in Paradise.'

'Oh yes.' Georgie's heart seemed to be beating between her legs.

Hermione, who detested Rannaldini chatting up anyone else, led the shrieks of praise for Guy's lobster mousseline, followed by quails *en croute* in ginger and yoghurt.

With great difficulty, Georgie wrenched her attention away from Rannaldini to talk to the horrific Ben.

'You have a very beautiful and talented wife,' she said.

'Julia is also a caring mother,' said Ben complacently.

At the end of the table, against the sooty black of the uncurtained window, Julia, her pale skin glowing like pearl, was listening to Guy's plans for the house.

'I'll knock this wall through into a conservatory, leading to an indoor pool,' he was saying. 'I mean, when does one get a chance to swim outside in Rutshire?'

And who the hell's going to pay for it? Only if I write another smash hit, which they're all so dismissive of, with their fucking classical music, thought Georgie.

Julia was telling Hermione how wonderfully she had sung in *Der Rosenkavalier*.

Having found out from Marigold the details of the Japanese record company Larry had bought into, Rannaldini was now discussing the sacked soloists across her with Bob. Georgie was dying to gossip to Marigold. How lovely if I had Rannaldini on the side, she thought dreamily, like Marigold had had Lysander.

As there was no broccoli, the salad was now being circulated. Alas, Hermione found half a slug in the lettuce; Georgie hadn't bothered to wash because it was Iceberg.

'I'm just worried that some poor person might get the other half,' Hermione was stage-whispering to Guy.

After that no-one wanted any salad, and conversation moved on to universities, which Kitty took no part in having left school at sixteen. Sitting between Ben and Meredith, who had both turned their backs on her, Kitty wished she was sitting next to Bob – goodness, he looked tired – or to Guy who'd read the lesson so beautifully in church on Sunday and who was being so sweet to that lovely painter. Kitty noticed that Rannaldini, as the Guest of Honour, had been put on Georgie's right, but did not feel slighted that she as his wife hadn't been put next to Guy. That privilege was naturally accorded to Hermione, the *maîtresse en titre*. Every night Kitty prayed not to hate Hermione, and to forgive those who trespassed against her. Georgie plainly had a crush on Rannaldini, too, but her demands on him, Kitty hoped, would be more rollicking, like a red setter wanting a long walk down the valley from time to time.

Rannaldini didn't really like Georgie and Guy, decided Kitty. That's why he had been subtly punishing her since the Bagley Hall concert, finding fault with everything, making her feel even more unsure of herself.

'I don't think one can beat the Backs at Cambridge,' Hermione was now saying.

Glancing down the table, Guy noticed Kitty's eyes were as red as her dress. Rannaldini's work, he thought grimly.

'Poor Kitty's having to put up with the backs of Paradise,' he said reprovingly. 'Turn round and talk to her, Meredith.'

'Sorry, love,' the Ideal Homo swung round. 'When's your sexy husband going to let me loose on the Valhalla dungeons?'

Kitty blushed scarlet, but thought once again, how sweet Guy was.

'I don't know how you put up with it,' she could now hear Hermione telling him, in her idea of an undertone, 'being dragged into the limelight in a pop song, when you're such a man of substance. I would never expose Bob to such publicity. My family is sacred.'

'I agree,' said Julia, leaving all her pastry and lighting a cigarette, at which Hermione looked pained, until the pudding of guava-and-mango ice-cream with kiwi-fruit purée reduced her almost to orgasm. Guy, however, was incensed that a bottle of Barsac had gone missing.

'Flora whipped it,' confessed Georgie. 'It's a good thing she's going back to Bagley Hall next month to dry out. Whoops, sorry, Miss Bottomley.'

Ben pursed his red lips and said he thoroughly disapproved of teenage drinking. Miss Bottomley's mouth was too full of guava and mango for her to do anything but nod in frenzied agreement.

'Oh, Flora's sixteen, going on a hundred,' sighed Georgie to Rannaldini. 'I get so worried about AIDS. I sat her down last week and said: "We must have a good talk about sex".'

The room fell silent.

'A good talk about sex, because I was worried,' went on Georgie, 'and Flora put her pretty head on one side, and said: "Oh, poor Mum, are you having trouble with Dad?"'

Georgie laughed so loudly at the sheer impossibility of such a thing that everyone joined in. But it was one of the few light moments of the evening. Georgie was dying to get into another heart-to-thumping-heart with Rannaldini, but, without a waitress, she seemed to spend her whole time leaping up to remove plates and filling glasses.

It was a relief finally to whisk the ladies off upstairs. On the way Miss Bottomley shot into the downstairs loo.

'I'll use this one.' Julie disappeared into another loo on the landing, whereupon Hermione vanished into Georgie's bathroom.

'Three old ladies got stuck in the lavatory. I wish Hermione would stay there.' Georgie collapsed on to her bed between Marigold and Kitty. 'Now we're alone, how are you?' she asked.

'Wonderful,' said Marigold, fluffing on face-powder with a red brush. 'Larry's faynally given Nikki the push and Pelham Crescent, it cost over a million, can you imagine? But he's bein' magic to me. He bought me these.' She turned her head to show off ruby earrings big as strawberries. 'And he's going to buy me a flat in London, and take me on a second honeymoon in Jamaica.'

'Lucky you,' said Georgie petulantly, thinking of herself nailed to the desk for months to come.

'I'm so pleased for you, Marigold,' said Kitty, who didn't feel there was much point in repairing her face.

'How's Lysander?' asked Georgie.

'Never off the telephone, the sweetie-pay. He's raydin' in a point-to-point in Cheshire this weekend, and wants me to go. Ay must say, I'm sorely tempted.'

When they went downstairs, Larry, who normally liked nothing better than to cap other men's achievements over a large glass of brandy, had already joined the ladies.

'What recession?' he was saying to Sabine Bottomley. 'If you're liquid, it's bonanza time. You can pick up companies, like shopping in Oxford Street.'

'Fed up with talking about wife avoidance?' Marigold asked him teasingly.

'Not at all. Rannaldini, Bob and Meredith all wanted to know what Guy had done to those quails. Not my board-game.' He sat down on the arm of Marigold's chair. 'This is, though.' He took her hand, then added to Georgie, 'Don't she look great? See the earrings I bought her?'

'They're lovely.'

'How's the album going?'

'Good,' said Georgie truthfully. 'I wrote a song today.'

Looking at the big red scented candle flickering on a side table, she suddenly found the answer for her lyric: *Swept by tempests, drenched by rain, I'll come burning back again.*

'Could we play one of your old albums, Georgie?' asked Kitty, as *Der Rosenkavalier* finally ended.

'Wait till Rannaldini goes,' said Hermione.

Georgie gritted her teeth.

To gain the ascendancy before he left, Larry bought three of Julia's paintings, and actually wrote Guy a large cheque. Bob, egged on by the Most Beautiful Voice in the World, put down a deposit on one of the smaller ones. Rannaldini bought the most erotic and said he'd talk to

Guy about money later. Proudly Guy went round putting red stickers on them. Julia was in heaven. She didn't say much, but her skin flushed faintly like the crimsoning on the underside of a wood anemone.

Larry and Marigold left immediately afterwards. They were followed by Rannaldini, who was flying to Milan first thing to do *The Barber of Seville* at La Scala.

Just for a second, as he and Georgie were alone in the hall together, he took her hands.

'I'd love to talk to you sometime about Flora's career,' she heard herself stammering.

'Of course,' said Rannaldini. 'Let us have lunch, and then we will have a chance to talk about ourselves.'

She felt he was just about to kiss her when Kitty came out, saying what a lovely evening it had been, and that Georgie and Guy must come over to Valhalla next time Rannaldini was home.

Georgie had the feeling that, with the departure of his boss, Bob would have liked to stay on and unwind, but that, for the same reason, Hermione felt the evening had lost all point, and dragged him away.

'Look after Julia,' Guy called out briskly to Georgie. 'I'm taking Ben and Meredith round the house.'

Georgie was a little alarmed about what grand redecorating schemes Meredith might lure him into, but it was bliss to kick off her shoes, throw another of their own logs on the fire, and relax with a bottle of Kümmel and Julia.

'How beautiful both Marigold and Hermione are,' said Julia. 'I'd so love to paint either of them.'

Feeling slightly deflated Julia didn't want to paint her, Georgie suggested Julia approached them through Larry and Bob.

'They both obviously love your work, and Larry's on such a high with Marigold at the moment, he'd commission anything. I do hope it lasts.' Georgie collapsed on the floor so she was level with Dinsdale on the sofa. 'Larry's been such a shit to her. I'm sorry I was so uptight this evening, but two couples cancelled at the last moment because their marriages had gone up the spout.'

Julia had chewed off her lipstick and her eyeliner had smudged beneath the fox-brown eyes, but her skin was unlined in the candle-light, and the scorpion glinted evilly between her breasts as though it might plunge its sting into the soft white flesh at any moment. She must be Scorpio, that most passionate and complicated of signs, thought Georgie.

'I'm so lucky to be married to Guy,' she went on hazily. 'I used to be very wild when we were first married,' and a bit now, she thought, luxuriating at the prospect of lunch with Rannaldini. 'I think Guy feels so much safer now I'm tucked away in the country. Even when I used to go into the West End from Hampstead, he used to police my every move.'

Dinsdale, half-asleep, grunted with pleasure as Georgie scratched his back.

'Guy's been so wonderful about my career,' she went on. 'So happy to bask in any reflected glory, but he's going to get glory himself soon – not just your exhibition which I'm sure will be terrific – but because of *Rock Star*. I know *The Scorpion*'s a rag, but they've nominated Guy Hubby of the Year, and if he wins, he gets ten thousand pounds. I expect Guy will insist on it going to charity, but it means he'll be a star in his own right. It's lovely that people have started recognizing him in the street and asking him for his autograph.'

Julia's eyes seemed to get bigger and bigger.

'It's so sad when marriages break up. You hang on to your Ben,' urged Georgie, then thought, I don't think she should at all, he's ghastly, I *must* be pissed. As she refilled their glasses, she noticed an adorable china puppy tangled in blue ribbon clambering out of a flowered bowl among the ornaments on a side table.

'How lovely! Victorian,' she examined it, 'I wonder where that came from.'

'Geraldine and the girls from the gallery gave it to me as a moving-in present,' said a returning Guy smoothly. 'I kept forgetting to bring it home.'

'The puppy's exactly like Dinsdale,' said Georgie enchanted. 'How clever of Geraldine.'

Saying they must go, Ben bore off Julia and Meredith whom they were going to drop off on the way.

'Nice, aren't they?' said Guy, gathering up glasses.

'Juliet's lovely,' said Georgie. 'Not sure about him though.'

'She's called Julia,' said Guy, 'and Ben's a genius.'

20

The next morning Guy and Georgie were woken ridiculously early by the telephone.

'Leave it,' mumbled Guy.

'Someone might have died.'

'Well, I wish they'd die later in the day.'

The sleepy smile was wiped off Georgie's face when she found it was Hermione, too lazy to write, but priding herself on her good manners.

'Thank you for a pleasant evening. We *so* enjoyed meeting Julia Armstrong.'

Hermione wanted recipes of everything Guy had cooked – anyone would think he'd had a baby or landed on Mars, thought Georgie irritably. Then, before ringing off, she announced, 'Sabine Bottomley has asked me out to lunch.'

She doesn't seem like a Sabine, thought Georgie as she put back the receiver. She's the one who'd do the raping.

For a few moments she tried to burrow like a mole back into the dark furry tunnel of sleep, but Guy was stroking her breasts and putting increasing pressure on her clitoris, like a stiff button on the cordless telephone, until grumbling Georgie lumbered out of bed, muttering that she must clean her teeth and wash, but Guy pulled her back. 'I want you now.'

Head turned and mouth clamped shut to divert garlic-and-wine fumes, she admired her bobbing body in a long dusty mirror, wondering if she should move more, and tried to remember to grip Guy with her inside muscles. She found it hard to come unless she was still and concentrating on her orgasm. Beneath her Guy looked tired, his face rumpled, and his white-blond fringe fallen back off his forehead.

'Tell me about the last time you went to bed with Tancredi,' he whispered.

So Georgie told him about the last time Guy thought she had been to bed with Tancredi.

Afterwards, he said, 'I'm sorry. That was selfish of me,' and he brought her breakfast in bed with grape hyacinths in a little vase. Only able to keep down the coffee, Georgie buttered the croissant for Dinsdale. When she staggered down, hungover to the hairline, everything had been cleared up, and once again she realized how lucky she was to be married to Guy, her rock star.

She felt less chipper when she opened their joint bank statement. The outgoings had been horrific and had almost mopped up the massive advance from Catchitune. The advance on *Ant and Cleo* had been spent months ago. Conciliatory before a screw, brisk afterwards, Guy was waving the bank manager's letter and just getting into his must-tighten-our-belts routine when all worry temporarily evaporated because *The Scorpion* rang to say Guy had been voted Hubby of the Year.

'To be quite honest there wasn't a lot of choice,' the reporter confided to Georgie. 'Faithful husbands are an endangered species. Can we come and interview you and him tomorrow for Monday's paper?'

At least the house had been bulled up for the dinner party, so Guy didn't have to spend the rest of the day tidying. Sunday was a lovely day. After the reporter left, they sat watching an orange sun setting like a tiger down the black bars of the wood listening to the Top Twenty on Radio 1, apprehensive almost to the end, until they heard the opening bars of Dancer Maitland's 'Recession Blues' at Number Two, and knew it hadn't knocked Georgie off the Number One spot. When 'Rock Star' came on, Guy turned up the wireless, so it blared round Paradise.

'I'm so proud of you, Panda,' he said opening the only bottle of Dom Perignon left from the dinner party.

'I wish I could really tell you how much I love you,' said Georgie.

Then, in a brief twilight wander round the garden, Guy outlined his long-term plans for the house and garden.

'A new heaven and a new earth,' murmured Georgie.

She must get on with *Ant and Cleo* tomorrow to pay for it.

Guy was in amorous mood again at bedtime.

'Don't be too long,' he urged Georgie.

But Georgie got stuck into the *Penguin Book of Narrative Poetry* in the bath, and by the time she'd finished *The Pied Piper*, marvelling at Browning's gift for rhyme, particularly as there were no rhyming dictionaries in those days, Guy was snoring with the light on.

Next morning he set off for London in his new BMW looking splendid. His blue-striped shirt and indigo tie brought out the light Messianic-blue of his eyes, as if he was some explorer setting out to discover new continents. Noticing his beautifully brushed pin-stripe jacket and his cases in the back and breathing in his English Fern aftershave as she hugged him goodbye, Georgie felt utterly desolate at being left on her own for five days. Flora was away staying with friends. But it would be nice to watch what she wanted on television, not tidy up and work all night if she felt like it.

It had rained heavily in the night, and where the valley was drying off, mist the same blue as Guy's eyes drifted upwards. Georgie wondered how far away Julia Armstrong lived and if she sent up smoke signals to some lover. She couldn't be in love with that fearful Ben.

Georgie was just looking at *The Scorpion* headline: 'CARING GUY, THE HUNKY HUBBY', when she realized he'd forgotten to take the little Hockney drawing to be framed for Flora's birthday which was on Sunday. Ringing him, she found his car telephone engaged. He must hardly have reached the outskirts of Paradise, but it remained engaged for the next thirty minutes.

Georgie was distracted by her agent ringing, saying the Gas Board were definitely firming up the offer for her and Guy to do a commercial, and that a champagne firm had rung to check out Georgie's availability.

'Better pay us in kind after Friday night,' said Georgie.

Remembering it was dustbin day, and Mother Courage wasn't due for half an hour, Georgie started to empty the waste-paper baskets. In the basket in Guy's study she found a pink envelope, torn up into pieces smaller than confetti. Was it practising for this that one did so many jigsaws as a child? thought Georgie. Having laboriously pieced the envelope together, she saw it was addressed to: GUY SEYMOUR, *private*, at the gallery.

'I must not let it put me off my work,' she told herself sternly. 'Women have always had crushes on Guy. Look at the way Kitty Rannaldini goes scarlet every time he speaks to her.'

All the same, she jumped as though she'd been caught snooping when the telephone rang. It was London Weekend asking how she was getting on with *Ant and Cleo* and whether there was anything they could see.

'It's going really well, but it's still in draft form,' Georgie told them airily, but starting to shake.

After they'd rung off, she decided to look for Act One. Perhaps Guy had picked it up. His study was so tidy, she was frightened of disrupting anything. Opening a desk drawer, searching for a sheaf of manuscript paper, she stumbled on the most charming nude drawing of a girl in a primrose-yellow bath cap with, except for the full breasts, a long slim, almost childish, body. It was a second before Georgie realized it was Julia. The drawing was unsigned, but it didn't have the narrow-eyed, scowling intense look of a self-portrait.

It was perfectly normal for Guy to buy drawings of artists he exhibited; but Georgie nevertheless felt her happiness seep away like water out of a crooked plughole.

There was the bloody telephone. How was she getting on in the country, asked the girl from the *Daily Mail*. Was she meeting lots of interesting people?

'I don't meet people down here, I meet fucking dead-lines,' snarled Georgie, then had to apologize to the reporter, who knew what hell deadlines were, and who congratulated her on Guy being voted Hubby of the Year, and asked if she could do a telephone interview with her about Guy.

Feeling guilty that she'd been harbouring jealous thoughts about pink envelopes and nudes, Georgie was even more glowing about her husband than usual.

The rest of the week was punctuated by thank-you letters for the dinner party praising Guy's cooking. Not to be outdone, Georgie wasted a whole workday making a fish pie for Guy's return on Friday night. Putting the first bluebells in his study and his dressing room, she welcomed him with clean hair and a rust angora jersey which he loved because it made her feel all soft and cuddly. As he came out on to the terrace after unpacking, he handed her the *Evening Standard*.

'They've given Julia's exhibition a terrific advance plug, I brought it down to show you. God, it's beautiful here.'

A week of sun had brought out the wild cherries and palest gold criss-cross leaves like kisses on the willows.

'*From you have I been absent in the spring*,' murmured Guy, sliding his hands up under the rust angora. 'Will that deliciously smelling fish pie keep for half an hour?'

Next day was just as beautiful, and Georgie decided to walk down to Paradise with Dinsdale, trying out the new path that had been hacked out through the wood. On either side, trees soared tall and gangling from being planted too close. Many of them were smothered to the top in ivy. Georgie noticed how many of the trunks had been daubed with silver paint, which meant they would soon be cut down to make more room for the others. Georgie felt really sad. Some of the condemned were really splendid trees, happily putting out palest green leaves, unaware of their fate. Would that make a theme for a song? She was about to scribble the idea on the back of her shopping list when she realized she'd left it behind, and calling to Dinsdale, who was baying in the woods after rabbits, ran back home.

Climbing back in through the low kitchen window, she found Guy on the telephone.

'All alone in a huge house,' he was sighing, 'God, if only you were here.' Then, seeing Georgie, without missing a beat, he said, 'I'm sorry, you must have got the wrong number. This is 284 not 285. OK, no problem,' and hanging up, 'Hallo, Panda, what did you forget?'

Georgie collapsed astride the window because her trembling legs wouldn't hold her up.

'Who were you talking to?'

'Wrong number.'

'But I heard you saying you were alone in a huge house, and if only whoever it was, was here.'

'I beg your pardon?' Guy's mouth gave a little pop of incredulity as he pronounced the 'B' of beg. His eyes were as innocent as a kitten's.

'Guy, I heard you.'

'Are you out of your mind? If I get a wrong number, you accuse me of having other women. You're spending too much time on your own. Ask Kitty over to supper next week, or get some pills from the local doctor. Benson he's called. Everyone swears by him.'

Such was his assurance that Georgie felt she was the one in the wrong. She ought to have left well alone, but she was badly frightened.

'Who were you spending thirty minutes talking to on the telephone within seconds of leaving the house on Monday then?'

'Harry,' replied Guy calmly. 'I was bringing him up to date about selling all those Armstrongs, and talking about a couple of British Impressionists Rannaldini's after. He *is* my partner and we had a lot to catch up on. I had a week off moving you, and a Friday off to organize *your* dinner party.'

'*You* asked Julia and Ben. No, stay outside, darling, I'll be with you in a sec,' Georgie added as Dinsdale's lugubrious face appeared at the window.

'And who sent that pink envelope marked "Private" which you tore up and threw in your waste-paper basket?'

'I haven't a clue,' snapped Guy, sliding a squeezed-out dishcloth along the runnels of the sink. 'Geraldine and the girls in the gallery probably sent it as a joke.' He extracted a piece of bacon rind and fish skin, both of which she supposed she should have removed from last night's fish pie, from the plughole.

'And what about the charming nude of Julia?' she hissed.

'That does it,' said Guy, losing his temper. 'You said you liked Julia, so I kept back that little nude for you for Easter. It'll be worth a lot one day, and I know how you like women,' he added nastily.

Georgie flushed. In her wild sixties days, she and Tancredi had had the odd threesome with other girls.

'And don't you get turned on hearing about it?' she said furiously.

The row escalated, until Georgie burst into tears and said she was sorry. Then Guy apologized. He hadn't meant to be ratty, but he was worried about their overdraft.

'We must pull in our horns.'

Cuckolds have horns, thought Georgie as she hugged him in passionate relief.

She was particularly glad the row was made up because Flora was coming home on Sunday for her birthday before going back to Bagley Hall for the summer term in the evening. Having forgotten to get the Hockney framed, Guy gave her a cheque instead. Georgie gave her a sand-coloured shorts suit from Jigsaw which she'd wanted. Dinsdale, who'd been decked out in a big blue bow for the occasion, gave her a basket from the Body Shop.

★　　★　　★

'I don't want to go back,' grumbled Flora, chucking all the clothes, which were marginally more crumpled after Mother Courage had ironed them, into her trunk, and putting two hundred Marlboros on the top.

'Ought you to take these?' asked Georgie. 'You'll ruin your voice. Do try and do some work, darling, and don't get caught drinking. You know how it upsets Daddy.'

Guy had seldom looked less upset as he walked in.

'Goodness, what a shambles,' he said. 'Panda, that's worked out really well. You remember that old boy in Wales whose private collection hasn't been looked at for fifty years? He's just rung. He's going abroad tomorrow, but he's invited me up to stay at the local and have dinner with him tonight.'

'Oh, a jaunt,' said Georgie in excitement. 'I'll come with you.'

'You can if you like.' Guy didn't sound too enthusiastic. 'But he's an old queen and doesn't like women, so I'd better go on my own. As I had to book at the last moment, I only got a single room.'

'When we were first married we slept on sofas,' said Georgie sadly.

'Darling, be reasonable. You've got to work and someone's got to look after Dinsdale.'

'Will you come back here on the way to London?' Georgie hated to plead.

'I really ought to get up first thing and bash up the motorway,' said Guy, removing one of his favourite jerseys from Flora's trunk. 'I've got a lunchtime meeting with an American collector. I can take Flora back to Bagley on the way to Wales. So get your finger out,' he added to Flora.

Georgie worked late that night until she was so tired that she slept through a massive thunderstorm which blew down several of the silver-painted trees in the wood. Then she had a marvellous morning's work, joyfully playing the piano, singing, scribbling and rubbing out. She could hear all the themes of the individual instruments in her head, and she kept doing different things to prove to herself that what she'd written in the first place was the right thing.

By a quarter-past one, she'd drunk so much black coffee she was beginning to jump, so she went down to the kitchen to get some lunch. Mother Courage had already left, so she decided to cook that ox's heart for Dinsdale. As she was looking for it, the telephone rang. It was Geraldine from the gallery.

'You don't know where Guy is? His lunch date's arrived and his car phone's on the blink. I rang The Leek and Daffodil. They said he checked out at eight-thirty.'

'Oh, help,' said Georgie going cold. 'You don't think he's had a shunt?'

'No, probably a tree across the road or something. They had force ten gales in Wales last night.'

'Will you ring me when he gets in?'

'Sure. How's the country?'

'Bliss. While you're on, Geraldine, you might be able to help me. A lovely puppy vase with blue ribbons turned up in the move. Someone must have sent it to us as a moving-in present, or to me for going to Number One. You've no idea who it could be?'

'Haven't a clue, sounds lovely though,' said Geraldine. 'I must go and force-feed Moët to Guy's disgruntled lunch date.'

Heart thumping, Georgie collapsed on the window-seat. Guy, who was so truthful he made George Washington look like Matilda, had been caught out in a second lie – first the wrong number, now the puppy coming from Geraldine. Feeling dizzy and sick, she found she had thrown all today's post in the dustbin. Loathing herself, she rang directory enquiries, and then The Leek and Daffodil.

'I'm awfully sorry, this is Georgie Seymour.'

'Oh, Mrs Seymour,' gushed the manageress, 'I'm so glad you rang. We're such fans, and it was lovely the way your husband signed you in under another name.

We all thought you looked so young and lovely. I expect you're ringing about your scorpion necklace.'

'That's right,' said Georgie numbly.

'My daughter found it in the bed. If you give me the right address, I'll post it back to you.'

'It's Angel's Reach, Paradise Lost,' said Georgie and hung up.

In the Exhibitions in Progress file in Guy's office, she found a formal letter from Julia and dialled her number.

'She's not back from Wales,' said a voice with a strong Rutshire accent. 'I was expecting her hours ago. Who's that speaking?'

But Georgie had hung up again. Her first emotion was passionate relief that she hadn't been going crazy, thinking Guy was up to something. He'd always been so adamant about his utter fidelity and now he'd been caught out. Wondering what to do next, Georgie decided to drive over to Julia's and confront her. It couldn't be very far with a Rutshire address. SHADOW COTTAGE, MILES LANE, ELDERCOMBE, said the letterhead.

On the way, it started to bucket down again. Georgie got terribly lost and nearly bumped into several cars. But finally she found the ravishing Stanley Spencer village, with a lazy, weed-choked stream meandering between the High Street and the faded red cottages. The rain had driven everyone in, so there was no-one to ask the way. On the right of the war memorial she found Miles Lane.

Getting out of the car, Georgie realized Dinsdale was still wearing his blue birthday bow and whipped it off, putting her belt through his collar, as she started to trudge through the deluge. She hoped Miles Lane wasn't miles long, and wished she knew on which side was Shadow Cottage. But the next moment, Dinsdale's nose had gone down and, sweeping her past three modern houses, tail waving frantically, he took a sharp right up the path of the prettiest garden filled with scillas, primulas and early forget-me-nots. Toys were neatly stacked on a table in the window, and someone had left a paper-bill addressed to Armstrong in the porch. Dinsdale's tail was really going, bashing Georgie's legs.

The door was answered by an elderly woman in a red mac and a crinkly plastic rain hat.

'Mrs Armstrong?' asked Georgie.

'No, she's out.' It was the same Rutshire accent that had answered the telephone.

'I'm Mrs Seymour.' Georgie tried to control her breathing, 'Guy's wife. He's putting on an exhibition of Mrs Armstrong's work.'

'Oh, right.' The woman in the rain hat looked suddenly more friendly. 'You must be Georgie Maguire. We've got all your records at home. Can I have your autograph?'

Somehow Georgie held the pen to sign the piece of paper.

'I'm expecting Julia any minute. She's so excited about her exhibition. She's just rung. She's been 'eld up four hours on the Severn Bridge. There were cross winds so they reduced the traffic to single line. I've just got to pop out and pick up the kids. If you want to wait, she won't be long.'

That woman doesn't know anything about Guy and Julia, thought Georgie, watching her splashing down the path. Perhaps I'm imagining things. Julia's cottage was absolutely gorgeous inside, a rainbow riot of pastel colour with her paintings on every wall.

If she's taken my husband, thought Georgie, I'm entitled to help myself to her drink. There was only elderflower wine, but it was better than nothing. Georgie took a slug, then opened the desk by the window, and nearly died. For there were a sheaf of *Rock Star* cuttings and the same *Express* picture of Guy in a handsome silver frame.

Slamming the desk shut, Georgie was pleased to see Dinsdale had left muddy pawmarks all over Julia's pale blue sofa, and when the telephone rang she answered it.

'Ju Ju,' said Guy's voice.

'No, it's Georgie.'

For a few seconds Guy thought he had rung home by mistake.

'Panda, hallo,' he said, cheerfully. 'I've only just got to London. I was stuck on the Severn Bridge for four hours.'

'I'm at Julia's,' said Georgie quite matter-of-factly. 'How long have you been having an affaire with her?'

Desperate to wriggle out of the situation, Guy found his mind moving as sluggishly as maggots in a dustbin surprised by a torrent of boiling Jeyes fluid. All he could manage was a feeble, 'Are you mad?'

'You're the mad one, mad about Julia,' Georgie's voice rose to a screech. 'You bastard, Geraldine didn't give you that puppy. And you took Ju Ju-fucking-Armstrong to The Leek and Daffodil last night, and passed her off as me. "You look so lovely and young, Mrs Seymour, you left your scorpion necklace behind, Mrs Seymour", and they've put it in the post to me at Angel's Reach, so you haven't got a clay foot to stand on. How long's it been going on?'

There was a long pause, during which Guy decided against bluffing it out.

'Well, I've taken her out once or twice in London.'

'Bed?'

'Not before last night. I'm sorry, Panda, we've been working very hard, getting ready for the exhibition. These things happen. She's only a child and she's got this terrific crush on me, probably because her marriage isn't very happy, and I'm getting her work recognized, and you know how gratitude turns into hero-worship. Dad had it all the time as a bishop.'

'I hope he didn't end up in the Leek and Daffodil. Do you want to marry her?'

'Of course I don't. Look, she'll be home any minute. Don't say anything that'll encourage her to blow it up into anything more serious. You've got to protect me. Go home and I'll come down. I'm leaving now. I love you.'

'How dare you bring Dinsdale into this bordello?' shouted Georgie.

She got even more lost on the way home. The torrential rain had let up, rainbows were lacing a sky the colour of Guy's cornflower-blue shirt. The white cherries were luminous in the unearthly light. Only when she got home did Georgie realize she was still wearing her pyjamas.

21

Georgie was so shivery that she had a bath and was just cleaning her teeth to get rid of the terrible sick acid taste when the doorbell rang.

Running to the window, she could see hair as red as dried blood. It was Julia. She must find out if her version tallied with Guy's. Throwing up the window, she said she'd be down in a minute. Having pulled on an old grey jersey and a pair of leggings, brushed her hair and slapped on a bit of base, she was amazed to see she looked rather beautiful. Scent, she decided, was pushing it. She would play the whole thing magnanimously. Running downstairs, she saw Julia in the hall dressed in jeans and a black polo-neck. Her hair was pulled back from her deathly white face into a pony-tail. She looked younger than Flora.

Georgie held out her arms. 'Julia, poor little duck, I'm so sorry.'

'Don't touch me!' Julia thrust her violently away.

'Well, at least let's have a drink.'

Only as they went into the drawing room did Georgie remember Julia's faceless pin-stripe lover in the paintings. Two of the paintings were still on the wall.

'I don't want a drink.' Julia was shuddering as though she had malaria, her eyes staring. 'How much has Guy told you?'

'That he went to bed with you for the first time last night, that he's taken you out one or twice in London. Guy's a kind man. Girls are always getting crushes on him.'

'A crush?' Julia collapsed on the gold corduroy sofa. 'Guy and I have been having an affaire for nearly two years. Since you moved to Angel's Reach we've spent virtually every night together when he's up in London.'

'Virtue doesn't seem to have much to do with it,' said Georgie, pouring herself such a massive Bacardi that there was only room for an inch of Coke.

'He loves me,' said Julia flatly. 'He's never had another woman since he's been married to you.'

'I know,' admitted Georgie. 'He's been a wonderful husband.'

'And you've totally neglected him. All you did at that dinner party,' reproved Julia, 'was burn the broccoli and leave slugs in the lettuce.'

Guy's been sneaking, thought Georgie, taking her drink to the window and admiring the pale green of the wood against the navy-blue thunderclouds.

'You don't take any interest in the gallery. You didn't even know my Christian name.'

'I hope now I may call you Ju Ju,' said Georgie gravely; she was getting rather a charge out of being bitchy. The Bacardi was beginning to put fire in her empty belly.

'You don't share any of his interests,' said Julia, flushing.

'Well, I certainly didn't share his interest in you.'

'And you had endless affaires.'

'I did *not*. I had the odd one-night stand when we were first married years ago,' said Georgie, thinking that Tancredi had been going on so long and so infrequently that he didn't count.

Dinsdale was slumped on a coral-pink chair on the other side of the empty fireplace, which still contained the ashes from the dinner party. Georgie crossed the room to sit on the arm.

'I had a wonderfully happy marriage with Ben,' Julia was saying bitterly. 'Guy pestered and pestered me to sleep with him. Ben used to joke about it and call him my Dirty Old Man. Finally I gave in, because I felt sorry for him, he seemed so lonely and bored with his marriage, and now I've fallen in love with him, and he's totally fucked my marriage.'

'And you too, by all accounts.' Georgie was nettled by the DOM reference. She was the only person allowed to slag off Guy. 'I can't imagine him pestering anyone. Guy and I love each other. Bored husbands don't police their wives' every moment.'

'You stupid idiot,' said Julia almost pityingly. 'The reason why Guy polices your every move when you're in London is because he doesn't want you to bump into him and me.'

Fumbling in the back pocket of her jeans, Julia brought out a red diary.

'Look!' She turned the pages. 'Georgie recording, Georgie Promo, Georgie recording, Georgie in America – that was a bonus.' The green pentelled arrow went through two weeks in February and into March.

'Guy told you he couldn't leave the gallery. It was me he couldn't bear to leave. Here's the key to Guy's flat.' Like a hypnotist, she swung it in front of Georgie's nose.

'Do you need a key?' said Georgie, taking another great gulp of Bacardi to fortify herself. 'I would have expected you to come in through the cat flap.'

'Stop taking the piss,' screamed Julia.

'And how does Ben fit into this?' asked Georgie, taking Dinsdale's ginger ears and putting them on top of his head like a Second World War pin-up. 'Is his software not hard enough for you?'

'Ben works in Chelmsford,' said Julia through gritted teeth, 'and he's abroad selling computers all week. It wasn't difficult.'

'The writing on the pink envelope.' Georgie examined the diary again. 'It's yours.'

'Of course. And I gave him the china puppy for his birthday, and when he's in the country he rings me the whole time, when he goes for petrol for the mower, when he's having drinks with the vicar.'

Julia was hissing down a bobsleigh run now and couldn't

stop. 'I saw Angel's Reach before you did,' she stammered. 'We slept in the spare room when you were in London with the *Mail on Sunday*.'

Letting Dinsdale's ears fall, Georgie shut her eyes and breathed in. The anaesthetic of shock was beginning to wear off. Getting to her feet, she tried to gather the shattered rags of dignity round her.

'I don't believe a word you're saying. Guy isn't like this.'

She felt strengthened by the sight of headlights in the drive and by Dinsdale's thick tail whacking her thighs once again. Guy was home. She was so desperate to run to him, that the bad dream should be over.

'He called me his second Peregrine,' said Julia quietly.

Georgie stopped in her tracks. The knitting-needle dipped in acid plunged straight into her heart.

'He what?'

'His second Peregrine.'

Peregrine had been a schoolfriend Guy had loved at Wellington, the one great unconsummated passion of his life. When Peregrine had drowned falling out of a punt at some wild Cambridge party, Guy confessed that it was only his faith that had kept him from suicide. It was this sadness, and the fact that for ages he didn't make a pass at her, that had drawn Georgie to him when they'd first met. Peregrine was sacrosanct, a love Georgie respected and of which she had never been jealous.

'I've got letters to prove it and photographs Guy took of me in the nude,' sobbed Julia.

'Hardly conclusive evidence, unless he's in them, too,' said Georgie as Guy came through the door.

He looked sulky and aggressive, like a small boy caught stealing sweets.

'It seems your affaire with Mrs Armstrong is more extended than you've admitted.'

Guy pursed his lips and looked proconsular.

'Well, if she says it is.'

'She does.' Georgie moved towards the drinks table.

227

'If you care to come upstairs with me, Ju Ju, and look into a suitcase under Guy-Guy's bed, you'll find a large folder of photographs Guy's taken of me with nothing on. Some, I hate to tell you, with Angel's Reach in the background.'

'You said you never slept with her,' Julia turned, screaming at Guy.

'Ah, but then he told me he'd only been to bed with you once. I think you two ought to get your stories straight.'

Grabbing the Bacardi bottle Georgie turned to Guy. 'You're a fucking hypocrite, and I'm leaving you tomorrow. I'm going to sleep in the spare room.'

On the kitchen table, she discovered a note Mother Courage had left earlier.

'Georgie – change in the envelope, heart in the deep freeze.'

Upstairs in the spare room, Georgie felt boiling hot. She took off her clothes and crawled under the duvet. Then she remembered that this was where Guy had slept with Julia. It was the repository of all their worst furniture, even a china Alsatian which Flora had won at the fair on Hampstead Heath at the age of eight. On the windows were ghastly curtains put up by a previous occupant, which clashed with the equally ghastly wallpaper. Would Guy have explained that this room hadn't been done yet, or had he been too busy bonking? She gave a groan and took a huge slug of Bacardi. She'd ring the Ideal Homo and order new curtains tomorrow morning – but what was the point when she was leaving anyway? Seeing the reflection of her flushed face on the pillow, she realized the mirror on the dressing table had been adjusted so that you could see what was going on in bed. Guy'd always liked watching himself. She heard a car starting up, and, rushing to the window, saw Julia's car lighting up the little green beacons of the poplar colonnade.

'Whore,' she screamed after her, and was so plastered and furious that she rushed downstairs in the nude and went completely berserk. First she smashed Julia's puppy and then she rushed into the kitchen and started breaking glasses.

'Stop it!' Guy came rushing in. 'Don't be infantile, Julia's a complete fantasist. It's all lies.'

'She knows my diary better than I do, and what about fucking Peregrine, or rather fucking your second Peregrine, you bastard?'

Georgie's yelling face was like a tomato that had been hurled at a rock. Guy ducked as a pint mug hurtled towards him. Finally, having taken down one of Julia's paintings, and tried to smash it over Guy's head, 'It's you in the pin-stripe suit, you disgusting lech,' Georgie raced off into the night.

In panic, Guy rang Larry who was in the middle of making love to Marigold.

'Julia came down and dumped.'

'Christ,' said Larry, who when he was with Nikki, had made up several foursomes at dinner with Julia and Guy. It was all much too close to home. 'We're off to Jamaica in a few hours,' he added, 'or I'd say come on over. Are you OK?'

'No, I'm not. Georgie's run off bollock-naked into the night.'

'No sweat,' said Larry. 'Snow's forecast. She'll come home when she's cold.'

'But what if people in the village see her?' spluttered Guy. 'The road goes straight past the vicarage. There's a meeting to discuss my election to the Parish Council on Friday.'

Larry tried not to laugh.

'I'd put your feet up, watch the boxing and have a large Scotch.'

'I can't. Georgie's broken every glass in the house, and plate, too, for that matter.'

'People who live in Cotswold-stone houses shouldn't throw glasses,' said Larry. 'At least it shows she cares. Take her away for a little holiday.'

'Guy's mistress has come down and dumped,' he told Marigold as he switched off the telephone and took her in his arms.

'Guy's got a mistress?' said Marigold, collapsing back on her ivory silk pillows in amazement. 'Ay can't believe it. Gay's not laike that. He's so upraight. Georgie must be shattered.'

'It's plates that are being shattered. She's throwing them at Guy,' said Larry, not displeased that Guy, who was always so sanctimonious, had been caught with his hand in the sexual till.

'Oh, poor Georgie!' Marigold climbed back on top of her husband, then gave a shriek of anguish as she impaled herself on his upright cock: 'Oh, may God!'

'What's the matter, Princess?' said Larry in alarm. 'Are you still sore down there?'

'No, they're our plates,' wailed Marigold. 'They were a matchin' set, Ay lent to Georgie for the dinner party.'

Sitting in the kitchen, Guy lined up all the milk bottles Mother Courage never put out on the kitchen table, so Georgie'd have something to smash when she came home.

Georgie actually burst out laughing when she saw them, then the laughter turned to tears, and although they rowed most of the night, in between sobbing on each other's shoulders, Guy felt by morning that he had calmed Georgie down enough to go back to London.

'I'll call you the moment I get to London,' he promised, but as she waved him off, Georgie felt like Demeter seeing Persephone disappear into the Underworld.

Slowly she began to piece together the horrors of the previous night. One moment she was freezing, the next boiling hot. She kept putting on and taking off jerseys. She still couldn't get rid of the sick taste in her mouth.

Mother Courage had laid out a page from the *Sunday Telegraph* under the cat's plate. As Georgie emptied a tin of Choosy on to it, she noticed a large piece by Peregrine Worsthorne about John Major.

You don't call a child who won't leave you alone, your second Peregrine, thought Georgie, and felt so furious she rushed into Guy's study and put a message on the ansaphone saying: 'Go screw yourself'.

Then she put on another jersey and cleaned her teeth again. She felt she was rotting inside. Half an hour later Mother Courage came storming up the drive.

'I've just had Mr Seymour on the telephone. He can't get through. Can you ring him urgent?'

Sulkily Georgie dialled Guy at the gallery.

'What the hell are you playing at, Panda?' thundered Guy. 'You're totally over-reacting. What happens if the Press ring, or, even worse, the vicar or Lady Chisleden?'

'I don't care,' screamed Georgie.

Out of the window she saw that a sudden fall of snow had covered the sweet spring promise of the primroses, and burst into tears.

22

The marriage limped on full of spats. Guy came down at midday on Good Friday looking wretched and carrying a box of glasses. 'To replace the ones you threw at me,' he said heavily, then, priding himself on his frugality: 'From the Reject Shop.'

'Why don't you put me in the window,' snarled Georgie.

Unable to suppress a craving for information that Guy was plainly not going to volunteer, Georgie asked if he'd seen Julia.

'We spoke briefly on the telephone,' said Guy, who had his back to her at the drinks table. 'I've talked to Harry, and because we've sent out the invites and done a lot of press lobbying and advertising, we've decided to go ahead with her exhibition.'

'Did Julia mention me?' asked Georgie.

'We didn't discuss you,' said Guy crushingly, pouring half an inch of whisky into one of his new glasses. 'Harry will deal with Julia from now on. But I shall obviously have to attend the private view.'

'Thought you'd viewed her enough in private.'

'Don't be petty. Julia wants us to be friends, as much as we can be. She'd like you to be there as well.'

If he says 'to err is human, to forgive divine', I shall scream, thought Georgie.

'To err—' began Guy.

'I'm not gracing her private view,' said Georgie flatly, 'just because she needs a celeb to pull in the Press.'

'That is the most horrible remark I've ever heard,' said Guy. 'It's my gallery and I make fifty per cent out of every sale. I would have thought you would have wanted to attract the Press.'

And Georgie had promptly burst into tears and run out of the house.

As she ran down the path Guy had cut out of the wood for her, she heard the cuckoo for the first time. The angelic third floating through the trees.

'*Unpleasing to a married ear, cuckoo, cuckoo,*' sobbed Georgie.

Ahead lay Valhalla. She was tempted to dump on poor Kitty Rannaldini, who had been endlessly cuckolded and survived – just. But as Rannaldini might be there, who would be amused rather than sympathetic, she stumbled on. There had never been anything like the pain.

Wandering aimlessly she arrived home to find the BMW gone. The red sun was disappearing over the horizon, a cricket-ball hit for six – like Guy over Ju Ju. Sunsets were only bearable because the sun would rise again tomorrow. If Guy never came back, she'd die. Leaping into her ancient Golf she set out to look for him. She didn't have to go as far as Eldercombe. There was the BMW crookedly parked in the churchyard, which in the twilight was still lit by daffodils. The church was decked for Easter. Breathing in the smell of narcissi and furniture polish, Georgie saw Guy slumped over the front pew, head bowed on clasped hands. When she touched his shoulder, his face was streaming with tears.

'Oh, Panda,' he sobbed, 'I've made such a cock-up of my life, but I love you so much. Please don't leave me.'

Georgie pulled his head against her belly.

'It's OK I love you, too. I nearly died when I saw the car gone. I thought you'd gone to her.'

'Never, never, never.'

Stumbling out of the church, they stopped to kiss each other in the doorway, and were seen by a photographer who worked for the *Rutminster News* on his way home from football. On Monday morning *The Scorpion* printed a picture of the happiest couple in England.

The truce was fleeting. In the weeks that followed Guy talked of commuting, but he never did. The weight fell off Georgie, who tried to glam herself up when he came home, but however quick she was in the bath, he was asleep by the time she came to bed.

Georgie was distraught. She couldn't stop crying, and, unable to believe Guy's protestations that he wasn't seeing Julia any more, she felt as venomous and rejected as ragwort in a field of cows. Not only had she lost her hero and her best friend, but her image of herself as a nice person, which Guy's great imagined love had given her.

The rows were terrible, with Georgie boozing and ranting into the night, then apologizing in panic in case she'd gone too far and Guy really would leave her.

The wastage was awful, too: milk going sour because it wasn't taken in; Dinsdale getting the casserole Mother Courage had made for the weekend, which no-one had touched; fuzzy potatoes on their third day in a saucepan of water; black volcanic shapes discovered in the Aga days later; and all the vegetables leaking in the rack. Even Dinsdale finally went off his food. The Press were also sniffing around. So many marriages were breaking up, they wanted to know the secret of a happy one.

'Ignorance,' Georgie told *The Scorpion* in an unguarded moment.

On automatic pilot, she managed to go up to London, talk about *Rock Star* on *Aspel*, open a supermarket and have a long session with the whizz-kid producer who was revamping some of her old songs for the new Catchitune album. 'Rock Star' still topped the charts, but every time she heard this celebration of Guy's dependability on the radio she felt sick.

She also had to live through the nightmare of Julia's exhibition. She didn't go to the private view, Guy didn't

234

want any more glasses smashed. But there was a large piece in *You* magazine. Julia, from the photographs, had cut her hair, and now had a head of russet curls rather like the Bubbles painting.

'*There is a wistful air about lovely Julia Armstrong,*' ran the copy. '*Slim as a boy . . .*'

More like the first Peregrine than ever, thought Georgie savagely. But it made her realize how awful it must be for Julia reading about her and Guy all the time.

Poor Guy wasn't having much fun either. Julia's paintings had sold well, but the art market had taken a dive and he'd also bought a couple of minor French Impressionists for a property developer, who'd suddenly called in the receiver. Guy was left with the bill.

But he could have put up with business being so awful, and Georgie's tantrums, and the nightmare of his marriage, if he'd still had Julia to lighten his darkness. He missed her terribly. It broke his heart when she rang up and tearfully pleaded with him to see her.

Nor were his men friends any help. Larry, in his now-married bliss in Jamaica, showed no interest in buying Guy's paintings, but insisted on being incredibly sanctimonious.

'If I can give up Nikki, why can't you give up Julia?'

'She's refusing to give *me* up.'

'Get an answering machine. That'll stop the dropped telephone calls.'

'I've got an answering-back machine at home,' said Guy. 'It's called Georgie.'

Rannaldini was vastly amused by the whole thing.

'Find another mistress, dear boy. There are plenty more fishwives in the sea.'

Guy was fed up. How could he find anyone else? He was desperately strapped for cash. There were all those pretty separated women who made warm eyes at him at gallery parties and in church on Sunday, but he could hardly afford to buy them a drink.

In the old days both Julia and Georgie had adored him, told him he was marvellous and asked his opinion on absolutely everything – two loves had he of comfort *and* comfort. Now they were both displaying all the venom of tabloid newspapers denied an exclusive. Hell certainly knew no fury like two women scorned. Guy felt like a worm done over by a blackbird.

23

Georgie couldn't work. There had been no rain in Paradise for weeks, and as the springs that had hurtled past her study window when they moved in had dried up, so had her inspiration. Trailing through St Peter's churchyard with Dinsdale towards the end of May, she noticed Queen Anne was losing her lace and the wild garlic its flowers. There were white petals everywhere, and yellowing leaves flattened probably by lovers, but not by her. Georgie's eyes were so full of tears she didn't see Kitty Rannaldini approaching with her arms full of huge scented pink peonies to decorate the church.

"Ow are you, Georgie?' Seeing she was plainly not all right and not knowing what to say, Kitty added, 'Come and 'ave dinner on Monday, about one o'clock.'

Arriving at Angel's Reach on Monday morning, Mother Courage persuaded Georgie not to cry off.

'Nice girl that Kitty. Rattledicky gives her the run around. She'll have cooked you something nice. Do you good to fatten yourself up.'

'Seven stone twelve on the scales this morning,' said Georgie.

Getting thin was the only good this terminally ill wind seemed to blow her.

'Make a nice day out for you,' encouraged Mother Courage. With Georgie gone she could help herself to the gin and slope off early. 'Be a tonic.'

'Only if she adds vodka,' said Georgie gloomily. 'However, I'd quite like to see inside Valhalla.'

'It's 'aunted,' said Mother Courage, getting a black

dustbin bag out of the cupboard. 'I don't know 'ow Kitty can sleep there on her own. She ought to get the vicar in to circumcise the ghost. Mind you that Rattledicky's pretty spooky. In his watch tower he's got one of them Ju-Jitzu baths.'

Had Guy ever had a Ju Ju-Jitzu bath with Julia? wondered Georgie.

At twenty-three Kitty Rannaldini was exactly half her husband's age (and his better half according to most people who knew them). Brought up in the suburbs of London, she had had a strict but happy childhood. Her father had been nearing retirement as a station master when she was born, and her mother, who took in ironing and minded other people's children, had been in her forties. Every Sunday, Kitty had been taken to St Augustine's Church round the corner, which her mother had cleaned for nothing. Nowhere else had brass gleamed more brightly. An industrious rather than a bright pupil, Kitty had left school with eight O levels at sixteen and taught herself to type. The family were staunch Tories – the only time Kitty remembered a bottle of wine being opened at home was when Mrs Thatcher first became Prime Minister. So it was natural that, as well as the Guides and the Youth Club, Kitty should have joined the Young Conservatives where she met a local bank clerk called Keith to whom she was engaged when she went to work as a temp for Rannaldini.

It took Rannaldini less than a week to realize Kitty's genius as a secretary. He was in the middle of a production of *Rigoletto*, everyone was walking out, writs were flying around like Valhalla bats at dusk. In twenty-four hours, Kitty somehow restored order. She was not only meticulous, conscientious, unobtrusive, worked till she dropped and exuded an air of absolute calm, but somehow, by listening patiently to everyone from soloists to scene shifters and sympathizing with their problems, she diffused the all-out warfare.

Exceptionally kind by nature, she was very shy and cautious. Decisions took a lot of thought. It had, therefore, taken Rannaldini a long time to persuade her to work for him permanently, involving as it did a long journey into London every day, and leaving her mother to nurse a sick father. One of the few impulsive acts of Kitty's life, and she never stopped feeling guilty about it, was to chuck Keith and all the plans for setting up house with him and her now-widowed mother, and run off with Rannaldini a week before the wedding.

But it was not until Rannaldini promised that her mother would at least be financially provided for that Kitty had agreed to leave home. In fact the financial provision was never enough, and Kitty had to scrimp constantly on the housekeeping and take in typing Rannaldini didn't know about to help her mother out.

Beneath her calm exterior, Kitty was not only a worrier but an incurable romantic. She admired people who were wild and free-spirited and stood up for themselves. Although her temperament and looks conditioned her to hold back, the moment her gentle heart was moved, she was the softest touch in the world. She didn't resent all she did for Rannaldini, but her greatest pleasures were the occasional hours snatched in church or in reading another chapter of Danielle Steel when she went to bed, which was often long after midnight.

Kitty had been desperately upset by the rumours about Guy and Georgie. Their apparent happiness had briefly restored her faith in marriage which had been shattered by the examples around her in Paradise, particularly her own.

Guy was so kind, thoughtful and thoroughly boy-scout decent. Seeing how he protected Georgie and did so much both at the *Rock Star* launch and at the Angel's Reach dinner party had convinced her he was an exceptional husband. Being married to Rannaldini, Kitty knew about living in someone's shadow. Happier in the shade herself, she felt it must have been difficult for a man as forceful and as charismatic as Guy. Although shocked to hear he was having an affaire with Julia, she could see he might need the boost to his morale, and working with someone was so seductive. She had only to remember the way she had given in to Rannaldini.

Guy had looked so wretched in church recently, and when he stayed praying long after the service, she had noticed there were holes in the soles of both his shoes. She felt he longed to talk, but thought it was a weakness to dump. Kitty didn't judge, but she felt Georgie didn't look after Guy as well as she might, and knew whose side she was on. Then she met Georgie trailing through the churchyard in tears and she felt so sorry for her that she asked her to lunch.

The boiled chicken in white sauce and the roast potatoes were now in the oven, the mint lying on top of the new peas, and the apple tart waiting to be warmed up. Kitty was a good, plain cook. Plain in all senses of the word, she thought, wiping her steamed-up glasses before glancing ruefully at her round, sweating face in the mirror.

The telephone rang and she guessed it was Georgie cancelling. But it was Guy.

'Darling Kitty!' Oh, that deep commanding voice. 'You're such a brick for having Georgie to lunch, I'm going to call you "Brickie". She's bound to be late. She's so unhappy and got everything so out of proportion. Please try and calm her down.'

Even on a hot, brilliantly sunny day, with white hawthorns exploding everywhere like grenades and cow-parsley still foaming up to touch the foliage of great trees, nurtured over the centuries, Valhalla looked sinister. Pigeon-grey, hidden from the road by a great conspirator's cloak of woodland, mostly evergreens, the house itself had originally been built as a medieval monastery, but had been considerably enlarged during the Restoration. The result was H-shaped, with rooms of all sizes on different levels, and low beams and doorways, which concussed every visiting male except Rannaldini.

Hurtling up the long drive because she was late and disappearing into the protective cloak of dark woodland, Georgie was shivering as she emerged. Ahead, through rusty iron gates, lay a mossy courtyard leading to the back of the house. Following the drive round the north side of the house, Georgie parked outside more ancient gates, with *Omnia vincit amor* written in rusty iron lettering across the top. Despite such an optimistic message, and a charming paved path up to the front door, which was overgrown with thrift, moss and saxifrage, and bordered by scented pale pink roses rising out of drifts of green lavender, the house gazed suspicious and unwelcoming out of its narrow mullioned windows.

Before Georgie had time to tug the ancient doorbell, Kitty came rushing out, looking comfortingly modern in a Ninja Turtle T-shirt and an overstretched grass-green skirt.

Although she kissed Georgie shyly, she actually put her lips to her guest's cheek, rather than merely clanking jaw-bones like the rest of Paradise. She also hid the fact that she wasn't wild about Dinsdale joining the party.

Not in a noticing mood, Georgie was only aware of a trek down scrubbed, winding flagstoned passages, past panelling dark and shiny as treacle toffee and hung with tapestries, crossed swords and the occasional family portrait. To left and right she caught a glimpse of rooms with leafy Jacobean ceilings and vast empty fireplaces.

'Rannaldini wanted rooms big enough for two grand pianos and sometimes entire orchestras,' explained Kitty, hastily looking the other way, as Dinsdale hoisted a red-and-white leg on some dark blue velvet curtains.

Finally they reached the tidiest kitchen Georgie had ever seen. Apart from the corkboard with the telephone numbers of Rannaldini's children's schools and a large smouldering poster of Rannaldini, there was nothing on any of the surfaces at all, except the newly bleached and scrubbed kitchen table which was laid for two at one end. At the other were two neatly stacked piles of envelopes and signed photographs of Rannaldini, which Kitty had been sending out to fans while she waited.

'How Guy would love this house,' said Georgie, 'everything so wonderfully ordered and lined up.'

She picked up one of the photographs in which Rannaldini was smiling slightly, a fan of wrinkles at the corner of each smouldering, dark eye.

'Beautiful man,' murmured Georgie, thinking how odd that she would have secretly nicked one of the photographs, had she come to lunch a couple of months ago.

Giving a deep sigh, Dinsdale lumbered on to the crocus-yellow window-seat which gave a glorious view of silver hayfields and sloping lawns, no doubt paced over the centuries by monks wrestling with temptation.

Rather gingerly Kitty poured out Georgie a large Bacardi and Coke, and made a cup of tea for Mr Brimscombe, who'd recently been poached from Larry and Paradise Towers by Rannaldini and who was now clipping a yew peacock out of the vast dark green side of the famous Valhalla Maze.

'I daren't face Marigold when she comes back,' said Kitty, 'particularly as Mr Brimscombe's tending a cutting of the Paradise Pearl in the greenhouse.'

Listlessly picking up a photograph of Rannaldini surrounded by adorable sloe-eyed children, Georgie asked Kitty who looked after them.

'Well, Cecilia, that's Rannaldini's second wife, she's livin' with a record producer at the moment. He's pretty wealfy, so she's got the kids wiv her and a couple of nannies, but if it breaks up, they might come back 'ere.'

'How awful,' shuddered Georgie. 'Are they monsters?'

'They're sweet,' said Kitty, 'but very Italian. Cecilia believes kids should 'ave supper and go to bed when they want to, and do what they like. Are you hungry?'

'A bit,' lied Georgie as Kitty poured white sauce on two slices of breast.

'Lovely house.' Georgie was making heroic efforts not to talk about herself. 'Mother Courage said something about a ghost.'

I shouldn't have said that, she thought, as the colour drained from Kitty's face.

'There was a young novice, very 'andsome evidently,' mumbled Kitty. 'He died here. Sometimes at night I fink I hear him crying, but it's probably the wind.'

Georgie shivered. 'Don't you get frightened here all by yourself?'

'I've got a panic button and the burglar alarm's wired up to the police station. Security's very tight, Rannaldini don't want his furniture or pictures nicked.'

'You ought to have a dog,' said Georgie, as Dinsdale, lured by a delectable smell of chicken, lumbered off the window-seat, and took up baleful drooling residence beside her.

'I'd be more scared if I 'ad them,' said Kitty, sitting down at the table. 'I didn't mean to be rude to Dinsdale. He's OK, but Rannaldini's guard dogs frighten me to deaf. Stupid livin' in the country and being terrified of dogs.'

'You ought to have someone living in.'

'Rannaldini doesn't want it. Cecilia had a living-in nanny, and when Rannaldini fired her, she went to the Press.'

Georgie was staring into space, so Kitty pushed the carrots, peas and mashed potato dishes forward so they were in a ring round her plate.

'Shall I 'elp you?'

'Oh, yes please.'

Georgie had finished her Bacardi and Coke, so Kitty gave her another one.

'Nice kitchen,' said Georgie, admiring the walls, covered with exotic brilliantly coloured flowers, snakes, humming birds and monkeys like a Malaysian jungle. 'I'd never have dreamt of having wallpaper like this in a kitchen.'

'Meredith did it,' said Kitty, 'but Rannaldini told him what to do.'

'Ouch, that hurt!' screamed Georgie, as Dinsdale scraped her skinny thigh with his paw, leaving great white tracks.

'Guy'll probably employ Meredith to wallpaper over the cracks in our marriage,' she went on bitterly. 'Nice wife, nice family, nice house in the country, nice BMW, nice mistress. He believes in the united front for the outside world.' She was twisting her napkin round and round.

'Try and eat, Georgie,' said Kitty gently. 'I don't mean to pry, but you looked so very unhappy in the churchyard.'

And like a burst water main, Georgie's misery came flooding out. Kitty was appalled when she'd finished.

'I can't believe Julia showing you her diary and telling you all those fings.'

'She was distraught. On balance, she probably loves Guy almost more than I do, but nothing's ever hurt me so much in my life.'

'It must have been a sort of fatal attraction.'

'Fatal distraction,' said Georgie in despair. 'I can't work, and we sink more and more in debt. I'll have to pay back the advance on *Ant and Cleo*. I thought I might re-title it *Octavia* and write it from the angle of the cuckolded wife.

'Every morning,' Georgie dripped white sauce all over the floor, as she gave a piece of breast to Dinsdale, 'I read Julia's horoscope, then Guy's and then mine. I bet Julia does the same thing. Then I feel sick. Guy and I are so terrified of touching each other, we keep bumping into the furniture. I know I should be sweet and loving with my legs permanently open, or he'll go back to her, but I can't stop sniping.'

Georgie was eating nothing because she was talking so much, and Kitty was reduced to giving herself second and third helpings. No wonder listeners got fat.

'I don't know what's got into men,' said Georgie despairingly. 'They're all at it, they ought to change the name of London on the map, and call it Bloody Adventure Playground. Doesn't Rannaldini hurt you?' she asked. 'Hermione must. She's such a cow.'

244

'Yes,' admitted Kitty, 'but I knew what he was like before I married him. I love him so much, Georgie, even a bit of him is better than nuffink. An' he's forty-six, he might settle down one day.'

'If only we could find nice lovers down here,' sighed Georgie, as Kitty removed her untouched plate. 'But men are so dire at the moment. Annabel Hardman went out with a quantity surveyor the other night, he just lay back on the sofa, said he wanted to hear all about her life from the age of two, and then fell asleep. Then he was terrible in bed, and expected her to drive him home afterwards.'

Kitty giggled, and put the kettle on. There didn't seem any point offering Georgie apple tart, but she cut a slice for a lurking Mr Brimscombe who was weeding the flower-bed outside.

'What are you going to do?' she asked Georgie.

'It's the duty of all prisoners of war to escape,' said Georgie, 'so I'd better start vaulting over a wooden horse. My problem is I can't stop telling people – ancient marinading I call it – I think I've gone a bit mad. It's such a comfort to dump, but you feel so disloyal afterwards, and it's bound to reach the Press soon.'

Kitty's wide-set eyes behind the thick spectacles were full of tears.

'I'm so sorry, Georgie. You and Guy are such lovely people, I can't bear you both being so unhappy. I'm sure you'll work it out.'

'You are nice,' Georgie hugged her. 'I'm awfully worried about you being lonely in this huge place.'

'I'm OK. Natasha and Wolfie come 'ome at weekends, bringing lots of friends. And you know Flora's coming to stay on Sunday. I'm so looking forward to meeting her.'

'Are you sure?' said Georgie. 'She always cheers me up, but it's a bit of a strain having to pretend everything is OK in front of her.'

'Wolfie adores her,' said Kitty, 'and Rannaldini says she's got a wonderful voice.'

24

Meanwhile, in counterpoint to this tragi-comedy, Rannaldini was taking advantage of the boiling hot summer and the collapse of Guy's and Georgie's marriage to pursue Flora. At first he made no progress. None of his witty postcards from all over the world were acknowledged. Flora was simply not interested. She was carrying a torch for Boris Levitsky, who was still teaching at Bagley Hall, but looking increasingly gaunt and miserable at having left his wife. She had loads of boys in the school after her; she had a hankering for Marcus Campbell-Black who was terribly shy and wrapped up in his piano playing, and she much preferred the tall blond Wolfgang, who was now cricket captain and a year ahead of her, to his father.

As part of his campaign, Rannaldini encouraged Natasha to make friends with Flora. Natasha, who was feeling neglected because of her mother's affaire with the record producer, was in turn gratified that Rannaldini was suddenly taking so much interest in her schooling, even rolling up to watch her play in a tennis match one Sunday which he'd never done before.

Longing to please him, she found she could always gain his attention by talking about Flora. How she was always climbing out of her dormitory window at night and running off to a night-club called Gaslight, and how Miss Fagan, their housemistress who was always pinging bras, far from being furious, looked really excited when Flora streaked through the house for a bet, and how Flora passed her French oral.

'The examiner asked her what her father did for a living. Flora said: "*Mon père est mort*," then he asked her what her mother did, and Flora said: "*Ma mère est morte aussi*," and burst into tears. The examiner spent the rest of the exam comforting her and gave her an A. It simply isn't fair. She's so sexy, everything falls into her lap.'

Including Rannaldini, who, on the day Natasha had a music exam, offered Flora tickets for a concert at the Albert Hall. Flora jumped at it. Anything to get out of Bagley Hall – particularly when Rannaldini sent the helicopter for her. Arriving at the Albert Hall, she found queues hoping for returns, coiled like an ancient lady novelist's plaits round the building.

Typically, Rannaldini delayed and delayed his entrance, so the packed audience would be panicked into thinking he wasn't coming on. When he finally appeared, women didn't actually scream, but they gasped, cheered, clapped, bravoed and then swooned at the incredible beauty of Rannaldini's back on the rostrum. The gleaming pewter pelt emphasized the wide muscular shoulders beneath the impeccably cut midnight-blue tailcoat. The beautiful sun-tanned hands were shown off by the Kitty-whitened cuffs with the silver cuff-links, which Leonard Bernstein, whose showmanship, if not his excessive emotion, Rannaldini had greatly admired, had given him for his fortieth birthday.

And if Berlioz conducted with a drawn sword, Rannaldini conducted with a newly sharpened Cupid's arrow. Flora was the only woman in the front row not wearing one of Catchitune's yellow-and-purple I LOVE RANNALDINI T-shirts. As he mounted the rostrum, she caught a whiff of Maestro and the white gardenia flown in for his buttonhole wherever he conducted.

The programme might have been chosen for Flora: Strauss's *Don Juan*, followed by his *Four Last Songs*, sung by Hermione. Every time Rannaldini turned to bring her in with Toscanini's ivory baton, the audience caught a tantalizing glimpse of his haughty profile.

He also took such liberties with a score, branding his own personality on it so forcefully, that afterwards his interpretation seemed to have become the true one. You felt it couldn't be bettered, and it couldn't be otherwise.

He and Hermione took bow after bow at the end of the first half. Her gushing ecstasy, blowing kisses and clutching Cellophaned roses to her heaving bosom, was in total contrast to Rannaldini's cold stillness which became even colder when, glancing down, he saw Flora engrossed in *Woman's Own*.

Strauss was followed in the second half by Stravinsky's *The Rite of Spring*, which portrays a virgin, who has been offered up for pagan sacrifice, dancing herself to death, and which is difficult enough to unnerve the most sophisticated orchestra.

Having told Hermione he couldn't see her later that evening because Kitty was in London, Rannaldini had left a note at the box office with Flora's ticket, saying that, if she met him at Daphne's in Walton Street at ten o'clock, he would buy her dinner.

Whizzing through *The Rite of Spring* even faster than Stravinsky himself, so that Toscanini's stick was a mere blur, in order to get to Flora sooner, Rannaldini's sexual excitement seemed to have transmitted itself to the orchestra. At the end the audience went berserk.

After a performance, Rannaldini always left the London Met rung out like a dishcloth, but there was not a drop of sweat on his forehead as he unsmilingly took his thirteenth bow. Only then did he deign to look in Flora's direction, anticipating delirious adulation – her little hands with their bitten nails sore and scarlet with clapping. But her seat was empty. The briefest scrawl on a diary page left at the box office told him she'd had to leave before the end to meet some friends.

Rannaldini was so furious, he went back to the green room and fired ten musicians, including Beatrice, the little blond flautist whose bed he'd been intermittently warming since March. But Flora's indifference only fuelled his lust.

Justifying his actions by saying Georgie and Guy needed space to sort out their marriage, he encouraged Natasha and the totally smitten Wolfie to invite Flora to Valhalla for half-term.

As Valhalla had many rooms on different levels, it was possible to look out of windows into rooms near by. An outraged Mr Brimscombe, who was increasingly tempted to go back to Larry, was told to leave the shaggy pink clematis montana round Rannaldini's dressing room which had long since finished flowering, so Rannaldini could peer through it into Flora's bedroom. But, far worse, Mr Brimscombe was then ordered to hack back from around Flora's window a rare honeysuckle just as it was emerging into its gold-scented glory. Such was his desire that Rannaldini would have ripped out the Paradise Pearl.

Valhalla, with its tennis and squash courts, cricket pitch, which the village team was occasionally allowed to use, and huge swimming-pool protectively ringed with limes, was a paradise for teenagers. There were also horses to ride and to add excitement, the famous Valhalla Maze planted in the seventeenth century, while the abbey was briefly in the hands of the laity, by Sir William Westall for the entertainment of his descendants. Now twenty feet high, with nearly a quarter of a mile of dark, convoluted alleys, it was alarmingly easy to get lost in.

Beyond the maze, deep in the wood was Rannaldini's tower, and beyond a path had been cut through the undergrowth to the edge of the Valhalla Estate near to Hermione's house. This was kept clear by Rannaldini's henchman, Clive, a sinister blond young man, given to black leather on his day off, who doubled up as his master's dog handler. Outside the tower, Rottweilers prowled, frightening off fans, trespassers and, most of all, Kitty.

★   ★   ★

When Flora arrived at Valhalla, Rannaldini was away recording Mahler's *Resurrection Symphony* in Berlin. A heat wave which had caught the country on the hop was into its second week. The darkening woods seemed to smoulder in the burning noon-day sun. The hayfields quivered. As though his battery was running down, the cuckoo called laboriously from a clump of horse chestnuts, whose candles were already shedding their white and bright pink petals. The dark maze drew the eye like a magnet.

'It's always more relaxed when Papa isn't here,' said Natasha, as she and Flora peeled themselves off the leather seats of the Mercedes in which Clive had collected them. 'Papa's wonderful, but when he doesn't get his way, the whole building shakes.'

Looking up at the house, grey, brooding and secretive with its tall chimneys, Flora noticed blinds drawn on most of the windows.

'Imagine Dracula's victims languishing behind them, unable to take the sun.'

'Papa likes them down during the day,' explained Natasha. 'Sun ruins pictures and tapestries. Beautiful, isn't it?'

'Quite.' Flora refused to be fazed. 'Bit Hammer House of Horror. In fact, extremely so,' she added, as Natasha led her in through a side door past a darkly panelled room containing rows of gleaming black riding boots and a daunting collection of spurs, bits with chains and hunting whips, many of them with lashes. 'I didn't know your father was into SM.'

Normality was restored by a delicious smell of mint and fennel drifting from the kitchen. Kitty, spectacles misting up, her face as red and shiny as a billiard ball, damp patches under the arms of her straining blue cotton dress, was cooking Sunday lunch.

'This is my stepmother,' announced Nastasha disdainfully, dumping two carrier bags of washing on the floor at Kitty's feet. 'And please handwash my purple flares. You shrunk my red pair last time.'

'I thought stepmothers were supposed to be wicked,' said Flora. 'My mother has never handwashed anything in her life. You're bloody lucky, Natasha. How d'you do?' she smiled at Kitty.

'Pleased to meet you,' Kitty wiped a red hand on her apron. 'Blimey, it's 'ot.'

'I'm afraid these melted in the car.'

Giving Kitty a squashed box of Terry's All Gold, Flora reflected that Kitty reacted as though they really were gold, going even brighter red with pleasure.

''Ow very kind of you, Flora, that's really fortful.'

'Not really,' said Natasha bitchily. 'Wolfie gave them to her, but she doesn't want any more zits.'

'That was another box,' snapped Flora.

'How are yer mum and dad?' asked Kitty.

'OK, but Mum's getting horribly thin. These are hers although she doesn't know it.' Flora held out the bottom of the slate-grey shorts she was wearing with a pale pink camisole top. 'They're part of a size ten suit, and they're already miles too big for her.'

'They're gorgeous.' Natasha took a bottle of wine from the fridge and sloshed it into two glasses. 'I wish I had a mother over here who was trendy enough to nick clothes from.'

Flushing, Kitty asked her how work was going.

'Boring, and even more boring talking about it.' Natasha handed a glass to Flora. 'I'll show you your room. I don't know why you're bothering about lunch, Kitty. It's much too hot to eat.'

'I'm starving,' said Flora. 'See you in a bit, Kitty.'

Later she and Natasha sprawled in the window-seat looking at old photographs.

'Isn't Papa ravishing?' sighed Natasha.

'Quite.' Flora examined a coloured photograph of Rannaldini shooting in the bracken. 'He's a bit urban, as though he pays some peasant to throw mud over his gumboots every morning, and tread in his new Barbour in the autumn like grapes. He is good looking for a wrinkly though,' she added kindly. 'What's his Christian name?'

'Roberto.'

'I shall call him Bob,' said Flora, draining a second glass of wine.

'I wouldn't,' said Natasha. 'An American baritone called him Bob at a dress rehearsal, and never made the opening night.'

'Bob Harefield's a sweet man,' said Flora giggling. 'That ghastly Hermione isn't short of a few Bobs, is she? Oh Christ!' Flora suddenly remembered Kitty, who fortunately seemed to be preoccupied, putting peeled prawns and sliced cucumbers round a sea trout.

'I'm starving now.' Natasha grabbed a chunk of Cheddar from the fridge and, removing the clingfilm, took a bite, before smoothing away the toothmarks with her thumb. 'Thank God! Here's Wolfie; we can have lunch.'

Having been given a Golf GTi for his eighteenth birthday, Wolfie Rannaldini insisted on driving everywhere. Blond, ruddy complexioned, beaky nosed, solemn and ambitious, when he wasn't training for various school teams, he was swotting for his A levels. He had taken after Rannaldini's German side, while the volatile, histrionic, over-emotional Natasha seemed all Italian. Unlike his sister, he gave Kitty a hug, before pulling Flora up from the window-seat, seeking her mouth and letting his hand slither under the pink camisole top for a quick squeeze. Having dismissed love as a girl's concern, he had been knocked for one of the sixes he was always hitting by Flora.

'Did you beat Fleetley?' asked Kitty.

'Slaughtered them.' Wolfie got a can of beer out of the fridge.

'Any runs?'

'A hundred and twenty, and three wickets.'

'But that's wonderful.'

Kitty is nice, thought Flora, who could never work up an interest in cricket.

'They were pissed off,' went on Wolfie. 'When we got out of the bus, the Fleetley XI sneered at us, and said: "What's it like being at a second-rate public school?" I said: "I don't know, I've only just arrived," and then we buried them. This is seriously funny.' He unrolled a long school photograph. Flora and Natasha screamed with laughter, for there grinning in the third row, just behind Miss Bottomley was Flora wearing a gorilla mask.

'They've printed six hundred and sent most of them out without checking,' said Wolfie in amusement. 'Bottomley will go ape-shit.'

'Gorilla-shit,' said Flora. 'Come and look, Kitty.'

Kitty giggled so much she had to remove her glasses and wipe her eyes.

She's not much older than us, thought Flora in surprise, and on closer examination decided that if Kitty wasn't remotely beautiful, she had a sweet crumpled face, and certainly wasn't the total dog Natasha made out.

'You look nice, Tasha,' she said, turning back to the photograph.

Too voluptuous at present, despite long thin legs, Natasha had shaggy black curls, Rannaldini's heavy-lidded dark eyes, a big pouting mouth like a frog, and a sly, sliding, slightly Asiatic face, giving off the possibility of great glamour to come. Watching the three of them laughing together and seeing Wolfie's hand creep round Flora's slim waist to find her breast again, Kitty felt a wave of envy. Then she turned in terror and nearly dropped the potato salad, as the room was plunged into darkness by the unexpected arrival of Rannaldini's helicopter blotting out the sun.

'Fuck,' said Wolfie, who'd been planning to spend the afternoon in the long grass with Flora.

Just then flew down a monstrous crow, as black as a tar-barrel,' said Flora.

*   *   *

253

Only Natasha was delighted when five minutes later the house was flooded with Mahler and Rannaldini stalked in. He was followed by Tabloid, his favourite and more ferocious Rottweiler, who would have plunged his teeth into Nastasha, when she rushed forward to hug her father, if Rannaldini hadn't shouted and given the dog a vicious kick in the ribs, which triggered off a serious of howls.

'Pavarottweiler,' said Flora disapprovingly. 'I heard you bullied your soloists.'

'Was the recording cancelled?' asked Natasha hastily.

'I made everyone rise early to beat the heat.'

Once home, Rannaldini established his ascendancy with the inevitable jackbooting. A brilliant imaginative cook, he often produced Sunday lunch himself, cooking as he conducted, keeping five saucepans going at once, mixing, tasting, stirring, ordering Kitty around like a skivvy. But today, as lunch was ready, he kept everyone waiting out of malice, sending Kitty scuttling to get him a drink, going through the synopsis she'd typed of his post, faxes and telephone messages, finding fault with everything, snarling like Tabloid, who lay panting at his feet, if she didn't know the answer.

In his post was a letter from some distinguished composer saying the concert in the Albert Hall, out of which Flora had walked, had been the most marvellous thing he'd ever heard.

'A peety you meesed most of it.' Rannaldini chucked the letter across to her.

'Expect the old sycophant wants you to commission another symphony,' said Flora unrepentantly. 'Basically I thought the *Don Juan* very self-conscious. You couldn't hear Strauss for Rannaldini, and I've never liked it as music. You keep longing for that divinely soppy theme tune to be repeated and it never is. And I'm not surprised those were Strauss's *Four Last Songs*, if he'd known Hermione was going to sing them. My mother's voice is far more beautiful than that gurgling canary.'

Terrified that Rannaldini might see her laughing, Kitty gave the mayonnaise a stir to check it hadn't curdled.

'You will never find a more exquisite voice,' said Rannaldini icily.

'Passion and thrust are what matters. Hermione's got no soul.'

Beneath the pale red fringe which was tangling with her sooty eyelashes, Flora's cool cactus-green eyes, a mixture of Georgie's seaweed brown and Guy's pale azure, were scornful and utterly unafraid.

I must get that girl into bed, thought Rannaldini.

'Are we never going to have lunch?' he snapped, turning on Kitty, and when she had laid out a beautiful pink sea trout, a huge bowl of yellow mayonnaise, which he complained should have been *sauce verte*, a green salad including the tiniest broad beans, and new potatoes, he made no comment, only rejecting the bottles of Muscadet and sending her scuttling back to the dungeons, of which she was terrified, to get some Sancerre.

'Why don't you have a little train to get your drinks for you?' said Flora, unfolding an emerald-green napkin. 'Then Kitty wouldn't have had to run around like a barmaid in Happy Hour.'

But Rannaldini was looking at *The Times* crossword which was normally faxed out to him wherever he was in the world, filling it in as easily as a passport form.

'Who, *Like a black swan as death came on, Poured forth her song in perfect calm*?' he asked the assembled company. 'Presumably none of you dolts know.'

'St Cecilia,' said Flora, accepting a plate of sea trout from Kitty. 'Yum, that looks good.'

'Correct,' said Rannaldini. 'Unlike my children, you read books.'

'I'm doing Auden for A level.'

Natasha was still studying the school photograph.

'Nice one of Marcus Campbell-Black. Have you snogged him yet, Flora?'

'Too shy. Wouldn't mind snogging his father though.'

'Rupert Campbell-Black was the man we voted we'd most like to lose our virginity to,' Natasha told Rannaldini. 'But you were second, Daddy,' she added hastily.

Rannaldini's vile mood returned. Although the food was delectable, he immediately emptied a sootfall of black pepper and a pint of Tabasco over his sea trout before taking a bite. Then, when he had taken one mouthful, snapped at Kitty that the fish must have died of natural causes, and gave the whole lot to Tabloid who promptly gobbled it up, then yelped, his eyes spurting tears, as he encountered the Tabasco and pepper.

'This sea trout's perfect,' protested Flora. 'You kept lunch waiting. You're lucky it's not old and tough, like certain people round here, and that was bloody cruel to that dog.'

Ignoring her, Rannaldini started talking in German to Wolfie. Kitty said nothing throughout lunch, as still as an extra on stage, not wanting to attract a second's attention from the actor who is speaking. There was another explosion when Rannaldini found the Brie in the fridge.

'I'm sorry, Rannaldini,' stammered Kitty, 'but it was running away in the 'eat.'

'Don't blame it,' said Flora, 'if it gets shouted at like you do.'

In the silence that followed, Natasha, Wolfie and Kitty gazed at their green ivy-patterned plates and shook.

Rannaldini glared at Flora for a moment, then laughed. 'You have to practise this afternoon, Natasha. You have homework, Wolfie. I will show Flora the 'ouse.'

Ducking unnecessarily so as to avoid hitting his sleek grey head on the low beams, Rannaldini whisked Flora through endless twisting and turning passages and dark-panelled rooms. Occasionally from the shadows grinned the white or yellowing teeth of a grand piano. On the way Rannaldini pointed out ancient tapestries, Tudor triptychs and family portraits, belonging to other people, because sadly, his left-wing mother had flogged off those of his own family. In the great hall with its minstrels' gallery,

Rannaldini had commissioned a red-and-gold mural of trumpeters, harpists and fiddlers, and a bust of himself in front of the huge organ.

'Something wrong there,' said Flora slyly. 'Surely you should be behind the huge organ?'

Ignoring the crack, Rannaldini led her up the great stone staircase, where sunlight poured through the stained-glass window of St Cecilia at yet another organ.

'*Blessed Cecilia appear in visions, To all musicians,*' murmured Flora. 'Is that Burne Jones?'

'A copy,' said Rannaldini. 'The original's in Oxford.'

Leading the way up to the attic, stepping over stray angels' wings and broken chalices left behind by the monks, Rannaldini pointed to a rope running down a groove in the thick stone wall.

'What's that?' asked Flora.

'The rope of the punishment bell,' said Rannaldini caressingly. 'The Abbot used to ring it from his study after vespers every Friday evening, telling the monks to return to their cells and flagellate themselves for the duration of the *misericordia*. This went on until a Father Dominic came up here and valiantly clung on to the rope, and the practice was finally stamped out.'

'How gross!' Flora fingered the rope with a shudder.

Through a narrow slit of window, she could see the valley lit by chestnut candles and beyond, green fields streaked with buttercups and dotted with red-and-white cows, like the backdrop to some medieval madonna. It was very cold in the attic. In some distant room, she could hear Natasha sulkily thumping out a Chopin *Nocturne*.

'I suppose you use the punishment bell on Kitty,' blurted out Flora.

'Only when she needs it,' said Rannaldini silkily.

Flora shivered, but was determined not to appear afraid. 'Mum said Kitty's terrified of a ghost here.'

'The Paradise Lad,' murmured Rannaldini softly. 'He was a very beautiful young boy. A novice here, and very loving and charming and not entirely sure of his vocation.

Then he fell in love with a village girl, and decided he wanted to leave the order. Denied this, he was caught with the girl. The Abbot loved the boy, and was so insane with jealousy that he threw him down in the dungeons before ordering him to be flogged and rang the punishment bell on and on, until finally the monks grew quite out of control and flogged the boy to death. Many people say they 'ave heard his ghost sobbing at night.'

Rannaldini's face was enigmatic, but there was a throb of excitement in his deep voice.

'That's horrific,' said Flora, utterly revolted.

'And probably apocryphal,' said Rannaldini, idly examining a battered cherub, wondering if it could be restored. 'The wind howl down the chimneys 'ere. That's probably all the screaming people 'ear. Let's go and play tennis.'

Rannaldini's passion for Flora was severely tested on the tennis court. Unaware of the honour of being his partner, she simply didn't try, and ducked, collapsing with laughter, each time Wolfie and Natasha, both powerful, much-coached players, hit the shocking pink balls straight at her. She and Rannaldini ended up in a screaming match.

'Your father's insanely competitive,' she grumbled, as she and Wolfie cooled off in the big blue swimming-pool which was tiled like a Roman bath.

When he simmered down, Rannaldini was reduced to watching her through binoculars while she sunbathed top-less, envying the Ambre Solaire Wolfie was rubbing into her high freckled breasts. At bedtime, peering through the montana, he caught a tantalizing glimpse of her undressing before she slipped on the outsize pyjamas which had come into fashion that summer. He imagined his hand stealing under the trouser elastic. With her cropped red hair, she'd be just like a schoolboy. Next moment he heard Wolfie's door open and shut, followed by creaking floorboards, then Flora's door opening and shutting. Then the light went out. Rannaldini was demented.

Stalking along the landing, he barged into Kitty's bedroom without knocking. She was wearing a high-necked white cotton nightgown and knitting a custard-yellow jersey for her mother's Christmas present. On the shelf were little bottles of shampoo, moisturizers and transparent bathcaps in cardboard packs which Rannaldini brought her from hotel bedrooms on trips abroad. She never threw out anything he gave her. Looking up at her husband in fear and longing, she waited for the next hammer blow.

'Time for the real thing,' said Rannaldini, dropping Danielle Steel on the floor.

Returning to the kitchen after waving goodbye to Natasha, Wolfie and Flora the following evening, Kitty gasped in horror. Flora had added a moustache, a squint, some long earrings and a mass of tight curls to Rannaldini's poster on the cork board. Underneath she had written: STOP BEING SHITTY TO KITTY. Kitty removed it only just in time.

25

Over the next few weeks the heat wave intensified and so did Rannaldini's obsessive passion; but whenever he flew home he found Wolfie and Flora wrapped round each other like Labrador puppies. He was in despair. Then, on the last Saturday in June, in the middle of Wimbledon fortnight, having despatched Kitty to stay with her excruciatingly dull, suburban mother, so he could install a two-way mirror between his dressing room and the spare room into which Flora had been moved, Rannaldini dropped in for a drink with Georgie and Guy.

As the sun had lost a little of its heat they sat out on the terrace, gazing down on a valley lit by white elderflower discs and garlanded by wild roses that shrivelled in an afternoon. Only docks, nettles and ragwort had been left by the ravenous sheep and cows. Both lake and river below it were dangerously low. Dinsdale panted gloomily under Georgie's deck-chair.

Georgie, in a pair of oatmeal Bermuda shorts and a sage-green T-shirt, which showed the skin falling away from her upper arms and thighs, gazed into space. She had dried up like the valley around her. Great cracks split the footpaths. The ivy round the house was showering down yellow leaves and the lawns of Angel's Reach, because Guy, unlike Rannaldini, observed the hose-pipe ban, had already turned brown.

Georgie and Guy were just reeling from another frightful row. While Guy was fussing around making Pimm's, Georgie unbuttoned to Rannaldini.

'Guy says he hasn't seen Julia since her exhibition. Then he buggers off for two hours this afternoon and returns with poor Dinsdale utterly exhausted and reeking of Je Reviens. The shoe-maker's children may be the worst shod, but adulterer's dogs have the sorest paws.'

'My dear, I cannot theenk why you're upset.' Rannaldini put a soothing hand on her razor-sharp shoulder. 'You are cross with Guy so he seeks approval elsewhere. Having an affaire is like going on television, one gets the chance to talk at length about oneself in front of an admiring audience.'

'But I don't understand,' pleaded Georgie. 'If he needs her, why does he insist on sleeping with me all the time? I locked myself in the spare room last night and he broke the door down.'

'Quite seemple,' Rannaldini smiled. 'He feel guilty and he know eef he stop fucking you, you will suspect something, and if he ees thinking so much of Julia, he needs the release.'

'Ooo!' said Georgie in anguish. 'Is that the reason?'

'My dear child, Guy will only really want you again when you find yourself a new man.' He paused as Guy came out with a clinking tray.

'Sorry, Rannaldini, I'd forgotten Pimm's takes such a long time. Do you think Becker's going to win?'

Guy, who always became more military when he sensed combat, had had a too short haircut. Rannaldini noticed with a stab of pain that Guy's newly revealed, rather pointed, ears were very like Flora's, as were his flat cheek-bones and square jaw. But Flora's luminous white skin, her earthy animal features and big sulky mouth were all Georgie's.

'How's my friend Kitty?' asked Guy, putting a piece of mint in everyone's glass.

'Staying with her mother, a pair of clacking false teeth in an armchair, and sorting out my VAT,' said Rannaldini.

'Kitty's a saint,' said Guy heartily. 'They always say behind every famous man there's a clockwork wife.'

'And behind every famous woman there's a wildly unfaithful husband,' snarled Georgie.

Turning puce, Guy shot a see-what-I-have-to-put-up-with glance at Rannaldini. Fortunately the telephone rang and Guy bounded in to answer it.

'I found a bill for Janet Reger under the lining paper of his pants' drawer,' hissed Georgie. 'Do you think he'll claim VAT – virtue annihilated tax – on that? When in silks, paid for by Guy, my Julia goes, Christ!'

'You are on form this evening,' murmured Rannaldini noticing Georgie go quiet, trying to work out if Guy was talking in code.

'Hallo, Sabine,' he was saying. 'Did you beat Radley yesterday?'

'Single-handed, I should think,' said Rannaldini.

Guy returned looking absolutely furious.

'Sabine's had to suspend Flora until the end of term for three offences: drinking in a pub, smoking in church – in *church*! – and being caught half-naked behind a combine harvester this afternoon with your son, I'm afraid, Rannaldini.'

'*L'après-midi d'un fornicator*,' said Rannaldini, enviously.

'Hell, it's only a few fags, half a bottle of Sancerre and a roll in the hay,' said Georgie, who thought it was funny. 'At least she's gone astray with the right sort of chap.' She clinked her glass against Rannaldini's. 'Has Wolfie been suspended, too?'

'Evidently not. He wasn't caught smoking and drinking and the XI's got a needle match against Marlborough tomorrow and Wolfgang still has two A levels to take. Flora shouldn't have got caught,' said Guy disapprovingly.

'That's always been your attitude,' said Georgie flaring up.

'I never did anything wrong,' snapped back Guy.

Rannaldini was ecstatic. At last a chance to get Flora on her own while Wolfie and Natasha were still incarcerated.

'And Sabine says Flora's got a singing exam in ten days,' said Guy, taking such a large gulp of Pimm's he tipped cucumber and apple over his face. 'I'd better go and collect her.'

And pop in on Julia on the way, thought Georgie despairingly. She shouldn't have made those bitchy remarks, she'd have to crawl later.

'Send Flora over to me,' said Rannaldini. 'I'll go through her songs and give her a bit of coaching.'

Returning from a tele-recording in a suffocatingly hot London studio two days later, Rannaldini went straight into the shower. On the white porcelain floor lay a huge spider. A second later Rannaldini had assassinated it with a boiling jet of water. In almost intolerable sexual excitement he took a long time choosing what to wear, then opted to show off the depth of his tan and the broadness of his shoulders with an ivory silk shirt, tucked into cream chinos. Having brushed his hair till it gleamed, combed his black brows, which could splay like centipedes, and drenched himself in Maestro, he went downstairs to the summer parlour.

Here the cheerful serenity of primrose-yellow curtains and walls and drained blue and white striped sofas and chairs was somewhat marred by savage hunting scenes of lions and bears fighting off packs of dogs and men with spears. Rannaldini had just switched on Wimbledon and his own magnificent recording of Shostakovich's *Tenth*, when Flora rolled up looking sulkier than ever.

'Christ, I didn't come all this way to watch Becker. He's got white eyelashes like Dad, and why'd you always listen to your own records? D'you spend hours conducting in the mirror?'

For a second Rannaldini listened to the growling brass.

'I'm playing this in New York next week. It's important not to repeat oneself. Shostakovich wrote thees music to encourage the Russians to resist the Germans.'

'You're half-German – I don't need any encouragement to resist you,' said Flora rudely.

263

Unfazed by her sniping, Rannaldini handed her a glass of Krug.

The sunshine, which had browned everyone else, had merely sprinkled a few freckles on Flora's turned-up nose. She wore no make-up, but at least she had washed her hair. Her cornflower-blue espadrilles were trodden down at the back. Her lighter blue skirt had been shredded round the hem by her bicycle. A black shirt of Wolfie's was knotted under her breasts.

'You look good in black.'

'Matches the blackheads. Where's Kitty?'

'With her mother.'

'Then I'm off,' said Flora crossly. 'I'm not staying here unchaperoned.'

'Don't be silly.' Rannaldini took her and the bottle of Krug down some stone steps on to the terrace around which the Valhalla garden had reached perfection.

Sprinklers undulated languidly like strippers casting off rainbows of light over the emerald-green lawns. Old roses in every pastel shade, tawny honeysuckle, regale lilies, single and double white philadelphus, pale yellow lime blossom all seemed to be dabbing their sweetest scent on the pulse spots of the valley. Like women in their Ascot finery jostling forward to watch a big race, the herbaceous border was overcrowded with white-and-pink phlox, dog daisies, red-hot pokers, foxgloves, yellow snapdragons and soft blue cathedral spires of delphinium. A strange, very clear light heightened every colour, the smell of each flower intensified by the hot muggy air.

For a while neither Rannaldini nor Flora spoke, watching black-and-white cows like scattered dominoes in the fields below and listening to the tetchy bleating of sheep and the rattling hoof-beats of Rannaldini's horses as, maddened by flies, they galloped about neighing. A red tractor chugged back and forth cutting Rannaldini's hay. Swallows dived after insects.

'It's going to thunder,' Flora said finally. 'Mum's got a ghastly headache.'

'Perhaps she doesn't want to sleep with your father.'

Rannaldini flipped through Flora's music. 'D'you want to sing to me?'

'No.'

On the inside page of 'The Magnet and the Churn' she had written Flora Seymour, Lower Sixth A.

'Beautiful trochaic name, Flora.'

'It's gross. How'd you like to have flat-stomached men mouthing your name across supermarket freezers? And as for Interflora, you can imagine what the boys at Bagley Hall made of that.'

Black clouds were edging round the sinking sun. Saying he had to walk his dogs, Rannaldini took Flora round the garden which seemed deliberately designed for love. Despite the drought, streams still hurtled through narrow ravines. Naked statues were strategically placed in sheltered glades. A little summer-house here, a white seat under a weeping ash there, beckoned dalliance. As he passed, Rannaldini let his hands rove suggestively over each romping nymph.

'It's like a nudist colony,' grumbled Flora.

She was more charmed by Rannaldini's Rottweilers who bounded ahead, muzzles covered in grass seed, soothing their thistle-pricked, nettle-stung paws in the streams, attacking clods of wet turf and wood, shaking and worrying them, emerging with dirty wet faces, giving skips in the air and bouncing fatly away.

'Avant-garde dogs – they're sweet.' Flora hugged Tabloid.

'To people who are not afraid,' observed Rannaldini.

Passing under a pergola fantastically entwined with pale pink roses and acid-green hop, they reached a frantically rushing stream, almost a river, but narrowed to a width of six feet between dark, drenched, very slippery rocks.

'*The sounding cataract 'aunted me like a passion*,' said Rannaldini softly, gazing down into the white churning water. 'This whirlpool is called the Devil's Lair. In the eighteenth century the young Westalls and their friends had bets eef they were brave enough to jump across. Several young men were keeled.'

Springing across like a great cat, Rannaldini turned towards her.

'Come, leetle Flora.'

'It's a hell of a long way,' snapped Flora, as the Rottweilers, distraught at being separated from their master, but not brave enough to jump, whimpered and barged round her legs. 'Unlike you, I'm much too young to die.'

'Life ees about taking risks,' whispered Rannaldini, his dark eyes glittering, his teeth gleaming in the half-light. 'Jump, leetle animal, or are you scared?'

Refusing to be beaten, Flora took a great leap, slipped on the damp moss and was only just pulled to safety in time. For a second Rannaldini held her shaking with fury and terror.

'Let me go, you fucker,' she screamed, 'I want to go home.'

Releasing her, Rannaldini trailed a warm caressing hand over the goose-flesh of her bare waist.

'Why you fight me?'

'Because I really like Kitty, because I'm not into gerontophilia and because I'm sleeping with your son.'

'And he satisfies you?'

'He's known as Trunch at Bagley Hall,' spat back Flora.

'Hush.' Rannaldini put a finger, which smelt of wild mint, over her mouth. 'I want confirmation not details.'

'And if that weren't enough,' went on Flora, 'you're utterly unselective. Natasha told me about Hermione and jumping on her mother every time she hits London, and bonking every female musician in the London Duodenal, not to mention choral sex with all those panting groupies in their I LOVE RANNALDINI T-shirts. You just pick them off.'

They had reached a little bank, covered in pink-spotted orchids. A blushing sun was retreating behind the wood.

Kicking off her espadrilles Flora cooled her dusty feet in the long wet grass. Like Rannaldini, his sprinklers went everywhere.

'I am Don Juan,' said Rannaldini, sticking to the path above which made him taller, 'or, being Italian, Don Giovanni. I seek the perfect woman and always despair of finding her because all women are the same. You would be different. You are not classically beautiful, but you light up when you smile.'

'Dad doesn't smile when I light up.'

'You shouldn't smoke when God has given you a voice.'

'I'd rather he gave me Boris Levitsky,' taunted Flora, disappearing into the fringed depths of a weeping ash.

'Boris not Goodenough,' said Rannaldini chillingly.

'Why did you marry Kitty?' Flora emerged from the far side of the weeping ash. 'Was it an act of deliberate sadism? Did they toll the punishment bell at your wedding? Did the Paradise Lad howl on the first night?'

Rannaldini gave a shrug. 'Kitty run my life. She was brought up by elderly parents so I seem like spreeng chicken, and she help her mother look after other people's children.'

'So she has no problem with your brat-pack?'

'Correct.' Rannaldini moved off down the ride, pausing to caress the upturned face and breasts of a naked wood nymph, then letting his hands stray downwards.

'Eef one is going to run more than one woman,' he continued, 'one must have a loving wife rather plain so one's mistresses don't get jealous, rather working class, so women think Keety is fortunate to be plucked from her humble origins and to have landed such a mesmerizing – ' Rannaldini paused mockingly over the word – 'husband that she cannot expect heem to be faithful to her.

'Above all,' he went on with a satanic smile, 'Keety is the perfect alibi. Eef Hermione is being difficult and I want to see Cecilia, I tell Hermione that Keety is in town so I cannot get away. Eef I want to see someone else, you, for example' – briefly he touched her cheek – 'I tell both

Hermione and Cecilia, Keety is in town. If I want to drop someone I say: "I am so sorry, my dear, Keety has found out, and I cannot 'urt Keety." If a woman suddenly refuses to get out of my bed or one of my 'ouses, I say: "Keety is due any minute, you must go." Finally eef any of them are foolish enough to want to marry me I tell them I cannot leave Keety, she do nothing wrong, it would be like throwing a freshwater fish into the sea.'

He has got the most beautiful voice, thought Flora, husky, caressing, anodyne. Perhaps it was an essential of adulterers because so much of their campaigning was done on the telephone.

'You're such a shit,' she said fascinated.

'Like Byron.' Gently Rannaldini fingered the crutch of the wood nymph. '*We love our men of genius not because they are perfect but because they are great.*' Then, running his hand over the wood nymph's bottom, 'Still warm from the sun as though she has been given a spanking, I would love to spank all the bad temper out of you, leetle Flora.'

'You bloody wouldn't.' Outraged, yet excited, Flora plunged back into another weeping ash. As she emerged Rannaldini drew two ropes of fronds round her neck, trapping her.

'I 'ave a 'ole in my heart from Cupid's arrow,' he whispered, tightening the fronds. Aware that he could throttle her, Flora gazed into his mocking, sensual, infinitely cynical, face.

'*My father was a Spanish Captain,*' she sang softly,
'*Went to sea a month ago,*
First he kissed me, then he left me,
Bid me always answer No.'

She paused so long on the high note that Rannaldini felt the hair rising on the back of his neck, then she smiled and went on:

'*Oh no Juan, no Juan, no Juan no.*'

Rannaldini's straight black eyebrows underlined a forehead almost without lines. Not a man who worries or who suffers from guilt, thought Flora. His lips were absolutely on a level with hers. She was sure he was going to kiss her and shut her eyes. Then he laughed and moved away.

'Come and see my tower.'

Flora could hear the distant hum of a tractor trying to get the hay cut before the storm. The sun had set, but the heat was still murderous. As they moved through the wood Rannaldini held back nettles and brambles and, having climbed a stile overgrown with elder, turned to help her. The starry elderflowers that fell into her hair were as creamy as her skin. Overcome with lust, Rannaldini let his hand stray over her right breast testing its soft springiness.

Leaping away, livid with her heart for pounding like the hoof-beats of Rannaldini's horses, Flora hurled a clump of goosegrass at him to lower the tension.

'Clinging but instantly detachable, like the perfect woman,' said Rannaldini, peeling it off his silk shirt and throwing it back at Flora who ducked and ran down the path. As she reached the clearing a crack of lightning lit up Rannaldini's tower, then thunder boomed like a twelve pounder. The Rottweilers collided against their master's legs in terror. Rannaldini just had time to kick them into their kennel and bustle Flora into the tower when the heavens opened.

The ground floor, where Rannaldini worked, was completely walled by records, tapes and editing equipment.

'It's soundproof, so however much you scream——'

'It won't sound as awful as Hermione,' mocked Flora.

As the soundtrack of Rannaldini's film of *Don Giovanni* flooded the tower and its surrounding woodland, Flora bounded up a sprial staircase into a sitting room furnished with pale grey sofas and chairs and two high footstools covered in buttercup-yellow and crimson silk.

Flora looked up at the bright scarlet walls and ceiling. 'Like being wrapped in the flames of Don Giovanni's hell,' she said.

On a side table beside a shoal of silver photographs of Rannaldini being congratulated by the famous, including Gorbachov and Princess Diana, stood a big yellow bowl overflowing with pink-and-green grapes, peaches, mangoes, persimmons and fruit so exotic Flora had never seen it before. A yellow Aubusson carpet swimming with roses and oak leaves caressed her bare feet. The only pictures were an Eric Gill panel of an ambiguous-looking madonna offering a perfect breast to a rather too-knowing and adult baby and a Picasso girl whose eye squinted over Rannaldini's ivory-silk shoulder as he opened another bottle of Krug.

The bathroom, also in pale grey and scarlet with a mirrored ceiling and walls, was dominated by a vast Jacuzzi.

'Mother Courage's famous Ju-Jitzu bath,' giggled Flora. 'I can't tell you how much I admire her, she makes my father's shirts look as though Dinsdale's slept in them and she told Mum that Mrs 'Arefield 'ad just had her back passage painted bottle green. You should know presumably.'

Even though a faint smile flickered at the corner of Rannaldini's mouth Flora decided not to tell him about Rattledicky.

'I could listen to her for hours.'

'Unlike Boris Levitsky's compositions,' said Rannaldini handing her a glass. 'To us.'

'To my guardian devil.' Trying to suppress her surging excitement Flora sauntered next door into a bedroom which was all bed, with a mural above it of an endlessly applauding opera audience, beautiful bare-shouldered women in wonderful jewels, handsome men in dinner-jackets, all cheering and clapping so realistically you could smell the carnations in their buttonholes and hear the bravoes ringing out.

'Christ, you're a narcissist,' snapped Flora. 'Do you delay your entrance even here? How'd you take out your teeth without a bedside table?'

She jumped as a huge clap of thunder burst overhead. Her heart was beating almost as loudly. Any moment Rannaldini would pounce.

'*Vile seducer,*' sang Hermione, '*like a fury I'll pursue you, haunt you to your dying day.*'

'Exquisite,' sighed Rannaldini and, going downstairs, he turned on Wimbledon to watch a replay of an excruciatingly boring women's singles match.

Feeling absurdly let down Flora slumped on one of the silk footstools, sulkily consuming an entire bunch of green grapes, pips and all, by which time Leporello was listing Don Giovanni's conquests to a distraught Donna Elvira.

Dark, blond, fat, thin, tall, tiny, all were fair game to the Don.

'*But his favourite form of sinning,*

Is with one who's just beginning,' sang Leporello.

Realizing that the rain was no longer machine-gunning the roof and windows Flora knocked back her Krug.

'Well, I can't stay here all night gazing up Miss Sabatini's knickers.'

'I'll walk you home. Are you tired?' Rannaldini switched off the television and the soundtrack.

'No, bored.'

'Ees the same thing.'

As they were leaving he flicked on his answering machine. Suddenly the tower was filled with desperate weeping.

'Rannaldini, it's Beatrice, I must see you, I love you so much.'

With an irritable shrug Rannaldini turned off the machine. 'Some stupeed flautist want her job back.'

'And you, too, by the sound of it,' reproved Flora. 'How can you hang a cross round your neck and behave so horribly?'

'Theenk how much worse I would behave if I didn't wear it. Women make such a fuss. As a sex, you will soon be expendable. The Japanese invent a robot that makes exquisite love. Afterwards you sweetch it off.'

'It must be called Hermione.'

Rannaldini laughed.

'You should scowl more often,' mocked Flora, going towards the door, 'you're too attractive when you smile.'

Rannaldini punched her gently in the belly.

'You wanna go 'ome?'

'While I still can.'

'Peety, you have no idea of the unimaginable pleasure you will miss. See these leetle footstools. They are very old. Italian voluptuaries used to kneel their mistresses up on them so they could spend hours licking their bottoms.'

'How disgusting.' Flora was rigid with shock.

She's a child, thought Rannaldini.

'Come, leetle wild thing.' Putting a warm hand on her neck, he drew her towards him and kissed her gently on each corner of her mouth, then slowly worked inwards, his mouth cool and tasting faintly of Krug.

Supported by the door, Flora just remained standing.

'Now I can tell them at Bagley Hall I've snogged Rannaldini.'

26

Outside night had fallen. The wood steamed like a tropical jungle. The rain had bowed the trees into a dripping green tunnel and pestled a rank sexy smell out of elder, nettles and the last yellow leaves of the wild garlic. As they emerged the maze reared up, a great jet-black wave waiting to topple over them. An owl hooted warningly, a bat swooped.

'Duck – it's the Count,' said Flora, through desperately chattering teeth.

'Go into the maze,' whispered Rannaldini.

'Give me a ball of thread, Ariadne. Although you're more like the Minotaur.'

'Keep your hand on the wall and you'll reach the centre.' Rannaldini buried his lips briefly in her neck. 'I geeve you a minute's start.'

Never one to resist a challenge Flora plunged into the maze feeling her way between drenched lowering yew cliffs. With a scream she ducked in terror as a sinister dark figure reared up ahead like a black cowled monk about to pounce on her. Then she gasped with relief: it was only one of Mr Brimscombe's yew peacocks. Shivering, yet pouring with sweat as her feet crunched on the wet, cold, pebble floor, she felt she was walking down an endless beach into a sea of no return.

Turning, twisting, falling to her knees, losing both her espadrilles in her panic, she could hear Rannaldini behind her like the Hound of Heaven (should be hell), his footsteps deliberate but relentless, stealthily drawing closer.

Oh Christ, she could hear breathing in front now –

someone else was in the maze, or was it the way it twisted back on itself? Terrified, she started to run, piercing herself as she crashed from one massed wall of sharp twigs to another. Twenty feet above, a thin strip of dun, starless sky gave her no direction.

Her breath was coming in such gasps she would have none left to scream for help. She'd never get out. Meeting a dead end she stumbled to the left, hands desperately searching. Rannaldini was going to murder her, the maze was a trick, there was no centre. She gave a sob as an owl hooted overhead.

Then suddenly she breathed in the headiest smell. The path seemed to widen. Her feet must have touched a pressure point because soft light suddenly flooded a bower of bliss in which an ancient stone bench was fantastically garlanded by great clumps of rain-soaked philadelphus and jasmine with white rambler roses clambering to the top of the yew ramparts, all wafting their sweetness. Flora gave a moan of relief and joy.

Next moment Rannaldini's arms were around her. She could feel the burning heat of his body, Don Giovanni in the flames.

'You made it, leetle wild thing.'

'I'm waiting for Mr Rite of Spring to come along.'

'You must not mock.'

This time he kissed her with real passion, quivering with tension, his tongue stabbing and probing her mouth, his hands untying the black knot of Wolfie's shirt. Laying bare her dove-soft white breasts, he covered them with kisses, murmuring endearments in Italian.

Then he seemed to gain control of himself and pushed her gently away.

'Now we play games,' he said softly. 'You must do what I say. You are leetle village girl who wishes to enter the great Convent of Paradise. But first the all-powerful Abbot of Valhalla must inspect you to make sure of your purity and innocence. It ees his privilege.'

His face was totally impassive.

'Are you some kind of nutter?' stammered Flora backing away.

'Take off your clothes,' said Rannaldini sharply.

Furiously Flora stepped out of her rain-soaked blue skirt and pink and white striped pants.

'Sit down.' He pushed her on to the stone bench. 'Now the Abbot will examine the leetle girl fully. He touches her breasts,' Rannaldini's warm hands were stroking, squeezing, searching, 'and he theenks what a tragedy that two such lovely theengs should be hidden for ever under a nun's black robes.

'The little girl is frightened now,' he went on, sensing Flora's apprehension, 'but just when she think the touching has gone on too long for decency the Abbot moves downwards. He is delighted to find her a little plump. Her puppy fat will protect her from the bitter cold of the convent.'

In time to the deep, husky, caressing voice Rannaldini's hands roved over her belly and thighs, slowly, meticulously, assessing and examining.

Once again Flora was appalled to find herself revolted but wildly, hopelessly excited.

'Sturdy legs, too,' murmured Rannaldini. 'Good for kneeling for hours on a cold chapel floor.'

Then, as he pushed her back on the bench, 'Now she must lie down and put her knees up to her breasts for the crucial examination to begin. The test of her virginity.'

'What sort of fucking pervert are you?' hissed Flora, but, powerless to resist, she lay back, raising her legs and giving a wail of pleasure as his fingers slid inside her.

'They go in too easily,' purred Rannaldini, 'the leetle girl try to tighten up to pretend she is still intacta but she is far too excited. As the Abbot explore probing her most secret places she cannot stop herself gripping his fingers. She is embarrassed how wet she is getting. She knows the Abbot is excited, too. He no longer care eef she is virgin.'

Rannaldini's iron-hard thigh was rigid against Flora's

bare leg. She began to gasp with helpless pleasure as his finger moved up to her clitoris.

'See the hood is back. From this tiny pink bud blossoms all female joy. It is so pretty. The Abbot will cure all her tensions, all her fears and geeve her such a lovely feeling.'

'Oh, you bastard!' Flora arched her back, went rigid and came.

'That was nice?' crooned Rannaldini, delightedly gathering her against his chest and stroking her hair.

'Bliss but utterly bent.'

'Is only the beginning. Tomorrow you can be little nun who has been caught in some wickedness.'

'And you'll be the Abbot of Valhalla ordering me to be flogged. Not bloody likely.'

Desperate to regain the upper hand, Flora dropped to her knees, unzipping his fly, lowering the blue silk boxer shorts and burying her face in the scented powdered hair flattened by the tight trousers, as the thick powerful cock flew up like a jack in the box.

'Oh, wow,' sighed Flora.

But, feeling her tongue, Rannaldini pulled away.

'I weesh to come inside you.'

'Pity, I wanted to have my cock and eat it.'

For a second she thought he was going to hit her.

'Stop taking the pees.'

Lifting her back on to the stone bench he roughly parted her labia and shoved his cock deep inside her.

'Aaaaaaah, lovely,' cried Flora, starting to move.

She was used to over-excited schoolboys who came in an instant. Rannaldini now totally in control, could have been a metronone for *The Rite of Spring*. His rhythm was so exact and so relentless.

'Keep your eyes open,' he ordered, his face satanical above hers, 'I want to see you come. Are you bored now?'

'Not as much as I was. Twelve bored more likely.' Ah, those deep slow thrusts, Flora was battling not to abdicate herself completely. 'For a pervert you're seriously good at straight fucking. Although this bench is even harder than you – oh my God, on second thoughts perhaps it isn't . . . Oh, Rannaldini, oh, Rannaldini.'

At the end of a week's suspension Flora was allowed back for the Leaver's Ball, because Wolfie Rannaldini, who'd won every cup and prize going, interceded with Sabine Bottomley.

Two days before the ball Flora, who was supposed to be practising 'Who is Sylvia?' with Rannaldini in his tower, was actually perched on his huge treble bed rubbing baby oil into him while he finished the crossword.

'Ah that's good. Deeper, deeper. You learn fast.' Later he combed back the hair between her legs.

'You are very charming, like a rose called *Felicia*. I cannot wait to shave you.'

'Do you shave all your women?'

'Usually. Cecilia 'ave a brush like Bernard Shaw's beard so I 'ad to.'

'You *are* decadent. You should publish a coffee table book of all your ladies and call it *Clitoris Allsorts*. Anyway you can't shave me until after the Leavers' Ball. Think of the raised eyebrows if we all go skinny dipping.'

'You are not going to Leavers' Ball.'

'I must. I feel so dreadful about Wolfie. I promised I'd go with him two months ago. I'm not letting him down in front of all his friends. I'm off backpacking soon, so he and I will just peter out without his knowing about you.'

'Eef you go to that ball, do not come back to me.'

It was her first experience of Rannaldini's intransigence. She knew she mustn't give in. She was horrified how difficult she found it.

Having persuaded Georgie to buy a slinky black dress covered in sequins for *The Clive Anderson Show* so she could borrow it for the ball, Flora discovered it was too tight on the hips. Resorting to half a packet of Ex-Lax she spent the day of the ball on the loo groaning that she was dying.

That makes two of us, thought Georgie.

Deathly pale, buckling at the knees, Flora managed to gird her ransacked loins to get ready. At least the dress fitted perfectly. Georgie was just fastening her own jade pendant round Flora's neck when Flora asked her point blank if she'd ever been unfaithful to Guy.

'No, of course not.'

As Georgie crossed her fingers the jade pendant slithered between Flora's breasts.

'And has Daddy ever been unfaithful to you?'

This time, as she crossed her fingers, Georgie held on to the pendant with her thumb.

'Of course not.'

'How very boring,' said Flora. 'Marriage must be like a prison.'

Next moment her mother had burst into tears, but denied there was anything the matter, just saying work was going badly.

As Wolfie was playing cricket against the fathers and going to be pushed for time, Guy – the ever-willing chauffeur – dropped Flora off at Valhalla where the roses were scattering pale petals all over the lawns.

Rannaldini, who'd just flown in from a wonderfully successful performance of Shostakovich's *Tenth*, was delighted to see Flora looking so wan. But she had the wonderful skin of youth where sleepless nights only put darker blue shadows under the eyes and made her look more appealing. He had never wanted anyone more, but icily he ignored her.

Before she left with Wolfie and Natasha, they paraded before the grown-ups in their finery.

Oh, I'd love to be beautiful and thin and go to a ball, thought Kitty longingly.

Wolfie asked his father to tie his tie. He had made another century this afternoon and looked bullish, very brown and handsome.

'None of our generation can tie bow-ties,' said Natasha.

'Family ties are more important,' said Flora pointedly.

For a second, as his father had to stand on tiptoe to see over his shoulder into the mirror and flick and slot the yellow Paisley tie in and out, Wolfie had a spookie feeling Rannaldini wanted to throttle him.

'You all look be-yootiful,' called out Kitty as they drove off.

As Kitty sorted through the mountains of washing from her stepchildren's trunks the following afternoon she felt really depressed – not only had she got the curse, which meant yet again she wasn't pregnant, but also because she'd just switched on Wimbledon and seen Hermione and Rannaldini sitting together on Centre Court.

She'd just removed the clothes which Natasha, who was flying to New York the next day, might need, when Wolfie tottered in still wearing his dinner-jacket. At first she thought he was drunk, then, as he collapsed at the kitchen table, she realized he was crying.

'Christ, I hate my father.'

Kitty went cold. Mindlessly she filled the kettle.

'Flora was impossible all evening,' said Wolfie, furiously wiping his desperately bloodshot eyes. 'Then she vanished and came back all lit up. I thought she was on something. She refused to dance, the sides of the marquee were up because it was so hot, she kept looking up at the stars. Then she gives this shriek of excitement and runs across the pitch leaving her bag, her shoes and her green jacket behind as my father's helicopter lands on the pitch.'

Wolfie couldn't go on. The wind from Rannaldini's blades had blown Flora's skirt over her head, and his last memory had been of her black legs and suspenders and her red bikini pants.

'She was so crazy about Boris,' he said despairingly, 'and Marcus Campbell-Black, but I thought I'd seen off the competition. But how can I compete when my father comes out of the sky like *Close Encounters*?'

Wolfie was a kind boy but so deranged with grief he'd forgotten who he was talking to.

'My mother's still in love with him and they've been divorced for years,' he went on bitterly. 'When we were in Salzburg Papa swanned up and put his hand on her shoulders: "You're looking lovely, Gisela," and Mum started shaking and shaking. He can have anyone. Why does he have to take Flora as well?'

Suddenly Wolfie realized the cup Kitty was putting down in front of him was spilling tea all over the table.

'Oh Jesus, Kitty, I'm sorry. I don't know what I'm saying. You must have known what a bastard he was when you married him.'

When his father returned, even browner, from Wimbledon, having been denied the satisfaction of seeing Boris Becker winning, Wolfie asked for five minutes alone. Expecting trouble Rannaldini was surprised when Wolfie bleakly announced that instead of an eighteenth birthday party he'd like the money to go round the world. Relieved to see the broad back of his son, Rannaldini wrote him a surprisingly generous cheque.

'I feel terrible,' said Flora, when Rannaldini telephoned to tell her, 'and I doubt if he'll ever forgive you.'

'Course he will. Sooner or later he'll need money or a leg-up in his career so bad he have to forgive a leg-over.'

'You've no fucking heart and I'm worried about Mum. If she's writing a musical called *Ant and Cleo*, why is she reading *Othello*?'

Returning to Paradise from her second honeymoon in Jamaica in late July, Marigold rang Georgie and suggested they went for a cheering-up lunch at The Heavenly Host.

'I can't face the outside world at the moment,' mumbled Georgie.

'Ay'll bring some smoked salmon and several bottles straight round. We've got to talk.'

Half an hour later Marigold rolled up at Angel's Reach looking gloriously suntanned but a bit plump with an apricot-pink shirt worn outside her shorts to cover the bulges.

'Ay'm so sorry,' she hugged Georgie. 'Kitty filled me in. Ay didn't realize how awful it'd been.'

She was horrified by Georgie's appearance. The magnolia complexion which men used to write songs about was all blotchy. She was desperately thin, her skin hanging like loose clothes on a skeleton. She couldn't stop shaking.

'Poor Dinsdale's aged more than I have. He's been walked so much as an excuse to get out of the house that he hides behind the sofa whenever his lead's rattled. Oh God, another single magpie.' Frantically Georgie crossed herself. 'I keep seeing them.'

'They're always single in July because the females are feeding their babies and protecting their nests,' said Marigold. 'Now where's the corkscrew? We both need a noggin.'

'He's still seeing Julia.' Georgie couldn't keep off the subject. 'I ought to get out, but I'm like a hotel coat-hanger, useless when detached from my moorings.'

'I was like that,' said Marigold. 'How are you and Guy when you're together?'

'Terrified. We never stop apologizing like British Rail. I bitched about him so much to Annabel Hardman the other day with the answering machine on that I had to record Dire Straits over the whole tape.'

'There.' Marigold put a huge blue-green glass of Chardonnay in front of Georgie.

'Thanks. Larry was so hellish to you I'd never have signed that Catchitune contract if I'd known about Nikki, but you look so stunning now. How did you ever get him back?'

'Promise, promise not to tell?' whispered Marigold. 'Ay paid Laysander.'

'You what!'

'Ferdie, Laysander's flatmate, orchestrated everythin'. They put me on an awful diet, took me joggin' and made me act totally unconcerned whenever Larry rolled up. Ay gave Laysander some lovely clothes and a Ferrari and we hired jewels for him to give me. Larry was so mad with jealousy he came roaring back.'

'It really worked!' Georgie showed the faint flicker of animation of the dying castaway hearing the chug of a helicopter.

'Far better than before,' said Marigold, taking the smoked salmon out of its transparent paper and laying it on a blue plate from the Reject Shop, which had presumably replaced her plates Georgie had smashed.

'You know how hopelessly undomesticated Larry was,' she went on, searching among the spice shelf for red pepper. 'Now he brings down his washing and even loads and unloads the dishwasher. Ay'm thinkin' of writing Nikki a thank-you letter. And he's become so marvellous in other ways.' Marigold unearthed a tired-looking lemon from the bottom of the fridge. 'Not just terribly loving and not being able to keep his hands off me, but he doesn't rev up any more or shout at me if Ay map-read wrong and he gives me the remote control when we watch TV and smothers me in YSL. That's why I'm looking so good and best of all I don't have to go to Masonic dinners any more.'

'Golly.' Georgie found herself peeling off a bit of smoked salmon. 'I wonder if it would work with Guy? How much did you pay Lysander?' she asked. Then, bleating in horror when Marigold told her, 'I can't afford that!'

'It's worth it,' urged Marigold. 'You'll never be able to pay back the *Ant and Cleo* money and Larry's hell-bent on having your album by Christmas. He's mean about deadlines. It'll be such fun having Laysander back in Paradise and he'll keep Larry on his toes,' she added dreamily.

'Did you sleep with him?'

'May word, no,' Marigold crossed her fingers. 'He's just there to rattle one's hubby. Do give it a go. He was in Cheshire bringing some drain billionaire to heel and now he's in Mayorca on some rescue mission. Ay promise he and Ferdie are brilliant.'

27

Feeling anything but brilliant, Lysander huddled in the only bit of shade on the burning deck of the motor yacht, *Feisty Lady*, as she chugged round the rocky Majorcan coast. He was seven days into the worst job Ferdie had ever found him: to rattle a fabulously rich arms dealer appropriately called Mr Gunn, who had brought his appalling bimbo on the cruise as well as his equally appalling wife.

Bloody Ferdie had also pooh-poohed Lysander's gloomy prognostications that he was bound to be seasick.

'That was rowing boats at school. Large boats are quite different.'

Large boats turned out to be infinitely worse. The minute *Feisty Lady* left the Hamble, Lysander started heaving his guts out. It was absolutely no consolation, particularly during a storm in the Bay of Biscay, that the busty, braceleted Mrs Gunn spent her time vying with the ship's crew who were all as gay as crickets (Mr Gunn was taking no chances) over who should minister to Lysander on his death bunk. Nor that Mr Gunn became so jealous of Mrs Gunn playing Florence Nightingale twenty-four hours a day that he dumped the bimbo in Gibraltar and was now bonking Florence Nightingale so vigorously in the master cabin below deck that *Feisty Lady* was pitching worse than in the Bay of Biscay.

It was Lysander's first day up. A molten midday sun blazed down out of a royal-blue sky and he felt too dreadful even to watch Goodwood on satellite or crawl to the telephone to ring his bookmaker. His wracked stomach was even more concave than that of the bronzed deck-hand in frayed hotpants who seemed to be spending an unnecessarily long time polishing the nearest life buoy.

'It's really kind, Gregor, but I honestly don't want anything,' mumbled Lysander.

He tried to concentrate on yesterday's *Sun*. But the cheery forecast for Pisces bore no resemblance to the horrors of the day before and he was depressed by a survey in which the majority of female readers said they preferred men to be well read rather than well hung. Lysander hadn't finished a book in years. Sick for a home that no longer existed, he longed for Jack or Arthur to cuddle. He was terrified once Mr Gunn stopped emptying himself into Mrs Gunn he would empty one of his Kalashnikovs into the catalyst. And wretched Ferdie, who had a maddening habit of going off air when he wanted Lysander to stay put, was always out of the office and refusing to return his calls.

Listlessly he gazed across a tie-dyed turquoise and navy-blue sea at the pine-spiked cliffs falling into the sea. They were so like hedgehogs he half-expected them to curl up, taking their tower blocks and hotels with them as the yacht approached. The buildings themselves were like the egg-box castles he used proudly to take home from playgroup for his mother who, to his father's irritation, always put them in the drawing room. He always missed her more when he was feeling ill.

They were approaching Palma. *Feisty Lady* was bucking ominously and Lysander was wondering if he had the strength to stagger to the side or anything left to throw up when a huge yacht overtook them.

'That's *Britannia*, Sandy, isn't she lovely?' sighed Gregor the deck-hand.

Raising his binoculars with effort, Lysander scoured the deck for Princess Diana or the Queen. He seriously admired the Queen, no-one knew more about racing. If she fell overboard he could dive in and rescue her, although in his weakened state he probably couldn't swim that far. Perhaps Princess Diana could rescue him. She was supposed to swim every day. He imagined her firm hands on either side of his head, her soothing voice saying: 'Not long now,' as she towed him towards *Britannia*. At the thought of her beautiful long legs doing a vigorous backstroke Lysander's mind misted over. He was roused by the ship's cook waving a cordless telephone smelling of garlic at him.

'Nice sounding man for you, Sandy.'

As Ferdie was the only person who knew he was on board, Lysander grabbed the telephone in a fury.

'Gemmyoutofhere, you bastard. Where the hell have you been? I've been propositioned by every bum bandit in the British navy.'

'Chill out,' said Ferdie, who had an irritating addiction to modern slang. 'What's the state of play?'

Lysander told him, then after a long pause in which Ferdie outlined his next assignment, Lysander gave a whoop of delight.

'Georgie Maguire, fucking hell, *the* Georgie Maguire. She's gorgeous. All right, I *am* keeping my voice down. I thought she was happily married . . . the bastard. I'll get the next flight out of Palma.'

'Wait till tomorrow,' said Ferdie, 'then I can meet you.'

The following afternoon as the temperature soared into the nineties Ferdie was amazed to see Lysander sidling through the Nothing-to-Declare doors at Gatwick, smothered in an enormous camel-hair overcoat, swathed in long scarves, sending fellow passengers flying as his trolley, hopelessly over-loaded with duty-free, polo sticks and expensive suitcases out of which protruded shirt-tails and legs of boxer shorts, veered out of control.

'Where's the fucking car?' he hissed to Ferdie.

'In the car park.'

'Well, take this trolley and move it.'

'You OK?'

'Move it, for Christ's sake.'

Even when he was shaking like a leaf with sweat pouring down a yellowing face, people stopped and gazed at Lysander.

Hell, thought Ferdie, he's picked up a fever, or worse.

It turned out to be worse. The moment they were alone and going up in the grey car-park lift Lysander parted his stifling coat to reveal a pink nose and a pair of totally crossed eyes. Tucked under his arm was a painfully thin, bedraggled, reddy-brown mongrel puppy who nevertheless managed to twitch its curly tail and stretch up to lick Lysander's chin.

'What the fuck is that?'

'What does it look like? Sweet little thing. I had to trank her so she's very dopey.' Lysander dropped a kiss on the puppy's head. 'All the way from Palma, Jesus, if another hostess asks if she can take my coat! I've never had so many women trying to get my clothes off. Isn't she adorable?'

'And probably rabid,' hissed Ferdie, then as the lift stopped, 'cover it up for Christ's sake.'

The row continued in the car.

'Have you ever seen anyone with rabies?' Ferdie was practically diving out of the window to avoid contact.

'No, nor anything like this puppy. She's got cigarette burns all over her back. Christ, people are bastards.'

'You could go to prison for ten years, so could I for abetting you.'

'Thanks for reminding me. I must have a bet.' Lysander reached for Ferdie's car telephone.

'Put it down. Don't change the subject. That dog could have rabies.'

'Course she hasn't. Her owners kept her locked in a cupboard. The boys from the boat took me clubbing and we heard her howling. We had to break in after-hours to rescue her. I really like gays. Basically they're so brave and so kind to animals. It took Gregor and me an hour to wash the shit off.'

'So it's stolen as well,' said Ferdie sternly. 'That's fifteen years.'

'Anything'd be better than that bloody boat. I am not into bateau-ed wives.'

Ferdie didn't smile. 'You're so fucking impulsive, like that time you hi-jacked the school cat. Jack will be wildly jealous.'

'Jack will be delighted – once he knows she's female.'

'Then they can have lots of rabid puppies.'

Lysander giggled. 'I've got you a huge bottle of Jack Daniels and some Toblerone for fat Jack and scent for Marigold. I can't wait to see her. God, it's bliss to be back. I hate abroad. People can't understand me and I can't understand the television. When are we going to see Georgie?'

'About half-past six.'

'How exciting. She looked so stunning at her launching party. Perhaps she'll write a song about me called "Cock Star"!'

'You are not allowed to bonk her.'

'No, well. I better have a shower before we see her. I've got pee all over my shirt.'

'What have you called that puppy, Death Threat?' asked Ferdie.

'Maggie.'

'After Thatcher?'

'No, after this girl in *The Mill on the Floss*.'

'What are you reading that for?'

Lysander, who was now marking runners in Ferdie's *Evening Standard*, his hand edging towards Ferdie's mobile, explained about the survey in the *Sun*.

'How far have you got?'

'Page three. He's quite a good writer, this George Eliot.'

Lysander was very hurt when Ferdie roared with laughter. He knew he was thick but he'd just executed a dangerous assignment with great skill and put a lot of dosh into Ferdie's pocket.

'Mrs Gunn was so grateful this morning, she's given me twenty grand to spend at Ralph Lauren so I can buy lots of sharp suits.' If he'd been bitchy he'd have added that Ferdie had put on a lot of weight and there was no way he could get into any of them. 'And she offered me a yacht with my own mooring at the Hamble whenever I want, which I told her I didn't.'

'You dickhead!' exploded Ferdie. 'Ring her up and accept and we'll flog it.'

Marigold was overjoyed to see Lysander.

'Chanel Number Fayve, oh you remembered, oh Laysander.'

As she flung herself into his arms, Lysander noticed that she had, like Ferdie, put on a lot of weight. But as they had been held up in traffic there was no time to do more than bath and change before setting off to Georgie's. Maggie the puppy, who was still dopey, having devoured a bowl of bread and milk and been inspected by Jack and Patch, had now fallen asleep on the sofa.

'Poor little thing came from the National Canine Defence Kennels in Evesham,' lied Ferdie, as Lysander, still a bit pale and black under the eyes, came downstairs rolling up the sleeves of a dark blue shirt.

'God, Gregor knows how to iron.'

'You look gorgeous,' sighed Marigold. 'Lucky Georgie.'

She wanted to come along to effect the introductions. It *had* been her idea. But Ferdie didn't want any feminine compassion softening the hard bargain he intended to drive.

'Well, at least nag Georgie about the village fête,' said Marigold. 'We desperately need any clothes she doesn't wear any more for the Nearly New Stall.'

Georgie watched a dying wych-elm showering yellow leaves on the burnt lawn. It hadn't rained since the storm that had delayed Flora the first day she'd had singing coaching with Rannaldini. Honeysuckle buds like bloody red hands clawed at the terrace walls. The hay had been cut for a second time in Rannaldini's field below, the bales like yellow coffins symbolizing the death of the summer. Georgie had had a terrible day – not a note of music or a word written. Having made a dropped telephone call earlier she had found out that Julia was back in the cottage at Eldercombe. So Guy's compulsive mowing, even though there was no grass, would go on.

She didn't know what had made her agree to see Lysander and Ferdie. The whole enterprise would distract her from work and cost a fortune and her confidence had taken such a battering she'd never pull it off. There's no way Guy was going to stop seeing Julia.

They were shooting clays across the valley in preparation for 12 August. Bang, bang, bang, like a relentlessly approaching army. She turned on the prom. It was the Tchaikovsky violin concerto, which Guy was always playing, probably because it was one of his and Julia's 'tunes'. Georgie started to cry.

'Marigold looks well, doesn't she?' said Lysander as they stormed up a drive lit by hogweed and dog-daisies. 'When you think what she looked like last February. I can't wait to see Georgie.'

In nervous excitement Lysander smoothed his windswept hair in Ferdie's wing mirror.

Georgie, however, was in a far worse state than Marigold had ever been. Even done up on their last notches, her belt and her watch hung loose. The stones of her engagement ring, fallen inwards, scratched against her wine glass. Like purple worms the veins rose on her thin hands. Her hair had lost its lovely Titian glow and had no life, like a dull village. She hadn't shaved the back of one of her emaciated legs and her ankles were scratched with brambles from wandering aimlessly through the woods. It also looked as though someone had grated coconut on the shoulders of her black T-shirt.

Getting drinks took ages.

'I'm sorry this tonic's flat,' she said when they'd finally sat down on the terrace. 'There's a bottle in the fridge,' she added as Ferdie leapt up. 'I'm sorry the place is a mess. Mother Courage, my cleaner, has gone to the Costa Brava for a week.'

'Lovely dog,' said Lysander, as Dinsdale wriggled along the bench until his head and shoulders were resting on Georgie's lap. She winced as the dog's elbows dug into her fleshless thighs.

'I spend my time taking grass seed out of his eyes.'

Which are only marginally more red-rimmed than your own, thought Lysander. 'We had a basset,' he told her. 'They're terrible at getting up in the morning.'

'You two should get along,' said Ferdie, returning with the tonic.

In the fridge he had also found blackening avocadoes, tomatoes spotted with grey, whiskery sweetcorn and mouldy cheese. All the plants in the kitchen were dying. Phlox and night-scented stock drooped round the terrace unwatered. This was definitely a house out of control.

Lysander loathed the moment when Ferdie told the wives where they were going wrong. Rannaldini's haybales reminded him not of coffins but of school trunks and sobbing into his pillow every night at prep school, until every boy in the dormitory had hurled their regulation black lace-up school shoes at him. No wonder he was brain damaged.

He was still smarting over Ferdie's amusement. How was he to know George Eliot was a woman? Down below he could see Rannaldini's horses seeking shade beneath a huge oak tree. He must get Arthur sound. Box rest had done no good. He'd turn him out when he'd got him back to Paradise.

'I can't afford that,' an aghast Georgie was saying as she rotated her leather bracelet. 'Marigold never said it'd be that much.'

'Inflation's gone up three per cent since we sorted her out,' said Ferdie, 'and Lysander must have a soft-top Ferrari.'

'I *am* due a big royalty cheque,' said Georgie. 'If it arrives when Guy's not here I suppose I could stash it away and pay you with that.'

'No sweat. The important thing is to get Guy back. He's away Monday to Friday, I presume.'

Georgie nodded. 'But the coast isn't always clear. Guy keeps telling his lady friends that I'm lonely. Last night bloody Hermione dropped in, had three whiskies and scrambled eggs, and I had to miss *EastEnders, The Bill, After Henry* and *Capital City*.'

Lysander turned even paler. 'How dreadful. Couldn't you have taped them?'

'I was buggered if I'd show her I'm hooked on soaps. She thinks I'm an utter philistine as it is. Then she had the cheek to tell me I wasn't unhappy, just suffering from rejection and hurt pride, the smug cow.'

'Well, if the lady friends roll up it doesn't matter.' Ferdie was anxious to get down to basics. 'It'll be no bad thing if they tell Guy Lysander was here.'

'But Guy's always been turned on by my having other men,' said Georgie, bursting into tears. 'When we were first married and I went on tour and had the occasional one-night stand he used to love hearing about it when I came home – although he made me promise never to see them again. I often made things up to excite him, so he thinks I'm far more promiscuous than I was.'

'But he's never faced serious competition on his own doorstep,' interrupted Ferdie. 'The first thing to do is to start eating, cut out the booze and get some sleeping pills.'

'I won't be able to work. They make me so uncoordinated in the morning,' said Georgie in panic.

'You're not working anyway. When he starts next week, Lysander will take you shopping. Don't buy anything strapless or sleeveless. You're too thin at the moment. And no minis, either, it looks too feverish. And,' Ferdie added sternly, 'you must do something about that scurf.'

'It isn't scurf.' Georgie frantically brushed her shoulders. 'It's sand from burying my head like an ostrich for so many years.'

Back at Marigold's house, Lysander sank into the blackest gloom. Even Marigold taping *EastEnders* and *The Bill* didn't raise his spirits. He'd last seen Marigold six months ago, when she'd been down to eight stone, looking terrific and was giving off sexual vibes like a mare in season. She had also provided him with comfort and a home when he desperately needed it. He had therefore carried an idealized picture of her in his head, which had sometimes merged with that of his mother. The reality was a let-down. Marigold was more matronly, bossier – all that fuss because they'd forgotten to ask Georgie about the Nearly New Stall – and much commoner than he'd remembered her.

She was now having a double chinwag with Ferdie as she painted bluebells on a pink chair.

'Gay, Ay'm afraid, has been rather a swayne to Georgie,' she was saying.

Part of Lysander's buzz at taking on Georgie had been that it would give him the chance to bonk Marigold again. Now he wasn't sure he wanted to. And Georgie had been harrowing. He was fed up with self-obsessed, desperately unhappy, married women. He wanted some fun. Clutching Jack, as he always did in moments of stress, he announced: 'I can't take Georgie on. She's too old and too far gone. She ought to be in the funny farm.'

'Oh, please,' said Marigold, who was secretly relieved Lysander didn't fancy Georgie. 'She's so low and you were so wonderful at bringing Larry back.'

Ferdie noticed the Picasso and the Stubbs had vanished from the drawing-room wall. He'd always suspected Larry was over-leveraged. It must have cost a bomb getting rid of Nikki, or keeping her quiet if he'd perhaps weakened and seen her again. Marigold might well need Lysander's services.

The puppy, who was stretched out beside Lysander on the sofa, gave a whimper and flexed her toes in her sleep. Her skin drooped between each rib. Ferdie knew how to touch Lysander's heart.

'Georgie's like that little dog,' he said gently. 'She may not have cigarette burns on her back, but she's in just as bad a way. Give it a try for a week.'

There was a long pause. Safe from the banging clays, pigeons cooed contentedly in Marigold's wood.

'Oh, OK,' said Lysander crossly.

'Come and have a look at the cottage I've found for you,' said Marigold, 'and then we'll have some dinner.'

Magpie Cottage stood in the far side of dense woods on the edge of Larry's land. Approached from the road by a rough cart-track, its front garden consisted of neat squares of lawn bordered by iceberg roses. Pink rambler roses and purple clematis swarmed over the door. Inside there was a kitchen, a dining room and drawing room knocked through and two bedrooms upstairs. Out at the back was another little lawn, a scented flower-bed filled with white stocks, pinks and tobacco plants, a pond and a white bench under a walnut tree. A four-acre field filled with dog daisies and red sorrel curved round the house and garden like a magnet.

'It's seriously nice. Arthur'll love it,' said Lysander, who had cheered up. 'He's so nosy he'll be able to put his head in through all the downstairs windows.'

'It'll need a few pennies spending on it,' admitted Marigold.

'Judging by the smell a few pennies have been spent in it already,' said Ferdie.

'A keeper had it,' explained Marigold, 'hence the pong of ferret. Ay'll get it painted and cleaned up and you'll need a cooker. Would you prefer gas or electricity?'

'Basically I don't cook,' said Lysander, 'but gas is better for lighting cigarettes.'

'You will keep the garden taydy, won't you, Lysander? Paradayse has won the Best-Kept Village award ten years runnin'.'

Marigold worked fast furnishing the cottage with, among other things, a large brass four-poster, blue-ticking sofas and chairs and a big wooden bishop's chair she'd found in a jumble sale. Eight days later, Lysander, Arthur, Jack, Tiny and little Maggie moved in. Loot from grateful wives now included six polo ponies which Lysander was keeping over at Ricky France-Lynch's yard at Eldercombe and Mrs Gunn's promised yacht which Ferdie had already swapped for a new soft-top dark blue Ferrari. He felt it was important for people to be able to see Lysander driving round Paradise and, besides, he wanted to appropriate the red Ferrari himself.

After moving in, he and Lysander went out to The Heavenly Host where they dined outside under the stars in the buddleia-scented dusk. Taking off his jacket Ferdie noticed Lysander's post which he'd left in his inside pocket.

'I forgot to give you these. Fan mail still coming in for Arthur and three letters from your father.'

'I don't want to see Dad. He was so horrible last time.'

'Well, at least open the one from your bank.' Ferdie chucked a thick white envelope across the red-check tablecloth.

'Are you determined to ruin my dinner? Gregor and I lost a hell of a lot of money in the casino at Palma. If only you'd let me come home straight away.'

'Open it,' said Ferdie, 'I promise you'll be pleasantly surprised.'

With shaking hands Lysander tore open the envelope and holding up a candle scanned the contents for a long time, his lips moving as he read, growing paler and paler.

'My God,' he whispered, 'I'm £102,000 overdrawn and

I've got to pay £750 interest. What am I going to do? The Ferrari'll have to go and the ponies and what about Arthur's vet bill? Oh Christ.'

'It's in credit, you jerk,' said Ferdie. 'And you *made* £750 in interest just last month. So you can bloody well buy *me* dinner.'

It took him several minutes to convince Lysander, who promptly suggested they went out later and blew some of it at the nearest casino.

'We will not,' said Ferdie tartly. 'I'll be fired if I don't put in some work at the office and you've got to move in first thing on Georgie. Here's the way I suggest you play it.'

28

A heavy dew silvered the parched fields. Invisible larks carolled joyously in a sky as blue as Mary's robes. However, as Lysander drew up at Angel's Reach the following morning, Georgie Maguire greeted him in a dressing gown and tears.

'I thought Guy'd left me a little love note on the kitchen table,' she sobbed, 'but when I looked it just said: *Don't forget the dustbins*. And even worse he's written Julia's number, without her name of course, on the inside of his Parish Council file.'

She waved a buff folder. 'I felt so miserable I've written *Cuckoo* beside it in biro, and now I can't rub it out.'

'*Pas de problème*.' Taking the folder, Lysander tore off the corner with Julia's number and chucked it in the bin.

'Guy will notice that even more,' said Georgie aghast.

'Say it's mice, or better still, moths. The waitress at The Heavenly Host says there is a plague of moths because of the drought.'

'There aren't any clothes for them to eat because they've all gone to Marigold's Nearly New Stall,' said Georgie, but she stopped crying.

'Go and have a nice long bath and get dressed,' said Lysander, dumping several carrier bags on the kitchen table. 'I'm going to make you porridge for breakfast. No, I promise it's delicious, with cream and treacle, and then croissants with black-cherry jam.'

'D'you know how to make porridge?' asked Georgie.

'I've made enough bran mashes in my life. You just read the directions. Then I'm going to take you to meet Arthur and then we'll have lunch at The Pearly Gates to get people gossiping and then go shopping for lots of glamorous clothes. Bath's better than Rutminster. Oh look, there's a little green van going up Marigold's drive.'

'That van goes to all the big houses in Paradise every Monday,' said Georgie sadly. 'It takes away old plants and replaces them with shiny new ones with flowers. They ought to do the same with wives.'

'Now, now,' reproved Lysander. 'You've got to stop sniping and cheer up.'

The ice was broken by Lysander reading all the directions wrong and making porridge so thick the spoon set in it like cement – so they had three croissants each and gave the porridge to Arthur. When they returned much later in the day they discovered that the video that Lysander'd thought was a jolly musical turned out to be an incredibly blue movie about rent boys.

As a result Lysander sat through the entire video in mounting horror with his T-shirt neck pulled up over his eyes, only lowering it occasionally when Georgie, in fits of laughter, said it was safe to look or when he wanted another drag at his joint.

'I really like gays,' he kept saying in bewilderment. 'Who would have thought my friend Gregor could do things like that? I'm sorry, Georgie.'

He's still only a child, thought Georgie, but certainly a very endearing one.

When Guy returned on Friday he was relieved to find the house a lot tidier and flowers in the downstairs rooms – but no little posy to welcome him in his dressing room. Nor any whisky, nor dinner on, nor any sign of Georgie. Usually the sniping started as he crossed the threshold. When she drifted down the backstairs from her study half an hour later she looked noticeably better, as though an iron had smoothed out her face.

'What are *you* doing here?' she asked in amazement.

'I usually come home on Friday,' said Guy nettled.

'Is it Friday? I didn't realize. O God, I haven't done anything for supper.'

'Work must be going well!' Guy was nonplussed. Coming home had recently been like being parachuted into an effing mine field.

Next morning Georgie rose early insisting she must walk a surprised and intensely irritated Dinsdale before it grew too hot. She put on a new and becoming T-shirt, and lots of lipstick and scent before she left, then stayed away for two hours reading *Billboard* and *The Face* under a chestnut tree. On the way home she carefully removed her lipstick with a Kleenex and rubbed into Dinsdale's fur some of Lysander's Eau Sauvage, which they'd hidden in an oak tree on the edge of the wood. This made her giggle so much she walked into the house looking happy for the first time in months.

Returning from a Sunday afternoon trip to get more petrol for the mower and ring Julia, Guy was disconcerted to find a note from Georgie: *Just popped down to The Apple Tree to get some milk.*

'You've lived here for over four months,' reproved Guy when she returned an hour later, 'and you hadn't realized The Apple Tree is shut on Sunday afternoon. They have to have some time off.'

'Aren't I stupid?' said Georgie blithely.

'And we've got plenty of milk.' Opening the fridge door, Guy confronted her with a regiment of white bottles.

'I must be going senile.'

On Sunday night Guy, who was getting edgy, heard Georgie singing 'Stranger in Paradise' in her bath. Christ, the whole village must be able to hear that raw, thrilling, yelping voice ringing round the valley. Georgie hadn't sung in her bath since Julia came down.

One of the great set-backs to Guy's amorous career had been having to sell the BMW to appease the bank and other creditors. Going to the station in a battered

Golf which had no air-conditioning didn't have the same kudos and the loss of his car telephone had really clipped Cupid's wings. At least he'd got a phone card with his own personal number so he could put any calls made from telephone boxes or from home on the gallery number. The new monitoring of calls was an awful bore.

He and Julia had made plans to travel up to London together the following morning, but it would mean him getting a later train than usual because Julia's babysitter couldn't reach her until half-past eight. Terrified of rousing suspicion he waited until Georgie emerged pink and reeking of Floris from her bath before announcing that he intended catching the nine o'clock train instead of the seven.

After a perceptible pause, Georgie said: 'I wouldn't. At least you'll get a seat on the seven. The nine's packed out on a Monday.'

'At least it gives me another hour in bed with you,' said Guy gallantly.

Thinking how much better Georgie looked as she slithered into her cream satin nightdress and climbed into bed, Guy edged up and slid a hand round her left breast. Feeling his cock stiffening, drowsy from a Mogadon taken half an hour ago, Georgie curled up like an armadillo, elbows on her hip bones, knees up to her wrists, shutting him out.

'Night, darling,' she murmured and was asleep.

Going into the bathroom next morning, after a sweatily sleepless night trying to suppress that churning guilty excitement which overwhelmed him whenever he was going to see Julia, Guy was brought up by a rim of fox-brown hairs round the bath. Why the hell was Georgie shaving her legs to write songs up in her turret? After bathing and dressing at lightning speed, a skill learnt through adultery, Guy tracked Georgie down in another bathroom. Thinking how vulnerable she looked with her water-darkened hair streaming away from her thin white neck and far-too-bumpy backbone, he asked her what on earth she was washing her hair for.

'Radio Paradise are coming to interview me at eleven.'

'Their two hundred listeners aren't going to see you.'

'No, but the interviewer will. I hate having dirty hair.'

Not for me, you don't, thought Guy. 'Well, I'd better go.'

'OK, see you Friday,' said Georgie, aiming the shower at her right temple to shift all the scurf.

Bewildered not to be clung to and exhorted to ring soon, or even made a cup of coffee, Guy had just gone into the utility room to get some Fairy Liquid soap and toothpaste for the flat over the gallery when the telephone rang in the kitchen. But when he picked it up and said, 'Hallo', it was promptly dropped at the other end. Having no idea that it was actually a dripping Georgie ringing him from her private line up in her study, Guy was even more rattled, which was what she had intended. Whoever had rung must have expected him to have left for the seven o'clock by now and meant to catch Georgie.

After an irksome week when he could hardly get Georgie on the telephone, he decided to catch her out by getting back earlier and was rewarded by having to stand all the way down in appalling heat, crushed against a woman who'd bought kippers for tea. Reaching home, sticky and bad-tempered, he found a dark blue soft-top Ferrari with A DOG IS FOR LIFE . . . NOT JUST FOR CHRISTMAS sticker on the windscreen parked outside the front door, at a contemptuous angle as though the owner had been in a frantic hurry to get inside. Despite its sleek exterior the car inside was a tip of tapes, race cards, chewed trainers, old copies of the *Sun*, cigarette ash, Coke cans and polo balls.

On the terrace Guy found a very suntanned, incredibly good-looking youth who looked vaguely familiar. Light brown curls clung to his smooth brown forehead and a black shirt to his marvellously elongated body. Georgie, who was totally transformed in a clinging leotard, which had just come into fashion and which flowed emerald-green into white-and-green flared trousers, was gazing into his eyes as though she'd like to be clinging to him as well. Her white ankles had turned a lovely gold and her toenails were painted softest coral. A shaggy, reddy-brown puppy lay between her thighs, and a half-full jug of Pimm's stood between her and the beautiful youth. Dinsdale thumped his tail but didn't rise; only a beady-looking Jack Russell went into a possessive frenzy of yapping.

It is my fucking house, thought Guy as Larry had done six months before.

'Hi, darling,' said Georgie happily. 'D'you remember Marigold's friend Lysander Hawkley? He came to the launching of "Rock Star".'

Resisting kicking Jack in the ribs, Guy became extremely hearty and, after discovering Lysander had moved into the area, said: 'You must meet my daughter, *our* daughter, Flora. You're about the same age. She's coming home this evening, isn't she?' he added to Georgie. 'She's been staying in Cornwall.'

'I'm expecting her to ring from the station any minute,' said Georgie.

'D'you want a drink – er – sir?' Lysander got to his feet. 'Shall I get another glass?'

Guy was not amused, by the slightly piss-taking 'sir', nor by the strength of the Pimm's when Lysander filled all their glasses.

'Been playing at the Rutshire?' asked Guy, looking at his dirty white breeches and bare feet.

Lysander nodded.

'Got any ponies?'

'Six,' said Lysander. 'I'm keeping them at Ricky France-Lynch's at Eldercombe. I've just been playing practice chukkas there.'

Guy flickered. Ricky France-Lynch's wife was a painter and a friend of Julia's. They pushed prams together. It was the sort of connection that might suddenly push Georgie into orbit.

'How was dinner with Larry?' asked Georgie idly, thinking how hot, middle-aged and crumpled Guy looked beside Lysander.

Guy flickered again. 'He cancelled.'

'What did you do instead?' demanded Georgie, suddenly feeling desperately insecure.

Gently Lysander's foot nudged her ankle. Ferdie's instructions were to be totally detached and never interrogate. But Guy was distracted by a huge emerald glittering on Georgie's newly manicured right hand.

'Isn't it lovely?' agreed Georgie dreamily. 'I liked it so much, I decided to buy it with my royalty cheque.'

Maggie the puppy wriggled to be put down. Already plumper, sleeker and gaining in confidence after a fortnight of human food and sleeping on Lysander's bed, she pounced on a yellow leaf from the dying wych-elm and, bounding up to Dinsdale, started swinging on his ginger ears. Raising a prehensile paw Dinsdale sent her flying. Covered in dust she righted herself, then seeing Charity emerge from the long bleached grass on the side of the lawn, took off after her.

'Magg-ee,' shouted Lysander.

'Named after Thatcher,' mocked Guy, who regarded himself as a champagne socialist.

'No, Maggie Tulliver in *The Mill on the Floss*,' said Lysander with all the authority of one who has reached page four.

Guy was fazed. An Adonis who read! Georgie had always been an intellectual snob. He was dying for a pee and a change into something cooler, but he was loath to leave these two together.

'Doing anything exciting this weekend?' Georgie asked Lysander, removing a rose petal from his hair.

'Playing cricket for the village on Sunday.'

'Oh really.' Guy perked up at a challenge. 'We're on opposing sides, I'm playing for Rannaldini.'

Lysander drained his glass. 'You play a lot?'

'Whenever work allows,' said Guy. 'I played for my old school and for Cambridge and the Free Foresters. What about you?'

'I haven't played since school. Georgie, I must go.'

'I'll get you a bag so you can take the Pimm's fruit for Arthur,' said Georgie. 'Lysander's horse,' she added to Guy. 'He's such a duck. Lysander's determined to get him fit for the Rutminster Gold Cup next spring.'

Standing up to hasten Lysander's departure, Guy suddenly noticed several holes in his beloved lawn.

'My God! Who did that?'

'I think Dinsdale's been trying to reach Melanie in Australia,' said Georgie.

Next minute Maggie shot round the corner with a regale lily corm plus plant in her mouth, pursued by a panting Jack and Dinsdale.

Grinning, Lysander bent to kiss Georgie goodbye. 'Thanks for the drink,' then lowered his voice, 'and remember be happy and distant and no sniping.'

'Oh, there's Rannaldini's helicopter returning,' said Georgie, as the great black crow landed on the other side of the wood.

Guy's temper was not improved when Flora sauntered into the house twenty minutes later wearing nothing but flip-flops and a ravishing shirt in Prussian-blue silk over bikini bottoms.

'Darling, you were going to ring from the station,' said Georgie, hugging her.

'I got a lift. Grania's father was driving up to London.'

'How was Cornwall?' asked Guy. 'You didn't get brown.'

'Too hot to sunbathe,' said Flora, who'd spent most of last week in Rannaldini's bedroom in his villa outside Rome.

'Lovely shirt,' said Georgie enviously.

'Grania's,' lied Flora who, as a leaving present, had been taken to Pucci.

'You're always nicking people's things,' exploded Guy finding a genuine outlet for his irritation over Lysander. 'Where the hell's my Free Forester's sweater?'

'How should I know?'

'You had it last at that dinner party—' Guy stopped as he remembered the occasion.

'When Julia Armstrong was the guest of dishonour,' said Georgie. Oh hell, she wasn't supposed to snipe.

'I gave it back the next day,' protested Flora.

'You did not,' spluttered Guy. 'I'm playing cricket on Sunday, and I need it.'

'No-one needs a sweater in this heat.'

'After one has been making a lot of runs, or bowling, it's easy to catch a chill.'

'Borrow my pink shawl,' said Flora kindly. 'I'm not stuffy about lending things.'

Guy found that Lysander's wide, untroubled smile like the Cheshire Cat seemed to linger unnervingly after he'd gone. He was further rattled by two dropped telephone calls which he'd no idea were Rannaldini, still in Rome, hoping to get Flora. Then he realized it would be too late for him to ring Julia. Ben would be home from London by now.

29

Rannaldini himself did not play cricket. An awkward ball on the hand could put him out of conducting for weeks, but he liked occasionally to distribute largesse to the village and flew in just before the match on Sunday to find that Kitty had been slaving all night preparing a magnificent tea and Bob Harefield had conjured up a formidable side consisting mostly of London Met musicians bussed down from London. These included a cellist who was a demon bowler and the horn player Rannaldini had sacked last March, who'd been hastily reinstated because he was a brilliant bat. Although the side would miss Wolfgang and his centuries, lustre had been added by Bob himself, who was a characteristically reliable wicket-keeper, Larry, who hadn't been tested but who boasted a trial for Surrey, and Guy, who was by all accounts a class player. Other London Met musicians would spend the afternoon playing in the blue-and-white bandstand right of the pavilion.

Having wandered around finding fault with everything and ensuring none of his orchestra had more than one glass of wine at lunch, Rannaldini stalked upstairs to change.

The villagers were already streaming in by car or on foot. They liked to gawp at Valhalla, jump the Devil's Lair, which had dropped two feet since Flora's leap, get lost in the maze and marvel at Rannaldini's famous all-delphinium bed whose blue spires seemed to touch the sky. Taking up position round the field, perched on car bonnets before they grew too hot, the men opened beer cans and the prettier girls stripped down to their bikinis in the hope that Rannaldini might claim droit de seigneur.

Of all the players Guy was the most anxious to make his mark. Determined to upstage Lysander, he also wanted to get on to the village cricket-club committee which would give him an excuse both to do good and to get out and ring Julia. He'd already joined the local Labour Party, the Parish Council and the Best-Kept Village committee.

His plans to ring Julia on the way to the match, however, were scuppered by Flora, who was desperate to see Rannaldini after a twenty-four hour absence, cadging a lift.

'I'll drive,' she announced with all the assurance of one who had been manoeuvring Rannaldini's Mercedes round Rome.

'You will not!' Guy snatched off the L-plates. 'I'm not risking our only car. Where's Mummy?'

'Working. She's coming later.'

Suddenly Guy had a feeling Georgie might be lingering to hear from Lysander. His worst fears were confirmed as he parked on the edge of the pitch and Natasha immediately joined them. Very tanned and wearing a sloppy black T-shirt and white shorts, which showed off her long slender legs, she looked unusually pretty and Guy told her so.

'Why, thank you, Mr Seymour. How was Cornwall?' she added to Flora.

'Brilliant. Christ, look at that.'

Following Flora's gaze, Natasha saw Lysander lounging against his blue Ferrari with a telephone glued to his ear and a Jack Russell and a shaggy reddy-brown puppy to each ankle. He was wearing his: SEX IS EVIL, EVIL IS SIN T-shirt.

'We're about to field,' he was saying, 'or I'd come over. Miss you too. You coming over? Or shall I nip over when he's in the field? Right. See you later.'

He's ringing Georgie, thought Guy furiously.

'Blimey, who's that?' said Natasha in awe, as Lysander stripped off his T-shirt to show a dark bronzed back, still a little ribby from seasickness, before he plunged into his cricket shirt.

Next minute Ferdie had roared up in Lysander's red Ferrari looking Mafiaesque in a white panama and dark glasses to oversee operations.

'Afternoon, Lysander,' called Guy. 'Remember I told you about Flora? Well, here she is with her friend Natasha.'

'Hi!' Lysander turned round from greeting Ferdie and over the din of Jack and Maggie's excited yapping introduced his mate.

'Lysander's taken Magpie Cottage just across the valley for the polo season,' Guy told the gaping Flora and Natasha, 'so I hope you young people get together.'

And bloody well stop pestering my wife, was the unmistakable implication as Guy strode off to the pavilion to find out the batting order.

Natasha had had a miserable few weeks. Aware of Rannaldini's increasing neglect, she had expected to go abroad backpacking with Flora during the holidays when Flora had suddenly dropped out. Natasha's mother was totally wrapped up in her new lover and her younger children. Bewildered, starved of affection, she gazed into Lysander's smiling untroubled face and thought he was the best- and kindest-looking boy she had ever seen. For the first time in weeks she removed her sloppy black T-shirt to reveal an orange camisole top which left her splendid suntanned breasts to their own devices.

'Can I look after this adorable puppy?' she said, scooping up a startled Maggie.

'That's really kind, as long as you keep her in the shade,' said Lysander. 'Keep an eye on Jack,' he added to Ferdie. 'He's rabbit-mad and they're moving so slowly – must be myxomatosis – he keeps catching the poor little things.'

'Some things like to be caught.' Natasha threw Lysander a trapping look, then, smiling at Ferdie, who was getting a picnic basket out of the Ferrari, 'Do come and watch with us.'

She had already noticed that Ferdie was red faced and sweaty beneath his dark glasses and panama and that, beneath his loose Hawaiian shirt, spare tyres billowed over his straining jeans, but she had enough of her father's manipulative nature to realize that a way to Lysander would be through his friend.

'Five minutes, Lysander,' shouted Paradise's captain, Michael Prescott. Landlord of The Pearly Gates and predictably nicknamed 'Archangel Mike', he had become great buddies with Lysander since he moved into Paradise.

'How did you and Lysander meet?' Natasha asked Ferdie.

'At school.' Kneeling down to lace up Lysander's other cricket boot, Ferdie murmured, 'How's it going?'

'OK. Guy's uptight, but Georgie keeps blowing it by showing how hurt she is.'

'Here comes another of your enemies,' said Ferdie as a large purple and yellow striped helicopter caused a ripple of interest as it landed by the pitch and out jumped Larry Lockton, jewellery flashing in the increasingly hot sun.

'If you come at me hostile I'll fight you all the way,' he was yelling into his mobile.

'Get padded up, Larry,' called Bob, who was opening the batting with the reinstated horn player. 'I've put you at number four.'

On his way to the pavilion, Larry bumped into Rannaldini who'd just emerged from the house.

'Who's that boy by the blue Ferrari?' asked Rannaldini, who knew perfectly well – his spies were everywhere – but who wanted to goad Larry.

Seeing Lysander for the first time, Larry snarled with rage.

'Got some poncy name like Alexander Harley. For some reason Marigold's let Magpie Cottage to him.'

In the old days Larry would never have allowed such a thing, but since his affair with Nikki he had less clout.

'Extremely glamorous,' remarked Rannaldini. No wonder Larry had been rattled.

Nodding to acquaintances, but not stopping, Rannaldini wandered over to the group round the Ferraris, which now included a slavering Ideal Homo wearing pale blue shorts and a little white sunhat.

'Papa,' Natasha hugged him joyfully, 'you must meet Lysander.'

While Flora had slept off their sexual excesses in Rome, Rannaldini had studied scores, dictated letters and even held auditions on the balcony of his Roman villa. A tan as dark as treacle toffee was now enhanced by a white suit of such impeccable cut and panache that it instantly set him apart from the crowd both as host and warlord of the manor. Lysander gave a sigh of pure wonder. Prepared to detest Rannaldini, he hadn't counted on such charisma or blazing vitality. He'd never met anyone as smooth or as sexy.

'That is the sharpest suit,' he stammered, 'where did you get it?'

'Some back street in Singapore,' said Rannaldini with a smile which softened the glittering, deadly nightshade eyes.

God, the boy was heartbreaking close up. With a competitive surge of excitement, Rannaldini wondered if Flora had fallen under Lysander's spell and ignored her, nodding on the other hand to Ferdie and the Ideal Homo, who said: 'I agree with Lysander. That suit is to die for.'

'Better watch out you're not run over by a snowplough,' mocked Flora, determined to disguise her longing.

'Where's Kitty?' asked Lysander.

'Organizing tea.'

'Doesn't she get to watch?' demanded Flora disapprovingly.

'Kitty doesn't understand cricket,' said Rannaldini.

'Didn't go to that kind of school,' added Natasha bitchily.

The umpires, Mr Brimscombe and Rannaldini's dog handler, Clive, neither of whom were paid to be impartial, were leading the players on to the field when Lysander was sent flying by two blond bullets, Marigold's sons. Jason was wearing a T-shirt saying: *I'm afraid of no-one in the world except my Dad*. Markie was carrying a cricket bat almost bigger than himself.

'We've got *Rocky IV* at home. Will you come and watch it after the match and will you bowl to us?' asked Jason.

'Wait till the tea interval.' Lysander tucked his billowing shirt into his white trousers. 'I've got to field. How was going back last term?'

'Fine,' said Markie. 'Mummy cried so much, I felt I should cry too, but only to make her feel better. How's Arfur?'

'Come and see him. He likes your father's grazing.'

'Come *on*, Lysander,' yelled the Archangel Mike.

He's sweet with kids as well, thought Natasha as Lysander loped on to a pitch as emerald-green due to illicit sprinkling as Georgie's new leotard which Flora was now wearing.

In the bandstand, sweating members of the London Met sawed their way through the *Trout Quintet*, wishing they, too, were under water. The group round the Ferrari were now joined by Marigold, who'd been working the crowd touting for the church fête.

She was feeling low because the jeans she and Lysander had bought in February were now within three inches of doing up. Telling herself they would have been too hot was no help at all.

'How's it going?' she whispered, accepting a glass of Ferdie's champagne.

'Not as well as you and Larry,' whispered Ferdie, 'but watch out for fireworks this afternoon.'

'I hope you girls are going to help at the church fête,' said Marigold.

'I'll be abroad,' said Flora hastily.

'So will I,' said Natasha.

'Shame. And I thought you could decorate a room for free, Meredith.' Marigold turned to the Ideal Homo. 'It would make a lovely raffle prize.'

'It would not,' said Meredith huffily. 'There's a recession on, dearie, if you hadn't noticed.'

Having met Lysander, he was not going to forgive Marigold for not calling him in to redecorate Magpie Cottage. 'Talk about the reincarnation of the Paradise Lad,' he muttered to Flora as he parked his small bottom beside hers on the bonnet of Ferdie's Ferrari.

The wine waiter of The Heavenly Host opened the bowling. Squaring his shoulders Bob hit him for four.

'Oh, well clouted,' said Marigold, who got very hearty on such occasions. 'Don't eat all Ferdie's Jaffa cakes, boys.'

'Is Hermione here?' asked Flora, who wanted to suss out the opposition.

'No, thank God,' shuddered Meredith. 'She's playing *Salome* in New York. When she gets to the seventh veil the entire audience rears up and yells: ' "No, no, keep it on!" '

As Rannaldini was now well out of earshot, everyone howled with laughter.

'Must be bliss for Bob having her away,' said Marigold.

'Bliss! Bobby's got a good body, hasn't he? Oh, well hit, that'll be a six.'

'Bob *is* nice looking actually,' admitted Flora. 'Pity he's losing his hair.'

'He's just receding to match the recession. Bobby's always been trendy,' giggled Meredith. 'Oh, good shot,' as Bob snaked a single past first slip. 'This is going to be a rout. Poor Paradise, more like Inferno in this weather.'

It was getting hotter. A silver haze writhed above the pitch. A sweep of mauve willow herb wilted beneath the smouldering ash-grey woods which bordered the ground. Birds, exhausted with feeding their young, were mute. Ferdie, running with sweat, wished he was thin enough to remove his shirt and get brown like all the other blokes. He couldn't take his eyes off Natasha – he'd never seen anyone so pretty. Full of patter normally, he was suddenly so shy he could only fill her glass and ply her with cherries as dark red and shiny as her lips.

A hundred for no wicket. The village were getting tetchy. They'd hoped for a glimpse of Georgie, who'd been singularly elusive since she'd moved in. Rumours of marriage problems, spread by Mother Courage, were circulating faster than greyhounds on a track. Guy, however, was much in evidence, looking very cheerful. Batting only at number seven, rather to his irritation, he was now being sweet to the wives of the fielding Paradise players, admiring their tans and their babies, making a manly show of reluctance when asked to sign autographs, intimating that he hoped to be playing for Paradise this time next year.

By contrast, Larry, who was going in at number three, was sitting in the shade furiously shaking *The Sunday Times* Business section. He'd run out of people to shout at on the telephone and it didn't look as though this stupid opening partnership would ever get out. He was livid to see Mr Brimscombe umpiring – the Judas. After the massacre of the honeysuckle round Flora's bedroom, Mr Brimscombe had been tempted to return to his old boss, but had decided that Larry was a bad-tempered bugger. The Paradise Pearl cutting had taken in Rannaldini's conservatory and the promise of a fat rise and an even taller mower from which he could look over the hedge at Natasha sunbathing topless by the pool had persuaded him to stay on.

The situation was getting desperate, a flustered Paradise had started dropping catches. Lysander's supporters had moved back into the shade under the mulberry trees and, when he was sent to field on the boundary near them, barracked him because his side was doing so badly.

'Can you ring Ladbroke's for me?' he shouted to Ferdie. 'My card's on the dashboard. Cover Point just told me Blue Chip Baby's a cert in the 4.15. Can you put on five hundred pounds on the nose?'

In the light of his new bank balance, Lysander had considerably upped his stakes.

'Rich as well,' murmured Meredith excitedly.

'Spoof you for him,' sighed Natasha.

'Bloody stupid putting on that kind of money,' snapped Ferdie.

'You got anything to eat?' called Lysander, who'd already accepted an iced Carlsberg.

'I'll make you a sandwich.' Natasha leapt down off the bonnet. 'Would you like chicken or smoked salmon?'

Mulberries were falling on the parked cars. The crowd were melting. Bob and the horn player had put on 140.

'If someone doesn't get out soon,' grumbled Marigold, 'Larry won't get a knock.'

'God, she's pretty,' mumbled Ferdie, as Natasha sauntered on to the pitch with Lysander's sandwich.

'Quite,' said Meredith, who'd hung two pairs of cherries over his ears like earrings, 'but an awful bitch.'

Lysander, however, only had time for one bite. Things were getting so desperate that the Archangel Michael beckoned him over.

'You bowl?'

'A little.'

'Can't do worse than this lot.' Mike lobbed the ball at him. 'Wicket's harder than Rannaldini's heart. Try and keep the ball up to the bat.'

'This should be interesting,' said Ferdie, as he finished off Lysander's sandwich.

'Bowler's name,' shouted the scorer.

'Hawkley,' yelled Mike.

The crowd, particularly the women, perked up. So this was the gorgeous man who'd moved into Magpie Cottage. The London Met, bored with playing classical music, launched into 'Hey, Goodlookin'.'

Meredith waved in time with a chicken drumstick.

'Hi, Teddy!' Lysander grinned at Mr Brimscombe as he paced out his run. The two had become great mates when Lysander was sorting out Marigold. Lysander had been a nice young lad, always prepared to carry logs or dustbins, even if he couldn't mow in a straight line.

His shirt billowing out, long-legged and loose-limbed as

a West Indian, Lysander loped up to the wicket. A split second later the ball had removed Bob's middle stump. The crowd exploded in joy and relief which turned to ill-disguised mirth as Larry came in to bat. He had padding on his thighs, chest and gut and he was wearing Ian Botham gloves, Astra-turf trainers with plastic studs, a short-sleeved cricket shirt that was much too tight for him, a helmet and a face guard. His bat had never been used. Fortunately the laughter was drowned by loud applause as Bob came back with seventy-eight runs on the board.

'What sort of a ball was it?' asked Larry pompously.

'I think it was a red one.' Bob mopped his brow. 'It's like a furnace out there.'

'And here's Larry Lockton,' said the commentator, 'who, we're told, had a trial for Surrey.'

As Larry made a prolonged fuss about taking guard, Lysander walked back rubbing the ball up and down his trousers.

'Oh, to be that ball,' sighed Meredith.

Lysander's second ball hit Larry on the snow-white pad.

' 'Owzat?' howled the Paradise slips.

'Out,' intoned Mr Brimscombe to the noisy chagrin of Marigold.

'Bollocks,' bellowed Larry, mouthing like a gorilla behind his face guard.

'Out,' confirmed Clive the doghandler, who didn't like Larry any better.

'Don't think you'll ever get your fucking job back,' roared Larry as he stalked back to the pavilion.

'Must have been a trial to Surrey, rather than for them,' giggled Meredith as Marigold rushed off to give solace.

Lysander had taken a devastating five wickets for nine runs and ended his second over with London Met looking suddenly in trouble, when Guy came in. Immediately the band launched into 'Rock Star'.

'Mum is clever,' admitted Flora. 'It does sound lovely played by a proper orchestra.'

'Mr Rock Star himself,' crackled the loudspeaker. 'No mean cricketer if my spies tell me right.'

With his athlete's stride, his powerful body, his strong handsome face and arctic-blond hair glinting in the sunlight, Guy looked worthy to have pop songs dedicated to him. He wished Ju Ju was watching and where the hell was Georgie? Who could blame him being unfaithful to a woman who never gave him any support? Then, just as he was taking guard, he saw her arrive with Dinsdale, wandering round the wooded side of the pitch, past Lysander who was now fielding in the deep again. Her newly washed hair was tied back with a blue ribbon and she was wearing a duck-egg-blue shirt tied under her slender midriff and yesterday's flowered trousers.

'And if I'm not mistaken, here's Georgie Maguire herself; Mrs Rock Star's just arrived in time,' said the commentator, and the band struck up again.

Guy kicked off with a wristy single to loud applause. Then the tenor, who had the reputation for being a big hitter, blocked four balls, then clouted a six over Lysander's leaping outstretched fingers deep into the dark midgy wood behind. Next moment, Lysander, Georgie and Dinsdale, followed by a racing-up yapping Maggie and Jack, disappeared in search of it. At first the players were happy to sit down and rest, then all eyes were turned to the wood as Dinsdale emerged carrying the ball. Waddling across the pitch he proudly dropped it to shouts of laughter at his master's feet.

As the field changed over, it was Lysander's turn to bowl again and all the Paradise fielders yelled for him to come back because the ball had been found. Then everyone waited and waited and waited until, finally, a good five minutes later Lysander and Georgie came out of the wood grinning from ear to ear. Lysander was ostentatiously wiping off the remains of Georgie's peach-pink lipstick with the back of his hand and Georgie's hair had escaped the blue ribbon.

Once more the whole crowd burst out laughing and the

band struck up: *'If you go down in the woods today, you're sure of a big surprise'* at Rannaldini's instigation. Guy was shaking so much that Lysander proceeded to bowl and catch him with his first ball for only one run.

Flora had wandered over to join Rannaldini by the pavilion as Guy stormed past.

'You're a single parent now, Dad,' she called out. 'As Lysander was being free in the forest with Mum, he should wear your sweater.'

Rannaldini's eyes sparkled with evil amusement.

Poor Guy was absolutely livid. Never had he needed his green-and-magenta sweater as a badge of former achievement more. A reporter from the *Rutminster News* who'd witnessed the whole scene wondered if it would be an idea to ring Dempster about the rocking of Rock Star. Larry had suddenly cheered up hugely.

'Your toy boy seems to have transferred his affections to Georgie,' he told Marigold nastily.

'Pity Wolfie's not here to make some runs for you,' Flora murmured to Rannaldini. 'Aren't you sorry now you pinched his girlfriend?'

'It was worth eet. Have you missed me a leetle?'

'No,' said Flora, then, looking up at him from under her thick eyelashes, 'I missed you a lot.'

'Once the London Met and your father are safely in the field we can slope off to the tower, Tabloid will keep watch.'

30

London Met was all out for 160 followed by tea in the great hall which was blissfully cool. White tablecloths had been laid over big oak tables. Huge vasefuls of red-hot pokers and early scarlet dahlias flamed like beacons in each corner. Kitty had provided a wonderful tea. Her sandwiches, made of smoked salmon, prawns swimming in real mayonnaise, scrambled eggs filled with herbs and the most delicate turkey breast, contained more filling than bread. There were also homemade scones to eat with mulberry jam and clotted cream, walnut, lemon and chocolate cakes, beautifully decorated on top and groaning with butter icing inside and a huge rainbow cake on whose white icing she had piped in blue: LONDON MET v. PARADISE 1990. Everything had been done to please Rannaldini. It was a pity that because of the heat more praising went on than eating.

'I can't go in there,' whimpered Georgie, who'd already been mobbed by autograph hunters, as she saw the crowds milling in the great hall. 'Guy's about to murder me for disappearing.'

'I'll stay with you the whole time,' said Lysander soothingly. 'Actually, I'm bloody hungry. Very Gothic this house, isn't it?'

Nor could the heat of hellfire put Percival Hillary, the vicar of All Saints, Paradise, off his grub. A consummate cadger of other people's food and drink, with a fish face redder than Ferdie's Ferrari and breath that could crack a safe at fifty yards, he was now piling his plate with sandwiches and crying in a fluting voice: 'What a wonderful, wonderful spread.'

'What a feast,' cried his wife Joy, who was always described as a 'tower of strength'. A bosomless chatterbox with a ringing laugh, she spent her time bullying the unwilling into charity work and hovering round Paradise flushing out lapses of behaviour like Milton's God.

'I always feel I should wear my fig-leaf outside my shorts when Joy's about,' grumbled Meredith.

It was a running battle between Joy, Marigold and Lady Chisleden who actually ran Paradise. Despite her high moral tone, however, Joy Hillary shared her husband's weakness for good-looking men and was potty about Guy. Guy was only prepared to be buttonholed by her for so long. Yanking Georgie from Lysander's side, hissing, 'How *dare* you show me up in front of the whole of Paradise,' he shoved her at Joy Hillary.

'Joyful, my dear, I'd like you to meet my wife, Georgie.'

A staunch vegetarian, who was systematically opening and casting aside sandwiches which contained meat, eggs or fish, Joy told Georgie that she'd just been saying to Guy that she couldn't understand why there were so many wild oats about this year.

'Symbolic of the times,' said Georgie bleakly and, when Joy Hillary looked blank, 'Men can't resist sowing them.'

'No-one sowed them,' said Joy patiently. 'The field behind us has been sprayed for twenty years, but we've still got wild oats.'

'At least it's better than that ghastly rape,' said her husband Percival, coming over on the pretext of introducing himself, but actually to cut a huge slice out of Kitty's utterly delectable chocolate cake. Alas, he was just about to plunge in the knife when Dinsdale lifted his big mournful face on to the table, and sucked in the entire cake.

Georgie burst out laughing. Then, seeing their horrified deprived faces: 'I better absent myself from the scene of the crime and go and congratulate Kitty.'

       ★   ★   ★

Even in her current state of self-absorption, Georgie was appalled by Kitty's appearance. She'd put on weight and her reddened eyes gazed into space as she filled cup after cup from a huge brown teapot. She was always quiet when Rannaldini was around, but she seemed to have lost all her warmth and her interest in other people. She didn't even smile over the story of Dinsdale's pilfering the chocolate cake and when Georgie ducked under the table to stand beside her and thank her for letting Flora spend so much time at Valhalla, Kitty said nothing, just lowered her eyes.

'You OK, Kitty? You're shaking.'

'I'm fine.'

How could she tell Georgie that her daughter was having a raging affaire with Rannaldini? A month ago, when poor Wolfie had sobbed all night like the Paradise Lad, Kitty had steeled herself to tell Rannaldini that he shouldn't pinch his son's girlfriend, particularly when she was thirty years his junior and still an impressionable child. Whereupon Rannaldini had launched into one of his petrifying tirades, screaming that Wolfie was an insanely jealous, paranoid fantasist who had to make up stories to justify Flora falling out of love with him and how *dare* Kitty virtually accuse him of child molesting.

He had punished her ever since by withdrawing all affection and Kitty was nearly at breaking-point. Almost worst of all, she had previously hero-worshipped Flora for sticking up for her so often, but in the end Flora had not just taken her part but her husband from her as well.

And now Kitty had spilt tea all over the snow-white tablecloth because Rannaldini and Flora were approaching. Flora, in fact, was starving. Georgie didn't feed her family much and it was a long time since breakfast.

'Hi, Kitty,' she said in delight. 'How *are* you?'

'OK.' Kitty spilled even more tea.

'Here, let me take that, Brickie.' Guy seized the teapot as though it was a large fractious baby Kitty couldn't quiet. 'I'll fill the cups. You chat to Flora.'

'I'll just get more 'ot water.' Frantically, Kitty seized a big silver jug. ' 'Ave a sandwich.' She shoved a plate at Flora.

'Oh yum, I'm so hungry,' cried Flora, then found that suddenly she wasn't, because fat, hopeless, red-eyed defeated Kitty looked absolutely wretched and couldn't even meet her eyes.

She knows about us, thought Flora in horror. And Kitty had been so sweet to her. But as she felt Rannaldini just behind her, surreptitiously caressing the bare sweating insides of her thighs, such was her longing, she couldn't stop herself pressing back against him.

'Rannaldini's little wife's done so well,' said Joy Hillary, taking a third piece of walnut cake. 'We must utilize her properly at the fête. Perhaps we should take her off bric-à-brac and put her in charge of teas.'

As Kitty bolted down the dark passages to the kitchen, Lysander, leaning nonchalantly on a suit of armour, blocked her path.

'D'you remember me? We met at Marigold's and at the *Rock Star* party. Here, let me take that jug. Stunning tea. I've stuffed myself so much I won't be able to bat. My mother hated doing cricket teas. She never produced more than a bought cake and curling Marmite sandwiches.'

He found it a relief to mention Pippa, even in a faintly derogatory fashion, and to find that it didn't hurt so much.

Kitty raised her eyes. The terribly strong spectacles magnified the inflamed lids and the red-threaded eyes grotesquely. God, she looked unhappy.

'Marigold told me about your muvver,' she stammered. 'She was so young. You must miss her somefink awful.'

Lysander, who often picked up vibes others missed, had noticed Rannaldini touching up Georgie's sexy-looking daughter. What chance did Kitty have? Rannaldini was a shit, after all, he decided, as he carried the jug of boiling water back to the hall.

Natasha, who couldn't imagine what Lysander could have to say to her boring stepmother, charged up with Ferdie, whom Lysander introduced to Kitty. Ferdie and Kitty might do rather well together, decided Lysander. Before they had time to find out, Guy had butted in with a plate of sliced rainbow cake.

'You must eat something yourself, Brickie.'

'Why d'you call her that?' asked Natasha.

'Because she's an absolute brick,' said Guy warmly.

'How many bricks are there in a tower of strength?' asked Georgie, earning herself a dirty look from Guy as she joined the group.

'We'll be eating this stuff for weeks,' Rannaldini told his wife as he glared at the still-loaded tables. People were lighting cigarettes and drifting back to the pitch. 'You've over-catered as usual, Kitty.'

'It'll all go,' snapped Lysander. 'I'll come and help you wash up, Kitty. It's nice and cool in here.'

'Lysander,' called out Marigold, 'you were going to bowl to the boys.'

'You're bloody not,' hissed Ferdie. 'You're being paid to rattle Guy. Stick to Georgie.'

But as soon as Lysander had sat down beside Georgie on a bench under a chestnut tree, the Archangel Mike ordered him to pad up and open the batting. Instantly his seat was taken by Larry whom Georgie had been avoiding all afternoon.

'How's the album coming on?'

'OK.'

'Guy said it was going really well and you might deliver early.'

'Pigs might fly,' snapped Georgie.

'My guess is that things are rough at the gallery,' said Larry, 'and you should help out by finishing as soon as possible. Guy's always looked after you in the past, Georgie.'

'It's a conspiracy. I'm being forced to rush things,' cried Georgie hysterically. 'Guy put you up to this over dinner.'

'Guy cancelled,' announced Larry. 'He had too much on.'

Georgie started to shake. In a sentence Larry had chucked her into the pits.

'You're psyching yourself into this block,' he went on bullyingly. 'All we want is something warm, sincere and happy, that kids and older folk can relate to. Just like "Rock Star".'

'I wrote "Rock Star" when I was happy,' hissed Georgie. 'How can I be warm, loving and sincere when my heart's breaking and my world's fallen apart?'

Taking the field, Guy noticed Georgie leaping up and sending a deck-chair flying as she stumbled away from Larry. Christ, he hoped Larry hadn't mentioned his cancelling dinner. He should have warned him, but, as a bishop's son, he found it tacky saying: 'Could you possibly tell Georgie it was you who ducked out?'

'Could you possibly donate half a dozen signed copies of *Rock Star* to the fête as prizes?' Joy Hillary met Georgie head on.

'No, I fucking can't,' screamed Georgie. 'Contrary to what you might think, I don't get my own albums free and I don't get the full whack every time a record is sold. Remind me to ask your husband to hand over the entire church collection to the Musicians' Benevolent Society next Christmas. Oh look, Lysander's batting. Excuse me.' And she walked off, leaving Joy unjoyfully mouthing.

Guy's lied to me yet again, thought Georgie. What's the point of finishing an album to appease their joint bank manager when he won't give Julia up. Sod Angel's Reach, she'd rather live in a council flat with Lysander.

It was a second before she registered that the field had changed over and Guy was bowling, holding the ball in that strong right hand that had given her so much pleasure, pounding up to the crease on those strong muscular legs that had once been nightly wrapped round her. Georgie gave a wail of misery.

A moment later, as if to avenge her, Lysander had hit the ball in the air, soaring like a lark into the rippling gold wheat fields, sending the London Met Players searching among the wild oats.

Paradise were in heaven. They'd never made a decent showing against the London Met before. Soon the London Met musicians, who relied on their hands, too, for their livelihood, had moved to the outfield and Guy, Larry, Bob and the big-hitting tenor were nervously surrounding the wicket. But to no avail. Whack, whack, whack went the ball over the boundary, and each time Lysander scored runs the cheers increased until even the London Met Players abandoned themselves to the voluptuous pleasure of watching a mortal become a God.

Having played 'See the Conquering Hero Comes', the band swung into 'The British Grenadiers'.

'Some talk of Alexander and some of Hercules.

Of Hector and Lysander

And such brave men as these,' sang the hard-hitting tenor, and all the crowd, particularly the vicar, joined in the chorus.

After fifty-five minutes Paradise were 130 for no wicket. Lysander had made a century, shaken hands with the opposition players and the two umpires and waved his bat at the ecstatic crowd. Then, almost contemptuously, as though he was saying: 'Now I'm off to romp with your wife,' he hit the easiest catch in the world to a crimson-faced, dripping Guy and sauntered, grinning, back to the pavilion before Mr Brimscombe had even given him out.

The local reporter was so busy racing back to the office to re-set the huge headline: PARADISE LOST, that he forgot to ring Dempster. Guy then had to field impotently in the deep for the next forty minutes, while Paradise somewhat laboriously made the remaining runs and Lysander wandered off into the woods with Georgie, trailing dogs. Both

Georgie and Guy were far too preoccupied to notice that Flora had disappeared with Rannaldini.

'I wish Georgie Maguire hadn't left so early. I was hoping to brief her about opening the fête,' complained Percival Hillary, who was actually much more interested in getting a closer look at Lysander.

'The sun must have unhinged her,' said Joy. 'First she rudely refused to give me any *Rock Star* albums; then I approached her again and asked her most politely for some very personal item that she doesn't want any more that we could raffle and she said: "How about my husband?" and flounced off.'

'I'm sure she was joking.'

'I'm not – and when you think what a tower of strength Guy has been. I didn't take to her – and as for that dreadful thieving dog—'

31

One of the hottest Augusts of this century resulted in Paradise drying up and the fields cracking open like vast jigsaw puzzles. Even the evenings were stifling as the music of the promenade concerts drifted down the valley. On the rare occasions Rannaldini was home to listen to a prom, he criticized non-stop, measuring the applause which would certainly never be as deafening nor as long as the ecstatic tearful ovation he would receive when he conducted the London Met in Verdi's *Requiem* at the beginning of September.

As Rannaldini was now perfectly confident of Flora's affection he decided to irritate Guy and Larry and distract Natasha from his own affaire, by inviting Lysander and Ferdie to lunch on the Sunday after the cricket match. Lysander, who wanted to go to the Gatcombe horse trials, only accepted for Ferdie's sake. Not that Ferdie was making any progress with Natasha. It was plain from the way she was gazing at Lysander, as he lounged on the terrace before lunch, drinking Bloodies and laboriously reading Mystic Meg in the *News of the World*, that it was him she was after.

By comparison Ferdie looked awful. There were black rings under his normally merry, calculating brown eyes. He had several spots, his gruelling schedule allowed him no time to sunbathe or take exercise. His ankles had swelled up in the heat and his chin spilled over the collar of his Hawaiian shirt worn outside his trousers to cover his gut. His chief asset – his fast line of patter – had dried up like the Paradise streams. He could only gaze and blush.

Piggy in *Lord of the Flies*, thought Rannaldini, then letting his hand stray briefly across Lysander's flawless, brown cheek-bones, he murmured: 'I'm amazed you've got so far in life without duelling scars.'

Lunch, laid out under a spreading chestnut tree, almost made up for missing Gatcombe: spinach roulade, lobster, vast langoustine and a huge plate of oysters ferried in from Bristol that morning by Rannaldini's helicopter.

'I've never had oysters before. They look like poached dishcloth,' said Flora, as Rannaldini tipped half a dozen on to her plate, and sprinkled them with lemon juice. 'Ugh! It's like swallowing one's own phlegm.'

'An acquired taste.' Rannaldini's leg moved against hers.

On his right sat Hermione, who, with Bob, were the only wrinklies invited and who spent most of the lunch happily reading out faxes from New York of her *Salome* reviews, which, despite Meredith's sniping, had been excellent. Bob, who never ate much, spent his time cracking lobster claws and peeling langoustine for Hermione and trying to bring Ferdie, and even more Kitty, into the conversation. This left Lysander at the mercy of Natasha who went on and on about her famous mother and the famous people she knew and how embarrassing it was having the name Rannaldini on her suitcases because everyone knew whose daughter she was and how Lysander must come and stay in the villa in Como.

Only when they'd eaten most of an incredibly light glazed-apricot tart made by Rannaldini and were drinking coffee and brandy did Lysander feel able to escape to watch the last horses at Gatcombe on television. But he found when he switched on that the competition was over and the leading riders were waiting for the presentation.

After the appalling heat and the terrible spills and thrills, they seemed blissfully happy to be alive. Lysander wistfully thought how young they looked in their dusty boots and breeches, many of them now wearing nothing above the waist but their coats and their white stocks.

There was Lysander's hero, David Green, so much the most handsome, his red coat not clashing remotely with his suntan, and there was Mark Todd, towering above the others with his charming lugubrious lived-in face. And there was the winner, Mary Thomson, crying with joy and hugging her brave horse in gratitude. Lysander wiped his eyes. What the fuck was he doing wasting his life hanging round rich bitches, who were far too self-obsessed to care about anything else? He started as he felt a hand on his shoulder. It was Rannaldini. For once his cruel sensual face was surprisingly gentle.

'Poor boy, you mees zee real work with horses. Come and see mine.'

The sun had lost its fiercest heat, so they'd decided to go for a ride, except Kitty who was petrified of horses and who would *anyway* be better employed clearing up.

'Leave her,' whispered Hermione, when Lysander tried to persuade her to come too. 'She's only sulking because I'm here.'

Lysander hoped the bloody bitch would fall off, but, irritatingly, Hermione, who had been brought up on a farm in South Africa, rode beautifully and as she rode she sang: '*Boot, saddle, to horse and away*,' with her lovely voice echoing round the woods.

Rannaldini obviously enjoyed dominating the vicious big black Prince of Darkness. A brilliant steeplechaser who had won many races, he had come second to his greatest rival Penscombe Pride, Rupert Campbell-Black's top National Hunt horse in last year's Rutminster Gold Cup. Having spent a summer resting and terrorizing any rambler, and particularly Kitty, who strayed into his field, he was being slowly got fit for the next season. He was now having a battle of wills with Rannaldini, who wanted to rub his leg against Flora's without The Prince of Darkness savaging the old gymkhana pony of Natasha's she was riding bareback. Lysander noticed Rannaldini put his hand right up Flora's skirt when he gave her a leg up.

Bob, who was competent, and Ferdie, who was petri-fied but determined not to show it, had been given two of Rannaldini's hunters, who were also getting fit, and who were less blown out with grass than in more fertile years. Sadly Ferdie's courage did nothing to further his cause with Natasha. A wobbling, mane-clinging lump of dough, he was a sad contrast to Lysander who rode with the dash of a Cossack and with hands even lighter than Rannaldini's pastry. Allotted Fräulein Mahler, a young bay mare who had already been very successful over hurdles, Lysander put her effortlessly over logs and little hedges.

'This is a seriously good horse,' he told Rannaldini. 'You ought to run her in the Whitbread or the Rutminster next year.'

'Perhaps you'd like to ride her,' said Rannaldini.

'Christ, I would, but basically I've got other plans,' and he told Rannaldini about Arthur.

'This is like something out of Tolstoy,' sighed Flora as they cantered across the platinum stubble. Rannaldini's farm workers were still harvesting. Tiny conkers were swelling on the chestnuts. Down drifted from thistle and willow-herb mingled with the blue hazy evening. Cows lumbered clumsily to their feet, like schoolboys when the headmaster comes into the room.

Finally they reached Rannaldini's lake at the bottom of the valley, its flawless azure surface being ruffled by splashing Rottweilers. The level had dropped dramatically, only at the water's edge were wild flowers: forget-me-nots, frogbit and soft mauve spearmint, still growing.

'My livestock is dependent on thees water.' Rannaldini told Bob. 'D'you think it will dry up?'

'Never has. I've no idea how deep it is in the centre.'

In answer, Lysander dug his heels into Fräulein Mahler's sweating sides and galloped her into the lake, with a huge splash, down, down, hardly rippling the water until Lysander had completely disappeared and all that could be seen were the Fräulein's brown nostrils just above the water.

'He'll drown,' screamed Natasha.

'That's a valuable horse,' said Hermione, outraged.

'Help him, someone,' pleaded Natasha.

Then both horse and rider emerged on the other side with Lysander roaring with laughter. Even when the mare shook herself like a dog, he didn't shift in the saddle.

His eyelashes were separated like starfish, his hair slicked back from his face, his bare brown back glistened, weed dripped from his jeans belt and from the Fräulein's bridle as he waited for them to catch up.

'Like Venus from the foam,' sighed Bob.

'But much more beautiful,' purred Rannaldini.

'We know who to use if we ever want to make a film of the Paradise Lad.'

It was so hot that both horse and rider were dry by the time they got home. Natasha was adrift with love. Flora and Hermione were equally diverted but both mildly irked that Lysander had shown nothing beyond politeness towards either of them. Rannaldini rode The Prince of Darkness home in silence, pondering how he could manipulate this charming but clearly naïve boy to his own ends.

Over at Angel's Reach, Georgie looked out of the drawing-room window in that particular despair that overwhelms unhappily married women in the country on Sunday nights, knowing there won't be anyone, even to row with, until Friday.

Guy had just announced he was going to London, she'd been so bitchy she couldn't blame him. For the first time since March, 'Rock Star' had dropped out of the Top Twenty. Nor were her spirits raised when a dark blue Ferrari drew up at the front door in a cloud of dust.

'Hi, Mum,' shouted Flora.

Elongated as a piece of asparagus between two slices of brown bread, she lolled between Ferdie and Lysander in the pistachio-green dress which Georgie had just spent hours looking for.

'*Boot, saddle to whore and away,*' sang Lysander in his high tuneless falsetto.

'See you lot in a bit,' said Flora as she clambered over Ferdie with much giggling.

'Georgie,' yelled Lysander, but Georgie had slammed down the window.

Babbling on about her gorgeous day, Flora met her mother in the hall.

'Lysander rides so well and poor Ferdie so badly, I'm afraid Natasha's been put off for life,' and she went on to describe the plunge into the lake.

'Stupid exhibitionist,' said Guy coming downstairs with his suitcase.

'As a result Rannaldini wants Lysander to ride for him.'

'Supper'll be ready in half an hour,' said Georgie, 'I thought we could watch *Howard's Way* and have supper on our knees.' Only possible because Guy, who disapproved of soaps, would be gone.

'Oh Mum, I'm sorry. I'm going out with Ferdie and Lysander. They want me to meet Arthur and then we're going to the cinema.'

'Good idea!' Guy was absolutely delighted. 'If you buck up I'll drop you off on the way.'

'That's really kind.' Not wanting to witness her mother's disappointment, Flora bolted upstairs.

'Still stupid exhibitionism,' said Guy, pouring himself a weak whisky. 'But I'm glad Lysander and Flora have got together. They're the right age.'

Somehow Georgie managed not to cry until they'd left. She knew Guy was off to see Julia. He'd deliberately played squash with Larry after tea as an excuse to shower and change before going to London. She was ashamed how depressed she felt that suddenly Guy and Flora were getting on. But most painful of all was that Flora had obviously got off with Lysander. Georgie had grown so fond of him over the past three weeks, although, despite Guy's suspicions, he hadn't laid a finger on her. Admittedly when they'd disappeared into the wood yesterday he'd squeezed her waist and, with his lovely infectious laugh, said, 'Shall we play it for real?' But she knew he was joking. Young boys didn't fancy hoary wrinklies, although it was clear from the suicidal way she felt now the reverse was possible. She couldn't even win Guy back like Marigold had recovered Larry. She was an utter, utter failure.

Ferdie returned to Fountain Street three days later in even lower spirits. He'd just taken Natasha out for a ludicrously expensive dinner. Her first course of two scallops had cost twenty-five pounds. She'd spent the whole evening quizzing him about Lysander and bitching about Kitty. Unfortunately Ferdie's increasing dislike did nothing to diminish his lust. Lunging with all the finesse of a grisly bear, he was rewarded with a slapped face.

It was after midnight but the telephone was ringing as he let himself in. Hope that it might be Natasha apologizing gave way to fury when it turned out to be Lysander.

'Oh Ferd, I'm so depressed. I don't think this campaign's going to work. Guy's showing no sign of giving up Julia and Georgie's really ratty with me and she's losing weight again. Basically I think we should scrap the whole thing and pay her her money back.'

'Don't be so fucking wet.' Ferdie had already invested his 10 per cent. 'Rome wasn't built in a day. Try a bit harder. Take Georgie on some decent jaunts. You've got the church fête on Saturday, haven't you?'

'The party of the decade,' said Lysander gloomily. 'I want to go clubbing, Ferd. I need some fun.'

'You're to beat Guy at everything – shooting, chucking coconuts, tug of war, guessing the weight of the pig.'

'You'll have to tell me how much Natasha weighs.'

'Shuddup, and you've got to win the best-chocolate-cake-made-by-a-man competition.'

'Don't talk bollocks, I can't cook.'

'Oh Jesus,' howled Ferdie. 'So I have to make it for you. I can't get down till late Friday. Get the recipe from Marigold.'

32

Georgie's mood did not improve the following week when Marigold kept borrowing Lysander to pick up stuff for the fête and then roping him in to set up stalls. Why the hell should she pay Lysander to give Marigold kudos?

Having savagely prayed for rain on the day, Georgie was ashamed to find her hopes fulfilled. But the rain only chucked down for a couple of hours, leaving puddles all over the rock-hard ground and the weather hotter and closer than ever.

Georgie found opening the fête even more frightening than her own launching party. Embarrassed to show the world such a diminished version of the abandoned beauty on the *Rock Star* album, she was also desperate to shine in front of Hermione, Marigold, Joy Hillary and, most of all, Guy – particularly as she had repeatedly refused both his and the vicar's offers to rehearse in front of them. If by some miracle she did it well, she didn't want them taking the credit.

Guy spent Saturday morning commuting between Angel's Reach and the vicarage. Every vegetable had been dug up in the garden to find longer carrots and larger marrows than Rannaldini's, Larry's and Bob's. He'd even tried his hand at some elderflower wine. But competition was at its fiercest in the class for the best chocolate cake made by a man. Guy had baked four cakes last night before he was satisfied. Larry was rumoured to have enlisted the help of Anton Mosimann and to be flying the cake down from London. Rannaldini had made his cake last weekend and Kitty, having removed it from the deep freeze, had just delivered it to the flower-tent wondering if she should leave Tabloid on guard.

She now despondently surveyed her bric-à-brac and was wondering how she was going to sell cracked 78s, single book-ends, cake knives, jigsaw puzzles of Norwegian fjords, purple plastic roses and a flowered vase she had given Hermione last Christmas, when Lysander came rushing up.

'Kitty, Kitty, help, help. Ferdie's going to murder me. He stayed up all night making me the perfect chocolate cake and I've just dropped it in a puddle.'

Kitty giggled. They decided against pinching a cake from Joy Hillary's stall next door in case the cook responsible recognized it. But by the time Kitty had found a clean plate and a white lacy paper mat, squeezed out the cake, shoved it together, disguised the cracks with Cadbury's flake sprinkled on top, and written a new card, Lysander's offering looked quite presentable.

'God, you're a star,' he hugged her. 'I don't know how you made all those cakes for that cricket tea. It took Ferdie and me till four in the morning.' He looked at his watch. 'Now, Georgie's opening the fête at two-fifteen. That gives us ages to have a bet on the one-thirty and a quick one or three in The Pearly Gates. Come on.'

'I can't,' said Kitty sadly. 'I promised Marigold and Joy I'd watch their stalls.'

She refused all Lysander's entreaties so he was reduced to boosting her turn-over by buying an old fox fur as a present for Jack and Maggie and insisting she kept the change from twenty pounds.

'It's for the spire. Oh Jesus, here comes Marigold. I don't want to blow up any more balloons.' And with that he shot into The Pearly Gates.

Back at Angel's Reach, Georgie was livid with Guy for insisting she wear a dress. Her only presentable one had disappeared with Flora. Why the hell Flora needed a pistachio-green silk tunic to go backpacking, Georgie

335

couldn't imagine. And she'd have to shave her legs and put Clinique on her varicose veins.

'I'll just ring Marigold to check everything's on target. We must leave by five to two,' said Guy as Georgie switched on her hair dryer.

Switching it off a second later to spray on some mousse, she heard Guy say, 'Hi, it's me.'

'Marigold OK?' Georgie asked later, as she ringed her eyes with dark brown pencil.

'Couldn't be bothered to ring her.'

'I heard you saying: "Hi, it's me." ' Then, as Guy put on his mental-nurse face, 'I *did*, Guy.'

'You must be going mad. I didn't ring anyone. Promise to go and see Dr Benson on Monday.'

Unearthed from a black dustbin bag in the attic, Georgie's grey denim midi was wrinkled like a rhino.

If I composed classical music it wouldn't matter, she thought savagely, everyone would say I looked charmingly eccentric.

'Why are you spraying scent on the back of your knees to open a village fête?' asked Guy.

'I might meet a ravishing dwarf,' snarled Georgie.

'You are not bringing Dinsdale.'

'No Dinsdale, no me. You can open the fucking fête yourself.'

Yellow leaves dislodged by the rain tumbled out of the limes around the village green. The high street was hung with red-and-white bunting. Parked cars glittered like shingle in the newly cut barley field next to the vicarage. Sheltered by high walls, seldom exposed to the winds which swept up from the Bristol Channel, the Hillarys' garden was a top-coat warmer than Valhalla or Paradise Grange. It boasted a yellow catalpa covered in big creamy white flowers and two massive horse chestnuts, whose leaves, touching the ground like cardinal's robes, added a suitable ecclesiastical note. A rainbow of different coloured clematis rose out of a bed of lavender against the ancient lichened walls of the house.

The crowds already milling round the stalls agreed on Joy Hillary's green fingers, but chuntered that the vicar must have been sprinkling illicitly to produce such a perfect lawn.

'Turning all that wine he drinks back into water,' suggested Bob Harefield, whose bald head had tanned as brown and freckled as a farm egg and who, in his quiet, steadily efficient way, had achieved far more than anyone else. Having set up most of the stalls, priced the goods and refereed squawking matches he was now taking money at the gate.

'You two ought to get in free,' he told Georgie and Guy, who insisted on paying.

'How good of you to come,' chorused the vicar's wife, Marigold and Lady Chisleden. As they all surged forward to 'receive the personality', the recently drenched grass pegged their high-heeled advance.

'We don't really allow dogs,' said Joy Hillary, remembering Dinsdale without enthusiasm.

'Well, at least keep him on a lead,' said Marigold.

'A quick whisk round the stalls to thank our caring helpers,' said Lady Chisleden, 'and then we'd better proceed with the opening.'

Poor Kitty was running bric-à-brac single-handed because last year's Miss Paradise, who was supposed to be helping her, hadn't turned up.

'What's this?' said Meredith, waving a cardboard disk.

'You put it at the bottom of your pans to stop fings boiling over.'

'Pity you can't stand Rannaldini on it. I've just bought a first edition of a book called *The Autobiography of a Cad* for 10p.'

'Written by every husband in Paradise,' said Georgie, pausing in front of them.

Joy Hillary shot her an alarmed look. Marigold had

promised that Georgie could be relied on to behave, but she had a wild look about her and she must have slept in that dress.

'I think you know Kitty Rannaldini,' said Lady Chisleden, 'a tower of strength.'

'An absolute bric-à-brac,' giggled Meredith. Grubbing around in a cardboard box he discovered the purple plastic tulips and handed them to Georgie. 'Just in case Marigold forgets your bouquet, dear.'

'Don't be silly, Meredith,' snapped Joy Hillary, bustling Georgie on to the plant stall where Marigold was urging people to buy plants to enhance their Best-Kept gardens.

'We've got some lovely heartsease,' she told Georgie.

'Take more than a plant to ease mine.'

'Come and guess the weight of the pig,' interrupted Joy Hillary hastily, 'and then I think we'll have your opening.'

' 'Allo, Georgie,' yelled Mother Courage. ' 'Ot isn't it? People are passing out like 'ot cakes.'

After the rain, the wasps were beginning to dive-bomb fruit and the jam tarts on the cake stall.

'I had a coffee cake in here a minute ago,' announced Lady Chisleden, gazing into a carrier bag in bewilderment.

On the way to the platform, Georgie caught sight of Ferdie who was having a ghastly afternoon giving pony rides on Tiny, who, maddened by flies and general ill-temper, had bitten him three times and lashed out at several small children.

'Where's your bloody little friend?' hissed Georgie. 'He promised never to leave my side.'

Ferdie was tempted to snap back that his bloody little friend had promised to be there to control Tiny, but, as there was so much money at stake, he murmured soothingly that Lysander would be here any second.

Guy, like his father the bishop, always whisked hither and thither at church occasions, big hand on bare elbows, telling willing helpers how splendid they were being. Now he was manning the loud speaker, his strong voice ringing round Paradise: 'Pray silence for our vicar.'

Everyone milled around patting Dinsdale, who was thoughtfully licking coffee cake off his whiskers. Percival Hillary then went into an orgy of platitudes about Georgie needing absolutely no introduction and how she and her husband Guy had been a most acceptable addition to our little community and how grateful they were to Georgie for taking time out from her busy schedule.

'Ladies and Gentlemen,' began Georgie.

The microphone let out an eldritch screech.

'Speak up,' yelled old Miss Cricklade who'd been home-made wine champion for ten years running.

'Thank you for making us so welcome.' Georgie sounded as though she was coming from outer space. 'It all looks absolutely lovely, but I know events of this kind do not spring up over-night like mushrooms. They take months of hard work and organization and I'd specially like to thank—'

She was interrupted by the doodle-bug chug of Larry's helicopter which landed in the next-door field blowing chaff over everyone. Miss Cricklade, who had been a fire watcher during the war, took refuge under a trestle table.

'As our opener was saying,' prompted Percival.

But Georgie had lost her place and couldn't remember whom she'd thanked. She could see that Mother Courage, her wisteria-mauve hair piled on top, her over-made-up face flushed from the pub, was holding Dinsdale and egging her on.

'I'd like to thank the Reverend and Mrs Hillary for lending us their lovely garden,' stammered Georgie, and was about to urge everyone to dig deeply into their pockets and spend, spend, spend and tell a little joke at the end when she realized she'd lost her audience. Looking down, she saw that Lysander's Jack had rolled up and was vigorously fornicating with Dinsdale's back leg.

'Don't, Debenham, that's rude,' squawked Mother Courage as her white plastic boot sent Jack for six.

'And I declare this fête open,' mumbled Georgie to very muted applause.

'I am going to murder Jack and Lysander,' vowed Georgie furiously. 'And Larry,' she added as she saw him scuttling into the flower-tent to get his chocolate cake in on time.

But there was no time for brooding.

Hissing, 'If only you'd allowed Percy and I to rehearse you,' Guy whisked her off to judge the fancy dress.

'She never thanked Produce, Nearly New or Coconuts,' Miss Cricklade was grumbling to Marigold.

'Well done. You'll need a bullet-proof vest,' murmured Bob as he ushered Georgie into a ring full of shepherdesses, gypsies, clowns and pop stars.

Georgie liked children and ear-marked Marigold's boys dressed as Margaret and Dennis Thatcher and Archangel Mike's two daughters sweating inside a white pantomime horse as Desert Orchid, as the likely winners, when a diversion was caused by Hermione, looking wonderfully cool in a cream Chanel suit and a big straw hat.

'I do hope we're not too late,' she was saying in her deep thrilling voice as she posted an angelic little boy in a sailor suit with a sailor hat on his dark curls into the ring. This must be Cosmo, Hermione and Bob's 'treasure'.

'Hallo, darling, you only made it just in time. Let's have a look at you.' Crouching down beside him, Georgie nearly dropped the clipboard with her markings on. For, looking out of a tiny version of Hermione's face, were the shiny black, deadly nightshade eyes of Rannaldini.

Next moment she gave a shriek as Cosmo kicked her sharply on the shin and then laid about Denis Thatcher with his telescope. This speedily concentrated Georgie's mind. She put Marigold's boys first, Desert Orchid a close second, Miss Muffet's spider third, Cosmo nowhere.

'Little Cosmo is very sensitive. He won't like that decision,' said Hermione ominously as she retrieved her bawling child.

'You're going to need that bullet-proof vest more than ever,' whispered Bob.

'Can we have all animals in the ring for the Best Pet shown by a child?' shouted Guy.

'Pity Rannaldini's in Geneva or we could have entered him,' said Meredith.

'Judged by our very own Hermione Harefield,' added Guy to loud cheers which temporarily assuaged Hermione's ire.

'I must have tubes of Smarties for everyone,' she was now insisting. 'I will not have any little one disappointed.'

'Hermione's so caring,' said Joy Hillary.

Seeing Ferdie give Tiny a great kick, Miss Cricklade reported him to the RSPCA who had a tent by the exit. Numbly Georgie signed autographs, still dazed by the fact that little Cosmo was Rannaldini's son. How did Bob and Kitty put up with such a constant public reminder? Finally, over the loud speaker, Guy announced that judging had finished in the flower-show tent and the public would be admitted shortly to see who'd won. Where the hell's Lysander? thought Ferdie and Georgie in murderous unison.

The hero of Paradise after last Sunday's cricket match had, in fact, fallen among thieves in The Pearly Gates. Everyone wanted to buy him drinks and, being Lysander, he promptly bought them back. Then Crooked Mouse, his hot tip for the 1.30, came in first and as he had told everyone to back her it was more drinks all round to celebrate, then at his suggestion they backed Georgie's Day for obvious reasons in the 2.15 and it came last so they had loads more drinks to cheer themselves up. By two-thirty Lysander was out of his skull. Hazily remembering he had to meet Georgie somewhere he staggered out wearing his fox fur and eventually found himself behind the vicarage. Hearing noise, he shinned over the wall, landing in a guelder rose bush at the back of a large tent. Wriggling through a side flap, he stumbled upon the home-made wine section on a nearby table with all the bottles open after the judging.

The winner had once again been Miss Cricklade. Last year after a couple of glasses of her elderflower wine the Archangel Michael, who normally drank for England, had driven straight through The Apple Tree's shop window after leaving her house.

Having finished the remaining half of this year's winning bottle, Lysander, who hadn't eaten since the previous evening and then only uncooked cake mixture, suddenly decided he was hungry and polished off an excellent spinach quiche and a plate of sausage rolls before starting on Miss Cricklade's prizewinning elderberry red.

By now people were flooding into the tent, shaking him by the hand and congratulating him. Really, thought Lysander, this is the nicest wedding reception I've ever been to. He must have another drink.

Outside, the RSPCA inspector, who had rolled up to prosecute Ferdie, having been bitten sharply by Tiny, was tempted to prosecute the pony instead.

The shadow of the spire fell over the vicar's garden as the sun started its descent. Disconsolate exhibitors were pouring out of the flower-tent. Rannaldini and Mr Brimscombe seemed to have won everything.

Having thrust cups of tea on willing stall holders and remembering that Hermione liked hers camomile and flavoured with honey, Guy led Marigold, who'd been up since six, off to the beer tent for something stronger. Now Georgie could see them laughing together. Traitor, thought Georgie, wishing someone would hurl a coconut at Guy.

Guy was less amused, as were Larry, the vicar and Meredith when they discovered that the still-absent Lysander had won first prize for his chocolate cake.

'It had a lovely damp texture and a delicious flavour we can't pin-point,' was the judge's comment.

It was time for Larry to run the auction and regain the ascendancy after not winning a single prize. He'd show who could drive a hard bargain and kicked off by getting eighty pounds for a signed copy of *Rock Star*.

Guy then impressed everyone by bidding an unheard of forty pounds for Hermione's posy of wildflowers. Consisting of marjoram, thyme, scabious and light and dark purple bell-flowers, they had been picked and arranged by little Cosmo's Nanny, Gretel. Hermione was in heaven.

'Guy Seymour is the most generous man in Rutshire,' she told everyone after kissing Guy several times full on the mouth.

Having only had the courage to open the joint bank statement that morning and seen the abyss of their overdraft, Georgie's smile fell heavily among the bric-à-brac. She knew she ought to roll up her sleeves and help Marigold or Kitty, but somehow she felt paralysed in her high heels and too shy to talk to people who were too shy of her fame to talk to her. She found Ferdie sitting on a haybale eating a choc-ice. All his bounce had left him.

'I'm sorry, Georgie. I'd go and look for him if he hadn't lumbered me with this fucking pony. I thought I'd cured him of bunking off.'

The fortune-teller was hidden in a little white tent under the taller of the chestnut trees. As Georgie's nails were clean after washing her hair and the queue had almost dried up, she decided to test her fate.

Outside, a sweet-faced woman with long dark hair was trying to quiet an adorable, but fretful, baby, and telling two pretty little red-headed girls, 'Mummy won't be long, then we'll go back to Robinsgrove and swim in the pool.'

Next moment a red-headed girl stumbled out of the tent, tears pouring down her cheeks.

'Oh Daisy, I can't bear it,' she wailed to the dark woman. 'He's not going to leave her.'

Georgie realized to her horror that it was Julia. There was no way of avoiding her. She was wearing a white shirt, blue schoolboy shorts and black pumps and the combination of tawny freckled skin and russet hair was absolutely stunning. *She* doesn't need to Clinique out her varicose veins, thought Georgie wearily.

'Oh Georgie – I'm so sorry. I tried to keep away today,' sobbed Julia, 'but I couldn't help myself. He's not going to leave you. You're so lucky to have him.'

'Come on, Julia.' Daisy put an arm round her heaving shoulders. 'Let's go home. I'm so sorry,' she turned to Georgie, 'I do hope you're OK.'

Georgie was not. Kicking off her beastly high heels she ran off to find Guy who was surrounded by eager helpers including Joy Hillary and Lady Chisleden, and having his photograph taken for the local paper as he pinned a tail on the donkey.

'Got a tenner?' he called out to Georgie.

'No, I have not,' hissed Georgie. 'If you're not worth a fortune, you're certainly worth a fortune-teller. I've just bumped into Julia and Daisy France-Lynch.'

'Julia and Daisy?' Guy didn't miss a beat. 'How good of them to look in. Perhaps they could sell some of their paintings here next year, Joy, and give you a percentage. D'you know Daisy? She's so sweet. There's so much local talent.' Then, turning to Lady Chisleden, 'I think cocoa gives a better flavour actually, Gwendolyn. My mistake this year was to use drinking chocolate.'

'I do not believe I am hearing this,' said Georgie. 'Guy, did you know Julia was coming?'

'Of course not, I haven't spoken to her for months. Settle down, Georgie.' Guy drew her aside. 'Think of other people rather than yourself for a change.'

'Time for you to draw the raffle,' interrupted Joy Hillary, whose eyes were on stalks.

'I'll make an announcement,' said Guy striding off.

'I do hope I win the Copenhagen dinner service,' said Joy. 'It's so good of Hermione to donate it.'

'Gives her another excuse not to invite anyone to dinner,' muttered Meredith to an exhausted Kitty. 'She's already got three sets in the attic. She gets one every time she sings "Wonderful Copenhagen" as an encore in the Danish Opera House.'

Among other raffle presents were a basket of fruit from The Apple Tree, a set of crystal glass donated by the local antique shop, dinner for two from The Heavenly Host and an array of bottles from The Pearly Gates.

Georgie was mindlessly scuffling round in the drum praying that she wouldn't pull out Julia's ticket when everyone was distracted by a piercing shriek from the flower-tent. Ancient Miss Cricklade, who had only just left her post at the Nearly New Stall to check how many prizes she'd won, came scuttling up to Marigold.

'All my wine's been drunk,' she screamed. 'That's three bottles and it's him what's done it.'

On cue out of the flower-tent, supported by Miss Paradise '89 and '90 with their crowns askew, came Lysander with his legs running away in every direction and his eyes crossing.

'*There is a green-fingered Hillary far away* – whoops – *without a city wall*,' sang Lysander waving a half-eaten rock bun in time. Georgie had never seen anyone so drunk. Suddenly Lysander turned his head with a superhuman effort.

'Georgie!' He tried to focus. 'Oh Georgie, darling, I've been looking everywhere for you. When are you going to make your speech?'

Then Georgie flipped.

'Piss off,' she screamed, advancing on him with her bouquet. 'Just piss off you little fucker to your play-pen and never come back again.'

There was an appalled silence.

'Georgie,' wailed Lysander.

Desperate to reach her, he lunged forward, tripping over a guy rope and lumbering into the raffle table, sending everything flying with a deafening crash. The Copenhagen dinner service was in smithereens, as were the Waterford glass and the bottles from The Pearly Gates.

'Put not your trust in princes,' murmured Bob.

'Time for a natural break,' said Meredith who was quite hysterical with laughter.

Hermione, who had hysterics of a different kind, was whisked inside the vicarage by Joy Hillary. Guy seized control of the microphone telling people to leave now to avoid broken glass, assuring them that the raffle would be drawn at a later date and all the winners would get their prizes in due course.

'And that little shit is going to pay for them,' he said grimly as he switched off the microphone.

After the broken glass and china had been swept up, organizers and helpers retreated to the vicarage for a well-earned drink while the money was counted. Georgie, who was shaking with mortification, only wanted to slope off home but Guy insisted she came too.

'You've made a complete fool of yourself, Panda. You owe it to the committee and to me to put in an appearance and show a bit of contrition.' The moment they entered the vicarage, he was off congratulating stall holders.

Hermione, as a result of smelling salts, two large whiskies and a vat of buttering up, was recovered enough to draw Georgie aside. Having misinterpreted Georgie's tight lips earlier, she said: 'I want to put your mind at rest. Guy admires me – very much indeed – it was so caring of him to buy my posy, but I'm far too much of a friend of yours to encourage him. Anyway he's not my type.'

'Why d'you kiss him on the fucking mouth every time you see him?' Georgie was appalled to hear herself saying.

'Oh Georgie.' Hermione put her head on one side. 'I thought by showing you everything was in the open, you'd realize nothing was going on.'

This time misreading Georgie's stunned silence for approval, Hermione went on: 'We all feel so sorry for Guy, he's such a darling man, so dependable and so different when you're not around glowering at him like a wardress. He may have lied to you, but men do lie when they're frightened. Anyway, any man of gumption keeps a mistress,' Hermione lowered her voice. 'You wouldn't want to be married to a wimp. Take a leaf out of Kitty Rannaldini's book and accept it. Brickie knows how to behave with dignity.'

'Because she doesn't kick against the lack of pricks,' snarled Georgie.

'Oh, I'm sure Rannaldini fulfils her every need.'

Stumbling away from Hermione, Georgie searched for a friendly face, but all the stall holders, holding their glasses of cheap wine like unexploded bombs, averted their eyes. Poor Guy to be lumbered with such a liability. Did liabilities always turn men into liars?

'I wasn't always like this,' Georgie wanted to plead.

'You all right?' It was Marigold.

'No, I'm not. That fucking Lysander!'

'Hush.' Marigold drew Georgie towards the window. The ledge was covered in dust. A vase of roses was dripping petals. Joy Hillary's thoughts had been elsewhere this week.

'And what were you doing letting Guy buy you drinks?'

'I was thirsty,' said Marigold apologetically, 'and Ay do like him. Oh, Georgie, we've made six thousand pounds and Ferdie's just given us a cheque for a thousand to pay for Lysander's breakages.'

'Where is the little beast?'

'Passed out in the field next door.'

'I hope they burn the stubble with him in it.'

But Marigold wasn't listening. 'We've made six thousand and, oh, Georgie, Lady Chisleden has asked me to call her Gwendolyn.'

33

Somehow, because Georgie was busy working out whether
to kill Guy with a bread knife or a carving knife they
managed to get home without a row. She had just fed
Charity and Dinsdale when he came into the kitchen
carrying a file.

'I'm off, Panda. I told Joy and Percy I'd help clear up.
Don't bother with supper. I'll grab a sandwich at The
Pearly Gates. I've got a Best-Kept Village meeting later.'

'Why don't you enter Julia in the Best-Kept Mistress
competition?' screamed Georgie. 'You might even beat
Hermione.'

Georgie cried and cried, had a large Bacardi, got down
her suitcase and couldn't think where to go. It was so
hot she put on an old denim bikini scrumpled up in the
ironing. Then she took a plum from the fruit bowl and
found she'd put the stone in her mouth and chucked
the fruit in the ashy muck-bucket. Everything turned
to ashes. Poor Julia had looked devastated, too. Georgie
found she didn't hate her any more. And maybe Marigold,
Hermione and all the ladies of Paradise were right and Guy
was different and really nice when he wasn't with her.
Why had Lysander let her down? Because she simply
wasn't important enough to him. She jumped as the
telephone rang. It was Flora.

'Where are you?'

'Lake Geneva – er – staying in a youth hostel. It's great
here.'

'And where the hell is my white silk shirt? No doubt

348

split across the back of one of your rugger-playing boy-friends, or being used to clean his car.'

There was a pause.

'Look behind the spare-room door,' said Flora huffily. 'You'll find it there. Go and look *now*.'

Belting upstairs Georgie found her white shirt, then remembered it was the spare room where Guy had adjusted the mirror to sleep with Julia, and started to cry again. By the time she got downstairs Flora had rung off. Georgie felt awful – poor darling Flora might jump in Lake Geneva.

I was beastly to her, said a small voice, because I was jealous of her and Lysander. She was overcome by a sick, heart-thumping, craving for information. She daren't snoop in Guy's study. She was a bit drunk and he'd notice if papers had been moved.

Loathing herself, she went into Flora's room. The radio and the record player were still on. Clothes carpeted the floor. On the wall was a poster of a gorilla; underneath it someone had written: FLORA SEYMOUR ON A GOOD DAY. Here was Flora's diary; Georgie's hands were shaking so much that at first she couldn't focus.

'*August 13: Read The Franklyn's Tale (not bad for a set book) about a man who sleeps with a disgusting old woman who turns into a beautiful princess. I can really relate to the Franklyn.*'

Would I turn into a princess if I went to bed with Lysander? wondered Georgie.

'*August 14: Sunday.*' Here it was. '*Lunch at Valhalla, Lysander and Ferdie there and Hermione being a pain.*' Then followed a lot of guff about Lysander riding into the lake. '*He's gorgeous but quite old. He and Ferdie really sweet and invited me over to Magpie Cottage. Daddy really nice, too, gave me a lift. We had a good chat. Later we had fantastic sex in the wood. I'm terrified I'm falling in love.*'

Giving a moan, Georgie turned the page. '*August 15: X made me come by just talking to me over the telephone. He's given me a tiny vibrator in the shape of a fountain-pen as a*

349

*going-away present so I don't miss him, but I know I will.
At least he's flying out lots to see me.'*

Georgie was so transfixed with horror that at first she
didn't hear the telephone. Sobbing at the sickness that
had made her pick the lock of Pandora's box she reeled
down the landing to her bedroom and snatched up the
receiver.

'Georgie, it's Lysander. I'm sorry I got pissed. I want
to come round.'

'Fuck off,' screamed Georgie.

'I know I let you down. Ferdie's just bawled me out.
I'll make it up to you.'

'You won't. Your bloody dog screwed up my speech,
then you make a fool of me in front of everyone and finally
you're fucking my daughter. How *dare* you! Keep your
rotten fee, but I don't want to see you or Ferdie ever again
and don't you dare contact Flora.' Slamming down the
receiver she raced round the house pulling out telephones
as though she were weeding tares out of her life.

She couldn't believe it was only eleven o'clock. Out on
the terrace the air was heavy with night-scented stock. In
the moonlight Rannaldini's strawbales encased in black
shiny bags looked like great slugs coming to eat her.

Undressed in her lonely double bed, she looked in the
big mirror over the fireplace and in her reflection, with
her red hair flowing over her bare shoulders, she could
only see Julia. Sobbing she swallowed two sleeping pills
and crashed out.

Next day she woke, as always after taking pills, feeling
calm and almost euphoric. What did a million mistresses
matter? In one of those bewildering volte-faces, she didn't
shrug off Guy's encroaching hands. Today she was going
to be like Brickie, who would never spurn a husband.

'Let's make love outside. Oh, Panda, I've missed you,'
said Guy, taking her down to a corner of the lake hidden
by willow trees and laying her on the scratchy yellow
grass. But just as he'd put his hand between her legs,

Dinsdale had barged through the willow fronds and was shoved aside so vociferously he had waddled off in a sulk to Mother Courage.

Georgie, needing the release so desperately, found herself wracked by sexual paralysis.

Too tense to reach orgasm that way, she started to cry and begged Guy to come inside her, but she was so tight down there, she nearly screamed out with pain.

'That was lovely, darling,' she mumbled afterwards, 'thank you so much.'

But as she got out of her bath, Guy came out of his dressing room with a cricket bag, kissing her on the cheek and announcing he was off to Oxford.

'You're always complaining you can't work, Panda, so I thought I'd give you a clear day.'

No doubt he and Julia would meet up in Ricky France-Lynch's woods and Guy would say, 'Things can't go on. Georgie's being so awful.'

It was terribly hot. The smell of dew drying on a nearby clump of fennel reminded Georgie of Wheeler's, London and fun. Whooping across the valley, Larry's farm boy was moving weary cattle in search of grazing. The bells of All Saints rang out, no doubt in grateful anticipation of a rebuilt spire. A young vixen sat motionless in the stubble awaiting victims disorientated by the combine harvesters – rabbits and field-mice so desperate for water that they lost their instinct for survival. Like me, thought Georgie with a sob. Oh please God, help me, she dropped to her knees.

God told her to get down to work. Getting into her bikini she took manuscript paper, pens and biscuits for Dinsdale, who'd come back but was still sulking, out on to the terrace.

Scraping back her hair in an elasticated band to get her forehead brown she whipped off her bikini top, coated her pale breasts with Ambre Solaire and started to think. Cleopatra was always ranting and raving at Anthony, who was charming, self-indulgent and adored by his men: a tower of strength with his willing helpers. To the west she could see a red glow beneath a mushroom-brown spiral of cloud. They were burning the stubble like Anthony's funeral pyre.

Georgie shut her eyes and hummed. Slowly a tune that her brain had been chasing for days took form in her head, almost as fast the words followed: '*I want to blaze with love once more before I die.*' Joyfully she started to write, but her biro refused to function where the paper was soaked with suntan oil. She took a fresh sheet; somehow she must capture the doomed folly of their love.

She didn't know how long she wrote, only that music was singing in her head and words racing as though the streams of Angel's Reach were carrying the rains off the hills once again. Like Hemingway, she was about to stop when she was 'going good' and make a cup of coffee when Dinsdale's bay rang out and Jack and Maggie raced across the lawn. Maggie was carrying an envelope which she dropped in her excitement. Georgie only had time to whip off her elastic band, fluff out her hair and clutch her bikini top to her sweating breasts when Lysander crept round the corner.

He was wearing Ferdie's dark glasses and carrying a bottle of champagne and a bunch of clashing pink-and-purple asters. It was hard to tell if he was shaking more from nerves or from hangover.

'Get out,' said Georgie.

'I've come to say I'm sorry. It's the worst thing I've ever done, but basically I got pissed and Jack's desperately sorry, too.' He reached down to pick up the envelope which Maggie had dropped. 'Jesus, my poor head! I can promise you there's nothing sham about this pain.'

As he handed over the bottle of Moët, he looked at Georgie under his lashes and was disappointed to see no flicker of amusement.

'Why aren't you playing in that polo final?' she snapped.

'I pulled out. You're more important and I'm not bonking your daughter.'

'I don't believe you,' said Georgie, wishing she wasn't so conscious of being hot, sweaty and middle-aged, when all she should be thinking about was Flora's honour. 'She didn't get back till four in the morning last Sunday, and I overheard her talking on the telephone.'

There was no way she was going to own up to reading Flora's diary.

'Flora stayed half an hour last Sunday and had one drink,' said Lysander, 'and what is more,' he went on indignantly, 'she wasn't remotely interested in Arthur, even when he lay on his side and snored and shook hands for a Twix bar and drank a can of Fanta. I was appalled.'

Not exactly the way, thought Georgie thawing slightly, to Lysander's heart.

'*And* she kept looking at her watch,' he went on. 'Then a car came to the bottom of our lane and she was off like a rat up a drain. You ask Ferdie.'

'He always covers for you.'

'He does not. He's just given me another bollocking.'

'Any idea who was in the car?'

'No,' lied Lysander. 'Where's the Ace Carer?'

'Gone to Oxford for an end-away fixture.'

'Am I interrupting you?' Lysander glanced at her paper. 'You *have* written a lot.'

'I've had a good morning.' Georgie suddenly felt absurdly happy. 'D'you want some lunch?'

'Don't think I could keep it down. Oh, Georgie, thank you for not being cross any more. I've been so miserable.' He followed her into the kitchen which was as cool and dark as a cave.

'I ought to get dressed,' said Georgie, putting the asters in the sink.

'Please don't. You're overdressed as it is.'

'How about some cold chicken or a bit of sea trout?' Georgie opened the fridge door.

'Unless you're starving. I'm honestly not hungry. Let's watch *EastEnders* first.'

'*You* ought to cook for *me*,' said Georgie, 'since you beat everyone in the chocolate-cake competition.'

Lysander opened his bloodshot eyes wide, then roared with laughter. 'I stuffed it with hash. No wonder the judges finished every scrap and couldn't identify the special flavour. Ferdie got livid because I kept taking spoonfuls while he was mixing it. Cakes are so much nicer before they're made.'

'Like women,' said Georgie acidly.

'Not all women,' said Lysander, handing her a glass.

Collapsing on to the dark gold sofa in the drawing room, Georgie wished Guy hadn't just cut back the rambler rose which had obscured the window. Now the bright sunlight streamed in showing up all her bags and wrinkles.

Dinsdale promptly heaved himself up beside her and refused to budge, so Lysander was reduced to sprawling on the shaggy rug at her feet, as her children so often did. From now on she must regard him as one of Flora's cricketing friends – delectable but out of bounds.

It was a gripping instalment of *EastEnders* and Georgie was so involved in Michelle's conversation with Sharon that she suddenly found to her horror she was stroking Lysander's hair.

'I thought you were Dinsdale,' she said aghast.

'If only I were,' Lysander trapped her hand, 'I'd like to climb into your bed every morning. Oh, Georgie, I've had my binoculars trained on Angel's Reach since first thing waiting for Guy to go out. And I stood watching you this afternoon while you were writing, you looked so gorgeous. I really fancy you.'

'Don't be ridiculous!' Georgie swelled with all the outrage of a cat startled by a dog.

'I nearly kissed you in the woods during the cricket match – and I know you fancy me.'

'I do not.'

'You do, too, or you wouldn't have been so furious about me and Flora.' Sliding his other hand round her neck he drew her towards him until their lips touched

and he kissed her with such alacrity that she fell off the
sofa on top of him.

'No, we really shouldn't.'

For a moment they were all deliciously sprawling limbs,
then his tongue slid inside her mouth and as she struggled
with increasing half-heartedness to escape, the safety-pin
holding her bikini top gave way and she was naked
except for her faded-blue denim bikini pants with her red-
gold hair flowing over her golden shoulders and youthful
rounded breasts.

'Oh, they're sweet!' Lysander kissed each nipple. 'You're
so beautiful.'

Laying her across his thighs, he pushed back her fringe
and adoringly kissed her forehead, her heavy eyelids,
her snub nose, and then, with a whoop of delight, returned to her mouth. All the time he was gently stroking
the back of her neck, her armpits, and her breasts an
inch below the nipples, every place where she was most
responsive, before tunnelling under her bikini bottom
until he could feel her heart bashing against his and her
thighs quivering with delight.

'I thought you had a hangover,' muttered Georgie,
struggling to keep a metaphorical foot on the bottom of
the pool.

'You could put Fernet Branca out of business,' whispered Lysander. 'God, I want to get inside you. I've got
a thing about women of experience.'

'Experience of retreating men,' said Georgie sadly. Oh,
why hadn't she kept up those exercises to strengthen
her internal muscles? 'Anyway we can't, not in front of
Dinsdale.'

Laughing, Lysander laid her on the rug. Switching off
EastEnders, he removed his dark blue shirt, threw it over
Dinsdale and turned a photograph of Guy to face the
wall. Then, dropping his jeans, he knelt beside Georgie,
gently easing off her bikini bottoms. Burying his face in
her breasts, breathing in Ambre Solaire, he mumbled, 'I
dreamt and dreamt this would happen. I'm going to be

the bridge over the ravine to your new happiness. Don't cry, it'll be so lovely. Lie on top of me if the floor's too hard.'

It had been such agony with Guy that morning that on seeing the splendour of Lysander's cock, Georgie was terrified he'd never get inside her. But having turned her sideways, with one thigh between his, he spat on his fingers and stroked her so delicately that she was soon bubbling like a hot churn of butter.

'Oooooh, that's heavenly,' she sighed as he slid easily right up inside her. 'We're tailor-made. God, what a wonderful cock.'

Lysander grinned down at her. 'It's an absolute tower of strength,' he whispered and Georgie got such giggles he came and she didn't.

'God, that was magic.' Lysander filled their glasses with tepid champagne. 'I'm sorry. I should have kept going. Ferdie always distances himself by reciting Shakespeare or Latin verbs, but I can never remember anything long enough to remember it. Anyway I can't think of anything but you. Oh, Georgie.' And he kissed her with such love, it was worth all the orgasms in the world.

As he lit them both cigarettes, a deep sigh came from the sofa. Jack, Maggie and Dinsdale, peering out from under Lysander's shirt, were watching them with the utmost disapproval.

'They look like Jack Tinker, Milton Shulman and Irving Wardle after the first act of a seriously bad play,' said Georgie, 'except it was seriously lovely.' Bending over she kissed Lysander's flat brown belly, then moving slowly upwards kissed each rib. 'You are desirability incarnate, but it *must* be the last time. You're less than half my age. It's obscene.'

'So what? Look at Rannaldini and—' Lysander just stopped himself saying 'Flora'. God, he must be careful. 'And – er – all those groupies he's always deflowering.'

'According to Hermione, Rannaldini fulfils a woman's every need.'

Chucking his cigarette into the fireplace Lysander stretched out on the rug, his cock pointing unambiguously heavenwards.

'Come and sit on my need,' he said, 'and this time you're going to come.'

Georgie's life changed. Feeling herself wildly desired by someone she found wildly desirable, her confidence flooded back. She started looking sensational. She had never enjoyed sex so much. She'd never believed lust and larkiness could be so entwined.

Ferdie, on the other hand, was livid. 'You're not supposed to bonk them,' he shouted at Lysander, 'you'll be done for enticement. Guy'll take you to the cleaners.'

'I don't care, I love bonking Georgie.'

'She's ancient,' snapped Ferdie. 'You're like a robin nesting in some rusty old kettle.'

Ferdie was somewhat surprised to find himself being shaken like a rat.

'Don't you ever talk like that about Georgie again.'

Guy was also seriously rattled. Georgie had cried wolf in the past, often threatening to walk out when she was plastered. But now she was never in when he rang. She claimed she was working, but he noticed exactly the same notes on her music-stand and the same words of lyric in her notebook on Fridays as there had been on Mondays.

'You're seeing far too much of Lysander Hawkley,' he told Georgie, who was wearing a scarf on the hottest day of the year to hide the lovebites.

'And you see too much of Julia Armstrong,' said Georgie blithely. 'Small tits for tat.'

'We're not talking about me. It's juvenile to try and get your own back.'

'Whoever said revenge was sweet was a smart cookie.'

Guy tried another tack. 'We must do more things together, Panda.'

'Right,' said Georgie. 'Let's kick off by getting a divorce.'

34

The impossibly hot summer sweltered on and people wore as few clothes as possible. Georgie and Lysander spent a great deal of time in bed and his presence at Magpie Cottage kept the husbands of Paradise more on their toes than Baryshnikov. In particular, Guy and Larry started ringing solicitously night and morning, cutting down their sporting activities at weekends and getting home early on Friday with bunches of flowers. In Guy's case it was dramatic how British Rail had suddenly improved their services.

Only Rannaldini carried on in his usual fashion making love to Flora in every possible position in every capital in Europe. Hermione and Cecilia, unaware of this new passion, joined Natasha in feeling more than a faint neglect and became increasingly demanding and histrionic – particularly towards Kitty, who was the one who had to cancel when Rannaldini was supposed to be seeing them.

The only pleasure afforded a chronically cuckolded wife, of witnessing the anguish of one's husband's current mistress when he moves on to a new one, was denied to poor Kitty because she felt that Rannaldini was far more smitten with Flora than any of the others.

A diversion was caused at the end of August by the launching of his film of *Don Giovanni*, promptly nicknamed Dong Giovanni because many of the leading characters appeared with nothing on. The critics, while full of praise for the production, pointed out that the wonderfully lit conductor appeared more than the Don. Paradise was electrified because their very own Hermione Harefield, and Cecilia Rannaldini, the ex-wife of their very own Rannaldini, appeared in the buff. Grin and Barefield, *The Scorpion* called it. Pirate versions were soon circulating Paradise with the sound turned down and much frame-freezing on Hermione's bottom.

At a private and raucous late-night showing in The Pearly Gates, pats of butter and even darts were thrown at the screen. Hermione was not quite so beloved in Paradise as she believed.

Having borrowed the tape to show Georgie, Lysander wandered down to Paradise the following morning to hand it over to ancient Miss Cricklade who was next in the queue. Since the arrival of a vast box of chocolates, Miss Cricklade had forgiven Lysander for drinking her home-made wine at the fête and was now taking in his washing.

It was a day fit for a wedding. After heavy rain in the night, a newly washed blue sky arched over gold fields. Every blade of bleached grass and already turning leaves sparkled in the sunshine. Apples reddened like blushing brides in the orchards of Paradise.

Lysander had meant just to take the dogs but Arthur had looked so bored and eager for a jaunt and Tiny made such a din if left behind that in the end they all went. Jack, strutting out proudly with Arthur's lead rope between his teeth, and Maggie, who was now three times larger than Jack, cavorted in front teasing Tiny and keeping out of the way of her gnashing jaws and lightning hoofs.

Lysander felt absurdly happy. Wearing just loafers and frayed denim shorts, he could feel the sun on his back which was now darker gold than the fields. He was in love. He had a mother to fuss over him once more and he adored living in Paradise. Since he'd mistaken the fête for a wedding reception and made the vicar's wife, Marigold and Lady Chisleden (all regarded as bossyboots) look silly, his popularity had soared even higher.

'*In a world where nothing seems real, I have found you, I*

have found you,' sang Lysander to Arthur, who waggled his big ears lovingly and didn't remotely mind his master being out of tune.

Passing Bob's and Hermione's, Lysander noticed a pair of sweating workmen hoisting very large, new-looking white balls on to the greying flat-topped pillars on either side of the gates.

He was so busy staring he didn't see anyone approaching. Giving a snort of irritation that Lysander's pack was spilling over the road and pressing herself into the hedge like a cat when the hunt passes, was a very tall, very thin girl. Startlingly pale for such a hot summer, she had very short spiky beige hair and a fine-boned foxy face dominated by angry eyes. She was wearing a loose, earth-coloured dress, which totally disguised her figure. Somehow she seemed familiar. Lysander heard her footsteps halt, but when he turned, she'd disappeared. She must have gone into Jasmine Cottage, the sweet little house belonging to Hermione, which was hired out for expensive holiday lets.

By the time Lysander had had a cup of coffee and a glass of parsnip sherry with Miss Cricklade and dropped off his washing and had a glass of Sancerre with Miss Paradise '89, who waited at The Heavenly Host and who'd saved the remains of last night's bread-and-butter pudding for Arthur, and had a bet and a pint of Flowers at The Pearly Gates and reached The Apple Tree, he was in fine fettle. But as Tiny had eaten his shopping list he'd forgotten what he'd come down for.

Wandering round the shop throwing smoked salmon, frozen Mars bars and a bottle of Moët into his basket as treats for Georgie, Lysander bumped into Eve the owner who was as short, plump and jolly as the unknown girl had been tall, thin and disapproving. 'Who's taken Jasmine Cottage?' he asked.

'Mrs Levitsky's come back,' said Eve with a sniff. 'She was married to Boris that Russian. They were so happy when they first lived here. She had two lovely kiddies

360

and hair down her back. Then he went off with another woman.'

'Ah. Is she called Rachel and plays the piano?'

'That's the one. She likes to be called Rachel Grant now.'

'I know her,' said Lysander in amazement. 'She was so beautiful she made me forget to go to an interview. Gosh, she's changed.' Lysander added Pedigree Chum, chewsticks and carrots for the horses to his basket.

'It's unhinged her,' said Eve, writing down Lysander's purchases in a red book. 'She's joined the Green Party and she's always in here complaining. None of the fruit's organic enough. I mean, we're not a health-food store. Then she says we've got the wrong washing-up liquid, the wrong toothpaste, the wrong shampoos.' Eve's sense of grievance boiled over. 'I hope her hair turns green and it all falls out. She's put off so many of my customers.'

'What's she doing down here?' asked Lysander, adding the *Sun* and *Sporting Life* to the pile.

'Come back to accompany Hermione. She'll get a pittance for that. She keeps grumbling Jasmine Cottage is so dark. Not surprising with all those Save the Whales and the White Rhino and the Rain Forest posters in the window. She could start by saving her breath,' added Eve putting everything into a carrier bag.

'I'll drop in and say hallo on the way home,' said Lysander.

Eve followed him outside giving a finger of KitKat to the dogs and breaking up a Twix bar for Arthur and Tiny.

'What did you think of Madam's video?' she asked.

'Well, basically I'm not into opera. I can never see how they can sing so loudly and for so long when they're supposed to be dying, and Hermione's got a bigger ass on her than Arthur. Talking of asses, I better get mine into gear. Here comes the vicar.'

The return journey took almost as long, with more drinks and bets and a long chat with Mother Courage returning from Angel's Reach with huge sweat circles under the armpits of Hermione's Jean Muir which she'd bought for £2.50 at the Nearly New stall.

'Take your time, Sandy,' she told Lysander. 'Georgie's playing and singing up in her tower like a lark. You 'aven't been missed. 'Allo, Jack, 'allo, Maggie, going to see Debenham? Yes, I know Rachel. Always flying off the angle. Her husband was a nice fellow, used to walk along the road composing. He'd always buy you a drink. People say he defecated all the way from Russia.'

Moving on, Lysander read in the *Sun* about a forest fire raging through France. It had probably been started by Flora tossing her fag into the bracken and crying, 'Encore, Rannaldini.' He wondered what Georgie and Flora would both say if they knew with whom the other was sleeping. He was dithering whether to pop in on Rachel when Jack took matters into his own paws. Seeing Rachel's tabby cat in the road ahead, he dropped Arthur's lead rope and took off, followed by Maggie.

When Lysander caught up with them the cat had been chased up an ancient quince tree hanging over the wall and the dogs were yapping hysterically round the base with Rachel swiping at them with a broom and screaming: 'Go away, you bloody animals.'

'Don't kill them,' begged Lysander. 'Here, hang on to Arthur and Tiny.'

He had grabbed Jack, when Maggie, unnerved by raised voices and any kind of violence, crapped extensively on Rachel's lawn, producing a further tirade.

'Are you trying to blind my children? Can't you keep your bloody dogs on a lead? Get them out of my garden.'

'I'm really sorry.' Tucking Jack under his arm, grabbing the horses and calling to Maggie, Lysander backed down the path until he had shut the gate firmly between them.

'Look, d'you remember me? Lysander Hawkley. We met in that chemist's and went back to your house. We were having a really nice time until your husband came back.'

Slowly, painfully, Rachel seemed to lug her mind out

of the horrors of the present into the far worse torments of the past.

'Boris left me.' Furiously she started dead-heading yellow roses.

'I know. I'm desperately sorry.'

'What are you doing here?'

'Living at Magpie Cottage – where are your kids?'

'A friend's taken them, I've got to go over to Hermione's. She's got a prom next week and needs to go through the score.'

Rachel was even thinner than Georgie had been. Her face was seamed with pain, her huge eyes dark with loss. Christ, what awful things men do to women, thought Lysander. As it was Friday he'd be at a loose end tonight because Guy was due home. He'd also had a lot to drink and heard himself saying: 'Why don't you come over to supper after you've finished?'

'No thanks.' Rachel's face shut like a trap. 'Hermione'll keep me for hours. She takes her kilo of flesh. Then I've got to put the kids to bed.'

'Oh, right,' said Lysander, relieved. 'Some other time.'

His skin was as smooth, dark and shiny as any of the rain-forest mahogany she was trying to save. His bleached hair flopped into his eyes. He was heartbreakingly pretty.

'You ought to put on a shirt or you'll get skin cancer,' snapped Rachel. 'The ozone layer's so thin. But I don't expect you care about that.'

Slamming the front door, she started to cry. It was a relief to be jolted out of her dry stony grief. Lysander had stirred up so many memories. That brief afternoon when they'd been so furiously and rudely interrupted was the last time she had been totally sure of Boris's love.

The marriage had started with such promise, after Boris caught sight of her slender bare back topped by shining piled-up brown hair as she played Beethoven's Third Piano Concerto in Moscow and had fallen so wildly in love that he could do nothing but defect. For a while, like the Gemini, they had been two glittering stars in the musical firmament: the broodingly handsome young conductor immediately snapped up by the London Met, and his equally dazzling young pianist wife.

Having shaken off the shackles of Communism, however, Boris, who already had a passion for red wine, red meat and red-blooded women, started amassing capitalist trappings: fast cars, designer clothes, CDs, tapes and electronic equipment – which was fine when he and Rachel were both working.

But with babies the trouble started. Because her mother had gone out to work Rachel had been determined to stay at home with her own children and on one income the money soon ran out.

Rachel also grew increasingly resentful at not being able to pursue her own career. As she pushed prams in the park with a green, *Guardian*-reading feminist, who indoctrinated her with her subversive ideas, Rachel started serving up vegetarian food and throwing Boris out of the house for smoking and drinking. Then, determined to return to work, she accepted an invitation to tour America, hoping that the totally undomesticated Boris, left at home to look after two small children and the house, would appreciate what she had to put up with.

But Boris, missing his homeland and family and fed up with Rachel's passion for the truth, which many people called tactlessness, suddenly felt a desperate need for warmth, approval and companionship.

Thus Rachel returned from America to find he had fallen in love with Chloe the mezzo, who was beautiful, bosomy, successful and only too happy to tell Boris how marvellous he was.

Finding himself unable to give up Chloe and too straight, unlike Guy, Rannaldini and Larry, to run two women, Boris had finally resigned from his marriage. Rachel, having lost touch with the music world, was getting no concert work. A couple of earlier recitals where she had loyally played Boris's compositions, which had meant half the audience leaving at the interval, hadn't exactly helped her career. Hermione paid her a pittance, as did her few pupils, and she was embittered at Boris's constant failure to keep up the maintenance payments. Her evenings were now spent festering and firing off letters on recycled paper to the prime ministers of foreign countries complaining about their treatment of the environment. At least it ensured that she occasionally got some post in return.

After smoked salmon, Moët, Mars bar ice-cream and a languorous, sweaty afternoon's lovemaking at Magpie Cottage rather than Angel's Reach, in case Guy or Flora, who was due home any time from backpacking, rolled up unexpectedly, Lysander was roused by the telephone. It was Rachel fulminating that Hermione had cancelled due to some mega-crisis and asking ungraciously if she and the children could come to supper after all. Lysander, who would rather have gone back to sleep or out on the bat with his Pearly Gates cronies, said: 'Of course.' He'd come and fetch her; only to be told: 'What's wrong with walking? It's only half a mile.'

'That was Rachel,' sighed Lysander.

'Isn't she fantastically young and pretty?' asked Georgie, jumping out of bed and scuttling into the bathroom so Lysander shouldn't get too long a sight of her droopy bottom.

'Used to be, but she's got seriously fierce. Oh dear, it didn't even seem a good idea this morning. Friday's my worst night of the week, knowing I won't see you until Monday.'

Following Georgie into the bathroom, he slid his arms round her waist, nuzzling at her shoulder.

'Promise to ring me every moment you can, and try and persuade the Ace Carer to play cricket on Sunday.' Then, turning on the taps, 'I'd better have first bath so I can nip down to The Apple Tree and get some supper and a video for the kids before they close.'

Suddenly Georgie realized why the mention of Rachel upset her.

'She was coming to dinner the night she and Boris split up. That was the night Guy fed Julia in,' she said.

'Don't think about Julia.' Lysander took Georgie back in his arms, stroking her hair.

'You won't fall in love with her, will you?' Georgie clung to him. One of the lovely things about Lysander was that she never had to try and be cool.

The day that had started so beautifully deteriorated. Returning from The Apple Tree, Lysander passed Rachel trailing two tired, fretful children, Vanya and Masha, aged four and three, who were only too pleased to jump into such a glamorous car and shrieked with excitement when Lysander drove at his usual reckless pace. Rachel was less amused.

'Any speed over 55 m.p.h. wastes energy.'

She then proceeded to castigate him for not using unleaded petrol, and for not having a catalytic converter to exclude carbon monoxide.

Lysander's hayfield of a front garden, however, temporarily cheered her up.

'How brave of you to flout the Best-Kept Village committee and grow your lawn. Those nettles attract the peacock butterfly and the thistles are a wonderful magnet for goldfinch, and, look, kids, lots of dandelions so we can make a salad for supper.'

The inside of the cottage was less of a success. There were plates, glasses and overflowing ashtrays everywhere, and a bowl of uneaten dog food, black with flies. When Jack and Maggie rushed to meet them, both children knocked their heads together burying their faces in their mother's skirt. Seeing Rachel wrinkling her long elegant nose at the smell of dog and game-keeper's ferret, which always surfaced on hot days, Lysander let rip with air freshener and fly spray and got a bollocking for using aerosols.

'This place is a bottle bank in itself,' Rachel went on in horror.

'I keep forgetting it's dustbin day. Basically, the dustmen come before I get up,' said Lysander apologetically. 'Let's have a drink.'

For a second, as Lysander took out some cans of Coke and a bottle of Muscadet, the children's eyes – sloe-black like their father's – lit up.

'They're not allowed Coke – sugar rots their teeth,' said Rachel. 'Water will do. Where are the mugs kept?'

'In the machine. It's just finished.'

'But it's only half-full,' said Rachel, opening the door. 'Can't you appreciate what a waste of energy this is?'

Masha and Vanya weren't allowed crisps either nor little chocolate nests filled with eggs.

'I'll have to re-educate you completely,' sighed Rachel. 'Those chocolate nests are at least eight hundred calories and when you think of the pesticides used on the cocoa bean. You must have some carrots and apples I can chop up.'

The fridge nearly finished her off. By not defrosting it, Lysander was completely responsible for global warming. Everything was past its sell-by date and he'd get listeria from the three half-full tins of pâté.

Getting some carrots out of the vegetable compartment she started ferociously chopping on a wooden board. Arthur, who always hung around touting for snacks when he saw people in the kitchen, frightened the life out of her by sticking his great face, half of it stained olive-green from rolling, in through the window. His wall eye lit up at the sight of the carrots. Really he was the muckiest horse.

'Arthur's joined the Green Party,' giggled Lysander.

'Must you trivialize everything? I hope to stand for the Rutminster Greens at the next election.'

'Oh, right,' said Lysander, 'or rather left.'

'Greens are not automatically left-wing.' Rachel put a plate of carrot matchsticks in front of her unenthusiastic children.

'Go and explore,' Lysander told them. 'There's a nice pond outside.'

'Who furnished this place?' Rachel's eyes roved over the ticking sofas and chairs and the bishop's throne.

'Marigold.' Lysander handed Rachel a glass of Muscadet. 'She's getting me a microwave, thank God,' he removed a dandy brush, a curry comb and a chewed trainer from the sofa, 'which'll help because I get bored and forget to eat waiting for things to heat up.'

'Trust Marigold!' Rachel was appalled. 'Microwaves are not only toxic to the liver but they kill off the brain cells.'

'My liver came out waving a white flag years ago,' said Lysander draining half his glass, 'and I've never had a brain cell to kill. Hallo, kids, I've got you a good video.'

Again the children's faces lit up, then faded as their mother said she didn't allow them to watch television, then getting some loo rolls and egg boxes out of her basket urged them to make a castle.

'Want to watch television,' grumbled Vanya.

'Well, you can't. I'll start you off,' said Rachel, getting out a bottle of glue. 'This place is a tip. Don't you ever clean it?'

'Mother Courage comes once a week but we seem to spend our time gossiping. She says she doesn't like to move things, so she doesn't.'

There was a pause. It was terribly hot.

'Perhaps you'd like a swim in the river,' suggested Lysander. 'I wouldn't mind one.'

'Polluted,' snapped Rachel.

'Well, we'd better have some supper.'

'Oh God,' Rachel clutched her head. 'White baps are the worst thing you could give them, and haven't you realized beef burgers are made from the pancreas, lungs and testicles of animals?'

Lysander looked at her meditatively. Easygoing to a fault, he was about to tell her he could see exactly why Boris had walked out. Then he caught sight of Masha and Vanya. They were like children on newsreels, so often photographed beside bomb craters and the dusty rubble of houses in foreign wars, children displaced because they'd been fought over.

'There are plenty of eggs,' he said gently. 'Your mother can make us something she considers suitable for supper and we can play football with Jack, and then I'll give you a ride on Arthur.'

This was a huge success. Jack could dribble a ball for hours and Arthur loved children. Sent to wash their hands before supper, Masha and Vanya came out shrieking with giggles.

'Rachel, Rachel, come and see the willies.'

Storming into the downstairs lavatory, Rachel found the artistic fruits of Lysander's drunken despair after the church fête when he had taken a can of red paint and sprayed cocks, balls and a vast nude lady with enormous tits and crossed eyes over the walls and then written I LOVE GORGY in huge letters.

'Oh God, I forgot about that!' Lysander tried not to laugh with the children.

'Not only are you damaging the ozone layer and adding to global warming,' stormed Rachel, 'but you're ejecting tiny particles of toxic paint into the environment.'

'And you make the worst scrambled egg I've ever tasted,' Lysander wanted to tell her as he emptied half a bottle of tomato ketchup, Rannaldini fashion, over the loose, tasteless mass. The only way Rachel used salt was to rub it into people's wounds.

The dandelion salad was even more disgusting. Lysander found the only answer was to drink as much as possible and even Rachel mellowed a bit after two glasses and allowed the children to watch a Donald Duck video.

'I identified with Donald like mad,' Lysander told Rachel as he loaded the machine. 'When I was a child no-one could understand what I said, like him.'

But Rachel was gazing across at Valhalla.

'There's that bastard Rannaldini's place. He was the

one who wrecked our marriage, persuading Boris it was *de rigueur* to have something on the side. He introduced Boris to Chloe.'

'How does she get on with the children?'

'Chloe? They adore her. Not surprising. She's filthy rich and fills them up with sweets and junk food and battery-operated toys every time they visit her and Boris. How can they ever learn to reject consumerism with that going on? And she lets them watch television all day.'

'They're sweet children.'

'I know. I just go crackers not being able to practise.'

To distract Rachel from the fact that both Jack and Maggie had climbed on to the children's laps, Lysander took her outside. The sun was setting; tobacco plants and stocks, fighting a losing battle with nettles, scented the evening. Owls were hooting in the wood. Not daring to risk mosquito spray, Lysander lit a cigarette.

After a long pause, Rachel stammered: 'I'm sorry. I've been bloody all evening. I've had to nag and nag Boris for maintenance. This morning a cheque arrived for the right money but signed by Chloe. It's so humiliating but I can't afford to tear it up.'

Lysander was shocked. 'You poor thing. I'll give you the money, then you can. I'm quite flush at the moment.'

But Rachel was too proud. 'I've got teaching jobs, and Hermione pays when she's around. God, she's awful! She never opens her mouth except for dollars and all her conversation is about money.'

'What's the point of those balls outside her house?'

'Self-aggrandizement,' said Rachel sourly. 'Rannaldini has griffins, Georgie Maguire has angels, Marigold has lions. Now Hermione has balls – probably Bob's. She emasculates him enough.'

'He's a seriously nice guy,' said Lysander. 'Good cricketer, too.'

'He's the most attractive man in Paradise,' said Rachel.

She looks beautiful again now, thought Lysander, with

her sad foxy face warmed by the falling sun and her beautiful fox's ankles beneath that shapeless dress.

'By the way,' he said, 'I discovered what Hermione's mega-crisis was.'

'How?'

'From Gretel, her hairy-legged nanny.'

'Why on earth should she shave her legs?'

'No reason at all, but if she wants me to be her Hansel, she better start waxing. Anyway, she told me that Rannaldini is making this film called *Fidelio* – should be called Infidelio – about some woman called Nora who dresses up as a boy and springs her husband from jug.'

'She's called Leonore – I know the story,' said Rachel crushingly.

'Of course you would. Sorry. Anyway, Hermione automatically expected to get the part, but Rannaldini told her: "You could hardly pass for a faithful wife, my dear, and with those outsize boobs no self-respecting gaoler would ever mistake you for a boy," so he's given the part to Cecilia.'

Rachel whistled. 'But I suppose it figures. Rannaldini would far rather put Catchitune's vast fee into the pocket of Cecilia, who's always pestering him for more alimony, than into Hermione's. No wonder Hermione's livid.'

'D'you think he'll make Cecilia strip off again?'

'*Fidelio*'s quite a different opera,' said Rachel patronizingly. 'On the one hand it's about an individual living in chains being rescued by a loving woman, but Beethoven raises the story to a universal level in which the human race is saved by the female sex.'

'Oh, right,' said Lysander. 'Rannaldini should love it. He's turned on by chains. Pity some loving man can't rescue poor darling Kitty.'

'Kitty could walk out if she wanted to,' said Rachel dismissively.

Yawning, surreptitiously looking at his watch, Lysander wondered how soon he could take her home. He looked longingly across at Angel's Reach, blank now the sun had set, straining his eyes to see Georgie and Guy sitting on the terrace and Dinsdale snapping at flies.

'If you never got to that interview,' asked Rachel, 'what are you doing for a living now?'

'Playing a lot of polo,' said Lysander evasively, 'and hoping to get Arthur fit for the Rutminster next year.'

'Lucky to have a private income. Are you in a relationship?'

'No, well yes.' Suddenly he desperately needed to tell someone. 'Basically I'm mad about Georgie Maguire, she and I, well, we're sort of an item.'

Rachel went rigid with disapproval.

'But what about her wildly uxorious husband?'

'He's been screwing around.'

'So, all that "Rock Star" rubbish is for commercial profit. United front for the world, screw like rabbits in private. I always thought Georgie was phoney.'

'She didn't know about the screwing around when she wrote "Rock Star". She was devastated,' said Lysander icily. 'She's the loveliest woman I've ever met.'

'Don't be ridiculous. She's old enough to be your mother!'

'That's probably why I love her. The video's finished.' Lysander picked up his car keys. 'I'll take you home.'

Rachel was horrified. Why had she been such an utter bitch? How could she explain that she'd been celibate for six months, that she felt like a fun-fair in winter, endlessly wondering if summer would ever come again, that it was desire that made her so cantankerous and the only thing she wanted was for Lysander to take her to bed?

35

Hermione's hysterics echoed round Paradise. She wasn't placated by the letters – fanny mail the Ideal Homo called it – that poured in after the release of *Don Giovanni*, nor even by offers to star in a musical of *Lady Chatterley's Lover*.

Being Hermione, however, within twenty-four hours she was telling everyone, including Kitty, that the only thing that shocked her was Rannaldini's appalling insensitivity to Kitty in casting an ex-wife as Leonore. Hermione had not forgiven Kitty for being the recipient of Georgie's and Marigold's confidences about their marriage problems. She might put down Georgie by praising Brickie's dignity, but she still wanted to exceed Kitty in everything, even in being more of a brick.

But she was not prepared to concede defeat. As Rannaldini had inconveniently buzzed off to Madrid and Flora, Hermione's first chance to confront him would be at the camera rehearsal for the Verdi *Requiem* which was already being trailed as the prom of the year.

Knowing Rannaldini would be stymied if she refused to go on, Hermione was determined to use this as a bargaining point to get herself the part of Leonore.

As usual Rannaldini rolled up at the Albert Hall when the rehearsal was nearly over, having left it to Heinz, the colourless Swiss, who didn't even have one variety, who had replaced Boris Levitsky as assistant conductor. Three of the soloists, a tenor, a bass and Monalisa Wilson, a vast black mezzo-soprano with a vast voice, were well into the 'Lux Aeterna', exhorting the Lord to let eternal light shine on them. Hermione, who was not needed in this penultimate section, had retreated to her dressing room venting her rage at Rannaldini's tardiness on her dressmaker. The poor woman had stayed up night after night finishing a ravishing low-cut dress made of panels of lavender and willow-herb-pink silk, specially for the occasion. Alas, she had not allowed for Hermione's misery bingeing over the weekend and the zip wouldn't do up.

'You've skimped on the material!' Hermione's screeches rose above the orchestra and other soloists. 'You cut it too small deliberately, so you'd have some spare for yourself. Those silks cost two hundred pounds a metre. Ouch! That pin stuck into me.'

Trying to appear not to be listening, the television crew wandered about looking for places to put their lights and cameras the following night. The London Met, used to Hermione's tantrums, were fed up. It was a blistering hot afternoon; outside in the park one could hardly breathe. They'd just returned from an exhausting tour of the Eastern Bloc with Oswaldo. Rannaldini earned three hundred thousand a year as their musical director. They hadn't seen him for three months and now he'd swanned in to impose his usual rule of divine right and brute force. They had vowed that they'd stand up to him, but now once more they were reduced to quivering jelly.

'Lux Aeterna' over, Rannaldini insisted on taking the orchestra without Hermione and the chorus through the final 'Dies Irae', with its deafening thunderclaps that came before the skirling descending flashes of lightning. The London Met knew the *Requiem* backwards, they had made the definitive recording with Rannaldini and Hermione in 1986, but he was determined to show even the oldest hand that their playing had become fuzzy and inaccurate. As he raised his baton, some of the orchestra started and some didn't and they started to laugh out of nerves, and were yelled at for inattention. But soon the brass fanfares were ringing thrillingly round the hall.

'Sounds like a completely different orchestra,' said Cordelia, the BBC's glamorous blond lighting camera-person.

Calling a halt Rannaldini got into a huddle with her and the director, persuading them to lower all the Albert Hall and television lights during the 'Sanctus' and 'Agnus Dei', then at the beginning of 'Lux Aeterna' at the words, '*Let everlasting light shine upon them,*' to raise them dramatically.

'What about Harefield? She's the star,' asked Cordelia. 'She'll need special lighting.'

'No, no.' Rannaldini gave a thin smile. 'Light her better than Monalisa and the men and you'll be accused of racism *and* sexism.'

'Oh, right,' said Cordelia, going pale.

'Not even in Mrs Harefield's last section, the "Libera Me" for soprano and chorus. In fact,' Rannaldini leant forward so Cordelia, who had already been mesmerized by his coal-black eyes, caught a whiff of Maestro, 'it is me who the audience have come to see. Tomorrow you will witness the rerun of the most successful classical record of all times.'

'Oh, right,' said Cordelia five minutes later. 'So we're really talking about "Rannaldini in Concert" and if the cameras focus on you throughout the evening with total darkness at the end except for your lit-up face, we won't go far wrong.'

'Exactly,' smiled Rannaldini.

'And we can always concentrate on Harefield's cleavage in the boring bits.'

'There will be no boring bits,' said Rannaldini icily.

The orchestra looked at their watches. In ten minutes they'd be into overtime. Determined to hold up the proceedings but disconcerted because she hadn't been summoned, Hermione finally emerged from her dressing room. For once she was wearing trousers, which emphasized her large bottom but covered up the bramble scratches on her ankles, caused by trying to force her way down the now unstrimmed path to Rannaldini's tower. Ignoring him, she took up her position for the final 'Libera Me' on his left, with Monalisa Wilson like a great bolster between them.

'Maestro and Maestress,' giggled the first flautist.

Breast quivering, eyes shining with unspilt tears, Hermione's mournful voice was soon soaring above the orchestra and chorus like a full moon above the stars, as she pleaded to be delivered from God's wrath.

'God's maybe – but not Rannaldini's,' murmured the leader of the orchestra.

What a beautiful voice, what a beautiful lady, thought Cordelia with a shiver of pleasure, but Rannaldini had called a halt.

'You're dragging, Mrs Harefield,' he said bitchily. 'We don't want the promenaders nodding off. There's nowhere for them to lie down. This is a requiem in memory of the greatest Italian writer since Dante, not a lot of old horses on their way to the knackers.'

But when Hermione opened her mouth to screech a reply, Rannaldini countered by pointing at the brass as though he were plunging a skewer into a well-done turkey and started up the music again. Hermione had a powerful voice, but, supported by the heavy artillery of the orchestra and the aerial bombardment of the chorus, Rannaldini was bound to win.

'Louder, louder,' he yelled raising the empty air with splayed fingers. 'I can steel hear Mrs Harefield.'

The screaming match that followed was so terrifying that the poor little tenor fell into the ferns and Monalisa Wilson snatched up the yellow duster belonging to the leader of the orchestra and tied it under her chin, mistaking it for her new Hermès scarf, before she fled.

The orchestra watched mildly interested and later heard Hermione and Rannaldini squealing in her dressing room like pigs in an abattoir, until Rannaldini stormed out.

★   ★   ★

When Hermione rang Rannaldini in his flat overlooking Hyde Park to continue the row the London secretary put her on hold so she had to listen to herself singing Donna Anna's aria from *Don Giovanni*: 'All my love on him I lavished', on the recorded musak which made her crosser than ever.

Rannaldini spent the rest of the afternoon auditioning singers and musicians for *Fidelio* who had to hump their instruments up eight flights of stairs because the lift wasn't working. He then read through a letter he had dictated to Rachel's husband Boris, who, having waded through a mountain of unsolicited scores sent into the London Met, had weeded out half a dozen of merit, putting Boris's *Berlin Wall Symphony*, dedicated to his new love Chloe, on top.

Rannaldini needed Boris. He was aware that a great conductor is assessed in part by the new music he brings into being. Boris had been invaluable on a freelance basis, pulling out the good stuff, often presenting it in a simplified form to save Rannaldini time. He didn't want to upset Boris too much.

'*My dear Boy*,' he wrote in black ink, then reading the typing, '*Thank you for the latest batch, from which I am returning your symphony. Since we are friends, I know you would prefer me to be frank. When I read your music, I do not hear it. For the enormous orchestra it requires, it is highly complex. No-one could sing the chorus correctly. One would have to hear it a dozen times to begin to understand it. Neither I nor the public have the time nor the inclination. The good news is that I have a series of lectures to do for BBC2 in the autumn. I shall need research done. I will call you. Best to Chloe.*'

His London secretary didn't type as well as Kitty but she was much prettier. As he scribbled '*Yours ever, Rannaldini*,' he felt he had been very good to Boris.

Showered and scented in a new grey satin dressing gown, having assembled some exciting sex toys, including a three-fingered vibrator bought in Paris on the way home, and several phials of amyl nitrite, Rannaldini waited for Flora. Clive was collecting her from Heathrow. Outside, the dusty plane trees were past their best and the bleached grass of the park was already covered in curled-up brown leaves and couples in T-shirts and shorts sharing a bottle before tonight's performance. Tomorrow you wouldn't see a blade of grass for crowds jostling to gaze at him and Hermione.

While he waited, he flipped through the *Requiem*. He had conducted it so many times but one must always try and bring something new and exciting to a work. His thoughts strayed to Cordelia, the blond camera-person. She was new and very exciting. Tomorrow Flora had to return to Paradise to get her trunk packed for the autumn term, so he would ask Cordelia out after the performance. Then he could invite her to light his bedroom with its shiny indigo walls and ceiling, its dark mirrors and its rich crimson four-poster. He might even offer her a job on *Fidelio*. He would have loved a threesome this evening, but Flora, despite her habitual cool, would never wear it. Even so he was roused out of the most erotic fantasy by crashes on the door louder than Verdi's thunderclaps. Through the spyhole he could see Hermione.

'Let me in, Rannaldini.'

Hermione could cry louder than she could sing, and as the editor of *The Scorpion* had installed a bimbo in the next-door flat, Rannaldini let her in at once.

'I cannot bear it, Maestro. Life is too short.'

Rannaldini agreed and opened a bottle of Krug.

'You have been behaving very badly, Carissima.'

'I know, Rannaldini.'

'You will 'ave to stand in the corner, and you know what that means.'

'Yes, yes.' Hermione's eyes glistened with excitement; he could smell the goaty reek of her body.

'What a peety Keety is due any minute,' Rannaldini smiled sadistically, 'and you must leave now.'

'Kitty won't mind,' protested Hermione, 'say we're rehearsing.'

'We promised to treat Keety with compassion, remember?'

Hermione remembered no such thing.

'When we get back to Valhalla,' briefly Rannaldini massaged her bottom, 'it will be the punishment bell.'

He was so worried Flora would arrive, as there was no late-night shopping to hold her up, that he was forced to get dressed and go down the eight flights of stairs and bundle Hermione into a taxi.

Flora arrived twenty minutes later wearing Georgie's emerald-green leotard, weighed down by carrier bags full of knickers and bringing him duty-free Armagnac, Givenchy for Men and a new biography of Swinburne, whom he admired. Rannaldini, who never wore any other scent but Maestro, was touched. Knowing him to be rich, women seldom gave him presents. Rather indiscreetly he told her about the screaming match.

'You need some Hermione Replacement Therapy.' Flora took a slug of Krug. 'The only time the silly old bag hits top E these days is when some journalist reveals her real age.'

'You should take your singing seriously. Then you can replace her. What d'you think of these?'

He threw half a dozen photographs on the little table beside her.

'Uck! Who are they?'

'You, my angel.' Rannaldini slid his hands over her breasts. 'Don't you recognize yourself?'

'My God!' Fascinated, Flora examined her own shining pink clitoris and glistening labia lips laid back like butterfly wings.

'I enter two prints anonymously in competition in German pornographic magazine,' announced Rannaldini proudly, 'you win first prize!'

'That's nice! As I'm obviously going to plough my A

levels I can put that in my cv when I start job-hunting. It might help in times of recession.'

At a rare loose-end Hermione went back to hers and Bob's house in Radnor Walk. Always grumbling that she never had an evening in, she now had absolutely no idea what to do with herself. Bob, still tying up all the details for tomorrow, wouldn't be home for hours. The maid, about to go out on her evening off, made Hermione a prawn omelette and was understandably irritated to find seven-eighths of it in the bin the following morning. Having sung a lullaby over the telephone to little Cosmo, who rudely told her to piss off, Hermione picked up the score of the *Requiem*. She'd show Rannaldini he couldn't do without her tomorrow when she moved the promenaders to tears and then frenzied applause. How dare he boot her out because Kitty was in London? On impulse, to reassure herself she rang Valhalla.

' 'Allo.' It was Kitty's breathless voice. ' 'Oo's that?'

Hermione thought she must have rung the London number. Dropping the telephone she re-punched the Paradise number, got Kitty again and hung up.

In a fury she rang Rannaldini, who had his head between Flora's legs and mumbled truthfully that he couldn't talk. Then when Hermione threatened to come round, he said he would take it in another room. Having put on the mute button while he brought Flora to orgasm, he proceeded to tell Hermione he had lied to her.

'I am with Cecilia not Keety, but I didn't want to upset you before your big night. I want you to sleep well and 'ave beautiful dreams.'

'Why are you seeing Cecilia?' demanded Hermione.

'A crisis about Natasha's future. We have to discuss UCCA forms.' Rannaldini lowered his voice. 'I must go, Carissima.'

'Why are you such a terrible liar?' asked Flora fascinated.

'When I was five I own up to stealing chocolate and my

mother beat me, which I didn't like. So I never bother with the truth again.'

Hermione had a terrible night. She went to bed early, passed the long lonely hours brooding about Cecilia, flicking channels and then ordering the maid and Bob to make her endless cups of camomile tea and honey when they returned. Having been persuaded by Bob to take a Mogadon she was wracked by nightmares about losing her place, forgetting the notes and arriving at the Albert Hall to find Cecilia singing in her place.

After another pill at five in the morning, she woke at midday when the maid brought her breakfast and the *Daily Telegraph*. The doctor would be coming round later with her Vitamin A and B jabs to give her stamina and keep the saliva going. She had just taken a large mouthful of fried bread when a picture of Cecilia on the Arts page, with a caption about a husband and ex-wife team in the forthcoming *Fidelio*, re-ignited her rage.

When she dialled The Savoy where Cecilia always stayed, a maid answered. Cecilia wasn't to be disturbed.

'Say it's Mrs Harefield and it's important.'

Finally, out of curiosity, Cecilia allowed Hermione to be put through and was very surprised when Hermione congratulated her with great warmth on getting the part of Leonore. 'I know how good you'll be.'

'Vy, tank you, 'Ermione.' Although placated, Cecilia was still suspicious. 'That is large of you.'

'Is Natasha all right?'

'Vy should she not be?'

'Did Rannaldini give you those tickets last night?' asked Hermione idly. 'I thought we might all dine together afterwards.'

'I did not see Rannaldini last night. I only fly een this morning,' said Cecilia. 'He was with Keety last night.'

'He was not,' screamed Hermione. 'Kitty was in Paradise. I checked. Rannaldini said he was discussing Natasha's UCCA with you.'

'The fucker! He no discuss UCCA wiz me,' screeched Cecilia. 'Ven did he tell you zat?'

But Hermione was gone, tugging on her clothes and roaring round to Rannaldini's. The lift was still broken and a cellist was lugging his priceless Strad up the stairs, when Hermione overtook him. Shoving aside Rannaldini's London secretary, who was holding the door open for the cellist, she barged inside.

'Rannaldini's not here, Mrs Harefield,' said the London secretary aghast. 'He's just slipped out.'

'Of whom?' screeched Hermione. 'Don't lie to me.'

Charging into the bedroom she met Rannaldini coming out of the shower wrapped in a red towel.

'You wicked liar,' screamed Hermione.

Terrified she was going to knee him in the groin, Rannaldini clapped his hands over his testicles, leaving his face exposed. Next moment Hermione caught his eye with a punishing right hook. Rannaldini would have hit her back had not the cellist appeared open mouthed in the doorway, followed by a screaming Cecilia.

Very Italian, with snapping over-familiar dark eyes, an oily, olive complexion, streaked blond hair and a muscular worked-out body, Cecilia was wearing an immaculate black suit with a long collarless jacket and a short pleated skirt and looked as though she'd come straight off the catwalk with every claw out. Gathering up a bust of Donizetti with a manic jangling of bracelets, she hurled it at Rannaldini, who ducked so it shattered the mirror behind him, which had witnessed so much of their lovemaking.

'*Scellerato, scellerato,*' screamed Cecilia, echoing Donna Anna as she started working her way through a bowl of alabaster eggs.

'Monster of vice, sink of iniquity,' screamed Hermione, echoing Donna Elvira.

'Bastard,' screamed Cecilia, just missing Rannaldini's left ear.

'She's right, you *are* a bastard,' yelled Hermione, kicking

Rannaldini's shins and rushing out of the flat.

'Not my Strad,' screamed the waiting cellist as Rannaldini ran into the living room and grabbed his cello to stem the bombardment.

Cecilia had not played cricket at school but she finally caught Rannaldini on the corner of his other eye with a powder-blue egg. Storming out, she sent flying a blonde in a white towelling dressing gown who'd just emerged from the flat of the editor of *The Scorpion* to see what the fuss was about. At which moment, laughing her head off, Flora emerged from the shower, having witnessed the whole thing through a two-way mirror.

'Oh dear.' She touched Rannaldini's two fast blackening eyes. 'Now there are two Pandas in Paradise!'

Rannaldini had conducted with peritonitis, with snakebite, even with a sprained right wrist before now, but he refused to expose himself to ridicule. Ringing Bob he croaked down the telephone that he was dying of pneumonia. Shrouded in dark glasses and a black fedora, he flew off to a retreat in the Alps.

Over in Richmond in Chloe's drawing room, Boris Levitsky wrestled with a two-hour lecture on Mahler, which he had to deliver at Cotchester University the following day and tried not to brood over Rannaldini's vile letter returning his symphony.

Chloe was out recording the *Alto Rhapsody*, one of her first big breaks. She would probably go out to dinner with the director and the conductor afterwards and not be home for hours.

Bearing in mind Boris's fondness for red meat and red wine and red-blooded women, she had left him a bottle of Pedrotti now being warmed by the evening sun, which he had vowed not to touch until he had finished his lecture. In the fridge was a large steak with instructions how long to grill it on each side and a pierced baked potato to put in the top right of the Aga an hour before he wanted to eat.

Chloe herself, however, had been less red-blooded since

Boris moved in. As he was hopelessly impractical, she had to look after him and, as he hadn't sold a single composition and had packed in his job at Bagley Hall, she had had to support him as well. Finally last week, with the thought: Why doesn't the stroppy cow get off her ass? ringing through her head, she had had to write a cheque for Rachel's maintenance.

This had been the greatest humiliation of Boris's life, which was why he had fired off his new symphony to Rannaldini. Groaning, he wrenched his mind back to his lecture.

'*God, I could endure anything,*' Mahler had written in despair to a woman fan, after paying the Berlin Phil to perform his second symphony, '*if only the future of my work seemed secure. I am now thirty-five years old, uncelebrated, very unperformed. But I keep busy and don't let it get me down. I have patience. I wait.*'

Boris didn't have patience – Chloe said it was like living with a good-looking bear – nor did he have the cash to pay the London Met to perform his symphony, which that shit Rannaldini had torn to shreds. Outside, the turning trees were casting long shadows of evening across the park. A young mother with a pack of dusty, happy children walked past carrying a picnic basket. Boris groaned again. He never dreamt he would feel so guilty or miss Rachel and his children so much.

Bob Harefield, having endured Hermione's hysterics, was now faced with the prospect of replacing Rannaldini, placating an enraged BBC and probably being lynched by a massive audience suffering from acute withdrawal symptoms. Oswaldo was in Moscow. Heinz the Swiss was on a plane to Rome. Bob was fed up with Rannaldini. There were other conductors he could have tried but he had always had a soft spot for Rachel and her husband.

Taking a deep breath, Bob dialled Chloe's number.

'Rannaldini's got his whores crossed,' he told Boris.

'Do you want to conduct the Verdi *Requiem* tonight? I'm afraid there's no time for a rehearsal.'

There was a long pause.

'Yes, I will come. Thank you, Bob,' said Boris, 'but I 'ave no score, no car, no tailcoat. He is at dry cleaners. Chloe's cat throw up on heem.'

'I'm sending a car for you with the score in,' said Bob, who knew Boris had been done for drink-driving and did not want to risk him getting lost, 'and we'll find you some tails. What size shirt are you?'

'I look.' Boris tugged the back of his collar round to the front. 'Size sixteen. I thank you, Bob, from the beneath of my 'eart.'

385

36

Boris was too busy mugging up the score to feel really
nervous until he saw the Albert Hall, enmeshed like
Laccoon in the cables of the BBC television vans, and
the vast crowds that had gathered without any hope of
tickets just to get a glimpse of Harefield and Rannaldini
arriving. Once in the conductor's dressing room, he had
great difficulty putting on the hired tails. When your
hands are trembling frantically it is hard to get the studs
through the starched shirt-front. He wished he could
stiffen his upper lip accordingly. The white tie took
even longer and was so white that his face and teeth
looked yellow by comparison. He felt as if he were in
a sauna and a straight-jacket already.

'Need any help?' Bob's gleaming brown head came
round the door.

'Eef my hand shake this much when I get up there,
we start prestissimo and the 'ole thing will be over een
ten minutes,' said Boris through chattering teeth, then
blushing, 'Is possible to let Rachel know?'

'I rang her,' said Bob. Then, thinking that at such a time
white lies didn't matter, 'She sent her love and wished you
luck.'

'Her love, oh God, if I make a dick-up, what will she
say, and how can I control Hermione?'

'Hermione's cried off,' said Bob grimly.

Despite his uncharacteristically enraged accusations that
she was being utterly unprofessional and bloody wet,
his wife had refused to go on.

'Christ! Who sing eenstead?'

'I thought, fuck it – so I rang Cecilia.'

'Omigod!' Boris went even paler. 'I control her even less. She raise skirt in middle of other soloists' arias to distract audience.'

Bob laughed. 'Tonight she'll play ball. She's got the perfect opportunity to upstage Rannaldini and Hermione. It's me who's going to end up out of a job and in the divorce courts.'

The shadows under Bob's eyes were as deeply etched as bison horns in cave paintings. The poor guy really has put his head on the block, thought Boris.

It was a stiflingly hot evening. Ladies with fans ruffled the fringes of those beside them. The London Met were tuning up like birds in a wood. Microphones hung like spiders tossed out of a window. In the dress circle, stalls and red-curtained gold boxes, people chattered away excitedly in a score of different languages. The promenade area was overflowing, mostly with young men with beards and their girlfriends, bright eyed and rosy cheeked like younger sisters in Chekhov. Many of them held up RANNALDINI RULES OK and WE LOVE HERMIONE banners. Paper darts were sailing through the air. The BBC had threatened to cancel. Richard Baker, who was covering the prom for television, and Peter Barker, for the radio, were frantically rewriting their scripts, as Bob mounted the rostrum and dropped the bombshell that both Rannaldini and Hermione would not be appearing.

With the storm of protest that broke over his head, it was a minute before he could announce that their places would be taken by Boris Levitsky, a young Russian composer and conductor, very well known in his own country, and by one of the greatest divas in the world, Cecilia Rannaldini.

'So at least,' Bob shouted over the uproar, 'you needn't fold up your Rannaldini banners.'

The audience glared at him stonily and started to boo

387

and catcall. Some of them had flown thousands of miles and threatened to demand their money back. Others walked out in noisy disgust.

'I 'ate them,' muttered Boris, waiting to go on.

'They'll hate themselves even more when they realize what they've missed,' said Bob, combing Boris's tangled pony-tail at the back, his calm exterior belying panic within. What if Boris really couldn't cope? The *Requiem* was one of the most complex and demanding pieces of music. The chorus, sitting up against their crimson curtains, slumped in disgust. All the young sopranos and altos had been to the hairdressers and bought new black dresses. They might never get another chance to sing, or whatever, under the great Rannaldini.

'O day of wrath, O day of calamity,' sang the front-desk cellist who'd nearly lost his Strad in Rannaldini's flat the day before. 'Bob'll get lynched if Boris cocks it up.'

'Boris is a good boy,' said his neighbour, opening the score they were sharing.

'And virtually inexperienced in public.'

'We'll be OK as long as we don't look up.'

Larry Lockton was so enraged he had to rush to the bar for a quadruple whisky. In anticipation of massive popular demand, Catchitune had just put on a huge re-press of Harefield's and Rannaldini's legendary 1986 version.

'The only thing that fucker can be relied on to do is to let one down. We're leaving at the interval.'

'There isn't an interval,' said Marigold, consulting her programme. 'They keep going for ninety minutes without a break. Poor Boris. I wonder what's happened to Hermione and Rannaldini.'

'I hope it's something serious,' snarled Larry.

It was bang on seven-thirty. Boris tried to keep still, take deep breaths and make his mind a blank, but the butterflies inside him had turned into wild geese flapping around.

'Good luck,' said Bob. 'And may God go with you,' he whispered.

The promenaders scrambled to their feet. Boris fell up the stairs as he and the four soloists came on and had to be picked up by Monalisa Wilson, enormous and resplendent in flame-red chiffon.

'I'm glad mega-Stalin is indisposed,' she murmured to Boris. 'He frightens the life out of me.'

Reluctant laughter swept the hall as she brushed the dust off his knees in a motherly fashion and straightened his tie.

'We show eem, we do better wizout him,' whispered Cecilia, who looked stunning, but more suited to sing in a night-club in clinging gold sequins. The boy's very attractive, she thought, and comparatively untouched by human hand.

The biggest audience ever squeezed into the Albert Hall were bitterly disappointed, but they saw Boris's deathly pallor and his youth and some of the *cognoscenti* remembered his defection from Russia. Goodwill began to trickle back.

Standing on the rostrum, all Boris could see below the soaring organ pipes were rows and rows of men and women dressed in black – as if for his funeral. He saw the pearly skins of the drums and the gleaming brass who would play such a big part in the next ninety minutes. The bows of the string section were poised above their instruments.

Boris looked at them all solemnly and searchingly. The notes of the score seemed to swim before his eyes – 278 pages of decision making and complexity. Bending his dark head he kissed the first page and with a totally steady hand gave the upbeat. The whispering nightingales of the 'Kyrie éleison' can seldom have been slower or more hushed. Alas, some gunman took off down Kensington Gore after a shoot-out and soon a convoy of police cars, sirens wailing sforzando and hurtling after him, could all be heard within the hall, destroying the mood of veneration and snapping Boris's concentration.

The first deafening crashes of the 'Dies Irae' were very ragged. Every hair of Boris's black glossy head was drenched in sweat. The audience were beginning to exchange pained glances. Twice he lost his place, pages fluttering like a trapped butterfly, but like kindly trusty old Arthur with a nervous young rider, the London Met carried him until he found it again.

His stick technique was ungainly. When emotion overwhelmed him, he slowed down dangerously. In the 'Recordare Jesu Pie' when Cecilia and Monalisa sang their first exquisite, divinely complementary duet together, their voices chasing each other in arrows of light like fireflies, he was so moved that he took his stick in both hands and began loudly to sing along with them, until he remembered where he was, and then had to wipe his eyes. But slowly both orchestra, chorus and packed crowd responded to his passion and terrifying intensity.

Back in Paradise earlier in the evening, Lysander, sounding like Neptune at the bottom of the sea, had rung Georgie from his car.

'I've really goofed this time,' he said. 'Rannaldini's ducked out of the prom so Boris is going on in his place – Verdi's Recreation or something. Rachel wanted to tape it on my machine, but it's fucked and I was stupid enough to say I was coming to see you and before I knew it, Georgie, I said, why didn't she come as well. I'm really sorry, I've screwed up Flora's last night.'

'It's OK,' Georgie stemmed the flow.

'We'll get a take-away. Rachel can have very dry vegetables,' said Lysander, reeling in gratitude. 'She's seriously fierce, but basically if she's watching Boris she won't have too much time to bang on about unleaded pet-food.'

Rachel was even fiercer. Overwhelmed with envy for Georgie's lovely house, her replete, indolent beauty and the obvious adoration of Lysander, only curbed by Flora's presence, she was driven into a frenzy of disapproval. She was also overcome with nerves for Boris, furious at having to watch him in front of strangers, ashamed how jealous she felt that he rather than she should be given this massive break.

A quick drink on the terrace before the programme produced a storm of abuse because the overflow from Flora's bath came splattering out on to the terrace and no-one did anything to save the water for the garden or even for washing the car. Trying to lighten things, Lysander said it was like Arthur peeing and then couldn't stop laughing.

Georgie, who was wearing an old sundress and a yellow chiffon scarf to hide yet more lovebites, was taken aback by how pretty Rachel was. Like one of those girls the upper fourth have crushes on at school, she carried understatement to an art form. Tonight her unmade-up eyes were hidden by big spectacles and, with loose black trousers and padded shoulders on her long black cardigan, you had no idea what shape she was, but could only think how marvellous she'd look with everything off.

On the way into the drawing room and the television, Georgie made the mistake of showing her the new yellow-flowered paper in the dining room.

'I wonder how many rain-forest trees were cut down to produce that,' said Rachel coldly. 'I prefer painted walls myself.'

Nor were matters improved when Flora wandered in with a huge vodka and tonic and wearing one of Guy's shirts with all the buttons done up to hide her lovebites from her mother, and promptly lit a cigarette.

'You shouldn't be smoking at your age,' snapped Rachel.

Having heard about Flora throwing up in Boris's trumpet and remembering him saying how sexy and talented she was, she was not disposed to like her.

'If I want to kill myself I should be allowed to,' said Flora, kissing Lysander hallo.

'It's the harm you're doing to everyone else's lungs. Move dog,' ordered Rachel, who wanted to sit on the sofa facing the television.

Dinsdale growled ominously.

'I'm afraid he won't,' said Georgie apologetically.

'The fleas are terrible, Mum,' said Flora slapping her ankles. 'Like dew leaping on the lawn.'

Very pointedly curling her long legs underneath her, Rachel sat in an armchair. Richard Baker was now telling viewers that Rannaldini and Hermione wouldn't be appearing.

'Why on earth d'you think Rannaldini cried off?' asked Georgie, emptying the remains of a bottle of Muscadet into everyone's glasses. Flora, who knew, couldn't say anything.

'Expect he had an offer he couldn't refuse,' remarked Rachel sourly. 'Like some girl he hadn't fucked before.'

Once in flow, she went on about Rannaldini's promiscuity.

'He was always trying to get me into bed, and he's had Chloe, Boris's present incumbent.'

Ultra-cool on the surface about Rannaldini, having enjoyed nearly a month in his company, Flora was now realizing how desperately she was going to miss him. Tired, and depressed that she hadn't done any of her holiday work, she wondered how on earth she would put up with the restrictions of Bagley Hall; and now this stupid bitch wouldn't stop slagging him off.

Once the *Requiem* was under way, however, Rachel's scorn was reserved for Boris. Why the hell was he wearing red braces? Why hadn't he cleaned his nails? Look at his hair halfway down his back. That must be Chloe's doing. Look how it was escaping from its pony-tail. Now he was taking things too fast, now much too slowly – he was so over-emotional – why the hell couldn't he beat in time?

'Why don't you shut up and listen?' muttered Flora.

'Boris is conducting marvellously,' said Lysander at the end of the 'Dies Irae', 'but it's a bit Inspector Morse for me.' Kissing Georgie and seeing they were supplied with drinks, he slid off to Rutminster to get a take-away.

'I'd no idea Cecilia had such a wonderful voice or was so beautiful,' sighed Georgie.

'Rannaldini bonks her every time she comes over,' spat Rachel.

I'll kill her soon, thought Flora.

'Oh, there's Marigold,' said Georgie as the camera roved over the audience. 'Doesn't she look gorgeous?'

'Anyone can look gorgeous when they spend that kind of money on clothes,' hissed Rachel, 'and the way her megalomaniac husband floodlights his house every night – such a waste of energy.'

She was panic-stricken that any minute the cameras would latch on to Chloe looking more blond and beautiful than anyone. There, dominating the screen, was the husband who had left her and who, after the performance, would go back to Chloe's arms.

The *Requiem* was drawing to a close. The television crew who'd come to mock were in ecstasies that a new star had been born. Boris had also been helped by Cordelia's superb lighting, although he had to muddle through the 'Agnus Dei' and the 'Sanctus' almost in the dark.

Arms stretched out like a young Christ, tears spilled out of his long dark eyes and poured down his wide, pale, tortured face, as he coaxed miracles out of orchestra, chorus and soloists. Even though they'd sung and played their hearts out for well over an hour without a break, both performers and audience wanted it to go on for ever.

After the thunderclaps, the lightning and the soaring brass, Cecilia was singing again, divinely mewing, making up in dramatic effect whatever she lacked in beauty of tone. The whispering nightingales had returned, as like a priestess she intoned, pianissimo, twenty-nine quavers on the same middle C: '*Lord deliver my soul from the doom of eternal death in the great day of judgement.*'

Then, against an ever-softening drum roll, the chorus joined in for the last two *Delivera Me*s and Boris, his stick like a scimitar, brought the work to a close. As the final brass sounded the last trump, the promenaders gathered themselves up like a great tiger. It seemed impossible that such a hush should be followed by such a deafening roar of applause as the entire audience, musicians, soloists and chorus rose from their seats shouting, screaming and cheering. The hall that had been so still was a churning sea of clapping hands. Richard Baker was so excited he could hardly get the words out.

Then Boris, who seemed in a trance, broke down and sobbed like a wild animal until Monalisa Wilson pulled him comfortingly to her bosom and the bass lent him a red paisley handkerchief to dry his tears as the bravoes rang out.

As he stumbled downstairs for the first time, Bob was waiting. His round, kind, ecstatic face told it all. 'Didn't you hear Giuseppi weeping with joy up in heaven? Oh, my dear boy,' and they were in each other's arms, frantically clapping each other's backs – but not for long, Boris was next being smothered in kisses. Cecilia only had time to wipe away her mascara before they were back on stage.

Running on, with a mosaic of red lipstick down the side of his face, clapping all the time like an excited child, Boris shook hands repeatedly with each of the soloists, then brought the section leaders to their feet, with as many of the orchestra as he could reach. To mighty roars of applause and thunderous stampings of feet, he made the entire chorus stand up again and again. Then there were more cheers for the chorus master.

But the applause was for him and when two huge bunches of yellow carnations and lilies arrived for Monalisa and Cecilia, everyone laughed and yelled approval when Cecilia promptly gave hers to Boris with a little curtsy.

'What are you doing later?' she murmured.

'More, more, more,' yelled the entire Albert Hall, stamping their feet.

'Vot shall I play? I breeng no music. I no expect,' said Boris.

Bob smiled. 'I took the precaution of getting copies run off of one of your songs.'

So Boris mounted the rostrum once more with Cecilia's flowers still under his arm and the hall fell silent.

'I no spik good English,' he said in a choked voice, 'but I zank you all. I feel the good weel. She carry me. I will have zee orchestra play leetle composition of mine in style of Russian folk-songs. That grass is not more green on other side of fence.'

Despite the orchestra and Cecilia sight-reading, the charm and haunting beauty of the little piece was indisputable and once more Boris was cheered to the rooftops and they were still applauding when Richard Baker regretfully bid goodbye to the viewers.

'That was the most wonderful programme I've ever seen,' said Georgie wiping her eyes. 'You really missed something,' she told Lysander as he came through the door weighed down with carrier bags.

'I saw a bit in the chip shop,' said Lysander. Then, turning to Rachel, 'You must be so thrilled.'

But Rachel was inveighing against Bob for not making Boris play one of his more ambitious compositions as an encore. 'Instead of that sentimental, derivative crap, and did you see the way Cecilia was pawing him? Talk about cradle-snatching.'

'That's a very ageist remark,' said Flora gently, as she removed a McDonald's cardboard box out of the nearest carrier bag. 'Your ex-husband is without doubt one of the sexiest men in the world. All he had to do this evening was stand up and women of both sexes would have swooned all over him. As it was, he produced the most exciting and beautiful *Requiem* people will probably ever be privileged to hear and Cecilia sang like an angel, too. Unlike you, Boris hears music with his heart, not his ears, and you're such a bitch, I can see exactly why he left you.'

'*Darling*,' protested Georgie.

'You have no idea the sacrifices we've made,' went on

Flora, getting out a burger and taking a large bite, 'I haven't had a cigarette for over an hour. You've wrecked my mother's and my last evening together and poor Lysander's had to miss *EastEnders* and *The Bill* and he can't even watch it later because we were taping Boris for you.'

'Oh, shut up, Flora.' Lysander leant forward to fill up Rachel's glass. 'Boris did so well, it's a pity Richard Baker can't interview him afterwards like rugger players.'

'I know.' Rachel's stony face crumbled in an avalanche of grief. 'He was absolutely miraculous, but I can't ring and tell him because Chloe'll be there.'

Bob had spread the word before the concert and the green room was absolutely packed with Press.

'Gimme a ring in the morning,' said Larry, who'd actually stayed awake throughout, pressing his card on Boris. 'I'll record that folk-song and anything else you've got at home.'

In the past interviewers had slit their throats because Boris had been so inarticulate, but tonight he had found his tongue.

'Why haven't you been discovered earlier?' asked the *Standard*.

'I didn't know how to beat when I start. The reviews were so terrible they almost depart me. I became Rannaldini's assistant. Rannaldini never go seek.'

'What happened to Rannaldini this evening?' asked the *Mail*.

Boris grinned. 'I think he ran into french window.'

'Why doesn't he programme more of your music?'

'He don't like eet. He no understand avant-garde music.' Then, as an afterthought, 'Rannaldini ees a vanker.'

The Press howled with laughter.

'That's enough,' said Bob hastily. 'Boris has had quite a night, give him a ring tomorrow morning.'

'I geeve lecture on Mahler in the afternoon.'

'Be the last you'll have to give,' said Bob.

Having extracted Boris rather reluctantly from Cecilia's

clutches he took him out to dinner at The Chanterelle in Old Brompton Road. Boris's wrist ached so much he could hardly cut up his steak – he wasn't very hungry anyway – but he drank a lot of red wine and talked a lot about Rachel.

'She geeve me a terrible cold shoulder. At zee end of our marriage she won't sleep wiz me because she tink I was carrying on, and I carried on because she wouldn't sleep with me. Is vicious triangle. She is beetch, but I love her. I 'ate Rannaldini living so near her. You know he 'ad Chloe at one time.'

'She's only a bitch because she's insecure,' said Bob.

'Chloe come home as I was leaving,' said Boris darkly. 'She could have come, but she was tired and her 'air was dirty. Rachel would have drop everything. But she would 'ave given me hard time because she was frighten for me. I once zink grass is greener on other side, but now I find eet cover een pesticide. Tonight was wonderful. I zank you, Bob, but I weesh Rachel and the children had been there. My new symphony is dedicated to Chloe. When I write it down in pencil, Chloe went over it in ink for me and put in the bars.'

'I should keep your options open,' said Bob. 'Why not dedicate it to Cecilia? I've read it,' he went on. 'There are fantastic things in that symphony. I didn't know such sounds existed. I'd send it to Simon Rattle. Rachel is miserable and she loves you. Why don't you try again? If you had money, and you certainly will after this evening, things would be very different.'

'Can I borrow the score?' said Boris as they went out a little unsteadily into the hot russet night. 'I like to go through and 'ighlight my mistakes.'

'You can keep it,' said Bob. 'You've made history, like the night Lennie Bernstein took over from Bruno Walter.'

This was confirmed by ecstatic reviews and news stories in all the papers the following day. The best notice came from *The Times* critic, whose wife Rannaldini had once taken to bed in revenge for a lousy review. Invitations to conduct, to compose, to appear on television and give press interviews poured in all day. Instead of lecturing his students about Mahler, Boris sat on the edge of a desk and told them about his night at the Albert Hall.

Rannaldini, who watched the video with two very black eyes, was insane with jealousy. Ringing up Bob, he screamed at him for replacing him with such a hopeless amateur.

'He was brilliant,' argued Bob. 'He had the longest ovation I've ever heard.'

'Promenaders 'ave no discrimination. Eef Tabloid come on in a white tie they cheer their 'eads off.'

Rannaldini was even crosser when the story, leaked by the bimbo next door, of the row with Cecilia and Hermione, was plastered all over *The Scorpion*.

The next time he confronted the London Met to re-hearse the *Missa Solemnis* they launched into 'Two Lovely Black Eyes' and, when he screamed at them, they refused to be intimidated and played it again. When it came to the public performance the front-desk cellist, whose Strad Rannaldini had endangered, deliberately played 'God Save the Queen' in the wrong key.

37

Machiavellian as ever, Rannaldini decided to avenge himself on Boris by laying siege to Rachel. This would not only enrage Hermione and Cecilia, with whom he was still furious, but also Flora who refused to take the whole eye-blacking incident seriously. She insisted on calling him Panda II and had been cheeky enough to insist that Boris's *Requiem* had been the best thing she had ever heard.

Rannaldini was further turned on by Rachel's animosity and the way she kept firing off incensed letters to the local papers complaining about his clay shoots, his closing of footpaths, and his spraying with pesticides.

Ignoring such bombardment, Rannaldini started dropping in at Jasmine Cottage, occasionally at weekends encountering Lysander, who was at a loose end with Guy at home and the polo season over. Rannaldini had also persuaded Catchitune to sign up Rachel to record the Rachmaninov piano concertos in the autumn with himself conducting. He knew it was too big a break for her to refuse. He was amused that, despite his largesse, Rachel kept an icy distance. And just as the husbands of Paradise had tried to make the best chocolate cake for the fête, now following Rannaldini's example, they vied, unknown to their wives, to be the first to comfort Rachel.

Lysander thought the whole thing hilarious and promptly picked up the telephone.

'Ferdie, Ferdie, you'll never guess. Rachel, my eye-gel friend has emerged in Paradise, and all the husbands are mad about her. They're all putting up shelves for her health foods and stalling their mowers with unleaded petrol. First they rolled up with trays of tomatoes for chutney, last week it was two-legged carrots, this week it's apples. Her cottage looks like Harvest Festival, and Rachel chucks out most of it because it's not organic enough, so Arthur and Tiny are doing terribly well.'

'Who's after her?' asked Ferdie beadily.

'Well, Rannaldini, Guy, Larry, Bob and the vicar for starters.'

'Larry and Guy bloody shouldn't be,' snapped Ferdie, thinking of Marigold's retainer and Georgie's fat monthly cheque. 'Your only justification for being down there is to keep them keen on their wives. You'd better come back to London and earn some serious money. I've got a terrific job for you in Kenya, beautiful rich wife, shit-of-a-parasite husband, stacks of polo and racing.'

'I'm happy in Paradise,' bleated Lysander in a panic at the thought of leaving Georgie. 'None of them is serious about Rachel. They just don't want each other to get her. Rachel's a crosspatch, but seriously good-looking. I wouldn't mind giving her one myself.'

'If you stopped at one, I wouldn't mind,' said Ferdie disapprovingly. 'I had to cope with your father yesterday, rolled up in a strop because you hadn't written. He's left you a letter.'

'I won't read it. It'll be just another lecture about getting a proper job. I've been working Rannaldini's horses,' said Lysander by way of mitigation. 'He wants me to race ride for him in the winter.'

'That won't keep you in fags.'

'Fags want to keep me; the vicar's asked me to go to the Holy Land.'

'Don't be fatuous. How's Natasha?' asked Ferdie. Even her name still caused him pain.

'Gone back to school. But she and Flora are home on Sunday for Rannaldini's famous tennis tournament. Do you want to play?'

'OK. I'll come down for the weekend.' It would be an excuse to see Natasha and protect his investment.

Poor Kitty, meanwhile, had been having a dreadful summer. Increasingly desperate for a baby, she had spent nearly all the running-away money she had saved in case things became too awful, hawking herself from one gynaecologist to another, putting up with the embarrassment of endless tests and internal probings. But even when her tubes were blown, no-one could find anything wrong.

'And it's not my husband, he's got loads of kids already,' Kitty kept telling the doctors.

Rannaldini, who bitterly resented any time Kitty took off, felt she should have been satisfied with her seven stepchildren – eight including little Cosmo.

'Concentrate on being a mother to them, and a secretary to me.'

But I'm almost the same age as your older children, thought Kitty, and the young ones, although very cute, made her feel guilty about longing so much for one of her own.

Her chances seemed less and less likely as Rannaldini slept with her so seldom. She had put up with Rannaldini and Flora all summer, and she had been upset and had to fend off the Press over the eye-blacking furore, but it had given her a faint hope that with Hermione and Cecilia out of favour, and Flora back at Bagley Hall, Rannaldini might have more time for her.

But immediately Cecilia, whom Rannaldini had to forgive because she was starring in *Fidelio*, turned up to use Valhalla as a base for the duration of filming, Hermione, who was still excluded from Maestro's presence, became even more histrionic.

Cecilia was easier than Hermione because she was less stupid and patronizing, and at least had a sense of humour. But she was just as demanding and narcissistic and there was also her total assumption that Rannaldini was still in love with her.

'I cannot understand, Keety, why he is so obsessively

jealous of all my admirers. He ripped out the telephone when I was talking to Carlo the other day, and I daren't tell him Luigi wants to take me to Thailand.'

Every time Cecilia went out she invited Kitty to her room pretending to ask her advice on what to wear, but really to show off how wonderful she looked in clothes. Often, to Kitty's embarrassment, she would greet her in the nude, taunting her with a body that was full-breasted but wonderfully slender elsewhere, and magnificent for someone well over forty. How could Rannaldini ever notice Kitty with that around?

It was the eve of Valhalla tennis tournament. Cecilia had mercifully disappeared to Paris in a ravishing pink shorts suit and Rannaldini's helicopter. Rannaldini, who was at home for once, had retreated to look at rushes of *Fidelio* in his tower. Kitty had hoped for peace to make cakes and sandwich fillings for tomorrow and to give herself a perm, but alas Rachel turned up trailing two fretful children who found making fortresses out of egg boxes insufficiently amusing during a hot summer afternoon.

Kitty had been very kind to Rachel, listening endlessly to her problems and looking after her children when Rachel needed to practise or see lawyers. Rachel felt it was only fair, in turn, to prevent Kitty poisoning herself and the environment.

'Why make a strawberry flan,' she was now complaining, 'when strawberries are out of season and there's a glut of apples? And tuna fish – *tuna* fish,' shrieked Rachel. 'Didn't you know tuna congregate beneath schools of dolphin, and the tuna fleets haul up dolphin at the same time? Nearly a quarter of a million dolphin die in the Pacific.'

'Poor fings,' muttered Kitty, appalled. 'I'll remember next time.'

'Good, though, to use brown flour,' said Rachel, feeling she'd been a bit sharp. Then, catching sight of a packet of Tampax in Kitty's shopping bag, 'but I wish you'd use STs. Tampons floating round in the sea take a hundred and twenty days to biodegrade.'

Shut up, Kitty wanted to scream. Normally as regular as clockwork, she was a week late and praying that at last she might be pregnant. Like taking an umbrella out on a sunny day, she had bought the Tampax.

Rachel was now glaring at a screen Kitty was secretly covering with photographs of Rannaldini and the famous for his birthday in December.

'Christ, look at him leering at Princess Di. Your husband is such a lech, Kitty. Why d'you put up with it?'

'I love 'im.'

'God knows why. I wish he'd stop dropping in on Jasmine Cottage. I wish all the husbands would. One's so defenceless being so close to the road. Everyone can see lights, or hear the radio.'

Not Rachel as well, thought Kitty hopelessly. On the dresser was a letter from her mother enclosing a postal order for three pounds and a card with a printed message wishing a wonderful daughter many happy returns tomorrow. Rannaldini was sure to forget it was her birthday.

As it was Mr Brimscombe's day off, she'd better water the new plants. The roots of older plants were supposed to go down far enough to find water. Emptying an entire watering-can over a bluey-mauve clematis against the wall, she reflected that new plants, like new or potential mistresses, required attention. Was this why Rannaldini was giving Rachel all this work, and insisting she came to the tournament tomorrow, and making sure Gretel looked after her children?

Dear God, help me to stop grumbling, pleaded Kitty. If I'm pregnant, I'll never, never grumble again, and at least Rannaldini hasn't taken Hermione back.

As Rannaldini's tournaments were so unbelievably competitive, Marigold and Georgie had arranged to play a warm-up foursome with Ferdie and Lysander the evening

403

before. Guy had gone to Salisbury to look at a private collection. Larry wasn't due back from London until later, so the coast was clear.

On the way over to Angel's Reach, Lysander had to pop in to Rannaldini's yard to pick up some worming tablets for Tiny and Arthur.

There had been no let-up in the weather. The authorities were even muttering about standpipes. Traveller's joy fell in creamy festoons over the hedgerows, which were weighed down with haws and shining scarlet hips. Ferdie could have leant out of the Ferrari and helped himself to huge ripe blackberries if Lysander hadn't driven so fast. A glut of crab-apples crunched beneath the wheels.

Lysander was unsettled by the tang of bonfires. In October his mother would have been dead a year. He clenched the steering-wheel to ease the pain. He must put some flowers on her grave. Perhaps he should make it up with his father.

Autumn had been daubing Rannaldini's woods yellow and orange. The Virginia creeper smothering the grooms' cottage had already turned crimson. Walking into the immaculate but deserted yard, Lysander heard a blood-curdling scream, like a rabbit caught in a snare. Whipping round, he was relieved to see Maggie and Jack still sitting beside Ferdie in the car.

'No, please, please no,' screamed a female voice.

For a horrified second Lysander thought it might be Kitty being savaged by The Prince of Darkness, but no, he was safely muzzled in his box.

There it was again. Another dreadful wail coming from the indoor school in which Rannaldini enjoyed being left alone to dominate difficult horses. His methods were very cruel, according to Janice the head groom, but, being well paid, she let well alone.

Beckoning frantically for Ferdie, Lysander loped round the corner and found the door of the indoor school locked.

'No more, please.' The moaning voice was too deep and throaty for Kitty's.

'You agreed to do everything I asked.' It was Rannaldini, spine-chillingly cold.

Clambering on to Ferdie's broad shoulders, Lysander straightened up and nearly fell off. He must be seeing things. For there in the centre, wearing shiny black riding-boots and the tightest buff breeches, stood Rannaldini. With one hand he held a hunting whip which he was cracking like a rattlesnake, with the other a leading rein, which was attached to a studded dog-collar round Hermione's neck.

Hermione was totally naked except for tight-fitting high-heeled boots. Her body ran with sweat. Her large, wonderfully firm breasts bounced as she trotted round in a circle, her big curved bottom was already slightly pink, her eyes glistened in terror and excitement.

'You're not going fast enough,' snapped Rannaldini, cracking the whip again, so the wicked thong caught her left buttock. With a neighing scream, Hermione broke into a canter.

Wrong leg, thought Lysander.

She was panting hard now; Rannaldini smiled, but his eyes were dead.

'Are you sorry for the way you behaved?'

'Oh yes, Rannaldini.'

'Sorry you made scenes?'

'Yes, yes.'

'What are you going to do about it? Head up, straighten your back.' With another vicious flick he caught the underside of her breast.

'I'm sorry,' shrieked Hermione.

'I said, "What are you going to do about it?" ' Yanking her towards him, nearly toppling her, he put a hand between her legs. 'You're getting bloody excited. Loving it, aren't you?'

'Yes, Rannaldini.'

'Then we'll try a few jumps. Come on, bitch.'

At this moment Lysander tumbled off Ferdie's shoulders and sent a yard broom flying.

'Who's there?' called out Rannaldini.

Just in time, Ferdie and Lysander leapt behind the mounting block. At least the Ferrari was parked round the corner. As Rannaldini came out they flattened in terror. Fortunately lust drew him back again.

'Must have been a horse,' they heard him say, as the key turned in the lock.

'What *was* going on?' hissed Ferdie. Lysander, bright red with shock, trying not to laugh, mouth wide open in amazement, couldn't utter, until they had hurtled to the boundaries of Rannaldini's land, and turned into the road up to Angel's Reach.

'Oh, Ferd, you never saw such a thing in your life! Talk about undressage. He was schooling her and she was bollock-naked except for her boots. She's got the most fantastic body! You can see exactly why he stays with her. She was giving excited little squeaks like Maggie when she gets on a rabbit trail. Give me a cigarette – and they were obviously about to have the most enormous bonk. God, it was gross, but seriously sexy. Wow! I've never seen anything like that.'

'You must have in a porn mag.'

'Dearie me, I'll never get rid of this erection.'

He took a cigarette from Ferdie, gave a long drag, and gasped in horror. 'You don't suppose he schools poor darling Kitty, do you?'

'She'd be a lot thinner if he did.'

Georgie looked better, really wonderful, thought Ferdie, as he and Lysander went into the kitchen at Angel's Reach. He felt distinctly envious, when, after pecking him on the cheek, she turned to Lysander, wrapping him in a warm, voluptuous embrace and kissed him quite openly on the mouth. She was wearing a torn grey T-shirt of Flora's and a pair of Guy's boxer shorts covered with bonking alligators. Despite chunkier legs, she looked twice as sexy as Marigold, who was all done up in a pleated white tennis dress with her hair in a pink bow.

'Ay'm afraid Ay always maintain the discipline of wearin' whayte,' she said apologetically.

Lysander wouldn't let anyone hit a ball until they'd drunk a bottle of Muscadet and he'd relayed every detail of his adventure.

The grass court was tucked away behind the house. Marigold was a good player. Having spent her youth aspiring to join a tennis club, she had been much coached in later life and as a non-working wife played all summer. Ferdie was overweight, but he had a good eye, and got most things back. Georgie had no backhand and was out of practice but she played with Lysander who was so soaringly better than anyone else that they beat Marigold and Ferdie 6–0, 6–1.

After that they started fooling around, pretending the ball was Hermione and saying: 'You've been a naughty girl, whack,' and giving a shriek, and getting so weak with laughter, that Maggie got excited and ran off with all the balls, with Jack yapping encouragement, so they packed it in.

Georgie seemed so happy that, as they walked back to the house, Ferdie dropped back and asked Lysander if she knew anything about Guy pursuing Rachel.

'No, I'm sure not. Why upset her?'

'God, this weather's bliss. If this is the greenhouse effect, long may it last,' said Georgie, emptying a watering-can over a panting Dinsdale.

'Don't let Rachel hear you,' said Marigold nervously, 'and don't let her see you wastin' water laike that. She's given me hell about Larry's floodlaightin' and our chandeliers in the lounge.'

It was the most perfect evening. Night-scented stock and tobacco plants mingled their sweet scents with the first autumnal waft of the poplars. A pale blue-and-cherry-red air-balloon drifted home into a rose-pink sunset passing the bright star Arcturus which had just appeared above the wood.

'Rannaldini's going to be livid Lysander's so good,'

said Marigold. 'He's so used to being the best player by miles.'

'You and I might beat him,' said Georgie fondly.

'Aren't you going to play with Guy?'

'No, I'm not. He gets so cross if I serve double faults.'

Lysander couldn't get the scene in the riding school out of his mind. It was the act of a seriously depraved man.

'Why doesn't Kitty leave him?'

Georgie shrugged, her face in shadow. 'Why doesn't anyone leave anyone? Mental paralysis, a belief in fidelity? Kitty's awfully religious. She worships the bastard, and he's sapped her confidence. Anyway, where would she go? Her mother's in a home.'

'Rannaldini won't let her go. She's far too useful,' said Marigold.

An owl hooted, pigeons cooed. Across the valley they were shooting clays. Georgie topped up everyone's glass and took another bottle out of the ice bucket for Lysander to open.

'I've had a brainwave,' she said patronizingly. 'Kitty's got a birthday this month. She's a Virgo, wouldn't you know. Why don't we club together and give Lysander to her as a present?'

She turned to Lysander. Her sludge-green eyes dark brown and mocking in the half-light. 'You're always talking about the need for a real challenge. Forget the Rutminster, try Kitty.'

'Don't be ridiculous,' said Lysander with rare ill temper. 'It'd be a farce. There's no way I could get Rannaldini back for Kitty. He was never hers in the first place. For Marigold, for you, for Hermione, not that she needs it, for Rachel even, no problem. But not poor little Kitty, for Christ's sake.'

With her sad, round, formless face, Kitty reminded him of the huge white moon hanging like a plate above Larry's woods, hardly discernible in the pale azure sky of the first dusk.

'Go on,' urged Ferdie, scenting more cash. 'Give it a try.'

If Lysander was refusing to leave Paradise and Georgie, this seemed a good way to supplement his income.

Lysander scooped up Maggie who was trembling at the bangs of the clay shoot, cuddling her to his chest.

'You just collect the ten per cent,' he said crossly. 'You get Rannaldini back if you feel so strongly. I'm having none of it.'

The others proceeded to get drunk and noisy. Lysander sat in silence, watching the moon rising, turning from a pale pinky-orange to butter-gold like one of Miss Cricklade's sunflowers, to incandescent mother-of-pearl, and then flooding the whole valley while the sky deepened from smoky-blue to sapphire as the doomed, menacing notes of Rachmaninov's third and most difficult piano concerto floated up from Jasmine Cottage.

'Rachel plays wonderfully well,' said Marigold. 'Larry says she's going to be a big star.'

'Might cheer her up,' said Georgie. 'Better than grumbling about junk food and fending off passes from Rannaldini.'

'You'd be a true knaight in shining armour if you rattled Rannaldini and made him naicer to Kitty,' said Marigold.

38

At six o'clock the following morning, Kitty was woken by the hiss of illicit sprinklers defying the hose-pipe ban. The floodlights of Paradise Grange across the valley had been switched off, which would delight Rachel, but to the left Venus blazed golden, and as Orion, followed by his yawning dogs, pulled on his boots and climbed up the sky, Kitty could see Mr Brimscombe wearily picking up discarded underclothes round the pool. Natasha and a crowd of friends had gone skinny-dipping in the middle of the night. Their shrieks must have roused the whole neighbourhood.

Glancing in the mirror, Kitty gave a wail. Desperate at the lankness of her hair, in her tiredness she had misread the home-perm directions and left the mix on too long. The result was a scorched, frizzy mass. If only she could hide behind the tea urn this afternoon, but, at the last moment, Rannaldini had asked the vicar, whose wife was away, and would expect Kitty to make up the numbers.

Falling to her knees, Kitty prayed to God to make her less vain.

'And let me not let my partner down too badly this afternoon and please don't let anyone find out it's my birthday or they'll be embarrassed.'

It was already hot and airless as she crept downstairs. Amid the chaos of dirty glasses, mugs, beer cans and overflowing ashtrays, there was a note from Natasha about not singeing her tennis dress. Kitty wanted to scream, but at least she hadn't got the curse and Mrs Brimscombe was coming to help with tea.

Matters were not improved by Cecilia wandering down at lunchtime wanting three exquisite tennis dresses she'd bought in Rome ironed, and Rannaldini arriving from a morning on the *Fidelio* set, finding fault with everything, and insisting she repack his suitcase should he decide to push off back to Germany tonight instead of early tomorrow.

Now, in accompaniment to Richard Strauss's *Arabella*, Kitty could hear the buzz of three hairdriers upstairs, as, fearful of Rachel arriving early and bollocking her for using aerosols, she gave a closet squirt of Mr Sheen to the dining-room tables before laying out the tea things.

The main tennis court at Valhalla lay some three hundred yards from the house beyond the swimming-pool. It was ringed by a thick high hornbeam hedge, which also encompassed grassy banks, where spectators could lie out, and a charming duck-egg-blue pavilion. Opposite this, a spyhole had been cut out of the hornbeam, giving a delightful view of the valley and Magpie Cottage. Although Valhalla was greener than anywhere else in Paradise on this stiflingly hot day, Rannaldini couldn't entirely stem the approach of autumn. Despite Mr Brimscombe's incessant sweeping, the lawn was strewn with gold leaves and chattering swallows lined up on the grey roof of the house. On the table in the pavilion Kitty had put a big blue bowl of greengages and plums from Rannaldini's orchard, a matching blue vase of yellow snapdragons and red dahlias and two big jugs of lemon barley water – but no alcohol. Tennis was taken deadly seriously at Valhalla. Pained by such a hideous colour combination, Rannaldini removed the red dahlias from the vase, chucking them on the grass to be trodden underfoot by the first arrivals.

As beautiful as the peacock butterflies crowding the Michaelmas daisies round the pavilion gathered the ladies of Paradise, their limbs as smooth and shiningly brown as the conkers hanging in their prickly cases on the great golden chestnuts on the edge of Rannaldini's woods. Cecilia wore the palest pink dress, with huge cut-outs at the waist, Natasha a zip-up white mini with her dark hair in a long plait tied with a scarlet ribbon. Marigold had covered her bulges with a broderie-anglaise shift and flaunted her lovely legs in the tiniest of white shorts. She was kicking herself for lending an adorable white cotton-jersey dress with a lace neckline to Rachel, which clung to Rachel's figure and showed off her even lovelier, long, lily-white legs, which Rachel loathed herself for shaving. Nor had being gratuitously rude about the monstrous expense of the dress deterred Rachel from wearing it.

Arriving late, Georgie instantly cursed herself for not making more effort. Touched because Guy had brought her breakfast in bed, exhausted but happy after a long, successful morning's work, she hadn't bothered to wash her hair. Unable to find the new white shirt and flowered Bermudas she'd specially hidden from Flora, she'd been forced to wear yesterday's grey T-shirt and a pair of cycling shorts which had looked fine in the bedroom mirror. Only outside did she realize how pallid the backs of her legs were. Flora looked her usual truculent sexy self in the baggiest of white T-shirts.

The male players on the whole looked less glamorous. The vicar, sporting a NAZARETH CARPENTER SEEKS JOINERS sticker in the back of his ancient Ford, rolled up in baggy greying shorts of just the wrong length.

'Tepid rather than hot pants,' murmured Georgie.

'Do I look like a bender?' asked Ferdie as he trained his normally slicked-back hair forward to cover a large red spot.

'Yes,' said Lysander, turning the Ferrari into Rannaldini's drive.

Feeling horrendously overweight, having eaten last night most of the large curry he and Lysander had ordered, Ferdie had kitted himself out at Lillywhites before leaving London. He was now appalled to discover he was wearing the same jokey orange shorts and white T-shirt covered with orange, red and mauve squiggles and orange-and-mauve sweat band as Larry. The only difference was that Larry had dressed up his outfit with a great deal of gold jewellery and was weighed down by six black Hammer Wilson racquets.

Guy was in stitches.

'I've got a non-figurative exhibition coming up next month,' he told Ferdie and Larry. 'I'll have to hang you both in the gallery.'

'Ferdie's certainly got a non-figure,' said Natasha, poking his beer gut with her tennis racquet.

'Ferdie's brilliant at figures,' said Lysander sharply, seeing the hurt in Ferdie's eyes.

Aware how white flattered his powerful body and ruddy, suntanned face, Guy was pleased with his appearance until he saw Rannaldini in a ten times more expensive cream polo shirt, shorts showing off his chunky, walnut-brown legs and a cream bomber jacket with terracotta piping flung over his muscular shoulders. No heat was ever too hot for Rannaldini. Getting into training for hell-fires, thought Guy sourly. At least that fucker Lysander looked hungover to the teeth, and had only taken the trouble to tug on a pair of trainers and frayed denim shorts.

Unlike Georgie, Lysander was dreading the afternoon. Not being married, he got no buzz out of situations where he had to conceal his feelings. He hated not being able to kiss Georgie and tell her how much he adored her, and she had warned him to be particularly careful today, because she didn't want Flora to suspect anything. Lysander's dogs showed no such reserve. Leaping out of the Ferrari, they threw themselves noisily on Dinsdale, Maggie swinging on his ginger ears, Jack chiding him for being away from them for at least eighteen hours, until they all took off into the wood.

By the time the stable clock struck three all the guests had arrived. Natasha, black plait flying, was knocking up with Marigold, Larry and Guy, the standard terrifyingly high, as Kitty tried surreptitiously to join the party. She was foiled by Cecilia.

'Keety, I never see you een shorts before, an' you change your 'air. Let's see you.'

Everyone turned to look.

'Thunder and lightning the size of your thighs is frightening,' sang Natasha.

Aware of Rannaldini's irritated indifference, Kitty wanted to turn and run. Guy made everything worse by charging off the court.

'Brickie looks terrific. We missed you at matins, didn't we, Percy? And you missed a splendid sermon.'

'Hell for you, Kitty darling, having Cecilia staying,' whispered Meredith, who was looking sweet in mauve shorts and his white Christopher Robin hat, 'worse than having the builders in,' he went on. 'At least you've got hot water and no Hermione, or rather you did have.'

'Manaccia,' swore Cecilia, swallowing a greengage stone.

Marigold and Georgie exchanged looks of horror.

I can't bear it, thought Kitty.

'Bloody hell,' murmured Flora, 'Rannaldini's forgiven her and not me.'

For Hermione had emerged from the path which had once more been strimmed through the wood to her house. Trampling heavily on chucked-out red dahlias, like a goddess in search of an apple, she was ravishingly dressed in a pleated white tunic which left one big golden shoulder bare. Her shining dark curls were arranged most becomingly over a flamingo-pink sweat band, which echoed the flush in her glowing brown cheeks.

'Hallo, Brickie,' cried Hermione, ignoring all the other women, then turning to curtsy to Rannaldini, 'Good afternoon, Maestro, sorry we're late.'

'Horsey, horsey, don't you stop,' whispered Lysander to Ferdie. 'Do you think Rannaldini's going to school her over the tennis net?'

And he had such difficulty in keeping a straight face that he had to wander off into the wood.

Following Hermione, carrying her bag and racquets as well as his own, came Bob, smiling as usual and looking elegantly old-fashioned in white flannels, braces and a panama shading his tired, deep-set eyes.

He really *is* handsome, thought Rachel.

Cecilia, who was livid to see Hermione, said: 'We better get started, Rannaldini, I've got to be on the set by ten o'clock tomorrow.' And she launched into 'Mir ist so wunderbar' from the first act of *Fidelio* to rub in that *she*, and not Hermione, had landed the part of Leonore.

His eyes glittering with malice, Rannaldini tapped the table with the handle of his racquet.

'Welcome to our tournament. The procedure is seemple. There are sixteen of us here. We divide into two groups, each consisting of four couples who each play one set against each other. Group One play on this court. Group Two on a court round corner. This means six sets on each court, then we break for a quick cup of tea, followed by the finals in which the best couple in each group play against each other.

'We then have proper tea, as much champagne as any of you feel fitting to dreenk on a Sunday night, then the couple who has lost the most matches will streep off and jump naked into the pool,' Rannaldini smiled evilly, 'and the punishment bell will be rung.'

'Who plays with who?' asked the vicar, gazing longingly at Lysander.

'I come to that. The man who draws longest straw has first choice of partner, him with second longest, second choice, and so on.'

Natasha came round with the straws. As Lysander, who'd temporarily stopped laughing, stretched out a lazy hand, Natasha deliberately let hers touch his.

'Lucky in love, you choose first,' she said as he drew the longest straw.

415

Lysander glanced round at the charming expectant faces: Flora looking sulkily sexy; Natasha smouldering with promise; Hermione radiating certainty – of course he'll choose me; Rachel trying to appear indifferent, but her eyes telling a different story; Marigold smiling at Larry who was ringing Japan on his mobile; Cecilia letting her pink slit-skirt fall open: 'I will excite you more than any of the others,' said her hot, lingering glance; and Georgie, fondly indulgent – Lysander's dear love, and to him even lovelier because she looked tired and not her best. Then at the back, her fat legs as brick-red as the squashed dahlias she was clutching, her face topped by that frightful frizzy perm and shiny from racing around all day, cringed Kitty. Her very white aertex shirt and her pleated shorts strained over her large breasts and bottom. Dying of humiliation, she gazed down at her racquet knowing she would be the last to be chosen. Georgie, whom he longed to please, had begged him to look after her.

'I'd like to play with Kitty,' said Lysander.

'You what?' said Rannaldini incredulously.

Smiling, mishearing, Georgie moved forward.

'I said I wanted to play with Kitty,' said Lysander firmly. Going over and putting his arm round her shoulders, he saw tears swimming behind the impossibly strong spectacles.

'Fank you,' she mumbled.

'The judgement of Paris,' murmured Bob. 'Well done.'

Ferdie was incensed. 'You're supposed to be getting Guy back for Georgie,' he hissed.

'What nice manners Lysander has,' said Hermione loudly. 'Anyone who says the young haven't got exceptionally nice manners doesn't know what they're talking about.'

Georgie was livid. Particularly when the vicar, who had the second longest straw, noticing her closeness to Lysander and desperate to get in there, decided to overcome his disapproval of her behaviour at the fête and chose her as his partner. She was even crosser when Guy, relieved of his duty as Ace Carer to choose Kitty, infuriated the husbands of Paradise by picking Rachel. Natasha, however, was crossest of all to be chosen by Ferdie who was getting redder and sweatier by the minute.

'I don't want my eyes blacked,' giggled the Ideal Homo, 'so I choose Flora.'

'Nor do I,' muttered Bob. Ignoring Hermione's furious stare, he chose Marigold.

Larry chose Cecilia, because Hermione'd just sent him a furious letter about an advance.

'Men are frightened of playing with really good women players,' Hermione told the empty air as Rannaldini, who'd drawn the short straw, bore her off to Court Two.

'Oh goodee, a cosy girls' foursome,' murmured Flora as she and the Ideal Homo also set off to the second court to play against Georgie and the vicar. A spitting Natasha then had to watch Kitty and Lysander drawn against Larry and Cecilia, both class players, on Court One.

'I'm 'orribly bad,' Kitty told Lysander miserably, clutching her ancient Prince racquet.

'Hurrah,' said Lysander. 'I've got a dreadful hangover, so if we get knocked out early we can slope off and watch Longchamps.'

A champing Larry kicked off, unleashing a thunderbolt at poor Kitty, who missed it completely. His next serve to Lysander came hurtling back. Picking up the ball on the half-volley, Larry whacked it cross-court to Kitty, who missed once again.

Returning to serve to Kitty once more, an over-eager Larry released another thunderbolt while she was still retrieving a ball from the long grass, hitting her hard on the bottom.

'You shouldn't be so large,' shouted Natasha.

'You OK, Kitty?' called Lysander sympathetically. 'She wasn't ready,' he yelled to Mr Brimscombe who was umpiring.

'Forty love,' said Mr Brimscombe, who, fed up with sweeping up leaves, thought he might allow himself to be lured back to Larry.

'Just lulling the opposition into a feeling of false security,' said Lysander, grinning at Kitty as he easily
passed Cecilia with his backhand.

'Forty fifteen.'

But poor Kitty was nowhere near Larry's next service.

'Game to Mr Lockton and Mrs Rannaldini. They lead
1–0.'

Kitty hung her frizzy head. 'I'm so sorry.'

'Doesn't matter.' Lysander peered through the spyhole
as they changed ends. 'I can see Arthur talking to some
children. I wonder where Jack and Maggie are. They've
been gone for ages. We've got sun in our eyes this end.'
He plonked his baseball cap over Kitty's perm. 'It can't
be much worse than Larry's jewels.'

Lucky Cecilia to have olive skin that never goes red,
thought Kitty as she cringed at the net waiting for
Lysander's serve.

'Watch zee ball, Keety,' called out Cecilia kindly.

'You won't even see this one, duckie,' muttered Lysander.
Bouncing the ball reflectively, he waited for Cecilia to get
into position, then curling over like a breaking wave, he
aced her.

Larry jumped from foot to foot awaiting service, blowing on his nails, twitching his orange-and-purple shirt. He
had all the Wimbledon tricks. He'd show the little bastard.
Another ace hurtled past his ear at 90 m.p.h.

'Game to Mr Hawkley and Mrs Kitty,' said Mr Brimscombe, two aces later.

Cecilia was so furious that she served a double fault
to Kitty, which gave her and Lysander a vital point,
Lysander only having to win his service to clinch the
next game.

Aware of everyone watching her and, she thought,
laughing, Kitty's hand was so sweaty that she promptly
served two double faults. On the second Lysander reached
out and caught the shocking pink ball as it veered off into
the woods, tossed it into the right court. He then turned
and gave Kitty a smile of such reassuring sweetness that

she served the next ball in. Cecilia pounded it straight to Lysander, who whipped it between her and Larry. From then on Kitty's dolly-drops went in and Lysander killed the return.

He was such a dazzlingly natural player, and his encouragement and kindness if she missed a shot gave Kitty such confidence that, having beaten the outraged Larry and Cecilia, they went on to thrash Natasha and Ferdie.

Flora and Meredith fooled about so much they lost all their three matches, which suited them both. Meredith wanted to drink lemon barley water and drool over Lysander. Flora was desperate for a word with Rannaldini, who, with Hermione, had slaughtered her and Meredith without the loss of a point or the flicker of a smile.

Now as he stood alone watching the needle match that had just started on Court One – Rachel and Guy v. Kitty and Lysander – to see which pair went into the final, Flora sidled up. Detesting herself, she slid a hand into his, whispering, 'Can't we slope off into the wood?'

'Too many people around,' said Rannaldini coldly, removing his hand.

'Never put you off in the past.'

'I weesh to watch. Hermione and I play the winner 'ere in final.'

Flora slunk off, despairing as a rescued dog returned to Battersea, and missed Rannaldini's quick smile. He had been recently glued to the serial about Vita Sackville-West and Violet Trefusis on television, repeatedly replaying the love scenes between the two women, which made him all the more eager for sexual variation. He was aware how crazy Flora was about him. If he made her desperate enough by freezing her out, she would agree to anything, even going to bed with Cecilia who loved to go both ways, or Hermione (that would humble the spoilt bitch), or Rachel (ditto). He glanced at Flora kicking the grass, puffing furiously on her cigarette. God knows, he wanted her, but he'd have to punish her a great deal more before he reduced her to an adequate level of submission.

Georgie wasn't enjoying the afternoon any more than Flora. Unlike Lysander, the vicar had been very shirty about double faults. He was enraged they hadn't made the final. How impressed his congregation would have been if that had been the reason for him to miss Evensong.

And although Georgie thought it sweet of Lysander to be so nice to Kitty, it had encouraged Guy to be even nicer to Rachel. Georgie experienced an excruciating feeling of *déjà vu* as Guy whisked about finding balls when Rachel was serving, putting strong brown hands on her slender back when she played well, gently guiding her in front of him as they changed ends, and shouting, 'Yours' commendably often if a ball were hit between them.

What a poppet, thought Guy, as Rachel bent down at the net to retrieve a ball. She had delightful legs. It was so hot he'd remove his shirt for the finals and ask her to rub in some Ambre Solaire to show his awareness of the ultra-violet rays. And as all the matches had ended on Court Two they now had an admiring audience to watch them thrash Brickie and that little pipsqueak who'd been fawning over Georgie. He was gratified Rannaldini was watching. Guy arranged his sweat band as Rachel waited for service. In deference to a woman, Lysander tempered his thunderbolt.

'Oh well hit, Rachie,' shouted Guy as she clouted it back to Kitty. So lost was he in admiration, he mishit Kitty's gentle lob. A split second later Lysander had murdered it.

From then on he had both Guy and Rachel racing all over the court. Rachel, upset at how aware she was of Rannaldini's smiling scrutiny, started hitting wildly. Lysander, who had an uncanny ability to guess when a ball was going out, took every advantage.

'Mr Hawkley and Mrs Kitty lead, 5–0,' announced Mr Brimscombe.

'*In a place where nothing seems real, I have found you,*' sang Lysander happily to himself as they changed ends.

'*Miss Saigon*,' said Kitty longingly.

'I've got the tape at home if you want to borrow it,' said Lysander. 'I'd stand further back for this game. The sun's tricky and Guy's going to step up the pace.'

He was right; but when even Guy forgot his Ace-Caring role so much that he served and hit really hard balls to Kitty, fired by Lysander she managed to get them back.

'Good li-el Prince,' she said, looking down at her ancient racquet at set point.

Guy was hurtling towards her, smiting a great shocking pink cannon ball in her direction. Shutting her eyes, Kitty stuck out her Prince and prayed. Next moment she heard cheers and clapping.

'Game, set and match to Mrs Kitty and Mr Hawkley,' said a delighted Mr Brimscombe.

Neither Rachel nor Guy could crack a smile as they all shook hands.

39

'Pile up on the motorway,' Lysander said to Kitty, as Bob, Guy and Larry all converged on Rachel two minutes later with cups of black tea and lemon.

Not that she was very grateful, and when they started to compete in telling the most grisly recession story, she stalked off to bend the vicar's ear about PVC coffin liners giving off noxious fumes. The vicar pretended to listen but was much more interested in eavesdropping on the frightful row Georgie was clearly having with Lysander.

'What the fuck are you playing at?' she hissed. 'You're paid a bomb to rattle my husband and he's been crawling over that ghastly vegan all afternoon. How the hell did he know she didn't have milk in her tea?'

'I'm sorry, Georgie.' Lysander was flabbergasted. 'I was so sorry for Kitty. I thought that was what you wanted. I wish we hadn't got into the finals. When's Guy going back to London? I miss you.' He tried to take her hand, but Georgie snatched it away.

'For God's sake, everyone'll see us.'

Flouncing off, Georgie found herself in a gaggle of women.

'How's *Ant and Cleo* going?' asked Hermione, radiant with smugness at being in the final.

'Fine,' said Georgie shortly.

'I just wonder if the musical is quite the right vehicle for Shakespeare.'

'*Kees me Kate* grossed a few million,' interrupted Cecilia. '*Brush up your Shakespeare*,' she sang softly. '*Start quoting him now*. When you 'ave a score for *Ant and Cleo*, I like to see eet, Georgie.'

'Oh – you'd be a wonderful Cleo.'

'I would enjoy eet. Kiri 'as been Eliza Doolittle.'

'The Verdi *Requiem* was fantastic, both you *and* Boris,' said Georgie in wonder.

Hermione was furious.

'It's amazing how you manage to inject sex into everything, Cecilia.' She gave a little laugh. 'Your "Libera Me" was more like Come and Get Me. You're not doing too much, are you? Your voice sounded tired in Rannaldini's rushes yesterday.'

This was a body blow. One only saw rushes in Rannaldini's tower.

'Don't talk crap,' said Flora rudely. 'Mrs Rannaldini sang wonderfully. She lifted the Verdi every time she opened her mouth. And at least she doesn't duck out at the last moment because of a lovers' tiff.'

'Why zank you, Carissima,' said Cecilia in amazement.

Abandoned by the vicar, who had beetled off on seeing Lysander looking miserable and standing by himself, Rachel was screwing up courage to ask Cecilia how Boris was, but, hearing arguing voices, didn't think this was a good moment. Putting her cup down on the table, she idly fingered a yellow snapdragon, squeezing its mouth open as she had when she was a child. Like a cloud over the sun, Rannaldini glided up.

'Enjoying yourself, Meesis Levitsky?'

'Not particularly.'

His smile was mocking, his thighs as hard and thick as the magnums of champagne that Mr Brimscombe was now opening for those who had finished playing. She'd never met a man who upset her more.

'This place is a disgrace,' she fumed. 'We're in the middle of a drought. Your garden is an oasis.'

'I know how to look after my own,' said Rannaldini softly. 'I thought you like things green.'

'Not at other people's expense. Don't be fatuous.'

Rannaldini noticed the slight down on her upper lip and the underarm hair inside her sleeve as she scratched a midge bite in her hair.

Smiling slightly, he edged a finger into the snapdragon's gaping, furry mouth. Instantly Rachel let go, and the mouth shut, gripping him.

'One day, *amore*, a more exciting part of you will greep me, and you will love every minute of it,' he said softly.

'Don't be disgusting.'

'In fact, you will beg for eet.'

'Your host not looking after you?' said Guy arriving with a magnum and two glasses. 'Presumably you want to keep your eye in until after the final, Rannaldini?'

'Won't make any difference. 'Ermione,' he called out, 'we'll start in five minutes.'

'The grass was very "Kitty" this morning,' announced Natasha, collapsing on the bank beside Flora to watch her fat stepmother make a fool of herself in the finals.

'Kitty?' asked Ferdie, squatting down beside her.

'Stands for "wet",' snapped Natasha.

'Why are you so vile to Kitty?'

For a second, real pain flared in Natasha's face.

'I can't bear to think of her in my father's bed.'

'I shouldn't think she is very often,' said Flora reasonably.

'Fancy Kitty, do you?' Natasha taunted Ferdie. 'If she rolled over in bed, she'd squash you flat. Although you'd probably do the same to her.'

Ferdie got to his feet.

'Can I give you a word of advice?' he said politely. 'If you're trying to pull Lysander, he's never been attracted to bitches.'

The sun dropped into the towering Valhalla woods, the shadow of the abbey with its tall chimneys stretched towards the tennis court like a great black hand as the players took up their positions. Rannaldini had service.

Trembling, Kitty waited to receive. Opposite her at the net, skipping from foot to foot in her Grecian dress like an avenging Juno, crouched Hermione.

Lysander had lost all his bounce. He wanted a stiff drink and this match to be over as quickly as possible so he could make it up with Georgie before she left. She'd already put on a cardigan and gathered up her racquets. He could see her pretending to listen to Meredith's patter as she watched Guy plying Rachel with champagne and compliments as they discussed saving the rhino.

In a quarter of an hour Rannaldini and Hermione were leading 5–0. They had followed a deliberate policy of hitting the ball at Kitty. Like a child fending off blows, she missed everything, apologies pouring from her whitening lips. Lysander simply wasn't trying.

'Your little friend certainly cracks under pressure,' Guy called out scornfully to Georgie.

As the players changed ends, Rannaldini beckoned Natasha.

'We'll be through in a few minutes. Run and tell Mrs Brimscombe to put the kettle on.'

Bastard, thought Georgie. Lysander and Kitty looked so cast down and Hermione so smug.

'Horsey, horsey,' she suddenly called out to Lysander as he slouched past her. Then as he swung round, she smiled, whispering: 'Don't let the old bat get away with it.'

Blissful to be forgiven, Lysander sauntered back to the base line. Next moment an ace whistled past Hermione's pink sweat band. Changing sides, Lysander curved into a perfect bow, threw up the ball and blasted it across the net – just out, which was lucky for Rannaldini who'd been staring at Rachel and hadn't even seen it. The second service was even faster.

'Out, fifteen-all,' snapped Rannaldini as he walked back to the base line.

Lysander didn't budge. 'That serve was in.'

'It was out,' snarled Rannaldini.

'It was in – sir. If you're going to cheat, there's no point in playing.'

Kitty quailed. Rannaldini's face contorted in rage. The spectators exchanged glances of gleeful anticipation.

'That ball was in, Rannaldini,' agreed Bob who was umpiring the final. 'I saw the chalk rise.'

On cue, Maggie came bounding on to the court, nose brown from digging, pink tongue lolling, frantically searching for her master. In a fury, Rannaldini picked up a ball and served it at her, only just missing, sending her fleeing in terror from the court. Instantly Lysander bounded over the net, seizing Rannaldini by the lapels of his cream polo shirt.

'I wouldn't do that if I were you.'

'*Vafuculo*,' swore Rannaldini. 'You should learn to control your dogs.'

'Not in the way you control your bitches,' retorted Lysander so only Rannaldini and Hermione could hear. 'You ought to be suspended for excessive use of the whip. Your partner can hardly sit down today.'

Hermione froze – speechless and open-mouthed – like a photograph of herself reaching top C.

'Keety 'as been sneaking,' said Rannaldini in a fury.

'Not at all.' Lysander scooped up a ball. 'You should keep the windows of your indoor school shut on hot summer afternoons.'

It took all Bob's tact to get them to play on.

To Lysander's relief that Georgie had forgiven him was added a cold fury with Rannaldini, and his game took on a sustained brilliance as, with great leaps, he intercepted the viciously powerful bombardment Rannaldini was directing at his terrified wife. Hermione, worried how much Lysander had overheard, had been totally put off her game.

'That tea's going to be very stewed,' crowed Georgie twenty minutes later. 'Hermione's quite fat, isn't she?'

'Kind Bob always turns down the scales when she comes

home from tours,' said Marigold. 'Oh, good shot, Kitty.' The spectators gave a great cheer. 'They've caught up at last.'

At six-all they went into a tie-break.

'Well done, Kitty. Take it slowly. You're doing brilliantly,' said Lysander, as, like a cat washing its ears, he wiped the sweat from his forehead with an inside arm.

Rannaldini kicked off and won his first serve. Watching his brute strength as he uncoiled like a cracked whip, Lysander was unpleasantly reminded of his behaviour in the indoor school. Fired up, Lysander served two aces, and somehow Kitty got Hermione's next serve back. Bounding in front of Hermione, Rannaldini poached her ball. But, in trying to pass Lysander, he left his own side exposed. Unpassed, Lysander powered the ball away into the farthest corner. Hermione now served to Lysander, promptly netted his return, and turned dark red as Rannaldini swore viciously at her under his breath.

'Kitty and Lysander lead 4–1,' said Bob, not without satisfaction. The spectators were cheering every point.

Kitty managed to lob her service in to Hermione, who was so upset by Rannaldini's invective that she hit it straight to Lysander who whipped a top-spin pass down the backhand. Rannaldini didn't get near it.

'Someone's soon going to have to save the Rhino-ldini,' drawled Flora.

The crowd, except Rachel and Guy, howled with laughter. Rannaldini was so furious that he ran in, hitting such a vicious return to Kitty's service that she ducked to avoid being killed.

'Temper, temper,' said Lysander. Then to Kitty, 'You OK, babe? We've got him on the run.'

Rannaldini promptly aced Kitty, making it 5–3. A heart-stopping rally followed, which had the crowd on their feet yelling with excitement. Seeing his wife quivering like a strawberry jelly in the middle of the court, Rannaldini opened his shoulders and fired the ball down the tramlines.

'Well played, partner,' panted Hermione.

'Run, Kitty,' begged Lysander.

Like a little hippo, Kitty lumbered across the court, slicing the ball with a stretched-out racquet, so it just toppled over the net, and Rannaldini, who was now reaching for a towel, had no time to catch it.

'6–3! Well done, we can do it,' whooped Lysander.

'Great play, Kitty,' called out Natasha who had taken Ferdie's lecture to heart.

How can I love a man who is such a terrible loser? thought Flora in despair.

It was Lysander to serve again. Crouching at the net, Kitty felt stabbing pains in her tummy, but was more aware of Hermione crouching on the back line. There was no goodwill in that beautiful face now, just hatred. Her return came straight at Kitty, hitting her glasses, sending them flying. Blindly Kitty groped for them.

'In front of you,' shouted the crowd.

Racing up, Lysander disengaged them from the net.

'You OK, sweetheart?'

She's got gorgeous eyes, he thought irrationally, as he handed her glasses back to her. Ferdie must get her into contact lenses.

Strolling back to the base line, he bounced the ball longer than usual, until a hush fell over the court. It was still set point. Rannaldini took service, blasting it at Kitty, who, shaken, mishit it. The pink ball sailed up in the air.

'Brilliant,' howled Lysander. 'Terrific return, Kitty.'

'Mine,' shouted Rannaldini, shoving Hermione aside and coiling himself up for a pulverizing smash. Alas, he was an inch too short. The ball cleared the top of his racquet, dropping a centimetre inside the back line. The crowd erupted.

'Game, set, match and tournament to Kitty and Lysander,' said Bob in ill-disguised delight.

Rannaldini's face was expressionless as he shook hands, but Kitty gasped with pain as his grip almost broke her fingers. With the sun gone, it was suddenly chilly. A screech owl screamed from the depths of the wood. As people gathered round clapping Lysander and Kitty on the back, the pavilion telephone rang. Only members of the family knew the number. Natasha got there first.

'Wolfie,' she gave a scream of delight, 'where *are* you? You got straight As, didn't you know? Bloody good. How's Australia? What time is it? You sound plastered. It's Wolfie,' she said to Rannaldini, who'd gone even stiller, his eyes boring into Flora.

'D'you want a word with Dad?' Natasha went on, as Rannaldini held out his hand. 'Oh, right.' Then, incredulously, 'You want to speak to Kitty? You've rung up to wish her happy birthday? Omigod.' Even Natasha was horrified. 'Is it today? I'll put her on.'

Everyone exchanged shocked glances, but no-one looked blacker than Rannaldini or redder than Kitty as she picked up the telephone.

' 'Allo, Wolfie. Well done with your Hay levels. We was so proud. It's ever so kind of you to remember. Well, I got a postal order from Mum, and a nice card.'

Flora's eyes filled with tears. Poor Kitty, and poor Wolfie, whom she'd treated so dreadfully. She was about to snatch the telephone from Kitty and ask him how he was, when Kitty said: 'Cheerio, Wolfie. We all miss you. Come back soon.' She put down the receiver to a chorus of, 'You should have told us. Shame on you, Rannaldini!'

'Happy birthday to you,' sang Flora's sweet, clear, piercing voice and everyone joined in, with Hermione's voice soaring above everyone else's, just to prove she should have been picked for Leonora.

'Many happies, Brickie.' As the singing ended, Guy hugged Kitty. 'I can't tell you how much we're all looking forward to tea.'

'You better come and organize it,' said Rannaldini, stalking off towards the house.

As Kitty panted after him, Lysander noticed a dark red stain on the back of her shorts. Snatching up Natasha's long scarlet cardigan, he sprinted after them. Where the hell were his dogs? Ferdie was useless at keeping an eye on them.

Entering through the french windows of the summer parlour, he heard Rannaldini saying in a chilling voice: 'Why didn't you tell me it was your birthday?'

'I'm ever so sorry, Rannaldini. I didn't want no fuss.'

'It's your job to remember birthdays. How dare you show me up as a sheet in front of all those peoples? You'll pay for eet.'

'Ahem.' Lysander joined them in the hall. 'You mustn't get cold.' And, putting Natasha's cardigan round Kitty's shoulders so it completely covered the bloodstain, he did up the top three buttons. He was just pondering how he could warn her that she'd got the curse without her dying of mortification when an even more piercing scream made them all jump out of their skins, and Mrs Brimscombe rushed in.

'It's Mrs Kitty's tea,' she screeched. 'Come quickly.'

Joined by the rest of the guests, swarming into the dining room in greedy expectation, they were greeted by a scene of total devastation.

Jack was on the table, paws in the smoked-salmon quiche, cocktail sausages hanging like fangs from his mouth. Dinsdale stood with his forepaws up on a chair, owlishly looking round like an old man disturbed in his club, a large chocolate Swiss roll drooping from his lips like a cigar. Plates of sandwiches and cakes had been upended all over the floor, and a great jug of milk dripped its last into a huge white puddle on the floor, beside which Maggie was languidly licking the last of the whipped cream out of Kitty's strawberry flan.

There was a terrible pause, then over the pandemonium, Rannaldini's voice could be heard saying: 'I shall be leaving in five minutes, Keety. There's a button needs sewing on my tailcoat.'

40

'Compared with Rannaldini's green and pleasant oasis, this place is like the Sahara,' grumbled Georgie as she sat on the terrace with Ferdie and Lysander the following evening, drinking Pimm's and surveying her parched garden.

All the little trees she and Guy had planted were dying. The only things that thrived were the wild oats growing outside the kitchen window which had turned as claret coloured as an old club roué's face.

'Why was Kitty crying so much?' she went on. 'She's such a trouper I was convinced she'd magic up Stroganoff and lemon meringue pie for twenty out of the freezer. I never dreamt she'd go to pieces.'

'She thought she was pregnant and found she'd got the curse.' Lysander put down the *Racing Post*. 'She's desperate to have a baby.'

'If she had Rannaldini's child,' said Ferdie, 'it would give her some financial hold on him.'

'She's not like that,' said Lysander quickly. 'She just adores children and wants one of her own. Then she wouldn't be lonely in that great Dracula barracks. I'd be scared shitless living there alone.'

'I'd be more frightened when Rannaldini was at home,' said Georgie with a shiver.

'She confessed he doesn't sleep with her very often.'

'You did get a lot out of her,' said Georgie, amazed.

'So you'll take her on?' asked Ferdie, suddenly business-like.

Lysander gazed moodily at the gold coin of the setting

sun on the dark horizon. It was as though Ferdie was putting a pound in the slot.

'OK. But only to annoy Rannaldini.'

'Improving her appearance is the most important thing,' said Ferdie briskly. 'We've got to de-prude her. Burn those terrible clothes and get the weight off. Mind you, I'm one to talk!' He squeezed the huge roll of fat above his agonizingly tight waistband. 'Sales of chocolate have rocketed since the recession.'

He was feeling guilty about skiving from the office, but at least he'd confirmed his suspicions that both Larry and Guy were desperately strapped for cash. Neither had bought a single round when the remains of the tennis party had retreated to The Pearly Gates last night. There was no point in Marigold and Georgie having quixotic and extravagant schemes for salvaging Kitty's marriage if there wasn't any money. Fortunately Georgie had received a large overseas royalty cheque that morning. She'd planned to give half to Guy, but after yesterday's pursuit of Rachel, she wrote a cheque to Ferdie instead, retaining Lysander's services for herself and Kitty until Christmas.

'Let's go and see Kitty,' said Ferdie, draining his Pimm's.

They found her in the garden talking to Mr Brimscombe. Her eyes were still red, but she greeted them cheerfully.

'Mr B. and I've been chasing a cow out of the vegetable garden. Must of stuffed hisself. Fank goodness Rannaldini's away.'

'How did it escape?' asked Georgie. 'I thought your husband's fences were everything-proof.'

'Must have come over the cattle grid,' said Mr Brimscombe. 'I've seen cows do it. They get so hungry, they stand sideways on the edge of the grid, then they lies down, and roll their legs over, and wriggle till their feets touch t'other side. Then they stands up and off they goes.'

'Isn't it brilliant?' said Kitty in delight.

'Reassuring, too,' said Georgie drily. 'Means you can get out of anything, if you want to enough. Done much damage?'

'Only a few footprints on the lawn and a lot of veggies,' said Kitty. 'But 'Arvest Festival comes up before Rannaldini's back, so we can blame that.'

Waving Mr Brimscombe goodnight, Kitty led them into the kitchen, where she had been making bramble jelly and listening to the tape of *Miss Saigon*.

'Heavenly smell.' Georgie gave the scummy dark crimson mixture a stir.

'I'll give you a jar,' said Kitty, 'and fank you for the lovely bouquet, Ferdie. I got a lovely azalea from Guy as well.'

We even send separate presents these days, thought Georgie wearily.

'And fank you for *Miss Saigon*, Lysander. I've been playing it all day.'

'What else did you get?' asked Georgie.

Kitty giggled. 'A solar-powered calculator from Rachel, and a jumper from Hermione. It's got a pattern wiv sheep round the bottom, which make my bottom look 'uger than ever.'

'Typical,' said Georgie. 'And what did Rannaldini give you other than a thick ear?'

Kitty blushed. 'Nuffink, but he's been filming all day.'

'Never mind,' said Ferdie. 'Marigold and Georgie are going to give you a special present. Let's you and me go into the drawing room.'

'*In a place that won't let us feel, I have found you*,' sang Miss Saigon.

'Just let me hear this bit,' pleaded Kitty.

'You can hear it later.'

Kitty was flabbergasted to learn that Lysander had been paid to make Guy and Larry jealous.

'But he seemed so keen, particularly on Georgie.'

'Things have got a bit out of hand there,' admitted

433

Ferdie, 'and I'm not sure it's had the desired effect on Guy.'

But when he explained that Marigold and Georgie wanted to give her Lysander's services, Kitty at first flatly refused.

'I couldn't do that to Rannaldini. It wouldn't be right. Anyway nuffing would bring him back when he wasn't there in the first place.'

'But you love him.'

'Oh, yes.' Kitty gave a sigh. 'I go weak wiv longing every time I sees him.'

'Then it's worth a try, just till Christmas. You'd like to be thinner.'

'Oh, I would.'

After a lot of persuading, Kitty agreed to let Lysander help her improve her appearance, but not to his hanging around pretending to be keen on her.

'It was realistic wiv Georgie and Marigold. They're both beautiful.'

'Not when he took them on,' said Ferdie. 'Look, I'd like to lose a bit myself. I'm going on holiday to the Algarve on Friday. I bet you a hundred pounds I lose more than you by the time I get back in the second week in October.'

That's the rest of my running-away money, thought Kitty wistfully. Oh hell, it was worth a try.

'All right, you're on,' she said, then blushing scarlet, 'd'you fink it might help if I talked more proper? Marigold suggested elocution lessons like she 'ad. Marigold talks so lovely.'

'No, no,' said Ferdie hastily. 'You don't want to end up talking like Mrs Thatcher.'

In appalling embarrassment, Kitty and Ferdie were then weighed in, with Lysander and Georgie as witnesses. Kitty was eleven stone one, Ferdie over fifteen stone, until Lysander discovered two Jaffa oranges in his blazer pockets.

'That's cheating,' he shouted, shoving Ferdie back on

the scales. 'You're only fifteen now. Enter it in the game book,' he ordered Georgie.

'Kitty's will-power is stronger than mine so she deserved a handicap,' grumbled Ferdie. 'And get that ghastly tight perm cut off,' he added taking Lysander aside. 'And I want her in contact lenses by the time I get back from Portugal.'

Rannaldini was away for two months filming and guest conducting. Georgie was working flat out on the album, seeing musicians and rehearsing for a concert in London the same week that Ferdie got home, which left Kitty and Lysander a lot of spare time.

He tried to cure her terror of horses by walking her round on Arthur who seemed slightly less lame, but although Kitty liked Arthur and took to making him his favourite bread-and-butter pudding, she still much preferred a fence between the two of them. She and Lysander also played endless tennis, worked out and swam. Seeing Kitty's vast thighs inside which the gusset of her black bathing dress practically disappeared, Lysander wondered if it was all worth it, but he carried on because she was so touchingly grateful.

The drought continued, and was now called an Indian Summer. Leaves were so dry they clanged down. More cows wriggled across the sheep grid into Rannaldini's woods.

One evening Lysander sat in the kitchen at Valhalla celebrating a large win on Rupert Campbell-Black's horse Penscombe Pride and watching Kitty iron.

'Rachel says it's a wicked waste of energy ironing underpants and 'ankies,' announced Kitty, 'but can you imagine Rannaldini goin' on the rostrum wiv a crumpled 'ankie.'

'Why did you marry him?'

'I was his secretary.'

'I know that.'

'It was the Wednesday. I asked him if I could have the Saturday off to go to a wedding. "That's very inconvenient,"

435

he said. "Whose wedding is it?" I said, "It's mine, Rannaldini." He was ever so upset, I fink he was worried he wouldn't find nuffing when I was on honeymoon. That night he turned up at our 'ouse at two in the morning. Mum was 'opping. Rannaldini drove me to Valhalla. Dawn was breaking, an' there was a white dew, and all the birds in the air was singin'. It was so beautiful. He was separated from Cecilia by then. He said I couldn't marry Kevin, because he was going to marry me. Just the same way he used to say: "Bring your book in". You know how forceful he is.'

'Christ,' said Lysander in awe. 'What happened to all the presents and the cake and things?'

'They went back.' Kitty hung her head. 'It was the worst fing I ever done. Mum was so upset, so was Kevin's mum and dad, Kevin was – ' Kitty went pink – 'he was 'eartbroken.'

'But you're Catholic, Kitty. It's a mortal sin to marry a divorced man.'

'No, I'm C. of E. Rannaldini's Cafflic. The vicar at 'ome was 'orrified. Rannaldini got a quickie divorce and married me three weeks later.'

'I'm gobsmacked,' said Lysander. 'Was it ever any good?'

'Was he faithful? No, never. I caught him phoning Hermione on our honeymoon. "Nuffing will change, my darlink," he was reassuring her. An' it didn't.'

'You're singeing that shirt,' said Lysander.

Kitty jumped and snatched up her iron.

'I just 'oped one day he might fall in love wiv me, like Mr Rochester. I've read too many romances. People say pack it in, but I 'ate frowing flowers away when they ain't all dead.'

'Oh, poor Kitty.' Lysander got up and hugged her. 'Once we get you glammed up, he'll get really jealous.'

'Some 'ope,' sighed Kitty. 'How's Georgie?'

'Suddenly terribly uptight about Rachel.' Lysander poured more Perrier for Kitty and Muscadet for himself.

'That Guy's keen on her?' asked Kitty. 'I expect he's just jealous because Georgie likes you so much, and Rachel's so pretty.'

'Pretty awful,' said Lysander. 'I hate Georgie being miserable. Do you think I should ask her to marry me?'

'Marry you!' said Kitty in amazement.

'We get on so well. I'd look after her.'

He was so touching in his total seriousness, his bluey-green eyes suddenly as vulnerable as Maggie's, his cheeks flushed with sudden excitement, that Kitty said: 'Oh, I know you would.'

Lucky Georgie, she thought, taking a grey silk shirt from the pile. 'The only problem,' she went on, 'is I don't fink Georgie could cope with your present job, hangin' round neglected wives. I mean she feels safe with me because I'm not a fret. But she had such a shock wiv Guy and Julia, I think her next hubby would need to do somefing which didn't involve women.'

'Then I must get Arthur sound,' said Lysander earnestly, 'and get a proper job.'

'How is Arfur?' asked Kitty fondly.

'The vet's coming tomorrow. I'm terrified he'll say he needs another year's rest. He loved those rock buns you made him.'

'Don't talk about food. I'm starving,' moaned Kitty.

'You've lost ten pounds,' encouraged Lysander.

'I wish I could climb into the tumble-drier and shrink myself down to a size eight like Natasha's purple flares.'

'Rachel doesn't approve of tumble-driers,' said Lysander. 'She'd peg you up on the clothes-line.'

Meanwhile the subject of such intense speculation was wrestling with the fiendish complexities of Rachmaninov's Third Piano Concerto. The recording was not until late October. It was not a work Rachel approved of – too flash and overtly romantic – but she was obsessively determined the London Met, and Rannaldini in particular, should find no fault with her. She was also desperate for her career to take off again to keep pace with Boris whose *Berlin Wall* symphony was being premièred in the Mozart Hall in November, and even more with Chloe who'd just opened in *Don Carlos* at the ENO to rave reviews.

Rachel was still burying herself in work, because, apart from her children, who got increasingly on her nerves, there was little cheer in her life. Her longing for Boris made her vile to him every time he came to pick up the children. She couldn't even bring herself to say anything nice about the *Requiem*, because Chloe had been sitting outside in the car. It was she, not the poor laboratory animals whom she was always campaigning to save, who should have had her vocal cords cut.

She had had high hopes of Lysander as the ideal dalliance, but, beyond kindness, he had shown no interest. She had hoped even more of Bob, who was on her wavelength intellectually. When Hermione was away, they'd taken the children for a picnic by the River Fleet. Bob was the only person who could control the appalling Cosmo, although yesterday the little fiend had disrupted all the wildlife along the river banks with a new toy speedboat.

When Rachel had tried to explain about noise pollution, Cosmo had told her to piss off, and her own disloyal children had roared with laughter, refusing to make daisy chains because they wanted to play with the boat, too. Realizing Rachel was worried about whirlpools, Bob had helped the children dam up one of the little tributaries still running into the Fleet, so they could paddle and sail their boat.

'I'm not eating this crap,' said Cosmo, when offered carrot cake and cauliflower quiche for tea.

Bob refused more politely. 'Honestly, Rachel darling, I never eat tea.' No wonder he kept that lean taut body.

Bob had also chucked away his cup of tea, flavoured with goats' milk, when she wasn't looking, and instead encouraged her to stretch out on the dusty bank with a cold bottle of Sancerre. After the second glass, seeing her children engrossed in their dam, Rachel had tried, over the appalling din of Cosmo's speedboat to discuss the far more appalling behaviour of Rannaldini and Hermione.

But Bob had deflected her. 'Not on such a lovely day. I truly don't want to talk about it.'

'But you must feel so humiliated. They're so odiously public. You ought to have some outlet. You can't dam the libido up for ever.' Rachel started to cry. 'I know I can't. I've been celibate for seven months now. Come over to supper after the kids have gone to bed.'

As if they had a separate life of their own, her pale slim fingers walked across the burnt grass and crept into Bob's.

'Dadd*ee*,' it was little Cosmo's screech. 'The boat's stuck.'

'Well, for Christ's sake, unstick it,' screeched back Rachel. But Bob's fingers, which had not returned the pressure, were gently withdrawn as he got up to help.

Wandering home along the river, when their eyes weren't meeting, Bob had said, 'Sweet of you, Rachel dear, but I've got to go back to London.' Then, smiling slightly to soften the snub, 'Let's take an acid-rain check on this one.'

And the hot flush of mortification had kept sweeping over Rachel ever since.

Even Rannaldini, who'd been so disgustingly suggestive at the tennis, hadn't been in touch so that she could reject him.

Hoards of men used to run after me, thought Rachel despairingly as she sunk her sweating, aching fingers once more into the keys, banging out the doomed, infinitely sorrowful opening theme.

'Dum, da-di-da, da-di-da, da,' sang Rachel. No-one will ever chase me again except married lechers who get a buzz out of deceiving their wives.

If only she could transmit the depth of her sadness to her playing, but she was hampered by the colossal technical demands of the piece, the explosions of notes which must be perfect.

Boris had warned her of the viciousness of Rannaldini's

criticism. Horrible man. Rachel had a vision of his face, heartless, cold, yet the black eyes blazing with lust and sensuality. Despite the punishing airless heat, Rachel shivered.

The church clock striking three brought her back to earth. She must collect the children at four. Lysander had given her a litre of gin some time ago, which she'd never drunk because she loathed the stuff, but had been intending to turn into sloe gin. Walking over to the tennis tournament at Valhalla, she'd noticed a bumper crop of sloes still green along the footpath which Rannaldini had closed to the public. They should be ripe now. Rannaldini was away. If she were quick she could make a detour on her way to school.

She had been concentrating so hard. Only when she went outside did she realize that it had been raining, a brief violent shower, which flattened the bleached grass and drenched the trees, but made as much impact on the rock-hard ground as spitting on an iron. As she ran up the forbidden footpath, Rannaldini's woods lay ahead pulsating and boiling like a jungle, incubating insects, dark greeny-grey beneath a white-hot sun which had already dried the tops of the trees.

'Dum, da-di-da, da-di-da, da,' sang Rachel, breathing in the rank stench of drying nettles, which had grown so tall they concealed the first PRIVATE – KEEP OUT notice. Blackberry fronds clawed her bare ankles and arms like importuning creditors. She could hear a rattle of distant thunder. Her head ached from gazing at little black notes all day.

Traveller's joy draped acid green leaves and lemon-yellow flowers over the NO FOOTPATH: TRESPASSERS PROSECUTED sign. Nature doesn't care about trespassers, thought Rachel. As she waded through waist-high grass, her shoes filled with water. Gretel had taken the children to school this morning, so Rachel had gone straight to the piano without bothering to wash. She supposed this was as good a bath as any.

To her joy, the blackthorn copse was groaning with sloes, shiny and dark like Rannaldini's eyes, but softened by the palest powdery-blue bloom. Holding her shopping bag underneath to catch the loot, she systematically stripped each branch, swearing as the sharp thorns plunged into her fingers. She glanced at her watch, she must go in ten minutes. She only need fill half the bottle. The recipe said white sugar, but she'd get unrefined brown from The Apple Tree instead. Just as she was reaching up to a high branch, she heard voices and started violently, shrieking as a particularly sharp thorn stabbed her arm.

'What was that?' said Rannaldini's voice sharply.

Rachel dropped to the ground, burying her face in the soaking grass, heart pounding, praying he'd go away. She cringed as a brown slug, big as a rat, edged towards her. How ghastly if Rannaldini caught her. Instead the sinister Clive jumped over a small wall just beyond the blackthorn clump and trained his rifle on her.

'Don't shoot,' screamed Rachel.

Rannaldini followed at a more leisurely pace.

'I might have guessed,' he said softly. 'Bugger off,' he added to Clive. 'I'll handle this.'

Lying flat on her face, Rachel was aware of sloes scattered all round her.

'Get up,' ordered Rannaldini.

Leaping down like a great cat, he still made sure he was on higher ground, when she scrambled, raging with embarrassment, to her feet.

'Can't you read? This is private property, you stupid bitch. You're trespassing as well as stealing.' The words came out like rifle shots.

'This is a public footpath.'

'Was,' snapped Rannaldini. 'And the wall was always mine. I didn't know you were a thief.'

Deliberately he stamped on half a dozen sloes, then, removing his shiny brown ankle boot, showed their wounded crimson flesh.

Rachel winced. 'You bastard!'

Looking down, she was appalled to see how transparent the wet grass had made her muslin shift and her cheap white rose-patterned trousers. She could see the moulded line of her breasts and sticking-out nipples, the pink flesh of her legs, and the dark GIVE WAY sign of her pubic hair. Rannaldini, however, had no intention of giving way.

'Today I not bastard. I forgeeve them who trespass.'

Rachel's heart pounded even more painfully, but she couldn't move as he reached out, testing the pudgy warmth of her breast through the drenched muslin.

'Bra-less in Gaza,' he mocked. 'You certainly advertise your wares.'

He couldn't tell if her thin face was wet with tears or rain, as his hand strayed downwards. 'No knickers either.'

'I got up first thing to practise,' stammered Rachel, 'then rushed out in a hurry. I didn't want to be late picking up the children.'

'You left plenty of time to steal my sloes.' Rannaldini clenched and unclenched his fingers.

With his other hand he drew her to him, kissing first her forehead, then both her unplucked eyebrows, then her mouth.

'No!' Suddenly aware she hadn't cleaned her teeth, and loathing herself for minding, Rachel clamped her lips shut.

'No?' Rannaldini moved away slightly. 'Do you have any choice?'

His hand slipped inside her sleeve, caressing its way up her arm, pulling at her long, silky armpit hair, before curling round to caress her breasts.

Rachel gave a moan, trying to duck her head away, as Rannaldini ruffled the slight down on her upper lip with his tongue.

'Leetle wild thing, eet will be like making love to an animal. A goat perhaps.'

'I hate you.'

'No, no, you 'ate yourself for wanting me so much, Mrs Levitsky.'

Rannaldini relished calling women by the names of the husbands he was cuckolding.

'I'm not Levitsky any more, I'm back to Grant now. Someone's coming,' gasped Rachel, hearing a snatch of 'For All The Saints' sung in a loud baritone.

Rannaldini pushed her back on to the ground, crouching beside her, holding his hand, which smelt faintly of Maestro, over her mouth, until the vicar had gone.

Then, when she tried to leap to her feet, mouth open in protest, Rannaldini plunged his tongue inside, until she forgot her uncleaned teeth and kissed him back. Rannaldini wanted to take her now, but the vicar might surprise them on his return.

'The kids! I must pick them up!' said Rachel, fighting to get free.

Back in his tower, it was Rannaldini who got the number of the school by ringing Kitty. Then he rang the school.

'Mrs Levitsky is stuck in traffic jam, and will be three-quarters of an hour late. She ask me to ring, she is very, very sorry. But she is not,' he added, switching off the telephone. 'You ought to get out of those wet things,' he said softly, then, sliding his hand down inside her trousers, 'and this is the wettest thing that I should eenstantly get into.'

'Let me undress myself, for fuck's sake,' snarled Rachel.

But so overjoyed was Rannaldini by the early conquest of something he thought would take him weeks, perhaps months, that his face assumed a quite uncharacteristic delight and tenderness. He also had a water diviner's skill in testing the depth of women's loneliness. He knew when to be kind.

'You have been so sad and lonely,' he crooned, drawing her into his arms and stroking her hair. 'You deserve some happiness. This time it will be queek, because of your children, but the next time . . . it will be ecstatic.'

In the long mirror, as Rachel lay back white and slender as a snowdrop against his mahogany chest, they looked wonderfully exotic. Some three inches shorter than her, perched on the back of a grey silk *chaise-longue*, it was simplicity for him to slide his iron-hard cock slowly in and out of her as he gently caressed her in front with the artistry of a Casals playing a cello concerto.

But the moment she came Rachel's moans of pleasure turned into wild sobs.

'Cry, leetle darling,' purred Rannaldini. 'Eet is what you need.'

'No, no,' wept Rachel. 'It's the wrong person in the mirror. You should be Boris.'

41

On Monday morning after Guy and Larry had left for the London train, Marigold and Georgie had got into a habit of ringing each other to grumble about their respective husbands – their Moan-day session, they called it. As September dragged on with no break in the drought and the recession deepened, Marigold's complaints were increasingly of Larry's stinginess, Georgie's increasingly of Rachel.

'He's stopped may account at Harvey Nicks,' announced Marigold indignantly the first Monday in October, 'and he's cancelled our box at Covent Garden and he won't let Patch have steak any more.'

'Better than Guy who's trying to turn poor Dinsdale into a vegan,' said Georgie darkly. 'And he's rigged up a washing-line. I mean, he's never let me hang out clothes even in our brokest days; said it was horrifically suburban. Now his Turnbull & Asser shirts are waving in the lack of wind for all at see.'

'He could be trayin' to save money.'

'Rubbish, the only thing Guy is saving at the moment is the whale and the rain forests.'

'But your marriage has been so much better since Laysander came on the scene.' Alarmed, Marigold detected the old obsessive rattle in Georgie's voice.

'It was, until Guy started pursuing Rachel. I can't cope, Marigold, it's like going through chemotherapy, then finding another lump.'

'Ay'm sure you're imaginin' things.'

'I am *not*. Guy's started using organic toothpaste, and

he won't have white loo paper in the house, because the "bleach pollutes our waterways", and worst of all,' Georgie's voice rose hysterically, 'Dinsdale came back from a walk smelling of a quite different scent. I'm certain it comes from the Body Shop.'

'Perhaps Guy wanted to test it on an animal.'

'Don't make sick jokes. I've lost my sense of humour, and even, even worse, because *Rock Star*'s selling so well overseas, your rotten husband's marketing Guy and Georgie T-shirts and key rings, and even Guy and Georgie balloons. What happens when people rumble how bad our marriage is?'

'They won't unless you tell them.'

'And to cap it all, Guy's off to the South of France for three days to look at some private collection, and he's picked the week of my concert so I can't go with him. I caught him admiring himself in the mirror in his new goggles and flippers yesterday. He jumped out of his skin. "Off to save the whales," I said. "The pollution's awful in the Med." He was livid and went into his "Are you mad, Panda? You must see a doctor" routine.'

Two minutes after ringing off, she rang Marigold back.

'Oh darling, I'm sorry to bang on. I must still love Guy for him to get so much under my skin.'

Lysander was so worried about Georgie he bought her a diamond necklace, a beautiful black backless Lycra dress and a book of Fred Basset cartoons. Then, deciding she was barn sour, he tried to take her away for a jaunt to coincide with her concert and Guy's trip to France. Kitty had lost over a stone and could be left unsupervised for a few days.

But Georgie was nervous of being recognized and only allowed Lysander to join her at the Ritz in her room overlooking Green Park where Catchitune had put her up for the night. Catchitune also sent a limo to collect her from Paradise. But, again to avoid the Press, she made Lysander drive up on his own to join her later in the day.

Having stayed with Marigold in the Ritz in Paris, Lysander promptly rediscovered the joys of room service. Georgie once again realized how young he was, as he ordered smoked salmon with gauze-wrapped half-lemons, club sandwiches and vast Bloody Marys, then played with the telephone in the bathroom and all the bottles of shampoo and bath gel before discovering a television where he could watch everything from blue movies to Donald Duck.

Most of all he wanted Georgie to romp with him in the big blue Jacuzzi and take advantage of a huge double bed, flanked by walls of darkened mirrors. But all Georgie wanted to do before a concert was to crash out with cold eye-pads, then spend an hour in trance-like silence making herself beautiful.

Bewildered that he hadn't satisfied her properly, Lysander took her face in his hands.

'Georgie darling, please leave Guy and marry me.'

Georgie smiled. 'That is the sweetest offer I've ever had, but can you imagine what *The Scorpion* would make of me and my child bridegroom?'

The concert was a massive success. Georgie sang all her old sixties songs which had just been issued as a CD and were racing up the charts, and then ended with 'Rock Star'. Having got well tanked up beforehand and during the interval in the private Catchitune box, Lysander nearly died of pride. Here was his darling Georgie, who had lain warm and naked in his arms a few hours ago, caressed now by thousands of coloured lights, skipping, dancing round the stage, with a great waving cornfield of clapping hands saluting her. It was so sexy the way her red hair tumbled down her bare back each time she threw back her head and how she seemed to suck, lick and even drink out of the microphone as she belted out these glorious heartbreaking songs in her yelping, husky, smoke-filled voice. In his diamonds, with her lovely suntanned shoulders rising out of his black

447

dress, she looked stunningly beautiful and about twenty-five.

She was backed by the same musicians who'd made *Rock Star* and a good deal of money in the past six months, and who were delighted to be on stage with her again.

Lysander liked it least when she sang 'Rock Star'. He barracked noisily and had to be shushed when Guy's handsome manly face was blown up on a screen for Georgie to sing to. The audience, however, cheered and yelled so much she had to sing it again – and still they wouldn't let her go.

Here is a talent that can cradle an audience in its hands, and hold them spellbound and captive for two hours, thought Lysander. How dare Rannaldini, Hermione and most of all, Rachel, patronize her.

She was going to do an encore. As she sat down on the edge of the stage with a guitar slung round her neck, a hush fell on the hall. One spotlight illuminated her; everywhere else was in darkness.

'Ladies and Gentlemen,' began Georgie in her soft voice with its faint trace of Irish, 'I'd like to try out a new song I've just written this week, which I hope will be part of my new album. At home I have an old dog, whom I love dearly. Like anyone in this situation, I dread the day he dies – so I dedicate this song to Dinsdale.'

Oh, she's so clever, thought Lysander, downing another glass of Moët. 'I never knew she could play the guitar so well.'

'*Old Dog,*' began Georgie, in her husky voice, '*you break my heart.*

How many days have I left with you?
Your muzzle whitens, your steps go slow,
But your tail still wags and your heart beats true.
Lie in in the morning, guard your strength,
Live as long as you possibly can,
For guys have come and guys will go,
But you've loved me more than any man.'

The haunting beauty of the melody redeemed the sentimentality of the words, and at the end, when Georgie bowed her head and waited for the storm of cheering, Lysander wasn't the only one who mopped his eyes.

It was after midnight before Georgie managed to tear herself away from the well-wishers in the green room. Larry was particularly ecstatic.

' "Old Dog" is going to be bigger than "Rock Star",' he said, chewing on his cigar. 'Naughty girl to jump the gun, but if that's anything like the rest of the album, we'll make a killing. We could rush it out as a single. I'll call you tomorrow.'

'Pity Guy wasn't here, he'd be so proud,' said Marigold.

'Better change that bit about Guys have come and Guys will go,' said Larry sardonically.

'That was my best bit,' muttered Lysander.

'Substitute the word "boy" or "man",' said Larry. 'But it's a great number.'

'And just the way Ay feel about Patch,' said Marigold, whose mascara had run.

After a concert, Georgie felt absolutely drained and preferred to go out for a gentle dinner with her agent, or people from the record company who'd talk shop, praise her, and go through every note of her performance, just as Lysander went through every stroke after a polo game. Instead, because she felt momentarily sky-high on adrenalin, adulation and champagne on a very empty stomach, she let Lysander bear her off to a party given by some of his friends.

'Won't it be over?' said Georgie as they drove through a recession-darkened Knightsbridge.

'It won't have started till after the pubs close,' said Lysander, noticing the full moon like a satellite dish topping Brompton Oratory. Was it only a month since he'd taken Kitty on? He hoped she was OK in her lonely fortress.

You could hear the din of the party six hundred yards away. The moment Georgie entered the big terraced house with its yelling jostling crowd hanging out of every window, she knew she had made a dreadful mistake. Still in her thick stage make-up, her diamonds and her backless dress, the halter neckline of which barely covered her breasts, she was ludicrously overdressed. Beside all the utterly ravishing girls in their T-shirts, leggings or occasional micro-skirt, she felt like boiled mutton dressed as lamb without even the aid of caper sauce.

And if she had been the star of the concert, Lysander was undeniably the star of the party. Everyone, particularly the girls, converged on him shrieking with joy.

'Where have you been?', 'We thought you were dead', 'London's dire without you', 'Lysander's back, everyone!'

'This is Georgie,' Lysander told them all proudly.

But although he stuck as close as he could, friends never stopped fighting their way over to talk to him, and whenever he fought his way to the kitchen, where a huge table groaned with every drink known to man, to fill up their glasses, it took him half an hour because everyone waylaid him.

It was a very wild party; most people were wasted with drink or drugs, and were already graffiting the walls. Seizing the aerosol can, Lysander wrote: I LUV GORGY, and everyone screamed with laughter.

Others were singing along to a Karaoke machine and videoing each other. Everyone wanted to video Georgie. They were charming to her, but in the same way they might gaze in wonder at the Taj Mahal, tick the guide book, and move on.

Georgie tried to get into the spirit of things, but drink only made her more tired. At the end of the sitting room, a group round a table were playing a game called Cardinal Puff, in which you recited a very complicated verse with endless subclauses. Every time you went wrong, you had to down a glass of booze. Lysander, being dyslexic and very drunk, couldn't get the hang of it at all, and kept making mistakes and reducing himself and everyone to hysterical laughter.

Georgie tried to match their mirth, but found her jaw aching. She longed to go back to her hotel, but didn't want to spoil Lysander's fun. Shrieks grew louder next door, as a blonde in a bright yellow sequined jacket and not much else rushed in.

'I've just emptied a saucepan of chilli con carne over the complete geek giving the party for not playing our kind of music,' she shouted, then seeing Lysander, '*Hallo*, sweet pea,' and grabbing him, she kissed him on the mouth, on and on to wild cheers.

'Anyone would think he was fucking Helen of Troy,' said a very suntanned stocky blond boy, who was drinking out of a bottle of vodka and taking alternate slugs out of a carton of orange juice.

'Seb!' In drunken delight, Lysander tipped the blonde off his knee. 'Oh, Seb, this is Georgie Maguire. Get her a drink and look after her for a sec while I crack this stupid game. Seb plays polo for England, Georgie, so does his twin brother Dommie. Where is Dommie?'

'Bonking some slapper upstairs.' Seb filled up Georgie's glass with vodka and orange juice. 'Love your album.'

'Thanks. Who owns this house?'

'Bloke called Mark Waterlane or rather his father does – Mark's a ghastly host: passed out by two in the morning. Where's Ferdie?' he asked Lysander.

'In the Aglarve,' Lysander never got the word right. 'Due home any minute. I thought he might be here.'

'He sent me a postcard saying he'd got off with a thirty-year-old wrinkly,' said the blonde, clambering back on to Lysander's knee. 'Must be pushed.'

Georgie tried to be a good sport, and return Lysander's apologetic grin round the blonde's jutting bosom. But when she escaped to the loo to check her own wrinkles, it was occupied.

'Someone's either bonking, throwing up, or passed out,' said a brunette in a crimson body-stocking who was painting her mouth rose-red in the landing mirror. 'They're organizing a search-party to climb in through the window, and get whoever it is out.'

Joining the girl at the mirror, Georgie gave a wail of despair. Beside that smooth fresh face, she looked like a raddled old tart of a hundred. Her heavy make-up sank into the lines round her mouth, and emphasized the weary red-veined eyes, and when she rubbed away a blob of mascara, the skin stayed pleated.

'Love your album,' said the brunette. 'I hope I meet a guy like your Guy one day. He's lush. He's not here, is he?'

'If he was, he'd adore you,' said Georgie wearily.

There was a crash and a tinkling of glass as a boy, climbing the creeper to rip down the satellite dish, put his biker boot through a window. The music was deafening. To stop complaints the telephones had all been pulled out.

Lysander waited in the hall with his arms out as Georgie came downstairs: 'Georgie! Let's get naked.'

A wild boy wearing a baseball cap back to front suddenly rushed up, squeezed both her breasts and shouted: 'Yippee, six, the big one!'

'What the hell are you doing?' said Georgie crossly.

'Tit cricket,' said the boy with an inane laugh. 'When you squeeze both you get a six.'

'Leave my woman alone,' howled Lysander, his right fist sending the boy crashing to the floor.

'Is he all right?' said Georgie anxiously when the boy didn't move.

'Fine.' Seb Carlisle kicked him gently out of the way. 'He was about due to pass out.'

'Just going to have a slash in the garden.' Lysander staggered out, cannoning off walls.

'Mrs Seymour?'

Georgie jumped out of her skin as she saw her husband staring at her. Beside him was herself looking twenty years younger. Then she realized yet another stunning girl was wearing one of Catchitune's new Guy and Georgie T-shirts.

'I bought it from Tower Records, Piccadilly, this evening,' she said. 'Will you sign it?'

'Will you sign mine, too?' said her even prettier red-haired friend. 'I temped for your husband last year,' she added. 'He's really sweet. Every morning he made the same joke: "Bring your book in, Lottie, and do your longhand, I want to look at your legs".'

'That's my husband,' said Georgie bleakly.

Much later, she was having great difficulty holding Lysander up on the dance floor, when over the din of the record player, she heard the wail of sirens.

'Quick, the pigs!' Seb Carlisle seized Georgie's arm. 'I'll get Dommie!'

Having retrieved his twin brother from upstairs, he led Georgie and a tottering Lysander through a kitchen three inches deep in beer out into a garden. The fresh air hit them like a fist. The twins had just given Georgie a leg-up over the wall when a policeman ran through the french windows, frantically blowing his whistle. Straddling an old rambler rose that ripped her tights to shreds, Georgie knew that he knew who she was.

'Now, where's my car?' said Lysander, scratching his head as he joined them on the pavement.

'You said you'd left it in Rosary Road,' said Seb.

As they rushed across the road, Georgie felt an unidentifiable pain.

'I can't see it,' went on Lysander.

'It's that BMW, you idiot,' screamed Georgie. 'The Ferrari's being serviced.'

'I was scoring with that brunette,' grumbled Dommie Carlisle, climbing sulkily into the back.

'Of all the ungrateful sods,' said Seb, climbing in beside him. 'Not sure Lysander's safe to drive,' he muttered to Georgie.

'I bloody am,' said Lysander, backing briskly into a parked Mercedes.

'I'll drive,' said Georgie, panicking the police would

catch up with them, triggering off some frightful scandal.
'For God's sake, move over, Lysander.'

The twins were now having a punch-up in the back.

'I would've scored.'

'Bloody wouldn't.'

'Would.'

'She was a slapper.'

'She was not.'

'For God's sake, stop them,' Georgie screamed at Lysander, as she set off with a jerk and furious revving.

'I can't. I'm navigating.' Lysander stared fixedly ahead. 'I'll be sick if I look round.'

'I'm going back to score.' Dommie leapt defiantly out, running straight into the arms of the police.

As Georgie drove towards Knightsbridge, the gutters were filled with brown plane leaves and the gardens with Japanese anemones and shaggy yellow chrysanthemums. Then she twigged. Rosary Road was where Julia had lived in London. How often Guy must have bowled down the Fulham Road in excitement and told the taxi to turn left.

She dropped Seb off at Sloane Square. Lysander, slumped beside her, was too far gone to notice the tears streaming down her cheeks all the way back to the hotel.

'Just walk in, don't look to left or right,' she hissed as she steered a buckling Lysander twice round the swing door.

'Good morning, Miss Maguire,' said the doorman.

As soon as his head hit the pillow, Lysander passed out. Georgie removed her hellish make-up and, suddenly icy cold, had a long, hot bath, waving two metaphorical fingers at Rachel as she wasted a great deal of water. Then she removed Lysander's flowered tie and took off his only pair of Guccis Maggie hadn't eaten. His brown lashes nearly covered the shadows beneath his eyes, there was a sprinkling of freckles on his sunburnt nose, and his big mouth was smiling as he reached out in his sleep for her. As Georgie nuzzled into his neck, he smelled as sweet and fresh as violets.

Too exhausted to sleep, she saw her bare shoulders, her long red hair and pale sad face reflected in the mirror opposite. Once again it was as though Julia was gazing back at her.

The next day, after a leisurely lunch and several Alka-Seltzers, as they set out for Angel's Reach in the BMW, Lysander handed her a copy of *Hello!*.

'To distract you on the journey. I used to buy one for Mum. She was so terrified of my driving.'

He didn't add that it was the anniversary of his mother's death. In their separate anguish, they didn't confide in each other. Despite *Hello!* Georgie had to bite her lip and cling on to the seat as the speedometer reached 120 m.p.h. The radio was playing the new tape of her sixties songs. Turned up fortissimo, it gave her a blinding headache. Even with all the windows open and in spite of the time of year, the day was impossibly hot and sticky.

Lysander, thought Georgie with infinite sadness, was adorable, but he needed children his own age to play with. Nor could she transfer her love to him. She lacked skins.

Back at Angel's Reach, longing to have a bath and change, she found a note from Mother Courage: *Cat's been sick, downstairs toilet blocked and water packed up. Got Debenham. See you later.*

'That's all I bloody need.'

'Hurrah, you can come and stay at Magpie Cottage,' said Lysander.

'I'll join you when I've got things together this end,' said Georgie, leafing through the post. 'Guy's sent me a postcard of a ruined abbey. Is that supposed to symbolize the state he's reduced me to?'

Upstairs, she turned on the ansaphone.

'Hallo, Panda,' said Guy's deep voice. 'Been thinking of you, hope everything went all right. Give me a ring. Miss you.'

The next call was from a jubilant Flora, who'd passed

her driving test. Clever little duck, thought Georgie fondly, but it was going to complicate things having her rolling up unannounced at any time of day. The third call was from Sabine Bottomley saying Flora wasn't working. The fourth was from Guy again saying he missed her and would she ring him back.

Perhaps I'm imagining things, Georgie felt suddenly happier. Then she went into the bathroom and saw Guy's organic toothpaste.

Craving truth, she dialled Rachel's number. If she was at home there was no need to worry. She was about to ring off when the telephone was picked up. Hell, thought Georgie, I'll have to ask her to something now.

'Hallo, Rachel.'

'No, it's Gretel. I'm just feeding the cat.'

'When's Rachel coming back?'

'Tomorrow, she's abroad.'

Georgie slammed down the telephone, hands shaking, heart pounding, body drenched in sweat. She was out of the house in ten minutes. Then the telephone started ringing and ringing.

42

The other man whose mind was very much on the late Pippa Hawkley on that heavy, thundery, suffocatingly close afternoon was her husband, David. Putting a bunch of tiger lilies, flowers as beautiful and exotic as Pippa herself, on her grave, he had prayed she was resting more in peace than he was in life. A year on he was still wracked by anguish and confusion. Despite overt offers from Mrs Colman and half the mothers who came to discuss their sons, he had remained celibate. But a couple of porn magazines, confiscated from a boy that morning and shoved in his desk drawer to burn later, had reminded him what he was missing. Glancing at the wanton, knowing girls with their tangled hair, hillocks of breast and buttock, and pink, glistening lips, he felt as parched sexually as the dusty dried-up pitches outside his window.

Slamming the desk drawer shut, he grimly turned to Catullus. A kindly letter from his publisher earlier in the week reminded him that his translation should have been delivered in January.

An earlier translator had written: '*Hard it is to put aside long-standing love.*' His sixth form would have probably put: '*It's a bitch to get over a long-standing relationship.*'

'How can I forget someone I have loved for ever?' wrote David Hawkley. Catullus might have written the poem specially for him. He was roused from his sad dreams by a knock on the door. It was 'Mustard' with a vase of bronze chrysanthemums.

'Thank you,' said David, thinking how Pippa had loathed chrysanthemums.

'Mrs Harefield's favourite flowers,' said Mustard reverently, who was the most awful star-fucker. 'You haven't forgotten she and her son Cosmo are due in five minutes?'

David had not. He even looked forward to Hermione's visit. Her exquisite voice had comforted him through many a long night of insomnia. Strange that even in the blackest despair, one searched for love.

Hermione was searching for a public school for little Cosmo. Having witnessed the dreadful rudeness of Flora and Natasha, she had no intention of subjecting her wunderkind to the co-educational anarchy of Bagley Hall. Fleetley had been top of her list because of its high academic record and David Hawkley's reputation as a disciplinarian.

Having been ushered into his study by a fawning Mustard, Hermione decided it would be extremely exciting to be disciplined by 'Hatchet' Hawkley, and that he was decidedly attractive in a brilliant, implacable High Tory way. Rannaldini had been neglecting her again. He never answered her calls. Hermione was consequently casting around for a new beau. This stern handsome widower would fit the bill perfectly – and might even allow little Cosmo in cheap.

One look at Cosmo, who was bursting out of his sailor suit like Tom Kitten, with his sailor hat atop his flowing black curls, and his evil black eyes rolling in search of diversion, convinced David that this vile child must never enter his school.

'Most of our boys are put down at birth,' he said truthfully, then less so, 'I'm afraid we're booked solid until AD 2000.'

'Come, come,' said Hermione skittishly. 'I know that powerful headmasters can always waive the rule for friends, and I know you and I are going to be very special friends.'

David knew no such thing as little Cosmo proceeded to lay waste to his office, overturning files, putting sticky fingers on first editions, scattering sweet papers, and finally pulling a penknife on Hesiod, the school cat, who was sleeping peacefully in a patch of sunlight. When chided fondly by his mother, Cosmo ordered her to piss off.

'Cosmo,' went on Hermione, 'is severely gifted, so he needs to be stretched.'

On the rack preferably, thought David, wondering how a woman so beautiful and so gloriously talented could be quite so awful.

As little Cosmo was now applying his penknife to the big oak table, David suggested a look round the school.

'That would be fun, wouldn't it, Cosmo?'

Cosmo said it wouldn't, and raising his mother's skirt, asked her why she wasn't wearing any knickers. Hermione was undeterred.

In the music room, where the choir was rehearsing 'How Lovely Are Thy Dwellings', she leapt up on the stage and sang along for a page or two, before telling the cringing music master he looked just like Paul Newman.

'You will be teaching my Cosmo.' She drew her wunderkind forward. 'Music is Cosmo's life.'

'Your flies are undone,' said little Cosmo loudly.

Instantly the hands of both headmaster and music master flew to their zips.

'April fool,' said little Cosmo, giving a maniacal cackle.

'Little Cosmo has such a sense of humour,' said a beaming Hermione.

Back in David's study, Mustard was waiting to pour.

'Camomile tea and honey or Earl Grey, Mrs Harefield?'

'How very caring,' Hermione clapped her hands. 'And flapjacks, too, my favourite. You *have* done your homework.'

She turned to David. 'You were going to show me your Oxbridge results, Headmaster.'

Mustard had just gone to find the file, when little Cosmo let out another maniacal cackle. Having discovered the porn magazines in David Hawkley's top drawer, he was now leering at the colossal breasts of a blonde in thigh boots and a cowboy hat.

'Confiscated at lunchtime,' spluttered David, snatching back the magazine, as Cosmo gave him a pull-the-other-leg smile.

'Mrs Colman,' yelled David, 'could you amuse Cosmo for a minute or two?'

'Ah sons, sons,' sighed Hermione, leaning forward in her pink Chanel suit to reveal a bosom just as splendid as the blonde in the porn mag.

'It must be difficult, with your exacting career, to spend enough time with Cosmo,' observed David.

'Quality time, I give him quality time,' murmured Hermione. 'I've been meaning to ask you – are you any relation of Lysander Hawkley?'

'My youngest son,' said David warily.

'You must be so proud,' said Hermione, who actually disliked Lysander intensely. 'I haven't discovered what Lysander does, but such a good-looking, clearly gifted boy. He gets all that from you, of course, but he's lucky to have such a generous father.'

'I beg your pardon?'

'He must have a massive private income to run a Ferrari,' said Hermione with her little laugh, 'and all those polo ponies, and he's always buying diamonds for his numerous ladies. What delicious flapjacks! I just assumed Fleetley was doing so well, you were able to give him a huge allowance, or perhaps he'd made a killing on the horses.'

David choked on his Earl Grey, turned purple, but made no comment.

The moment Hermione left, Mustard, unaware that little Cosmo had emptied his Ribena into her word processor, came bustling in.

'What a lovely lady. She wanted the recipe for my flapjacks. And what a dear little lad. Didn't he look sweet in his sailor hat?'

'Only if he wore it over his face,' snapped David.

'You know I never read the tabloids,' went on Mustard,

in almost orgasmic excitement, because of her pathological jealousy of Pippa Hawkley, 'but Matron just showed me this.' She handed David the *Evening Scorpion*. With a deep sigh, he put on his bifocals.

Across pages four and five were slightly blurred photographs of Lysander kissing Georgie on the dance floor at last night's party and of Georgie showing a lot of leg as she straddled the wall at the bottom of the garden. There were clearer photographs of Martha Winterton and Guy and Georgie together.

'FALL GUY,' said the huge headline. '*Hunky Hubby of the Year Guy Seymour,*' ran the copy, '*is such a tolerant husband he allows wife, singer-songwriter Georgie Maguire to kiss and cuddle in candle-lit restaurants night after night with Lysander Hawkley, the man who makes husbands jealous. Last night they were spotted escaping from a Fulham rave-up during a drugs raid.*

'*Fun-loving Lysander is the youngest son of "Hatchet Hawkley", headmaster of snooty Fleetley (fees £14,000 a year with extras).*'

With a bellow of rage, David scrumpled up the paper. Lysander must be pushing drugs to make the kind of money Hermione was talking about. Degenerate rock stars like Georgie Maguire were always into that kind of thing.

Picking up the telephone, he dialled the deputy head.

'I'm desperately sorry, Headmaster. I've seen the article.'

'I better take twenty-four hours' leave and try and sort things out.'

'Absolutely. We'll hold the fort till you get back.'

Alone at Valhalla, Kitty welcomed the prospect of a free evening. She had missed Lysander a lot – he was so lovely to have around – but he'd be pleased she'd lost another eight pounds, and had cheek-bones, ribs, ankles and flapping waistbands for the first time in her life. She must keep busy and not weaken. She had contracts to go through for Hermione, Rannaldini, and now Rachel; and darling Wolfie, having sent her a boomerang and a furry duck-billed platypus for her birthday, deserved a long chatty letter.

Yesterday, in a fit of despair, she'd taken the scissors to her fiendish perm. Shorn of its frizzy halo, her face looked even thinner, and all her features, the wide grey eyes still slightly inflamed by the contact lenses, the squashed nose and the sweet and generous mouth, much bigger. Peering in the mirror, she tugged tendrils of hair over her forehead and down her neck. It was dreadfully short, what would Rannaldini say? Probably wouldn't notice. Someone was leaning on the bell. On the doorstep stood a distinctly attractive man.

'For you,' he said, handing her a bunch of carrots.

'Ferdie,' squealed Kitty in delight. ' 'Oo my goodness, you look terrific.'

The prospect of winning a bet had concentrated Ferdie's mind and will-power amazingly. He had lost so much weight he was almost unrecognizable. He was also black-brown from the Algarve sun, with his dark hair streaked blond, and his bone structure re-appeared. The Laughing Cavalier was slowly turning into Mel Gibson.

'Oh, Ferdie,' sighed Kitty.

'You don't look so bad yourself.' Ferdie whistled in amazement, as he walked round her. 'Your hair's so much better, and you've got your contact lenses in. Oh, Kittywake, we're on our way. Let's have a huge drink to celebrate.'

'Lysander'd be ever so shocked,' said Kitty.

'I'll take care of Lysander.'

Neither of them had touched alcohol for a month, but Ferdie persuaded Kitty to bring up a bottle of champagne already chilled by the dungeons.

'We've got to weigh ourselves in a minute, so it's only fair if you drink with me,' said Ferdie, thinking how sweet she looked, not pretty at all, but appealing like his mother's Boston Terrier.

By the time Kitty had filled him in with local gossip and Ferdie had produced his holiday snaps, they'd had another glass, and Kitty, who hadn't eaten since breakfast, had become incredibly giggly. As they danced upstairs for the great weigh-in, they started squabbling over how much their clothes weighed.

'Men's clothes are heavier than women's,' said Ferdie, removing his shoes.

'Not that much,' said Kitty, kicking off her white high heels.

Ferdie took off his shirt to reveal a suntanned chest, solid as a bull terrier's.

'Oh, Ferdie, you look like Arnie Swart's what's it. 'Ave you been working out?'

Ferdie nodded. 'Nearly killed me, I've still got love handles,' he seized two chunks of flesh above his waist, 'but they're going.' He filled both their glasses. 'That dress must weigh a lot. Let's have it off. Gosh,' he gasped, as, after a little persuading, Kitty pulled her blue shirtwaister over her head, 'you're very voluptuous.'

'That's a nice way of saying I'm fat,' came a muffled voice.

'It's a way of saying you've got gorgeous boobs.'

'Have I?' Kitty emerged scarlet.

'Sure you haven't hidden tangerines in your bra?' Ferdie squeezed the ends. 'No, blimey, it's all you.'

Kitty screamed with laughter.

'Tangerines would make me 'eavier, you dope, I want to be lighter than you.'

It was thus giggling hysterically with Ferdie down to his Ninja Turtle boxer shorts and Kitty in a very white bra and knickers that Lysander, dropping in after his jaunt with Georgie to check on Kitty's weight loss, found them.

'You've got a fantastic body,' Ferdie was saying admiringly. 'Take off your bra, it must weigh at least seven pounds.'

Lysander was absolutely livid. Ferdie had always been so stuffy about not bonking clients, and here he was almost

463

at first base with Kitty. Only just managing to control his temper, he supervised the weigh-in. Kitty had lost a stone and a half, Ferdie a stone and five and a half pounds.

'Bloody good,' Ferdie conceded. 'Rannaldini will have to eat his words.'

'I wonder how many calories there are in them,' said Kitty shrieking with laughter. 'I've won the be-het, I won the be-het.'

'You are both plastered,' said Lysander icily, as Ferdie, forgetting what day it was, wasted three cheques, giving Kitty her hundred pounds. Having no intention of leaving them alone together in this state, Lysander insisted they come over to Magpie Cottage for supper.

'I'm only allowed half a grapefruit and a boiled egg,' said Kitty.

'Georgie was thinking of doing a barbecue,' said Lysander.

Knowing Georgie would get no further than thinking about it, Kitty put her blue shirtwaister back on, and returning to the kitchen, was loading cold chicken, tomatoes, baking potatoes and a big bag of peaches into a cardboard box, when an explosion shook the corridor outside.

'Ferdie's shot himself for losing the bet,' cackled Kitty.

But he was only opening another bottle of Rannaldini's champagne.

'That's more than I've eaten in a month,' he said, peering into the cardboard box, then burst into song. '*Join me dancing naked in the rain . . . cover me in ecstasy,*' and started bopping round the kitchen table.

'I *love* that song,' said Kitty. 'D'you think it will ever rain again?'

Outside it was even hotter, with finches fluttering over the burnt stubble, like fleas crawling on a lion's pelt. For the first time in her life, Kitty felt thin enough to sit on someone's knee.

I'm under ten stone, she told herself hazily.

'Rest your whole weight,' encouraged Ferdie, taking

464

a slug out of his bottle. 'You're as light as a fairy. Although, talking of fairies, the vicar must be over seventeen stone.'

Why the hell was Kitty suddenly finding Ferdie so funny? thought Lysander furiously. They were both being too silly and plastered for words. It must be tiredness and hangover that made him so down, and guilt about not putting flowers on his mother's grave today.

Alone at Magpie Cottage, Georgie stepped out of the bath and, leaving cannibal footsteps, went in search of a towel. She found one curled up like a hedgehog under Lysander's bed. Overwhelmed by another fiendish compulsion to snoop, she found herself going through the pockets of the trousers, shirts and blazer he was wearing last night. As a reward, she found dozens of cards girls must have slipped him with their telephone numbers with Home and Office written in brackets. One of them, Georgie noticed indignantly, belonged to the Catchitune publicity girl, another to the girlfriend of one of Georgie's musicians.

She started to shake, frantically frisking his drawers and cupboards, but found nothing. I'm sick, she thought. I know Lysander isn't the answer, but I can't bear to think of him with someone else. But looking like he does and being so sweet, how could he not be propositioned wherever he goes? Would she always die of jealousy whoever she was with? Was that the heritage Guy had left her?

Detesting herself, she started on Lysander's wallet and was gratified to find a nice picture of herself, and ones of Jack, Maggie and Arthur. Then she was brought up short by a photograph of a heartbreakingly pretty woman, laughing and sitting bareback on a big grey horse. She breathed again when she found Lysander had written: MUM AND ARTHUR, 1989 on the back. The leaves were turning in the photograph – it must have been taken just before she died. Oh, poor Lysander. Shoving the photograph back, Georgie, who was dry now, draped herself in a sarong covered in huge gold sunflowers, which Lysander had bought her on his way to London, and started to redo her face. How restful to return to pre-Julia days when, convinced Guy loved her for herself, she didn't have to spend her time getting tarted up.

Thunder was rumbling round the hills, but despite the punishing heat, the smell of moulding leaves and bonfires drifted in through the dusty window. Season of mistresses, thought Georgie sadly. She could see Tiny and Arthur waiting by the gate for their master's return. Standing head to tail, they were whisking the flies off each other's faces and nibbling the itches out of each other's necks. Symbol of a happy marriage, thought Georgie even more sadly.

Kitty had drunk enough champagne not to faint over Lysander's cottage. You had to beat back the nettles to get to the front door. Inside the place was a shambles with a Snowdon of washing-up in the sink, and Maggie's ripped-up victims – shoes, cushions and the fox fur Lysander had bought at the bric-à-brac stall – carpeting the floor. Kitty clutched on to her boomerang and her duck-billed platypus.

'You must have the spider franchise for the West of England,' said Ferdie, his arms full of Rannaldini's Dom Perignon. 'Hi, Georgie.'

'Whatever are Marigold and the Best-Kept Village committee going to say?' wondered Kitty as she tried to find a space to unload the goodies from her cardboard box. Stretched out on the sofa, Dinsdale opened a bloodshot eye as he smelt chicken. In the almost entirely frosted-up fridge, she found the three tins of pâté Rachel had inveighed against when she came to supper.

'Listeria leads to hysteria.' Ferdie peered over her shoulder, thrusting bottles through the ice like an Antarctic dredger. *'Come away from this squalor and join me dancing naked in the rain.'*

'And cover me in ecstasy,' sang back Kitty. At least she could replace Rannaldini's champagne with Ferdie's cheque. 'You haven't got any buttons on that shirt.'

'They popped off when I was fat,' confessed Ferdi, 'but I like the shirt.'

'I'll sew some on for you.'

Lysander was too irritated to praise them for losing all that weight, but Georgie was delighted.

'I cannot get over how marvellous you both look.'

As the back garden was even more crowded with nettles, they dragged the garden table and chairs out into Arthur's and Tiny's field. The sun had set, leaving a primrose-yellow horizon, but to the east huge black clouds were gathering.

Putting an arm round Georgie's shoulders, Lysander gazed down into Paradise.

'If I had a line of coke, I'd fly across the valley.'

Instead Ferdie produced some really strong dope. He had also rigged up an angle-poise lamp with an equally strong bulb, which threw their shadows, like late arrivals at the cinema, on to the trees that reared up at the end of the field. Above the wood, the stars rose like a fountain. The radio was blaring out pop music. Sewing on Ferdie's buttons between alternate swigs of Dom Perignon and puffs of Ferdie's cigarette, Kitty found, for the first time in her life, that she wasn't terrified when Arthur leant his great whiskery face over her shoulder.

'It's getting very dark,' complained Lysander, drawing on a joint like a maiden aunt throwing up a window and breathing in the morning air.

'It's night-time, you berk.'

It seemed to be getting hotter and closer. Midges were assaulting their scalps and their ankles. The grass was covered in little cobwebs and swarmed with spiders.

'Why are they called daddy-long-legs?' asked Kitty, biting off a thread.

'Because daddies need long legs to run away from all the trouble they cause,' said Georgie bitterly, 'and talking of trouble, Miss Bottomley is threatening to suspend Flora again. The moment Flora passed her test, she was caught driving four friends off to the pub in

Rutminster. Miss Bottomley has invited me to lunch to discuss it. Oh well, Gomorrah is another day. I've never had a woman make a pass at me.'

'Nor have I,' said Ferdie wistfully.

Everyone giggled.

'You will now,' said Kitty warmly.

'I never recognize lesbians,' said Ferdie. 'Do they have moustaches?'

'No, it's gays who have moustaches,' said Georgie.

'The technique with the opposite sex,' announced Lysander, refilling everyone's glasses, 'is to tell beautiful really stupid people—'

'Like you,' said Ferdie.

'Like me,' agreed Lysander, 'to tell beautiful, thick people how clever they are and tell clever plain ones how beautiful they are, then they always roll over.'

'What 'appens if they're both plain *and* fick like me?' asked Kitty.

'You're not,' said Georgie, Ferdie and Lysander in unison.

'Lysander means you've got to find a person's Achilles' heel and then praise it,' explained Ferdie. 'You've got a wonderful heel, Mrs Rannaldini.'

'And he's called Rannaldini. Whoops, sorry Kitty,' said Lysander.

They all grew hysterical with laughter at the stupidness of their own jokes. When the Dom Perignon ran out they moved on to peach schnapps. Having sewn on Ferdie's buttons, Kitty was fooling around with him, trying to make Wolfie's boomerang come back. Every time she threw it, it went up in the air. Once she nearly hit Arthur.

'That's a valuable horse. I don't mind if you hit Tiny,' shouted Lysander, who was now beached like a whale across two chairs with his head in Georgie's lap.

Ferdie was laughing all the time now, looking like a Chinaman with slit eyes and a huge inane grin. Against the towering trees, their shadows danced like the naughty boys dipped in great Agrippa's ink-well.

'Look how we get smaller as we approach,' cried Kitty, waving her arms.

'Wish dieting was as easy,' yelled Ferdie.

'Aren't they sweet together?' said Georgie, stroking Lysander's forehead. 'Ferdie's very taken. He's as lonely as she is. Wouldn't it be perfect if he took her off Rannaldini?'

Even in his present stupor, Lysander was conscious of a distinct disquiet. If Ferdie started looking after Kitty, and Kitty after Ferdie, who would look after him?

'Even the boomerang looks stoned,' he said sulkily.

'Will it ever rain again?' sighed Georgie.

They were all too preoccupied to realize it had clouded over and the stars had rushed in. The tape had worked its way round.

'*Take me dancing naked in the rain and cover me in ecstasy,*' sang Blue Pearl.

I'm under ten stone, thought Kitty, capering round to the music. I'm having fun for the first time in years.

'I haven't enjoyed myself so much since I went Sharon-shagging in Benidorm with the cricket XI after A levels,' said Ferdie, lighting another joint.

'You probably met me there,' screamed Kitty. Suddenly she stopped laughing. 'Listen everyone.'

At first it sounded like a faint rustle of silk, or a distant scream, then a rattle of machine-gun fire. Gradually they felt the first drops on their hair, soothing the midge bites. Suddenly as they turned their faces upwards, it was like stepping into the shower.

'Rain,' yelled Georgie, joyfully leaping to her feet. 'It's raining. Our little trees will be saved after all.'

Trying to hold her back, Lysander grabbed her sarong. Next moment she was naked, dancing wildly round the field, her writhing body glistening like a seal, her wild red mane flattened and dripping down her back.

'*See me naked dancing in the rain,*' the glorious husky voice echoed across the valley, '*and cover me with ecstasy.*'

Letting out Tarzan howls, Lysander and Ferdie whipped

off their clothes and raced after her. They were followed by Kitty, who removed her shirtwaister, but kept on her bra and knickers, which bobbed in the half-darkness like white rabbits.

Off they all charged into the deluge and an ecstatic conga round the field, leaping to avoid the thistles. Jack and Maggie frisked round their heels yapping hysterically, with Dinsdale working off Kitty's cold chicken, which he'd just eaten whole, waddling behind them. Arthur and Tiny cantered alongside, snorting, with their tails in the air.

'*I'm not frightened of Arthur*,' sang Kitty, swaying in front of him, stroking his whiskery nose. '*See me naked dancing in the rain, boo-be-doo.*'

Lysander was just noticing what a surprisingly good dancer she was, and how sweetly her plump body bounced along – like Pigwig in Pigling Bland – and how he could see her nipples now her bra had become see-through, when a car screeched up to the cottage.

'It's the fuzz,' giggled Georgie.

'No, you're the fuzz,' said Lysander, tugging at her sodden bush, and they all collapsed again.

Finding the house unlocked, David Hawkley walked straight in. The sight that greeted him compounded his worst fears, a drunken orgy, possibly bestiality and witch-craft, led by that decadent hippy, Georgie Maguire, who was now bopping with a basset, and with that degener-ate, overweight ruffian Ferdie Fitzgerald bringing up the rear.

Nor were matters improved by a second car roaring up decanting a deputation from the Best-Kept Village committee, including Marigold, Lady Chisleden and the vicar, to do a spot check on Magpie Cottage.

Glimpsing naked dancers, Lady Chisleden clapped her hands over the vicar's eyes, crying: 'Don't look, Percy,' in a ringing voice.

Whereupon the vicar, having seen Lysander and a much-improved Ferdie in the buff, and being convinced he'd finally arrived in heaven, tore down Lady Chisleden's fingers, crying in an equally ringing voice that the Church must face up to its obligations.

'*See me naked dancing in the rain,*' sang Ferdie waving a nearly empty bottle of peach schnapps. 'Come and party, you guys.'

'*And cover me with ecstasee-ee-ee,*' joined in Kitty.

'Put on your clothes at once,' ordered Lady Chisleden. 'Your vicar is present.'

'Oh, piss off,' said Lysander in a bored voice.

Painfully reminded of little Cosmo earlier, David Hawkley lost his temper.

'Lysander,' he thundered, 'stop this disgraceful pantomime at once.'

It was a voice that chilled Lysander's blood. For a second he froze, then gathering up his junior dog and holding her in front of himself like a fig-leaf, he turned to Georgie.

'Darling, I don't think you've met my father.'

43

The party broke up very quickly after that. A frantically giggling Kitty, Ferdie, Georgie and Dinsdale spitting out splinters of boomerang were driven away by a very irate Marigold.

'You've really let the sayde down, Georgie, conductin' black-magic orgies. You must have realized what a pigstay Lysander had reduced Magpie Cottage to, probably contributed to it yourself. And you and Lysander are plastered all over *The Scorpion*. Gay's been on the phone all day, trying to faind you. He's standin' bay you, bay the way. Ay can't think way, and all the Press are doorsteppin' Paradise Grange to get the Catchitune angle from Larry.'

'It's all Larry's fault,' screamed Georgie, 'for putting out mugs and T-shirts with Guy and me looking lovey-dovey. I'll get him under the Trade Descriptions Act. And what's all this about *The Scorpion*?'

She couldn't take in what Marigold was saying. She could only think how embarrassing it was that such a handsome man as David Hawkley should have caught her running around all wobbling and naked.

Having discovered that his youngest son was far too drunk to make any sense and refused to explain how he'd come by any of these amazing perks, David Hawkley drove off into the deluge. After a few minutes he calmed down and decided to put up at a nearby hotel and try a different tack in the morning. As every room within ten miles of Paradise was double-booked by reporters, he ended up at The Bell in Rutminster, an old coaching inn overlooking the River Fleet. The kitchen was closed, but noting his pallor and good looks, the landlord's wife insisted on sending up to his room a bottle of whisky and a plate of Welsh rarebit, which gave him outlandish dreams of naked ladies frolicking in meadows.

One of them was Georgie Maguire, white feet dancing on the greensward, red hair flying like a maenad, but close up she turned into Mustard wearing nothing but a pie-frill collar, and he woke up drenched in sweat, shaking in horror.

Next morning the papers were full of the chinks in Georgie's marriage with lots of jokes about Paradise Lust and On-the-Rocks-Star. 'Caring Guy' was much quoted from the South of France, insisting that there was no question of divorce and that Lysander Hawkley was a friend of the family, particularly his daughter Flora. At least Lysander wasn't going to be dragged through some messy court case.

Feeling slightly more cheerful, particularly after some excellent kippers and three slices of toast and Oxford marmalade, David decided to have it out with Lysander. He found Magpie Cottage locked and deserted, except for Arthur and Tiny who were standing gloomily by the gate in the continuing downpour. Paradise Village swarmed with reporters splashing round in the flooded High Street, desperate to find Lysander and a story. More of them were doorstepping Angel's Reach waiting for Georgie to emerge.

Receiving a tip-off from Miss Cricklade, who was unblocking a drain clogged with leaves outside her cottage, David approached Angel's Reach from the south side, crossing the Fleet a mile upstream and walking through the woods. The rain had stopped, but the downpour continued as the water sifted and worked its way through twigs, leaves, traveller's joy and dog mercury to the leafy floor below. The weather was still in the seventies, but not stifling like yesterday. Robins were singing, beech masks and acorns crunched beneath his feet like shingle, but a drenched blackberry he picked was as tasteless as his life.

Reaching the edge of Georgie's land, he could see the house with its soaring angels turned amber by the rain, and the lake flanked with bulrushes, glinting in the sunshine. Beech trees, stingingly red as Georgie's hair after yesterday's deluge, trailed their leaves in the water. Statues gleamed seal-like, red hips glittered on rose bushes puffed out by their weight of water like enraged tomcats. Saffron and sea-green lichen on the flagstones as he walked up the path were almost luminous. The rain seemed to have given the garden back its youth.

In a clump of drying lavender, he found a page of pink flimsy on which Georgie had scribbled some lyrics.

'You're a snake on the make, a minx of a sphinx

You're a wog, I'm a wop, but I can't give you up,' he read, then jumped at a Baskerville bay. Dinsdale trying to look fierce at the front, but waving his tail, kept looking back at the potting shed. Here David found Georgie. She was perched on a garden roller, wearing a grey T-shirt and yellow trousers, reading *Antony and Cleopatra*. Yesterday's downpour had brightened her pale cheeks (David thought of Lavinia in *The Aeneid*) and fluffed up her hair, which was tied back with a yellow ribbon.

'How did you get in here?'

'Miss Cricklade, rather a fan of Lysander's, told me a short cut,' said David, removing his flat cap. Even a red rim across his forehead didn't diminish his fierce, dark glamour.

'You don't know where he is?'

'Over the hills and far away. Ferdie's packed him off to Australia on a job. We thought it better to get him out of the country until the dust, and there's plenty of that in Magpie Cottage, settled. He's distraught at going – leaving the horses and the dogs.'

And you, too, presumably, thought David. 'Look,' he added brusquely, 'I need your help. I beg you to lay off him. We've got to get him back and into some drug rehabilitation centre before it's too late and with all due respect, you're much too old for him.'

'That doesn't show respect, due or otherwise.'

'It isn't funny.'

The deeply etched lines on either side of David Hawkley's tightly clamped mouth reminded Georgie of an H-block. For a second she dickered, then said: 'Can you keep a huge secret? Lysander's not peddling drugs. He hardly smokes dope at all. You cut off his allowance and ordered him to get a job, so he got one. He's employed by women like me to make their erring husbands jealous and he's making a bomb.'

'You mean a sort of gigolo?' asked David with a shudder.

'No, no, he just hangs around looking heavenly and rattles our husbands. They're such an unfaithful bunch, but they don't like their wives playing the same game, so they come to heel.' Georgie's eyes suddenly filled with tears. 'He's such a sweet, kind boy, you should be really proud of him. He's saved far more marriages than Relate.

'I'm really sorry the Press picked on him and me,' she went on humbly, 'it must be awful having your name dragged in. Schoolboys so love that sort of thing. I feel desperate about my own children as well.'

She's beautiful, thought David, touched by her concern. Pity her eyes were obscured by that thick fringe. He itched to trim it with a pair of secateurs.

'Are you all right?' he asked.

'I'm in hot water,' sighed Georgie, 'but I have none. I hoped you were the plumber, but at least you're not Guy. All that sanctimonious claptrap about standing by me, particularly when he's out in France bonking his brains out.' She didn't know for sure but why else would Rachel be in France? 'I hope *The Scorpion* catches him.' She lobbed a Bonio at Dinsdale.

'I found this.' David handed her the soaked bit of paper.

'Oh, lovely! I wondered where it had got to.'

'What's it for?'

'A musical called *Ant and Cleo*. I'm trying to think of a word to rhyme with "asp". Look, I know that party last night must have looked the last word in decadence, but it's the first time anything like that's happened.' And she explained about Ferdie and Kitty celebrating losing weight, and then Ferdie producing this amazing dope.

'That boy's always been a pernicious influence.'

'He is not,' protested Georgie. 'He's saved Lysander's life. He fusses over him like an old nanny and he's got two horses and two dogs to look after now.'

Unable to banish the memory of Georgie's rain-soaked body, David suddenly said: 'I'm staying at The Bell in Rutminster. You're very welcome to come and have a bath, then we could have lunch. If you're worried about the Press, I'm sure they could fix a private room. I'd like to talk about Lysander.'

'I'm not going to bore him by banging on about my marriage,' vowed Georgie half an hour later, as she lay in a foot of scented water, shaving her legs and downing a large Bacardi and Coke.

David was drinking whisky and soda in the lounge when she came down and reading a small black leather-bound book. Georgie peered at the spine. It was Catullus.

'*Odi et amo*,' she said bitterly. 'Just like my marriage. How've you translated it?'

'Loving and hating someone at the same time is excruciatingly painful,' said David, 'but I'll have to improve on that.'

The dining room was practically empty. The head waiter gave them a table overlooking the river and flooded water meadows. Like the black tassels of a widow's shawl, rain was pouring out of approaching clouds, people were running over the bridge under buckling umbrellas. On the far bank hawthorns, groaning with berries, rinsed their bloodstained fingers in the water. Georgie felt heady, detached and very much in need of the second Bacardi and Coke he ordered her. She didn't want the mood to slip. Guy got furious when she dithered over menus, so she quickly chose hors-d'oeuvres and a Dover sole because they were the things she saw. As she gouged out pink mayonnaise with bits of raw carrot and cauliflower and gazed at the river, David noticed her eyes were the same sludgy green as the water and her nipples which had been sticking up through her grey T-shirt had retreated after a hot bath.

Unable to stop himself touching her freckled cheek, he said: 'Why do you look so young?'

'Because I thought I was loved,' said Georgie sadly, and proceeded to tell him all about Guy, Julia and Rachel.

Melba toast stiffened in a cooled pink napkin, rollmops, asparagus, egg mayonnaise and tiny sweet corn lay untouched on her plate half an hour later.

'I married a bishop's son who's turned into a chess bishop always sliding off at angles,' sighed Georgie. 'Now I've been caught out, he'll feel more justified in catting around than ever.'

David, who'd finished his oysters ages ago, waved to the waiter to remove her plate and fill up their glasses.

'And Lysander didn't help?'

'Not really. He jolted Guy to begin with, but it was like putting Band-Aid over a boil. Guy still has the capacity to make me more suicidally unhappy than anyone else.'

'Then you'd better get out.' David leant back as the waiter placed two huge soles in front of them with the green-flecked pats of butter already melting.

'Guy won't change,' he said when they were alone again. 'He may still love you, but he's lost that unqualified adulation he's so dependent on, and he won't rest in his search to find it again. And you've lost your hero. It needn't be the end of the world,' he added gently. 'Divorce may not guarantee you happiness, but it might be an end to unhappiness.'

'It's the duty of prisoners of war to escape.'

477

'You'd better start tunnelling. You don't have to eat that.'

Thinking how surprisingly nice he was, and that Lysander had got his father totally wrong, Georgie blurted out: 'It's a compliment really. I can't eat when I fanc . . . I mean . . . find someone attractive.'

David flushed.

'And Guy always says I'm the worst boner of soles,' she giggled, the drink taking effect. 'I'm a better barer of them.'

'I'll do it for you.' Pulling her plate towards him, he plunged his knife into the crisp brown-speckled skin. Lovely deft hands, thought Georgie.

'What about you?' she asked tentatively as he chucked the transparent bones on to a side plate. 'Have you got over Pippa at all?'

David handed her back her plate.

'She was the most beautiful woman I've ever known.'

'I know.' Georgie hung her head. 'I saw a photograph when I was snooping through Lysander's wallet. I was madly jealous until I twigged who she was.'

He's got the most gorgeous hair, she thought hazily, striped grey and black like morning-coat trousers and a gorgeous aquiline nose and even more gorgeous eyes, hard and unblinking. His only similarity to Lysander was the long, lustrous, curly eyelashes and Georgie felt he would have straightened these if he could.

'She was also the most promiscuous.'

'What?' Georgie was shaken out of her reverie.

'Grindy pepper,' said the landlord's wife, brandishing a huge wooden pepper-pot.

Frantic to discover if she'd heard right, Georgie waited until they were alone once more.

'Promiscuous?' she repeated incredulously.

'She slept with my elder brother, Alastair, even when she was engaged to me. He trained racehorses. He was the one who sold that hopeless horse Arthur to Lysander for such an outlandish price. Alastair was a constant, but she always had several others on the go – junior masters, senior boys.'

'Pippa?' said Georgie bewildered.

'She was insatiable,' said David harshly. 'When I was head of a school in Yorkshire, before I took over Fleetley, she left me for a month to live with the local vet. All the masters had a whip-round for her leaving present, a rather expensive fridge. The sixth form all sent her a telegram saying: WHAT'S WRONG WITH US?'

He was perfectly in control of himself, except for his hands like rigid claws clamped on his knee.

'Oh, my God,' said Georgie in horror. 'It was so public! How did you cope?'

'Pride, stiff upper lip, gritted teeth – all the clichés. Men tend not to dump, women do. That's their strength.'

Georgie shook her head. 'I've dumped too much. It's a drug. I don't believe it, she looked so sweet and innocent. Why didn't you chuck her out?'

'Everything all right?' said the head waiter, looking at the untouched plates. He always wanted to make a pie from the uneaten fish and call it Lovers' Leftovers. Nixon, the hotel cat, was going to have a field day.

'For the same reason you don't leave Guy,' said David. 'I suppose I loved her.'

'And you had Lysander and the other boys.'

'Christ, I was jealous of Lysander.' It was all coming out now. Georgie felt she ought to be wearing a dog collar and have a grille between them.

'Pippa worshipped him,' muttered David, 'gave him everything when it seemed she gave me nothing. She used to cover him with kisses deliberately. I was too proud to beg. It didn't help Lysander. Alexander and Hector beat him up, because they were jealous, too. I sent him to a different school, because they were so bright, I didn't want them to show him up, but he was so unhappy, he ran home along the railway track to Pippa all the time. Then in his second term a horsebox rolled up outside the school. He'd only gone out and bought a racehorse.

It had to go back, of course, and he was so heartbroken he ran away again. So I let him stay at Fleetley. I know I was vile to him. He hates me and blames me utterly for making his mother miserable.'

'It wasn't your fault,' said Georgie indignantly. 'Anyway,' she lied, 'Lysander doesn't hate you, he's just in awe of you. Someone must tell him the truth.'

'Christ, no!' David was really shocked. 'He must have that untarnished image to cling on to.'

'But it's totally false! He ought to be falling for girls his own age.'

This time Georgie had eaten most of her sole, and David's was untouched. Seeing she'd finished, he clashed his knife and fork together.

'D'you mind if I smoke?'

Watching two middle-aged matrons trying not to water at the mouth as they inspected the pudding trolley, Georgie was reminded of the way women looked at Lysander. She wondered why she found his father so much more attractive. Perhaps Lysander was too sweet, too easygoing. She'd never be able to push David around, yet Pippa obviously had. Neither of them wanted pudding, but Georgie was shocked how happy she felt when he ordered two glasses of Armagnac.

'Should we? We'll be running round the water meadows with nothing on at this rate.'

'*And all my days are trances, And all my nightly dreams, Are where thy grey eye glances, And where thy footstep gleams,*'

murmured David. 'I dreamt about you last night.'

Flustered, absurdly flattered, Georgie felt able to ask what happened to Pippa at the end.

'She fell hook, line and stinker,' David circumcised the end of his cigar with grim relish, 'for our local MFH, Tommy Westerham, a terrific womanizer. He got bored with her, and then had the gall to ring me and tell me to tell *her* to get off his back. His wife's very rich and he was terrified of being kicked out.'

Georgie's mouth opened in horror. 'Oh, God!'

'I broke it to her as gently as I could, but she didn't believe me, she thought it was a ruse to stop her seeing him. So she rode straight over to his house. Car backfired on the road. Horse went up. She wasn't wearing a hard hat.'

The flame flickered over his tormented face like hellfire, as he tried to hold a match still enough to light his cigar.

'I keep reproaching myself. If I hadn't told her then, had let things take their course, she might be still alive. Did I want to spare her humiliation, or was I secretly enjoying humiliating her by telling her Tommy wanted out?'

For a moment he rested his eyes on the balls of his hands.

'You couldn't see the churchyard for flowers at her funeral and the church was full of her lovers, clapping kind hands on my shoulder. They must have thought me a cold fish. Hector, Alexander, Lysander and I carried her coffin. Lysander stumbled once. It was like Christ collapsing under the Cross.'

He glared at Georgie. 'I've never told anyone this,' he said slowly, 'because I felt so ashamed, but as they lowered her into the grave, such a slim coffin, I felt only relief that at last she was sleeping alone.'

'Oh, God!' Tears were flooding Georgie's flushed cheeks. 'I'm so desperately sorry.' She put a hand on his. 'And Lysander knew nothing?'

'Nothing. He was so on her side. He never realized my intransigence stemmed from frustration. I should have risen above it, but I was strait-jacketed into my misery.'

'*Break, my heart, for I must hold my tongue.*' Georgie shook her head.

'Lysander was deranged with grief. I thought he'd drive over a cliff, or drink himself to death. I didn't know how to comfort him.'

Taking a slug of Armagnac, he choked slightly. Patting him on the back, Georgie encountered muscles, and fought a temptation to run her hand upwards and stroke his sleek head.

'More coffee, Miss Maguire?' asked the head waiter, who'd been reading *The Scorpion* in the kitchen and had put two and two together.

Georgie shook her head. Seeing a fat woman splashing through the water meadows in the wake of a jolly black Labrador, she said regretfully, 'I must go home and walk Dinsdale.'

'Shall I come with you?'

'Oh, please.' Georgie beamed up at him. 'My world's tumbling about my ears. Why on earth do I feel so happy?'

'Probably booze,' said David drily, then suddenly he had a horrific vision of having Georgie as a daughter-in-law. 'It isn't serious, you and Lysander?'

Georgie's pony-tail flew as she shook her head: 'No, no, it's utterly platonic. We're just terrific friends.' She had conveniently forgotten that Lysander had asked her to marry him two days ago, and how distraught he'd been when he'd left for the airport that morning. 'Ferdie insisted no bonking from the start,' she went on. 'Lysander's suffering slightly from calf-love maybe. Anyway, toy boys are like tadpoles. If you're sporting you throw them back at the end of the season.'

'All the same, he ought to get a proper job,' said David, making a writing sign to the waiter.

'Shouldn't give it up too lightly,' said Georgie. 'He's the only person I know making serious money in the recession.'

'I'm still trying to think of a word to rhyme with asp,' said David, getting out his cheque book.

'When was Catullus supposed to be handed in?'

'January.'

'That does make me feel better.'

'D'you read poetry?'

'Not since I picked up Herrick the other day, and found Guy had marked all the poems to Julia. I'm sure Herrick praised Julia's leg for being white and hairless because it meant she wasn't always pinching his razor.'

'D'you mind coming upstairs a minute?' asked David as they left the restaurant.

For a second, when he produced a pair of scissors from the dressing table, she backed away in terror thinking he was some kind of maniac, but he laughed and said he only wanted to cut half an inch off her fringe so he could see her eyes.

David had had a wretched year of insomnia, apathy, exhaustion and terrible migraines from bottling up his emotions. He was a man who liked to have control of himself and other people; he shrank from physical displays of affection; was often brusque and offhand to hide his feelings, but, once smitten, he went truly overboard.

Half an hour after Georgie got home, the telephone rang.

'I'm not *The Scorpion*,' said David. 'If you use worm instead of asp, there are lots of words that rhyme with it.'

'Poisonous worm, you'll end my term. Goddit,' said Georgie. 'You are marvellous.'

'I hope I see you before the end of term.'

'It's half-term next weekend,' said Georgie.

44

The streams came back to Paradise and so did Guy Seymour. He was photographed looking handsome and suntanned at Heathrow and repeated his vows to stand by his errant wife, adding with a manly, slightly crooked smile, that as a Christian and father, he didn't believe in divorce. In fact he couldn't afford to be anything but magnanimous. His French trip had cost a bomb. Half the galleries in the West End were going belly-up, and he needed financial help from Georgie to keep going. And, utterly perversely, Georgie had suddenly started looking fantastic, and he found himself fancying her rotten once again. As Lysander was in Australia, he felt less threatened and that Georgie was genuinely trying to save the marriage. They got on better than they had in months and the Press, increasingly preoccupied with the Gulf War, drifted away.

As autumn gave way to winter, Georgie found she was looking at her own and David's horoscope long before Guy's, Julia's, Lysander's or even Rachel's. Guy was delighted Georgie was burying herself in work. Marvellous tunes floated from her turret room like banners, and she sang even more beautiful versions in her bath.

Lysander, however, was stuck in the outback, rattling a sheep farmer who'd been cheating on his wife and playing a lot of polo. Missing Georgie constantly, he grew increasingly frustrated when she never answered his letters which admittedly were pretty short, and always seemed out when he rang. If he didn't get her, as Rannaldini was still away, he'd ring Valhalla.

'Kitty, Kitty, Kitty. It sounds as though I'm calling a cat in the dark. Did I wake you? What time is it? Five-thirty? Oh shit, I'm sorry.'

'Don't be. It's the nicest wake-up call I've ever 'ad. Now I can read.'

'What are you reading?'

'A book called *Love's Young Dream*.'

'Tell me what it's about. I've got to page twenty-five of *The Mill on the Floss*, so you can tell how bored I am. Where's Georgie? I daren't leave a message on the machine in case Guy Fucks picks it up.'

'Probably pulled the phone out. She's working ever so 'ard.'

'Will you call round and beg her to ring me, please, Kitty? I miss her so much. Have you heard from Ferdie?'

'Only that Maggie's in season, and 'alf the dogs in Fulham are baying outside the door.'

'Oh God, poor Ferd. I'll ring him. Jack'll be in there. He's such an operator. They'll have gorgeous puppies. I'll give you one. How much d'you weigh now?'

'Eight stone eleven, but it's 'ard to diet when the wevver's cold. Wasn't it sad about Mrs Fatcher?'

'I know. I really cried when I saw her leaving Downing Street in her crimson suit.'

'Awful 'aving to move 'ouse in three days.'

'I sent her a good-luck card.'

'That was kind. John Major seems nice.'

'Are you sure Georgie's OK? Is she missing me?'

'I'm sure she is.'

'Well, I'll be home for Christmas. I've got you a present to make up for Dinsdale chewing up your boomerang. Bye, Kitty darling.'

Putting back the telephone, Kitty thought how empty Paradise seemed without Lysander. Out in the night, a sharp frost was bringing down the last leaves. She felt sad there was no-one to witness their fall, like soldiers dying alone on the battlefield. How awful if Lysander or Wolfie or Ferdie got sent to the Gulf.

Australia grew hotter and Lysander, missing Arthur and his dogs, and having restored the errant sheep farmer to his lovely wife, decided to fly home and surprise Georgie whom he missed most of all. He spent the twenty-four-hour flight gazing at her photograph, which had grown cracked and faded in his wallet and landed on a bitterly cold morning in the first week in December. Collecting an ecstatic Jack and Maggie, who seemed to have put on a lot of weight, from Fulham, he found Ferdie leaving for work and extremely disapproving.

'You can't go back to Paradise. The Press are still sniffing around. Everything'll blow up again.'

'I must check if Arthur and Tiny are OK. My stuff's all at Magpie Cottage, and I'm frantic to see Georgie.'

'Well, for God's sake, ring first. You don't want to bump into Guy.'

Lysander left a message on Georgie's ansaphone, and then played Georgie's sixties tape, which he'd nearly scrambled, all the way down. He was so tired, the drive seemed longer than the flight. He remembered how, after any time apart, his mother used to race out of the house, arms open wide, eyes wet with tears of joy, and tug him into a warm, scented embrace. If he had Georgie, Christmas wouldn't be so bleak.

Stripped of its green leaves, Paradise was as he remembered it on his first visit. Crows cawed morosely, the stone of the houses had lost its lustre, everything was blanketed in mist. Grey and sullen, Valhalla had retreated into its trees like a murderer with a gang of retainers. The only colour came from the last saffron of the larches and the faded red of the Turkey oaks. Georgie's soaring angels looked in need of thermal underwear.

Anxious to get into the house out of the vicious wind, Lysander parked the Ferrari across the drive and loaded himself up with a koala bear, a huge bottle of Giorgio, a pearl necklace and twelve bunches of pale pink roses he'd bought on the way. Dinsdale welcomed him and the dogs with great delight. The Rover outside, as highly polished as an elderly army officer's shoes, looked vaguely familiar, but Lysander was in too much of a rush.

'Georgie, it's me,' he yelled, letting himself into the house.

His heart was hammering with excitement, he was so dying to hold her in his arms.

'Georgie, where are you?'

After too long a pause, she came downstairs, wrapped in a dark brown towel. She looked so terrified that Lysander thought for a ghastly second that Guy might be at home. There was a faint smell of fish. She must be cooking Charity's cod.

She wore no make-up, except mascara smudged under her eyes, and, although her hair was tousled, she was growing her fringe out and wearing it brushed sideways off her forehead. Having gazed at a very glamorous photograph of her for two months, Lysander thought she looked much older.

'I was having a bath,' she stammered.

Clutching his presents, his curls flopping over his bruised eyes, his chin resting on massed pink roses, Lysander looked like some Bacchante strayed out of an all-night revel.

'D'you want a drink?' she said nervously.

'No, I want you.' Dropping the presents on the hall table which was so small that half the roses fell to the floor, he hugged her. 'Let's go to bed. God, I missed you.'

Looking down at her feet, bare on the flagstones, he felt weak with love. 'You've got chilblains. You must wear slippers. I'll buy you some. Chilblains means it's going to snow. I'll take you tobogganing. You don't seem very pleased to see me,' he added in bewilderment.

'Of course I am. I wasn't expecting you, that's all, and Flora drives now, and – er – as she's broken up, she might roll up at any minute. Come on, let's have a drink.'

'OK. You put on something warm. I'll get a bottle.'

'I'll get it.' Georgie's eyes flickered.

But as she went towards the kitchen, there was a crash and the sound of a window being slammed. Jack bristled and barked.

'What's that?' Pushing her aside, Lysander sprinted into the kitchen and froze.

For out of the banging window he could see a man in his trousers and socks, carrying his shoes and jacket and frantically buttoning up his shirt as he hotfooted across the garden round to the Rover.

Lysander couldn't move. He would recognize that broad-shouldered, ramrod-straight back anywhere. Jumping into the Rover, David Hawkley drove off in a flurry of leaves, unaware that his son had seen him.

Lysander thought he was suffocating. On the kitchen table lay a copy of his father's translation of Ovid. Flipping it open, he saw his father had written on the fly leaf: TO DEAREST GEORGIE, and followed by some incomprehensible Latin tag. By the recipe books he found three of his own letters unopened.

Georgie was sitting on the stairs, surrounded by pink roses, looking sulky, dead eyed, caught out, but not nearly sorry enough.

'Tell me this is a bad dream.'

'It's a bad dream.'

'How could you, Georgie?' whispered Lysander, clutching the door for support. 'How could you? You were so unhappy. I worked and worked to get you over Guy and I find you bonking my father – like a couple of bloody dinosaurs. He's a geriatric, for Christ's sake.'

'He's only five years older than me,' said Georgie, flaring up.

'He's a bastard. Guy's a saint by comparison. You're revolting, Georgie. I don't understand you.'

A combination of guilt at being caught out, or fierce protectiveness towards David, and blazing jealousy of the dead Pippa, unleashed Georgie's legendary Irish temper.

'Your father is the dearest man in the world, and what's more he's been a wonderful father to you.'

'Bullshit,' shouted Lysander, so loud that Maggie cringed terrified against the door, and Jack started to yap.

'He's incapable of love. He was *diabolical* to Mum.'

'Rubbish,' screamed Georgie. 'Your mother was a whore. D'you know how many lovers she had when she was married to your father?'

At the top of her voice, saliva flying, face engorging and disintegrating like beetroot in the Moulinex, she proceeded to scream chapter and worse. Lysander couldn't stop her, he'd never been quick enough for back chat. He just mouthed at her, utterly shattered, fists clenched, rigid but trembling.

'Did you know,' yelled Georgie finally, 'your Uncle Alastair was her lover for years and she was having an affair with Tommy Westerham? His picture from *Horse and Hound* was found in her bag the day she died, galloping down the main road to plead with him not to dump her.'

'I don't believe you,' whispered Lysander. 'My father told you this to get you on his side, to poison you against me and Mum. The lying, lying bastard! I'm going to kill him when I catch up with him.'

For a second, as he grabbed Georgie's shoulders, shaking her like a rat, his beautiful face contorted into frenzy, Georgie was terrified he was going to kill her as well.

Then he caught the reek of cod again, and recognized the smell of sex, and with his father, and threw her back against the stairs. As he stumbled out, trampling the roses underfoot and slamming the front door behind him, Georgie realized what she'd done. She tried frantically to trace David, who now would never forgive her. Nor would Lysander, who would probably kill either himself or his father.

Lysander's only thought was to find someone who had known his parents well enough to refute Georgie's horrific accusations. Hurtling out of Paradise with Jack

489

and Maggie huddled together on the seat beside him, he frantically punched out numbers on his car telephone, repeatedly getting wrong people because he kept mis-reading his address book and misdialling. By the time he had narrowly avoided crashing into several stone walls, he had learnt that his brothers were both out of their offices, his grandmother was whooping it up at some bridge party and his mother's sister was in the Seychelles. In despair, he decided to drive down to Brighton to see Uncle Alastair's widow, Dinah, a tetchy old soak, who spent her life outwitting a succession of companions paid by the family to keep her off the booze. If he hurried, he might catch her while she was sober enough to make sense.

Brighton looked its least seductive. An icy wind savaged the tamarisk bushes along the front, a sullen grey sea pummelled the shingle. Aunt Dinah's flat stank of tom cat, long-term dirt and stale booze. Lysander remembered how his mother had referred to her mockingly as an auntie-depressant. Mrs Bingham, the paid companion, tweed-suited and tight-lipped, had the same gaoler's eyes as Mustard.

'Mrs Hawkley's in the lounge. Would you care for some refreshment?'

'I'd love a drink.'

Mrs Bingham offered tea or coffee.

Lysander said he'd prefer a large whisky.

'Oh, we don't keep alcohol in the flat, I'm afraid.'

Looking at this wild-haired young man, totally inadequately dressed in a Foster's Lager T-shirt and dirty white jeans, clutching a koala bear and with shakes even worse than his aunt, Mrs Bingham deduced alcohol must run in the family.

'Who's there?' came Aunt Dinah's gin-soaked yell.

Lysander found her in the sitting room, reading Dick Francis with a huge magnifying glass with the television roaring. She was wearing a grey wool dress so tight it had ridden up to reveal stocking tops and thighs like unbaked suet. Although her black wig was worn at a rakish angle, her once-fine features had collapsed with the booze. Beneath eyelids swollen like shiny white maggots, however, her bloodshot eyes had the craftiness of an old hippo.

A large tabby cat covered most of her lap. Fear of her dashing husband leaving her had kept her sober and reasonably attractive for thirty-five years, but when he did go, albeit to another world, she had given up. Even in his state of shock, Lysander felt huge pity, and wished he had brought her a box of chocolates.

'It's Lysander, Aunt Dinah.'

As he leant forward to kiss a cheek on which red veins tangled like candy floss, he caught a waft of stale sweat and Gordon's. The paid companion wasn't being as efficient as she thought.

'Just been watching a flick called *The Bengal Lancers*.' Aunt Dinah spoke in a very precise voice to conceal the slurring. 'Everything wrong as usual. They never had pig-sticking on the Frontier, but Gary Cooper was certainly a dish. Sorry, I can't get up – cat on lap.'

'I'm sorry to barge in. I need to talk to you.'

'She offered you a drink?' said Aunt Dinah as the paid companion sidled in, plonked her tweed bottom on the sofa and got out her knitting.

'I'm OK.' Collapsing into the armchair nearest the electric fire, Lysander noticed a cat's earth box beside his aunt's chair. From the smell, it hadn't been cleaned out recently. He suppressed a wave of nausea.

'You get more and more like your mother.'

Glancing up, he was disconcerted to see both Dinah's crossed eyes concentrating on him.

'It's Mum I came to talk about.'

A long sigh ruffled the tabby cat's fur.

'I wondered how long it would be.'

Lysander turned to Mrs Bingham. 'Look, d'you mind awfully if we talk alone?'

'My job is to stay with Mrs Hawkley.'

'Oh, bugger off,' snarled Dinah. 'I'm not likely to get up to anything with my nephew. No doubt you frisked him before he came in.'

As Mrs Bingham flounced out, the cat started to purr.

'Common, isn't she? Doesn't like Thatcher,' yelled Dinah over the television. 'The one coming next week, according to the hand-out, has wide experience with handicapped children.' She gave a cackle of laughter.

'D'you mind if we turn the television down a bit?'

Jane Asher was in her kitchen talking about Christmas cake. She looked so fresh, pretty and alien to his current squalid surroundings that Lysander wished he could climb into the set with her. After turning her face bright orange and changing channels twice, Dinah found the mute button.

Ramming his hands between his knees to stop them trembling Lysander took a deep breath. 'About Mum. I honestly don't want to upset you, but basically Dad's got a new woman.'

'Mrs Colman. I've met her. That voice would drive me cuckoo.'

'No, a newer one. Basically she's been slagging Mum off, I don't believe her, but I just wanted proof that she was lying.'

'What sort of things?'

'That, that – I'm really sorry – that she was having an affaire with Alastair.'

'Ah.' Dinah's dirty-nailed fingers stopped stroking the cat.

'And loads of other people.'

Outside he could see two gulls and a boat with a red sail battling desperately with the gale. The pause seemed to go on for ever.

'She was rather unfaithful,' said Dinah.

'She was?' Lysander was aghast. 'Then Dad drove her to it. He's such a shit.'

'Your father put up with a lot. They were never suited. He brought her to stay when they were first engaged. He was dotty about her. The first afternoon he went to his room to write a review for *The Spectator* and Alastair offered to show her the garden. Looking down from my bedroom, I saw them kissing in the orchard. All the blossom was out. It was like a Barbara Cartland book jacket.'

'I don't believe it,' hissed Lysander.

'It's true.' Dinah's words were slurring now. 'I caught them out so many times. Christmas, birthdays, your grandfather's funeral – even your christening. Some people even thought – no, forget that. Alastair and Pippa would be the life and soul of every party, but suddenly they'd vanish like gypsies' lurchers.'

Lysander had put his head in his hands. Now he looked up, his eyes cavernous in horror and bewilderment.

'It was a pity Alastair died so suddenly. Didn't leave his affairs in very good order.' Staggering to her feet, tipping the cat on to the carpet, Dinah lurched towards the desk and after pulling out several drawers, took out a salmon-pink file on which the words: TWO YEAR OLDS, 1983 had been crossed out.

'It's all here. When I want a masochistic charge of adrenalin late at night I go through it.' Her voice dropped to a whisper. 'And wish they were both alive, so I could kill them.

'Alastair was crazy about her,' she went on. 'In the beginning he blamed the male menopause. Twenty years later Pippa was an old man's folly. But there were always others. She loved collecting scalps, then telling him about them.'

Opening the file, she emptied it out on to a nearby table, knocking over a dying cyclamen and a Staffordshire dog. Photographs, bills, letters fluttered everywhere all over the carpet.

With a stab of anguish, Lysander recognized his mother's scrawl on a piece of blue writing paper.

'*Darling Alastair,*' he read laboriously. '*That was the best fuck I've ever had.*'

493

'As your father got crosser and grimmer, your mother got wilder,' mumbled Dinah picking up the *Radio Times*. 'Nice lunch party I went to yesterday, with even numbers for a change. All the men were queer of course, but at my age, you have to expect queers.'

This isn't happening to me, I can't read any more, thought Lysander.

'Here, give that back,' said Dinah as he chucked the letter on the electric bars of the fire.

'Time for your medication, young lady.' Mrs Bingham, dying to know what was going on, marched in with a glass of water and two yellow pills on a plate.

Trying to shield his mother, Lysander hunched himself over the letters and photographs, as he frantically gathered them back into their file. For a second they were all distracted by the giant tabby cat lumbering into its earth box scattering cat litter as it rose like a Deux Chevaux, and noisily evacuated.

Then, as Lysander shoved the file viciously back into the drawer, he caught sight of a photograph that had fallen on to the floor and nearly blacked out. It showed Uncle Alastair with a great grin on his face, lounging in an armchair with a cigar in one hand, and his mother kneeling at his feet and laughing as she held his rampant cock towards her mouth between two fingers as though she were about to smoke it. They were both naked.

Lysander gave a sob. For a second his distress jolted Dinah out of her stupor. 'Damn, I thought I'd burnt that one.'

Mrs Bingham gave a crow of triumph.

'Why, you naughty, naughty girl,' she gloated.

For scraping away in his earth box, the cat had revealed a green bottle of Gordon's gin, three-quarters empty.

'Turn up the telly,' said Dinah airily. 'There's William Morris on *The Animal Road Show*.'

Lysander only just reached the lavatory in time, before he threw up and up and up.

* * *

Stumbling down three flights of stairs and rushing out into the street, narrowly avoiding being mown down by cars trying to get home before the rush hour, he took Maggie and Jack for a run on the beach at dusk. He was acutely conscious of the indifference of the sea, as it reared up in a long white wall of foam, then collapsed at his feet. The pier was already lit up against a darkening sky. Ahead the little fairground where Pippa had often taken him had closed down for the winter. The red train rested on its buffers. No children whizzed, shrieking with delight, down the blue-and-yellow helter-skelter. The merry-go-round horses had been zipped away in their leather covers. Even the ghouls on the ghost train had fled.

'Oh no,' pleaded Lysander, as he frantically wiped away the tears. 'Oh please, Mum, oh no, no, no.'

But he knew that his childhood had gone for ever.

45

Wearily Kitty made lists for a Christmas she dreaded. All Rannaldini's Christmas cards had to be sent off and presents bought for his numerous children and each member of the London Met. Rannaldini had to compensate for his chronic bloody-mindedness somehow. Even more lavish presents had to be bought for his multitude of mistresses, but the London secretary, who had better taste, dealt with that. Kitty wondered if Flora or Rachel had been added to the list. He'd been away so long, she wasn't *au fait* with the latest developments. But the deep freezes still had to be filled. Rannaldini liked to have Cecilia and all his children for Christmas, and Hermione, Bob and little Cosmo came over for Christmas dinner. Kitty was also desperately trying to cover her screen with photographs of Rannaldini and the famous, and had just cut out one of him gazing admiringly up at Princess Michael.

It was nearly midnight on the wildest of nights. Everything rattled and creaked. Creepers clawed at the windows, the wind moaned down the chimneys like women desperate to get at Rannaldini. Kitty had already had three dropped telephone calls, and didn't know if she'd rather it were burglars checking anyone was at home or mistresses checking Rannaldini's whereabouts. She'd also had increasingly distraught calls from Georgie trying to trace Lysander.

'We had a stupid lovers' tiff and he stormed off. You know how impulsive he is. Make him ring me at once if he rings or turns up.'

Kitty had been jumpy all evening. The wind was really wailing now. Suddenly she heard a jangling of bells and a distant pounding on the front door. Terrified, she seized a saucepan and crept along the dark, panelled passages, guided by the rough slither of a tapestry, or the sharp blade of a hanging sword, edging round cannon-balls and suits of armour, not daring to betray her identity by turning on a light. The pounding grew louder, and was now accompanied by terrible spine-chilling sobbing. Kitty gasped with terror as she saw an anguished shadowy face at the hall window.

'Oh, God!' Frantically she crossed herself – it was the Paradise Lad.

'Go away,' she screamed.

'Kitty, Kitty, let me in.'

'Oh, fank goodness.'

As she unbolted the door, Lysander fell inside, clutching a koala bear, followed by a very subdued Maggie and Jack. He was absolutely plastered and blue with cold beneath his suntan, his teeth chattering convulsively, his eyes crazy, his face drenched with sweat. Kitty had never seen anyone shake so much.

'Help me, Kitty. Georgie, it's her fault, not Mum's. She's a bitch, and Dad's a bastard, and Uncle Alastair, oh Christ.'

Putting her arms round him, propping him up, Kitty steered him two steps forward, one step sideways or back until, knocking over several suits of armour and the screen, they finally reached the kitchen, where she steered him into an armchair by the Aga.

'Why did she do it? Jack, Maggie, I haven't fed them. Oh, Kitty,' he started to cry.

'There, there, my lambkin, I'll see to them. Let me run and get one of Rannaldini's jumpers, then I'll make you somefink hot. Wherever 'ave you been?'

'Don't go.'

'I won't be a sec.'

But when she came back with jerseys, including Guy's

lost Free Forester's cricket sweater, and blankets, he had passed out.

Tucking them round him, she fed the dogs, who appreciated the steak and kidney she was about to freeze for Boxing Day far more than Rannaldini's faddy family ever would.

She then curled up on the window-seat. She didn't want Lysander falling into the Aga, or waking terrified and not knowing where he was. He and Georgie had plainly had far more than a lovers' tiff.

It was a good thing she stayed. Two hours later he was awake and screaming the house down, and she only got him to the loo in time, where she had to hold his head for the next quarter of an hour until she thought he'd heave his entrails out. Somehow she managed to get him upstairs to bed, but he continued to rave and gabble incoherently, begging her to stay with him. Only when she gave him one of Rannaldini's Mogadons did he finally fall asleep.

Next day Kitty abandoned the hundred and one things she had to do, including making a dozen sets of angels' wings for the annual Valhalla nativity play, and nursed Lysander, feeding him dry toast and clear chicken soup, and letting him talk. She didn't fill in the silences as he frantically tried to get his image of his mother into some kind of shape.

'She was so kind, Kitty,' said Lysander. 'We had a really awful groom, who bullshitted her way into the job. She couldn't even ride and she was vaguer than me. Mum finally screwed up courage to sack her, but four hours later Mum had said so many nice things to her to soften the blow that the groom thought she'd been promoted.'

'Kind people find it ever so hard to say no,' said Kitty who was cutting out a picture of Rannaldini shaking hands with Donald Duck. 'Your mum was so beautiful, and so many men must 'ave wanted her, she must 'ave felt unkind refusing them.

'I expect Georgie's infatuated with your dad,' she went on. 'As he's almost as 'andsome as you, I don't blame 'er, and that makes her ever so jealous of your mum. I mean you know how huptight she was about Rachel and Julia. She's worse than ''im.' Kitty pointed to Jack who was sitting on the kitchen table glaring at Maggie who was now lying like a baby in Lysander's arms.

'I don't 'spect she meant half the fings she told you. Some people just need extra frills in marriage,' Kitty added sadly, as she dipped her brush in glue and pasted Donald Duck and Rannaldini under Princess Michael.

'Christ, it's a horrible world!' Lysander, who was still wearing Guy's cricket sweater, dipped a ginger biscuit in his tea and handed it to Jack. 'I don't understand why everyone plays games. I loved Georgie so much, we were having terrific sex, twice a day at least, but it wasn't enough for her. She had to have Dad as well.'

As Kitty was reflecting that if Georgie were working really hard she might have preferred the perhaps lesser sexual demands of David Hawkley, Lysander noticed Donald Duck.

'God, I'm jealous of Rannaldini meeting him. Did he get Donald's autograph? This screen is lovely. You're brilliant at cutting out. Can I have a go?'

'What d'you really want from life?' asked Kitty, passing him the scissors and a picture of Rannaldini laughing with Pavarotti.

'I'd like Arthur to make a come-back and win the Rutminster with me riding him. I want a job with horses. I'd like a place of my own, a wife who loved me as much as I loved her, and,' he added on reflection, 'I'd like some kids. I'm bored with racketing around. D'you know, I asked Georgie to marry me, and she's bonking my father.' He started to shake violently again. 'Oh Christ, I've cut Rannaldini's head off. I'm sorry, I can't do anything right. Can I possibly stay with you until I get myself together?'

In fact it was highly inconvenient. Kitty had so much to do and, instead, had to listen to Lysander banging on and on with all the egotism of utter despair and extreme youth. As a very truthful person, she hated having to lie so much on Rannaldini's behalf, and now she had to lie for Lysander, as Ferdie, Marigold, an increasingly frantic Georgie, and even David Hawkley and Aunt Dinah (in the morning admittedly) rang or rolled up to ask if she'd seen or heard from him. And then Mrs Brimscombe, who'd had to be let into the secret, went down with flu so Kitty had to cope on her own.

Having hidden Lysander in an attic bedroom in the oldest part of the house, Kitty felt like the monks living at Valhalla harbouring some Cavalier during the Civil War: Astley perhaps, or Rupert of the Rhine, or even Charles I. With his flopping hair, his gentleness and his beauty, Lysander made the perfect Cavalier, and would certainly have been dashingly fearless in cavalry charges. No Cavalier seeking sanctuary, however, would have had the diversion of the sixty-two instalments of *EastEnders* and *Neighbours*, which Kitty had taped for him while he was away. After four days almost concentrated viewing, some excellent plain cooking, and a very good 100–1 win at Lingfield, Lysander was beginning to perk up. At least Kitty managed to finish the screen and the angels' wings as she listened to him.

He only left in the end – and then reluctantly – because Natasha was coming home from Bagley Hall; and that had been another of Georgie's lies, that Flora had broken up the day he'd returned from Australia. Anyway he didn't want that bitch Natasha drooling over him, and he felt he'd traded on Kitty's hospitality enough.

Within a couple of hours of his departure, however, he was on the telephone.

'Kitty, Kitty, Kitty, come and have dinner at Magpie Cottage tomorrow night.'

' 'Ow lovely. Shall I bring Natasha?'

'God no! Don't say a thing to her. I'm going to cook you a wonderful dinner.'

Alas, Lysander woke the next morning with a blinding

headache and the shakes. In fact he ached all over. He must have caught Mrs Brimscombe's flu. He wanted to collapse into bed, but he couldn't let Kitty down.

What followed was not just a chapter but a whole book of accidents. The avocados he bought were harder than hand grenades. The *coq au vin* took five hours and tasted disgusting. He cooked the spinach early and boiled it away to a grit purée. For pudding, he tried to make syllabub. One just followed a recipe, but after hours of whisking and even more hours in the fridge, the syllabub separated – like everything else in Paradise, he thought sourly.

The sink was by this time blocked solid with the food he'd chucked out. There were saucepans all over the lawn and he'd singed his beautiful eyelashes when he realized Jack was missing and set out with Maggie, a spade and a torch into the freezing night to find him. After twenty minutes, with every fox, badger and rabbit for miles around rustling in the wood to distract them, a demented Maggie finally located some faint yapping, and Lysander and she spent a further twenty minutes digging Jack out, after which the little sod wasn't remotely grateful and tried to shoot back down the hole again.

Hearing her master's language, Maggie fled home in terror. Following her, Lysander found the chicken burnt out. How did people run restaurants? He'd have to take Kitty out. He was feeling so shivery, he better have a hot bath. All his problems that day had stemmed from feeling he ought not to ring Kitty every five minutes to ask her how to do things.

Unfortunately a frantic Georgie had just returned from London and, seeing lights in Magpie Cottage, chose that moment to ring. By the time Lysander had told her to fuck off, and his father had rung and been told roughly the same thing, and Ferdie had rung and been told Lysander was pushed for time, the bath had run over and flooded the light fitting below. Getting electric shocks every time he touched a switch, Lysander tried to mend the fuse and blew the lights.

                      *   *   *

Kitty was so behind with her Christmas preparations
that she felt dreadfully guilty going out, particularly as
she was abandoning Natasha on her first night home.
To her amazement, Natasha couldn't have been more
amenable, even when they met on the landing, both
reeking of scented bath oil with their bodies and their
newly washed hair wrapped in towels.

'I'm just popping out, Natasha.'

'Have you got a meeting?'

'Sort of.' Kitty stood on one pink leg.

'Have a nice time. Don't hurry back.'

Natasha was also unbelievably complimentary about her
appearance, saying, 'You've lost so much weight. Papa
won't recognize you,' that when Kitty found Magpie
Cottage in total darkness, she suspected some fiendish
practical joke to get her out of the house. As she stumbled
up the overgrown path, she was knocked sideways with
relief and by the stench of burnt chicken.

'Oh Kitty, Kitty, talk about coq-up au vin!' Nearly in
tears, Lysander greeted her with a candle and was just
thinking how sweet she looked despite the awful beige
dress, when the wind blew the candle out. They had
just groped their way to the fuse box when the telephone
rang.

'I'll get it,' said Lysander, knocking over a stool. 'It's
bound to be Natasha.'

'I'm desperately sorry, I can't make it,' Kitty could hear
him saying. 'Basically I've got the flu. Honestly, I'm best
on my own. I'm really infectious. I'll just crash out with
a dozen Anadin Extra. See you in a bit.'

'You are awful,' said Kitty, who had found some
matches and was pushing in plugs.

As the lights came on, she saw Lysander was once more
pouring with sweat and shaking. Thinking it was probably
delayed shock, she tucked him up in bed once more.

'I'll make it up to you, Kitty, I'll take you to *Miss
Saigon*, I know a bloke who can get tickets.' And he

drifted off to sleep, but spent most of the night crying out for his mother.

Staggering down the following afternoon, he felt woolly legged, drained, but normal. It was as though the devil had left his body. The cottage was unrecognizable. Kitty had unblocked the sink and cleaned everything. As Jack had been muddy after his tunnelling, she had even given him a bath, and was drying him in front of a glowing crackling fire, as she chatted to Arthur who was peering in through the window. A delicious smell of shepherd's pie reminded Lysander he hadn't eaten for two days.

'Oh, you angel. God, it looks wonderful and smells even better.' Lysander hugged her. 'I don't know how to thank you, but please don't get too thin.'

'Chance'd be a fine fing,' said Kitty, blushing.

Putting his fork down after a second helping, Lysander said, 'What shall we do this afternoon?'

'I thought you was ill,' chided Kitty.

'I'm too ill to do anything I don't want to do, if you know what I mean.'

It was the first time he'd giggled since he'd come back from Australia, and it was such a lovely sound that Kitty giggled, too.

'I've got to go back to Valhalla,' she sighed. 'Rannaldini's bound to 'ave rung and I've got so much to do, and I promised Rachel I'd pick up her kids from school and keep them overnight. Poor fing's got to go to London to see her solicitor.'

As she waited outside the school playground, Kitty was overwhelmed with tiredness. She'd have to spend the evening wrapping up the dozens of overseas presents to be despatched before the last day for posting. She could have done without Rachel's children. For someone always banging on about the wickedness of nannies and not bringing up one's own kids, Rachel was remarkably adept at palming her own off on other people.

'Kitty, Kitty.' Masha emerged from the coloured stream of children flowing out of the gates. 'We learnt about the olden days today. You know when Jesus was alive and you were a little girl.'

'Lo, Kitty,' said Vanya. 'Is it OK if Cosmo comes to tea as well?'

Sighing, Kitty agreed. Rachel's children had speedily sussed out little Cosmo's advantages as a companion. There was no way he'd put up with health foods or building castles out of loo rolls.

'Mummy says we've got to practise our carol for the nativity play,' said Masha, as she and Vanya got into the back.

'I hate music.' Little Cosmo clapped his hands over his ears, as he jumped into the front. 'All I hear in my house is fucking music.'

Over increasing clamour, Kitty drove wearily back to Valhalla to pick up some cash to get some supper that Cosmo would approve of. But as she came out of the house, Lysander's Ferrari stormed up the drive, and he jumped out clutching an armful of Super Macs and chips, a video of *Pretty Woman* and a huge round tin of toffees.

'Here you are,' he said chucking the tin at the children. 'Have some Quality Street time, and if you're good you can play football with Jack in the chapel.'

They all adored *Pretty Woman*. Lysander alternately roared with laughter, wiped his eyes, or said, 'Bastard, *bastard*, how dare he treat her like that?' But by the end he liked Richard Gere very much indeed.

'*Pretty Woman*'s rather like Mummy,' said Masha.

It was unfortunate for Rachel that on his way home to Magpie Cottage after the children had been tucked up in bed, Lysander saw a light ahead in Jasmine Cottage. Crawling past, because of a car casually parked outside, he saw a couple in a clinch in the doorway. Then the man ran down the steps. Turning, blowing a kiss to the woman, he was spotlit for a second in Lysander's headlights. It was a triumphantly smirking Rannaldini.

Having dropped off the three children at school the following morning, Kitty set out for Tesco's. As she staggered out half an hour later, pushing two groaning trolleys of food for supper after the nativity play which she was going to cook and freeze that day, she suddenly saw that a big pot of yoghurt was leaking. Leaning forward to remove it, she took her hand from the right-hand trolley which veered off with a mind of its own. Gathering speed it rolled down a small slope and, narrowly missing an ancient pensioner with a string bag, went slap into a dark green Porsche, scraping it down one side, then toppling over with a sickening crash of broken glass.

'Oh, God,' screamed Kitty, surveying the debris of pastry cases and cracked eggs, floating in a disgusting goo of double cream, yoghurt, Hellmann's, whisky and red wine. 'It's not fair, it's not bloody fair.'

It took her ages to clear up the chaos. Then she put a note on the Porsche's windscreen: *'Dear Driver, I'm ever so sorry about your car. I will pay all damage. Could you write to me at Valhalla, Paradise? Yours truly, Kitty Rannaldini.'*

That's all my running-away money and more, she was thinking despairingly, when the note was whipped away.

'Car looks much better that way. Gives it character,' said a voice.

Springing round, Kitty saw Lysander. 'Mrs Brimscombe said you were here,' he said, opening the door of the Porsche for her.

'That's not your car,' stammered Kitty.

'Garage lent it to me,' said Lysander. 'Ferrari's got engine trouble. Honestly, it couldn't matter less.'

He was feeling very virtuous. Finding Georgie's paying-in book under the bed at Magpie Cottage, he'd written her a cheque for fifty thousand, the sum she'd paid him overall for his services, and despatched it to her bank. He thus cancelled any debt between them.

'Look what I've got!' He waved two tickets for *Miss Saigon*. 'You and I are going on a seriously good jaunt.'

'I can't. Rannaldini came 'ome unexpectedly last night, and buzzed off this morning to LA, leaving me so much more to do. Anyway,' she sighed, 'I'm married. I don't fink I should.'

'Pretend you're going Christmas shopping.'

They took the train to Paddington. The restaurant car attendant was so taken with Lysander that he ran them up some bullshots.

'They're heavenly,' said Kitty, taking a great gulp. 'What's in them?'

'Oh, clear soup and tomato juice,' said Lysander, conveniently forgetting the huge tots of vodka and sherry. 'Have another.'

'Oh, yes please. I've never travelled first class before.'

Kitty gazed in ecstasy at the silver foam of blackthorn dividing the frozen fields and the furry white-antlered branches of the trees tossing a glittering yellow sun as it bowled along with the train. What was the point of life where she was always rushing and never had time to look at beautiful things? She didn't even worry when they bumped into the vicar's wife as they got off the train.

Lysander took her straight to Harrods.

'I'm going to buy you a dress,' he said as he went down the rails pulling out clothes and being gazed at by Way-In shop assistants, not over-busy because of the recession.

He finally chose one in dark grey-green wool, which matched Kitty's eyes and showed off her bosom and now so-much-slimmer waist, but which had a flowing skirt which disguised her still plump hips.

'Lovely,' he said, looking at her in delight. 'Like ivy clinging to a beautiful statue.'

The dress was followed by black tights and flat, black pumps.

'You're never to wear those flesh-coloured horrors again. Now we better buy something to keep you warm.' And ignoring her cries of protest, he chose her a blanket

506

coat in a rainbow riot of colours, three pairs of leggings and two huge, sloppy jerseys.

Whisking her past the baby-wear department: 'You don't want to look at them – only depress you. It'll happen one day, I promise,' he bore her off to the toy department to admire huge stuffed donkeys, giraffes, tigers, lions, gorillas and teddy bears.

'They always remind me of a dogs' home,' said Lysander. 'I used to try not to catch their eyes when Mum brought me here as a child. We ought to go to Battersea and get you a puppy to protect you at Valhalla.'

Instead, when she was looking at computer games to keep Cosmo quiet at Christmas, he bought her a vast fluffy life-size collie with a shiny black plastic nose.

'Here's Lassie, to guard you.'

'Oh, Lysander,' Kitty was overjoyed, 'you shouldn't 'ave, but I love her.'

'*In a place that won't let us feel,*

in a life where nothing seems real,' sang Miss Saigon as they passed the record department. Next minute they were brought up short by Rannaldini's cold unsmiling face, looking out from a montage of his record sleeves, as the haunting strains of the first movement of Mahler's *Fourth* with its jangling sleigh-bells swept through the store.

Turning right, they saw huge blow-ups of Cecilia and Hermione as Donna Anna and Donna Elvira and even a cardboard cut-out of Georgie clutching a rock.

'Fucking hell,' said Lysander in outrage, and before reality could reassert itself, he dragged Kitty off to lunch at San Lorenzo.

Here her calm, sweet unmade-up face and full body were in total contrast to the slender, painted beauties around them, who all seemed to be wearing scarlet and crimson suits, lots of rouge, red lipstick and red nails, and seemed never to draw breath. They were obviously fascinated to see an utterly stunning man with such a nondescript girl.

They're all so beautiful, thought Kitty.

She's so peaceful, thought Lysander protectively, like a leveret, or a female mallard.

He also noticed, as her face, used to Rannaldini's cold house, grew pink in the warm room that her spots had gone.

'I do hope Joy Hillary tells Rannaldini she saw us on the train,' he said, 'and makes him seriously jealous.'

With a start, Kitty remembered they were only here because Lysander was being paid by Georgie and Marigold to glam her up. How very kind, she thought humbly, of him to make everything such fun.

'It's driving me crazy.' A blonde paused at their table on the way out. 'What part in *EastEnders* do you play?' she asked Kitty.

But later when the helicopter landed on the stage of the Coliseum, she forgot everything except *Miss Saigon*, as she and Lysander cried their eyes out and went through a whole box of Kleenex and a box of Belgian chocolates.

'That was the best fing I've ever seen,' she said, as they had supper together afterwards in a Fulham wine bar. 'I fink this is the nicest day I've ever had.'

She's so sweet to take out, thought Lysander.

'I wish you weren't so terrified of horses, then we could ride together.'

'I'm not frightened of Arfur,' said Kitty, tucking into her cottage cheese salad. 'But the way he drinks coffee, and snores wiv one eye open, and gets hisself dirty, he's not really an 'orse, he's more of a 'uman.'

'I think that's the nicest compliment Arthur's ever been paid,' said Lysander gravely. 'Thank you, Kitty.'

They talked so long and drank so many cups of coffee, Kitty suddenly realized they'd missed the last train.

'We'll go back to my old pad,' said Lysander. 'I've still got a key. Ferdie's away this evening. It's all right,' he added, seeing the look of panic on Kitty's face, 'you're quite safe with me and there are two bedrooms.'

I'm chaperoned by my own plainness, thought Kitty sadly. No-one looking like me could cause talk.

'No-one will see us,' said Lysander as the taxi turned into Fountain Street. But as he rushed in to switch off the burglar alarm, the gays opposite parted their damask curtains and started waving frantically.

'What a lovely little 'ouse,' said Kitty, thinking how easy it would be to keep a place like this nice, 'and you could put camellias in tubs in the little patio at the back.'

Lysander put Kitty in Ferdie's room with the big bay window looking over the street. She could see the gays peering in as she drew the curtains. Lysander had found her a glamorous cream silk nightdress left behind by one of his girlfriends. It slithered over her like a skin. If only she could take on the beauty of its original owner.

All the same, she thought, as she set Ferdie's alarm clock for six-thirty and snuggled down in bed with the toy Lassie stiff-legged beside her, it *had* been the nicest day of her life. Lysander had made her feel like one of the romantic heroines she so loved reading about, not a drag, nor a dog, nor even a brick. With a guilty start, as she was falling asleep, she realized she'd forgotten to say her prayers. Perhaps for once God would forgive her if she did it lying down.

'Please God, bring Lysander happiness and find him a nice girl who'll look after him and not take advantage of his sweet nature.'

Unused to London traffic crashing along the end of the street, Lysander woke at six, and was horrified to hear Ferdie coming in from a night on the tiles. Not wanting to get shouted at and still half-asleep, he pulled the duvet over his head, hoping the trouble would go away. He heard Ferdie's bedroom door open, then after a long pause while he waited for an explosion, it shut again. Relieved, Lysander went back to sleep.

A couple of hours later, aware that they were supposed to get an early train back, he staggered downstairs, nursing his hangover, expecting to find Ferdie furious at having to sleep on the sofa, probably frozen stiff from not having a duvet. But to his horror there was no-one there; the cushions of the sofa were still smugly plumped up. Ferdie must have gone to work. But, opening the sitting-room curtains, Lysander saw the red Ferrari, which he'd bloody earned for Ferdie, and Ferdie's black brogues were sitting on the kitchen table, together with the Ferrari's car keys.

Lysander was appalled. Kitty was an innocent girl in his care. How terrible if Ferdie, in his new slimline sexual awareness, had come home tanked up and taken advantage. He remembered how he'd caught them half-dressed and giggling together over the weigh-in at Valhalla. Ferdie had always liked Kitty. In a fury, Lysander pinched one of Ferdie's Marlboros and put the kettle on. His worst fears were confirmed when his old flatmate came down in a towel, showing off a still suntanned and increasingly svelte torso and smirking worse than Rannaldini emerging from Jasmine Cottage.

'Black and no sugar for me,' said Ferdie, getting a carton of unsweetened grapefruit juice out of the fridge. 'I've got a terrific job coming up for you in Brazil in a couple of weeks.'

Lysander refused to admit how furious he felt.

Kitty was not the kind of person one got jealous about. He was even more irritated at the relief which overwhelmed him when Kitty rushed downstairs ten minutes later.

'I feel shockin'. Poor Ferdie 'ad to sleep in the armchair in his room, an' he must have turned off his alarm clock, because we've really overslept.'

When they finally got back to Valhalla around midday, she found the tape on the answering machine exhausted by increasingly outraged calls from Rannaldini.

'Where zee fuck are you, Keety? Ring me at the Beverley Wilshire the eenstant you get in. Zee next time you rush off to your mother's, leave a number.'

Even thousands of miles away, he terrorizes her, thought Lysander angrily, watching the frantically fluttering pages as Kitty fumbled through the Los Angeles telephone directory. Then she stopped, remembering it would be 2 a.m. in LA and Rannaldini would be asleep or more likely coiled round some female musician.

The last message on the machine, however, made Lysander forget everything. The voice was clipped, light, drawling and decidedly amused: 'This is Rupert Campbell-Black ringing from Venturer Television for Rannaldini. We gather you're doing a nativity play at Valhalla. We were wondering if we could come and film and put it out on Christmas Eve?'

Lysander gave a Tarzan howl of joy. 'At last Rupert will have a chance to meet Arthur.'.

46

Paradise was thrown into a complete tizz. Suddenly, at the prospect of millions of viewers and Rupert Campbell-Black in the audience, what Hermione airily described as 'Making sweet sacred music together for the delight of a few friends' had become a Steven Spielberg spectacular. Rannaldini, who'd always been insanely jealous of Rupert's success both with money and women, was driven to a frenzy of rivalry. The rows were pyrotechnic.

'You cannot put hanging baskets outside the Inn in the middle of winter. Bethlehem's not competing for the Best-Kept Village,' screamed Meredith who, in charge of sets, was now dragging the manger an exciting shade of raspberry pink.

'Well, your stable's more like the braidle suite at the Ritz,' screamed back Marigold who'd been unusually ratty of late.

'This play is supposed to be topical. With a recession on, Mary and Joseph would have been able to get into any hotel they chose,' snapped Meredith, twitching the pink damask curtains flanking the stable window into place. 'But we're not having those,' he went on, tugging down a washing-line and four towelling nappies Rachel had strung across the set. 'Baby Jesus has only just been born in this scene. There's no way he'd have got through four nappies.'

'Put those back,' shouted Rachel furiously. 'We've got a chance to tell millions of viewers, perhaps twelve million if it's networked, that disposable nappies take five hundred years to biodegrade, whereas cotton towelling ones can be—'

'Oh, shut up,' screamed Marigold and Meredith in unison.

Kitty, who as usual had to do everything, had retreated to the kitchen to retype, on recycled paper, Georgie's script which everyone kept changing.

Ten minutes later Lysander rushed in hidden inside the front half of the donkey with Jack and Maggie hanging, furiously growling, on the uninhabited back half.

'Oh Kitty, Kitty,' he cried despairingly from his furry depths, 'the vicar and Meredith and Natasha all want to play my back half. I don't want to be groped by any of them.'

Wrenching off the donkey's head he fumbled for a cigarette. Even scarlet with indignation, his hair all ruffled, he looked adorable.

'Don't worry.' Kitty handed him a lump of sugar on the flat palm of her hand as he had taught her. 'Rannaldini's due back tonight and he'll change everyfink.'

'Oh dear.' Lysander's face fell. 'Then it won't be nearly such fun.'

There had also been furious spats over the casting, with all the Paradise ladies angling for the coveted role of the Virgin Mary in order to wow Rupert Campbell-Black. Hermione got the part – natch – and insisted on four changes of blue silk robe and a becoming gold halo designed by David Shilling. In the only moment during the entire production when Hermione was in agreement with Rachel, they decided Mary must be seen to breast-feed the doll which had been flown down from Harrods with the Christmas caviar, to play Baby Jesus.

'Trust the old tart to grab any chance to flash those great tits in public,' grumbled Meredith.

Rannaldini had turned down the suggested role of Herod and was leaving the conducting of the orchestra (hand-picked members of the London Met) to Bob. Instead, he insisted on riding in on the viciously volatile Prince of Darkness as the First of the Three Kings.

He had co-opted Rachel, because of her long legs and because she looked disturbingly sexy with a cork moustache and beard, to play the Second King, but had vetoed Rachel's suggestion that she should hand over a free-range turkey instead of frankincense. Lysander was able temporarily to forgive Rannaldini who, having cast Marigold, also because of her great legs, as the Third King, then because of Marigold's nervous disposition, had signed up Arthur to play her horse.

Guy, who had a fine bass voice and a lifetime of singing loudly in the church choirs, was cast as St Joseph, which gave him a legitimate excuse to grow a beard and no longer use plastic razors, which took even longer than nappies to biodegrade.

At Hermione's suggestion, the script had been rewritten to portray Joseph as 'deeply in love with his young wife' and now included several long clinches under the mistletoe and Guy's repeatedly professed delight at being present at the birth.

'Why don't you have a bonk and make it really authentic?' snapped Georgie, who was playing the chief shepherd and was fed up with her script being messed about. If Guy was absolutely not Hermione's type, as Hermione had told Georgie after the church fête, she was concealing her prejudice extremely well.

Larry, who'd been cast in the key role as the innkeeper, kept cutting rehearsals due to the 'pressure of work' which explained Marigold's increasing twitchiness.

The casting of the vicar reduced Meredith to more hysterics.

'You can't let that fat queen play Gabriel. Give Lysander the part. He's got the angel's face.'

'Lysander's tone-deaf and he really can't act,' said Georgie kindly.

'Then he can play one of your shepherds,' said Hermione pointedly. 'He and you are *such* friends.'

'Not any more,' spat Lysander, glaring at Georgie.

It was at this point that he was demoted to the front legs of the donkey. Lysander, in fact, was feeling as though his life had been churned up like a ploughed field. After the things Georgie had said about his mother, he couldn't bear to be in the same room with her, but he was desperate for Rupert to meet Arthur and increasingly felt the need to protect Kitty from everyone.

As Kitty had predicted, Rannaldini breezed in that evening, completely rewrote the script, re-arranged the music and, taking one look at the furry ox and the donkey, whose front legs were doing a soft-shoe shuffle at the time, replaced them with real animals to give the play authenticity. By the following day there were also live sheep. Maggie, Jack and Dinsdale had got parts as sheepdogs and even Tabloid was enrolled to guard the Inn. At Rachel's prompting, chickens and a fearsome turkey were freely ranging the set.

'Are we staging St Francis of Assisi as well?' grumbled Meredith as he trod in a cowpat.

Sacked as the front of the donkey, Lysander was relegated to turning Rachel's pages when she played the piano for early rehearsals. But he was so distracted by the sight of Kitty in the green dress he'd bought her that he totally ignored Rachel's repeated nods and was demoted to shifting scenery.

Bob admired the green dress, too.

'Kitty's getting prettier,' he observed.

'Where?' said Natasha, who was fed up with her tiny part in the angelic choir.

Suddenly Georgie realized that Kitty hadn't got a part.

'I'll write you in as the innkeeper's wife.'

'Kitty's *forte* is being a back-room girl,' said Hermione firmly. 'Who else could play the innkeeper's wife? Natasha's too young and pretty.'

'What about Mother Courage?' suggested Georgie. 'She so longs to get on telly.'

'Certainly not,' Hermione was shocked. 'Let's keep it simple. Just our set. We don't need an innkeeper's wife. Your daily can sit in the audience, because the crew are bound to cut to them some time during the play. I hope Rupert Campbell-Black's been invited to stay on for supper after the performance,' she added to Bob.

'Rupert won't be able to refuse once he sees Brickie's spread,' said Guy, smiling warmly at Kitty.

'Lully, lully, breast is best, lully, lully, baby rest,' sang Hermione, flashing a blue-veined boob at her sleeping Harrods doll.

'I still think Kitty should be in it,' said Georgie stubbornly.

'Kitty is needed at home,' hissed Rannaldini, who was trying on a totally anachronistic purple velvet doublet. 'Theengs are getting very slack 'ere. There are lights on everywhere, plants go unwatered.' He pressed the earth of a huge ficus. 'The second post hasn't even been opened and I hardly think my study is the right place for a roll of lavatory paper.'

Lysander's face tightened with anger.

'As you talk so much shit, *sir*, I would have thought it was very appropriate.'

Rannaldini looked at Lysander in amazement as though the manger had spoken.

'Particularly white lavatory paper,' he went on. 'I told you not to buy white any more, Keety. You know bleach pollutes the rivers.'

Hearing Rachel-speak coming straight out of his mouth, everyone exchanged uneasy glances. Kitty had gone puce with mortification.

'I'm sorry, Rannaldini,' she stammered.

'Don't apologize. Do better next time,' said Rannaldini chillingly.

'And you still haven't sewn up my robes where the ox trod on them,' grumbled Hermione.

'Perhaps the Kings could give Mary a year's subscription to the Nappy Service,' suggested Rachel.

'Then they could all wish the Holy Family a very Nappy

Christmas,' giggled Meredith, 'except it's Epiphany by the time they roll up.'

'Stop taking the piss,' howled Rachel.

'Shut up, Meredith,' ordered Rannaldini.

From the summer parlour next door, Larry could be heard yelling: 'Someone else must have guaranteed the loan, for Christ's sake.'

'Nice if your husband could put in an appearance except to use my telephone,' snarled Rannaldini.

'Nice if you could put in an appearance except to bully everyone – sir,' said Lysander, putting an arm round a sobbing Marigold.

Kitty was amazed how much less she minded Rannaldini's tantrums. Lysander might have been passed up as the Angel Gabriel but, suddenly, he seemed to have drawn a halo around her life, which became increasingly brighter as he brought in logs for the great hall fire, carried her shopping in from the car and nipped down to Paradise to get her some Anadin Extra when she got her period. Lysander also helped her staple together the retyped scripts, even if he did put them all in the wrong order because he was chatting so much and she had to retreat discreetly into the larder to restaple them when he wasn't looking.

And it was bliss to have someone to amuse everyone's children when they were dumped on her, and to giggle with when Hermione complained Kitty had mended her robes with the wrong blue thread or Natasha hit the roof about shrunk washing.

Natasha wasn't the only one who noticed how Lysander's face and voice softened when he was with Kitty.

'You don't need to pay her so much attention when Rannaldini isn't here,' snapped Marigold. 'It's him you're being paid to rattle.'

Two days before D-Day, Lysander sat in the back row of the stalls, pointedly reading a porn mag to discourage Natasha and the vicar, who was gallumping around in a long white nightgown from Cavendish House trying to secure his halo with Velcro.

Hermione, about to do the Annunciation scene, was making a very short list of Christmas presents she simply had to get.

'What can I give Bob? Men are so difficult,' she asked Lysander. Then, suddenly remembering her visit to Fleetley, 'I forgot to tell you I met your father last term.'

Across the gangway, Georgie, clad in the unglamorous robes of chief shepherd, stopped writing her Christmas cards.

'Rather a charmer,' went on Hermione. 'What are you going to give him?'

'A bottle of arsenic,' snapped Lysander, returning to Chantelle 42–22–35.

'Good idea,' said Hermione who wasn't listening because Kitty had staggered in with a tray of coffee and home-made flapjacks, which Lysander leapt up to carry for her.

Huddling back in her robes Georgie returned to her Christmas cards. She was fed up with the number of Guy's parents' friends – who'd all been shown *The Scorpion* by their dailies – who sent Christmas cards addressed solely to Guy with tender messages inside about how they were praying for him.

Wistfully, Georgie remembered Christmases earlier in her marriage when she had signed every card: *Love from Guy and Georgie* with Guy's name first because men should be deferred to. Now she just signed her own name. Under the lining paper in her desk at Angel's Reach was a pretty little Victorian card that she was dickering whether to send to David Hawkley.

Although Lysander totally froze her out now, he had behaved honourably. He had never sneaked to David – admittedly because he couldn't bear to repeat the horrific things Georgie had said about Pippa – but he had bawled David out for stealing Georgie, the woman he loved, and

David had been shattered. He was mortified that Lysander had caught him and Georgie virtually *in flagrante*. He had risked bringing scandal on Fleetley by dallying with a pop star, but, worst of all, Georgie had lied to him – as Pippa had so often before – that her relationship with Lysander was platonic, thus luring him into cheating on his own son. At whatever heartbreak to himself, David had refused to see Georgie again.

Utterly devastated, Georgie had thrown herself into work. *Ant and Cleo* was nearly done and, to her great relief, Larry had stopped nagging her to finish the album. Guy, on the other hand, was playing her up again. Only last night she caught him cleaning St Joseph's sandals with non-toxic shoe polish and, later, when she had been so carried away at the moment of orgasm that she'd ripped his back with her long nails, he'd yelled: 'Don't do that, for Christ's sake.'

'Are you worried,' Georgie had yelled back, 'that your mistress might discover you actually sleep with your wife?'

And Guy had retreated into his usual orgy of hurt outrage.

It was 21 December and Georgie hadn't bought a single present nor had she done any cooking. Guy, who'd taken three days off from the gallery, could bloody well do that. Only her bank statement cheered her. Opening it this morning she found she was an amazing fifty thousand pounds better off than she'd expected. It must be more forgotten foreign royalties.

Guy, who had snooped and also read Georgie's bank statement, was relieved they wouldn't starve. Things were desperate at the gallery – another backer had gone belly-up last week – but, unlike Georgie, he had thumbed through the statement and found one dated 10 December for fifty thousand from Lysander and was racking his brains to work out what it was for.

Remembering times past when he had, in public, studiously ignored women with whom he was having affaires in private, he construed Lysander's total avoidance of Georgie as evidence of an ongoing affaire. His suspicions were fuelled that morning when Lysander marched in wearing his Free Forester's jersey.

Matters were not helped by Flora's return from Bagley Hall and then jumping on every telephone call. Because of her ravishing voice, Bob had persuaded her to give the play a homely touch by appearing from time to time to sing unaccompanied carols.

Flora had only agreed because she was so desperate to see Rannaldini again. All summer she had basked in the gold sunshine of his love, then as relentlessly and inevitably as leaves coming off the trees, after Boris's success in the *Requiem* he had withheld it. Now she was stripped bare of all affection.

Rannaldini had never rung her again and apart from the few messages she had left with his London secretary, Flora had been too proud to pester him. She refused to become one of the distraught, tearful, pleading creatures whom Rannaldini got a sadistic charge out of listening to on his answering machine.

'Think not for whom the lack of telephone bell tolls,' sighed Flora.

Rannaldini, in fact, had not become bored with Flora. He still wanted to reduce her to such abject longing that she would take part in his fiendish games, but more importantly, the New World Phil in New York had come up for grabs. Rannaldini wanted the job of Musical Director very badly. He had never regained the same ascendancy over the London Met after the Lovely Black Eyes incident. Hermione was still giving him earache. He wanted to start a new life in a new country. Then, to his rage, he learnt that the New World Phil were also considering Boris Levitsky.

American orchestras, and their social benefactors, like their musical directors to live in the city and lead regular lives. It was vital for Rannaldini, therefore, to avoid any scandal and present a happily married front with Kitty, while doing everything he could to prevent Boris and Rachel getting together again – a challenge that appealed to his machiavellian nature. He had kicked off by ringing Boris with words of warm encouragement.

'I will talk to the right people, Boris. I will smooth your path. I am right behind you.'

'With a fleek knife,' said Boris slamming down the receiver.

Although Rannaldini felt it prudent to soft-pedal his affaire with Rachel, he found himself more and more addicted to the demanding crosspatch. Her ability to massage essential oils into all parts of his body was beyond anything. Flora, who'd been trailing them in her father's car, had also noticed Rachel's increasing dominance over the play and was in a dangerous kamikaze mood.

Only Marigold was more miserable than Flora. She had wrapped all her Christmas presents, over-loaded the deep freeze, despatched her cards and decorated the house so early that the mistletoe was already shrivelling under the huge chandelier that was no longer switched on as it wasted precious energy. Larry was behaving in an increasingly suspicious fashion, coming home later and later, pouncing on the telephone, then shutting the door or going out to his car when he rang out, rising early to intercept the post and eating nothing.

In earlier years he had relished taking part in the Christmas play and never missed a rehearsal, conducting business in the wings on his mobile. This year, in the plum part of the innkeeper, he had hardly showed up. Marigold was sure he must be back with Nikki or having an affaire with Rachel who was looking utterly radiant. Marigold felt she was having a leg broken and reset without an anaesthetic.

47

Tempers were not improved during the dress rehearsal by the arrival of a film crew with a sleek, glamorous but very aggressive director from Venturer Television called Cameron Cook. The continual stopping to re-adjust cameras and microphones threw the entire cast – even such old hands as Georgie and Hermione. Lights fused, lines were forgotten, cues missed. Cameron decided to put two cameras on either side of the hall and one up in the minstrels' gallery from which the vicar, as the Angel Gabriel, would descend to address Mary and later the shepherds. The technicians stood around yawning, looking bored and tripping over Mr Brimscombe as he peered into the chapel, which had been turned into a women's changing room, while he pretended to fiddle with the fuse box.

Lysander had taken refuge at the back of the stalls. He was laboriously ploughing through a really sad piece in the *Express* about Rupert Campbell-Black and his wife who had just lost a test-tube baby at four months and were both utterly devastated.

Oh, poor Rupert, thought Lysander, and his wife was so beautiful and not much older than himself. He wished he could do something to help them.

The rows on stage were getting worse.

'Don't forget not to look at the camera,' Hermione was hissing at the shepherds.

'With so many cameras one can hardly help it,' said Meredith fretfully.

The star fused again.

'If it blows on the night, Larry can leap on to the roof and flash his medallion,' said Flora.

'If he turns up at all,' said Natasha bitchily. 'Talk about a never-in keeper.'

Marigold burst into tears again. Dropping a huge bunch of holly, Kitty ran to comfort her.

'Lully, lully, breast is best,' sang Hermione, nearly taking the vaulted roof off.

'You can't say that shit,' said Cameron Cook, consulting her script. 'And what's a Christmas tree doing in the stable? They weren't invented in those days. And why isn't it decorated?'

'Because it's demeaning for trees to be hung with baubles,' explained Rachel earnestly.

'For God's sake,' snarled Cameron. 'Now Holy Joe's arrived, we better go back and do the Annunciation.'

Up in the gallery like some vast white bird in his Cavendish House nightgown, the vicar cleared his throat and straightened his halo.

'Hi, Charismatic Mary,' he called out in his fluting voice. 'I've dropped in from heaven to tell you your pregnancy test is positive.'

'How wonderful,' cried Hermione, gazing down at her Harrods lily. 'Joseph will be absolutely, absolutely—' She turned to Meredith who, instead of prompting, was gazing at a butch cameraman.

'Joseph will be absolutely?' repeated Hermione, snapping her fingers.

'Gobsmacked,' suggested Lysander, who was still reading about Rupert.

'Absolutely delighted.' Meredith had found his place.

'I'm afraid Joseph isn't the father,' said the vicar as he slowly descended on a wire attached to a buckling beam in the ceiling.

Hermione bowed her head. 'It could be no other.'

'It is – God Almighty!' screamed the vicar as he landed on a free-range hen.

'Well, I know Joseph will make a caring stepfather,'

said Hermione, launching loudly into 'Behold a Virgin Shall Conceive'.

'Stop, stop! Who wrote this shit?' shouted Cameron Cook.

'This bit, Handel and Jennings,' said Bob helpfully. 'The rest of it is Georgie's.'

'It is not,' stormed Georgie. 'Not a line of mine's left in.'

'I'd take your name off it sharpish then,' advised Cameron.

A diversion was created by the arrival of Ferdie who had dropped in to discover if Natasha still had the power to hurt him and why Marigold's last cheque for Lysander's services had bounced twice and Georgie's retainer not been paid at all. As Larry was still AWOL, Ferdie was promptly co-opted to play the innkeeper.

'You've lost even more weight,' said Lysander, coming through the big door at the back, leading Arthur – looking very smart in a jewelled bridle.

'I've been working out and cleaning up,' said Ferdie, giving Arthur a Polo. 'The gym is packed with bored housewives walking very slowly around the running track so their make-up doesn't run. I'm telling all of them I'm about to be sent to the Gulf and pulling everything in sight.'

'Here's the script.' Bob handed it to Ferdie. 'I don't think Larry's up to it, even if he does show. It's not a huge part, but key. Can you learn it by tomorrow? Ad lib if you like.'

'Ferdie was brilliant as Shylock at school,' Lysander told Kitty.

'How are you anyway?' he asked Ferdie.

'Exhausted with electricity privatization, I've been stagging all week.'

'I've been staggering all week, moving scenery,' said Lysander. 'But Rupert Campbell-Black's turning up tomorrow and I know he and Arthur are going to get on. Aren't you, boy?' He gave Arthur a hug.

'What's happening?' hissed Ferdie, drawing Lysander aside. 'No-one's paying. Not a bean out of Marigold, nor Georgie. If they don't cough up soon, we should cut our losses and pull out. The Brazil job's still open – and that's serious dosh.'

But Lysander was watching Kitty who had climbed up a ladder to put pieces of holly around a huge oil of one of Rannaldini's alleged ancestors. She was wearing the black leggings and huge black-and-purple sloppy jersey he'd bought her in Way-In. He'd never seen her in trousers before. There was something infinitely touching about her plump little legs. As she stretched up he could see three-inch gaps of white calf above her Father Christmas socks. He suddenly longed to touch them. Just as he always wanted to stroke Arthur, Jack and Maggie, who was now chewing up a stray shepherd's crook, he told himself firmly.

Putting down the *Express* he walked over to hold her ladder.

'It's Lysander, not electricity, who ought to be privatized,' drawled Flora. 'Having exhausted the other ladies of Paradise, he's moved on to Kitty.'

'Don't be ridiculous,' snapped Rachel, Hermione and Natasha in unison. With their deep involvement in Rannaldini and Lysander, they found it impossible, as well as unbearable, to concede that Kitty had any pulling power.

However often Lysander banked up the fire in the great hall it was definitely getting colder. People's breath rose in thick white plumes.

'Cameron will be able to send up smoke signals from the back of the hall,' said Meredith to his pal Flora. 'I do hope she gets the script back to your mother's version.'

But Flora was glaring at a new and splendid fur coat which Hermione had put on over her blue robes, which could only be a Christmas present from Rannaldini.

'I'm going to report her to Animal Rights,' she said furiously. She also noticed Rachel had disappeared and

Cameron was yelling into a telephone in the summer parlour which was a good thing, as neither of them would have enjoyed Ferdie's début as he welcomed Mary and Joseph to the Inn, script in one hand, litre of red in the other.

'Come in, come in,' he was saying cosily. 'Of course we take Amex. Just give me the keys to your donkey and I'll park him. Sign in here.'

The orchestra, all in their overcoats, were in stitches. Kitty nearly fell off her ladder laughing.

'I've got the video of *Dirty Dancing*,' murmured Lysander, handing her up another branch of holly.

'There's a lot of shepherds in the next room who keep ordering pie on room service,' Ferdie was now saying. 'Bang on the wall if they get too noisy.' Then, handing two room keys to a very disapproving St Joseph, 'Oh, well, I better go back to watering the wine.'

'Oh, please, don't waste precious water,' interjected Hermione, who was revving up for the birth of her Harrods doll.

Bob, who'd been laughing a lot, told Ferdie in future he'd better stick to the script.

'And it's about time for you to sing "Oh, come all ye faithful",' he shouted to Flora.

'No-one's faithful in Paradise except you and Kitty,' shouted back Flora. 'As we're heavily into realism I better sing, "Come both ye faithful".'

'That is quite uncalled for,' thundered Guy, turning brick red above his blond beard.

Flora strolled towards the stage, hands in her pockets. '*Oh, come all ye faithful, joyful and triumphant,*' she sang softly.

'Oh wow,' murmured the leader of the orchestra to a neighbouring oboist, 'eat your stony heart out, Hermione.'

They had reached the part when the Angel Gabriel appeared to the shepherds abiding in the fields.

'You ready, Perce?' called Bob to the vicar in the gallery.

'Ready,' called the vicar, adjusting his halo in the window.

Outside it was snowing. How very appropriate in the bleak midwinter. He was glad he was wearing his thermals under his nightgown.

'Chat amongst yourselves, shepherds,' said Bob consulting his script.

'What are you doing on New Year's Eve, Reuben?' asked Meredith who, as second shepherd, was holding Maggie.

'That's not in the script,' hissed Georgie, burnous askew as she clung for grim death on to a terrified ewe.

Suddenly, like sulphur and brimstone, a waft of Maestro swept through the great hall, far stronger than frankincense or droppings of sheep or donkey.

Instantly the nearest flautist whipped the curly blond wig off Rannaldini's bust. Georgie let go of her ewe, which bolted into the wings sending a peeping Mr Brimscombe flying. The star fused again.

Rannaldini, the astrakhan collar of his black coat turned up, framing a face white with barely controlled fury, strolled towards the stage.

'I thought I told you all to be word and note perfect by the time I came back.'

'My fault.' Ferdie stubbed out his cigar and stood up in the stalls. 'I was standing in for Larry and thought I'd jazz things up a bit.'

'Well, don't,' said Rannaldini witheringly. 'Hermione?'

'Maestro?' Hermione smiled at him, awaiting praise.

'*Piano*, for God's sake,' snarled Rannaldini. 'That lullaby would have woken every bambino in Judea and babies are fed every four hours not every four minutes, so put those boobs away. You're playing the Virgin not Delilah.'

Then, not giving Hermione time to scream at him, he turned on Guy who was eating a flapjack in the stalls.

'You're even more wooden than that ludicrously over-decorated manger, Joseph. Your young wife's having a baby, then everyone rolls up bringing him presents and ignoring you. Show some pride or some jealousy, and as for you, Percy,' he looked up at the vicar who was still swaying helplessly from his beam, 'talk about Fat Tum of the Opera.

'Your belly's too large and your voice too small. You're being drowned by Hermione and Georgie and you couldn't instil mighty dread into any mind, troubled or otherwise. I'm afraid you'll have to join the angelic choir instead.'

Normally suntanned, Rannaldini's extreme pallor was infinitely more sinister. The jet-black eyes glittered like holes into hell, but there was an air of purring satisfaction about him, not just due to the pleasure of bawling people out. Ignoring the equal hysterics of the vicar and Hermione, Rannaldini picked up Cameron Cook's mobile and punched out long distance.

'Carissima,' he launched into a flood of Italian, only the occasional word like 'network' being comprehensible. Then, with a vicious smile, he changed to English so everyone could hear over Hermione's squawking.

'It only means arriving a day early for Chreestmas. The script? Eees excellent. I'll get Keety to fax you a copy so you can learn it tonight. Ciao.'

Switching off his telephone, he turned evilly to face the cast. 'Cecilia arrive tomorrow to take over Gabriel.'

Artistic integrity overcoming terror, Georgie tore off her head-dress.

'The script is not excellent, Rannaldini,' she protested. 'We'll be a laughing stock. Rachel's wrecked it, Cameron Cook agrees with me. Someone's got to tell Rachel.'

'I will, my dear Georgie,' said Rannaldini gently. 'To me the scripts are much improved, more topical, more relevant, less trite.' He turned to the back of the hall. 'Well done, Rachel.'

Everyone, particularly Georgie who thought Rachel was miles away, jumped out of their skins as Rachel drifted through the door.

She was wearing a very new-looking, pale fawn cashmere jersey, softer than the belly of a Persian kitten and

528

she looked absolutely beautiful, as though all her anger had been ironed out.

'Christ,' murmured Meredith, letting Maggie off her lead so she shot back to Lysander, 'if Rannaldini likes that script, he must be hooked.'

'I shall be working late in the tower,' Rannaldini called to Kitty who, up on her ladder, was now filling the window-ledge with big branches of yew. 'I do not weesh to be disturbed.'

As he walked past Rachel, like a bat in his black coat, he shielded her from the others' view. Only Flora, stiller than a shadow in the window-seat, saw him reach out for Rachel's breast as Rachel put a quick hand on his crotch.

'My leetle Quaker,' whispered Rannaldini, 'my leetle earthquaker. You will come soon to the tower?'

'The moment I've found a babysitter.'

And he was gone.

The best-laying plans of maestros and men, however, can go astray. Wandering into the kitchen to make Arthur a bowl of coffee, Lysander found Rachel writing a note.

'Where's Kitty?' she demanded.

Picking up the note, Lysander scrumpled it up.

'She can't babysit,' he said flatly.

'Why ever not? What else has she got to do?'

'She's taking Christmas presents over to her mother.'

'Oh, right – well, perhaps you could? The kids adore you so much.'

'I couldn't.' Lysander's sweet face hardened like wet clay cast in bronze. 'I'm not looking after your kids so you can get fucked by Rannaldini.'

'What d'you mean?' Rachel gave a gasp of horror. 'I've been celibate for nine months.'

'Not with Rannaldini, you haven't. December 9th, wasn't it? I was driving home from Kitty's, Rannaldini was kissing you on the doorstep. Your towel was slipping. And you told Kitty you'd gone to see your solicitors – soliciting more likely.'

'We were discussing cadenzas,' said Rachel, frantically casting round for excuses.

'Cad's a better word,' said Lysander bleakly. 'Kitty was so bloody tired that night.'

Rachel was shattered by his anger.

'Come and have a drink this evening. I'll explain.'

'No thanks, and don't ever do that to Kitty again.'

Poor Rannaldini. Hermione was so livid she decided temporarily to emulate the purity of the Virgin that night. Kitty was in Sidcup and Rachel was confined to barracks minding her own children. Faced with the appalling prospect of a loveless evening, Rannaldini decided to forgive Flora. Ringing up Guy and Georgie, he suggested he dropped by after supper to show them the video of the dress rehearsal and have a last-minute script conference.

'Maybe Rachel make it a leetle too green.'

It was snowing heavily by the time he arrived at Angel's Reach. Shivering in the icy wind like a slaughtered ostrich, a large Christmas tree lay on its side.

Rannaldini was livid to discover that Flora had gone out to a party. Georgie was livid because the video showed Guy's hand disappearing more than once into the billowing blue depths of Hermione's robes.

'It's good acting,' protested Guy. 'A pat on the bottom is just the kind of friendly gesture a wife receives from any husband.'

'Particularly someone else's,' snapped Georgie.

Guy had been twitchy all evening because wretched Flora had pinched the car without asking and there was no way he could escape.

They worked in the kitchen because it was warm by the Aga and by the time they'd gone through the script and toned down Rachel's worst excesses, Rannaldini had drunk enough red wine to risk dropping in on her on the way home. He had just picked up his car keys when Flora walked in. She betrayed no trace of surprise at seeing him. Her red hair, darkened by snow, had grown since last summer. A thick strand had blown round her white neck like a leather strap.

She was wearing a black leather jacket over a gunmetal-grey satin camisole top and black velvet shorts above black-stockinged legs that had lost any trace of puppy fat.

'We were worried about you, darling,' said Georgie. 'The roads must be hell. Was it a good party?'

'Great.' Flora crouched down beside Dinsdale, giving him a crumbling sausage roll out of her pocket.

'Ask, next time you borrow the car,' said Guy angrily. 'I can now get some more red.'

'We've got some,' said Georgie, 'there's a crate in the utility room.'

Guy jumped as the telephone rang.

'I'll take it next door,' said Flora, running across the hall into the drawing room to answer it. There was something stark and unwelcoming about her parents' house, not a coloured ball nor a string of tinsel yet in sight.

Hearing the happy Tennyson's brook sound of continuous laughter, Guy reflected that at least he wasn't paying for the call.

'It's Melanie,' said Flora, a quarter of an hour later. Then, smiling sweetly at her father, 'She's reversing the charges from a Perth call-box.'

Somehow Guy kept his temper and when Georgie rushed off and because Rannaldini showed no sign suddenly of leaving, he went off to get another bottle.

Bidding a tearful farewell to her adored elder daughter five minutes later, Georgie noticed the copy of Catullus David Hawkley had sent her and pulled it out of the bookshelf.

'*It is hard to put aside long-standing love,*' she read sadly.

If only she could see David – he was so straight compared with Guy. A bad sleeper, he'd probably be awake now. His number was engraved on her heart.

Surreptitiously she picked up the second telephone and heard Guy's voice saying: 'I couldn't get away, Ju Ju. Flora took the car without asking and Georgie suddenly remembered a crate of booze, so I had no excuse. I daren't risk it, sweetheart. I'm really sorry, I'll ring you first thing. Sleep well, my darling.'

'Which is more than you're fucking going to do,' screamed Georgie down the telephone.

'I'm sorry I didn't speak to you this afternoon, little one,' murmured Rannaldini. 'You sing very well.'

'Wailing for my demon lover,' said Flora drily.

Outside Rannaldini could see the dark snowless shadow under his car and the ostrich's white feathers fluffing up. Through the gloom a light still shone in Rachel's cottage. He had a vision of Rachel in bed with Flora, languorously smoothing oil into each other's bodies, growing increasingly slippery inside and out as they waited for him to join in.

'I mees you,' he said softly. 'Wheech is your room?'

Out in the hall, under the mistletoe she had put up that morning, Flora could see her parents furiously mouthing at one another.

'Oh, Maestro,' she said in a tremulous voice, 'I thought you would never forgive me.'

'Ees good for little girls to be punished sometime.'

'I deserved it,' Flora admitted. 'If you go up the stairs and turn left, I'm the fourth door on the right, up three small stairs, but don't turn on the light as it shines right into Mummy's and Daddy's room. Don't be too long.'

She slid out of the room.

Rannaldini could not keep the grin off his face. He felt sure Rupert Campbell-Black couldn't pull seventeen year olds any more.

As Guy bustled in, his face redder than the bottle of claret he was carrying, Rannaldini yawned and said it must be jet lag. Could he borrow a toothbrush and crash out in the spare room? Once alone he had a quick wash, plucked out a grey hair from his chest, rubbed one of the samples of eau-de-Cologne Guy had brought back from France into his neck and shoulders, and waited half an hour until the house was so quiet you could hear the snow padding like a white cat outside.

Clad in a dark red towel, scratchy from Mother Courage's washing, he tiptoed along the landing. The creaking was awful. He jumped as Dinsdale in his basket let out a great snore. One, two, three doors. Rannaldini thought he would explode with lust. Feeling his way up the three uncarpeted stairs with his bare toes, he opened and softly closed the fourth door on the right.

'Come to me, lovely creature,' whispered a voice.

'Leetle darling, it is I,' answered Rannaldini.

Taking a flying leap in the direction of the voice, he found that Flora had shrunk and grown in the most improbable places. Next moment he realized his arms were full of naked Guy, who'd been banished to the spare room by an enraged Georgie and who'd been drunkenly rehearsing his lines. Guy was sober enough, however, to be extremely stuffy.

'Flora's only seventeen. How dare you run after schoolgirls like a dirty old man?'

'And I saw you coming out of Langan's with that painter girlfriend of yours on Monday,' spat back Rannaldini. 'I'd keep your trap shut if I were you.'

533

48

Both Rannaldini and Guy were furious with Flora, but had little opportunity to vent their rage on the day of the play.

Members of the cast, however, continued to spat. Cecilia, in her new role as Gabriel, had gone off to Valentino and bought a seductive, but totally inappropriate, thigh-length gold tunic and an even bigger halo than Hermione. In revenge, Hermione spent two hours in make-up, leaving little time for anyone else.

Marigold cried all day because Larry hadn't come home the previous night. He must have gone back to Nikki.

Rachel was totally unsympathetic.

'If you have a remotely attractive husband in the nineties,' she snapped as she buttoned up her Second King's velvet tunic, 'you have to be prepared to share him.'

'*Rock Star, you are the rock, the star that guides me,*' sang the wireless.

'Shut up, you bloody thing,' screamed Georgie.

But by six-thirty the great hall was decked with greenery and hundreds of candles and camera lights were reflected in the gleaming dark panelling. The crew were ready, the London Met tuned up. A vetted collection of villagers, a sprinkling of local gentry including Lady Chisleden, the odd talent scout and a crowd of Meredith's gay friends were among the audience. Mother Courage, thrilled at the prospect of appearing on television, was holding forth noisily.

'Rattledicky stayed the night and Guy was furious that Flora delapidated herself all over the bath, and I only cleaned it yesterday, and Melanie's sending Georgie a duck-billed platitude for Christmas.'

Standing in the wings, all dolled up in his red plumes and gemmy bridle, Arthur was itching to get on stage.

'Don't forget to look at the camera,' Lysander urged him. 'And whenever you see Rupert, wave a hoof. I'm really nervous for him,' he told Cameron Cook as Arthur rested his head lovingly on his master's shoulder.

'Ever thought of becoming an actor?' asked Cameron, handing him her card. 'D'you mind sitting in the audience when it starts? Marigold can look after Arthur.'

She was determined to get reaction shots of him whenever they cut to the audience.

'D'you actually know Rupert?' pleaded Lysander.

'You could say that.'

'Is he seriously wonderful?'

Cameron thought for a second. 'Only if he likes you. For Christ's sake, see all the telephones are switched off,' she added to her PA as her mobile rang.

'Bloody hell,' she whispered to the chief cameraman two minutes later. 'Rupert's not coming. He's buggered off skiing.'

'Well, don't tell anyone,' whispered back the chief cameraman. 'We don't want the entire female cast going on strike.'

But at last the cameras were rolling and the London Met were appropriately playing like angels, enjoying the novelty of the occasion and the relief of being conducted by Bob, whose bald head gleamed like a bathing cap above the dark river of the orchestra pit.

Everything, in fact, was going wonderfully. Neither Hermione in her blue robes nor Cecilia in her figure-hugging mini would have looked so radiant if they had known Rupert wasn't going to make it, even for 'Brickie's spread', which included two vats of *boeuf bourgignon*, whose delicious smell was stealing up from the kitchen.

'Hail Mary, Full of Grace,' called Cecilia who preferred the beauty of the old language, 'thou art with child.'

'Joseph will be very supportive, and present at the birth,' said Hermione who did not.

Kitty caught Lysander's eye and giggled.

'There's a Christmas tree with nothing on,' said Mother Courage as the curtains jerked back on the stable at Bethlehem.

The play was nearing its end. Although the shepherds and inn staff had been rather too reminiscent of Iraqi and Saudi agitators in the Gulf, Meredith's gay cronies were in ecstasies over the sets and the beauty of little Cosmo as a shepherd boy unaccountably trying to strangle Hermione's white cat. The animals had all behaved impeccably, except Dinsdale who had lifted his leg twice on the manger.

Flora had sung 'O come all ye faithful' and 'O little town of Bethlehem' so magically that she had earned a round of applause each time. But the real *coup de théâtre* was when Rannaldini, Rachel and Marigold, singing the most ravishing three-part arrangement of 'We Three Kings', cantered in on their splendid bejewelled horses.

Rannaldini and Rachel looked so glamorous that the audience hardly noticed the reddened eyes and streaked moustache of the Third King, whom Arthur carried with such sympathy and gentleness.

'Look at the old boy really acting,' said Lysander proudly. 'Don't look at the camera, Arthur.'

'Will you be quiet,' hissed Lady Chisleden.

The Prince of Darkness, who'd had a good win at Lingfield the previous week, was jumping all over the place as Rannaldini, perfectly capped teeth flashing above his black beard, bent down to hand Hermione a gold casket.

'Bet Hermione pockets it,' whispered Lysander.

'I'd give that Prince of Darkness a wild berth if I was 'er,' said Mother Courage.

As everyone lined up to gaze at the Virgin and Child, Hermione brandished a large breast in the direction she imagined Rupert to be sitting.

'Wasted on us,' chorused Meredith's cronies in unison.

As the Kings remounted their horses, Flora, hovering in the wings, noticed Rachel shoot Rannaldini a smile of uncharacteristic lasciviousness.

For the final tableau, Flora came forward to sing 'Once in royal David's city'. She was wearing black jeans and a black polo-neck with her hair slicked back off her incredibly pale face.

Playing Death *and* the Maiden, thought Bob, raising his baton. The poor child looked extraordinarily bleak.

The orchestra gave her the introductory bars, then put down their instruments in anticipation of a treat. Guy folded his arms, happy to claim ownership when Flora brought him credit. For a second she glanced around, waiting for total silence. Her voice, cool as an icicle, was so exquisite it was several seconds before anyone took in the words.

'*Once in Rannaldini's watch-tower,*' sang Flora,
'*Stood a king-size double bed.*
Where the Maestro bonked Hermione.
Once her Chanel suits she'd shed.'

Horror, amazement and delighted expectation were slowly creeping over the faces of the audience. The leader of the orchestra put his head in his hands to hide his laughter.

'Stay on Camera Two, for Christ's sake,' hissed Cameron Cook.

'*Rannaldini drove her wild,*
Little Cosmo is his child,' sang Flora emphasizing every word.

'*And through Cosmo's wondrous childhood,*' a beatific smile spread over Flora's face.

'*Maestro popped in every day,*
Just to bonk the fair Hermione,
In whose hulking arms he lay.
And he bonked his ex-wife, too
Rachel Grant's just joined the queue.'

Laughing himself sick, then suddenly noticing the

distress on Kitty's face, Lysander took her hand, warming it with both his own. The otherwise mesmerized paralysis of the entire room was broken by an animal howl of rage from Rannaldini.

'Cut, for Christ's sake, cut.'

This so overwhelmed the overbred Prince of Darkness that he crapped all over the stage, whereupon, Jack, who'd been licking his chops, took off after Hermione's cat, followed by an hysterically barking Maggie, Dinsdale and Tabloid. Hermione opened her mouth and screamed and screamed. Arthur, who loved babies as much as hay, shuffled forward to inspect the manger and was just about to nudge Baby Jesus when the Harrods doll was snatched up by Cecilia, halo askew.

'*Scellerato*,' she yelled, laying into Rannaldini with it.

'Oh,' sighed a visiting talent scout from Virgin Records, consulting his programme, 'Flora Seymour has the most beautiful voice I have ever heard.'

As everyone started yelling at Flora she burst into tears.

'Please don't cry.'

Running forward, Kitty clambered clumsily on to the stage, putting her arms round Flora and, with Lysander's and Bob's help, carried her out through the wings, up the steps into the summer parlour, where she collapsed on to the blue and white striped sofa on which she had first scorned Rannaldini's advances.

'You spoilt our nativity play,' shouted Guy rushing in, tearing off Joseph's head-dress, then turning to Georgie who had followed him.

'Now see where your sloppy permissive attitude has led.'

Next minute they were joined by Meredith and his twittering cronies who swooped on Flora, trying to comfort her, when Rannaldini stalked in, his face incandescent with rage.

'You bitch,' he screamed.

'Are you talking to us?' chorused Meredith's cronies.

Staggering to her feet, Flora lurched towards Rannaldini.

'You're drunk,' he snarled.

'No, pregnant,' said Flora tonelessly, 'and you're the father.'

'That's not true,' screamed Natasha. 'How could you, Flora?'

'You lying slut,' hissed Rannaldini. 'How dare you tell such fucking lies?'

'It's true,' sobbed Flora.

Calmly, Rannaldini walked over to the telephone.

'Get me James Benson's number,' he called over his shoulder to Kitty. 'He'll soon do a few tests to see who's right.'

Kitty paused. She knew James Benson's number by heart, having rung him so often about her own tests, but she suddenly felt so sorry for Flora. As if reading her thoughts, Flora slumped at Rannaldini's feet, sobbing that she'd made the whole thing up, clinging hysterically to his purple-stockinged thighs.

'I love you,' she wept. 'I can't help myself. I'm so sorry, Kitty. It's all my fault.'

'*And* you've broken the Official Secrets Act,' hissed Rannaldini viciously, wriggling out of her frantic clutches as though she were a pair of tight breeches. He seemed oblivious of the crowd around them.

'You should have cut my vocal chords at the beginning,' said Flora falling pitifully to the floor.

Kitty, rushing forward to comfort her, was almost pushed sideways by Georgie.

'Oh, darling, I'm sorry I've neglected you. I've been so worried about work and everything. It's not your fault. Let's go home.'

Utterly appalled that she'd been too locked in over Guy's philandering and the loss of David Hawkley to notice what was going on, she started to cry.

'It's all your fault, you bastard,' she sobbed at Rannaldini.

539

Guy was longing to castigate Rannaldini, too, but didn't dare in case Rannaldini shopped him about Julia. Instead he proceeded to vent his fury on Flora.

'Look how you've upset your mother.'

'Not nearly as much as you've upset her,' screamed back Flora. 'She'd never have gone to bed with Lysander if you hadn't been carrying on with Julia all this time.'

'Dear, dear,' said Meredith, looking from a speechless Georgie to a flabbergasted Guy. 'Turnbull & Asser are going to do a roaring trade in hair shirts this Christmas.'

Very, very reluctantly and only because Rannaldini threatened to close all the electric gates and doors and imprison them, Venturer signed a hastily typed-out agreement that they would cut Flora's outburst.

'If Rupert hadn't fucked off skiing, we could've made a fight for it,' said Cameron furiously.

'The Kings just mounting their horses make a shitty ending.'

'Very shitty in The Prince of Darkness' case,' giggled Meredith.

'Who's talking of endings?' said Rannaldini, admiring Cameron's snarling sexy face. 'Let's have dinner in the New Year. Now bugger off everyone.'

If anyone was more distraught than poor Flora that evening it was Marigold, who didn't seem to have taken in any of the dramas. All that mattered was that Larry hadn't turned up. She refused to join Meredith, his friends, various euphoric members of the London Met, most of the crew and Ferdie and Lysander in The Pearly Gates for a pissed mortem.

As he first had to box Arthur back and feed him, Lysander insisted Ferdie drive Marigold home.

'Ay wish they made husbands laike you, Arthur,' Marigold said, having sobbed off most of her stage make-up into his grey shoulder.

As they trooped out into the snow they passed Hermione. Completely oblivious that Little Cosmo, who'd been at

Kitty's sweet sherry, was systematically removing tenners from her bag, she was screeching, 'How dare Flora call my arms hulking?'

'I think the Virgin Mary's suffering from post-natal depression,' muttered Ferdie.

'And what happened to Rupert Campbell-Black?' demanded Hermione.

'I'd forgotten about him,' said Lysander in dismay as he helped Marigold into the car. 'I so wanted him to meet Arthur. Look after her,' he urged in an undertone as he shut the door against the swirling snow. 'She's worried sick.'

'Not as worried sick as I am,' said Ferdie, scooping up a ball of snow from the top of the car and hurling it at a departing harpist. 'Larry, or rather Marigold, owes us thirty thousand pounds.'

'Forget it,' said Lysander. 'You don't think Rannaldini will take it out on Kitty, do you? I didn't get a chance to say goodnight to her. Promise to go into the house with Marigold and see she's OK.'

Even Ferdie couldn't bring himself to talk finance to such a shuddering, desolate wreck. Ahead, through a snowy tunnel of bowed trees, Paradise Grange reared up darkly, its great battlements and turrets lit by the wannest of moons.

'Since Rachel moved in, the laights have been goin' out all over Paradise,' said Marigold sadly. 'Ay'm sure Larry gave her that lovely cashmere jumper.'

'Rachel's being bonked by Rannaldini,' said Ferdie gently. 'Your husband's far too deeply into filthy consumerism to appeal to Rachel. Aren't you going to ask me in for a drink?' he added. 'You shouldn't be on your own.'

'I've obviously got to get used to it,' said Marigold.

She had got through the performance. All she wanted to do was crash out in her lonely bed and sob out her broken heart.

★ ★ ★

She was amazed to find the front door open. She was so off the wall, she must have forgotten to put on the burglar alarm when she left that morning.

As she put down her costume in its carrier bag, her gold crown fell on to the floor, a symbol that her Ritzy life had gone for ever.

Catching sight of her blackened, red-eyed, miner's face, she went into the downstairs loo and washed away the streaked mascara and the remains of her cork moustache. Now, wanner than the moon itself, she switched on the drawing-room light, and gave a scream for there, slumped on the sofa, was Larry. He looked utterly wretched. He was neatly dressed in a white shirt and a pin-striped suit. Only his face was unironed and rumpled.

Marigold wanted to yell at him for not showing up, for humiliating her, for being unfaithful like everyone else in Paradise, but the words withered on her white lips.

'I tried to grapple back up the tree,' said Larry, as though they were in the middle of a conversation, 'but it was like using fungi as 'andholds. They kept givin' way.'

As he put his head in his hands she noticed all his gold rings and the bracelets had gone and how grey his dark hair had become.

'I don't know 'ow to tell you, Princess, but I'm finished, up the spout,' he croaked. 'I guaranteed a big electronics project, borrowed a 'uge amount of money, used some of Catchitune's assets as well, an' it bombed. The bank's pulled the plug. I'm ruined, skint.' He tugged his empty pockets out of his trousers like a conjurer.

'I didn't want to worry you.' He gave a groan. 'I've been trying to raise the dough from everywhere, but there isn't any about.'

As Marigold opened her mouth to speak, he put up his hand.

'But I can't blame the recession. I was greedy. An' this afternoon they voted me off the Board.'

'They can't have,' said Marigold aghast.

'So I'm broke, belly-up. I've got nuffink.'

Marigold couldn't speak the lump in her throat was so huge, the tidal wave of tears ready to smash the lock gates, as Larry hung his head.

'I understand if you want to leave me, Princess.'

'Oh Larry, Larry, Ay thought you'd gone back to Nikki.'

Incredulously, Larry looked up.

'All those phone calls,' sobbed Marigold. 'An' you've lost so much weight and never turning up to rehearsals.'

She moved towards him with her arms open.

'Ay don't mind where Ay live so long as it's with you. Ay never really laiked this mansion. It's a naightmare to clean, and Ay've never felt comfortable with servants and the boys will be delaighted to leave boarding-school and we've got enough food in the freezer to live on for ever.'

'You don't mean it? You'll stand by me? Ow, Princess, ow, Princess.'

'Oh Larry, Larry,' said Marigold crying and laughing all at once as she flung herself into his arms. 'Ay love you so much, Ay'd follow you to the hend of the earth.'

49

As President Gorbachov kept going abroad to distance himself from the growing domestic crises in Russia, so Rannaldini abandoned all thought of Christmas at Valhalla. He knew Venturer still had the clip of 'Once in Royal David's City' and that he couldn't silence blabbermouths like Mother Courage and Lady Chisleden. Harassed by enraged mistresses and a baying Press, Rannaldini decided, as a gesture of family solidarity, to take Kitty and his many children skiing and made sure that a delightful photograph of them all arriving at the airport was circulated worldwide.

Lysander felt sick when he saw it reproduced on the front of the *Sun*. He had been appalled, the morning after the play, to find Valhalla deserted except for Mrs Brimscombe who was sourly freezing *boeuf bourgignon* and who handed him a Christmas present from Kitty beautifully wrapped in red paper covered in polo ponies. Inside were chewsticks for the dogs, Twix bars for Arthur and Tiny and a dark blue jersey with Donald Duck on the front which Kitty had knitted for him. A card enclosed said: '*Dear Lysander. This is to thank you for your many kindnesses. I hope you don't miss your Mum and Georgie too much over Xmas, yours sincerely, Kitty Rannaldini.*'

Lysander was utterly desolate. Earlier in December, Kitty had given him an Advent Calendar. Now he felt all the doors were closing on him. Returning to Magpie Cottage, he found Ferdie bemoaning his excesses the night before in The Pearly Gates and examining a green tongue in the mirror. On the strength of his success as the innkeeper he had managed to score with Miss Paradise '90, the barmaid.

'I told her I was off to the Gulf, too.'

'That's bloody dishonest. She's a nice girl.'

'What's bitten you?' said Ferdie in amazement.

'Rannaldini's taken Kitty skiing.'

'That is terrific,' said Ferdie. 'I have to congratulate you. I never dreamt you'd get Kitty looking that good, almost attractive, in that green dress the other night – and to get Rannaldini back as well. He's never taken her on holiday before. I'm going to give you a massive Christmas bonus,' he added as Lysander's face blackened. 'You're off to Brazil. Bastard coffee billionaire giving his ravishing young wife the run-around. Here's the ticket.' Ferdie reached for his brief case.

'I don't want to go to Brazil,' said Lysander mutinously.

'You'll get some seriously good polo.'

After Christmas in the extremely fashionable French ski resort of Monthaut acquiring a suntan and being photographed on every piste surrounded by children, Rannaldini was bored rigid and decided to fly home. Christmas, like the snow, had temporarily blotted out all gossip. Natasha left with him. To shake her out of her shock at his affaire with Flora, he despatched her to Barbados for a holiday.

Kitty got no such compensation. She was to stay on in Monthaut over the New Year to keep an eye on Rannaldini's children and the au pair, who was very pretty and expected to go out skiing and clubbing in the evenings, leaving Kitty in charge. At no time had Rannaldini apologized in any way for Flora's revelations.

Wearily, Kitty drove back from dropping him off at the airport. Rannaldini had been particularly ratty over Christmas. In her distress at not being able to say goodbye to Lysander, Kitty had left several scores and clothes that he needed in Valhalla, although she felt he would have complained whatever she had picked. She was desperately short of clothes herself. She hadn't brought anything for the evening, no ski clothes and no boots for walking on the polished ice, so, as Rannaldini loathed her spending money, the drive to the airport was her first outing. Even with chains on the wheels, she had been terrified of the winding, treacherous roads.

She felt safer when she reached Monthaut. Horses with bells jangling on their bridles, which reminded her of Arthur, were pulling sledgefuls of tourists along the High Street. Beautiful girls with vivid brown faces and enviably narrow hips strode purposefully over the frozen pavements. The Hotel Versailles, where Rannaldini always stayed, was the best in Monthaut. South-facing, yellow-stoned, overlooking the village square with its statue of President de Gaulle and a wonderful view of the mountains, it was two minutes' walk from the main ski lifts. Snow and icicles glittering from the gables were melting slightly in the sunshine.

As Kitty crept in through the swing doors, every table in the foyer was occupied by glamorous, chattering, sunburnt people. It was several seconds before she recognized the most glamorous of them all. He was wearing a Donald Duck jersey and knocked over his glass of Kir as he jumped to his feet.

'Lysander,' whispered Kitty.

Her delight was so unmistakable that Lysander nearly kissed her properly, but, as she ducked her head in embarrassment, he made do with hugging her.

'I fort you was in Brazil.'

'I got bored and I missed you. I'm going to teach you to ski.'

'I 'aven't got any gear.'

'I'll buy you some. I haven't given you a Christmas present. Thank you for the Donald Duck,' he looked down, 'he's the best present I've ever had. I hope he doesn't have to go into quarantine when we go back to England.'

Tucking his arm through hers as he led her towards the lift, he asked her if she had been given anything nice.

'Rannaldini gave me a filing cabinet and Hermione some chopstick 'olders,' Kitty giggled, 'an' a red sloppy jumper big enough for a helephant. "I know you like them baggy, Kitty." Ooo, I am 'appy to see you, Lysander.'

Feeling dreadfully guilty about abandoning Rannaldini's children to the sulky au pair and feeling embarrassingly ostentatious in a lime-green, violet, harebell-blue and shocking pink ski suit, 'I look like a rinebow 'ippo,' Kitty took to the slopes.

'You must have lots of protection,' said Lysander, rubbing Ambre Solaire into her pink cheeks and painting her mouth with mauve lipsalve before dropping a kiss on her squashed nose.

He was looking very flash in a tight daffodil-yellow bomber jacket and ski pants, and a kingfisher-blue sweat band keeping his curls out of his eyes, which were covered with black wrap-around glasses. He'd streaked his face and his beautiful big mouth with different coloured lipsalves like an Apache. Behind him, dazzling white peaks reared up against a sapphire sky. Chalet girls, PAs from Knightsbridge, glamorous divorcées on the prowl, au pairs who'd escaped, gazed at him in wonder.

'I feel like a new-born foal wiv a banana skin attached to each hoof,' protested Kitty. 'Ooooh – I'm going to fall over again.'

'No, you're not,' encouraged Lysander. 'Stand on the edge of your skis, that's right, now lean forward, sticks behind, sticks be*hind*! Don't cross them! Well done, Kitty.'

'Weeee, I can do it.' Kitty got so carried away, she skiied several yards. 'Ow, my legs are going, 'elp, 'elp.'

Soon her suit of many colours was covered with snow. It was true what they said about the mountains making you feel all tingly and excited. All her tiredness had vanished.

Lysander had taken her to a comparatively deserted slope, and such was his total preoccupation with teaching her and his growing awareness of the delicious curves of her body since she'd lost all that weight that neither of them realized that the snow around them had been invaded by photographers and reporters, sliding all over the place, gabbling into telephones and tape recorders. For a horrific moment, Kitty thought they were on to her and Lysander, but they were all gazing up the mountain.

'He's on his way down,' announced a reporter from the *Daily Mail*, switching off his telephone.

'James Whittaker says the kid's got a strong American accent, so Rupert must have got it from Texas,' said a predatory blonde.

'I thought he and Taggie were going to adopt from Bogotá.'

'Probably decided he wanted something more Aryan.'

'Evidently the kid's the spitting image of Rupert. It's amazing how these adoption societies match them up.'

'They must have got it very quickly. Taggie's miscarriage was only a few weeks ago,' said the *Sun* photographer.

'Could be an illegit of Rupert's he's trying to palm off on Taggie,' suggested the predatory blonde.

'Oh, Beattie, you would think that.'

'Taggie looked miserable last night and she hasn't skiied since she's been out here,' said Beattie Johnson of *The Scorpion* shirtily.

'She's just lost a baby, stupid.'

'If it is Rupert's,' Beattie was not to be deflected, 'it means that he has been unfaithful to Taggie, because Nigel says the kid can't be a day over three and he's been married to Taggie nearly six years.'

'Hush, here they come.' The world's Press adjusted their long lenses and switched on their tape recorders as a very blond child in huge dark glasses and a striped blue and white ski suit came whistling down the slope. For a second, it looked as though he was going slap into an elderly American in fuschia-pink who was gingerly picking herself up.

'Move your ass, grandma,' yelled the child as he shot past.

'Come back, Eddie, for Christ's sake,' yelled a voice loud enough to start an avalanche and over the white brow of the slope like a shiver of lightning came a tall man in faded jeans and a thick dark grey jersey. Slithering to a spectacular halt beside the child, he hid them both for a moment in a fountain of snow. As they emerged, Lysander took in the smooth brown forehead, the thick gleaming blond hair, the beautiful Greek nose thrown into relief by the dark glasses, and the curling mouth now set like a trap.

'Rupert Campbell-Black,' he whispered to Kitty in wonder. 'Just think, I come here to see you and he's here as well. Oh, Kitty, isn't he handsome?'

'I fort Taggie'd just had a miscarriage.'

'They must have adopted this one. Isn't he sweet?'

'Don't you run away from me like that, you little sod,' yelled Rupert. 'And you can all fuck off,' he added as the Press closed in with a frenzied clicking of cameras.

'Where you get him from, Rupe?' demanded the *Express*.

'What's your name, darling?' asked Beattie Johnson.

'Edward Bartholomew Alderton,' said the child politely. Then, turning to Rupert, 'Move your ass, Grandpa, I'm starved.'

As the howls of laughter subsided and Rupert disappeared in a towering rage, Beattie Johnson could be heard saying: 'Of *course*, he's Perdita's child.'

'Who's she?' asked *Paris Match*.

'Where've you been for the last four years?' said Beattie as they trooped back to their hotels to file copy. 'One of Rupert's illegits. That's why her kid's the spittin' image of him. She married an American polo player called Luke Alderton.'

'Fancy Rupert being a grandad,' said the *Mirror*.

549

'Not very good for his super-stud image,' said Beattie in amusement. 'I wonder if I can get Grandfather Cock into the copy?'

Sitting in the bar at the Hotel Versailles watching the mountains turn from rose-pink to glittering electric-blue as the gold lights came on in the village square, Rupert ignored his beautiful wife Taggie, drank whisky as brown as his face, in a mood as black as his name. He was trying not to lose his temper with Mr Pandopoulos, the rich Greek owner, who'd flown in specially to complain that his best horse hadn't even been placed in a big race that afternoon.

In the past Rupert had notched up more conquests than Don Giovanni. The Press, deeply sceptical about his apparent fidelity to Taggie, were determined to catch him out. *The Scorpion* employed two reporters whose sole job was to tail him night and day. Their last scoop had indeed been four and a half years ago when the tempestuous Perdita Macleod, England's best woman polo player, had turned out to be Rupert's daughter. After passionate initial antagonism, Rupert had eventually recognized her as his child and given her considerable emotional and financial support. Since then the paparazzi had had nothing to go on, following him warily, aware that Rupert was rich enough to sue them witless if they stepped out of line.

But a scoop in the *Daily Express* about Taggie's heart-break over the miscarriage had triggered all the speculation off again. Apart from the loss of the baby, which had affected him just as badly as Taggie, Rupert had had a pulverizing year. Even successful owner-trainers had been stymied by the recession. Rupert's yearlings didn't auto-matically fetch six figures any more. For the first time he was having to put up with indifferent horses if the owner was rich enough to pay for them. Hence the post-mortem today. As a founder director of Venturer Television he should have made a killing but advertising was right down and they'd been forced to lay off staff.

Nor were his three children giving him much joy. Marcus, who was at Bagley Hall with Flora, was a wimp whose only ambition egged on by his mother, Rupert's first wife, was to be a concert pianist. Tabitha, with whom Rupert had enjoyed an adoring, almost too symbiotic relationship, had suddenly turned into a brat who questioned Rupert's every decision and attitude and who had recently, at the age of fourteen, fallen madly in love with Rupert's tractor-driver. Removed out of temptation to Monthaut, she had sulked so badly that Rupert, in a rage, had packed her off home to her mother. Finally, Perdita, with whom Rupert had an erratic relationship – only her husband Luke could really handle her – had added a last straw heavier than a crowbar.

His wife Taggie, though young enough to be his fourth child, adored him and longed to have his children. After an almost fatal miscarriage early on in their marriage when she had been told she couldn't have children, she had endured several painful and disappointing attempts to have a test-tube baby. Finally getting pregnant to universal rejoicing in August, at four months she had had a ghastly and inexplicable miscarriage.

Nothing in the world would bring back the baby. Dismissing Rupert's anguished protestations that he must be bringing Taggie bad luck, James Benson, who was also Rupert's family doctor, told him to take Taggie away for a holiday.

'And then go to South America, or Texas, or even Romania, and adopt. There are plenty of babies if you wave your cheque book.'

Having endured innumerable sleepless nights worrying about Taggie, Rupert was desperately in need of a break himself. A dashing skier all his life, the mountains always recharged his batteries and Taggie would get brown and strong again.

Then all had been sabotaged by Perdita ringing Taggie from Palm Beach; she had deliberately chosen the moment just before Christmas when Rupert was in Ireland.

Announcing that it was high time he and Taggie got to know their grandchild, she asked if she could dump little Eddie on them for a fortnight while she and Luke flew to Kenya to play polo.

'It's the chance of a lifetime, Taggie,' she had begged. 'All expenses paid. Luke and I have been working our asses off keeping the barn and the ponies going. The recession's been far worse in America. We really need to spend some time together.'

And sweet, gentle Taggie, of course, had agreed and Rupert had returned from Ireland to find little Eddie *in situ*, totally American, utterly adorable but as self-willed as his grandfather, who never stopped asking when Mom and Dad were coming back. Outraged with Perdita for lumbering Taggie with a child when she'd just lost her own, Rupert had promptly employed a French girl to look after Eddie. But, infuriatingly and stubbornly, Taggie had insisted on caring for him herself, getting up in the night whenever he cried, even allowing him to come into their bed, so there had been no holiday and even less sex.

He had taken Eddie skiing to give Taggie a break and the little sod, who had learnt to ski before he could crawl, had given Rupert the slip and showed him up as a grandfather in front of the entire world Press – the Misconstruction Industry, as he always called them.

Rupert actually liked his new grandchild. He knew it was desperately uncool to mind about being a grandfather, or even worse, to go round saying that he had only been eighteen when Perdita had been conceived. But, at the moment, he felt a failure as a grandfather, a father, a husband and a trainer, particularly with Mr Pandopoulos bellyaching beside him.

Most of all Rupert despised himself for biting Taggie's head off yet again because she had allowed *his* grandchild to wreck their holiday. She looked utterly ravishing this evening in a crimson angora jersey and a straight black, sequined skirt, showing off legs far more beautiful than any tiresome owner's colt. Rupert was about to take her hand and tell her he loved her and was only livid with himself, when he noticed a couple at the next table. A plain girl whose pink face clashed with her brilliantly coloured ski suit and a miraculously good-looking boy, whose clear bluey-green eyes were unashamedly gazing in his direction. Rupert was quite used to admiration from his own sex, but the boy didn't look gay, so he must be after Taggie, hardly surprising if one was lumbered with a dog like that.

Five minutes later when Kitty went upstairs to read a bedtime story to Rannaldini's children, Lysander paid the bill. For Arthur's sake, he must do it now. Knees knocking, mouth dry, unaware of every woman gazing at him hungrily, he approached his great hero. Looking down at the wonderful chiselled features, the cold lapis-lazuli eyes, he wanted to give Rupert some amazing present, to kneel down and kiss his hand. Instead he stammered, 'Excuse me, I hope you don't mind my butting in?'

'If you're a journalist, piss off,' snapped Rupert.

'Oh no, no, no, I'm absolutely not. My name's Lysander Hawkley.'

Rupert's eyes narrowed in half-recognition.

'Basically I live in Paradise,' went on Lysander, 'I'd hoped to meet you last week at the Valhalla nativity play.'

Rupert looked fractionally more friendly.

'We were hoping to go,' said Taggie, feeling horribly sorry for the poor boy. 'Do sit down for a minute and tell us about it.' She winced as Rupert kicked her on the ankle.

'Thank you.' Lysander beamed at Taggie and nearly knocked over the water jug in his efforts to appear calm.

'I gather Georgie Maguire's daughter – last seen throwing up into a trumpet at Bagley Hall – went berserk and listed Rannaldini's mistresses,' said Rupert lightly. 'Roberto Rannaldini, this is one of your nine lives. Cameron said it was seriously funny.'

'Not for Kitty,' said Lysander quickly.

'Kitty?'

'Rannaldini's wife,' said Lysander proudly. 'She was with me just now.'

'Ah.'

The penny was beginning to drop. This must be the boy that Cameron had been raving about. 'We've got to sign him up, Rupert. He's to die for.'

'What part did you play?' asked Taggie, aware of the menace of Rupert's mood.

'Oh, I just shifted scenery, but my horse, Arthur, carried the Third King. He was seriously good in the part, but that was only a sideline. It's Arthur I wanted to tell you about.' He looked at Rupert fair and square.

After five minutes he realized that Rupert was yawning and tapping long fingers on the table.

'Sorry. I'm talking too much.'

'I wouldn't argue with that.'

'He sounds really sweet,' said Taggie quickly, wishing Rupert wouldn't be so vile.

Comforted, Lysander turned to her. God, she was lovely with all that cloudy dark hair and her soft, pink mouth and her kind, silvery-grey eyes and sweet, shy face.

'You're so much prettier than your picture in the *Express*,' he stammered, 'and we saw your little boy. He's adorable. He'll be skiing for America soon and he looks just like you.'

'Odd,' said Rupert coldly, 'he's no relation of Tag's. He's my grandchild.'

That's torn it, thought Lysander. 'I know it sounds crass,' he stumbled on, 'but you don't look anything like old enough to be a grandfather.'

Little bastard, patronizing me, thought Rupert.

'He doesn't, does he?' Taggie put a hand over Rupert's clenched one. 'Eddie's parents are playing polo in Kenya, so we're looking after him for a few days. Good practice because we're hoping to adopt our own baby from South America soon.'

Rupert was looking thunderous. He didn't like Taggie discussing their private life. The boy could easily be stringing for *The Scorpion*.

'I spent Christmas in South America. Brazil actually,' Lysander told Taggie, 'in an incredible house with a swimming-pool and a polo field, running into the sea at one end and the mountains at the other. We were drinking on the terrace one evening and I pointed out that the mountain was dotted with stars. Gina, my hostess, just laughed. "Your stars are lights from the shacks of the poor," she said. "Don't ever grumble about being rich." '

'That's really sad,' said Taggie.

'Isn't it? I thought what the hell am I doing here?'

Rupert yawned pointedly. 'One might ask the same question.'

'Rupert!' reproved Taggie.

Flushing, Lysander jumped to his feet.

'I'm really sorry.'

Suddenly Rupert twigged. This must be the boy who had cut such a swathe through the Paradise wives. There was no way he was leaving him on the loose to run after Taggie.

'How well d'you ski?' he asked Lysander.

'OK. I'm a bit rusty.'

'I'll take you off-piste tomorrow if you like. Down the Chute des Fantômes, Chute d'Enfer, Descente des Diables – it's got a lot of names. We could stop for lunch on the way down and talk about Arthur.'

'That's seriously kind.'

'I'll pick you up about nine-thirty then.'

50

Lysander went up to his room to find lots of messages. Then he hung up on Georgie because he was still furious with her. Next Marigold rang scolding him for staying out there.

'Rannaldini's back in England. He doesn't need rattling any more. We've got to talk, Lysander.' But he had hung up.

Ferdie was even more disapproving.

'Why the hell aren't you in Brazil? That's a half a million pound deal,' he shouted.

'Go and sell some more houses,' snapped Lysander.

'The market's dead. Gina's just called. She's hopping you walked out, and Martha rang. Remember Martha, your first success? She needs a Refresher Course because Elmer's straying again. You can go on to Florida from Brazil. Gina said it was working fine when you buggered off. And office parties at Christmas have triggered off lots of unfaithful husbands who need bringing to heel when you get back from Martha's. Loadsamoney, boy.'

'I'm not interested.'

'This is a partnership,' said Ferdie angrily. 'I've worked my ass off for you. I deserve my cut. There's no way you'll be able to hold down any other job earning this kind of money. Remember the mess you were in this time last year. And you don't want to take on Rannaldini, he's a dangerous bugger – you won't have any kneecaps left – and Kitty's sweet, but frankly, she's not the right class and certainly not good looking enough. You shouldn't be giving her ideas.'

'You're always grumbling I never have any. And shut up about Kitty.'

'I'll ring you when you're in a better mood.'

Outside it had started to snow, whitely blurring the gold lamps and windows lighting the town square, wrapping the church spire in cotton wool. Realizing he hadn't been to sleep for forty-eight hours and in need of Kitty's cheerful company, Lysander wandered off to the vast President de Gaulle suite which Rannaldini had taken for his holiday. He found her plumping the cushions of a huge dark green velvet sofa and in floods of tears. He was appalled. The only time he'd seen Kitty cry was after the tennis tournament when she'd discovered she wasn't pregnant. Perhaps she'd just got the curse again. Hell! He'd been hoping to get her into bed that evening. Then he felt furious with himself for being selfish.

'Oh, Lysander, I'm in such a muddle.'

Lysander was about to take her in his arms when the telephone rang. It was Rannaldini in a rage because Kitty hadn't cancelled the President de Gaulle suite. Why, after he'd left, should she live in the style befitting a great maestro?

'I'm sorry, Rannaldini. We'll move into other rooms first fing.'

Lysander was so angry that Kitty was being so placatory that he retreated to the vast bathroom next door, gazing stonily at the dewy bank of ferns and the red velvet steps leading up to a raspberry-pink Jacuzzi big enough to accommodate an entire string quartet. And the bastard wanted to move Kitty into some pokey little hole! He was tempted to pick up the telephone and join in the row. Instead, despite Kitty's frantic waving, he pulled the chain noisily and then turned up the television – some French rock band – far too loud.

'What's that noise?' asked Rannaldini sharply.

'Nothing, one of the children,' stammered Kitty over the din.

'They should be in bed.'

Lysander had sulkily eaten all the strawberries in the fruit bowl and was starting on the nectarines when Kitty put down the receiver.

'How dare you make all that noise,' she said furiously.

Lysander looked up in amazement.

'Kitty, you can actually be cross!'

And like a bullet between the eyes he realized that he was in love with her.

'I just hate you being so nice to him,' he mumbled.

Wiping his hands on his jeans, he pulled her towards him. Despite her wriggling away like a piglet, he kissed her and she tasted so clean and sweet and her young skin smelt so like a wild rose that he went on kissing her until the wriggling stopped.

'I haven't got any knees left.' Catching her off balance, he pulled her down on to the green velvet sofa and, kissing her again, began to explore her body.

Beneath a dress drenched by the children's bath water, he discovered wonderfully full, bouncy breasts and a waist no longer belted by spare tyres.

'Oh Kitty, I'm mad about you.'

Then the wriggling started again.

'You don't have to be nice to me,' sobbed Kitty. 'Just to rattle Rannaldini and give me a sheen.'

'This had nothing to do with Rannaldini.' It was Lysander's turn to be outraged.

Trapping her face between his hands, he forced her to look at him, 'I'm doing this because I can't not. I love you, Kitty. It crept up on me in Brazil. I was Kitty-sick, not homesick. From now on, you're where I belong.'

Then seeing her utter amazement. 'You're as irresistible as Cambozola, you're' – he snapped his fingers trying to be really poetic – 'as comforting as a baked potato full of butter on Sunday night. As-as-as welcome as a glass of cold water in the middle of the night when the ham's been too salty. Oh, Kitty, I can't say clever things but

I want to be the hot-water bottle that melts your frozen heart.'

'Oh, blimey!' Kitty was fighting back the tears as she gazed up at him. 'You're so 'andsome, you oughta be on every Mills and Boon jacket but the girls the 'eroes gaze at don't look anyfink like me.'

Now it was Lysander's turn to grit his jaw.

'Of course they don't. They're pretty.' He ran his hand wonderingly over her blushing, squashed little face. 'But you're beautiful. And you're beautiful inside, too, like Arthur.'

Realizing how huge a compliment this was, Kitty managed not to laugh.

Encouraged, Lysander suggested they romp in the Jacuzzi. But Kitty's face clouded over.

'We shouldn't. I'm married.'

'Don't be ridiculous.' Lysander only just stopped himself cataloguing Rannaldini's women.

'Anyway, it was so lovely, kissin' you,' sighed Kitty. 'I couldn't stop.'

'That's the general idea.' Lysander began to unbutton her dress then, seeing her apprehension, 'Let's discuss it over dinner. Go and change.' He yawned. 'I love you, Kitty.'

But when she came out, jet lag had overtaken him. He was slumped, fast asleep, on the sofa, red juice running down his chin, a half-eaten pomegranate on the floor.

'Good night, Suite Prince,' murmured Kitty, who had done *Hamlet* at school, wrapping her duvet round him. She was going to allow herself the luxury of watching him all night.

At dawn she drifted into a heavy sleep in her armchair and was woken by the telephone. She remembered the clipped, contemptuous drawl from Rannaldini's answering machine.

'I thought Lysander was coming off-piste with me,' said Rupert.

The fact that Lysander was apologizing sleepily on the same telephone a few seconds later did nothing to assuage Rupert's suspicions. Lysander could use the money Kitty paid him as a gigolo to run after Taggie.

'Where are you going?' asked Kitty, feeding Lysander croissant spread with apricot jam as he groggily tugged on his yellow ski pants.

'Somewhere he called Chute des Fantômes, Shoot to Kill, I dunno. I'll ski down as fast as I can. At least I can bend Rupert's ear about Arthur.'

It had snowed heavily in the night, blotting out yesterday's footprints and ski tracks, putting five inches on the parked cars and President de Gaulle's cap in the town square. Glancing out of the window, Kitty saw Rupert's dark blue Mercedes draw up. Getting out, he looked as chill and menacing as the day. Suddenly Kitty was frightened.

'Please be careful,' she said, brushing crumbs off Lysander's chin and handing him his sweat band.

Gazing down a cliff face steep as a lift shaft, three-quarters of an hour later, Lysander wondered why the hell he'd come.

Deliberately sitting two seats away from Lysander in the helicopter on the way up, Rupert hadn't spoken a word. The putty-grey skies, liverishly tinged with yellow, presaged further heavy snow. A howling blizzard chucked glass splinters in their faces. Below, the skein of ski runs and the fir trees herring-boning the side of the valley blurred as the visibility grew worse. Far, far down, the houses of the village, one of them containing darling Kitty, lay like ants on the snow. Lysander's yellow ski clothes were the only note of colour in the black-and-white magpie landscape. Rupert's slit eyes through his dark glasses were anything but friendly.

'OK?' he asked Lysander.

Lysander nodded, teeth chattering far more from terror than the bitter cold.

'I'll lead the way,' and Rupert was off, hissing down the valley like a falling meteor, hidden in a permanent spray of snow.

'I love you, Kitty,' shouted Lysander to the whirling snowflakes. 'Dear God, take me back safe to her.'

And he was off, careering after Rupert, crouched like a jockey so low over his skis that his hands were higher than his face, furiously stabbing with his poles as he tried to recapture his old skill and adjust to the rhythm.

Within seconds, as Lysander streaked past him, Rupert realized he was outclassed. Although once almost Olympic standard, he was now nearly twenty years older and lacked the boy's suppleness, extreme fitness and split-second timing. Rupert really had to force himself to keep up and all the time was aware of going far too fast as trees rushed to meet him and crevasses loomed below. Only by straining every muscle did he avoid catapulting to his death. Almost more goading was that, once in his stride, Lysander started enjoying himself, showing off his miraculous control by going into a series of long, bounding jumps like a lurcher trying to see over the barley, each time landing perfectly. Going so fast round the final bend, he lost a ski and carried on with one, shooting straight into the bar three-quarters of the way down the mountain.

He was waiting when Rupert arrived, giggling with nervous hysteria, his cheeks flushed, his hands round a glass of Kir.

'Jesus, that was hairy. I thought the wind was going to pound me to bits. Thank Christ we're in one piece. I got you a whisky.'

Rupert was absolutely furious with himself. He might never have seen Taggie, the children or his dogs again – just because he wanted to scare the daffodil-yellow pants out of this cocky little sod.

'You come down the Ghost Valley today?' asked the barman incredulously, putting a bowl of pretzels between them. 'Mad Englishmen and dogs! You know why eet called that?'

Lysander shook his head.

'Because so many people been keeled. At night their ghosts ski down mountain. Local people no go near it.'

The sun was hot now, melting the snow which splodged every fir tree like soap suds. Rupert clutched his glass of whisky to stop his hand shaking. The boy's languid beauty, his rumpled brown curls, his big, generous mouth emphasized by white lipsalve, his endless legs up on the wooden table, only increased Rupert's dislike and jealousy.

Not understanding why Rupert was looking marginally less friendly than a rattlesnake with a hangover, but desperate to placate him, Lysander said: 'I thought Taggie, I mean Mrs Campbell-Black, was seriously beautiful.'

'Which is more than can be said for Mrs Rannaldini.'

Refusing to be goaded, Lysander gazed into his glass. Mistaking stillness for passivity, Rupert became almost chatty.

'Your hotel's dripping with gigolo fodder. Surely you could have found someone more glamorous than that cow to pick up your bills. I appreciate there's a recession on and you have to take what you can get.' Draining his glass, Rupert waved to the barman to refill their glasses, adding to Lysander, 'It's OK, the rest of the run's a doddle. I'm amazed Rannaldini's married,' the drawl was becoming slower and bitchier, 'to such a boot. Did her face get stuck in a lift door? No wonder he doesn't let her out before sunset. Still I suppose there's no accounting for lack of taste.'

Next minute, Rupert found himself on his back on the floor of the bar.

'Don't ever speak about Kitty like that again,' yelled Lysander. 'She's the nicest, sweetest, loveliest woman I've ever met.'

As Rupert fingered his jaw and pondered whether to throw Lysander out of the window down the precipice, he decided there was no way Lysander could be after Taggie if he leapt to Kitty's defence like that.

After that, Rupert and Lysander skiied down the rest of the mountain and, in the course of getting rather drunk together, Rupert even confessed to his reservations about being a grandfather and cramping Taggie's style.

'I feel I've stolen her youth, but I hate any man that looks at her. I wanted to kill you this morning.'

'That's OK,' said Lysander. 'I'd have killed you if you'd gone on bitching about Kitty or tried to take her off me. Did you really think I was after Taggie?'

'You couldn't stop staring at her last night.'

'I was staring at you.' Lysander blushed furiously. 'I've always hero-worshipped you – even more than Donald Duck. Look what Kitty made me.' Proudly he unzipped his yellow jacket to show off his jersey.

'Anyway, to go back to you, my parents had a terrible row because my father thought I was too young to be allowed to stay up and watch you win your bronze in the middle of the night at Colombia.'

'How old were you?'

'Seven.'

'Gee, thanks.' said Rupert wryly.

Swearing Rupert to secrecy, Lysander explained, in his confiding way, how he had amassed quite a fortune, admittedly totally masterminded by Ferdie, making husbands jealous.

'But now I'm in love with Kitty I've got to find a proper job so I can support her.'

'You could be a presenter at Venturer,' said Rupert. 'All you have to do is to read an autocue.'

Lysander shook his head. 'You're really kind, but I'm dyslexic. It takes me all morning to read the runners in the *Sun*, or DO NOT DISTURB notices on hotel bedrooms.'

Rupert was touched. Taggie was dyslexic and he knew what heroic efforts she had made to overcome it.

'What I really want to do is work with horses,' went on Lysander. 'I'm going to get Arthur sound, and have one more crack at the Rutminster.'

'Penscombe Pride's going to win that,' said Rupert. 'But Arthur was a good horse, I remember him winning in Ireland.'

'He still gets fan mail and Twix bars in the post.'

The sun was setting as Rupert dropped Lysander off at the Hotel Versailles. The next moment he was knocked sideways by Kitty, blue with cold and hysterical with worry, shooting across the icy pavements into his arms.

'I was so worried. You was so long. I fort you might have been killed. Fousands of people 'ave died in Ghost Valley.' And she kissed him over and over again. 'I was so worried Rupert took you there deliberately.'

'No, no, he's been wonderful and so are you.'

Delighted with her response, Lysander pulled Kitty through the revolving doors, kissing her on and on until the porters, the receptionists and all the glamorous people grouped round the tables stopped chattering and drinking and gave them a round of applause.

'I should have rung.' Oblivious of the attention they were causing, Lysander led her towards the lift. 'I didn't mean to frighten you. Let's go and try out that Jacuzzi before I stiffen up.'

*'In a place that won't let us feel,
in a life where nothing seems real
I have found you, I have found you,'* sang Lysander tunelessly as he lay in eighteen inches of warm, scented, churning water soaping Kitty's breasts as they gently juddered above the surface. At first she had been desperately embarrassed because Rannaldini had shaved off her pubic hair.

'I was the only person 'ere for 'im to sleep wiv,' she confessed. 'The au pair's father works for *Le Monde* so he couldn't risk it.'

Lysander hid his anger by saying she looked adorable and more like a little piglet than ever and Rannaldini was obviously obsessed with strimming paths to exciting places. Kitty then said Rachel would disapprove of such deforestation, and laughed and felt better. Glancing in the darkened mirrors lining the wall, she felt almost beautiful for the first time in her life and put her hand under the water.

'It's no good, I *have* stiffened up,' admitted Lysander as his rampant cock reared above the surface.

'It's like a periscope,' said Kitty, stroking it.

'Looking for its target. Come on.'

Rising out of the bath, he carried her, dripping, next door, drenching the pink chintz roses as he dropped her gently on to the counterpane of the huge four-poster.

They didn't bother to draw the curtains. Outside, duck-egg-green shadows lay on the snow, the stars were brilliant in the clear, frosty night. The ring of silent, blue mountains beyond seemed to protect them.

'I love you,' murmured Lysander as he slowly stroked her pink wet body into a state of ecstasy. Then, as he sat up and drew her between his thighs and slithered inside her, 'A-a-a-ah, ooo – it's heaven. Like the soft, pink fingers of a milkmaid squeezing me. Oh help,' he wailed, 'I can never hold out if I really fancy someone and I want you more than anyone ever. Oh God, oh help, I'm sorry, Kitty darling.'

The difference between Rannaldini and Lysander, reflected Kitty, was that although Rannaldini played with her and kept going for hours, she always felt he was like a pianist polishing his technique for a big concert which wouldn't be with her. With Lysander she felt she was the big occasion he had practised for all his life.

'Oh, Kitty,' he echoed her thoughts, 'I've fucked so many times in my life, but this is truly the first time I've ever made love. Now it's my turn to give you pleasure. Promise to tell me exactly what you like.' Then, when she was embarrassed, he said, 'I always wanted to be a Brickie-layer when I grew up,' and collapsed with such laughter that she joined in too, and started to relax.

Afterwards, she said truthfully, 'That was ubsolutely mudgic, Lysunder.'

'Let's do it all over again at the gallop,' he said, kissing her, 'but if we're not going to die of rheumatism we better sleep in one of the other beds. I'm just going to have a pee.'

Tottering, dizzy with love, into the bathroom five minutes later, Kitty saw that Lysander had taken the hideous crimson lipstick Cecilia had given her for Christmas and scrawled across the mirror: KITTY IS FOR LYFE NOT JUST FOR KRISTMASS.

Next door a five-eighth moon with a white, wistful nun's face was peering in through the window at the sprawled naked beauty of a waiting Lysander. Running into the room, Kitty flung herself on him, burying her face in his silvery chest.

'All my life,' she whispered, 'I've longed to have moonlight and someone I loved at the same time.'

'I keep wanting to ring Mum and tell her how wonderful you are,' said Lysander.

51

But as Shakespeare's Lysander pointed out four hundred years before, *'the course of true love never did run smooth'*. The Press, trailing Rupert and clocking everyone who spent time with him, took photographs of Lysander kissing Kitty in the foyer. Plied with a fat bribe the hotel porter revealed that the President de Gaulle suite was now being paid for by a Mr L. Hawkley. The picture-desk promptly identified Lysander as the man making husbands jealous and Kitty, from her brief appearance at the airport, as Rannaldini's wife.

Coming out of the Abbey Road recording studios with Rachel the following evening after they'd recorded the taxing first movement of Brahms' First Piano Concerto, Rannaldini was confronted by a reporter and a photographer.

'Mr Rannaldini, we wondered what you thought about these photographs of your wife in France.'

A swift inspection was enough.

'What paper are you from?' exploded Rannaldini.

'Today.'

Rannaldini raised his fist. 'You'll be from Yesterday if you're not careful.' Shoving them furiously aside, he dived into the waiting Mercedes. Clive, who'd had plenty of practice, slammed the doors and, racing round to the driving seat, took off into the night leaving Rachel with hardly a penny to get home.

In Monthaut, Kitty was reading *Pigling Bland* to Rannaldini's children – very slowly – so they could understand the English. Lysander lounged at the end of the bed listening. He had always loved the story which his mother had often read him and he thought how alike were Kitty and Pig Wig, the little black pig heroine, with her double chin and her blue-flowered smock. How nice if he and Kitty could escape to freedom together away from Rannaldini over the county boundary. He wished he was as noble a character as Pigling Bland.

'*Over the hills and far away, she danced with Pigling Bland,*' read Kitty, closing the book. 'Now you must all try and go to sleep.'

As she kissed each of them, Lysander wandered back into the sitting room and without thinking picked up a ringing telephone.

'Who's that?' yelled Rannaldini.

Lysander hung up.

'Who was that who answered?' demanded Rannaldini when he rang a second time.

'No-one. You must have dialled the wrong number.'

She's learning, thought Lysander, but as he sloshed vodka into two glasses he could hear Rannaldini's tantrum right across the room, and, as Kitty clumsily replaced the receiver and glared at him in anguish, he could hear the slither of magic carpet crashing back to earth.

'I've got to go back. It's all over the papers.'

'So what? It doesn't matter. We're what matters.'

'You're Natasha's boyfriend.'

'Bullshit, I hate her. I've never paid her the slightest attention. That's Rannaldini stirring it.'

'And I am 'is wife.'

'You can't stay with him.' Aghast, Lysander bounded across the room but, as he took her in his arms he could feel her distancing.

'He's old and evil.'

'He needs me.' Kitty took a tangerine from the fruit bowl and having peeled it threw the pigs into the waste-paper basket and started to eat the peel.

'You're like that spare blanket in the cupboard.' Taking the peel from her, Lysander shoved a vodka into her shaking hand. 'Rannaldini gets you down when he's cold. I'll look after you, Kitty. We can run over the hills and far away. I know you love me.' Her face, when he forced it upwards, was as pale and filled with longing as last night's moon.

'That was infatuation.'

'No, it wasn't. Why did you waste an entire suitcase bringing Lassie out here?' Triumphantly Lysander pulled a case from under the bed and unearthed the collie he'd bought her in Harrods toy department.

Kitty went scarlet. 'I fort the kids might like to play wiv her.'

'Why haven't they then?'

'I've got to go home tomorrow,' whispered Kitty.

'Then I'm coming with you.'

He wished Rupert hadn't flown back to England, or he would have enlisted his help to persuade Kitty not to return.

The journey home was crucifixion, worse than going back to school, worse than his mother dying. Surrounded by children incensed to be going home four days early, aware of the Press everywhere, Kitty and Lysander didn't touch each other and exchanged not a word. Both grey beneath their suntan, neither had slept.

In duty-free Lysander bought a large bottle of Diorissimo. Despite the number of times he'd bought it he still pronounced it 'Diorimisso', and the girl behind the counter smiled because he was so handsome.

'It was Mum's favourite scent,' he said, handing it to Kitty. 'I want you to wear it because,' his voice broke, 'because now I love you more even than I loved her.'

After the champagne air and the dazzling white and blue of the mountains, Heathrow was grey and bitterly cold. A vicious wind whipped Kitty's green dress over her head as she stepped out of the plane. She was trembling so badly Lysander gave her his coat.

Worst of all, the customs men took one look at Lysander's

polo sticks and the mass of chattering Italian children and, opening everything, finally discovered Lassie.

'Oh, please not,' whispered Kitty.

'Funny thing to hide in a suitcase,' said a brutish-looking customs man.

'I gave it to Mrs Rannaldini,' snapped Lysander.

'Pull the other leg.'

'Leave it fucking alone.'

'Don't you get lippy with me, sunshine.' The customs man took out a penknife, and with relish plunged it into Lassie's defenceless fluffy white throat and proceeded slowly to rip her brown-and-white body to bits, finally even cutting off her shiny leather nose and gouging out her eyes.

Rannaldini's children were all screaming hysterically. Lysander thought Kitty was going to faint. Only her desperate pleading stopped him leaping across the table and beating the customs man to a pulp, particularly when without a word of apology he handed back Lassie's remains.

'I'll get you another one to replace her, and I'll get you, you bastard.' Lysander was nearly in tears, too. 'Oh, Kitty, please don't go back to Rannaldini. Let's get a taxi to Fountain Street.'

Out in the airport they went slap into a cauldron of Press, seething for a story. But the ubiquitous Clive was waiting to pounce and soon had bundled Kitty and the children into a suitably funereal-black limousine and out on to the M4.

Rannaldini had had a nasty shock. He had never imagined anyone fancying Kitty. But in the photographs plastered all over *Today* and in the later editions of most of the papers, he noticed her gazing up at that winsome little snake with such happiness that she looked almost pretty.

He felt his publicity getting worse and worse. He was sure that shit Campbell-Black wouldn't be able to resist circulating the pirate version of 'Once in Royal David's City'. He knew he was favourite for the New York job but

Boris Levitsky's *Symphony* had just won a prize for the best-orchestral work of the year (and Boris had conducted it himself at the Mozart Hall to ecstatic reviews and puzzled, but enthusiastic, applause). While Rannaldini had been skiing, according to Clive, Boris had also been over twice to see Rachel and the children. The last thing Rannaldini wanted was these two getting together.

If he was going to clinch the New York job he must mend his marriage at once.

He therefore curbed his initial instinct which was to beat Kitty up on her return. And when she came through the front door just holding back the tears and waiting, trembling violently, for the tolling of the punishment bell, Rannaldini promptly despatched the children to Mrs Brimscombe and roast chicken and chips in the kitchen and drew her into the red morning room.

After the bleak, bitter day, nothing could have been more welcoming. Apple logs crackled merrily in the grate, side lamps cast soft light on huge dark blue bowls of white hyacinths, and on the soft red roses and peonies of the Aubusson which flowed over the entire floor. Instead of the usual deafening Stockhausen or Shostakovitch the stereo was playing *My Fair Lady*. Even Rannaldini himself looked more approachable in old brown cords, a yellow-checked shirt and a dark brown cashmere jersey, which seemed to bring out softer brown flecks in the hard black eyes, and he was smiling at her with such tenderness.

'I'm ever so sorry, Rannaldini,' Kitty's teeth were chattering so frantically she could hardly get the words out.

'Hush, hush, all that matters is that you are home. Come here, my lovely child.'

Taking her blue frozen hands he drew her close, gently stroking her cheek, which was rigid with tension, as she waited for the first blow from the back of his hand.

'I'm so sorry about the Press and fings.'

'What does the stupid Press matter?' sighed Rannaldini. 'Seeing you in Lysander's arms bring me to my senses. I 'ave the worst twenty-four hours of my life.'

571

Expecting screaming abuse, the thumbscrew, the stapler punched through the hand, Kitty looked up in bewilderment.

'*I've grown accustomed to her face, she seems to make the day begin,*' sang Rex Harrison.

'My sentiments entirely,' said Rannaldini, kissing her forehead and then her trembling lips.

'You're not angry?'

'Only with myself for neglecting you. All my cheeldren adore you, even Natasha. She reeng me in such distress this morning. Papa, don't let Kitty go. She is very upset, of course. Lysander 'ave often tell her he love her, and keep ringing up from Switzerland.' That hurts her, thought Rannaldini with satisfaction, seeing Kitty flinch.

'Of course he chase Natasha,' he went on. 'She will be very rich woman eef I die. So will you, Kitty, and that ees not so impossible.' He waved away her protests. 'Theenking you might not come back, I contemplate ending it all.' Pulling open a desk drawer he pointed to a black pistol.

'Oh no, Rannaldini!' Kitty was horrified. 'You mustn't do anyfing like that.'

'Not eef I have you.' Banging the drawer shut Rannaldini went to the drinks table and poured Kitty a large brandy. 'But I have many problems. Catchitune have gone belly-up. Larry is ruined.'

'Oh, poor Larry and poor Marigold.'

'Poor me,' said Rannaldini fretfully. 'Catchitune owe me meelions of pounds. We will have to find a new record company, theenk of the new contracts to be drawn up.' Then, seeing the exhaustion on Kitty's face, 'But forget that. Theenk only of us, my Keety, and come with me to the tower.' His hand slid round her waist, sliding upwards to caress her breast with infinite gentleness, then down to stroke her bottom, giving it a quick vicious pinch.

'You are made for love, Keety, and now perhaps a

leetle punishment for being such a naughty girl. Drink up your brandy and I will blot out all memory of that promiscuous greedy little gigolo.'

'He's not,' gasped Kitty.

'Oh, my dear!' Picking up a woodlice crawling across the hearth, Rannaldini tossed it into the fire. 'Don't make me shatter any more of your illusions. You must promise never to see him again.'

Even worse was Lysander's return to Magpie Cottage. Paradise had never looked bleaker. A sadistic east wind whipped the last leaves across the sallow fields. The frantically threshing branches of the trees tangled like antlers. Rannaldini, the wily old buck, was despatching the young pretender into the forest. He never should have let Kitty go. It was his fault. If he'd been able to keep his hands off her in public they'd have got away with it. He was terrified of Rannaldini's vengeance and for a sickening moment over the wind and rain thought he could hear the punishment bell tolling at Valhalla, then realized it was only the church clock striking twelve. It seemed like midnight. How could he get through the rest of his life?

The cottage smelt damp and sour. The doormat was covered in letters, mostly brown envelopes. In the fridge he found a half-eaten pheasant crawling with maggots and, shuddering, threw it in the bin. Pouring himself the dregs of a bottle of vodka he topped it with tonic as flat as his life and only bothered to open three letters, each of which plunged him into deeper despair.

The first was from the vet saying he was 99 per cent sure Arthur had contracted navicular disease which meant he was a write-off for racing.

'Oh, poor darling Arthur.' But Lysander couldn't really absorb such a bodyblow in his present shell-shocked condition. The second letter didn't need a stamp. Marigold wrote:

Dearest Lysander,
I'm terribly sorry but poor Larry's been voted off the
Catchitune board so we won't be able to pay you
your monthly retainer any more, but I hope Georgie
is still paying you, and we've got to put The Grange
and Magpie Cottage on the market at once. You can
stay until we sell it, but please try to keep it tidy
because agents will be showing people round. Don't
worry about Larry and me, we're OK.

On a happier note, although I can't afford the
£10,000 bonus, congratulations on getting Rannaldini
back for Kitty. He was really rocked by those pictures
in Today. *Larry, who saw him afterwards, said he*
minded much more about them than Catchitune going
belly-up. And you managed to look really in love with
Kitty – you are a good actor. Rannaldini's so jumpy
he'll be dropping all his mistresses soon, even that
old bat Hermione. Hope to see you at Rachel's party
tomorrow evening. Love, Marigold.

Rain was sweeping down the valley like a ghost cavalry
charge. Lysander started to shake; all his old insecurities
came hurtling back. He had lost his true love. If he
moved out of the cottage, where would all the animals
and, hopefully, Kitty, live? Poor Marigold, too – going
up the spout. He'd had a lot of money from her. His
trembling hand had great difficulty in writing her a cheque
for thirty thousand pounds. He didn't want to be paid
a bean for saving Kitty's marriage. He'd better ring his
bank sometime and find out how much he'd got left. Or
perhaps Ferdie could do that for him. He must ring up
and get the dogs back and talk of the devil, here was a
letter from Ferdie. How odd, Ferdie never wrote letters
and his handwriting on the envelope looked really crazy.

Dear Lysander, I'm afraid Maggie's dead. Lysander
gave a moan of horror. *She wasn't getting fat like*
we thought, she was pregnant and pining so much for

*you she wouldn't eat. She had no strength and died
giving birth to three puppies. Two were still born.
I'm feeding the third with a bottle.*

'Oh God,' whispered Lysander; he read on: *I just
want you to know that you can't go on fucking up people
and animals like this and dodging your responsibilities.
You plucked Maggie out of hell, made her fall in love
with you and dumped her. And from those pix in* Today
*you've done the same to Kitty. I'm fed up with picking
up the pieces. I'll leave Jack with Marigold. I don't
want to see you any more. You're on your own.*

Lysander was distraught. Poor darling, little Maggie, the
most adorable dog in the world, who'd given him nothing
but love, starving herself to death, and sweet darling Kitty,
and Ferdie, his dearest friend, whom he'd totally taken for
granted. How could he have behaved so appallingly to all
of them? Shivering, he threw himself down on the damp
grey sheets and sobbed himself to sleep. Waking two hours
later, the light was already fading and he felt so desolate
he dialled Valhalla even though he'd promised not to. At
first he thought Kitty was a recording machine, her voice
was so high, stilted and unnatural.

'I can't see you any more.'

'I can't live without you,' he jibbered in panic, 'and
Maggie's dead.'

'Oh, Lysander.' For a second, Kitty's voice faltered,
'I'm ever so sorry, but I still can't see you. Rannaldini's
forgiven me. I've got to save my marriage.'

'What marriage? You're married to Saddam Hussein.'

'He's frettening to kill hisself if I leaves 'im. Fank
you for everyfink. God bless you and I'm sorry about
Maggie.'

It took Lysander five dials to get Rupert's number
right.

'Oh, Rupert, Rupert, I'm really sorry to bother you, but
Kitty won't see me any more and Rannaldini's threatening
suicide.'

'That old trick,' said Rupert scornfully. 'No doubt he'll get Kitty to run off suicide notes on her word processor for all his mistresses. I've just been watching the tape of the nativity play. Christ, it's funny. I must send Flora some flowers.'

'And Arthur's got navicular,' said Lysander despairingly.

'Bring him over tomorrow. I'll have a look.'

'Are you sure? D'you mind having Tiny as well? She's such a bitch, but Arthur pines without her.'

52

The only reason Lysander went to Rachel's party was in the hope of seeing Kitty. It was another mean night. Black ice gripped the winding Rutshire roads. A savage wind chivvied woolly sepia clouds across the stars. Rachel's barrel of rainwater was frozen solid. Although Jasmine Cottage was, if anything, colder in than out, the party gave an initial illusion of success because the twenty-five odd guests crammed into a small room, dominated by a large black grand piano, had to yell to be heard, par-ticularly as Rachel had turned up Rannaldini's CD of Shostakovich's *Fifth* fortissimo.

'Thank God you've come – I need spare men,' shouted Rachel, her welcome vanishing when she saw Jack tucked inside Lysander's coat.

'I hope that beast won't chase Scarlatti. Can't he stay in the car?'

'He'd freeze to death. Happy birthday,' said Lysander, unable to meet her eyes he disliked her so much, as he handed over a bottle of Moët.

'You spoil me,' said Rachel mockingly. 'I've had so much booze, anyone would think I had a drink problem.'

Lysander's hopes that he might get one decent drink were dashed when she promptly put the Moët in the cupboard with the other bottles, saying she'd keep it for special occasions.

Your next bonk with Rannaldini, thought Lysander in disgust. He was sure that the huge brown mohair jersey and the thigh boots in softest mushroom-pink leather she was looking so good in were more presents from the Maestro. Glancing round the room he noticed an elaborate new stereo system, shelves filled with Rannaldini's tapes and records and a piano stool exquisitely embroidered with yellow pansies. And poor darling Kitty got a filing cabinet for Christmas!

'Hot apple punch or exotic fruit cup?' asked Rachel, brandishing a ladle.

'Whichever's the strongest.'

'People seem to prefer the cup.' Rachel handed him a green glass of fruit salad. 'Come and meet some of my London friends.'

Such a description presupposed some degree of glamour and sophistication, but Lysander found himself faced by a row of all-time dinginess: Anita Brookner heroines with long pale faces and longer pale cardigans desperately trying to warm dirndl-skirted bottoms in front of a desperately anaemic fire.

'This is the local stud I told you about,' Rachel whispered.

Already dominating the group was Guy. Still high on his television success as St Joseph, he had received stacks of fan mail and been the subject of an *Independent* profile comparing the ways Joseph took Mary away privily and Guy the *Rock Star* had stood by Georgie.

'You made so many statements in *Nativity Green*,' said one of Rachel's friends, displaying armpit hair that was a positive fire hazard as she reached for her glass. 'I liked the bit when you calmly changed Baby Jesus's nappy during the shepherd's visit.'

Guy smiled in acknowledgement, then, turning to Lysander, towards whom he now felt quite well disposed since he had proof he wasn't after Georgie: 'How was skiing?'

'Lovely.'

'Don't you feel guilty,' reproved another London friend, 'about the way skiing disrupts the ecological balance.'

'I didn't know it did,' said Lysander, longing to spit out his first mouthful of fruit cup.

'Skiers hurtling down the mountains trigger off avalanches and disturb the wildlife,' he was told earnestly. 'Not to mention deforestation.'

Deforestation! With a stab of anguish Lysander remembered giggling over Kitty's shaved bush. He hated all these long, pale supercilious faces for not being round, pink and smiling like hers.

'Have some blotting paper,' interrupted Rachel, handing round sausage rolls.

'Thanks.' Lysander broke one in half, giving it to Jack.

'Are you sure they don't contain meat?' asked a London friend nervously.

Jack promptly confirmed this by spitting his all over the carpet.

'Excuse me,' said Lysander, 'I must go and talk to Meredith,' who, with his airborne curls and merry blue eyes, seemed the nearest thing to Kitty in the room.

'Hallo, baby boy,' said Meredith.

'I go to parties to dance and get wasted,' sighed Lysander. 'What the hell's in this drink?'

'Most of Rachel's Body Shop concoctions I should think. Certainly no booze.'

'Christ, I wondered why I was getting lower.'

'Hallo, you sweet thing.' Meredith stroked Jack's rough white head but the little dog could hardly wag his tail.

'He's pissed off. To him parties mean chops, chicken and sausages, proper human food. He'll eat Rachel's cat in a minute.'

'I'm sorry about Maggie. Poor old you.'

Lysander nodded, not trusting himself to speak.

'How's Arthur?'

'I took him over to Rupert Campbell-Black's yard this afternoon.'

'Did you now? What's it like?'

'Seriously impressive: swimming-baths, solarium, computers, a resident blood analyst and such terrific horses. I actually patted Penscombe Pride. God, what a beautiful horse, but he's really small. Rupert's going to try and sort Arthur out.'

'Lucky Arthur,' sighed Meredith. 'Rupert's to die for and dye for.' He patted his blond curls in the mirror.

'He can be quite fierce,' said Lysander.

'Oh, I love that. Treat 'em mean, keep 'em keen.'

'Taggie, Rupert's wife, was really sweet. She made Arthur a bowl of coffee to make him feel at home, but he still sulked dreadfully when I left. I don't think I'm very good at making anything happy,' he added dolefully.

'Mrs Rannaldini looked pretty cheerful in *Today*,' said Meredith, noticing the way Lysander's bloodshot eyes kept darting towards the door.

'She *is* coming this evening, isn't she?'

'Well, Hermione and Bob have just arrived,' said Meredith. 'And Madam wouldn't grace a grisly jaunt like this unless she was expecting Maestro.'

'Christ, it's cold,' said Lysander. 'No wonder Rachel doesn't bother with a deep freeze.'

'Here are the lovers,' said Meredith as a battered Marigold and Larry entered hand in hand. 'Go anywhere for a free drink these days. All the same it's sad to see the FOR SALE sign outside Paradise Grange. Your friend Ferdie's got his board up already. Whoever buys it can't not want to redecorate it. I better get in there early and give Ferdie a ring.'

Lysander couldn't bear to talk about Ferdie either. He missed him dreadfully and was trying to screw up courage to ring him and apologize. Oh God, here was Hermione.

'Hallo, Mary,' said Guy, turning from the admiring circle of London friends to waylay her.

'Hallo, Joseph,' said Hermione skittishly, 'I've just been talking to the *Independent* about Me and My Cat.'

'What a coincidence,' laughed Guy. 'I've just done a long interview with the *Guardian* on Me and My Work Station.'

'I am going to leave Guy,' hissed Georgie to Marigold. 'He's been so uppity since the play. Look at him being drooled over by all those dreary friends of Rachel's.'

'Well, he is charming,' protested Marigold. 'How's Flora?'

'Desperately low. Oh, Marigold, I made a New Year's resolution to look after her and make my marriage better and I'd broken it by Christmas Eve when Guy insisted a little unsigned Victorian love note on his desk had come from some picture framers.'

'I made a New Year's resolution not to maind about not havin' any money,' sighed Marigold, 'but the boys have decided they rather like boarding-school. And every taime I see the FOR SALE sign swinging outside Paradise Grange, Ay burst into tears.'

'I can't think why you're making such a fuss, Marigold.' Hermione, who was still wearing Rannaldini's mink Christmas present and quite oblivious of the glares of Rachel's Green friends, barged between them.

'You were always telling me how blissfully happy you and Larry were when you were poor. It's far worse for me having to renegotiate all my contracts. Larry might have warned us he was going bankrupt.'

'If you and Rannaldini hadn't screwed such vast advances out of him, never maind the jets and the ten-star hotels, it maight never have happened,' said Marigold furiously.

'Oh, don't over-react,' sighed Hermione. Then, turning to Georgie, 'I must tell you what a wonderful man Guy is, so caring and supportive.'

'He was certainly supporting your bum pretty often in the video of the nativity play,' snarled Georgie.

A hot apple punch-up was avoided by Rachel staggering in with a huge casserole dish. All the husbands except Guy, who was too frightened of Georgie, leapt to her assistance.

Bob got there first. 'Looks good. What is it?'

'Organic oat risotto,' said Rachel, 'with artichokes and haricot beans. Take a plate, Meredith.'

'I'm OK at the moment,' replied Meredith who was

blue with cold. 'When it's a toss-up,' he murmured to Lysander, 'between dying of hypothermia and farting like a drayhorse all night, I choose the former. Shall I get some more logs, Rachel?'

'I'm as warm as toast,' said Hermione smugly. 'I've got my thermals on and I had a nice hot bath before I came out.'

'Baths are a waste of water,' snapped Rachel, piling food on to plates, 'you should have a shower, or share the bath water with someone.'

'I'd share a bath with you any time, Rachie,' joked Guy, getting a black look from Georgie. 'You've got a terrific crowd here.'

'Oh, people are so bored with cooking over Christmas they'll go anywhere for a free meal,' said Hermone airily.

Fascinated by Lysander's beauty a London friend edged forward to stroke Jack.

'I suppose you use him for digging out foxes.'

'No, only for fouling footpaths and children's playgrounds,' said Meredith. 'Cheer up, it may never happen, Lysander.'

'That's what I'm frightened of,' said Lysander dolefully.

'I'm off to raid that drinks cupboard.' Meredith lowered his voice. 'Like Captain Organic Oates, I may be gone some time. Keep our hostess occupied.'

But Lysander didn't have to bother for, as Meredith sidled off, Rannaldini walked in. He looked feral and aggressively decadent in a black shirt and cords which matched his predatory eyes and a vast, almost floor-length coat made of wolf pelts which seemed an extension of his hair and set off his Monthaut suntan. And like a wolf entering the fold he mesmerized the room.

I can't wait for everyone to go, thought Rachel, then he can make love with me in front of the fire.

Rannaldini nodded at Hermione and Bob, then, running his eyes over the long-faced carecrows from London, found nothing to interest him.

'Where's your much better half, Rannaldini?' asked Meredith, sliding a cup of neat whisky into Lysander's grateful hand.

'In bed.'

'Is Brickie ill?' asked Guy.

'Just pleasantly exhausted, she sent her apologies.' Rannaldini smiled evilly at Lysander. 'All Keety need was a leetle loving.'

Jack gave a yelp then understandingly licked Lysander's face when his master apologized for gripping him so hard.

'It's disgusting the way they boil the roots of Christmas trees so they can't be replanted,' chuntered a London friend.

Looking at Lysander so white and distraught, Bob remembered the larky, radiant young blood who'd stopped even the music in its tracks at Georgie's *Rock Star* party.

'Come and have supper one day this week.' He put a hand on Lysander's arm. 'Hermione's off to Rome.'

'Thanks, but I gotta go.' Lysander emptied his cup of whisky. Through in the kitchen, he could see Scarlatti scraping his litter tray and, reminded of Aunt Dinah, nearly blacked out. Next moment Jack had wriggled out of his grasp and, scattering cat litter, chased Scarlatti out through the cat flap.

'That's no way to save planet earth box,' giggled Meredith. 'Shall I open a window and let in a little hot air? There's a bit of a pong.'

'I told you not to bring that dog,' snapped Rachel. 'You can't go yet. The party hasn't started.'

'Sorry, I've got to. Bye, Bob, bye, Meredith, bye, Marigold,' muttered Lysander and, gathering up his long coat from the hall chair, he rushed off into the night.

'Well, we know who *he* likes,' said Rachel, furious at losing her only heterosexual spare man, although it was good Rannaldini had come on his own, not that Kitty ever really inhibited him.

'I'm not going to drink this goat's piss,' said Rannaldini,

pouring his exotic fruit cup over a depressed-looking yucca. 'Get me a whisky, Rachel.' Then, turning to Larry, 'How are things? I assume your tiny assets are frozen.'

Feeling neglected because Rannaldini hadn't even come over and kissed her, Hermione decided to check her face before approaching him. Crossing the hall as she went upstairs to the bathroom, she found a letter on the carpet which a distraught Lysander had dropped on the way out. Seeing the letterhead: PARADISE GRANGE she read on. Ignoring the posters about banning additives from school dinners and protecting the natterjack toad, she sat down on the edge of the bath. A smile spread over her face and a glow suffused her body as she read.

Hermione had always been irked and mystified that Lysander had never made a pass at her, nor even chatted her up. Now she knew why. She was about the only wife in Paradise who hadn't paid him to. Stepping into the bath she used the shower to wash between her legs and cleaned her teeth with Rachel's organic toothpaste. Returning to the party, she whispered in Rannaldini's ear, then turning to Rachel triumphantly: 'Lovely do, darling. Must go. I've got work to do on *Wozzeck*. See you later, Bobbie.'

Almost immediately, to Rachel's fury, she was followed by Rannaldini.

Half an hour later in the blissful warmth of the tower Hermione sipped a glass of Krug and watched Rannaldini reading Marigold's letter to Lysander for the second time.

'Well done,' he said softly, as conflicting emotions of fury, excitement, passion, hatred and jealousy flickered across his face.

'What a very silly letter to drop. So Georgie and Marigold paid little Mr Hawkley to retrieve their husbands; and Martha Winterton as well presumably. It always puzzled me how he lives so well.'

'Georgie and Marigold must have paid him a fortune to make up to Kitty,' said Hermione smugly. 'I mean the others are at least attractive. And just to make you jealous. But Kitty must have collaborated.'

'That was naughty,' said Rannaldini. 'Like Cavaradossi, Keety must be tortured. No-one makes a fool of me.'

Unplugging himself from Hermione after a rather perfunctory coupling he plugged in his telephone. He was going to enjoy this game.

Machiavellian as ever, Rannaldini planned an orgy at Valhalla. January was such a dreary month and everyone was so worried about impending war in the Gulf that they needed distraction. First he sent out the invitations: MRS ROBERTO RANNALDINI AT HOME ON TWELFTH NIGHT FOR A *fin de siècle* TOGA PARTY.

Then he offered Hermione the part of Lady Macbeth in his next film if she succeeded in seducing Lysander during the evening.

Rannaldini was not an unperceptive man. Lysander might have been paid vast sums to pretend to be in love with Kitty but it was clear from his increasingly desperate messages on the ansaphone and his illiterate passionate faxes which spewed out of the machine like tapeworm that the boy was utterly infatuated. Nor was there any doubt that Kitty was smitten, too. Yesterday she had singed his best shirt when they played *Miss Saigon* on the radio, and, typing out the list of acceptances, which didn't include Lysander, she misspelt half the names and changed several people's sexes.

Even though caterers and florists had been hired to save her work, she cleaned obsessively so the place would be sufficiently spick and span. More tellingly, Rannaldini had failed to bring her to orgasm since her return and helpless tears gushed out of her eyes throughout. His digital wife was on the blink.

Rannaldini did not upbraid her. He realized increasingly how dependent on her he was for his comfort and what other wife would run his life so efficiently and allow him such freedom? Certainly not Hermione. Just doing the seating plan together made him want to throttle her.

'I want you to look pretty and enjoy yourself this evening

and leave everything to me,' he told Kitty on the afternoon of the party as he watched her dazedly digging up a poinsettia some fan had sent him and freeing its roots from the cruelly constricting plastic cage before repotting it.

'I want to make a beeg sum of money over to you, Keety,' he went on. 'The royalties on *Fidelio* perhaps, to give you independence. I know I 'urt you horrible in the past, but let us try again. In the States we will leave all the eediots in Paradise behind and eef you cannot 'ave children, no matter, we will adopt.' Which made poor Kitty feel more confused and guilty than ever.

Over at Magpie Cottage a despairing Lysander saw helicopters bringing Krug and most of Harrods Food Hall, landing all day as he kept his binoculars trained on Valhalla. By dusk snow was falling thickly, turning Georgie's blond willows grey before his eyes, icing Rannaldini's maze and weighing down his fruit nets like trampolines. Like a black tie of mourning the dark waters of the River Fleet halved the white valley.

Unable to remember when he'd last eaten, Lysander opened a tin of sweetcorn, then, after a spoonful, put it in the fridge. For the thousandth time he checked if the telephone was on the hook. Jumping violently at a pounding on the front door, he prayed as he never stopped praying that it might be Kitty. Instead in marched the next best thing.

'Oh, Ferdie!' Lysander stumbled forward, flinging his arms round his friend, drawing comfort from his solid bulk. 'I'm sorry I've been such a shit. I didn't mean to use you. Poor darling little Maggie.' His voice broke.

'My fault.' Ferdie patted Lysander's shoulder, shocked how bony it was. Then, bending down to scoop up an hysterically excited, yapping Jack. 'Came on too strong. Choked about Maggie. Had to take it out on someone.'

'Everything you said was right. I just couldn't bear not to see you any more. I've missed you so much. Did Maggie suffer terribly?'

'No,' lied Ferdie, 'and her puppy's doing really well.'

For a second Lysander's haggard face lit up.

'He's still alive! That must be an omen.'

'It's a bitch.' Ferdie opened the fridge. 'Christ, don't you ever have any food? My mother's got her this weekend. Bottle-feeding her on goat's milk, but Mum's got to go back to work on Monday.'

'I'll take her. I'll give her to Kitty to replace—' His voice faltered again. 'Oh, Ferdie what am I going to do?' And the story of his great love came pouring out.

'Kitty and me are an item. It's the real thing,' he said finally.

'You said that about Georgie,' said Ferdie, reduced to putting the kettle on as there was no drink in the house.

'Georgie!' said Lysander, outraged. 'That boring, self-pitying slag. I even remember Kitty's postcode.'

'It's the same as yours,' said Ferdie unimpressed.

'Is it?' asked Lysander in surprise. 'I don't know mine. I can't concentrate on *EastEnders* and I haven't had a bet since I came back.'

'My God,' said Ferdie in alarm. 'Ladbroke's will go into receivership. I'll give you my opinion of this situation after the orgy tonight. What are you going as?'

'NFI,' said Lysander sulkily. Then, when Ferdie raised his eyebrows, 'Not fucking invited?'

'You sure?' Ferdie rifled through the post which Lysander hadn't bothered to open because none of it contained Kitty's neat round handwriting but which included several letters marked PRIVATE AND CONFIDENTIAL from his bank and three marked URGENT from David Hawkley.

'Here you are.' Ferdie slit open the thick cream envelope: MRS ROBERTO RANNALDINI AT HOME.

'No-one could feel at home at Valhalla,' shuddered Lysander.

'You've got to dress up as a Roman,' said Ferdie, 'preferably a decadent one. Most people'll go in sheets and Duo-tan.'

'I loathe fancy dress.' Lysander had gone whiter than

the snow outside at the thought of seeing Kitty again. 'And I've got a zit.'

'First time in your life. I can't see it.' Then, as Lysander lifted the curls off his forehead, 'That's nothing.'

'It's massive. If I stood in Paradise High Street, I'd stop the traffic.'

'You better start eating.'

'I can't. I must go into Rutminster and get Kitty some flowers before the shops close.'

'You could go in the buff as an Ancient Brit,' suggested Ferdie. 'You'll be so blue with cold at Valhalla, you won't have to bother with woad.'

53

The thunder and surge of Schoenberg could be heard all
the way down the valley which glittered in the icy light
of a moon hardly softened by a rusty halo presaging
storm. Outside Valhalla the Press stamped their feet,
desperate for the latest on Kitty and Lysander. But,
determined to prevent any drawbridge crashers, Rannaldini had posted a fleet of minions and guard-dogs on
every gate. Only guests with invitations were allowed in
and, directed by Mr Brimscombe, who was almost more
desperate to join the orgy than the Press, to park their
cars and helicopters on the lawn.

Rannaldini had laid his plans with care. The scarlet morning room and the yellow summer parlour were
radiant with candles and carpeted with pink rose-petals.
The central heating, most uncharacteristically, was turned
up to tropical, huge banked logs smouldered like the fires
of hell in every grate so anyone who had turned up in
anything hotter than a toga was soon stripping off.

Great vases of lilies, roses and jasmine poured forth their
overpoweringly voluptuous scents, recalling Rannaldini's
garden during last summer's heatwave. The air was blue
with many kinds of smoke as soothsayers, slaves, emper-
ors, Mercurys in tinhats and fig-leaves and goddesses,
holding in their tummies and wishing they'd cut down
on the turkey left-overs, got stuck into the Krug.

Having frozen at Rachel's party, Larry had made the
mistake of wearing a lion's costume and was now twitching
a yellow tail as he yelled into his mobile.

'He's trying to set up a new business with some Japs,'

explained Marigold, who'd come as Minerva. Having fallen asleep under the sun lamp she was redder in the face than Percival Hillary who, as Julius Caesar, had recycled his Cavendish House nightgown and put a laurel wreath on his wispy grey curls.

'Julius Seize-him, more likely,' giggled Meredith, lissom in a beige tunic. 'Rannaldini is not promiscuous, Marigold, just terribly, terribly frightened of the dark, so he cannot sleep alone.'

'What are you on about?' said Marigold, adjusting the owl on her shoulder.

'I've come as a Christian,' said Meredith, folding his hands piously, 'so I can't bitch about anyone. Isn't Hermione a sweet person? Hasn't Percy got lovely breath? Doesn't Rachel cheer one up? How the *hell* did Gwendolyn Chisleden wangle an invite? She could have come as Caligula's horse without dressing up. Whoops, I've sinned again!'

'Ay think Gwendolyn looks very dignified in that midnaight-blue shirtwaister,' signed Marigold. 'Ay wish Ay hadn't bothered with fancy dress.'

Most chillingly sinister of all was Rannaldini as Janus, the two-faced Roman God, guardian of the gateways and appropriately of January. A best-selling item at music shops round the country was a Rannaldini mask, so lifelike that musicians crossed themselves when they suddenly encountered it. Tonight Rannaldini had attached this second face to the back of his head so wherever you were in the room the black hypnotic eyes seemed to follow you. With his smooth brown torso, black loincloth, and thick gold snake coiled round his arm, he looked menacing and terrifyingly sexy.

Belle of the ball, however, was definitely Hermione as the Botticelli Venus with her glorious figure barely disguised by a flesh-coloured body stocking and her serenely beautiful face framed by a long curling strawberry-blond wig looped back with a silver ribbon.

'You can count every hair on her pubes, silly old tart,'

fumed Meredith, 'I don't know why she didn't come as herself. She's so lifted no-one would have recognized her. Doesn't Bobby look divine as Brutus?'

'The nobbliest Roman of them all,' said Bob deprecatingly, looking down at his bare knees. 'Christ, it's hot in here. Shouldn't someone open a window?'

Poor Georgie had felt absolutely stunning in gold robes and a black wig as Cleopatra until Natasha rolled up totally unexpectedly after ten days in Barbados, as an infinitely more seductive version in her mother's Angel Gabriel gold tunic and with her own dark curls straightened and cut in a fringe.

'Two Cleos! You should have come as Georgie's daughter,' said Hermione laughing heartily.

'Bags I be your asp,' said Guy, who was showing off his splendid legs as a centurion.

Unlike most fathers, Rannaldini was not remotely inhibited by his daughter's presence. Seeing a miserable, utterly upstaged Georgie retreating into an alcove, he went over to fill up her glass: 'Hallo, Georgie.'

'Oh hi, Rannaldini. God, I'm unhappy. I screwed up courage to go to Relate in Rutminster last night and came home full of resolutions to be nicer to Guy only to find he'd gone round to see Rachel and what is more—'

'Georgie,' Rannaldini cut into her monologue mockingly, 'I only came to say Hallo. Talk of zee devil.'

Leaving Georgie squirming with humiliation he sauntered across the room to kiss Rachel, who, having been to a candle-lit peace vigil to protest against the Gulf War, had arrived in an embattled mood. Dressed as Ben Hur, she was brandishing a large whip.

'Ah, Dolores, Lady of Pain,' he said softly, sliding a brief caressing hand inside her thighs just below her tunic, 'let me pull your chariot.'

'I loathe fancy dress,' snarled Rachel, but she had lost her audience, because Lysander had just walked in and as usual brought the room to a halt.

He wore ripped jeans, a dark blue shirt and Kitty's

Donald Duck jersey. His deathly pallor set off by the dark stubble and the purple shadows beneath the cavernous eyes, which searched endlessly for Kitty, only made him stand out more from the gaudy yelling revellers swarming around him.

'Hi, Trouble,' said Meredith, tossing a handful of rose-petals over him. 'Calves in Ancient Rome were always garlanded with flowers before they were sacrificed.'

Lysander was followed by a tottering, leering Ferdie, who, as Bacchus, had draped himself in a wine-stained tablecloth. His mouth was smeared dark purple with one of Lysander's lipsalves and a wreath of plastic vine leaves borrowed from The Pearly Gates fell over his nose.

'Hic,' said Ferdie, lifting a flagon of red to his lips.

'*Haec hoc,*' added Meredith. 'Hermione should have come as Frontus. Any moment Guy will tumble down her cleavage.'

Kitty was so used to staying in the background that Rannaldini had the greatest difficulty in dragging her out of the kitchen. He certainly didn't want Lysander sloping off there. Because she had no idea Lysander was coming, she had listlessly acquiesced when Rannaldini insisted on dressing her as a Vestal Virgin in clinging pleated white, which only emphasized her lack of colour, her swollen reddened eyes and her dumpy little figure.

Now she was carrying a big terracotta bowl loaded with green grapes and crimson cherries past the red morning room along to the dining room.

'Kitty, darling, how are you? Let me take that,' called out Bob, but next minute he had been waylaid by the leader of the orchestra, who'd come plus fiddle as Nero and who was already half-cut.

'Where's this famous toy boy who got off with Kitty?' he demanded, not realizing she was within earshot.

'I want to shake him by the hand for rattling that shit. I've never known him so histrionic, screaming down the telephone about deps at four o'clock this morning: "Those were completely deeferent musicians to zee ones I saw in rehearsal." So I said: "It's not surprising, Rannaldini. The first lot were so fucking frightened of being shouted at." That must be him in the Donald Duck sweater. Jesus, what a beauty. It's going to be like the first day of the sales once we start orgying.'

Hearing this, Kitty shot into the room and found herself looking straight at Lysander. He was clutching Jack and a huge bunch of snowdrops. Next minute the terracotta bowl crashed into the rose-petals.

'Oh, Lysander,' she whispered.

Unable to speak, Lysander stumbled forward thrusting the snowdrops into her hands, closing her fingers round them and stroking them. For a second they gazed at each other, stunned by the devastation both had wrought.

'I can't go on,' stammered Lysander.

'Welcome to the Underworld, Orpheus,' murmured Rannaldini, gliding up. Then, snapping his fingers at a couple of waitresses to clear up the broken pieces, he turned to Kitty. 'I want you to come and meet Rudolpho who's going to play Macbeth.'

Dropping her snowdrops contemptuously on a side table, he frogmarched her across the room.

'I thought you'd promised to geeve up Lysander,' he hissed, squeezing her arm till she gasped with pain. Switching to purring conciliation, he introduced her to a very fat tenor covered in white make-up and his harpist boyfriend whose costume consisted of brown curling leaves. They had come as Decline and Fall.

'Rudolpho, *caro*, I would like you to meet my wife, Keety, who'll be sorting out your contract. Ring her eef you have any problem.'

From then on Kitty kept her eyes firmly down, deliberately avoiding looking at Lysander, who had collapsed dolefully on the sofa, muttering to Jack.

'I assume you'd rather talk to that dog than me,' said Hermione archly.

'Yes, I would,' snapped Lysander, holding out his glass to an admiring waitress for a refill.

The party was hotting up. Gluck's *Orphée* was pouring out of the speakers. Ravishing female musicians and handsome gay opera stars, realizing that spare heterosexual beefcake was in short supply, hovered hungrily around Lysander, hoping he'd tread on their togas.

'I wouldn't mind a house down here,' said Rudolpho, the very fat tenor.

'I have secret information,' said Ferdie in an undertone, 'that Paradise Grange across the valley might be coming on to the market. I could show you around tomorrow if you like. Goodness, that's nice,' he added as a stunning blonde, inadequately clad in a pale blue cot sheet, appeared in the doorway. Perhaps she could jolt Lysander out of his despair.

'That's Chloe, Boris Levitsky's girlfriend,' said Rudolpho. 'I did *Aïda* in Cardiff with her. Marvellous voice.'

'Chloe, *carissima*.' Rannaldini dropped a kiss on her bare brown shoulder, licking off wild strawberry and rose-hip body lotion. 'How did you give Boris the slip?'

'He's working on his *Requiem*,' said Chloe petulantly. 'He didn't even notice I'd gone out.'

'Silly boy to neglect something so exquisite.' Beckoning to a waitress, Rannaldini put a beaker of Krug in each of Chloe's little hands. 'You 'ave catching up to do. We are about to dine.'

'I'm not sitting next to Rachel?'

'No, next to me. That will upset everyone.'

Kitty's snowdrops gave a long despairing hiss as he tossed them into the fire.

Dinner was served in the blue dining-room which was more intimate than the great hall. Guests lounged on multi-coloured silk cushions piled round low tables on which was arranged suitably Roman fare: great fishes swimming in herbs and butter, lobsters, barbecued geese, sucking pigs, great flagons of wine and big bowls spilling over with grapes, cherries and pomegranates.

Wrapped in imperial purple paper beside each gold plate was a condom and an Ecstasy pill. Rannaldini's version of

Ravel's *Bolero*, said to be the sexiest ever, was pulsating out of the speakers like a great heartbeat, with the leader of the orchestra playing along.

'I wish Rannaldini would spend as much on church flowers,' grumbled Joy Hillary, glaring at the cliffs of freesias.

'Who did the seating plan?' grumbled Georgie who was stuck between the vicar and Rudolpho.

'Rannaldini and I,' said Hermione smugly. 'I've put Guy next to the two prettiest women in the room – Rachel and Natasha. Is your phone out of order, by the way? I saw Guy coming out of the call box in Paradise High Street this afternoon.' Then, suddenly furious, 'What the hell's Chloe doing next to Rannaldini? She must have gatecrashed. He was supposed to have Gwendolyn Chisleden on his right.'

Lysander, who was already absolutely plastered, found himself between Hermione and a really ugly female double-bass player who'd come as Caesar's wife, Calpurnia.

'Wouldn't get a chance to be anything else but above suspicion with a face like that,' said Meredith, who was sitting opposite and sucking a lobster claw.

At the same table were Guy, Rachel, Natasha, whose cat's eyes beneath her black fringe were devouring Lysander, and Ferdie on her right who was depressed that he still wanted her so desperately.

Rannaldini, who had deliberately put Kitty at his side, had also arranged it so that Lysander was gazing straight at the back of Kitty's head with the evil, mocking Janus mask beside it. Throughout dinner Rannaldini deliberately caressed his wife, stroking her very clean neck as though he was an executioner pondering where to drop the axe, fondling her breasts and her back as though he were working in suntan oil, and all the time kissing her and whispering in her ear.

Lysander had to exert every ounce of self-control not to get up and hit Rannaldini across the room. Looking washed-out and not remotely pretty, Kitty moved him more than ever. Putting the Ecstasy pill in his mouth, he washed it down with half a pint of Krug.

'You don't seem very happy, Lysander,' said Hermione, putting a hand on his leg.

'I'm not,' said Lysander, removing it. 'Kitty's gone back to Rannaldini and she's the only truly good person, apart from Arthur, I've ever met.'

'That's because she's young and hasn't experienced life,' said Hermione dismissively.

'It isn't.' Furiously Lysander pulled off a piece of goose and gave it to Jack. 'She's good because she's good.'

'Your friend isn't in a very cheerful mood,' Hermione shouted across to Ferdie.

Not wanting to blow themselves out before orgying, people were drinking more than eating, already openly necking and beginning to undress one another. As the Ecstasy struck home Hermione engineered the conversation on to favourite fantasies.

'I'd like to be playing Desdemona to Domingo's Otello at Covent Garden,' she began, 'and to charm him into making love to me instead of killing me in front of a huge audience.'

'That's quite a rewrite,' said Meredith. 'I'd like to be raped by Mel Gibson – very slowly.'

'I'd like to see three gorgeous women making love,' Guy smiled at Hermione, Rachel and Natasha, 'and be invited to join in.'

Natasha, who was chucking grapes at Lysander to rouse him from his black gloom, said she'd like to be abducted and seduced by a highwayman.

'My name's Turpin. Call me Dick,' offered Ferdie, topping up her golden goblet.

Even Natasha laughed. 'What's yours then?' she asked.

'I'd like to have a woman in love with me,' said Ferdie simply.

'Aaaaah,' said everyone at the table except Rachel, who now was staring at Rannaldini's table with as much horror as Lysander.

'What's Chloe doing here?' she whispered to Guy.

Although Rannaldini was publicly stroking Kitty with his left hand, his right hand had disappeared under the table.

'And what's your secret fantasy, Lysander?' asked Hermione.

'No secret. I want to marry Kitty,' said Lysander flatly.

There was a pause. Then Natasha led the howls of derisive mirth.

'You're beautiful,' sighed Ferdie, unable to keep his eyes off Natasha's soft gold thighs.

'Marry me then,' taunted Natasha. 'As Lysander only lusts after married women, it's the one way I'll get him into bed.'

Georgie got lower and lower. On her right Rudolpho and his boyfriend were busy pulling grey hairs out of each other's heads like chimpanzees and the only man who'd come dressed as Anthony was a counter-tenor who displayed a cock the size of a three-year-old boy when his toga fell open. She was only too aware of the shrieks of laughter coming from Guy's table. To her right the vicar was gazing at Lysander who was looking so grim that he reminded her for an agonizing second of David Hawkley. If only David would forgive her.

Across the table Lady Chisleden was getting very uncorked and had undone nearly all the buttons of her midnight-blue shirtwaister.

'I want to go somewhere that will give me new horizons and widen my experience in life,' she was telling Bob.

'Why not try Bexley Heath?' said Meredith, plonking himself down between them.

Drunken dining was followed by even more drunken dancing. Hermione opened the ball with Guy, rocking and rolling just to show the younger generation that they'd invented the dance, and when Guy hoisted Hermione in the air she clasped him with her body-stockinged legs.

Hermione's smug smile was wiped off her face, however,

when Rannaldini led Kitty on to the floor. A mesmerizing serpentine dancer, he was soon practically raping her, his body writhing against her, kissing her shoulders and then her mouth, sticking his tongue down her throat until she nearly gagged, letting his hands wander over her body, yet his feet never losing the rhythm of the music.

Deliberately he danced past Lysander, so close that the hem of Kitty's pleated skirt brushed Lysander's foot and he could smell her hot frightened body and caught a faint agonizing waft of the Diorissimo he had given her at the airport, a scent he would now associate even more with loss.

'Oh Mum, oh Christ, oh Kitty, oh Maggie,' he muttered hopelessly and drunkenly.

Daring to glance at him, Kitty thought how desperately ill and diminished he looked. His jeans were ripped everywhere. There were buttons off his shirt. The tip had been eaten off one of his shoes. He needs me, she thought in anguish, not feeling Rannaldini's fingers until they were pinching really hard.

Unable to bear any more, Lysander stumbled from the room.

Now's my chance, thought Natasha leaping up.

For a second Kitty dropped her guard.

'You don't think he's going to blow his brains out?'

'With that little brain,' sneered Rannaldini, 'he'd have to be a bloody good shot.'

54

The orgy roared on.

'Toga, toga, burning bright,' shrieked Marigold tossing her sheet into the morning-room fire and rushing pinkly up the stairs pursued by a man in a Neil Kinnock mask.

It didn't occur to any of the guests as they charged in and out of bedrooms that there was something odd about Mr Brimscombe pruning the Valhalla honeysuckle in the middle of winter.

Downstairs Rannaldini was dancing with Rachel, bopping through the rose-petals and fixing her with his deadly stare. Utterly suicidal Kitty was being lugged round the floor by the vicar – the hostess with the leastest. If she'd known Lysander was coming she'd have tried to look prettier, but at least he'd brought her snowdrops. If she were truthful, what she dreaded most was his no longer loving her. Last thing at night when she lost control of her thoughts, she dreamt she was a little mole (with its blind eyes, pink hands and lack of waist – the two of them had a lot in common) and she was tunnelling under the gates of Valhalla, beneath the River Fleet, not stopping until she joined the other molehills on the lawn of Magpie Cottage.

Seeing Rannaldini had disappeared, Kitty left the vicar in mid-foxtrot and escaped to the summer parlour. Unable to find Lysander's snowdrops to put them in water, she crept up the main stairs, tripping over entwined couples and her own long skirt, praying she might bump into Lysander.

Through a landing window she noticed the moon's

increasing halo, mother of pearl now and ringed with darkened rainbow colours. Kitty was reminded of Lysander who shone like an angel in her dreams. Next moment Lady Chisleden rushed shrieking past in her bra and roll-on pursued by a man wearing Lysander's donkey head.

'Take me dancing naked in the rain,' roared the loud speaker, *'and cover me in ecstasy.'*

Suddenly it was October again and she was dancing round the field at Magpie Cottage. It was no good. She'd have to find Lysander.

'Mrs Rannaldini,' a defeated-looking caterer called up the stairs, 'there's a policeman down here come to complain about the noise.'

'Hooray, a spare man at last,' called back Kitty. 'If he's handsome introduce him to Rachel or the vicar.'

Giggling hysterically, she felt light with happiness. She and Lysander loved each other – nothing else mattered.

'Take me dancing naked in the rain,' sang Kitty as she rocked down the gloomy landing.

She could hear terrible sobbing but to hell with people's problems. Then she realized it was coming from Natasha's room. Tiptoeing to the doorway she found her step-daughter crying so hysterically that her whole bed seemed to heave.

'Sweet'eart, what's the matter?'

'Everything. I'm going to die. You'll be pleased because it means Dad and Hermione are caput.' As Natasha looked up, Cleopatra's kohl and mascara were streaked down her face like a yashmak. 'Oh, Kitty, I can't bear it. I love him so much.'

'Poor lambkin.' Seizing a handful of pink tissues, Kitty put an arm round Natasha's shuddering shoulders, drying her eyes and glad to be allowed for once to comfort.

'What is it? Tell me.'

'Lysander's fucking Hermione.'

'What did you say?' The pink tissues fell like rose-petals from Kitty's hand.

'Making love, if you prefer it,' howled Natasha.

'I *don't* believe it.' Kitty sat down very suddenly on the bed, her lips were trembling so much she could only mumble, 'L–l–lysander l–loathes H–h–h–ermione.'

'Funny way of showing it. Go into Papa's dressing room. They're all watching him.'

Narrowly avoiding crashing into the open door, sending a big vase of dried poppies flying, Kitty stumbled along endless winding passages up and down stone steps, cold beneath her bare feet.

'The Ride of The Valkyrie' was now pounding out of a different set of speakers, more and more menacing.

It couldn't be true, it couldn't.

For a terrifying second she thought Rannaldini was defying her to enter his dressing room. Then she realized it was his mask and that he and Bob, who was using a video camera, and Meredith, who was dabbing Maestro behind his ears, and Rudolpho and his boyfriend, who were both down to their boxer shorts, were all gazing excitedly through a two-way mirror. Moving closer, clinging on to a bust of Schubert, Kitty could now see Lysander and Hermione both naked in Rannaldini's big pale grey four-poster with the little Renoir and Watteau girls looking indifferently down from the faded cherry-red damask walls. Jack, beadily glaring at his master, had taken up sentry duty in an armchair.

Rannaldini turned smiling viciously.

'Come een, Kitty.'

'Two-way mirror on the wall,' giggled Meredith, 'who is the fairest of us all?'

'No doubt about that,' said Rudolpho, taking hold of his boyfriend's cock. 'Can we have him next, Rannaldini? Hell, did you ever see anything so beautiful?'

Collapsing against the mirror Kitty was amazed her anguish didn't shatter the glass. How could Lysander not see her? Although entwined with Hermione there was a slumped, utterly defeated look about his pale body on those silken red sheets.

'Oh God, please help me,' she whispered.

'Peety, you mees a wonderful performance,' said Rannaldini, 'your boyfriend make love with all the brio of a youth orchestra. A few wrong notes but such energy.'

It's the Paradise Lad, thought Kitty in horror, as Hermione slid down Lysander's still body and took his limp cock between her beautiful, smiling lips.

Screaming, Kitty fled to her bedroom where she found Lady Chisleden lying on her flower-patterned duvet doing exactly the same thing to a man in a donkey's headdress.

Slamming the door, Kitty leant against it for a second, trying to ride the pain, which was far, far worse than anything she'd suffered from Rannaldini's infidelities. Of all his mistresses, Hermione had used, abused, patronized and humiliated her the most and now she had calmly stolen Lysander, the only man, Kitty knew now, that she had ever loved. You could stop torturers by telling them what they wanted, but there was no way to end this agony.

'I've never known such breakages!' One of the caterers was scratching her head over the broken glass which glittered among the trampled rose-petals, as Kitty rushed out into the snow. She was dimly aware of the vicar, followed by a trail of screaming Bacchantes, chasing a panic-stricken police constable, naked except for his helmet, into the Valhalla Maze. But as she looked up at the moon, howling in anguish, she noticed that, like Lysander, it had lost its halo.

The party showed no sign of abating. Salt lay like patches of snow over the wine stains. Even worse howls came from Lady Chisleden when she discovered that the man in the donkey's head, whom she'd enjoyed for the last hour, was none other than a leering Mr Brimscombe.

Joy Hillary, who'd been kept very busy failing to stop couples coupling, stiffened with delight as she saw Marigold disappear giggling into the broom cupboard followed by the naked man in a Neil Kinnock mask.

Wrenching open the door she chucked the contents of a rusty firebucket over them, crying: 'How can you bring such disrepute on the Parish Council, Marigold?'

'Ay'm makin' love to may husband, you stupid cow,' shrieked Marigold, who was straddling a drenched Larry, who'd received most of the deluge.

'But he came in as a lion,' said Joy in bewilderment.

'And he's not goin' out laike a lamb,' said Marigold, and throwing a dustpan at Joy, kicked the door shut.

'I want my mother,' sobbed Natasha.

'Where is she?' said Ferdie, stroking her tear-drenched hair.

'In New York, I think,'

'I'll take you to her,' said Ferdie. 'The moment I've shown Rudolpho over Paradise Grange.'

'If I were you, Gwendolyn,' said Joy Hillary, trying to regain some ascendancy, 'I'd get that nice shirtwaister dry cleaned.'

Over in his tower, lying in his other huge bed surrounded by cheering opera crowds as he listened to his own recording of *Salome*, Rannaldini drew heavily on a joint.

'According to Sade,' he murmured, 'enjoyment increases in proportion to the intensity of the sensations the imagination receives. The most intense sensation' – he groaned in ecstasy, as Chloe plunged a long-nailed finger deep inside him – 'ees produced by pain. The true voluptuary will impose the greatest amount of pain.'

He smiled round at Chloe, drawing on the joint until it glowed, then placing its burning end within a millimetre of her smooth brown face.

'Don't be frightened,' he said softly as she winced away. 'Listen.'

Straining her ears, Chloe could hear the faint tolling of a bell.

'How would you like to play Lady Macbeth, Chloe?' asked Rannaldini.

Lysander woke around ten with a murderous headache. Groaning, he tried to focus on a strawberry-blond wig flowing down from one of the posts of a big double bed.

There was Jack asleep on his Donald Duck jersey, and several pink nude girls looking down at him from the pictures, and a strong scent that boded evil. Slowly his aching eyes took in scarlet toenails, smooth brown waxed legs swelling to plump cushiony thighs and glossy brown pubic hair trimmed in the shape of a heart.

Like a massive electric shock he realized something was dreadfully wrong. Kitty's bush had been shaved in France and would now only be sprouting stubble. Dragging his eyes laboriously up over billowing breasts he reached Hermione's smug satisfied face, a fat tabby who had just wolfed a side of smoked salmon.

'What in hell happened?'

'We made love,' Hermione stroked his forehead, 'and it was wonderful.'

'It couldn't have been. You must have spiked my drink. I've never wanted to go to bed with you. I like Bob too much anyway.'

'How ungallant!' Hermione still smiled, but her nails raked savagely across Lysander's scalp.

'Ouch, don't. I love Kitty.'

'Oh, come, we all know you were being paid.'

'The love was real, damn you.'

'And did she say afterwards: "That was ubsolutely mudgic, Lysunder"?'

'Whadyamean?' Lysander, totally awake now, leant up on his elbow, glaring into Hermione's lovely spiteful face.

'That's what Kitty always says; 'Thut was mudgic, Rannaldini." You've been putting a lot of marriages asunder, Lysunder.'

Suddenly frightened, she waved a hand in front of his murderous, bloodshot eyes.

'D'you mean Rannaldini tells you about him and Kitty in bed?'

The bastard. How horrible that Kitty should say Rannaldini was 'mudgic' too.

'Oh, come. Pillow talk. Rannaldini doesn't pretend to

be a gentleman. He loves stories and he adored watching you and me through the two-way mirror last night.' She gave her deadly little laugh. 'So did Kitty.'

'Kitty!' Lysander froze. '*Kitty*. The poor angel. What did she say?'

'She'll be OK,' said Hermione, irritated by his sudden desperate concern. 'The working-classes don't feel pain like we do. I can't think why you're making such a fuss, you must have made a fortune out of the whole thing. Come on,' she patted the red silk sheets enticingly. 'Let's try again now you're sober. You'll soon forget Kitty.'

Revolted, Lysander leapt out of bed, clutching his head as waves of nausea almost floored him, and, tugging on his jeans, ripped them even further. Hermione lost her temper.

'Why should Kitty leave Rannaldini?' she hissed. 'Look at this beautiful house and all this beautiful land.'

Out of the narrow windows Lysander could see snow-covered chimneys soaring to a brilliant blue sky. Across the valley, like a Brueghel, people were already skiing and tobogganing in the sloping fields below Paradise Grange, hurtling downhill with dogs barking joyously after them – a scene so reminiscent of Monthaut and Kitty that Lysander had to cling on to the window-ledge.

'Think of her thrilling lifestyle, married to a man of genius.' Hermione's voice was now tolling like the punishment bell. 'Think of her future in New York. What the hell have you got to offer her?'

'Only my heart.'

With Hermione's mocking laughter ringing in his ears, he went in search of Kitty. The landing was deserted except for the odd bra and pair of knickers. Downstairs, wading through sandals, daggers, laurel wreaths, fallen fig-leaves, place cards, cigarette ends, condoms and burst balloons, Lysander breathed in a stench of sex, stale tobacco and half-full glasses.

Not wishing to wake the vicar, who was stretched out on a sofa with a bunch of dried poppies in his arms, Lysander finally stumbled on a cheerful, bleary-eyed group having a post-mortem round the kitchen table.

'I never knew Gwendolyn Chisleden had had a tummy tuck,' said Georgie, who was actually holding hands with Guy.

'And the first decent bonk in forty years,' said Meredith. Then, noticing Lysander. 'Hallo, duckie. How are *you*?'

Seeing Bob at the end of the table deep in the music pages of the *Observer*, Lysander went scarlet and mumbled: 'Where's Kitty?'

'Not herself, poor lamb. She put salt in all our coffee. Then, when I asked her very politely for some butter for our croissants, she got two pounds out of the freezer and chucked them down on the table like bullion.'

'I should think you, Larry and I are the only people who didn't catch Aids last night,' said Marigold, pushing Kitty into a chair against the Aga and handing her a cup of black coffee to warm her numb frozen hands. Her teeth were rattling between blue lips. She was wearing an old sheepskin coat over her torn vestal virgin dress.

The few maiden ladies, waiting in vain in All Saints, Paradise, for the vicar to take Matins, had been electrified instead by the sight of poor little Mrs Rannaldini, always so quiet and retiring, wandering in in a white ball dress with bleeding feet and collapsing in a back pew, piteously sobbing, 'Oh, please God, help me, help me.'

Miss Cricklade had run out to ring Marigold from the telephone box, much used by Paradise adulterers, begging her to come and collect Kitty.

'I think the poor little soul's finally gone off her head.'

Now Marigold was half-tidying up, as Rudolpho the tenor was due to see over Paradise Grange in a minute. It did look beautiful with the big rooms lit up by the snow. If only all the pictures hadn't gone off to Sotheby's. Larry was fast asleep upstairs. They both agreed they hadn't enjoyed a party so much in ages. Relieved that Kitty seemed calmer, Marigold was now being very practical.

'Ay know Lysander went to bed with you, Kitty dear. He laikes you very much, but he also went to bed with Georgie and me, yes Ay'm afraid he did, he just can't resist a bonk, and yes he's a genius in bed. He makes you feel so desirable and funny and, well, beautiful.'

Aware that Kitty was flinching at every adjective, Marigold felt one had to be cruel to be kind: 'And he was about to go to bed with Rachel and he did with Martha in Palm Beach and God knows who else when working away from Paradise, and now Hermione. I know it's a shock, but let's face it, he's a playboy, out for what he can get and whom he can bonk.'

Kitty took a gulp of coffee so scalding her eyes watered. 'I fort he'd changed.'

'Men don't change,' said Marigold, 'except their partners. Lysander wouldn't be any more faithful than Rannaldini, but at least if you stay put, you live in luxury.'

Kitty started to cry. 'But I love him, Marigold.'

'Because he was so kaind. That's another thing. He gets ladies not just by the saize of his winkle, but by his ears, because he's so good at listening.'

Restored to Rannaldini's arms later in the day, Kitty was allowed one incoming telephone call. It was all she needed.

'Go away,' she screamed, cutting through Lysander's hysterical pleadings. 'You're worse than all the uvvers. All you fink about is sex. Leave me in peace. I never want to see you no more.'

Half an hour later Lysander's hopes flared for a second as he heard steps coming up the path of Magpie Cottage, but when he ran to the door he found only a note in the porch from Bob, summoning him to lunch in London the following day: '*You and I have to do some serious talking about Hermione.*'

55

Sick with terror Lysander rolled up at Radnor Walk the following day. Was Bob going to cite him as co-respondent or to call him out for bonking Hermione? The house was absolutely beautiful inside and seemed far too subtly decorated to be Hermione's taste. The drawing room had burnt-orange curtains, a big white carpet strewn with blue flowers and drained blue walls covered with musical books, scores, Hermione's records and tapes, a mournful Picasso clown, not unlike Bob, and a Cotman of a soft gold wood in autumn.

A huge portrait of Hermione as Donna Elvira was reflected in the big gilt mirror over the fireplace. Lysander turned his back on both of her, but couldn't avoid photographs of the awful old bitch everywhere. Delicious smells of wine and herbs drifted from the kitchen. Despite the bitter cold of the day, the house inside was warm enough for Bob to be wearing a grey striped shirt tucked into jeans showing off the flattest stomach and neatest hips in Gloucestershire.

Lysander, who seemed to have been cold for days, felt a passionate, almost tearful, relief at the equal warmth of Bob's welcome.

'Come in, dear boy. You look frozen and in need of a whole fur of the dog. Morning, Jack. Put him down. There aren't any cats.'

Pushing Lysander towards a pale orange and blue striped armchair beside a crackling leaping fire he opened a bottle of pink champagne.

'How were the roads?'

'Awful, until I got to Rutminster and they'd started gritting.'

'More gritted teeth than roads the other night,' observed Bob, as he carefully eased the cork out. 'What a remarkable evening. I had terrible problems getting the orchestra sobered up in time for today's rehearsal. We're playing a fiendishly difficult piece by Villa-Lobos at the Festival Hall this evening. Chloe was supposed to be singing *Les Nuits d'été*, but she's done in her back, or so she says.'

Bob gave Lysander his weary charming smile as he handed him a glass. 'You enjoy yourself?'

'No.'

Idly Bob straightened the yellow Chinese silk shawl draped over the piano and removed a browning flower from a bowl of light blue hyacinths. Then, sitting down opposite Lysander, he raised his glass: 'To my deliverer. This should really be Dom Perignon Rosé 1982 because it's such a red-letter day. I cannot tell you how grateful I am. I've been praying for someone to take Hermione off my hands for fifteen years.'

Lysander's jaw clanged like a gangplank.

'Rannaldini's always been far too fly to offer the old thing marriage.' Bob carefully smoothed out the gold paper of the champagne cork with a beautifully manicured thumb. 'Anyway he *is* my musical director and if I cited him as co-respondent he'd probably fire me and the orchestra doesn't need any more scandal. Beside,' he added gently, 'I've got you and Hermione on video so I'm home and dry.'

'Oh, my God!' Lysander choked on a huge gulp of champagne. 'Basically I don't think Hermione and I would suit. She's a terrific singer and a terrific-looking woman and all, but honestly she'd find me such a thicko and hopelessly unmusical – and I doubt if I could afford her.'

'You should have thought about that,' Bob said, suddenly cold. 'Hermione could certainly afford you. You'd never have to work again. And you'd be a much more arresting accessory than a chain handbag on her arm; and she's sensational in bed – as, of course, you know.'

Lysander had gone green, his face glistened with sweat.

'I don't remember. I promise you, Bob, I was set up. One of the reasons I feel dreadful is you've always been seriously nice to me. I never wanted to bonk her.'

'So, you're telling me you've got no intention of standing by her.'

'N–no, please not,' bleated Lysander.

'After you've compromised her so appallingly. You realize she can afford the toughest lawyers in the world.'

For a long moment Bob glared at Lysander's terrified face, then he started to shake with laughter.

'What a pity! I suppose I'll have to hang in there. She couldn't cope on her own and Cosmo does need a putative father.'

'But I thought you adored her?' said Lysander in utter bewilderment.

'I take care of her,' said Bob flatly.

Getting up, smoothing his remaining blond hair in the mirror, he perched on the arm of Lysander's chair: 'The other night when you and Hermione were in bed you reminded me of Matthew Arnold's white violets plucked by the little children then, when the nurse calls them home, thrown down to die on the woodland floor. You're wasting yourself on women, you know,' Bob added softly.

Lysander's eyes widened. He felt himself blushing and tried to make himself as small as possible. Even so, Bob was seriously close. Glancing up he noticed the smoothness of Bob's recent shave, his hairless nostrils above the long wide upper lip, the big kind, almost lashless eyes.

'You were probably too drunk to remember anything about your performance the other night.' Bob put a light hand on Lysander's hair. 'But I promise you it was the most exciting thing I've ever seen.' Slowly he stroked Lysander's rigid cheek with the other hand. 'I know you'd be turned on to watch yourself on the video.'

'I bloody would not!' Lysander jumped to his feet so fast he nearly tipped Bob on to the floor.

Jack stopped inspecting a stuffed bear in the corner and barked furiously.

'Are you quite, quite sure?' Righting himself, Bob moved towards his quarry.

'Quite.' Backing away panic-stricken, Lysander was blocked by the piano.

'What a shame,' sighed Bob. 'You'd find men so much more rewarding and far less hassle. Oh well, we better have lunch. Meredith!' he shouted through to the kitchen.

And in bustled Meredith. Swamped in a butcher-boy apron, he was bearing a big blue Delft dish of lobster pancakes smothered in the palest white wine and anchovy sauce.

Collapsing on to the keyboard with a crash of notes, Lysander opened his eyes the widest ever.

'You and him?' he mumbled incredulously.

Bob nodded, filling up a glass for Meredith. 'Been going on for fourteen years. I'd never have survived marriage to Hermione if it hadn't been for Meredith.'

'Does Hermione know?'

'Course not, silly bitch. She's so unobservant and self-obsessed,' said Meredith. 'Can you get the bread from the oven and the salad, Bobbie? I'm sure you'd enjoy the video, Lysander,' he went on cosily. 'I loved it. You're so photogenic you'd make a fortune in blue movies.'

'You really are kind.' Starting to giggle in relief, Lysander found he couldn't stop until they all joined in until the tears were pouring down their cheeks.

'I'm so sorry,' gasped Lysander finally, wiping his eyes on his sleeve. 'It's so nice to laugh, but I love Kitty.'

'Tush, tush,' chided Meredith. 'There's a world of possibility out there,' he tapped the window, 'called London. Three thousand miles away there's New York. With those God-given looks, why throw yourself away on a plain Jane?'

'She is *not*.'

'Who is married to someone else,' went on Meredith laying a blue napkin across Lysander's thighs, 'who is determined not to relinquish her.'

'I must rescue her.'

'You won't, duckie. Now eat up that pancake before it gets cold. You're much too thin. Don't worry,' he added when Lysander drooped like one of Kitty's snowdrops, 'you've got to move out of Paradise and give it time.'

'Kitty's doing time with that shit. How can I abandon her when I know how happy I can make her?'

'She's a treasure,' agreed Bob, forking radicchio and cêpes shining with tarragon dressing on to Lysander's side plate, 'but she'll never leave Rannaldini. He terrorizes her and appeals to her conscience. A lethal combination. He's got her mother into an expensive home which Kitty couldn't afford on her own. As it is she sends her money every week.'

'I could pay for that,' said Lysander quickly. 'Kitty's mother could live with us, then it wouldn't be so expensive.'

'Well, you'd better abandon this gigolo lark and win her properly.'

'I find it mystifying,' said Meredith, gobbling up the untouched three-quarters of Lysander's pancake as he loaded up the machine. 'What's Kitty got that we haven't?'

'She's touched his heart,' said Bob. 'Lysander's quite uncomplicated despite those wondrous looks. Like Papageno all he wants is enough to eat and the woman of his choice. Fighting's not his business.'

Natasha had been so distraught she had fled Valhalla, while Ferdie was showing Rudolpho over Paradise Grange, and sought sanctuary with a girlfriend's parents in Pimlico. She left her address with Kitty just in case Lysander asked for it.

The worst part of the nightmare for Natasha was that

her own father had actually been drooling over Lysander and Hermione in bed together.

'Papa knew I was crazy about Lysander,' she sobbed to Kitty. 'How could he do that to me and get a buzz out of it? And how could Lysander bonk that gross old wrinkly?'

Deranged with grief herself, Kitty had comforted Natasha as best she could and, although neither Rannaldini nor Lysander had shown the slightest interest in Natasha's whereabouts, the fifth time Ferdie rang Valhalla Kitty had given him the Pimlico address.

Two days later, having bored the girlfriend and her parents rigid with her obsessive monologue, Natasha was forced to return to Valhalla as she was due back at Bagley Hall that evening. She and Flora would be like war casualties. At least Kitty would have packed her trunk. Since the orgy, Natasha had decided there was something definitely to be said for her stepmother. Arriving at Paddington, she bought Kitty a box of Black Magic and a book on tapestry. But as she slouched miserably along the platform, thinking of Mocks in two weeks and all the holiday work she hadn't done and how unbearable Bagley Hall would be if she couldn't while away lessons dreaming of Lysander, she felt a hand picking up her suitcase. Swinging round she found herself looking into the square, blushing face of Ferdie.

'Oh, go away. You remind me of Lysander. I'm sorry, Ferdie, that was bitchy, but the bottom's fallen out of my world.'

'The world's fallen out of my bottom,' grumbled Ferdie. 'I should never have eaten that curry last night.'

A slight smile lifted Natasha's big mournful red mouth. 'You're a dickhead. What are you doing here anyway?'

'I've been put on commission only. I thought I'd come and see you off.'

'You better find yourself a rich girlfriend.'

'I've got one in my sights,' said Ferdie, taking her arm. 'Now let's find you a seat.'

For reasons best known to themselves British Rail had

scrapped the normal open-plan express and replaced it with an old-fashioned train with small carriages and, even worse, no bar or heating. Somehow, with a fat tip, Ferdie managed to inveigle a large brandy out of a dining-car waiter on the next-door train.

'This'll warm you up,' he told Natasha, emptying the bottle into a paper cup, 'and here's *Tatler* and *Hello!*.'

'Thank you,' said Natasha listlessly.

'I'll come and take you out from school.'

'If you like.'

'And I'll write.'

Natasha felt so low and was so determined not to break down that she didn't even look up and wave to Ferdie as the train pulled out. Slumped in her seat to avoid the low-angled sun she noticed the train had the same hoot as the first notes of the last movement of Beethoven's *Violin Concerto*. Next door to her a pale girl was writing an essay on The Future of Marriage. Opposite, a fat woman seemed to be deriving far more enjoyment from Maeve Binchy and the rest of the carriage was occupied by three lawyers in black and white on their way to the court at Swindon, talking most indiscreetly about their cases.

Natasha tried to read *Hello!* but on page twelve found a big piece on Bob's and Hermione's marriage, so she put it away. Gazing out of the window at the cheerless landscape and the leafless trees she started to cry and found she couldn't stop, even when the door slid open and a voice said: 'Tickets, please.'

'I don't know where mine is,' sobbed Natasha.

'In your coat pocket on top of the rack,' said the voice.

'Oh, Ferdie,' howled Natasha, 'go away.'

Charmingly relentless, Ferdie ordered everyone out of the carriage, getting down the fat woman's suitcase, explaining that there had been a death in the family. Then, sitting beside Natasha, he emptied another bottle of brandy into her paper cup.

'I'm such a bitch, how can you possibly still love me?'

'The torch I carry for you has a rechargeable battery. I'm thinking of signing up for the Gulf.'

Natasha looked up suddenly. 'Oh, please don't.'

'Would you mind?' Ferdie started to wipe away her tears with a British Rail napkin.

'I would,' said Natasha in amazement. 'Actually I seriously would.'

Ferdie got out his wallet and handed her two hundred pounds in cash.

'What's that for?'

'It says: PENALTY FOR IMPROPER USE: £200, and I want to use you improperly! Oh Natasha, my darling,' said Ferdie, taking her in his arms.

By the time Lysander returned to Magpie Cottage the rosy dreams of winning Kitty, induced largely by Bob's Dom Perignon, had faded and he collapsed into a deep despairing sleep. Woken by his alarm clock set for two in the afternoon so he could back Hannah's Uncle in the 2.30, he was outraged to find his Ladbroke's account had been suspended. Transferred to the accounts department, he learned that his December cheque had bounced. Only utter disbelief induced him to open one of the numerous letters from his bank, whereupon he nearly died of shock. He was on to Ferdie in a trice.

'Does OD at the bottom of the page always mean one's overdrawn.'

'Or over-dosing. It certainly does.'

'By twenty thousand pounds?'

'Jesus! Did you buy Paradise Grange or something? You had a hundred grand in there in November. Look at your cheques.'

Laboriously Lysander started to decipher them.

'Well, there's fifty thousand to Georgie.'

'Georgie? She was supposed to be paying *you*.'

'I hate her so much I paid her back. I didn't want to be be – whatever it is – to her. Anyway I didn't get her husband back.'

'Sale and no return,' sighed Ferdie. 'Carry on.'

'And thirty grand back to Marigold. No, she's honestly on her uppers, and I had to pay my return fare from Brazil, and give Gina a diamond bracelet because I'd walked out on her.'

'Oh, Lysander,' said Ferdie wearily.

'And ten thousand for the Hotel de Versailles. Christ, that's steep.'

'You were only there three days.'

'I know, but Rannaldini wanted Kitty to move into a pokey little room so I picked up the tab for her suite. The Jacuzzi was sensational. Hang on, I'll ring you back. There's someone at the door.'

In fact quite a crowd had gathered, stamping their feet on the snowy doorstep, including the owner of The Heavenly Host who hadn't been paid for four months, a man in a duffle-coat with a drop on the end of his red nose and Marigold, swollen with indignation and a blue Puffa, who was accompanied by a disdainful camel-faced couple in Barbours.

'Oh, Marigold,' Lysander pulled her like a lifebelt into the cottage. 'Is Kitty OK? Please put in a good word for me.'

'You keep away from Kitty,' whispered Marigold furiously. 'You'll only upset her and Ay don't think this is funny.' She thrust a large sign saying BOTTLE BANK, which Ferdie had put in the porch, into his hand. 'Ay left a note sayin' Ay was bringing Gwendolyn Chisleden's nephew and his fiancée to see over the cottage. They're getting married in April. You mayte have shaved and got dressed.'

Then she gave a gasp of horror as she took in the chaos behind him: overflowing ashtrays, glasses on every table, a floor littered with clothes, chewsticks and newspapers turned to the racing pages and washing-up rising out of the sink and along the window-sill to meet an army of mouldy green milk bottles.

Worst of all, poor Jack, unable to contain himself after

a long night's confinement, had crapped extensively in the kitchen doorway.

'You promised to keep the place taydy.'

'It wasn't Jack's fault. You know how good—'

'It's your fault, you aydle lad, for oversleeping.'

'Look, I'm really sorry. Have a drink, everyone,' Lysander called over Marigold's shoulder. 'No, actually I haven't got any. Why don't you all go down to The Pearly Gates and chalk up a stiff one on my account while I get dressed and clean the place up?'

'No thanks, I'm driving,' said the man in the duffle-coat. 'I've come to repossess your TV and video machine.'

'I'm about to watch the 2.30,' said Lysander furiously. 'And there's *EastEnders* and *The Bill* this evening. Look, if you're popping down to The Pearly Gates you can put twenty quid on Hannah's Uncle,' he yelled after the camel-faced couple who were belting down the path to their car.

After they'd all departed, Lysander was reduced to listening to the race over the telephone, which cost a bomb because Hannah's Uncle wouldn't go into the starting gates for ages, before storming home, five lengths clear at 25–1. Lysander was about to ring up Ladbroke's and shout at them that he could practically have settled his account if he'd been allowed his bet, when he was distracted by a photograph of Arthur on the mantelpiece.

He'd been so miserable about Kitty that he'd forgotten to ring Rupert to find out how poor dear Arthur and utterly bloody Tiny were getting on.

56

As Lysander drove through Penscombe past grey-blond houses, and a little Norman church where generations of Campbell-Blacks were buried, he noticed a betting shop. Rare in such a tiny village, it was no doubt patronized by all the locals putting their shirts on Rupert's horses. In the village-store window was a poster advertising a British Legion cheese-and-wine party to raise money for the Gulf. Lysander knew he ought to take an interest. The radio banged on and on about the liberation of Kuwait, but he was only interested in liberating Kitty.

Below Rupert's beautiful blond house, with its halo of magnificent beech trees, a long lake like mother of pearl in the falling sunshine was freezing at the edges. Across his rolling fields patches of snow lay like the spilt milk over which there was no use crying. All the birds were singing, trying to disguise the dull constant roar high above the clouds of B52s carrying bombs south from RAF Fairford.

Rupert was not surviving the recession and alarming set-backs at Lloyd's by altruism alone. Although beguiled by Lysander in Monthaut, he had noticed the boy's effortless extravagance. By smiling at the receptionist at the Hotel Versailles, Rupert had also ascertained that Lysander was picking up the massive bill for the President de Gaulle suite. The reason, therefore, that Rupert had offered to get Arthur sound was because he regarded Lysander as an engaging dolt awash with cash, who could easily be coaxed into buying other much younger horses for Rupert to train.

Rupert loathed droppers-in. Even the richest owners disturbed the horses' routine. He was not running a Harley Street nursing home. But when Lysander rolled up shivering uncontrollably with Donald Duck glaring out between the lapels of his long, dark blue, dog-fur-matted overcoat, Rupert actually stopped placating Mr Pandopoulos, whose horse hadn't been placed last week either. Leaving the apoplectic Greek to Dizzy, his extremely glamorous head girl, Rupert bore Lysander off to the yard kitchen for a cup of tea.

'Put him down,' said Rupert, as a pack of dogs swarmed round trying to reach a bristling Jack. 'They're quite safe, and the two Jack Russells are bitches.'

Enviously Lysander examined the photographs which crowded the walls of Rupert and his daughters, Perdita and Tabitha, winning world championships at show jumping, brandishing polo cups and leading in winners on the flat and over fences.

'I'm really sorry not to ring first,' he mumbled, 'but my telephone's stopped working.'

'Hug the Aga,' said Rupert, putting on the kettle. 'You look frozen.'

You could tell when a horse was in pain by its eyes; Lysander's were bright red, but the pupils and the irises were drab and lifeless. He was as pale as the Christmas roses Taggie had arranged in a dark green vase on the table. Jeans, skin-tight when he was skiing, were really baggy now.

'How's Arthur?' asked Lysander.

'King Arthur of the round belly,' said Rupert. 'God, he was cross when I cut down his rations. He ate every blade of straw, so I've put him on shredded newspaper. I expect he and Tiny are busily piecing together lurid stories about you and Mrs Rannaldini. How is she?'

'Oh, Rupert!' Once more, with all the egotism of heart-break, Lysander launched into his tale of woe.

'How can I convince her that I'm serious?' he pleaded finally, as he dipped a fifth piece of shortbread into his tea before handing it to a slavering Jack. 'I'd like to get a medal in the Gulf to show her I'm not just a cheap gigolo. The Yanks are paying people a thousand pounds a week just to put up tents.'

'I thought you were paid ten times as much as that for erections in England,' said Rupert, who'd been doing the entries for next week's races and working out who was going to ride out which horse tomorrow morning as he listened. 'All right, joke, joke,' he added, as Lysander's face blackened. 'Anyway, I've got news for you. Bunny, the vet, and I think we've sussed Arthur's problem.'

Rupert half-rose to look out of the window. 'That's her now.'

Arthur as usual was lying flat out snoring with his eyes wide open to get attention.

'I ought to move Penscombe Pride from the next-door box,' said Rupert as he opened the half-door. 'He isn't getting any sleep with that racket going on, but he's got a bit of a crush on Arthur.'

Arthur lurched to his feet in delight when he heard his master's voice. Whickering like Vesuvius, he nudged Lysander in the belly, grumbling about the dreadful starvation diet to which he'd been subjected. As usual he looked like nothing on earth, his face, back and quarters smeared with green, his mane and tail strewn with pieces of pink *Financial Times* like confetti. Having tried to eat Donald Duck, he went sharply into reverse and shook ostentatiously when he saw Bunny the vet.

'He's a terrible drip,' said Lysander apologetically. 'A programme seller in a white coat has him all of a tremble.'

Rounded, sweet and smiling, with long, soft brown hair and a gentle comforting voice, Bunny reminded Lysander for a fleeting agonizing moment of Kitty.

'We've discounted navicular,' she told Lysander. 'It's easy to make a mistake on an X-ray, but those lesions are actually normal synovial recesses.'

'Oh, right,' said Lysander, not knowing if that was good, and hanging tightly on to Arthur's headcollar as he kept trying to edge away.

'Will you trot him up now,' asked Bunny.

Even Arthur's delight at putting as many yards as possible between himself and Bunny soon disappeared as pain overwhelmed him. Miserably, he stumbled across the yard. Lysander could hardly bear to look. Arthur seemed worse than ever.

'He's certainly lame on both front legs,' said Bunny, when they had both returned. 'But I think the pain's coming from his coffin joints. Arthur,' she added, picking up his near-fore, 'has abnormally shaped feet with very long toes.'

'Sounds like Lady Chisleden,' said Lysander, giggling out of nerves.

Bunny raised her eyes to heaven.

'I have the misfortune to look after her lunatic Arabs,' she sighed.

Having clipped back the hair and scrubbed both Arthur's front feet, she filled a syringe with local anaesthetic: 'I'm going to do a nerve block in the near-fore coffin joint,' she explained as she plunged the needle into the front of a wincing Arthur's foot.

In his brief stay at Penscombe, Arthur had endeared himself to everyone. Now all Rupert's grooms left their charges, stopped sweeping up and cleaning tack to gather round. They were soon joined by farm workers, gardeners, the estate carpenter, a man delivering feed and Mr and Mrs Bodkin, the ancient couple who seemed to have always looked after Rupert.

Snow was drifting down as though it had all the time in the world. Even when Lysander lit a cigarette, which was strictly forbidden in the yard, the autocratic Rupert didn't snap at him.

'OK. It should be dead now. Trot him up,' said Bunny.

Tail whisking, pleased to have an audience, Arthur once again shambled off up the yard after Lysander, who was running backwards in order to look down at his legs.

'He's only lame on the off-fore now,' said Rupert. 'Trot him back.'

It took all Lysander's strength to stop Arthur taking off towards the house. He'd had enough of vets and his disapproval turned to megasulks when Bunny plunged another needle into his off-fore coffin joint.

'If he trots out sound now,' she told Lysander, 'it means all the pain's inside the joints and we can cure him with a combination of intra-articular injections and corrective shoeing.'

It seemed the longest ten minutes of Lysander's life. Penscombe was very high up. In winter, Rupert's horses wore dark blue hoods at night and often three rugs against the cold. Now, sensing something was up, like medieval chargers waiting for the start of Agincourt, they leant over their half-doors.

The yard had fallen silent, except for the sweet liquid carolling of a single robin and the occasional outraged protest of Tiny who was being held out of the way by a nervous stable lad. Lysander lit another cigarette. The girl grooms grew closer. Arthur's master was even more adorable than Arthur. Rupert lounged deceptively still against the lichened wall of the tack room. Only Jack, oblivious for once of the tension, was wagging his little tail and raising his ginger ears as he stepped round Taggie's black-and-white mongrel, Gertrude.

'Please God, make Arthur sound,' pleaded Lysander. 'I promise I'll get up in the morning and drink less – a lot less.'

Arthur, bored, tried to eat Bunny's Rolex.

'I need that to tell the time,' she cuffed him gently on his green nose. 'All right, if you'd like to trot him up the yard in a straight line.'

As Arthur set off, Jack streaked after him, and Tiny broke away from her stable lad. Like outriders, they flanked Arthur as he shambled through the snowflakes, first gingerly testing his off-fore, anticipating pain, then putting it down again. No, it really didn't hurt any more, nor, miraculously, did the other one. Then, joyfully, he was striding out, clattering up the cobbled yard, growing more and more confident, then out on to the gravel path until he reached the beech hedge round the tennis court. Swinging him round, with a Tarzan howl of joy, Lysander trotted him back, running backwards, nearly toppling over an uneven stone as he gazed in ecstasy at Arthur's great platey feet, shooting out sparks as they flew over the ground.

'Oh, Rupert, he's sound, he's fucking, fucking sound!'

A huge cheer went up from the crowd, which sent all the horses neighing and the dogs barking with excitement.

'I cannot believe it.' Lysander wiped his eyes with the back of his hand. 'Just one more time, Arthur.'

Turning, he sprinted back to the beech hedge, and Arthur bounded after him, even putting in a gallumphing buck of delight.

'Oh, thank you!' Lysander kissed Bunny, all the grooms, ancient Mrs Bodkin and very nearly Rupert, before flinging his arms round Arthur, and kissing the bits of his great ugly face that weren't green. Jack yapped excitedly round their feet, until Lysander plonked him on to Arthur's back, where he balanced still yapping to even louder cheers and screams of laughter, as Lysander trotted him up and down one more time.

'Arthur has a bilateral coffin joint problem due to poor foot balance,' explained Bunny, as Rupert opened a bottle of champagne, 'so he'll need egg-bar shoes, which are closed up in a circle where the heel ought to be. Then the heel will grow. You'll gradually be able to cut the toes back and his feet will become a normal shape again.'

Lysander hugged her again. 'It's a miracle! I can't tell you how grateful I am. Could Arthur have a small glass of champagne, Rupert? He really likes it – ouch,' he yelled as Tiny bit him. 'And can this bitch have one, too?'

*   *   *

When he and Lysander were back at the house in Rupert's office, Rupert got out the whisky decanter.

'Let's have a proper drink. It's things like this that make the job worthwhile. I must say Arthur's a sweet horse.'

'He's so clever.' Lysander admired the sleek, Stubbs horses over the fireplace and hoped, as he smelt Taggie's *boeuf Provençal* drifting from the kitchen, that he might be asked to stay for supper. 'And he's brilliant at getting himself out of trouble.'

Which is more than can be said for you, thought Rupert, as he reached for the soda syphon. Aloud he said: 'If you're on, let's give him one more crack at the Rutminster.'

Lysander swung round. 'D'you think there's time?'

'Course there is. He'll need a month on the roads. Then we'll start cantering and doing a bit of jumping by the end of the second month, then galloping for the last month, slowly building him up. We've got till the beginning of April.' Rupert flipped back the calendar. '6 April to be exact.'

'Oh, my goodness.'

Gazing at Rupert's wonderfully handsome face with the skiing tan heightened by the cold, the sleek blond hair darkened by melting snowflakes and the cornflower-blue eyes for once gentle and without mockery, Lysander felt a wave of adoration. Once again he wanted to kneel down and kiss Rupert's hand and to win his approval almost as much as Kitty's love. God, he was turning into a wimp.

'D'you mind awfully if I ring Kitty?' he said, reeling euphorically towards the telephone.

'We'll have to get the right jockey,' said Rupert, handing Lysander a glass. 'Arthur needs cajoling, but not too much.'

In horror, Lysander came reeling back again.

'But I'm going to ride,' he protested.

But Rupert was glancing from his diary to the list of horses on the wall and wondering who to send to Lingfield later in the week.

'If you're pouring out all this money for training, you might as well have an experienced jockey,' he said, then added: 'Christ, what a day. Tabitha, my daughter, is supposed to be going back to school this evening. And she's buggered off with a ghastly, bearded, animal-rights tractor-driver who thinks trainers are something one wears on one's extremely dirty feet. And Taggie's already paid the school fees. Honestly, with children at boarding-school, you're talking about wrapping a new BMW round a tree every six months and walking away from it.'

Glancing up, he saw Lysander was mouthing desperately, trying to get out the words.

'Look, basically, Rupert, I think we're at cross purposes. I honestly didn't mean to mislead you, but I can't possibly afford to put Arthur into training.'

It was as though the whisky was sliding right back into the decanter.

'Basically,' stammered Lysander, 'I opened my bank statement this morning. It was surprisingly depressing. I thought I had seventy-five grand, but actually I don't. Rather the reverse.'

'So, what do you have in mind?' said Rupert softly, his long fingers curling round his glass of whisky, eyes narrowed, every trace of friendliness gone from his face. Lysander was suddenly aware of the explosive menace of the man.

'Arthur's been staying here ten days,' went on Rupert, 'which is almost more expensive than the Hotel Versailles, not to mention that man-eating Shetland. The vet's bills alone have been astronomical. This isn't Donkey Rescue,' he added bitchily.

'I can see that.' Lysander put up a placating hand. 'But I have won point to points, and my uncle Alastair—'

'That drunken lech.'

Lysander winced. 'He knew about horses. He said I could ride anything.'

'And take anyone for a ride.'

Rupert's cold, dead face and icy, bullying voice

reminded Lysander of his father and made him stammer worse than ever.

'B-b-basically if you give me a job riding your horses at work and in races, I'll do it for free. I'll even clean tack although I'm not very g-g-good at it. I always put on too much saddle soap, and if we get Arthur sound, and I win the Rutminster on him, Kitty would realize I wasn't just a playboy, and I could afford to marry her.'

It took a lot to silence Rupert. The clock ticked, the fax machine squeaked and regurgitated. His secretary rattled away next door. There was a faint whirr from the kitchen as Taggie turned on the mixer. A ginger tom crashed through the cat door. A car drew up outside, and a door banged, before Rupert said: 'This is the top yard in the country and you expect me to train some clapped-out dinosaur for nothing and pay its entry fees?'

'I thought you might.' Lysander stared at his bitten-off toes. 'A big win would be good for your yard. People will be impressed that you've got Arthur. He still gets Christmas Cards and he got a jar of humbugs only last week. I can ride, I promise you.'

'You've got to be joking. There's no way I'll let an airhead like you loose on my horses. We're busy,' he added with unusual sharpness as Taggie popped her head round the door.

'I'm sorry,' she blushed, 'but Tab's home.'

'Let me get my hands on her.' Rupert drained his whisky. 'No, you don't,' he howled, as a blue streak topped by ruffled blond curls hurtled past the door.

Catching his daughter as she reached the bottom of the stairs, Rupert dragged her snarling like a Jack Russell into the office.

'I'm not going back to Bagley Hall,' screamed Tabitha. 'I hate you.'

'How *dare* you sneak off with that bloody leftie?'

'If Ashley was the son of a duke you wouldn't give a stuff,' yelled back Tabitha. 'You're such a snob. When you were young you pulled everything: Dizzy, Podge, Marion, there wasn't a groom unbonked in the South of England, and what about Perdita? The world must be strewn with your illegits.'

Tabitha had erupted into the room like a Catherine wheel, eyes narrower and bluer than Rupert's, skin the thick creaminess of elderflowers, blond curls bouncing off the same smooth forehead, her face delicately modelled despite the huge screaming mouth. Lysander had never witnessed such rage, such bristling antagonism, such passion between two people. Any moment, they'd set fire to each other. Jack, allergic to rows, started yapping.

'You ought to write your autobiography and call it *The Stud Book*,' taunted Tabitha.

'Shut up,' yelled Rupert, 'and don't you start laughing.' He turned on Lysander. 'Get out, and shut that fucking dog up.'

As Lysander and Jack slid out into the hall, they found Taggie clutching her head.

'Oh dear, oh dear.'

'Hi.' Lysander kissed her on both cheeks. 'Oh wow, I don't blame the tractor-driver.'

'Rupert's under a lot of pressure,' said Taggie defensively. 'He's worried about the war. Having been in the Army, he feels he ought to be out there, and he's worried about business; the Saudis and Kuwaitis own a lot of his horses.'

'Lovely house,' said Lysander, admiring the yellow flagstones, the tapestries and the huge oil of a rotund black Labrador.

'When it's quiet,' said Taggie.

The screaming was escalating.

'Don't you touch me. I'll ring Esther Rantzen and get you for child battering. I've had to live through one lousy newspaper scandal after another. No wonder I'm disturbed. Ashley says I ought to be in therapy.'

'You ought to be in a chastity belt,' yelled Rupert. 'You've always had everything you wanted.'

'So've you – mostly women.'

'Not since Taggie, and you know it.'

'She doesn't trust you an inch. That's why she tags (ha, bloody ha) along to everything. Never lets you out of her sight. I used to see something of you before you married her.'

Putting her hands over her ears, Taggie ran back to the kitchen.

'Shut up!' Rupert was shaking Tabitha like a rat. 'You've gone too far this time. You can go and live with your mother. And I'll sell Frankie, Sorrel *and* Biscuit.'

This was the red-hot poker on Tabitha's back.

'You wouldn't dare,' she sobbed hysterically. 'I'll report you to the RSPCA and the NS what's it. You promised Biscuit could end her days here! You promised!' She was banging her fists frantically against Rupert's chest.

'If you ever see that hairy little wimp again, and you don't go back to Bagley Hall tonight, Biscuit'll be in a can, or shipped abroad for horse meat.'

Rupert had always insisted on an office with two doors, so he could escape from importuning women in the old days and now from tiresome owners.

'Bastard!' Tabitha ran screaming through the door leading upstairs.

Lysander jumped guiltily and fell into the office as Rupert opened the second door. His face was expressionless, but there was a glint in his eyes.

'Where were we?' he said amiably. 'Oh yes, you wanted to race ride for me.'

Picking up the telephone, he dialled the yard.

'Dizzy darling, can you tack up Meutrier?'

Lysander could hear Dizzy's squawk of disapproval down the telephone, but he was too excited about proving himself to notice.

Horses, their blazes and stars gleaming in the dusk, hung out of their boxes whickering in delight as the grooms put scoops of oats and nuts in each manger. Meutrier, a beautiful chestnut, showing a crescent of white below both eyes, came out with a clatter, not amused at having to postpone his supper.

'Hang on, he's as quick as lightning,' muttered Dizzy in defiance of her boss, 'and his mouth's gone, and he's got a horrific stop.'

'No-one asked your opinion,' snapped Rupert, as he gave Lysander a leg up.

'I ride long,' said Lysander, gathering up his reins.

'Not on my horses, you don't.' Rupert tugged up the stirrups until Lysander's long thighs were level with Meutrier's back.

'Goodbye, world,' giggled Lysander.

Like a jewelled hairnet he could see the lights of Penscombe tangling with the bare trees.

'This is a beautiful horse, Rupert,' he said as he rode off.

'Why d'you put him on Meutrier?' asked Dizzy furiously. 'He's a sweet boy.'

'And needs hacking down to size.'

Having bawled her head off in her room, incensed that not even Taggie, whom she really adored, had come up to comfort her, Tabitha stopped crying. She couldn't go back to Bagley Hall. She'd never see Ashley again and feel the tickle of his beard. She wished he washed more, but he despised deodorants, thinking the skin ought to be allowed to breathe.

Looking out of the window, she saw her father and Dizzy walking towards the all-weather track that ran for a mile and a half over Rupert's rolling fields. They were following a rider on – Christ, it was Meutrier. No other horse walked with that fluid grace or that innocence. Tab picked up her binoculars. She couldn't identify who was on his back, but he rode wonderfully. She'd never seen anyone move so naturally with a horse. For Meutrier, it must have been like dancing with Fred Astaire.

In gratitude the big vicious chestnut put in a terrifying buck. The rider grabbed his mane but didn't shift in the saddle, then he swung the horse towards the floodlit track, and he was off, hurtling towards the first fence. Meutrier's ears were flat to the head. He was taking off too near. Meutrier was going to stop. Tab gripped her binoculars in horror. The rider would be killed going at that speed. Then amazingly Meutrier put in a terrific cat jump and sailed over.

Kicking his feet out of the stirrups, stretching his legs, the rider was over the next fence, his body folding beautifully, as he disappeared over the brow of the hill.

Down by the finish, Dizzy forgot the cold and the racing snowflakes and gave a cry of relief as Lysander appeared round the corner. Coming up to the last fence, he dropped his reins and folded his arms, laughing as Meutrier hoisted himself upwards and cleared the birch twigs by a foot. As Lysander pulled up, for a second Rupert's antagonism, overdrafts, unemployment, even the loss of Kitty were forgotten.

'This is the most wonderful horse I've ever ridden. I'm sure he'd stay twice the distance. I'd give anything to ride him at Cheltenham.'

At that moment Taggie came slipping and sliding down the snowy path. She hadn't even bothered to put on a jacket.

'Rupert, you didn't put Lysander on Meutrier? He was going back tomorrow.'

'Well, he may not now,' said Rupert.

His rage had subsided, but, not prepared to be conciliatory, he stalked ahead of them back to the house.

Lysander was sitting at the scrubbed kitchen table eating miraculously light cheese-straws hot from the oven when Tabitha slid round the door like a cat, took one incredulous look at him and shot out again. Then, as Taggie handed him a glass of whisky and settled herself on the window-seat opposite, Tabitha's amazed face reappeared outside the window.

He couldn't be real, thought Tabitha, he couldn't.

Such thick brown curls, such a wonderful curving mouth pulled upwards by the short upper lip and such big, kind, laughing eyes.

'Oooooooh,' she wailed.

'Has anyone seen *Horse and Hound*?' she muttered as she slid back round the kitchen door a minute later.

'Hi, darling,' said Taggie. 'Help yourself to a drink.'

'Thanks.' Tab reached for a sherry glass and filled it up with Coke so it spilled over and over as she gazed at Lysander.

'Come and sit down,' Taggie patted the seat beside her.

'Sorry,' muttered Tabitha, sliding in beside her step-mother, and putting her chin on Taggie's shoulder. 'Didn't mean it.'

'I know you didn't.' Taggie hugged her. 'You two haven't been introduced, have you?'

'Not properly,' said Lysander. 'You look just like your father. D'you ride as well as he does?'

'Um.' Tab had gone crimson and opened her mouth and shut it, when Rupert marched in, dangling the cordless telephone between finger and thumb.

'It's Ashley,' he said softly.

There was a long, tense pause.

'Tell him I'm not here,' stammered Tabitha. 'That I've gone back to school, make up something. Arthur's fantastic,' she turned adoringly back to Lysander, all thoughts of tractor-drivers forgotten. 'Can I do him when I come back at weekends?'

Looking from Tab to Lysander, Rupert gave Taggie the faintest smile.

'All right, you're on,' he told Lysander, after he had dealt with Ashley. 'Three months' trial, but if you step out of line just once, you're fired. You can ride out for me, and if any of the other jockeys don't want a ride in a race you can have it. You'll need ten wins or places to qualify for the Rutminster.'

Tabitha got up and hugged her father. 'I love you, Daddy.'

'Oh gosh, thank you so much. That's seriously, seriously kind,' Lysander was able to stammer out at last.

'You'll have to lose a stone – which you can ill afford. So you'll have to build yourself up at the same time. And remember, no booze.'

Lysander turned green. 'Surely the odd glass of wine wouldn't matter?'

'It would be odd if you stopped at one,' said Rupert. 'Not a drop till after the Rutminster.'

57

Lysander was so unhappy that the weight dropped off him. He had never been up at six in the morning before unless he'd been partying all night. Nor had he ever been worked so hard. Rupert immediately moved him into Penscombe, putting him up in a little room under the eaves with low beams – 'one can't concuss him more than he is already' – a patchwork quilt and paintings of Rupert's old ponies on the whitewashed wall.

'I'm not having you mooning around in Magpie Cottage with your bins trained on Valhalla,' he told Lysander. 'I want you here where I can keep an eye on you.'

Lysander would never have survived without Rupert's girl grooms. Once they realized they weren't going to get him into bed – and he rejected their offers so sweetly – they stopped squabbling over him and covered up for him instead.

Every morning they would shake him awake, practically dressing him, forcing extra jerseys over his diminishing frame, frogmarching him to whatever difficult horse – Lysander could never remember – that Rupert had earmarked for him the night before.

But however difficult the horse, he seemed to steal into its head and heart before arriving somewhat to his amazement on its back. Horses really wanted to go well for him and seemed delighted by their own capabilities.

His problem was concentration. If he started thinking of Kitty when he was three lengths clear in a gallop, he'd be trailing the field in a matter of seconds. He was also a chatterbox, talking constantly on the gallops and even when jumping fences. If a jockey or a horse had a fall he had to pull up instantly to see if they were all right, and walking Arthur round the Gloucestershire lanes took hours because he stopped to chat to everyone – anything to avoid going back to clean mountains of tack or spend hours dunking hay in icy water to get rid of the dust.

Having lost an efficient if truculent tractor-driver in Tabitha's boyfriend Ashley, Rupert made an early mistake of handing over the job to Lysander. Flying home the following evening Rupert was appalled to see lines that should have flowed straight over the rich brown earth tangled together like a kitten's ball of string. A very harrowing experience, admitted Rupert, when he'd regained his sense of humour and put Lysander back to cleaning tack.

Taggie was the person who really saved Lysander's life. If he hadn't been so hopelessly in love with Kitty he would have certainly been smitten. Worried about his pallor and dramatic weight loss, while the other riders were joyously guzzling fried eggs, sausages and bacon sandwiches after the gallops, Taggie tried to tempt Lysander with grilled soles, or steaks dripping with herbs and butter. She put slimming biscuits in a flowered tin in his bedroom and made him hot chocolate with skimmed milk at night to help him sleep, which he surreptitiously emptied down the sink because he couldn't stand the stuff.

And Taggie listened when he banged on about Kitty – the grooms restricted him to five minutes an hour. Still numb at the loss of her own baby, when she was not cooking for Rupert's staff, she was always bottle-rearing calves and lambs, or feeding hens and ducks, or Rupert's dogs, or topping up the birdtable, or smuggling forbidden toast and marmalade to Arthur when he hung forlornly out of his chewed-down half-door.

Owners bored Rupert, but Taggie was always ready with a sympathetic ear, a cup of tea and home-made chocolate cake.

This led to problems. Checking on Arthur one after-noon, Lysander was amazed to discover Taggie cringing at the back of the box, stroking an outraged Tiny.

'What *are* you doing?'

'Hush!' Taggie went scarlet. 'Mr Pandopoulos is here, and he keeps groping me. If Rupert found out he'd hit him across the yard and tell him to take his horses away, and we really can't afford it at the moment.'

Lysander's face fell. 'And Rupert's keeping me and Arthur and Tiny for nothing. Oh, when's he going to let me race ride, so I can start earning my keep?'

'You're doing that already. Rupert's really pleased with the way the horses have improved. Being tough is the only way he feels he can get results.'

Lysander had never met a couple so aware of each other, as they drifted together, watching, touching, like each other's shadows. Their love filled Lysander with envy. But Rupert was very tricky. Lysander had to be careful not to be too friendly to Taggie. The only thing male and beautiful Rupert really wanted in his yard was horses.

Lysander hardly noticed the war, as bulletins came and went on the tack-room radio, but, reeling from one of Rupert's tongue-lashings, he often felt like Baghdad after a night's bombardment.

In the second week in February he was just schooling a vastly improved but still cussed Meutrier over a row of fences. The setting sun, like an exploding ball of flame rising into a thick black nuclear cloud, seemed to symbol-ize everyone's worries over the approaching land war.

Planes had roared overhead all day. Rupert, who was in a particularly foul mood because King Hussein, a fellow old Harrovian, appeared to be supporting the Iraqis, called Lysander over.

'Why the fuck don't you use your whip?'

'My Uncle Alastair said it was a lazy way of riding,' said Lysander, quaking but defiant. 'Meutrier was really trying, so it's stupid to hit him. And when horses are exhausted, it only slows them down. Honestly, Rupert, it makes me sick to see jockeys flogging horses. There's no need to hit them so hard.'

This was an oblique reference to Jimmy Jardine, Rupert's second jockey, who'd just begun a fortnight's suspension for excessive use of the whip – probably at Rupert's instructions.

'So, you think Jimmy's had nearly ninety winners this season just by feeding his horses sugar lumps. If you ride for me, you use your whip.'

For a second they glared at each other. Lysander lowered his eyes first. He couldn't face that cold dismissive contempt. Swinging Meutrier round, he rode wearily back to the yard. Overtaking them in the Land-Rover, Rupert was on the tack-room telephone when Lysander got back.

'OK, Marcia, Jimmy's been suspended, but I'm not sure he and Hopeless were twin souls. Anyway, I'm putting a new boy, Lysander Hawkley, up on him. You'll like him, Marcia, he's better-looking than Jimmy. Yes, the 2.30 tomorrow, Maiden Hurdle, Worcester.'

Putting back the telephone, Rupert saw Lysander mouthing helplessly in the doorway, hanging for support from Meutrier's sweating chestnut neck.

'You heard me,' said Rupert. 'And you'd better take a whip or you won't get Hopeless off the starting line.'

Unplaced in her last eight races, Hopeless was an appropriately named chestnut mare with spindly legs, wild eyes and a punk mane, too sparse even to plait. Her owner, Marcia Melling, a glamorous but ageing divorcée, only kept the horse in training because she had a massive crush on Rupert, who in turn only trained the horse, and then with minimum effort, because he charged Marcia three times as much as any other owner.

It was not with any hopes of victory that Lysander set out with Samantha and Maura, two of the girl grooms, in Rupert's lorry on the thirty-five mile drive to Worcester the following morning. To distract him from his desperate nerves, Rupert had given him the responsibility of loading the five runners and their tack.

It was a beautiful day, with soft brown trees sunlit against the khaki fields, catkins hanging like golden Tiffany lamps, and coltsfoot exploding in a sulphur haze on the verges.

'Arthur always enjoys being read to,' said Lysander, as he turned the lorry towards the motorway. 'He likes the *Sun* better than the *Independent*, but he likes *Dear Deirdre* best.'

'*Dear Deirdre, I am in love with a married woman who will not leave her husband*, Arthur must be quite sick of that one,' said Samantha, handing Lysander her last cigarette. 'You can't stop here,' she said in horror as Lysander screeched to a halt to much honking and fist-waving.

'I've got to. I took half a bottle of Cascara last night to lose the last three pounds and I'm about to explode. Open the fucking door.' Lysander leapt across them out of the lorry and bounded up the hard shoulder.

Rupert and Taggie were flying to Worcester from London with Mr Pandopoulos and Freddie Jones, the co-owner of Penscombe Pride. Tabitha, back for half-term, was being given a lift by Dizzy, Rupert's tough, blond, glamorous head girl, who had recently returned to work for him after getting a divorce.

Racing into the yard, Tabitha greeted her own ponies, then, armed with a Twix, rushed off to see Arthur. Coming out of his box, just avoiding Tiny's teeth, she gave a gasp, for in the next box, rugged, bandaged, plaited up and fast asleep was Penscombe Pride.

'Dizzy,' screamed Tab, banging on the groom's flat window.

'What is it?' said Dizzy, who rather fancied Mr Pandopoulos as a sugar daddy, turning off the hair drier.

'Isn't Pridie running in the 3.15?'

'Certainly is. He should be halfway to Worcester by now.'

'The hell he is, he's still in his box.'

'Jesus.' Dizzy dropped the hairdrier. 'That stupid fucker must have forgotten to load him. Sam and Maura are so in love with him, they wouldn't have noticed.'

'We've got to get him there,' said Tabitha in panic. 'Daddy'll boot Lysander straight out if he finds out.'

One of Rupert's lorries was in for a service, the other had gone to Folkestone. There only remained the trailer used for ferrying pigs, calves and Tab's ponies around – transport ill-fitting the winner of the Cotchester Gold Cup two years running and the yard's biggest earner.

'I daren't risk it,' said Dizzy. 'We could borrow one of Ricky France-Lynch's lorries.'

'Ten miles in the wrong direction,' urged Tab. 'Pridie'll enjoy the fresh air and at least his tack's gone on already.'

'I'm going to be sick,' said Tabitha, hanging out of the window as the speedometer hit sixty miles an hour along the narrow, winding high-banked country lanes.

'I'm going to be sacked,' said Dizzy. 'Is Pridie still there?'

'He's fine.' Leaning round Tabitha could see his lovely dark bay head, with the instantly recognizable zigzag blaze, and large, wide-set eyes looking over the top of the trailer at the russet cottages and orchards.

As they rattled through Pershore, two women with shopping bags cheered in amazed excitement. As they hit race-day traffic, more and more people started laughing and waving to see little Pridie so close.

'Like the Pope in his Popemobile,' giggled Tab.

'I've backed that horse in the 3.15, so get a move on,' said a man in a Jaguar drawing alongside them at some traffic-lights. 'What are you two doing for dinner tonight?'

'Someone's bound to tell Daddy,' said Tab despairingly.

'He nearly killed Lysander for forgetting Mr Sparky's bridle last week,' said Dizzy, drawing the attention of the man on the gate to the green trainer's badge on the windscreen.

'If only Lysander weren't so lush,' sighed Tab. 'D'you think there's any hope for me?'

'Doubt it,' said Dizzy, bumping over the muddy track. 'seems so set on this Kitty, he's determined to practise being faithful.'

'My brother Marcus only practises the piano for eight hours a day. Oh, thank God! There's Dad's lorry.'

Ahead, beside horse boxes belonging to Martin Pipe and Jenny Pitman, was parked the familiar dark blue lorry with RUPERT CAMPBELL-BLACK in large letters on the side. Stamping could be heard from within. With the cough and viruses about, Rupert preferred to leave horses in the lorry which was about as luxurious inside as the Ritz.

'If we can reload Pridie, we might get away with it,' said Dizzy, leaping out.

'Oh, hell, there's Lysander,' muttered Tab. 'Have you got a comb and some blusher, Dizz?'

Leaning against Rupert's lorry as white and elongated as a piece of spaghetti tested on a wall, Lysander was chatting to Penscombe Pride's champion jockey, Bluey Charteris. Tough as hell – you couldn't kill him with a machine-gun – Bluey worked hard and played hard.

'Hi, Tab,' called out Lysander. 'You got here quickly. We've only just arrived. Not a bush unleapt behind.' He patted his concave belly. 'Bluey's giving me a few tips.'

Tab trotted a skittishly leaping Penscombe Pride right up to Lysander's nose.

'Who the hell's this?' she said accusingly, as Pridie whickered and left white dribble on Lysander's blue overcoat.

'It's Pridie.' Lysander scratched his head. 'How did he get out?'

'You forgot to load him, you asshole.'

'Omigod!' Lysander looked from Bluey to Tab in horror, then started to giggle. 'How did he get here?'

'Dizzy's trying to hide the trailer.'

639

'Kerrist!' The grin was wiped off Bluey Charteris' swarthy, cadaverous features as he shot round the horse, feeling his legs. 'You fuckwit, Lysander.'

'He liked the fresh air – like a day at the seaside,' said Tab.

'And what's Rupert going to say?' demanded Bluey.

'Say about what?'

Everyone jumped. It was Rupert in a pale brown overcoat, with a dark brown velvet collar, and with a brown trilby tipped over his Greek nose. With him was Taggie, ravishing as ever in a pale grey trench coat, shiny black boots and a scarlet beret, and Freddie Jones, the electronics billionaire, who had red hair and a jaunty smile and was the most popular owner in the yard. Rupert never minded Freddie dropping in.

' 'Allo, Pridie,' Freddie greeted his very famous prize winner with affection. ' 'Allo, Tab, 'allo, Lysander. Gather you've got your first race in a minute. What is it?'

'Maiden hurdle,' said Lysander, starting to shake.

'Lysander's principal hurdle is a married woman,' said Rupert acidly. 'What the hell's Pridie doing out of the lorry?'

'He sweated up. We were just walking him out.' Tabitha returned her father's blue-eyed stare blandly. 'He does look well, doesn't he?'

'I'd better get changed,' said Lysander, anxious to escape interrogation.

Fortunately Rupert was sidetracked by the arrival of Mr Pandopoulos, leering in a massive belted camel-hair coat, together with Hopeless's owner, Marcia Melling, wafting Joy.

'Hallo, Rupert,' she said petulantly, leaving crimson lipstick on both sides of his face. 'I'm a bit choked. You've put a complete novice on Hopeless.'

'This is Lysander,' said Taggie quickly.

'Oh, oh, oooo.' Suddenly Marcia looked as delighted as a large bear let loose in Barbara Cartland's larder. 'My word, aren't you tall for a jock? Lysander, d'you say?

Mystic Meg said only this week that luck would come from a man whose name began with L.'

'Meg's brilliant,' Lysander smiled weakly. 'How d'you do? Must go,' and he fled to the changing-room lavatories.

'What a charming, intelligent face,' said a bemused Marcia.

'Hasn't he?' said Rupert. 'Makes a battery hen look like Stephen Hawking.'

In the same race as Lysander Bluey Charteris was riding a brilliant five year old called Turkish Hustler, whom Rupert had brought off the flat and who was odds-on favourite. Hopeless was 100–1. 'Lives up to her name,' said *Timeform* succinctly.

The crowds hanging over the paddock railings, studying their racecards and *Sporting Life*, laughed at Hopeless. Even wearing the thick blue rug with the initials RC-B on the side, which generally inspired terror in the most phlegmatic bookie, Hopeless looked like a child dressing up in her mother's overcoat.

Lysander, weighing-out in the tiny chair beside the huge red clock, discovered he'd lost three pounds overnight, which was nice and light for Hopeless and meant he hadn't anything left to throw up. He had spent last night pouring over videos of Hopeless's earlier races. An inexperienced horse, she was not used to being in front and weaved all over the place. He must keep her straight and behind Turkish Hustler to the last moment. He wished he could wear his Donald Duck jersey instead of Marcia's olive-green colours, which he supposed matched his face. He'd got to be brave for Kitty's and Arthur's sake. Even if he were only placed, it would help notch up his quota of races needed to qualify for the Rutminster.

In the paddock, Taggie put her coat round his shuddering shoulders as Rupert gave him last-minute instructions.

'Start slowly. She's most unlikely to last the distance, and build up,' he added finally. 'And I'd get down to the start as early as possible. She gets upset if horses come thundering past her.'

Rupert wants her out of the paddock as quickly as possible, poor old Hopeless, thought Lysander indignantly. We'll show him.

Rupert turned to Bluey who was eyeing a redhead in a group clustered round the second favourite.

'I don't need to tell *you* anything, Bluey. Just sit on his back. Let's go and have a drink,' he added to Freddie. 'This race is a foregone conclusion.'

'I put two pounds on Hopeless,' said Tab.

Rupert was busy discussing viewing figures with Freddie, who was also a director of Venturer, when he heard the flat, patrician voice of the course commentator echoing round the ground.

'And Hopeless jumped that extremely well, and is moving up to join the leaders.'

Running to the balcony, choking on a turkey sandwich, Rupert looked through his binoculars at the shimmering garland of colours moving above the rails and the centipede of frantically galloping legs below, as they came to the second hurdle from home.

Hopeless was in fourth place, making it look really easy and Lysander was riding beautifully, his hands almost touching the horse's flickering orange ears, urging her on, his body moving with her like a lover's, encouraging her every inch of the way.

Only a grey gelding and a fence were between Hopeless and the finishing post as she caught up with Turkish Hustler and Bluey.

Together they cleared the last hurdle.

'Hang on. You're going a bit quick. Don't want to wear her out,' called across Bluey. 'There's a long run up.'

Wide and emerald-green, the course loomed ahead. As the grey gelding's tail drew nearer and nearer, Bluey picked up his whip, only allowed ten whacks before the finishing-post.

Crack, crack, crack; down they came on brave Hustler's heaving flanks.

'Come on, Hopeless,' shouted Lysander. 'Good girl, go for it.'

Turkish Hustler hurtled forward, galvanized but frightened. Hopeless's competitive spirit flared. She must keep up with her stable-mate. Scrawny mane and tail flying, spindly legs flailing, galloping her no-longer-timid heart out, she chased Hustler past the grey. Then Hustler seemed to tire and go backwards as Hopeless shot forward.

'Go on, angel,' begged Lysander.

'Pick up your bat, you stupid fucker,' yelled Rupert from the balcony.

Marcia, blue mascara streaming, was too excited to speak.

'He's going to do it,' shrieked Tabitha. 'I've won two hundred fucking pounds,' as Hopeless slid past the post a quarter of a length ahead.

Down they all surged into the winner's enclosure. A huge cheer and much laughter went up as Lysander rode in with a great grin spread across his face, leaving white stripes of foam on a bemused but happy Hopeless's chestnut coat as he patted her over and over again.

Marcia couldn't stop kissing Lysander, and only relinquished him when Taggie turned up to give him a big hug.

'Oh, that was wonderful! I'm so proud of you, and darling Hopeless.'

Ecstatically, Lysander hugged her back.

There were photographers everywhere.

'I made two hundred pounds,' said Tab, feeding Hopeless a Polo. 'It was a toss up between a bet and a packet of fags.'

Over Taggie's shoulder, Lysander's eyes met Rupert's.

'You didn't obey a single instruction,' he said coldly.

'Basically,' Lysander edged away from Taggie, 'I thought she needed encouraging. I'm really sorry.'

But Rupert suddenly laughed, and clapped him on the shoulder.

'Fucking marvellous; only another nine races and you qualify for the Rutminster.'

'And don't go drinking champagne now,' said Bluey, adding his congratulations. 'If you've been wasting, you're better off with a cup of tea.'

It was Rupert's day. Meutrier won by three lengths, Penscombe Pride by ten. Mr Sparky came second, but only after a photo-finish. Afterwards Bluey took Rupert aside.

'I don't like competition, but that boy is bloody good. Meutrier's improved out of all recognition since he's been working on him. Mr Sparky's a different horse. He's loving it. He can see a stride.'

'Marcia feels the same,' said Rupert. 'She wants to buy Lysander.'

Over at Valhalla the following morning, Rannaldini, who hadn't liked Lysander having such a powerful ally as Rupert, delightedly handed *The Scorpion* to Kitty.

'Your little friend's up to his tricks again.'

On page three was a large picture of Lysander and Taggie embracing ecstatically.

HAS RUPERT TAKEN IN A TROJAN HORSE? said the caption.

Rupert pretended not to mind the picture in *The Scorpion*, but he was livid underneath and took it out on everyone, particularly Taggie. Lysander made himself as scarce as possible. Dusk saw Rupert howling round the house in search of yesterday's *Racing Post*.

'Some bloody idiot's chucked it out. How many times do I have to tell you I need to keep them?'

'It's probably in the study,' snapped Taggie, who was exhausted.

'I've looked.'

'Go and look again.'

Clenching his fists, Rupert stormed out, then paused

in the hall in front of the huge oil of his beloved, late Labrador, Badger. Badger would have understood how he felt about *The Scorpion*, providing solid, silent, black sympathy.

Then Rupert heard the crash of the pedal dustbin, followed by a rustling noise, and sidled back towards the kitchen.

As he opened the door very slowly, he found Taggie frantically wiping baked beans off the front of yesterday's *Racing Post*.

'Gotcha!' Rupert grabbed her from behind.

'You startled me.' Jumping like a kangaroo, Taggie turned crimson. 'Someone must have, I mean, *I* must have thrown it away. We can't keep everything,' she said defensively.

Turning her round, Rupert glared down for a second.

'Of course we can't.' He pulled her towards him. 'If you weren't here,' he said roughly, 'the entire house would disappear in a mountain of rubbish in a week. I'm only terrified you'll throw me out one day.'

As he took her tired, dirty, unpainted face between his hands, her hair smelt of bonfire smoke. Looking down, he noticed blood all over her clothes.

'What have you done?' he asked in horror. 'Are you OK?'

'Yes, yes,' Taggie smiled proudly. 'Passion went into labour, I pulled her calf out all by myself.'

'You shouldn't,' said Rupert appalled. 'You might have strained yourself or got knocked over.'

'I'm fine, and it's the sweetest little calf. Come and see it.'

'I know sweeter calves.' Rupert ran his hands down her thighs. 'I'm sorry I've been such a shit. Tomorrow's Valentine's Day.'

'I know. I love you so much.'

'And we're going to Paris tonight.'

'Wow,' squeaked Taggie in excitement. 'Can we leave the yard?'

'Of course we can, for thirty-six hours.'

'Have I got time to wash my hair and have a bath?'

'More important, we've got time to go to bed,' murmured Rupert.

Peering round the door, Lysander felt a great wave of longing and loneliness as he saw them locked in each other's arms. They looked so beautiful, straight out of *Dynasty*. In the corner, Jack was sharing a basket with Gertrude the mongrel, so besotted he could hardly bear to leave her to sleep on Lysander's bed at night. Everyone's shacked up but me, thought Lysander. He'd just posted a second Valentine to Kitty, because he couldn't remember if he'd posted the first. Rupert was going away tomorrow. Lysander had a brainwave.

58

Clive, Rannaldini's leather-clad henchman, intercepted both Valentines which Lysander had drawn himself. The first was of a leopard with tears pouring down its face as it tried to scrub off its spots, in the second the same leopard tried desperately to climb into a washing machine. Clive hid them in a file with all Lysander's other letters he'd whipped and any press cuttings that had appeared about him. Rannaldini had instructed him to tail Kitty, so on Valentine's Day he followed her into Rutminster when she did the week's shopping.

The moment Rupert and Taggie left for Paris Lysander sloped off to London where he picked up Maggie's puppy and enlisted Ferdie's help in writing Kitty a letter. Next morning, Valentine's Day, he had to crawl back to Rutshire because the whole West of England was blanketed in fog. Risking his neck by missing the morning's gallops, he prayed that none of the grooms would grass on him. As he reached Paradise his heart started jumping and his hands became so sticky he could hardly swing the wheel enough to navigate the winding lanes. A florist's van was parked outside Rachel's cottage. Delivering Rannaldini's roses, thought Lysander savagely. Avoiding the electric gates and guard-dogs at the main entrance to Valhalla, he bumped up a little-used ride through the woods, stretching a hand back to steady the little creature on the back seat beside Jack.

Only the passionate hope that one day he and Kitty would be together enabled him to part with Maggie's puppy. Pale fawn, striped like a tiger, she had a white belly, speckled paws and a sweet frowning striped face with a very direct stare. Despite long legs, her tail practically trailed on the ground. A cross between a flying fish, a bird and a deer, she glided into rooms and leapt on to chairs with the grace of a ballet dancer.

It was clear that neither Jack nor Dinsdale, nor even Tabloid had a paw in her parentage. Lysander put his money on a greyhound.

'You're going to cheer up my Kitty,' he told the puppy who cocked her head on one side, 'for not having a baby, and don't let her get pregnant. Sleep on her bed and bite Rannaldini's willy whenever he comes near her.'

The silence was eerie. Valhalla was strangled by thick veils of floating grey fog. At the edge of the park Lysander could distinguish rusty iron railings and ancient trees looming up like bison or great horned stags. His heart was pounding his rib cage, a lunatic trying to escape from a padded cell. Then Jack and the puppy started yapping furiously as the fearsome Prince of Darkness in a New Zealand rug galloped out of the mist and thundered away. Ahead the woods reared up like cliffs, treacherous to mariners, and there was the house, greyer than the fog itself, with its gables, tall chimneys and small secretive windows, as though the stonework between the panes formed prison bars.

Gathering up the puppy, Lysander went up to the great front door, resting against it for a second before setting the rusty bell jangling mournfully. If Kitty answered the door, he was tempted to kidnap her. But the nose that peered out was long and red-veined.

For a second Mrs Brinscombe's face lit up, then she looked terrified.

'You mustn't come here, it's more than my life's worth. Oh, the sweet little duck.' She put up a red, roughened hand to stroke the puppy.

'Where's Kitty? Please, please, Mrs B, I've got to see her.'

'She's gone shopping in Rutminster.'

'Then I'll wait.'

'No.' She shrank from him. 'Clive's being paid to follow her and he's a villain. Please don't risk it. Rannaldini'll sack me and Mr B, and he'll take it out on Kitty.'

'Is she OK?'

Mrs Brimscombe loved Lysander and hated to see him so thin and ghost-pale. She had endured enough of Mr Brimscombe's indiscriminate lechery to have huge sympathy with Kitty.

'She's all right on the surface.' Mrs Brimscombe thought for a second. 'But she reminds me of one of those prisoners of war that Saddam Hussein keeps parading on TV, that looks all bruised and beaten and dazed, but keeps on telling you what a good man Saddam is, and how wicked the Allies are to fight him. She don't seem natural.'

'Oh, God!' Lysander was frantic. 'Poor little Kitty. Is he bullying her?'

'No. That's what don't seem natural either. He's being so nice.'

'Well, give her this, and this.' Lysander shoved the puppy and his letter into Mrs Brimscombe's unwelcoming hands. 'Tell Clive she's a stray wandered in from the wood, but please see that Kitty gets her.'

Stumbling in despair back to his car, he reminded Mrs Brimscombe of one of those poor wretched seabirds, helpless and paralysed by oil in the Gulf. With no other thought but oblivion, Lysander headed for The Pearly Gates.

Returning from Rutminster, Kitty was greeted by a very over-excited Mrs B, who managed to slip her the letter. 'Put it in yer bra, m'duck,' and whispered that the puppy came from Lysander before Clive walked in buckling under the two trays of Bounce for Rannaldini's guard-dogs.

'What's this?' he said, as the puppy padded trustfully towards him. 'Gorgeous little thing.' He put out a hand ringed like a knuckle-duster. 'Where's it come from?'

'It's a stray. Mrs B found it wanderin' outside,' said Kitty quickly.

'Doesn't look like one.' The puppy yelped as Clive picked it up by the scruff of the neck. 'It's well fed, and its paws aren't marked. I'll pop it down to the local rescue kennels.'

'No you won't,' said Kitty with surprising sharpness.

'You're scared of dogs,' said Clive rudely.

'Not this one. Give it to me.'

'Rannaldini don't like dogs in the house.' Clive's pale fleshless face was alight with malice, his pale grey eyes had the innocence of a psychopath. 'Canine dogs, that is.'

'I'll deal with Rannaldini.' Kitty was fired with sudden courage. ' 'And it over. Now clear off.'

As she grabbed the puppy from Clive, it covered her face with little licks. Shutting her eyes, Kitty breathed in its sweet, fresh oatmeal smell. It was the first Valentine she'd ever had.

Only when the puppy had been fed and watered and they'd both retreated to the safety of her bedroom did she open Lysander's letter kindly dictated by Ferdie. She read:

> *Darling Kitty,*
> *This is Maggie's puppy, Lassie II, to replace the one from Harrods those bastards at customs ripped open. Unless you have a dog that needs taking out, you never get out at night. But when you look up at the moon, and the great Bear and Orion the Hunter with his dogs, think of them looking down on me and Jack who both love you, Lysander.*

Kitty gave a sob. Her dark little room, which faced north into the wood was lightened today by sheets of snowdrops which reminded her unbearably of the nursery slopes at Monthaut. She should have burnt Lysander's letter, but she read it over and over again before hiding it under the lining paper of her tights drawer.

Jumping at the knock on the door, she shoved the

drawer shut just in time. It was Clive bearing a huge bunch of dark red roses and a jewel box wrapped in shiny red paper. Inside was a ruby brooch in the shape of a heart.

To my Valentine, said the card, *whose price is far above rubies, with all my love, Rannaldini.*

Marigold was in despair. Although Larry was trying frantically to build up some kind of business again – you don't go from 10p to ten million by stroking the cat, was one of his favourite sayings – no-one wanted to buy Paradise Grange, or Magpie Cottage or the villa in France, and all the pictures had gone for knock down prices.

But far, far worse, Larry hadn't sent her a Valentine. Last year, when he'd been with Nikki, was the only other year he'd forgotten. Maybe he'd gone back to her to boost his ego. Marigold had so little confidence, any little thing triggered off the panic. She must keep calm, but when Larry rang just before lunch, she found herself shouting at him, 'I thought we were traying to mend our marriage, you beast.' Then she burst into noisy sobs.

'Princess, princess.' When Larry finally could get a word in, he said rather smugly, 'If you go and 'ave a butchers be'ind the mirror in the 'all.'

Rushing out, Marigold found a large box of chocolates, a card with a red heart on the front, and a page of kisses inside. There was also a letter. *Dear Mr Lockton*, read Marigold incredulously, and felt the blush of joy creeping slowly over her.

Down the telephone Larry could hear her scream of delight.

'Oh, Ay love you, Sir Laurence,' she said in a choked voice as she picked up the telephone. 'No-one deserves a knaighthood more.'

'I thought you'd be pleased, Lady Lockton. But Mum's the word till it's in the papers.'

★ ★ ★

Behaving like the ideal husband on the surface, Rannaldini put a coded Valentine message in the *Independent*: *Little wild thing, the big leopard longs for you.*

As he called all his mistresses 'Little wild thing', Hermione, Chloe, Rachel, Cecilia, even for a giddy second, Flora, and most of the ladies of the London Met thought Rannaldini was sending secret signals to them.

Returning from the Highlands where he had been looking for locations for *Macbeth* with Cameron Cook, Rannaldini was decidedly unamused to find Lassie *in situ*. She had already made herself thoroughly at home romping along the passages after Kitty and peeing everywhere.

'Let her go to the stables with Clive.'

'No, she's mine.' Kitty's eyes were terrified.

Lassie got up and stretched, turning her toes backwards, trailing along, then attacking the red-and-yellow rose-patterned Aubusson in the morning room, and shaking it furiously.

'Stop that,' snapped Rannaldini, aiming a kick at her.

Instantly Lassie flattened her ears, and seemed to become half her breadth, as she fled to Kitty's side.

Having already read Lysander's letter, which Clive had tracked down and photostated while Kitty popped out to the post, Rannaldini suspected the hand of Rupert Campbell-Black. According to the ubiquitous Clive, who frequently bunged the Rutminster florists, the roses sent to Rachel that morning had come from Boris, who had just returned from a successful tour of his homeland. The New York job wasn't in the bag yet, so even when Kitty forgot to provide him with a white gardenia for the Gulf concert that evening, Rannaldini didn't bawl her out, and Lassie was allowed to stay.

Returning from an equally successful but nerve-racking tour of Israel where she'd expected to be flattened by a Scud missile in the middle of a piano concerto, Rachel felt horribly depressed.

The war grew more dreadful. Only the night before

the Allies had bombed a bunker full of civilians. The Americans intended to use napalm to ignite the Iraqi oil ditches on the front lines and the Iraqi hospitals had no electricity, so the baby incubators couldn't function and syringes were having to be used several times.

Rachel knew she ought to go straight out that evening to a peace vigil in Rutminster, but she felt so tired, and the children, whom she had to collect from Gretel, would kick up if she left them again.

Perhaps the most nightmarish part of being a single parent was that she had no-one to tell things to – to boast that she had taken seven bows last night.

'I had to take these in for you,' said Gretel, handing Rachel a huge bunch of the palest peachy-pink roses.

Rannaldini or Guy? thought Rachel wearily, then read;
Dearest Rachel, Happy seventh wedding anniversary, all love, Boris.

To Gretel's amazement Rachel burst into a flood of tears.

'Oh Gretel, he remembered,' she sobbed. 'He really, really remembered.'

Rising late on Valentine's Day after a long stint the night before, Georgie wandered round the garden. The lake was as flat and grey as washing-up water. In the tub outside the kitchen window a lone mud-spattered daffodil swayed in the wind. She and Guy had been getting on so much better since the orgy. He'd shaved off his beard, so she didn't think he was pursuing Rachel any more. But suddenly last Friday he was up to his old tricks again – coming back to Paradise early to go to the doctor about his headaches. Returning to Angel's Reach an hour and a half later, he explained that the surgery queue had been so long that he couldn't be bothered to wait – but he had the jubilant air of an aircrew flying in from a successful raid over Iraq without loss.

Georgie simply couldn't cope with a return to the old uncertainties. She'd got to get out. *Ant and Cleo* was so nearly finished, then she'd make plans. Looking at the kitchen clock she decided to start work soon, but she'd promised to mince up the remains of Sunday's leg of lamb for a shepherd's pie. She felt she ought to practise wifely duties for when she was living alone or shacked up one day with someone less domesticated than Guy. At first, she didn't hear the telephone over the Moulinex.

'Georgie, it's David Hawkley. Hallo, hallo, are you there?'

'Just,' stammered Georgie, wiping her hands on her jeans.

'Thank you for your Valentine card. It was sweet. You did send it, didn't you?'

'Unless you know some other Georgie. Look, I'm really sorry I lied to you about me and Lysander, but I was so frightened of losing you.'

'It's OK. How's Lysander?'

'I haven't seen him, but he's in love. She's married and even more common than me, but at least she's the same age as him and got the sweetest nature.'

'I can't get him on the telephone and Magpie Cottage is deserted.'

Georgie felt an air of gloom. David must have visited Paradise without coming to see her. He was only ringing to pump her about Lysander.

'Where's he living?'

'With Rupert Campbell-Black.'

'Good God!' exploded David. 'That's worse than peddling dope.'

'He won a good race yesterday. Didn't you see *The Scorpion*?'

'I don't read *The Scorpion*,' said David tartly. Then, he started to stammer, 'I miss you – a lot. Let's have lunch.'

In a daze of happiness, Georgie watched Dinsdale remove the leg of lamb from the kitchen table.

'Are you still there?'

'I'd adore to. How about the end of next week?' She

needed the time to give up booze, lose seven pounds and finish *Ant and Cleo*.

'Fine. Where d'you want to go?'

'What about L'Escargot?' It was a restaurant Guy and she had frequented when they were first married.

'Good idea, I'll book. D'you know Rupert Campbell-Black's address?'

It was still pitch black when Dizzy's alarm clock went off the following morning. Cocks were crowing through the mist, horses knocking over their buckets as she staggered into the yard. Going from box to box, she felt each horse's legs for fullness or bumps, before giving it a bucket of fresh water and a scoop of racehorse nuts. When he was at home Rupert preferred to perform this duty and decide which horses should be pulled from the gallops and merely walked round the village or rested in their boxes. He was due back from London at midday. Taggie had arrived from Paris very starry-eyed last night. At seven-thirty the rest of the grooms would arrive to muck out and tack up the horses for everyone to ride out at eight.

But long before the grooms, Taggie had erupted into the yard wearing nothing but a red silk kimono covered in gold dragons.

'Oh, Dizzy, Lysander's bed hasn't been slept in and he didn't come home last night.'

'And men are missing,' intoned Dizzy, echoing the Gulf War bulletins.

'What the hell's Rupert going to say?' she went on. 'We had enough trouble covering up for him yesterday and when he left Pridie behind at Worcester. He's a fucking liability.' Dizzy slammed Penscombe Pride's stable-door shut.

'But such a sweet one,' pleaded Taggie, 'and he's been such an interest and a morale boost for Rupert. Rupert was desperately upset about the baby,' stammered Taggie.

'I know.' Dizzy put an arm round Taggie's shivering

silk shoulders. 'But Rupert'll have to sack him if he doesn't turn up. He can't risk such irresponsibility with the horses.' Then, noticing Taggie's blue, bare feet, 'get dressed, I'll finish feeding the horses. Then we'll look for him.'

They both jumped as deafening snores rent the air from the direction of Arthur's box. Both doors were bolted to stop Arthur chewing them. Opening the top one, Dizzy and Taggie found both Arthur and Lysander stretched out. Lysander was asleep. Arthur was not and was snoring to get attention and breakfast.

Giving a great rumbling whicker, he waved a hoof at them. Arthur was so lazy, and pretended to be exhausted by all the trotting up and down the Gloucestershire hills, that he often managed to persuade the grooms to feed him his racehorse nuts and even his bucket of water lying down. From the back of the stable, Tiny glared down on such debauchery with more disapproval than the vicar's wife at the Valhalla orgy.

'I hope he's not ill from all that wasting. He's awfully still,' said Taggie alarmed.

Dizzy sniffed: 'Not ill. Drunk and passed out cold. Wake up, you stupid fucker.'

When shaking Lysander had no effect, Dizzy turned the hose on him.

'Go and get some warm clothes and some black coffee,' she urged Taggie. 'We've got to try and sober him up enough to ride out.'

'Kitty won't leave Rannaldini,' mumbled Lysander.

'Can't say I blame her if you carry on like this,' said Dizzy tartly.

It was a pity that Rupert's helicopter had engine trouble, so no-one was alerted by the chug, chug, chug of his approach. Instead, arriving in the dark blue Aston Martin, he was mistaken for Jimmy Jardine or Bluey Charteris rolling up to ride out. His first sight was of his beautiful wife, still wearing nothing but a drenched, gaping red kimono frantically trying to dress a half-naked paralytically drunk Lysander in the kitchen. Rupert had no option but to sack him on the spot.

Rupert spent the afternoon venting his rage on owners who owed him nearly a million and whose alleged cheques-in-the-post would rival the mail on Valentine's Day. He had already received tearful deputations from every groom and estate worker, Mr and Mrs Bodkin, even Jimmy and Bluey, and his own sweet wife who was now sobbing into the batter she was about to freeze for Shrove Tuesday pancakes. Any moment Beaver, Gertrude, Jack and the rest of the dogs, the stable cat and all the horses would troop out of the twilight waving banners in some candlelit protest march.

He was brought back to earth by Taggie knocking on the door.

'*You* magazine are just going to press. They want to know what you're giving up for Lent.'

'Lysander Hawkley,' howled Rupert. Then, as Taggie burst into tears, 'Oh, for Christ's sake, are you and my entire staff and livestock bewitched by this cretin?'

'No,' sobbed Taggie. 'It's just that he hasn't got a mother any more and his father's a pig to him, and he's nowhere to go if we chuck him out.'

Shooting across the room, knocking over his out-tray, Rupert took her in his arms.

'There, sweetheart, I'm sorry. Of course he can stay.'

Pulling her head against his shoulder, he stroked her hair. She'd been so incredibly brave since the baby died. She needed something to fuss over, and Lysander had been such an interest and a morale boost for her.

'I love him, too,' he muttered. 'But he's such a dickhead.'

At that moment Lysander appeared round the door hanging his head, clutching a large bottle of whisky as a peace offering. He could hardly move for hangover and misery.

'I'm sorry, Rupert. I've made such a fool of myself.'

'Get out,' said Rupert irritably. Then, as Lysander

shuffled desolately out again, 'Go to bed, I want you on parade at eight tomorrow morning.'

Lysander turned in desperate hope. 'Pridie needs more work,' Rupert went on, 'and Arthur's come on so well he can start on the gallops tomorrow.'

59

With a huge lump in her throat, Georgie wrote THE END in capital letters on the score of *Ant and Cleo*. She had a faint, faint hope that it was the best thing she had ever done. Her head, her hand and her back ached dreadfully but not for once her heart. At least tomorrow she could go up to London to meet David with a clear conscience. Tonight she would spend several hours de-slagging herself.

Having steeped her hair in coconut oil, waiting for a mud pack to dry on her face, she noticed that the rain which had been lashing the windows all day had finally stopped. Outside the sun had broken through behind the woods and flooded the opposite side of Paradise in rosy gold light, turning the fields a brilliant, leaping emerald-green, and a lone grey horse and the departing clouds the softest pink. Then, as she watched, a rainbow soared between the clouds. My life is on the up, thought Georgie.

Picking up the telephone, she rang Relate.

'I'm terribly sorry, I can't make it this evening. You've been so kind. I'm sorry I've talked so much about myself.'

That's fifteen pounds saved, she thought in jubilation, I can buy a new T-shirt from Miss Selfridge, something clinging and sludgy to match my eyes.

Money was dreadful at the moment. It was a good thing she hadn't bothered to finish the album for Larry. Catchitune were in such deep trouble, despite the new board, that they would never have paid the rest of the advance on it. But as she was leaving for the station her agent telephoned saying that Dancer Maitland was interested in playing *Ant* and could they see an early score. Then Guy rang, delighted that she'd finished.

'We'll celebrate this evening, Panda.'

He was having lunch at the Athenaeum with his father, he said.

That's far enough away from L'Escargot, thought Georgie, floating off to London.

Arriving at Paddington on the next train after Georgie, David Hawkley felt the need to stretch his legs – a headmaster's favourite phrase – and decided to walk to Soho. The first daffodils waving at him from Hyde Park put a spring in his step. Overtaking a traffic jam in Oxford Street, he was amused to pass a taxi in which Georgie was frantically powdering, combing, scenting and trying to re-assure herself in a tiny smudged hand-mirror that her new khaki T-shirt wasn't too juvenile. All the girls in Miss Selfridge had been so sweet about her records.

Feeling happy and excited for the first time in months, David bought an *Evening Standard* and a bunch of daffodils and followed a trail of Giorgio into L'Escargot.

Having been told that his lunch guest had gone to the Ladies, he sat down at the table, ordered a glass of sherry and was soon engrossed in the racing pages, which described Lysander as Campbell-Black's golden boy, and suggested people put their money on him and Mr Sparky the next day. Torn between pride, disapproval and sudden sharp envy of Rupert, he turned to the front pages and the war.

The land battle was about to start any minute, all Kuwait was aflame, burning the midnight and the midday oil.

David was so engrossed he didn't notice a charming redhead sit down in an alcove round the corner, and then everything was forgotten because Georgie arrived with the price tag still on her T-shirt, but looking as beautiful, scented and shining as a woman in love.

'How gorgeous!' She took the daffodils from him.

'Not as gorgeous as you.' Cursing himself for being corny, David kissed her warm, scented, freckled cheek.

'I'm manic. I've just finished *Ant and Cleo*.'

'Oh Eastern Star, that calls for champagne.' David waved to a waiter.

Although a place had been laid for her opposite him, Georgie wriggled between the tables so she could sit down on the bench-seat beside him. Sod being recognized.

'Oh, it's lovely to see you. Isn't the war terrifying? Do you think the Israelis will retaliate?'

David shook his head. 'The Americans have paid them too much money.'

'Mother Courage was so funny this morning: "Oh, Mrs Seymour, the Iraqis are copulating." '

David laughed, his face losing all its daunting sternness.

'I liked Duck-billed Platitude best.'

'You remembered!'

'I remember everything about you. Look.' He brought a little silver box out of his pocket, and for a worried moment Georgie thought he was about to inhale snuff. Instead she saw it was full of hair.

'Do you remember the day I cut your fringe?' Putting the box away, he broke a roll in half but didn't eat it. 'How's Guy?'

'Not great. We lie side by side at night not touching like apples in the attic because we're so frightened of bruising.'

'Sounds like Sappho.'

'Did you finish Catullus?'

'Yup. How's Flora?'

'Absolutely devastated,' and she told him about the affair with Rannaldini. 'He's destroyed her,' she said finally. 'I wish you two could meet.'

'We will soon.'

Flooded with happiness, Georgie felt they were talking in certainties.

'Tell me about Mrs Rannaldini, I assume she was that plump little thing bouncing around like a rubber ball in a bra and pants last October?'

Georgie laughed. 'She's so sweet.'

David took her hand. 'I'm so glad you sent me that Valentine card. It arrived during a staff meeting, I had to rush out and ring you.'

'I was about to ring you at Christmas, but when I picked up the telephone Guy was talking to Julia.'

'My poor darling.'

But as she leant sideways to kiss him, she suddenly heard a familiar voice saying: 'Darling, I'm so sorry I'm late, the traffic's appalling,' and as painful as electrolysis on the bikini line, she realized it was Guy and he was speaking to Julia, who had leapt out of the alcove as beautiful, scented and shining as herself to embrace him.

The proprietor, coming over to ask if they'd chosen yet, turned green, but was too late to warn Guy, as over Julia's shoulder he caught sight of Georgie and the tender smile froze on his handsome face.

'It's Guy,' whispered Georgie.

'Rock Star in person,' said David acidly, and with great presence of mind he downed his glass of sherry, gave the waiter a tenner and whisked Georgie down the road and took a room at the Mountbatten.

'Guy said he was lunching at the Athenaeum with his father,' sobbed Georgie as they entered the lift.

As David led them into a room that had framed photographs of Lord Mountbatten playing polo all over the walls, Georgie turned to face him.

Taking her hand, he pulled her down on to the bed. 'I'm not going to assault you. It's all right. Please don't cry.'

Georgie felt buttons against her face. There was something comfortingly upright about a man who wore a waistcoat.

'Now Guy knows about us it's all in the open.'

'Are we an "us"?' asked Georgie.

'I think so, don't you?'

* * *

That night, because it was Friday, out of habit both Georgie and Guy returned to Paradise.

'You took him to our favourite restaurant,' said Guy furiously.

'So did you,' snapped Georgie. 'And I'd just struggled to pay the poll tax and you go squandering money on Julia.'

'You bought a new T-shirt.'

'Out of my Relate money. Anyway it was the first time I've ever lunched with him,' she lied.

'It's the first time I've had lunch with Julia since Christmas,' lied Guy. 'Who is he anyway?'

'I'm not going to tell you,' hissed Georgie.

Alas, there was a feature in the *Daily Telegraph* the following day on the headmasters of the top schools in England with a large picture of David, looking stern and handsome.

Devastated how jealous he felt, Guy rushed off to play squash with Rannaldini, who was feeling very smug because he was behaving comparatively well at present.

'What am I going to do? Georgie's having an affair with Lysander's father. He's got two inches in *Who's Who*.'

'And presumably eight inches in Georgie,' said Rannaldini evilly. 'I thought she was looking good.'

'But headmasters shouldn't behave like that,' spluttered Guy.

Rannaldini laughed. 'Like father, like son. If Georgie can keep her Head, when all about her are losing theirs.'

'Oh, shut up. Julia thinks that lets me off the hook, but I can't afford to leave Georgie. Another backer went belly-up last week. Anyway I don't want to.'

'You should have thought of that before.'

'Have you heard the latest Saddam Hussein story?' Dizzy asked Lysander at the beginning of March as they drove home after another highly successful day at Sandown.

663

'What do Saddam Hussein and nylon knickers have in common?'

'I don't care.'

'They both rub Bush the wrong way. Ha, ha, ha. Have you totally lost your sense of humour?'

'Totally. I don't care if the war is over. Stormin' Norman should have been allowed to go in and crucify Saddam Hussein for starving all the Kuwaiti bloodstock to death. A lot of them came from this yard. And if Allied prisoners of war are being released, why can't Rannaldini release Kitty?'

Still pinching herself with joy at the prospect of being the future Lady Lockton, Marigold was also delighted to see Boris's clapped-out Fiesta parked at an angle outside Rachel's cottage. Perhaps, as was rumoured, they were getting together again. On the other hand, Marigold was getting increasingly worried about Kitty whom she'd just bumped into outside the village shop. Kitty had been wearing odd shoes and her coat was done up all wrong. She was also as white as a sheet, but explained it away as a tummy upset.

Kitty, in fact, was almost certain she was pregnant. Although she hadn't dared go to James Benson, she had missed three periods. But the thing she had longed for most in the world had only brought her desperate worry and unhappiness because she had no idea if the baby was Lysander's or Rannaldini's. She felt overwhelmed with guilt. What would happen if the baby popped out in September, another little Virgo like herself, but with Lysander's wide blue eyes? She couldn't stop crying, and she was feeling appallingly sick. Thank goodness Rannaldini was too tied up with *Macbeth* and the machinations of the New York job, which still hadn't been confirmed, to notice.

Like a pickpocket, Kitty's hand kept edging towards the telephone, longing to dial Rupert's number, just to hear Lysander's voice. She was watching him win a small race at Cheltenham that afternoon when Clive marched in, so she hurriedly switched over to an Australian soap opera.

Lassie was her only comfort. Getting up in the middle of every night to carry her outside, feeling the little creature covering her face with gentle licks, as she lay warm and sleepy in her arms, Kitty thought she had never loved anything except Lysander so much.

At night Lassie curled up against her on her counterpane. Running her hand along the tiger-striped back, as smooth and silky as a banister, Kitty dreamt of racing down the great Valhalla staircase out of the front door across the valley into Lysander's arms.

60

In the second week in March doughty little Penscombe
Pride trounced The Prince of Darkness in the Cotchester
Cup by ten lengths, bringing great glory to the yard, and
putting a welcome forty thousand pounds into Rupert's
pocket. Rannaldini, who'd watched the race on satellite,
while attempting to hammer out terms with the New
World Phil, was so furious he promptly faxed his trainer
to say he was taking The Prince of Darkness and his other
horses away and would also be seeking a new jockey.

The two equine Titans were due to meet next in the
Rutminster Gold Cup in the first week in April. Arthur,
who had been reluctantly heaving his whale-like bulk over
Rupert's fences, had also been entered, but not declared.
It was still a question of Lysander having enough races
in the bag to qualify. Spirits at Penscombe plummeted
when, ten days before the race, he had a punishing fall
from Mr Sparky, putting his shoulder out and breaking a front tooth. Laid off for a week, he was nearly
sacked on the Saturday before Mothering Sunday. His
mind was so much on Pippa, as well as Kitty, that
he forgot to pack the colours.

With only forty-eight hours left to qualify, however, he
exonerated himself by winning a selling plate at Leicester
so brilliantly that the owner was forced to buy the horse
back for three times what he'd paid for it. Then he came
third in the 3.15, and finally notched up his quota by
finishing, as he thought, second in the handicap hurdle.
But he was so elated he raised a clenched fist to punch
the air, whereupon a startled Hopeless, thinking he was

going to whack her, shot past the dark brown gelding in front to win by a nose.

The only person in the yard not overjoyed was Rupert. 'How many times have I told you to get past before you start waving your arms about like a fucking politician,' he yelled at Lysander as he caught up with him on the way to the winner's enclosure. 'And where was your head during the first circuit? Between Mrs Rannaldini's fat legs, I suppose.'

A very nasty punch-up was averted when a pretty brunette from *The Scorpion* shoved her tape recorder under Rupert's nose.

'Is Penscombe Pride going to beat The Prince of Darkness on Saturday?'

'Not a question of whether he'll beat him,' snapped Rupert, 'but by how many lengths.'

'Is he the best horse you've ever had?'

'Yes, now buzz off.' The prettier the reporter, the more Rupert distrusted them.

'We do have another runner in the race,' protested Tabitha indignantly, as she gave Hopeless a congratulatory hug.

'Oh, right, King Arthur, 200–1.' The brunette consulted her notebook. What had *Timeform* said about him that morning: '*Campbell-Black's white elephant, gigantic grey gelding of little account.*'

'Fucking hell!' Lysander, on his way to being weighed in, swung round glaring at the brunette over Hopeless's saddle. 'How dare they?'

'He's your horse, Lysander,' she said slyly. 'How d'you rate his chances?'

'Negligible if he rides like he did just now,' snapped Rupert. Then turning to Lysander. 'Piss off and get weighed in.'

'People are saying the Rutminster's a grudge match between you and Rannaldini,' the brunette quailed slightly under Rupert's chilling ice-blue glare, 'for taking Lysander under your wing.'

'So?'

'You were in Monthaut with Lysander and Kitty Rannaldini.'

'Don't you say anything against Kitty,' said Lysander coming back again.

'Fuck *off*,' hissed Rupert.

'Why are you entering Lysander on a no-hoper just to irritate Rannaldini?' asked the brunette, delighted at what she'd stirred up.

As Lysander opened his mouth, desperate to think of a really crushing reply, Rupert spoke first.

'Arthur isn't a no-hoper,' he said coldly. 'He's a stayer. He stays even longer than my mother-in-law.'

'Don't worry,' Tabitha whispered to Lysander. 'Daddy's always in strop before a big race.'

Daddy got stroppier. On the last gallops before the Rutminster, little Penscombe Pride was so well and above himself that he carted Bluey off the end of the all-weather track across two fields of barley on to the Penscombe–Chalford Road in the rush hour. Arthur, by contrast, didn't try at all, slopping along at the back of the field, listening to the larks singing in a cloudless sky. He was still outraged that because caffeine was a banned substance, Rupert had stopped his morning cup of coffee. Far worse, having despatched Lysander to the dentist yesterday to get his tooth capped, Rupert had taken the opportunity to sharpen Arthur up himself, giving the old horse a good hiding when he refused to jump a row of fences at the gallop.

Lysander was in despair as he rode back to the yard. The cracks in the paths were as bad as last summer. Rain, which would make the going soft enough for Arthur, had been forecast for days, but showed no sign of appearing. Wild garlic was spreading over the floor of the wood like a thousand green hangover tongues. Lysander hadn't had a hangover since the morning after Valentine's Day. Nor a drink, nor any dope, nor magic mushrooms, nor even a fuck. Last night he had reached his target weight of nine stone six, but what was the point of all this self-denial if Rupert wasn't going to declare Arthur? He glanced at his watch. It would be too late in half an hour. In the distance he could hear Tiny yelling her head off because Arthur had deserted her. She'd give him hell when he got back.

'Can't someone strangle that fucking Shetland?' Rupert stalked into the kitchen where Taggie was turning sausages and frying eggs.

'There are about thirty press messages on the machine,' she said desperately, 'asking if you're going to run Arthur.'

'Not after the way he went this morning,' snapped Rupert, pouring himself a cup of black coffee and disappearing into his office.

The morning's papers didn't make Lysander any happier. There was a lot of guff about Rupert's 'Rutminster raiding party' and how many winners he would get during the meeting. The tabloids all concentrated on the contrast between Penscombe Pride and Arthur. ' *Beauty and the Beast*,' said the *Mail*. '*David with an Exocet faces Goliath with a sling*,' quipped the *Sun*. '*Why do the handsomest men choose the ugliest horse?*' wrote the brunette from *The Scorpion*.

'How dare they pick on Arthur?' Lysander was practically in tears. 'I'll sue them.'

'Hush.' Shoving a piece of fried bread spread with marmalade into Lysander's protesting mouth, Taggie led him to the door of Rupert's office. 'Just listen.'

'It's Race 31161,' Rupert was saying in his flat drawl, 'Rutminster Gold Cup, King Arthur, owned by Lysander Hawkley, ridden by Lysander Hawkley – that's right. You still don't know who's riding The Prince of Darkness yet?'

Coming out of his office on his way to a Venturer board meeting back at the house, he found Lysander leaning against the wall, fighting back the tears again.

'Thank you, Rupert. I won't let you down.'

'I've declared him, but I won't run him unless it rains. And go and have a haircut. You can't ride in the Rutminster with a pony-tail.'

Everyone grew increasingly tense. Danny, Penscombe Pride's Irish lad, had been throwing up all morning, even Taggie was shouting at the Press. Rupert, in his board meeting, was trying to concentrate on plummeting advertising revenue, when there was a thundering on the door and Lysander barged in, white-faced.

'Oh, Rupert, Arthur's lame. He's going short on the off-fore.'

'Probably knocked himself this morning, just poultice him. Now get out,' said Rupert curtly.

'Just come and see him. Per-lease.'

So the entire board trooped down to the yard to have a look, only to find Arthur dramatically recovered.

'He's winding you up,' Dizzy chided Lysander. 'He does it to get sympathy and Polos now.'

Although the yard was running down at the end of the season, and most of the young horses had been turned out, Rupert hadn't wanted to waste a valuable stable-lad on Arthur. To keep Tabitha out of mischief, he let her do the horse. She had proved both responsible and efficient.

Wearing a navy-blue jersey, which brought out the famous Campbell-Black eyes, but was already coated with white hairs, she stood on a bucket that afternoon to wash Arthur's mane.

'We've got to stop you rolling and getting yourself mucky before tomorrow,' she told him, as Arthur nudged her jeans' pocket hopefully looking for Polos.

Lysander, sitting on the edge of a stone tub of white narcissi, holding Arthur's lead rope with Jack on his knee, had been laboriously reading Ivor Herbert's life of Red Rum to inspire Arthur, but had given up with the effort. Trapped in her stable, Tiny watched them beadily.

'Arthur has a look of Rummy,' said Lysander. 'I wonder

how many more stable-boys The Prince of Darkness has eaten. I tried to help one of the grooms at Valhalla clip him once. Jesus, he went ape-shit. I jumped on to the manger. The groom shot out of the door. I want to know who's going to ride him. I bet Rannaldini's got some nasty surprise. God, I hope he lets Kitty come to Rutminster tomorrow.'

He was really upset that, unlike most of Paradise, Kitty hadn't sent him a good-luck card. He had even driven over to Magpie Cottage in the lunch hour to check.

'Have you got a picture of her?'

'It's a bit cracked.' Lysander took a photograph out of his trouser pocket.

After a long pause, Tabitha said kindly, 'I expect she looks better in the flesh.'

Lysander scratched his head. 'No, she doesn't really. Jack's very plain, particularly on his white-eyed side, but he's got such a dear little face, and Arthur isn't classically beautiful either, although I hate the Press saying it, but I love him to bits too.'

'But you don't want to go to bed with Jack and Arthur,' said Tabitha. 'Shut your eyes, darling,' she added, as she hosed the soap out of Arthur's forelock. 'Not bed-bed, I mean. I suppose you're beautiful enough for two.'

'I feel safe with Kitty,' confessed Lysander. 'Since I lost weight I'm always cold. The only thing that could make me warm would be her arms around me.'

Suddenly noticing the expression of desolation on Tab's face, Lysander realized how tactless he was being. Taking her grubby little hands, he pulled her off her bucket.

'If I wasn't so hopelessly hooked on Kitty, I'd fall madly for you, Tab. There isn't a single man in the world that won't slit his throat for you in a year or two. Like your father, you're irresistible.'

'Not to you,' said Tabitha dolefully.

'I got you a present.'

It was a silver horse-shoe brooch and he pinned it on her jersey.

'Oh, thank you, it's lovely.'

'It's going to bring you special luck. Mystic Meg said your destiny was linked with the initial I. God, I'm nervous about seeing Kitty.'

Returning at dusk from the second day of the Rutminster meeting with two wins and a couple of places, Rupert was in a much better mood. The raiding party was turning into a rout. But the smile was wiped off his face when he went into the tack-room and found Dizzy, Danny and the stable cat poring over the *Evening Scorpion*. They all jumped when they saw him.

'You're not going to like this,' said Dizzy warily. 'Bloody Beattie's dumped again.'

RANNALDINI'S REVENGE, said the front-page headline.

'*Once again Rupert Campbell-Black's past has come back to haunt him and perhaps rob him of a third victory in the Rutminster Cup tomorrow,*' ran the copy.

'*In 1980,*' it continued, '*top show-jumper Jake Lovell shocked the world by running off with the charismatic trainer's beautiful first wife, Helen, in the middle of the Olympics. Eleven years later, Rupert's neighbour, jet-setting conductor, Roberto Rannaldini, has brought Jake Lovell's twenty-year-old son, Isaac, over from Ireland to ride the brilliant but vicious Prince of Darkness in tomorrow's race.*

' "*I was impressed by Isaac when I saw him winning a race recently in Ireland," enthused the Machiavellian Maestro from Valhalla, his Rutshire mansion. "He and The Prince of Darkness will annihilate Penscombe Pride."* '

Without a word Rupert turned to page three.

'*In a Mafiaesque move worthy of his Latin ancestors, Rannaldini could be paying back Rupert for taking Lysander Hawkley under his wing. Fun-loving Lysander (son of Hatchet Hawkley, headmaster of posh Fleetley – fees £16,000 a year), nicknamed the Man Who Made Husbands Jealous because of a string of relationships with married women, was caught cuddling and kissing Rannaldini's much younger wife, Kitty, in Monthaut in December.*'

Rupert was deceptively calm and, as the stable cat, who loved newspapers, padded across the page, he gently removed her so he could read on. But as Tab wandered in, putting her arm round his shoulder to see what he was reading, she caught a glimpse of Isaac Lovell's thick, dark, sombre, gypsy's face and gave a moan of wonder: 'Wow-wee, he is gorgeous.'

Turning on her like a cobra, Rupert grabbed her shoulders, shaking her until her bones rattled like castanets.

'If you ever have anything to do with that little shit,' he hissed, 'you're disinherited, out of here, never coming back, see?'

'I don't see at all,' said Tabitha, flaring up. 'You never approve of the men I like.' Then, as Rupert stormed out, 'Is he worse than Ashley?'

'Much worse,' sighed Dizzy. 'I'll tell you about it.'

'Bastard, bastard, bastard.' Eyes narrowed to slits, Rupert paced up and down the bedroom, neat whisky in one hand, cigar in the other.

Helpless in the face of such volcanic fury, Taggie lay on the faded patchwork counterpane of the huge Jacobean four-poster in which Rupert had made love for so many years to his beautiful first wife.

'Pridie'll win it with two legs tied together,' she stammered. 'A new jockey won't make any difference. You're the best trainer in the world. No-one's heard of Isaac Lovell over here.'

Rupert got hopelessly uptight on the eve of big races. It affected the whole yard. He had hardly ever been nervous when he was show-jumping because he was so confident of his own riding, but now he could only mount the best jockeys on the best horses and pray. It was the one time when he had to be kept really calm.

'It all happened such a long time ago,' muttered Taggie. 'You're the most utterly g-gorgeous, glamorous, faint-making m-m-man in the world. Jake Lovell's a little squit, so's Rannaldini. I'll probably trip over both of them in the paddock.'

Taggie never bitched about anyone. Rupert looked down at her in amazement, as she stood up, and putting her hands on both sides of his rigidly clenched face, pulled his mouth down to meet hers.

'Kiss me. I love you so, so much.'

'Oh, Tag,' groaned Rupert, burying his face in her thick dark hair. 'Thank God for you. You're absolutely right. It's all in the past. Jake did me such a good turn. I'm such a boring old reactionary, and I'm so against divorce, I'd probably still be miserably unhappy with Helen if he hadn't walked off with her, and never married you and been so divinely happy. It just destroys me because he beat me in the Olympics and sex, if you know what I mean. But if I lost the war, I won the peace.' Pulling her down on the bed beside him, he reached inside his jacket pocket.

'I've got something for you.' He handed her two open-ended first-class tickets to Bogotá. 'We're going baby-hunting.' Then, when Taggie looked up in incredulous hope, 'The nuns have accepted our application. If we fly out to Colombia and stay there for six weeks, really convincing them we're serious about wanting a baby, they'll find us one.'

Taggie couldn't speak. Like the moon's reflection in a lake ruffled by a wakeful carp, her pale face suddenly disintegrated. Rupert could feel her tears as she covered his face with kisses.

'Oh, I love you. A real baby. I can't believe it. Oh, d'you think they'll like us enough?'

'They'll like you. I'll have to behave myself.' And give them a fat cheque, thought Rupert.

'I wonder if it'll be a he or a she, blond or black hair, oh, Rupert.'

'It'll certainly be black market,' said Rupert, 'Our little black-market baby.'

'And six weeks together, what bliss! But I hope you

won't be too bored,' she added anxiously. 'What'll you do?'

'I can think of one thing.' Rupert slowly unbuttoned her harebell-blue cardigan and unhooked her bra, so, like cream boiling over, her wonderful breasts spilled out. Putting his lips to one nipple he sucked gently. Just as desperate for her attention and love as any baby, he thought wryly.

'I'm terribly sweaty and unwashed,' mumbled Taggie, as he pushed up her scarlet skirt, and burrowed under the dark purple tights and skimpy knickers.

Rejoicing that he could get her that wet so quickly after five years of marriage, finding it always as exciting as pulling a groom in the back of a loose box for the first time, Rupert moved his fingers upwards as Taggie's hands fumbled with his zip.

Naked, white-skinned, utterly gorgeous, her dark hair tickling his belly, she kissed him everywhere, her tongue as delicate and subtle as a lurcher's.

'Oh, my angel.' Wriggling down, he slid inside her, hearing her gasp of joy, as he warmed her with his body and constantly moving hands.

'Oh, Rupert, Rupert, Rupert.'

'Rupert, Rupert, Rupert!' Taggie's voice had suddenly got deeper, and was accompanied, he realized, by someone hammering on the door, and then – good God – opening it.

'Rupert, I'm really sorry to bother you. Oh, Christ!' Lysander clapped his hands over his eyes. 'I mean *really* sorry, but I think Arthur's been nobbled. He keeps yawning and he hasn't eaten his last feed.'

'I'll nobble you, you little fucker,' howled Rupert, scooping up a shoe from the carpet and hurling it in Lysander's direction. 'Get out, *get out*. Arthur's exhausted because you keep waking him up to see if he's OK, and he's not hungry because the entire Press have been stuffing him with Polos.'

In the end, chivvied by Taggie, Rupert tugged on a

675

pair of jeans and ran barefoot across the parched lawn to the yard. In his box, he found Arthur lying flat out, waving a huge foot in the air, snoring loudly, one eye open. Seeing his tormentor, however, he lumbered up and hid behind Tiny shivering with terror in the corner, his newly washed coat, and particularly his mane, once more stained with green.

'Oh dear,' Lysander blushed. 'He's made a lightning recovery. I do think,' he went on hastily, 'Arthur ought to have a security guard tomorrow. Pridie's got a guard and closed-circuit television in his box, and The Prince of Darkness'll have all Rannaldini's hoods around him.'

'He's got Tiny,' said Rupert, avoiding the Shetland's darting teeth and deciding not to blow his top. 'Now will you please stop wasting my time.'

'I'm sorry.' Lysander hung his head. 'I gather all this Isaac Lovell business has upset you. Bloody unfair. Can't make head nor tail of it myself. Who is Isaac Lovell anyway?'

'His father ran off with my first wife.'

'Bastard!'

'Like you want to run off with Kitty Rannaldini,' said Rupert, bolting the half-door.

'Not at all,' said Lysander indignantly. 'Rannaldini's an utter shit, and a bully who beats up horses and women and never stops humiliating poor darling Kitty by screwing around. You were never like that.'

'Hum, your faith in me is touching. You didn't know me in the old days.'

'Old days is old days.' Lysander blushed again. 'I used to be a bit of a stud myself in the past. But I want you to know you and Taggie have really restored my faith in marriage as an institution.'

'Ta very much,' said Rupert. 'I had better go back and – er – institute it. What are you going to do with yourself this evening?'

'Watch the video of last year's Rutminster again, and

then play poker with Danny and Dizzy. We're teaching Tab.'

'She'll beat you all,' said Rupert. 'But I want you in bed early.'

Lysander slept fitfully and woke at a quarter-past three. In twelve hours exactly, if by some miracle he got to ride, they'd be lining up at the start. In twelve hours, ten minutes, it would all be over. And after tomorrow, would Rupert kick him out? Despite his misery over Kitty, he'd been happier living at Penscombe than anywhere else. Desperate for some sign of rain, he opened the window, and was mocked by a million stars. The lawn was lit by daffodils and a clump of white cherry trees already in bloom, it had been so mild.

The constellation of Leo the Lion was romping off to his lair in the west. But any moment Lysander expected his great shaggy face to appear back over the top of Rupert's beechwood to bite the Great Bear in the bum. Longing as never before for Kitty's arms, he collapsed into an armchair.

He must have drifted off again, for the next minute he was galloping up Rupert's track, and Arthur was going gloriously, and he could hear, far more menacing than Rannaldini's tympani, the thunder of hoofs behind him. But no-one was going to catch Arthur. The stands were rising to cheer him.

'Go on, go on, go on,' yelled Lysander.

'Lysander, Lysander, wake up! It's tipping down.' It was a few seconds before he realized Tabitha was shaking him, and the thunder of hoofs was torrential rain, machine-gunning the roof.

Leaning out of the window into Niagara, he could see the downpour flattening the daffodils, stripping the white cherries, flooding the gutters, sluicing the valley.

'Yippee, yippee, Arthur's in with a chance.' Lysander let out a great Tarzan howl, hugging Tab until she screamed for mercy and Jack began yapping with excitement.

677

'When you come back to earth,' announced Tab, 'the tooth fairy's been.'

Under Lysander's pillow, still in its polythene wrapping, lay a vast blue rug, braided with emerald green and with the initials RC-B which always brought bookmakers out in a cold sweat, embroidered in the corner.

'Daddy had it made up specially. Any of the normal rugs look like saddle blankets on Arthur.' Then, as Lysander buried the balls of his thumbs in his eyes, 'It's OK, Daddy really likes you, Lysander.'

Few would have thought it later in the morning, as Rupert shouted at everyone in the yard. Danny was throwing up in the loo. Even Bluey was silent and pre-occupied during the gallops, on which Rupert had insisted, to give an air of normality to the day. Only Arthur was unmoved, as he breakfasted on carrots, oats and a handful of dandelions newly picked by Taggie.

'Have you got Arthur's passport and your medical card?' nagged Tabitha.

Lysander was packing his bag, putting in pain killers because his shoulder was still giving him hell, and his own beautiful colours, which he'd chosen himself: white sleeves, black-and-white body and brown cap, because they were the same colours as Jack. He was wearing his Donald Duck jersey, which Taggie had finally dragged off his back yesterday and hand washed.

The morning seemed endless, but at last the lorry containing Penscombe Pride, Arthur, Tiny and three younger horses splashed down the drive, splitting the pack of Press outside the gates with their Barbours over their cameras.

'Charlie's going to do a runner,' said Tabitha, as they passed Penscombe's betting shop. 'Everyone's put so much money on Pridie, and on Arthur for a place, his odds have shortened from 200 to 100–1, and you should see the champagne they've got on ice for a mega piss-up this evening at The Goat and Boots.'

'I'm going to be sick again.' Hanging out of the window,

Danny came back inside absolutely drenched. 'If it rains any more it's going to be too wet for Pridie.'

Water was pouring in a tidal wave down the High Street.

'Ouch,' grumbled Lysander, as he bit his cheek instead of his chewing gum. 'I'm injured before I get to the course.'

He felt even worse as he read the horoscopes in the *Sun*.

'Arthur's going to have a good day for shopping.'

'I hope that isn't a misprint for stopping,' said Tab.

61

The ancient town of Rutminster, with its splendid cathedral and russet Queen Anne close, lay in a bowl of hills covered in thick, rain-drenched woodland. In a sensible marriage of secular and ecclesiastical, the race-course was only divided from the cathedral water meadows by the River Fleet, which was rising steadily as Rupert and Lysander walked the course.

Despite the relentless downpour and the lurking fog, it was very mild and the ground was already filling up. Helicopters were constantly landing and the bookies were doing excellent business under their coloured umbrellas. Lysander never dreamt the fences would be so huge. Not for nothing was the Rutminster called the Grand National of the South.

Down by the start Rupert turned up the collar of his Barbour: 'You must push Arthur on. No-one misses the beat. You've got a very short run up to the first fence. If you're not at the front at this stage, you can get boxed in or squeezed out.

'From then on your best bet is to hunt Arthur round in the middle, letting the leaders exhaust themselves trying to pass Pridie. This is a sod,' he went on, as they stopped at five foot of closely stacked birch and gorse with a huge ditch on the other side. 'If you hit it below six inches, Arthur'll turn over. If he drops his legs in the water, it'll slow him up. Meet it right, and you won't know he's jumped it.'

'I wish Arthur were walking the course,' sighed Lysander. 'He's got a better memory than me.'

'Give him a breather here,' said Rupert as they climbed a steep hill to a fence Lysander could hardly see over, 'and you must stand back at this one. It's known as The Ambush because there's a terrific drop on the other side. Yummy Yuppy unshipped his jockey here last year. He tried to pop over on a short stride and bellied into it. Piss off,' he snapped as two men approached with a camera.

'Could you take a picture of us beside this fence?' said the first in a strong Irish accent.

'No, we can't.' As Lysander reached out for the camera, Rupert hustled him on. 'Concentrate, for Christ's sake.'

They had reached the top of the course now and three-quarters of a mile away could see the stands and the cathedral spire soaring above its scaffolding.

'If a favourite moves up here, you can hear a great cheer from the crowd. It's quite eerie.'

'And I've got to go round twice,' said Lysander in a hollow voice as they squelched down to the bottom of the hill.

'This is where you fork right for the final run in,' explained Rupert. 'And the horse sees the crowd in all its yelling glory for the first time. Paddywack lost the race here last year. His head came up, he saw the crowd and Jimmy Jardine felt him coming back. Pridie passed him and it cost Jimmy the race, so keep a hold of Arthur.'

'Arthur loves crowds. He'll accelerate if he gets this far.'

'This is a tricky fence,' said Rupert as they rounded the bend into the home straight. 'If you go flat out, you'll turn over; take a pull and you lose momentum; jump it wide and you'll lose a few vital yards that could cost you the race. Bluey'll be taking the paint off the rails. From now on, if Arthur's still on his big feet, it's a chance of surviving home.

'Bluey's so experienced, he'll be on automatic pilot now, but you're likely to tense up with nerves and miss a vital gap. If Bluey comes to a bottleneck, he just pushes his way through, freeze for a second and you've had it, and if you come up on the inside, even Bluey'll squeeze you out.'

Glancing at Lysander's vacant stare, the shadows under his eyes, the pale translucent skin not even tinged with pink by the lashing rain, Rupert was worried he'd pushed him too hard.

'What have I just said?'

'That even a mate like Bluey will try and squeeze Arthur out.'

'Good boy. For eleven thousand pounds in his pocket, any jockey will kill his mother. All that matters from here is to get your whip out and your head down and go like hell. You'll hear a roar like you've never heard, you'll ride into a tunnel of yelling faces, and you'll think the post will never come, but don't let up till you're past the post. When you hear Tab screaming with relief in the stable-lads' stand, you'll know you're OK.'

'Thank you, Rupert.' Lysander felt overwhelmed with gratitude that Rupert should take the whole thing so seriously. 'We won't let you down.' Then, as an ambulance screeched by, 'When I was at the dentist's the other day, I popped into a solicitor's and made a will. It's in my bedroom drawer. If I don't come back, I'd like Tab to have Arthur, and you to have Jack. He's had such a ball since he's been at Penscombe.'

'As long as you leave Tiny to Rannaldini,' said Rupert.

Rannaldini had a household staying for the Rutminster, including the chairman of the board of the New World Phil, a squat, jolly businessman called Graydon Gluckstein, whom he was determined to impress. As a result Kitty had hardly had a moment to think. Having bought a Donald Duck good-luck card for Lysander, she had torn it up. It was immoral to send it if she were trying to save her marriage. Having not been allowed to see *The Scorpion*, she hadn't realized the connection between Rupert and the pale, watchful jockey, Isaac Lovell, whom Rannaldini had singled out to wrestle with The Prince of Darkness. He had dropped in for a drink last night.

'All that matters is that you annihilate Bluey Charteris and Penscombe Pride,' she heard Rannaldini saying as he shut the door on them both.

Kitty longed to look her best on the day of the race, but as she'd been wracked with morning sickness worse than Danny, and the rain that suited Arthur only crinkled the hair she'd blow-dried straight, there wasn't much hope.

Although Rutminster was only fifteen miles away, Rannaldini insisted on ferrying his party, which also included Hermione and Bob, Meredith and Rachel and Guy and Georgie, by helicopter. Terrified of throwing up over the dove-grey suede upholstery, Kitty pleaded last-minute shopping in Rutminster for the celebration party the utterly confident Rannaldini was planning for that evening, when everyone would drink Krug out of the Rutminster Cup.

Having bought some home-made pâté and a side of smoked salmon from a delicatessen in the High Street, Kitty drove past the russet houses of the Close, peering out behind their fans of magnolia grandiflora, and, parking her car, popped in to the cathedral.

The numbers of the hymns were up for Palm Sunday tomorrow. In a side chapel, pinned to a green baize screen, Kitty noticed children's drawings of Jesus riding into Jerusalem on donkeys even more outlandishly shaped than Arthur.

Would the baby inside her, which could so easily be Lysander's, one day draw pictures like that? she thought despairingly, as she sunk to her knees on a faded crimson hassock.

'Please, please, dear God,' pleaded Kitty, 'let him get round, I don't care if he wins. Just let him come back safe, he's so brave and reckless.'

Surely it wasn't adultery to pray for someone's safety?

Through the clear-glass lattice window to her right, fringes of rain were falling out of dark purple clouds on to the palest green leaves, just emerging from the chestnut trees.

'Rain's good for Arfur, God, but please don't let him slip.'

Beside her lay the stone effigy of Robert, Lord Rutminster, who died in the crusades. He had pudding-basin hair and his nose broken off, but he was flanked by stone angels, with a little dog like Jack at his feet. Kitty ran a finger down his pale battered translucent face.

Oh, let angels ride on Lysander's shoulders, too. Wiping away the tears, she quickly lit a candle for him. Walking towards the door, she saw a man standing beneath the tattered colours of the local regiments. He looked vaguely familiar, so she smiled, then went absolutely scarlet as she realized the last time she'd seen him she'd been in her bra and knickers, bopping in the rain. As she scuttled out, however, she looked round.

'Good luck,' she stammered.

'Good luck, Kitty,' said David Hawkley.

Any comfort she might have felt evaporated as Clive slid forward out of nowhere to open the door of the Mini to take her to the races.

Rutminster racecourse on the final day of the meeting had never been fuller. Anticipating victory for Rupert, who was a huge local hero, and forgetting the recession, the multitude were drowning their sorrows. Penscombe Pride would get them out of trouble, pay their mortgage arrears, their poll tax and their daughter's wedding. As the beautiful little bay with his bright questing eyes and his zig zag blaze, who had never fallen in his life, or lost in his last eight races, strutted round the paddock like a bantam cock, no-one would have thought he carried top weight and the expectation of hundreds of thousands of punters. Ten-deep, they gathered round the rails to admire him.

He was followed at a respectable distance by The Prince of Darkness, who was a hand bigger. He looked magnificent with his blood-red rug rolled back to show rippling muscle worthy of a black middle-weight champion. But his evil eye rolled and his jaws strained against his muzzle

684

and everyone kept clear of his hoofs because he could lash out with all four of them.

Of the thirty other runners, the most serious contenders were Camomile Lawn, a fleet chestnut mare so flashy Tab said she ought to wear an ankle bracelet, Male Nurse, a stocky brown gelding who jumped and stayed well, Yummy Yuppy, the handsome dark bay who had fallen last year, Blarney Stone, who had won the Irish Grand National, Paddywack, who was third to Penscombe Pride and The Prince of Darkness last year and Fräulein Mahler, Rannaldini's second horse, whom Lysander had ridden into the lake last summer.

A ripple of delighted laughter ran through the crowd as Arthur entered the paddock. A hand bigger than any other horse, shambling round like a great circus elephant, his coat gleaming like an iceberg, he was plainly delighted at the attention he was causing. The crowd, particularly the men, admired his slim blond stable-girl with her exquisite bone structure and arrogant eyes, and, seeing RC-B on Arthur's new blue rug, made the connection and nodded wisely.

'That horse couldn't win if it started last week,' yelled a wag on the steps.

'Don't be so fucking sure,' yelled back Tabitha.

The crowd roared, in no doubt now that she was Rupert's daughter, and they were delighted when Georgie Maguire, ravishing in a suit of grass-green silk, sheltered by a pink peony-patterned umbrella gave Tab the two-hundred-pound prize for the best turned-out horse.

Up in the private boxes, after excellent lunches, the rich and sometimes famous and their satellite freeloaders looked down on the runners. The noisiest, most glamorous, throng inhabited the Venturer Television box. They included Freddie Jones, Pridie's co-owner, as plump and as jolly as his writer wife, Lizzie, and Taggie's parents, Declan and Maud O'Hara, who hadn't forgiven Rupert for his crack about Arthur staying longer than she did. Billy Lloyd-Foxe, Rupert's old show-jumping crony, who was doing the commentary for Venturer, and his wanton, blond wife, Janey, who was covering the race for the *Daily Post*, and finally Ricky France-Lynch, polo captain of England, who'd had Lysander's ponies at livery, and his adorably pretty, painter wife, Daisy, who was busy sketching everything in sight.

By ghastly irony, Rannaldini's box was bang next door, and Rannaldini ignored them icily. But he couldn't stop Freddie Jones gossiping to Larry about the way the recession had stymied the electronics business, nor Meredith and Hermione, radiant in squashy blond furs, casting covetous eyes at Rupert, nor the chairman of the New World Phil, who was enjoying the hospitality more than the horses, gazing at Taggie, who echoed Rupert's colours in a dark blue suit with an emerald-green turban, and whose navy-blue-stockinged legs were longer than any of the horses'.

'I fancy Male Nurse,' said Meredith, taking his eyes off Rupert for a second to study his racecard.

'That figures,' said Guy. 'I fancy Busty Beauty.'

That figures, too, thought Georgie.

Georgie didn't care, because she'd had glorious sex with Guy that morning, because people had shoved Hermione aside to mob her and get her autograph when she'd arrived at the course, and because she'd been asked to present the turn-out prize, and because down below on the grass, watching his son go round the paddock, looking aloof and Byronic, stood David Hawkley. They had just managed to avoid the Press and snatch a blissful two minutes together behind the hot dog stand.

Why, therefore, was she so upset when she caught Guy giving Julia's friend, Daisy France-Lynch, a discreet wave? Had Ricky and Daisy had cosy foursomes with Julia and Guy?

'Oh, look,' Meredith broke into her reverie. 'Rannaldini and divine Rupert have both come into the paddock. Very dirty of Rannaldini to have raked up Isa Lovell. Perhaps Rupert will challenge him to a duel.'

Weighed out, dressed in his black, white and brown colours, Lysander huddled in the jockeys' changing room, trying to keep down half a cup of sweet tea. His knees were knocking, his mind a blank. He couldn't remember any of Rupert's instructions. Around him jockeys hid their nerves in hectic skylarking. Rushing to the lavatory when he arrived, he had found a note pinned to the door in Bluey's handwriting: '*This bog is reserved for Lysander Hawkley for the next two hours*,' and smiled feebly, but he couldn't join in. All he could think was that he might see Kitty again in a minute, but she was probably too frightened of horses to venture into the paddock, and he mustn't let Rupert, Tab and Arthur down. At least this morning's shaving cuts had stopped bleeding.

As tense as a sprung trap in the woods, Rupert didn't hear a word Freddie Jones was saying as he waited for Isaac Lovell to come out with the other jockeys. He was trying to be rational, but in his head he was back in 1980, with Isa's father, Jake, winning his silver, and Rupert coming nowhere on the most expensive show-jumper in the world.

There was that shit Rannaldini in his black astrakhan coat and poor little Kitty looking as bombed as a stuffed fox in a glass case. And there, Rupert gave a hiss, was Isa Lovell, a couple of inches taller than Rannaldini, but with the same dark gypsy stillness as his father – which always captivated women and horses. For a second Rupert's eyes met Isa's, then slid away, as he felt all the old black murderous churning.

'He *is* a little squit,' whispered Taggie.

Squeezing her hand until she winced, Rupert was relieved when the other jockeys spilled out as if from a conjurer's coloured handkerchief into the paddock. The safety pin holding Lysander's high black collar had come undone. Taggie refastened it. Like Arthur, he towered over his rivals, but he was thinner than any of them. Even his brown-topped boots were loose.

Like Scarlett O'Hara being laced into her stays, Arthur groaned as his girths were tightened.

'It's all right, darling,' Tabitha kissed him on his whiskery nose. 'Tomorrow you'll be turned out to get fat and eat as much grass as you like.'

Having seen Bluey safely mounted on Pridie, Rupert came over to give Lysander a leg up. Indignant at being ignored by his master, who was desperately scanning the private boxes for a glimpse of Kitty, Arthur deliberately stood on Lysander's toe.

'Fucking hell, Arthur, after all I've done for you!' Lysander gathered up the reins.

'Stop looking for Mrs Rannaldini, or I'll put you in blinkers,' chided Rupert, checking Arthur's girths. 'Now take it slowly, although you haven't got much option on Arthur, and remember no black power salutes until you're ten yards past the post, and don't forget—'

But Lysander never heard what he was going to say because Arthur, who never forgot a hand that fed him, had given his great Vesuvius whicker and carted his master and Tab, hauling helplessly on his lead rope, across the paddock to lay his great hairy face against Kitty's and start eating her racecard.

'Oh, Arfur!' Kitty hugged the only horse in the world of whom she wasn't terrified.

For a second she and Lysander gazed at each other. Her little pug face was flushed from the hospitality tent. There were raindrops in her hair which crinkled unbecomingly. Her eyes were red, but, to Lysander, she had never looked more adorable. Kitty only noticed how the weight Lysander had lost showed off his beautiful bone structure, his huge eyes and his long, brown curly eyelashes, and how his hips had gone to nothing but his shoulders were still wide.

Stunned by the intensity of their passion, neither of them could speak.

Tab, meanwhile, was gazing at Isa Lovell, who was as dark and slender as a Tuscany cypress in the moonlight,

688

and who was about to mount a plunging Prince of Darkness. Swinging round, Rannaldini was temporarily distracted by her disdainful beauty. The little Campbell-Black child would be an amusing conquest.

He was about to introduce her to Isa Lovell, which would be an even more amusing one, when suddenly he caught sight of Lysander and heard him mutter: 'Me and Arthur are trying to win this race for you, Kitty.'

'That's very unlikely,' interrupted Rannaldini. 'With your track record you'll be lucky to get off at the start. And this must be Arthur. I didn't know Rupert was reduced to training carthorses.'

Lysander would have ridden Arthur into him, if Rupert hadn't called him back.

'Good luck, Lysander. Come 'ome safe and Arfur, too,' cried Kitty defiantly.

Arthur gazed back at her most reproachfully for not producing any bread-and-butter pudding.

Lysander looked so thin and pale on the great white horse that, for a second, David Hawkley was reminded of the skeleton Death in Dürer's etching of 'The Four Horsemen of the Apocalypse'.

'Good luck, God bless you,' he called, as his son clattered past, but the wind and rain swept his words away.

Tabitha gave Arthur a last hug as she released him on to the course. 'Please come back safely,' she said shakily, then smiling exactly like her father, 'and in front. I'm off to put all my turn-out money on Arthur.'

Leaving the paddock, Rupert nearly collided with Isa Lovell. Pale and expressionless and now astride the fearsome, leaping Prince of Darkness, he could have been the Jake Rupert had first battled with on the show-jumping circuit twenty years ago.

'Hallo, Isa,' he drawled. 'I owe your father actually.' Then, turning to Taggie, stunning in her slim blue suit, 'Don't you think I got the better bargain? I gather Jake's still lumbered with the same clapped-out model.'

'Rupert!' said Taggie in horror.

Isa would have had no scruples about riding The Prince into Rupert, but he had a race to win. Instead, hissing a gypsy curse, he spat neatly at Rupert's feet, before thundering after the others.

The Press were going berserk.

The jockeys, as was traditional, showed their horses the first fence. A rampantly impatient Penscombe Pride nearly jumped it. As it was a long time since breakfast, Arthur started to eat it. A prat-in-a-hat then brayed through the downpour for the jockeys to line up. The Prince of Darkness, lashing his tail like an angry cat, flattened his ears and tried to take a chunk out of Arthur.

'I wouldn't.' Lysander lifted his whip.

'You shouldn't take up so much room,' mocked Isa Lovell in his flat Birmingham accent.

A summer meadowful of butterflies was fluttering in Lysander's belly. His black, brown and white colours were drenched with rain and sweat. The reins slipped through his stiff, trembling fingers. The rain drummed impatient fingers on his helmet. What the hell had Rupert said about the first fence? Gigantic gelding of little account, white elephant, no-hoper, carthorse, he thought furiously. We'll show them, Arthur.

No-one could see anything beyond the second fence. Several over-eager runners, including Pridie and The Prince of Darkness, were pushing their noses over the tape.

'Turn round, jockeys, get back,' brayed the prat-in-a-hat. 'I can't get it up.'

'That's nothing new, you asshole,' muttered Bluey as they all swung round and realigned.

Starting to giggle, Lysander was petrified he wouldn't be able to stop. They were all bunched together. Snap went the tape and the 1991 Rutminster Cup was under way.

62

Lysander never dreamt it would be so fast. The Light
Brigade hurtling into the Valley of Death didn't have
to stop and jump huge fences. His face and colours
were instantly caked with mud kicked back from horses
in front, but, heeding Rupert's words, he managed to
keep up with the hurtling, barging leaders over the first
fence, and then, as they fanned out and rattled over the
Rutminster–Cheltenham Road, he and Arthur settled into
an easy stride, bowling along in the middle of the field.

Meanwhile little Penscombe Pride, who loathed being
overtaken, had set off at a cracking pace, but as he took
the lead over the first fence, Fräulein Mahler, The Prince's
stable-mate, who never lasted more than a mile and a half,
revved up beside him, forcing Pridie to go even faster,
unsettling and muddling him, so he hit the second fence
hard.

'Fucking hell,' muttered Rupert.

He stood apart from the others in the box, tense as a
waiting leopard, cigar between his long first and second
fingers, binoculars flattening his dark blond eyelashes.
Taggie knew better than to talk until the race was over.

Penscombe Pride was still out in front, but having seen
off Fräulein Mahler who had dropped back, the gutsy little
bay was now being challenged by The Prince of Darkness,
which denied him a breather as he climbed the hill, forcing
him to gallop on. Isa Lovell sat absolutely still and let
his horse have its head, just the same technique as his
father, thought Rupert savagely. The Prince was going
really well. Rupert chewed on his cigar. All this would

rattle Pridie and wear him out. He winced as that most careful of jumpers hit The Ambush hard; that would shake his confidence even more, and now The Prince was dropping back for a rest, and Fräulein was storming down with the last of her strength to challenge and rattle again. Shit, thought Rupert in outrage, these were just the sort of spoiling tactics with which he'd won races himself.

Lysander hoped Arthur wasn't going too fast. He seemed to be enjoying himself. It was like a jigsaw. You saw a gap and slotted in when you could. Now the big ditch was racing towards him. He searched his brains. What had Rupert said? Take off about eight feet away. He steadied Arthur, who flew over like a huge white swan. Beside him Blarney Stone only realized there was a ditch when he was on top of the fence, dropping his legs in it and knocking the stuffing out of himself. Rupert was right. Arthur had nearly reached the next fence by the time Blarney Stone had recovered.

'You're doing brilliantly, Arthur,' said Lysander.

Arthur flapped his ears, relishing the cheers of the drenched crowds at each fence.

Coming up to The Ambush, five solid feet of birch and gorse, with a drop on the other side, which had caught out Yummy Yuppy last year and so shaken Pridie first time round, Lysander stood back again, but Camomile Lawn, half a length behind, was encouraged to take off at the same time, hit the fence smack on the way down and slipped on landing, rolling over and over.

'Bad luck. You OK?' shouted Lysander.

He was able to give Arthur a breather, as instructed, as they climbed the now hopelessly churned-up hill, so he was able to gallop down like a three year old. They must be lying about fifteenth now, over the road and into the second circuit. But alas, the fog, reluctant to miss such an exciting race, had come down. Lysander couldn't see more than a fence in front.

'Better put your fog lamps on, Arthur.'

*　　*　　*

'No sign of Lysander,' said Hermione with her horrid laugh.

She was bored by racing. For seven minutes all the attention was focused on someone else.

Peering through the fog at the riders' colours bobbing along the rail like a long-tailed Chinese New Year dragon, Kitty strained her eyes to identify Lysander and strained her ears, which were full of water from washing her hair, to hear the commentary. Every so often she glanced fearfully back at the monitor, which was now showing Penscombe Pride and The Prince of Darkness slogging it out about ten fences from home.

'Oh, Guy, I know he's fallen,' she whispered. 'Oh God, look!' She froze with terror as a loose horse appeared out of the mist and, circumnavigating helicopters and ambulances, hurtled across the centre of the course.

'There's Lysander, lying about thirteenth,' said Guy. 'Look, he's going really well. Come on, Lysander.'

'You wouldn't recognize him, nor Arthur,' said Georgie. 'They're both covered in mud.'

'Arthur was always a mudlark,' said Kitty in a shaky voice. Then, aware of her husband glaring at her, she added meekly, 'The Prince is going very well, too.'

Isa Lovell had been brought up to detest Rupert Campbell-Black. He couldn't overtake Penscombe Pride, but he knew the horse was tiring. Bluey had shifted him on to a different leg to wake him up and he wasn't running totally straight now. They were coming up for the second time to The Ambush, only six fences from home.

Pridie was very tired, unsettled and encased in fog, with rain lashing his face, but he didn't stop battling. Glancing round, Bluey saw Isa Lovell's white and mud-spattered face blazing with hatred and almost crossed himself. Pridie was aware of a dark shape stealing up on the rails, sinister as a shadow on the lung. Concentration flickering, he took off too late. Half a ton of horse-flesh hit the massed panel of gorse and birch six inches too low. Penscombe Pride and the punters of Rutshire and Gloucester gave a grunt of pain as he went head over heels for the first time in his life. Next moment, as The Prince overtook them, Yummy Yuppy was in the air. He swivelled to the left to avoid Pridie, landing awkwardly and crashed with a sickening thud. Busty Beauty, Paddywack and the following horses, joined the pile-up a second later. The fog was thickened with swearing, horses' legs thrashed the air, bits of gorse and birch lay everywhere. Fräulein, exhausted anyway, took one look at the pandemonium on the other side of the fence and decided enough was enough.

As the closed-circuit television picked up the disaster with not very good pictures, Rupert was absolutely stunned.

'I do not believe this,' he said, very slowly tearing up his betting slips. Then, turning to a distraught and tearful Freddie Jones, 'We were fucking robbed. I'm going to object.'

'Good old boy, clever old Arthur.' Blithely unaware of this catastrophe, Lysander came trundling through the fog into what indeed looked like the remains of the Light Brigade, with mud-coated horses and riders picking themselves out of the quagmire with varying degrees of success. Holding Arthur steady, standing back once again, Lysander jumped to the right. Seeing a huddled jockey motionless beneath him, Arthur veered to the left in mid-air, like a Zeppelin changing course, and though pecking on landing, was brilliantly picked up by Lysander. As Arthur flatfooted carefully through the chaos, Lysander was aware of a grimy drenched figure running along beside him.

'Bluey,' Lysander shouted in horror. 'Are you OK?'

'Sure. Pridie's buggered off home. Go get that fucker on The Prince of Darkness.'

We will, thought Lysander, as he cantered Arthur up the hill, waiting for the great roar from the crowd which would tell him that the leaders had emerged from the fog. But it never came. They couldn't be too far ahead.

'Sock it to them.' It was Jimmy Jardine, cadging a cigarette from someone in the crowd as he walked an utterly knackered Blarney Stone back home.

'Come on, Arthur,' urged Lysander. 'We've got a train to catch.'

The further the old horse galloped the better he seemed to go, like a Volvo that needed a long run. Dying with pride, Lysander was riding like a dream now, sitting very quietly, letting Arthur choose his own pace and the place to jump, his great stride devouring the ground.

Then Lysander gave a strangled whoop of joy as, through the mist, he glimpsed Isa Lovell's blood-red colours and the sleek black rump of The Prince of Darkness only a fence ahead. Male Nurse was beside him harrying him, giving him a taste of his own medicine.

Hitting the next fence, The Prince of Darkness veered to the right, went wide round the corner and lost a few yards, as Arthur pounded up on the inside, hugging the rails. Male Nurse was at last in the lead, but, just as Rupert had predicted, he was a young horse, and when he saw this huge yelling mass of faces, waving their arms and making more noise than he'd ever heard, his head came up and his jockey felt him coming back, and both Arthur and The Prince of Darkness passed him.

Arthur loved crowds. Now was the time for a bit of showing off, but The Prince was still three lengths ahead. They were into the home straight with two fences to go.

Lysander could see the hoof marks of earlier runners. He must keep his nerve. Ahead, The Prince, furious at being challenged, was looming over from the right determined to squeeze him out. If he froze for a second, it would cost him the race. For a second, Isa Lovell glanced round, his face torn with hatred.

'Campbell-Black's bumboy,' he hissed.

That did it. Remembering the ride-offs in polo, Lysander asked Arthur to push through. White elephants don't forget. Not wanting to be bitten again, Arthur put on an incredible burst of speed, just grazing The Prince as they drew alongside, thundering neck and neck to the last fence. Meeting it spot-on, Arthur took a great kangaroo leap.

That must put us two lengths ahead, thought Lysander, but soon The Prince'll rally and catch up.

'Oh, go on, Arthur,' he begged.

And Arthur gallantly slogged on up the hill as fast as his great raking stride would take him. But now there were only the ghosts of previous winners to challenge him because The Prince of Darkness had fallen, brought down by the last fence.

'May I borrow your binoculars, Kitty?' asked Hermione. 'This bit looks rather exciting.'

'No, you may not,' said Kitty, snatching them back. Her hands were shaking so much she could hardly hold them still. Oblivious of Rannaldini's howl of rage when The Prince had fallen, she was now screaming her head off with excitement. Arthur cleared the last fence and, with a vigour utterly belying his thirteen years, gallumphed towards the post. Lysander had no need to pick up his whip.

David Hawkley thought his heart would burst with pride and there was never such a roar of amazed delight at Rutminster as Arthur came up the straight, his great feet splaying out, rolling along like the bull terrier at the end of *The Incredible Journey*, lop ears flapping, to catch every word his young master was saying.

'My Christ,' said Rupert, who'd completely recovered his good temper, putting his arm round a joyfully sobbing Taggie. 'Is that the same old donkey who was always last on the gallops? *Come on, Arthur*. He's fucking going to do it.'

'God, the boy rides like an angel,' said Ricky France-Lynch in delight.

As if someone had tossed a match into a box of fireworks, the entire Venturer Box erupted in ecstasy.

'Come on, Arfur, you can fucking do it,' screamed Kitty, to the amazement of Hermione and the chairman of the New World Phil, and the white-faced, quivering fury of Rannaldini.

'Come on, Lysander,' howled Guy and Georgie clutching each other.

Glancing round, Lysander saw Male Nurse ebbing away in the distance. Realizing it was in the bag, and with the post only fifty yards away, he gave a great Tarzan howl of joy that was drowned in the deafening roar of the crowd.

'We've done it, Arthur!' he yelled and, completely forgetting Rupert's warning, he punched a fist in the air.

This seemed to startle and unbalance Arthur, who'd always veered to the left when he was tired. Suddenly he stumbled, and to the collective horror of the crowd, he reeled, utterly punch-drunk for a second, then lurched quite out of control towards the rails. Crashing into them, he hurled Lysander over his head within a yard of the finishing post.

For a moment Lysander lay still. Then, dragging himself groggily to his feet, he staggered over to Arthur, collapsing on top of him. Flinging his arms round the horse's great white motionless body, he pummelled at him with his fists, sobbing his heart out.

The racecourse fell silent. There was hardly a cheer as Male Nurse slid wearily past the post. It was as though the mute button had been pressed on the whole crowd. Utterly appalled, many in tears, they watched the so-recently joyful and youthful conqueror, blood and phlegm pouring from his nose on to his muddy shirt and breeches, as he slumped crying piteously over the huge ugly horse, whose gallant best in the end had not been enough.

The next moment Tabitha had raced up from the stable-lads' stand and, collapsing, sobbed dementedly beside Lysander.

'Oh, Arthur, darling Arthur, wake up! I don't believe it.'

Walking quietly back, leading a shaken but unharmed Prince of Darkness, Isa Lovell dropped a sympathetic hand briefly on her shoulder as he passed.

Before Rannaldini could stop her, Kitty had fled from the box, clattering down the grey stone steps, shoving her way through the boiling cauldron of crowd.

'What 'appened, me darlin'?' asked an Irishman.

'Arfur's dead, broken his neck,' sobbed Kitty. It seemed to take hours to battle her way round the paddock, where Arthur had shambled so jauntily only half an hour ago. Barging into the changing room, she pushed past jockeys in various stages of undress and some with just coloured towels round their hips, but all utterly shocked as they looked on helplessly.

Lysander sat huddled in a chair, his head in his hands. Rupert in a mad rage was yelling at him.

'You fucking bloody idiot goofing off like that. If you'd kept him straight, he'd never have crashed into the rails. Why didn't you bloody listen to me?'

'Shut up, Rupert,' yelled Kitty back. 'It weren't Lysander's fault.'

Lysander looked up. His face was a chaos of tears, blood and mud.

'Oh, Kitty, I let him down.'

'No, you didn't, my lambkin.' Kitty flung her arms round Lysander's frantically shuddering body, cradling his head against her breasts. 'You rode the most wonderful race in the world. They forget winners in a week, but Arfur'll be remembered for ever. He won really. His great 'eart just gave out.'

'Don't be fatuous,' roared Rupert. 'He broke his fucking neck.'

'How d'you know it was that, you great bully?' screamed Kitty. 'It might have been his 'eart, or his legs givin' out, and then he broke his neck fallin' into the rails. There hasn't been a post-mortem. It's all right, pet, it wasn't your fault.' She clung to Lysander trying to warm him and still his sobs.

'What the hell's going on?' A chill had entered the room, a waft of Maestro mingled with the stench of sweat and antiseptic. Beneath his icy calm, such was the gale force of Rannaldini's fury that the jockeys drew back.

'Do you want to make a complete fool of yourself?' he hissed at Kitty, then nodding icily at Rupert. 'Sorry about the horse. It was bad luck to lose like that. Come, Kitty, you are needed in the box. We have guests to entertain.'

Lysander looked up in bewilderment.

'Don't go,' he said, hanging on to Kitty in anguish. 'Please don't leave me.'

Clamping Kitty's arm like a vice, Rannaldini almost dragged her out of the changing room. On the way they passed David Hawkley.

'Where's Lysander?'

'In there. Please look after 'im,' begged Kitty. 'He needs you so badly.'

For a second, David took her rough, frozen hands.

'You OK?'

'Yes, yes,' sobbed Kitty. 'But I should 'ave lighted a candle for Arfur as well.'

Only when they were outside among the crowds did Rannaldini let rip a lethal lava of invective, far worse than any of his screaming tantrums to the London Met. Hypnotized by his frenziedly yelling mouth, his black-maddened flashing eyes, sickened by the smell of frying hamburgers and the animal reek of wet sheepskin coats all round her, Kitty started to sway. Suddenly she crumpled and was sent flying by a fractious crowd, deprived of the result they wanted and pushing through to watch the next race. As she was trampled underfoot she lost consciousness.

Desolately empty of Arthur, Rupert's lorry rolled back to Penscombe. In respect of such a death, the curtains had been drawn along Penscombe High Street. The streamers, bunting and flags had been put back in their boxes. For once Charlie the bookmaker was heartbroken to make a killing. Everyone had got to know and love Arthur as he'd shambled along the lanes. At The Goat and

Boots, where he had stopped for his daily pint, the champagne had gone back to the cellar.

Stony-faced, the stable-lads and girls unloaded the remaining horses. Taggie tried to comfort an inconsolable Tab, who lay on her bed, sobbing, Arthur, Arthur, over and over again.

Sacked by Rupert, Lysander was so deranged with grief he had to be given a shot by the course vet. Now crashed out at Magpie Cottage where he'd been put to bed by his father, he lay curled up with a watchful, worried Jack in his arms. Having tidied up the mess as best he could, David made himself as comfortable as possible in an armchair and waited for his son to wake.

Unable to sleep, Rupert padded down to the yard to check Pridie, who was a bit stiff, but would live to despatch any opposition another day. But he seemed cast down at the loss of his wise old friend. None of the horses would get any sleep with that Shetland keeping up such a din.

Hardly able to bring himself to go into Arthur's box, Rupert found Tiny crouched in a far corner, the picture of furious hysterical desolation.

'Come on,' said Rupert gently, stretching out a hand, then hastily withdrawing it as Tiny let out a squeal of misery and lunged at him.

Bloody minded when unhappy, just like me, thought Rupert.

63

Having got rid of his guests, Rannaldini remembered his role of faithful, loving husband and rolled up to see Kitty where she had been kept overnight at Rutminster Hospital. He was greeted by Dr Benson, who was in an excellent mood having had a thousand pounds each way on Male Nurse.

'How is she?' asked Rannaldini, as James drew him into Matron's office for a drink.

'Shaken and a bit bruised for a start, she needs rest and she shouldn't lose any more weight. Been overdoing things.'

'Anything else the matter with her?' asked Rannaldini irritably, thinking of the New York job where Kitty would need all her energy.

'Well, this should be champagne,' said James handing Rannaldini a glass of red. 'Kitty's pregnant. Congratulations.'

'*What?*' It was like the first great crash in the Verdi *Requiem*.

'About three months, I'd say.' James smiled happily. 'Best thing that could happen to her. Been longing for a baby since you two got married. Endured all those tests. Always felt inadequate when all your other wives dropped children so effortlessly. Sweet girl, worth ten of all the rest, if you don't mind my saying.' Then, seeing Rannaldini's utterly bleak expression, 'Don't need me to tell you, women need a lot of love at times like this.'

'But we're probably moving to New York next month.'

'No problem. Just see you're well insured, dear boy.'

Rannaldini was a seriously rattled man. He was furious at not winning the Gold Cup and at the very public humiliation of Lysander and Kitty clinging to each other in front of Rupert and all those jockeys. He needed Kitty as never before to smooth the path for him if he were to conquer New York and tame the toughest orchestra in the world – but not with a squawling brat around.

He left his glass of red. He needed a clear head.

'You're right, James,' he said, jumping to his feet. 'Kitty is a wonderful girl. I 'ate being without her. Eef I wrap her in cotton wool, can I take her 'ome this evening?'

'I don't see why not.' James was delighted by this unexpected display of affection.

Following Rannaldini into Kitty's little room where she lay whiter than her pillow, he was further gratified to see Rannaldini take Kitty's hand and stroke her forehead.

'My darleeng, you're coming 'ome with me so I can look after you.'

There was no way he was going to leave her vulnerable in hospital with Lysander Hawkley on the prowl.

Leaping and pirouetting in delight, Lassie greeted her mistress when they got back to Valhalla. Rannaldini instantly sat Kitty down on the blue and white striped sofa in the summer parlour, banked up the fire, poured her a glass of brandy and turned on *Hansel and Gretel* pianissimo which he knew she loved. He didn't even kick up when Lassie joined her on the sofa. There were more important issues – like persuading Kitty to have an abortion.

'But I couldn't. It'd be wicked,' she whispered in horror.

Rannaldini sat down beside her stroking her hair.

'It is wonderful news that we know you can get pregnant,' he said soothingly. 'It means we can have loads of other cheeldren later, my Keety. But I do not know eef this kid is mine or Lysander's. I am macho-man,' he shrugged engagingly but menacingly, 'I would find it hop-lessly deeficult to love another man's child, or at least to be in doubt.'

And what about your pack of children that I've tried and tried to love, thought Kitty bitterly.

'I can't 'ave an abortion,' she said, trembling at her own courage.

'We'll discuss it some other time. At least promise not to tell anyone about the baby until we decide what to do,' said Rannaldini sharply. Then, changing tack and becoming conciliatory, 'You are cold, you must 'ave a nice hot bath and I weel come and dry you like a leetle girl.'

Oh please, please no, thought Kitty in horror. Fortunately Rannaldini was distracted by the telephone. Emerging from the quickest bath in history, Kitty found that Lassie had shredded a roll of lavatory paper all over the landing carpet – white horses on an olive-green sea. Very pleased with herself, she bounced up to Kitty, seizing the bottom of her dressing gown and tugged it open to reveal her mistress still wet and naked.

'My child.' Rannaldini moved forward to touch her.

'No,' Kitty shrank away. 'I still feel queer.'

'Of course, I just wanted to 'old you in my arms. I bring you sleeping pill.'

Sulphur-yellow, it lay on the palm of his hands.

'I don't like takin' those fings.'

'My dear, James said complete rest.'

Kitty longed for time alone to mourn the passing of Arthur, but within a couple of minutes sleep engulfed her.

Downstairs, Rannaldini planned his next move.

The sooner Kitty was removed from Lysander's clutches the better, but maddeningly Graydon Gluckstein had whizzed back to New York at Rannaldini's expense without confirming his appointment. Having made himself a smoked-salmon sandwich, Rannaldini choked on his glass of Pouilly Fumé as, catching up with the papers, he discovered a large piece in the weekend *Times* on the relative merits of his and Boris's candidacies. The damaging implication was that while Rannaldini's fame and explosive personality would draw the crowds, Boris was a far more interesting and creative musician.

How could they possibly think that? fumed Rannaldini as he turned up the new CD of *Fidelio*. No-one else made brass sing like that.

The pictures accompanying the weekend *Times* piece were even more damaging. Rannaldini, marvellously lit in perfect profile and exquisitely cut tails, was conducting on the rostrum. Boris, looking twenty years younger, had been photographed without a tie with his arm round Rachel, each holding a happy child by the hand. In a fury Rannaldini scrumpled up the page and, flipping through his address book, punched out a number.

'Beattie, my leetle wild thing, we need to talk.'

Lying in Boris's arms the following Thursday Rachel slowly came back to earth.

'I must get up.' She buried her lips in her husband's shoulder.

'No, no.' He held her tightly.

'I must practise for Saturday.' She had a concert at a girls' boarding-school in Sussex. She was going to play Chopin and Schumann's *Scenes from Childhood*.

'Play them for me now as you are.'

With the curtains drawn and one lamp casting a golden glow over his wife's body, which was as smooth and as ivory as the keys over which she was running her fingers, Boris felt totally happy. *Dreaming, The Song of the Reaper, Soldier's March, Little Orphan, Child Falling Asleep, The Rocking-horse Knight*, they were the charming little pieces his mother had played to him as a child.

'Go on please.'

'*The Merry Peasant*'s been re-titled *The Happy Farmer*,' said Rachel flicking over the pages, 'Quite right, "peasant" is much too demeaning and "merry" has connotations of alcohol.'

'They'll all know that one,' said Boris.

There was a new passion to Rachel's playing that Rannaldini must have unleashed. His wife, Boris decided, had the most beautiful body in the world, the longest neck, the slenderest waist, the softest bottom swelling out over the pansy-embroidered piano stool. He could see the gleam of her unpainted toenails as she worked the pedals. Chloe always painted hers.

Boris hadn't told Rachel but on the way to Heathrow this evening he was going to pop in on Chloe to pick up some clothes and a pile of scores. He hadn't seen her since they broke up several weeks ago. He knew she was in a bad way and she needed compassion and consideration, but he was determined not to start the affaire up again. Chloe was beautiful and would soon find someone else.

Rachel had launched into *Important Event* which entailed vigorous staccato octaves in the bass, with the right hand going right down below middle C. This meant she had to turn sideways and he could see her breasts jiggling in the firelight. Appropriately Rachel moved straight on to *By the Fireside*, but she got no further than the opening bars. Boris had pulled her down on to the carpet.

'I swear I vill nevair love anyone else but you. Pleese one more time before I leave for the airport.'

The following evening Beattie Johnson sat in her large office at *The Scorpion* flipping through some photographs of Boris going into Chloe's flat and embracing her tenderly on the doorstep as he left. Then she dialled a number and flicked on the recording machine.

'Hallo,' her voice thickened slightly, 'Rachel Levitsky? I'm sorry, I know you like to call yourself Rachel "Grant". It's *The Scorpion* here. OK, OK, I understand, but before you ring off I wonder if you've got any comment about a story that your husband's gone back to Chloe. Oh dear, she's hung up.'

Beattie turned to the good-looking boy perched on her desk. 'OK, Rod, you ring her now. Ask the same question and pretend to be the *Mirror*. Give it five minutes and you pretend to be the *Mail*, Kev. Then you can put on a posh voice and be *The Sunday Times*, Mandy, and finally I'll do my refined Islington twang and be the *Independent*. That's her favourite paper. That'll really rattle her. She'll soon crack under pressure.'

Rachel hadn't cracked, but she hadn't been able to get Boris in Italy because he'd checked out of his hotel and was obviously on his way to Israel. Despite a sleepless night she didn't really believe the papers – they were just chasing old rumours – until she came out of Jasmine Cottage with the children on her way to Sussex. It was one of those perfect daffodil-lit mornings when the cuckoo might make his first appearance. Breathing in the sweet air Rachel suddenly noticed a bug-eyed blonde getting out of a car.

'Rachel Grant, can we have a chat?'

'No, go away,' said Rachel, shoving the children and her music case into the back of her car which unfortunately was cold and took a bit of time to start.

'What d'you think of this story about your husband and Chloe?' The girl thrust *The Scorpion* through the window.

'*Cheating Boris fakes happy marriage to clinch New York job*,' read Rachel.

'It's not true,' she whispered, driving off with a squeal of tyres.

'Look at the pictures,' yelled the blonde.

Half a mile away in Valhalla Kitty was in an increasing turmoil. For a week now she had been cut off from the outside world. As James Benson had prescribed complete rest, Rannaldini had employed a temp, a Miss Bates, who had very nice ankles and who fielded all telephone calls and visits.

Now up and dressed for the first time, Kitty sat in an armchair in the summer parlour gazing listlessly at a little copse of young poplars thrusting their acid-green branches upwards in victory salutes and reminding her agonizingly of Lysander. Out in the park in their New Zealand rugs all Rannaldini's horses, except The Prince of Darkness, who was still confined to box rest, were enjoying the spring grass. But not Arthur, thought Kitty in despair – and wondered for the millionth time whether Lysander was all right.

Lassie was her one comfort. Already in trouble that morning for having pinched Mr Brimscombe's paintbrush, peed on Rannaldini's Aubusson and chewed one of Miss Bates's green suede shoes, she had now collapsed in front of the fire and was showing off her white belly, with her speckled paws folded over like a model wearing smart new gloves.

As the front door banged she rose with a lot of woofing, shot between Kitty's legs, then bounded forward pirouetting with joy as her old friend Ferdie walked in with Natasha.

'Kitty, you poor thing!' Natasha ran across the room and kissed her. 'We've only just found out how ill you've been. Are you OK? You look so pale and thin.' She thrust a vast bunch of red tulips into Kitty's hands. 'And we've brought you some mags and some scent. Hasn't Lassie grown?' Leaving Kitty, she crouched down beside the puppy who was still trying to lick Ferdie to death.

Kitty had never seen such a change in two people. Natasha looked utterly ravishing in a clinging campion-pink shorts suit and high-heeled black shoes. The heavy make-up had gone; dark-lashes and sparkle were enough, and what was the point of lipstick when it kept being kissed off? And the beady, calculating dead-pan Ferdie was grinning from ear to ear, which were mostly hidden by a curly new cherub's haircut.

'I took him to Schumi's,' said Natasha proudly. 'Doesn't he look gorgeous?'

'Wonderful! You both do,' said Kitty in amazement. 'And *so* thin, Ferdie.'

'Forget Special K and Lean Cuisine,' said Ferdie patting his concave gut. 'Love's the answer.'

'You don't think he's too thin?' asked Natasha anxiously.

'No, no. When did you two get togevver?'

'Beginning of last term.' Natasha collapsed on the sofa and pulling Ferdie down beside her, started nibbling his ear. 'Ferdie started taking me out from Bagley Hall. Papa's stopped bothering now he's bored with Flora. Oh Christ, sorry, Kitty.'

'I'm sorry we didn't take you out. I fort when you didn't come 'ome,' Kitty blushed, 'you preferred it that way.'

'Oh, I did.' Natasha was ruffling Ferdie's hair. 'I've always grumbled about Papa and Mama neglecting me. Now I realize how wonderful it is. Ferdie and I have just had the most gorgeous ten days in France.'

'We fort you was with Cecilia,' said Kitty.

'Mama thought I was with you,' giggled Natasha. 'No-one checked. And Ferdie takes care of me so much better than either of them. Oh hi, Papa.' She edged closer to Ferdie as she noticed Rannaldini in the doorway.

'I thought you were with your mother,' he snapped.

'Basically, no. She's got a new boyfriend. You can read all about it.' Natasha waved *Hello!*. 'The last thing she wants is me around.'

'And what about your A levels?' said Rannaldini coldly.

Natasha smiled. 'Well, Ferdie's been helping me with Business Studies and even more with Human Biology. And as for Ancient History – I ought to study Lysander.'

Rannaldini was looking thunderous but fortunately rushed back to his study to answer the telephone. He was expecting confirmation from New York any second.

Just for a second colour spilled over Kitty's grey face. 'How's Lysander?' she whispered the moment he'd gone.

'Absolutely miserable,' whispered back Ferdie, thrusting a letter into the pocket of her grey cardigan. 'Almost as miserable as Tiny who never stops crying and running to the gate looking for Arthur. So most of the time Lysander lets her into the house. He's back at Magpie Cottage by the way. Marigold rolled up with some prospective buyers and was not amused to find Tiny eating carrots in front of the fire.'

'Lysander's still wiped out about the Rutminster,' added Natasha who was entwining her fingers with Ferdie. 'He blames himself totally.'

'It wasn't his fault,' flared up Kitty.

'Course it wasn't. Rupert's had to apologize,' said Ferdie, who was very shaken by Kitty's appearance. 'They did a post-mortem. Arthur had a massive heart attack. From what I gather some old worm larvae got into the gut and migrated through the wall of the artery into the aorta and died there leaving a lesion which couldn't cope with all that blood racing round.'

'You are clever to explain,' said Natasha fondly.

'So they've decided Arthur crashed into the railing and broke his neck as a result of the heart attack, so Lysander's in the clear.'

'Oh, fank goodness.' Kitty's eyes filled with tears. 'I'm so frilled, but poor Arfur.'

'Wonderful way to go,' said Ferdie. 'Leading the field by twenty lengths, cheers echoing in his ears, his beloved master in ecstasy. He wouldn't have known anything.'

'Are you quite sure?' Kitty gave a sob. 'Lysander loved him so much.'

'He loves you much more,' said Ferdie with a furtive glance at the door. 'He's lost his Eurydice.'

Kitty was about to ask him to explain when Rannaldini marched in, singularly unamused to see Natasha still wrapped round Ferdie, who was no doubt acting as a go-between for Lysander.

'You better push off now,' he said coldly. 'Kitty gets very tired.'

'She looks terrible,' said Natasha. 'Have you been feeding her on Paraquat?'

'Don't be infantile,' hissed Rannaldini so evilly that even Ferdie shivered.

Lassie was barking again. There was a knock on the door. It was Miss Bates with her normally bold grey eyes cast down.

'Dr Benson to see you, Mrs Rannaldini.'

Before Rannaldini could stop him, James had swept in.

'Natasha,' he said kissing her on both cheeks, 'I haven't seen you for years. You've grown even more lovely than your mother.'

'Why, thanks. This is my boyfriend, Ferdie Fitzgerald,' said Natasha proudly.

'Lucky guy.' James shook Ferdie's hand, then glancing from this glowing buxom child to her desperately pale, red-eyed stepmother. 'Aren't you pleased about the new addition to the family?'

Natasha looked blank.

'He's talking about Lassie,' cut in Rannaldini. 'Now buzz off you two and have a drink in the morning room.'

'I wasn't talking about Lassie,' said James Benson smoothly. 'Hasn't your father told you that your step-mother's expecting a baby?'

'She can't be,' whispered Natasha, utterly aghast. Then, fielding a laser-beam of warning from Rannaldini, 'I mean, that's great. How *very* exciting,' she added in a strange high voice.

'We're not telling anyone,' said Rannaldini grimly, 'not until the New York job's in the bag. Now bugger off you two. James wants to look at Kitty. He hasn't got all day.'

Natasha seemed so shattered that she walked out without even saying goodbye.

'Look after yourself,' said Ferdie, hugging Kitty. Seriously worried, he hated leaving her.

Natasha can't bear my having her father's child, thought Kitty hopelessly. Oh God, another dreadful complication.

Rannaldini jumped up and rushed out as the telephone rang. He had been unbelievably edgy all morning. A long time talking, he met James Benson on his way out.

'Not very happy about Kitty,' James told him. 'Not responding at all well, almost clinically depressed. I've put her on anti-depressants and some iron and vitamins to boost her up. But I cannot recommend TLC too strongly, Rannaldini. She needs a proper holiday.'

'She has one,' said Rannaldini, who was quite incapable of controlling his orgasmic elation. 'That call confirm the New World Phil job. It is all I have dreamt of and worked for.'

'Well done, great,' said James, 'brilliant, but that's hardly a holiday for Kitty.'

'It'll be a change of scenery.' Most uncharacteristically, Rannaldini kissed his doctor on both cheeks. 'If you'll forgeeve me, James, I must break the news to Kitty. That will be the best tonic.'

What a victory! He wanted to shout to the rooftops as he bounded upstairs. How dare that little Russian upstart challenge his throne. The best man had won – even if he had had to fax *The Scorpion* piece on Boris and Chloe anonymously to Graydon Gluckstein the moment it came off the press.

'It'll be a new 'eaven and a new earth, my kitten,' he told her joyfully.

The early afternoon sun flooding his face made him look young and extraordinarily handsome.

'We will leave our problems behind and start our marriage again. You will adore New York. It pulsates like an animal.'

Cecilia lives in New York, thought Kitty bleakly, and once she's dumped this latest boyfriend she'll want Rannaldini back and me as a dogsbody. And if I go to the States and want to come back Lassie will have to go into quarantine for six months. And Hermione will come and stay for ages and little Cosmo will break the place up. At least in England they live in their own house.

'They are so delighted to 'ave me,' Rannaldini was saying, 'they 'ave already release the news worldwide. Next week we can fly over and look at 'ouses. Oh, sheet,' as his mobile rang again. 'Why can't people leave us alone? 'Allo, 'allo.'

His face went utterly still, so instantly drained of colour

and joy that for a second Kitty thought the job had been withdrawn. For a couple of minutes he listened, just interjecting the occasional '*sì*'. Then he said: 'It was good of you to let me know. We'll talk later, *ciao*.' He switched off the telephone.

Only then did the rage erupt, as he launched into a stream of Latin expletives.

'What's the matter?' Kitty clung to a cringing Lassie.

'The stupid, stupid beetch,' screamed Rannaldini, 'driving over a fucking cliff and we've only recorded the first two movements of the *Emperor*.'

'What *are* you talking about?'

'Rachel. She kill herself driving off the road.'

Kitty gave a moan. 'Oh my God! Poor Rachel. 'Ow terrible. What 'appened? Did the brakes fail? It couldn't have been suicide.'

Rannaldini shrugged. 'She was found clutching a copy of *The Scorpion*. They'd run a piece about Boris going back to Chloe.'

'Oh no, I can't bear it. Oh, the poor li-el kids.'

'Rachel left them with Gretel. Stupid, selfish beetch.'

'Oh, poor Boris. Does he know?'

'Ees in Eesrael,' said Rannaldini contemptuously. 'That was Bob. He's trying to trace him.'

'Oh, my God.' Kitty's face crumpled up with tears. 'She was probably just distracted by the 'orrible article and drove off the road.' Groping in her pocket for a handkerchief, she nearly pulled out Lysander's letter. 'She dropped me a line only this week sayin' 'ow 'appy she and Boris was.'

Again the telephone went. The *Telegraph*, having been tipped off, was ringing to congratulate Rannaldini about New York and wanting a comment on Rachel's death.

'One of the most tragic losses to the music world,' Kitty could hear him saying as he walked back to his study, 'Rachel Grant had an individual talent which I personally . . .'

Guessing he would be tied up for some time, frantically

brushing away the tears, Kitty took the note out of her cardigan pocket. It was full of crossings out. A demented Lysander had clearly struggled over it himself without any help from Ferdie or Rupert.

Darling kitty,

I wonnted to proove i cud do sumthing, well arthur and i allmost did. I havent got a big howse or a jetset life but i give you my hart wych feals as if its been tramsplarnted withowt any annisetik. please wring i am dieing of missery.

your luvving Lysander.

Kitty felt as though the jagged teeth of a steel trap had closed into her leg, holding her back. Darling sweet Lysander. How could she ever even respect, let alone love Rannaldini, after he'd been so monstrously insensitive about Rachel?

'Mrs Rannaldini?'

Whatever was wrong with Miss Bates? She'd been so bossy and uppity yesterday, now she couldn't meet Kitty's eyes, as she handed her the second cordless telephone.

'Mr Rannaldini's still on the other line, it's Natasha. She says it's desperately urgent.'

' 'Allo,' said Kitty, steeling herself for abuse.

'Are you alone? Promise you won't leave Papa.' Natasha's Italian-American accent was coming in gasps. 'Wolfie won't come back to Valhalla because Dad took Flora off him and I'm living with Ferdie now. Papa'll be so lonely living on his own. I shouldn't be telling you this – Papa'll kill me. Promise you won't tell him.'

'I promise,' said Kitty fearfully, 'but be quick, he'll be back in a second.'

'Your baby isn't Papa's. It's Lysander's.'

'How d'you know?' whispered Kitty. 'I slept with your dad the night before Lysander came out to France and the night I got back.' She shuddered as she remembered Rannaldini's ice-cold anger as he practically raped her. 'I only slept wiv Lysander twice.'

'Papa has had a vasectomy.'

'He *what*? When?'

'Just after he married you. He didn't want any more children, what with seven of us and buckets of illegits. He was fed up with the expense and the hassle. But there's a 28 per cent chance of reversing the operation, so you still could have babies together. Kitty, Kitty, are you still there?'

'Yes – are you sure?'

'Certain. He had the op in America. Not even James Benson knows.'

'Oh my God.' Kitty gave a sob.

'You will go on being my friend even if you leave him,' pleaded Natasha. 'But try not to. He loves you in his funny way, and he needs you. You're the best wife he's ever had.'

'I've got to go,' mumbled Kitty, switching off the telephone and slumping back on the blue-and-yellow cushions, clutching Lassie, who stretched up, long pink tongue frantically trying to staunch her mistress's tears. Outside, Rannaldini's horses were lying down in a patch of sunlight close together to keep warm, folding up one after another like camels.

Kitty couldn't stop crying as she remembered the way Rannaldini had complained so bitterly when she had all those horribly embarrassing and often painful tests – not to mention the devastating disappointment each time her period came. Now he was bullying her non-stop to have an abortion and all the time he'd made her bear the full guilt and humiliation of being the infertile one.

'The stupid bitch drove off the road,' she muttered, 'an' we've only recorded two movements. Oh, poor Rachel, oh dear God.'

Kitty had no idea how long she sat, her thoughts churning, but suddenly the door flew open and in bounced Hermione, smothered in leopard skin.

'Come on, Brickie! We're off to the bird sanctuary at Slimbridge. We've always vowed we'd go. Such a lovely day and what better way of celebrating Rannaldini's wonderful new job.'

He must have rung to tell her straight away, thought Kitty dully.

'You must wrap up warm.'

Marigold, following Hermione into the room, thought how really ill Kitty looked.

'But what about Rachel?' said Kitty bewildered.

'It's terrible. We're all devastated,' said Hermione briskly. 'Bob was crying when he rang from London to tell me, but crying won't bring her back. We'll all have to rally round Boris and the children. Gretel's being a tower of strength. Mind you, spare men are lucky, they get snapped up very fast.'

'We can't go on a jaunt,' said Kitty in horror, 'not when she's just passed away.'

'Rachel was mad about conservation,' said Marigold gently. 'It's a sort of memorial to her if we go. Come on, Kitty, it'll do you good.'

64

So off they went in two cars: Marigold and Larry, Georgie and Guy rode in the first. Hermione, reluctantly accompanied by Meredith, because Bob was still in London coping with the ramifications of Rachel's death, drove with Kitty and Rannaldini, who was resplendent in a new, long pale-fawn cashmere coat from Ralph Lauren.

The clouds had rolled away. Primroses, violets and blue hazes of speedwell crowded the hedgerows from which the first green flames of hawthorn and wild rose were flickering brightly.

'Dark glasses and head scarves, chaps,' said Hermione, tying a rust silk square over her dark hair. 'We don't want to be mobbed by autograph hunters.'

There was hassle even before they got inside Slimbridge when, ignoring a sign saying NO ENTRY FOR FURS MADE FROM SPOTTED CATS OR TIGERS, Hermione tried to force her way through the turnstile.

'Is that coat fake leopardskin?' asked the girl on the till.

'Certainly not,' said Hermione in outrage.

'I'm afraid you can't come in.'

So Hermione threw a moody and as Rannaldini showed no signs of relinquishing his splendid new cashmere, kind Guy had to lend her his old army greatcoat.

'It looks better on a man,' joked Guy as he did up the brass buttons. 'D'you remember that advertisement, Brickie?'

Kitty didn't. She was thinking of the contrast between the noisy, self-confident sophistication of the Paradise party – excluding herself of course – and the scruffy excited crowds, mostly parents and children in anoraks, retired couples or earnest men in shorts and hung with cameras and binoculars.

'Dreadfully suburban,' shuddered Meredith, as he whisked Kitty past bright pink double cherries, weeping willows, little concrete ponds and pebble-dash islands crowded with birds.

'I fink it's beautiful,' said Kitty, admiring the little teals with their glossy blue, green and chestnut heads and the black swans whose necks unfurled like ferns.

' 'Ooo, 'ow sweet.' She bent down to stroke the little brown striped Hawaiian geese who wandered round soliciting bread and rubbing against people's legs, tame as Lassie.

'That bird with a white collar looks just like Percy,' said Meredith.

'It's called the common shoveller.' Marigold was eager to show off her ornithological knowledge.

Guy, who'd been a keen birdwatcher during the walking tours of his youth, was equally eager.

'The courtship of the ruddy duck is absolutely fascinating,' he was telling Larry.

Seeing a notice which said GO QUIETLY, TREAD GENTLY, Kitty thought it sounded like a prayer. There must be a god to produce such a marvellous variety of different coloured birds, and what a wonderful quacking and honking and hooting they make. From every bush came scuffling like a teenage party.

'Interior designers could pick up a few tips.' Meredith was studying the black, rust and white plumage of a passing eider duck.

'Listen to what it says about the courtship pattern of the great whistler,' cried Marigold putting on her spectacles to read another notice: *The male arches his body and neck, flinging up droplets followed by head up, tail up. Usually several males frantically display before one female.*

'Sounds like the husbands of Paradise showing off to

Rachel,' said Georgie sourly. 'Oh my God, I forgot she was dead.'

Noticing Kitty's glazed eyes suddenly spilling over with tears, Meredith mouthed to Marigold, 'Is she OK?'

'I don't think so,' mouthed back Marigold.

Picking up this exchange, Hermione turned to Rannaldini: 'Wouldn't it be wonderful if Kitty could adopt a Canada goose? They've got a scheme here. It would give her an interest. I'll go and jolly her up.'

Showing off her deeply caring nature and her charmingly curved legs, she moved forward putting her arm through Kitty's.

'I'm so delighted about Rannaldini's new job. I know he's been a naughty boy, but when you think of stags, stallions and male dogs, and how much more glamorously the male birds are kitted out than the females, it's no wonder men are different. Bitches, does and female birds are gentle, sit on their nests and stay at home. Sex really isn't *that* important.'

It is with Lysander, thought Kitty sulkily.

She noticed a mallard, his emerald head gleaming in the sunshine as his tabby wife nestled beside him in married contentment.

Like Lysander and me, thought Kitty, I'm plain and tabby, he's beautiful and resplendent, but he loves me.

'I know you've still got a crush on Lysander.' Marigold took Kitty's other arm. 'He's so sweet. We all had one on him once, just like the flu.'

'Some of us still do,' sighed Meredith, admiring the blond hairy legs of a hulking German tourist.

'Don't be silly, Meredith,' reproved Marigold. 'And don't be rash, Kitty. Valhalla's a beautiful place and Rannaldini'll buy some gorgeous apartment for you in New York. It's no fun lowering one's standard of living.' Marigold sighed even more deeply. 'And think of the travelling you'll do.'

And the packing, thought Kitty wearily.

'*He will not always say what you would have him say,*'

sung Hermione warmly, so crowds turned and gawped at her, *But now and then he'll say something wonderful.* They're holding an Infertility Workshop in Rutminster next week,' she went on. 'Why don't you go along, Kitty? A problem shared is a problem solved.'

Surging ahead Larry, Guy and Rannaldini turned off to look at the flamingos. Soft orange and Barbara Cartland-pink they stood about on one leg making a very unmelodic, jangling din.

'Sounds like one of Boris's symphonies,' said Rannaldini bitchily.

'Poor bastard,' said Larry.

But Rannaldini was deep in thought, anticipating the wonderful tussle he would have, knocking those bolshie but stunningly talented New York musicians into shape. The concert at which he'd raised so much money for the Gulf had been good for his image. Before he left he might do the same for the Royal Society for the Preservation of Birds. They could do an ornithological programme. There were so many composers – Delius, Respighi, Sibelius – to choose from. In the tower was a serenade to the lost birds of Italy which he'd written in his youth. He'd get it out and have a look this evening.

'Guy is such a pig,' Georgie was now whispering to Marigold. 'A girlfriend rang me yesterday to say I must read *Love in The Time of Cholera* because its whole premise is that you can only keep a wife happy by lying and lying to her. And that was the bloody book Julia gave Guy for his birthday.'

At least, she comforted herself, Guy was being really sweet to her at the moment and David had rung while Guy was out getting the papers and presumably ringing Julia this morning, and she and David were having dinner on Monday.

'I'm so lucky with darling Bob,' said Hemione smugly as they moved towards a small wood. 'He is so devoted. Oh, aren't those coots sweet – I wonder if coots really are queer.'

719

'I want to go to the Wild Goose Hide-away,' giggled Meredith, bounding up some steps into a wooden hut. 'Well, perhaps I don't,' he said shooting out on discovering a lot of bearded men with knobbly knees peering through binoculars.

But the Paradise party, who'd already started up the steps, pushed him jovially back into the hide-away. Inside, wide windows looked on to the Severn estuary which stretched out like a great white luminous STOP sign. In front little lakes were dotted with birds. To the right on the far shore, pylons and cranes rose out of a smoky haze.

'Look at the Canada geese,' cried Marigold.

'There's a beautiful Bewick swan,' observed Guy, then raising his voice for the benefit of the *cognoscenti*. 'The Bewick's call during flight is "tong, tong, tong, bong, bong, ongong, ongong".'

'Jourdain describes the call as a "varied din of honking notes",' volunteered one of the men with knobbly knees.

Kitty caught Meredith's eye and, in order not to laugh, turned to examine a wall chart listing sightings, together with descriptions of the species and the numbers seen.

Running her eyes down the list which included great-crested grebes, all kinds of swans, ducks and geese, herons and even a kingfisher, she suddenly started to shake with helpless laughter, until she was gasping and clutching her sides.

'Whatever's the matter?' asked Marigold alarmed.

'Look.' Kitty pointed to halfway down the list where in a very round hand someone had written DONALD DUCK. As a description they had put: *Blue coat, yellow beak*, and under the number recorded they had written, *Sadly none*.

'That's not really funny, Brickie,' reproved Guy. 'People take birdwatching very seriously.'

'Lysander could have been here.' Kitty wiped her eyes on her sleeve. Having started laughing, she found she couldn't stop.

'Better take her home,' whispered Marigold.

'Come on, old girl.' Larry put his arm round her shoulders, 'Don't want to overdo it.'

'Off her trolley,' mouthed Guy to Meredith.

'Wouldn't you be,' said Meredith with unusual sharpness, 'if you were married to that?' He nodded at Rannaldini and Hermione who were straightening their clothes and smirking as they emerged from the Goose Observation Tower next door.

The birds look so happy, thought Kitty, meekly allowing Larry to lead her back. They've done their bonking and now they've got their little families. She watched a drake and a duck striking out from the shore, proudly leading a convoy of tiny fluffy ducklings.

They had sanctuary here at Slimbridge but they could leave when they want to. Suddenly she remembered the cow loose in the barley during the drought last summer who had rolled its way over the cattle-grid. It had looked so carefree. Anyone could get out if they wanted to enough.

'Tong, tong, tong, bong, bong, ongong, ongong,' muttered Kitty.

Larry glanced at her nervously.

'I'll take over,' whispered Georgie, taking Kitty's arm. 'David Hawkley is so attractive,' she told Kitty, lowering her voice. 'If you can imagine a macho, intellectual Lysander.'

'Lysander's perfect as he is,' said Kitty indignantly.

A sharp breeze was already scattering pink cherry blossom over the dark water like confetti.

'You know I really love Guy,' admitted Georgie. 'The most important thing in marriage is companionship and a huge bit on the side to cheer one through the bad patches. Divorce is so damaging for children.'

They were passing the Slimbridge shop which still had a Mothering Sunday sticker in the window.

I don't want no bits on the side and I'll never even have children to damage if I stay married to Rannaldini, thought Kitty numbly, and a Canada goose that flies in and out of a bird sanctuary isn't enough.

A pretty young mother was coming out of the shop. She had a sweet child who was trailing a black toy pig by the hand.

Over the hills and far away she danced with Pigling Bland, thought Kitty, biting her lip to stop herself crying.

'The most important thing,' Hermione came up on the left, 'is that Rannaldini needs you. It's wonderful to feel you are indispensable to a genius.'

'Bob must find it a huge comfort,' snapped Georgie.

Hermione bowed her head. 'He does, he does.'

I'm not their age, thought Kitty. I don't remember advertisements about things looking better on a man. I'm still young and I love Lysander.

Rannaldini, Guy, Georgie and Hermione, bored with anonymity, were not displeased when a big party of foreign tourists stopped them for autographs. Where foreigners had rushed in the shy English were not slow to follow.

'We really must go,' laughed Hermione five minutes later.

I love Lysander, he is the father of my child, thought Kitty. Rannaldini had lied and cheated and betrayed her and been utterly, utterly reprehensible. Now he was asking a busty Swedish girl her name so he could personally inscribe her autograph book.

'We're having our sixteenth anniversary in October,' Marigold was saying. 'Ay suppose we should be awfully grateful to Lysander. We maight not be havin' it at all if he hadn't made Larry so jealous.'

'Home for tea at Valhalla,' said Rannaldini, putting a warm caressing hand on the back of Kitty's neck as they walked towards the cars.

'What a lovely afternoon,' cried Hermione, smirking as he stroked her bottom with the other hand. 'Let's make a regular thing of it.'

Georgie shivered. 'It's getting cold.'

'How d'you think I feel with no coat,' murmured Guy,

then smiling at Kitty. 'The best part is going home to crumpets and Brickie's chocolate cake.'

They were all smiling at her now, some of them realizing the extent of her unhappiness and trying to boost her spirits.

'You look tired, Kitty,' said Rannaldini when they got back to Valhalla. 'Miss Bates will get tea. You sit by the fire. Come and see my new toy,' he added to the others.

65

They all trooped off to admire Rannaldini's new helicopter.
As Kitty went wearily into the house, Lassie danced
towards her, striped body weaving and snaking, black-
rimmed eyes full of love, peeing on the flagstones in her
delight.

I can't leave her, thought Kitty.

Not even pausing to wipe up the puddle, she ran down
the dark passage. Outside Rannaldini's boot room Lassie
had chewed up what Kitty first thought was a twig.
Then she realized it was the baton Toscanini had given
Rannaldini on his death bed.

'It'll be your deaff bed, Lassie, if we don't get out of
here.'

Gathering up the puppy in panic and rushing into the
kitchen, she found Miss Bates still looking dreadfully
embarrassed.

'Mrs Rannaldini, there's something I must tell you.
Then I'll get you all tea.'

'You've looked after Rannaldini and me so well,' stammered Kitty, terrified of any delay, 'we're so griteful.
Can't it wait till tomorrow?'

'No!' Miss Bates was so insistent that in the end Kitty
sat her down at the kitchen table.

'Mrs Rannaldini,' said Miss Bates, frantically rotating
the gold bracelet on her slender wrist. 'I have to tell
you that while you were fast asleep in bed, knocked
out by one of Mr Rannaldini's sleeping pills, I went
to bed with Mr Rannaldini.' Her voice faltered. 'I'm
desperately sorry, he's just so attractive.'

For a minute Kitty looked at Miss Bates incredulously, then she burst out laughing.

'Is that all? For an 'orrible moment I fort you was going to 'and in your notice. Promise to stay and look after 'im.'

In the utility room Kitty found an ancient cat basket and, wiping it down, shut a quaking Lassie inside, who was convinced she was going to the vet.

'Bong, bong, bong, tong, tong, ongong, ongong, this is the flight call of the female Rannaldini.' Shrieking with helpless laughter, Kitty raced across the lawn, past the glowering maze and turned left to the stables. As the garage was next to Rannaldini's helicopter pad she couldn't steal off unobserved by car. The only answer was the kindest horse in the yard.

'Bong, bong, bong, tong, tong. Nuffink venture nuffink win.' She was already shaking with nerves worse than Lassie, she must try and keep her courage up.

But as she ran into the yard she gasped with horror. She'd forgotten that all the horses had been turned out except The Prince of Darkness who glowered out of his box as sinister as his name, evil eyes rolling as he scraped and gnawed at his half-door.

He'll go for me if I try and put a bridle on him, thought Kitty, almost fainting with terror, then froze as the door of the groom's cottage opened. But instead of Clive, Janice the head groom emerged.

Janice was very fond of Kitty; she might not shop at Valentino like Cecilia, but she always saw that the grooms were paid on the nail.

'You do look poorly. You shouldn't be up,' she said, noticing Kitty's violent shakes and her face grey and glistening with sweat.

'Could you please tack up The Prince?' stammered Kitty, kicking Lassie's cat basket behind the mounting block. 'Rannaldini wants to ride him.'

'At this hour?' Janice looked at her watch.

'He's got friends over.'

'And he wants to show off,' Janice sniffed. 'And I was just off to get the other horses in. What was that?' She paused at a piteous whine from Lassie.

'Nuffink, 'spect it's a bird. We was at Slimbridge today,' said Kitty desperately.

'More like one of the Rottweilers got stuck in somewhere.' Janice glanced round the yard.

'Please tack up The Prince.' Kitty tried to disguise her panic.

The wait seemed interminable, particularly as she had to keep up a tuneless singing to drown Lassie's increasingly aggrieved whining, but at last Janice put her head over the half-door.

'God, he's a dangerous bugger. Where d'you want him taken?'

'Leave him for a sec. Rannaldini fort he left his silver-topped whip in the tack room,' said Kitty.

She would rot in hell for such awful lies.

'I'll look,' said Janice.

Kitty was nearly frantic with terror.

'Please God take care of us,' she prayed.

Taking a huge breath she unbolted The Prince's door and just grabbed his reins as he shot out like an Exocet. Not giving herself time to have doubts, she gathered up Lassie's basket, clambered on to the mounting block and somehow scrambled astride the vast black back which was pitching like a top deck in a force ten gale. With a manic clatter The Prince tore out of the yard, down the rough track in search of his friends. At least he couldn't savage her if she was on his back. Alarmed by Janice's screams to come back, however, he broke into a gallop.

'*Oooh*, it's worse than the big dipper,' moaned Kitty, twining her fingers in the thick mane, as trees, bushes and telegraph poles flashed by. All this jolting must be bad for the baby, but far, far worse, Kitty gave a sob, if it had ended up a bloody mangled foetus on the abortionist's table. The thought made her cling on even tighter.

Oh, heavens, she suddenly remembered she was hurtling towards the West Gate which was chained and bolted. If she had to get off The Prince to undo it she'd never get on again. Thundering towards a clearing on her left she loosened her grip on the mane to tug the near-side rein. Miraculously the big horse cornered at Rutminster Cup speed into a woodland ride.

'Oh, good boy, Prince, please keep straight,' begged Kitty. If he carted her under the branches, she'd had it.

The wind was lifting her hair, tugging at her grey cardigan and her old grey check skirt. To right and left on the woodland floor, bluebells battled to push through the dog mercury, little primroses were stifled by brambles and pale-faced anemones were being drowned like bathers in a rising sea of garlic, which gave off pungent wafts of aioli as it was pounded by The Prince's flying feet.

They had reached open fields now. Again Kitty knew she was finished if The Prince's stable-mates came pounding down to join him. But ahead like the Berlin Wall lay the River Fleet and freedom.

'Go on, Prince,' yelled Kitty as they slithered down the bank.

Only baulking for a second, the brave black horse plunged into the swirling brown water. A terrified whine reminded Kitty that if she slid off or let go of the cat basket Lassie was as good as drowned.

'Our farver which art in 'eaven,' cried Kitty, ' 'allowed by thy name.'

For a nightmarish few seconds The Prince was out of his depth, swimming boldly, battling with the cross-currents, then he was lurching up the other side.

'Oh, fank you, good old boy,' cried Kitty.

It was as though Magpie Cottage was pulling them towards it. Staying on going up hill was much easier. The south side of Paradise was far less advanced. The trees brushing the clouds were still bare. They were tearing past great banks of blackthorn that looked as though they'd been dipped in flour, and there was poor Rachel's cottage.

An' flights of angels sing thee to thy rest, thought Kitty.

But the present was more important. Glancing back, fearful of seeing Rannaldini's helicopter rising like a malignant hornet, Kitty wondered how much longer she could cling on. Then, like the heavenly city, she saw the Paradise Road which passed Magpie Cottage. Again untwining her aching fingers from The Prince's mane she tugged the offside rein and the horse swung to the right.

'I can ride,' called out Kitty in ecstasy.

But nothing prepared her for galloping along tarmac at a breakneck speed. What happened if they met a car? She ducked to avoid a low-hanging sycamore branch. Having lost both her shoes, she felt she was about to lose her teeth.

As she tried to swing left up Lysander's track, she and The Prince parted company. The lures of Paradise were too strong for him and he kept on going. Kitty landed gently amid the white violets on the verge. All her life she would associate their sweet smell with relief that she wasn't hurt and even greater relief when she opened the cat basket, and Lassie jumped out, pirouetting in glee, raking her mistress's legs with her striped paws.

'Quick, quick, my lamb.' Urging them both on, Kitty panted up the lane, oblivious of the sharp stones ripping her soaked tights.

Then she gave a cry of despair. The curtains were drawn. Three days' milk hadn't been taken in. The FOR SALE sign shivered despondently in the chilly wind. Heart crashing, gasping frantically for breath, she raced up the path and pounded on the door. No answer. She pounded again. Nothing. Perhaps Lysander was in bed cheering up some sad beautiful girl whose husband was about to become jealous.

'Oh, Lassie, what will become of us?' wept Kitty.

In answer came a shrill outraged yap. Pushing open the door Kitty tripped over a mountain of post. LYSANDER

HAWKLEY, OWNER OF ARTHUR, ENGLAND, was written on one of the top envelopes. Jack, who from his caked brown nose had been rabbiting, greeted her in noisy ecstasy. He then discovered Lassie timidly hovering on the threshold, strutted round her on poker legs, sniffing and assessing. Realizing she was female he started to twitch his stumpy tail, then ran into the sitting room barking importantly.

Lysander sat slumped on the old blue corduroy sofa staring hopelessly into space, oblivious of a wildly exciting photo-finish on the television. There was a quarter of an inch of stubble on his haggard cheeks and black, black half-circles beneath his eyes. His Donald Duck jersey was inside out and he was wearing odd socks.

'Lysander.' Kitty could hardly get the word out.

He looked round dully, then started incredulously.

'Lysander, it's me,' she whispered, shakily holding her hands out. 'Over the 'ills and far away, she danced with Piglin' Bland.'

As though struggling from the bottom of the sea Lysander staggered to his feet.

'Are you a mirage or a miracle?' he mumbled.

'I'm me. I love you,' sobbed Kitty. 'I'm sorry to barge in. I can't live wiv Rannaldini no longer.'

Lysander's stubbly jaw dropped, his bloodshot eyes opened wider and wider as he gazed at her. Then a great smile split his face and he gave a great whoop of joy and, vaulting over the sofa, fell into her arms kissing all the life out of her – but only for a few seconds because they were both so gasping and breathless they had to come up for air.

For an enraptured moment Lysander touched Kitty's windswept hair, and ran his hands wonderingly over her pale frozen little face to prove he wasn't dreaming.

'I thought I'd never see you again,' his voice broke. Then, reluctant to let her go for even a second, he dragged the hefty bishop's chair across the room and shoved it against the front door.

'We're not letting Rannaldini in here.' He collapsed into the chair, pulling Kitty onto his knee.

'You escaped. Oh, Kitty darling, you really escaped. You are brave.' Kissing her between sentences, he said, 'I got you an engagement ring just in case. It's in a case actually.' He giggled helplessly and, leaning back, scrabbled amid the chaos of the desk drawer and produced a little crimson leather box containing an enormous diamond.

'It's a bit flash but diamonds are for ever. Who said that? Shakespeare?'

They were both shaking so much it took a long time for him to slide the ring on to her finger.

'It's 'eavenly,' breathed Kitty, 'ow, Lysander you shouldn't, I mean it must've cost—'

'Hush.' Lysander put his lips on her forehead. 'Georgie gave me back the diamond necklace I gave her to get the clasp fixed so I flogged it. You and me are what matters. How the hell did you break out of Valhalla?'

'I rode The Prince of Darkness,' said Kitty proudly.

'You what?' said Lysander, utterly aghast. 'Oh, Kitty, you couldn't have. You're so frightened of horses, and I'd be petrified of riding him.'

'I was more frightened of not getting to you,' confessed Kitty.

'But you're soaking.' Lysander suddenly took in her dripping skirt and her ripped tights. 'Oh my God, you didn't come over the river? You could have been drowned. You did that for me. Oh, Kitty darling, you're so brave, I can't believe it. Where's The Prince now?'

'Dunno,' Kitty shrugged. 'Pushed off to Paradise. He needed some fun. Probably openin' an account at The Apple Tree, or havin' a sherry at The Pearly Gates, or wiv any luck wrecking Percy's garden.'

'Kitty!' said Lysander in awe, 'I never thought you were capable of such irresponsibility. Oh, I love you.'

Tipping her head back he buried his mouth in hers, kissing her more and more passionately; and his stubble lacerating her cheeks was the sweetest pain she'd ever felt.

'I can't believe this is happening to me. Let's go to bed. I just desperately need to prove you're real.' Dazedly he started to undo her grey cardigan.

But Kitty couldn't give in to joy just yet.

'There's somefink I've got to tell you.'

Taking in her lack of suitcases, Lysander began to tremble. 'You only came for a few minutes.' He grasped her hands until she winced. 'You're going back. I can't handle it, honestly I can't.'

'It's not that. I don't want to trap you, but I'm expecting a baby.'

'I don't believe it!' Lysander's face was flooded with relief and happiness. 'That's fantastic. I'll take care of both of you. I love babies. Doesn't matter if it's Rannaldini's. If we bring it up, it'll be ours.'

Kitty was frantically wiping her eyes.

'It's yours,' she whispered.

'Mine?' said Lysander incredulously. 'How can you tell?'

'Rannaldini's 'ad a vasectomy, so it can only be yours.'

Lysander gazed at her, gradually absorbing the enormity of the truth, horrified disapproval battling with overriding pleasure and pride.

'My baby! God, that's great, but that bastard Rannaldini letting you think you couldn't have kids. Christ, the bastard. I'll give him an Iraqi manicure, then I'll kill him. D'you mean it's really my child, I mean, our child?'

As he took her hands kissing each finger, she could feel his tears.

'You could have lost it,' he said in a choked voice. 'You might have had a fall on the road, like Mum. Oh, thank God you're safe.'

'It was nuffink. I wasn't frightened once we got going because you was at the end of it.'

'You mustn't cry.' Lysander reached for his handkerchief and dried both their eyes. Then he said slowly, 'It's *our* baby, God, I feel fantastic. Shall we ring Dad? No, let's open a bottle first.'

He was so desperately thin that Kitty couldn't wait to feed him up with jam roly-poly and treacle pudding.

'I can work right up until the birf,' she said, not wanting him to feel pressured financially, 'and afterwards I can take up typing.'

'You will not.' Lysander stuck out his chest. 'I've got a proper job starting on Monday, working for Rupert, breaking and schooling horses for him. He thought it was too much hassle me keeping the weight down so he's going to try me on eventing or even show-jumping.'

'That's wonderful,' said Kitty overjoyed. 'I'll forgive 'im for being so 'orrible.'

'He's been wonderful. He's actually taken Tiny back to live with Pridie, because both of them were missing Arthur so much. He and Taggie have gone to Bogotá for six weeks to get a black baby. No, I'm not sure that's right – anyway Dizzy's going on holiday so Danny and I are in charge of the yard. I was shit-scared, but now I've got you I can do anything.'

'You always could,' said Kitty proudly.

'And Rupert's lent me a cottage. It's really sweet, but only because you're going to live in it. Oh, do look.'

Following his gaze Kitty saw that Lassie and Jack had curled up in the dog basket together and Jack was busy licking Lassie's eyes and nose.

'*Jack shall have Jill.*'

'*Naught shall go ill,*' Kitty's voice broke again.

'He'll need a step ladder when she reaches her full size,' said Lysander.

'An' I'll need a social ladder marryin' you,' giggled Kitty.

'Don't be ridiculous!' he said furiously. 'You're so good and so far above me, Kitty. I really will be the man who made husbands jealous now, because every man in the world's going to die of envy because I've got you.' He kissed her small squashed nose. 'I'd forgotten how beautiful you are.'

Then suddenly his flawless brow wrinkled.

'I can't figure it out. Basically twenty minutes ago I was going to shoot myself. Now I'm the happiest man in the world and I'm going to be a father.'

When the Tarzan howls had finally subsided, Kitty said timidly: 'I fort if it was a little girl we could call her Pippa after your mum.'

For a few seconds Lysander couldn't speak, then he said: 'She'd have loved that. And if he's a boy we'll call him Arthur.'

THE END

APPASSIONATA
by Jilly Cooper

Abigail Rosen, nicknamed Appassionata, was the sexiest, most flamboyant violinist in classical music, but she was also the loneliest and the most exploited girl in the world. When a dramatic suicide attempt destroyed her violin career, she set her sights on the male-dominated heights of the conductor's rostrum.

When Abby gets the chance to take over the Rutminster Symphony Orchestra, she is ecstatic, not realising the RSO is in hock up to its neck and is composed of the wildest bunch of musicians ever to blow a horn or caress a fiddle. Abby finds it increasingly difficult to control her undisciplined rabble and pretend she is not madly attracted to the fatally glamorous horn player, Viking O'Neill, who claims *droit de seigneur* over every pretty woman joining the orchestra. And then Rannaldini, arch-fiend and international maestro, rolls up with Machiavellian plans of his own to sabotage the RSO.

Effervescent as champagne, Jilly Cooper's new novel brings back old favourites like Rupert and Taggie Campbell-Black and his son Marcus and ends triumphantly with a rampageous orchestral tour of Spain and the high drama of an international piano competition.

Appassionata – the most swooningly romantic and heartwarming novel of the year.

'Triuphant ... a boisterous tale of sex and Chopin amongst Rutshire folk'
Tatler

'*Appassionata* – the divine Jilly Cooper's latest and greatest novel'
Jane Procter, *Sunday Times*

9780552156387

CORGI BOOKS